Inside the
Castle
in the Glass

By Bob Siegel

ISBN-13: 978-1535514033
ISBN-10: 1535514035

Author's Preface

Inside the Castle in the Glass is part of a novel series united by a common theme and a recurring story arc. Not every novel has the same characters, but they each relate to each other, and readers will clearly see their connection when the entire epic is completed. The full collection is entitled *The Crown and the Crystal.*

Certain novels in the series can be read alone, without their sequels and prequels. However, that is not true with every book. *Inside the Castle in the Glass* falls somewhere in between, offering enough exposition to be read without its predecessor should the reader so desire. However, it will be best enjoyed if it follows *The Dangerous Christmas Ornament.*

Some of the conflicts and mysteries will be resolved at the end of *Inside the Castle in the Glass,* but the story still ends in suspense, and its characters continue their adventure in subsequent novels.

In the dedication, you will read about some inspiration from my life, but modest inspiration notwithstanding, this novel is pure fiction, a fantasy story from start to finish. It is not my intention to teach any new theology about God, angels, or the supernatural.

Dedication

To my loving and encouraging wife, Dana,
To the real Aunt Loureen,
And finally,
To the real Caligula, who, in reality, was my daughter's cat,
Shadow. He never actually spoke, but he often looked like he
had something to say, especially when I was annoying him.

Table of Contents

Part One: The Writer

Part Two: The Other World

Tempted by wickedness,
All of you will,
Two turn to evil,
The others hold still,
One turns again,
So his soul can be crowned,
The other stays lost,
And can never be found.

Part One: The Writer

Chapter One

How I Became Famous at Sixteen

In the year 2003 …

Most kids aren't famous at sixteen, unless they're movie stars or rock stars or something like that. I'm no star, but by accident, I did stumble into some attention I wasn't expecting — enough attention to at least be called "a little bit famous." And I was glad, too, because otherwise I would have been miserable in high school.

Up until recently, I hadn't liked being sixteen. I always thought I would, and I grew up looking forward to it, but after my sixteenth birthday, I realized that I really didn't feel much different than when I was fifteen.

Oh sure, I was in Driver's Ed now, and I would have my license soon. That would help a little. That would be better than having my parents drive me places. There's nothing worse than when your parents drop you off at school or at basketball games and your friends catch you. Yeah, the license would make a difference, but not much, because I was still afraid of girls, and there isn't much point in having a car if you're afraid of girls.

I'd been afraid of them ever since the first time I fell in love. I had been only twelve then, in the sixth grade. I could barely even talk to girls back in those days, but my Aunt Loureen told me it would get easier as I grew older.

"So be of good cheer, Nephew," she said. "Sweet sixteen comes to all of us."

Well, it came all right, but there was nothing sweet about it. And girls weren't the only problem. There was also a thing about sports. I tried out for sports, but I couldn't get on any team except cross-country, and they took practically anyone because most people hate cross country. I hated it too, but I wanted to be in sports. I'm not sure why. Probably because it sounds good to tell people you're in sports, even if you're not having a good time, and in high school, how you look to others is more important than how you feel. I might have had more fun with football. I did good at football when we played it in PE, but I didn't make the team because the other guys who tried out were giant compared to me, and I'm not even that short.

But the worst thing about being sixteen was that I still felt like a kid, and nobody wants to feel like a kid when he's only a few years from being an adult. I would be twenty-one in just five years, and I wasn't ready. Some of my friends said that eighteen is the real age of turning adult since you get to vote at that age. I guess eighteen *is* the legal age, but if people were gonna expect me to act like an adult at eighteen, I was in real trouble. I already had questions about how much I would change by twenty-one, but I knew for sure I wasn't gonna change by eighteen. Besides, I had always thought of eighteen as still being a kid since you're still a teenager. But anyway, whenever it was supposed to happen, I was not ready to become an adult.

The main reason I didn't feel ready was because I still had a lot of my old childhood problems. In sixth grade, my adventure with Aunt Loureen's magic Christmas ornament had taught me that I was a coward. It was hard to face at first, but I figured I would at least learn from the experience, like Aunt Loureen said I would. I counted on getting over it when I got older. Now I was in high school, I was still a coward, and anyone who's still a coward in high school may just stay a coward his whole life.

I did manage to keep it a secret. Nobody knew besides me. What helped the most was that I had always been kind of average. I wasn't real popular, but I wasn't a nerd either, so jocks and tough guys never picked on me. Also, a lot of kids from elementary school grew up with me, and they remembered how I had once clobbered that bully Joe Blankenship. Only my two best friends, Cliff Reynolds and Ben Robinson, knew the truth: that it was really some magic from the ornament which had knocked him over. Still, between that one time of popularity and my average look today, I was pretty much left alone in high school and not picked on. So how did I know that I was still a coward? Because I never defended the people who *were* picked on, even when I wanted to, even when one of them was my friend Cliff, who had been a nerd since way back in grade school and who had stayed a nerd all these years.

Only one good thing came from being a coward. It gave me an idea, and my idea made me famous. That must sound hard to swallow, that an ordinary guy like me could come up with an idea so unusual that every kid on campus suddenly knew his name. Well, believe me, no one was more surprised than I was. But anyway, once my idea made me famous, being sixteen wasn't a hassle anymore. It was actually fun! I guess I would have been glad to be famous at any age, but when you're famous at sixteen, it makes you kind of a big shot to all the other kids. It made the girls like me too, even though I still had trouble talking to them.

Who could have thought that a sophomore would end up on television talk shows or be interviewed by magazine writers? But that's exactly what my idea did for me. It was very exciting, even though they asked hard questions, like "Mike, how about telling us where you get your inspiration from?"

When you're in high school, you usually don't think much about stuff like inspiration, but this time, I actually had a good answer. I guess I'd have to say that the idea first hit me one day at school when I found Cliff crying during lunch hour.

Like I already said, Cliff was the classic nerd. I could tell he hated being viewed that way. Unfortunately, the poor guy fit the description: skinny, weakling, glasses, horrible at sports, but brainy in science and a straight-A student in every other subject too. He also belonged to the chess club. I never understood why nerds liked chess so much, but yeah, Cliff belonged to the chess club too. You'd think he would have stayed away from the chess club just to keep at least one "nerd feature" off his list. But he did join the chess club, maybe for a chance to hang out with people more like him. Anyway, to top it off, Cliff also had red hair and freckles, not that I care what a person looks like and not that red hair would bother me even if I did care what people looked like. In fact, the first girl I ever got a serious crush on had red hair. I had known her briefly in sixth grade, and I thought she was really pretty. As for Cliff, he was my friend, and his hair color didn't concern me one way or the other. Probably most of my classmates didn't really care either. But you would never guess from the way they teased him. You'd think the poor guy had leprosy or something. This was high school! In high school, once a guy got a reputation for his looks or for anything else, he kept it. My Aunt Loureen used to talk with me about this kind of thing. She was a teacher herself in another city, and she'd made many observations about what she called "school etiquette."

"It's like the story of the Emperor's New Clothes," she once explained. "People wish to blend in, so they go along with the crowd. If some fellow student is dubbed 'homely' or 'nerd,' it sticks. Few will trust their own opinions, and few will have the courage to speak out even if they *do* know otherwise."

Before graduating from middle school, Cliff had made one major attempt to improve his social life. He changed the spelling of his name, hoping that it would make a difference. It hadn't, but I guess changing your name is easier than changing your looks or changing your coordination.

Actually, he never really changed his name legally. To do that, he would have needed his parents' permission. His legal name, the one typed on his birth certificate, said "Clifford." Since most people go by abbreviated names, Cliff's mother taught him early on to spell his name as *Cliffe*. The *e* was supposed to be silent, but good luck explaining that to grade-schoolers and middle-schoolers. Everybody pronounced his name "Cliffy," as if the *e* wasn't silent. Cliff finally got tired of arguing about silent *e*'s with kids who could care less and would find a way to put him down one way or another anyway. And so, when he entered high school, he just started spelling his name the more normal way, *Cliff*, without the so-called silent *e* at the end. His mother went on and on about how he didn't need to do this and what a beautiful name *Cliffe* was, but he just ignored her and wrote it the way he wanted on all his tests and papers.

I'm not sure why Cliff thought that would make any difference. I guess it eliminated one way of taking a ribbing since *Cliffy* always sounded like such a baby name. Unfortunately, once the name got straightened out, there was still plenty of other ammunition, like the stuff I already mentioned. With or without an *e* at the end of his name, Cliff remained a nerd to the students of Valley View High.

Anyway, back to the day I caught my poor nerd friend crying during lunch hour.

"What's wrong?" I asked him.

"Nothing. I'm fine."

"No you're not. You're crying."

"I am not!"

"Well, not this second maybe, but you've *been* crying. Your eyes are all red."

"That's just because I have a cold."

I decided not to argue the point. I knew he was lying, but I understood. I wouldn't wanna be seen crying either, especially at school. "OK. I believe you. But *something's* wrong."

It took Cliff a couple of minutes to admit the problem. Finally, he said, "Aw … it's just Doug DeWorken. He was giving me a rough time again. I wish I could stand up to these guys the way Ben does."

You may remember that Ben Robinson was my braver friend, the opposite of Cliff in every way. As he got older, he got more and more popular, and in high school, they made him captain of the basketball team. Usually guys like Ben wouldn't give a brainy, redheaded, freckled faced, chess player the time of day. But Ben did. He was the first person in grade school who had been willing to be Cliff's friend, and they stayed friends, all the way up through high school. A lot of folks didn't understand their friendship. Some of the guys on the basketball team even told Ben he could be more popular if he would stop hanging out with Cliff, but Ben didn't care much what people thought, and for some reason, his friendship with Cliff never did seem to get in the way of any popularity.

My Aunt Loureen explained it to me once. "Ben has a lot of positive self-esteem. When a person likes himself, he never feels that he has to go around proving things to others. People around him sense this, and they respect him for it. You'd do well to learn that lesson, Nephew."

But I hadn't learned jack diddly squat. Oh sure, I learned to admire Ben, but that was all. He was the kind of friend you could count on. *I* always let people down. Oh sure, I was also willing to stay friends with Cliff, but unlike Ben, I never really defended Cliff. And unlike Ben, my popularity wasn't on the line for hanging out with Cliff because I wasn't popular anyway. Like I said, I was just kind of average. But in high school, *average* is better than *nerd*, and I was always afraid that might change if I ever tried to protect Cliff to the point where they decided to start picking on me too!

I remember one time in a ninth grade PE class, Scott Pierce had stood up on a bench in the locker room while we were changing into our gym clothes. "Raise your hand if you like Ol' Freckled Nerd Cliff!"

5

he shouted. "Hold your hand up high if you like the dork!"

Nobody raised their hand, including me. I could hardly look Cliff in the eye. He was standing right next to me, feeling betrayed.

I never did understand why I failed him that day. I've thought a lot about it since, and my behavior really didn't make much sense. For one thing, people always saw me hanging around with Cliff anyway, so they already knew that I *did* like him. Of course, a lot of the times when we were together, Ben was with us too, and nobody was gonna hassle Ben. Ben wasn't in the same PE class, so maybe that's why I felt scared to stick up for Cliff by myself. But it was still weird because only a few guys in the PE class scared me. When I say I'm a coward, I don't mean that I'm scared of everyone. I just mean that I never stand up to the ones I *am* scared of. But Scott Pierce wasn't one of the scary guys. He was just an idiot with a big mouth, almost as skinny and weak-looking as Cliff. And the few in the room who *did* scare me might not have cared if I raised my hand for Cliff.

I tried to make it up to him. After PE, I slapped Cliff on the shoulder. "Don't worry about Pierce. The guy's a loser."

"I'm all right," Cliff muttered. I could tell he didn't wanna talk about it.

"Hey … ah … the only reason I didn't raise my hand is that I was just kidding around. I mean … they all know we're friends, right?"

"Sure, Mike. No problem."

He knew I was lying, but we were both too embarrassed to talk about it anymore. It would have served me right if he said he never wanted to see me again, but Cliff couldn't afford to lose a friend, so I knew that was never gonna happen.

Now, here we were in the quad at lunchtime, a year later. He was still being picked on, still confiding in me as a friend, and still aware that I would only be his friend up to a point. But I wanted to at least try. I needed to stop thinking about the locker room incident and find out more about *today's* mess.

"Well, what exactly did DeWorken do?"

DeWorken was a huge football jock, definitely on the list of guys who *did* scare me.

"He grabbed my lunch out of my hand and got nailed by a teacher. Now he says he's going to be waiting for me after school."

"How did he get in trouble? You didn't narc on him, did you?"

There were certain understandings in high school, kind of like unspoken laws. No one was ever to rat on a bully. It only made stuff worse because now the bully was madder than ever. Besides, none of the principals could protect you twenty-four hours a day, so you were better off just keeping your big mouth shut and hoping that sooner or later they got tired of picking on you and moved on to somebody else.

"Narc on him? You think I'm crazy? No. You see … one of the teachers caught him swiping my food and gave him detention on Saturday. But DeWorken is still blaming me, even though he knows I didn't say anything!"

We could actually see DeWorken sitting with his friends while we talked. He and his slick buds always hung out in a special place on the lawn during lunch. This was another unwritten high school law: Certain places on the grass were reserved for the "cool people," the big clique. Everyone understood this. Good luck to any new kid if the poor schlemiel accidentally sat down in a "restricted quarter."

DeWorken and his friends were looking at Cliff and laughing at him. I thought they might have been laughing at me too, but I wasn't sure.

Ben always joined us for lunch, so I looked toward the snack bar line to see if he was around yet, to see if I could get him over here faster. Yeah … there he was.

"Hey, Cliff, why don't I go get Ben? He'll protect you."

"It's after school. The fight's after school. He's not going to bother me now. Too many teachers around."

I disagreed. Usually bullies like to scare people and brag all day about what they're gonna do, long before the time of the actual fight. Doug DeWorken was the kind of guy who could come up with a whole wagon load of hassles that wouldn't technically be considered fighting. He could make threats and digs. He could also get a little bit physical — stuff like grabbing Cliff's collar, stepping on his foot. The small things — small enough to keep him out of trouble, big enough to get a lot of attention and scare the snot out of poor Cliff.

"I'll get him anyway." I hurried toward the snack bar line.

Ben saw me coming from a distance and was frowning by the time I arrived. "What's up?"

"Cliff may need some help. DeWorken called him out after school."

"Jeez …" Ben was shaking his head. "All right. I'll be there in a minute."

"But I think DeWorken's gonna bother him now. They're all laughing and pointing at him."

"I'll be there after I get my lunch."

"That'll take forever. There's five people ahead of you."

"And about ten behind me. I don't wanna lose my place in line. Can't you go protect him till I get there?"

"Well … ah … sure … yeah … I guess."

"Then get over there."

"Look, Ben! They're moving toward him. A bunch of guys! Not just DeWorken!"

Ben started grumbling something under his breath. But I knew he wouldn't let Cliff down, even if it meant missing his lunch. Ben always talked kind of gruff, but deep inside he cared, and he put others before himself … Not too many high schoolers like Ben. I didn't understand him. My whole life, I'd never learned to put others first unless the cost was low. True, I fetched Ben because I *did* care about Cliff, but "fetching Ben" was about all Cliff could ever expect from me. What a relief to see DeWorken making his move now, while Ben could witness it with me. Now I wouldn't have to go over by myself. It was like being saved by the bell.

"Let's go," Ben said.

I felt pretty scared, even though I knew that nothing was likely to happen once Ben entered the scene.

As we moved closer, we heard DeWorken barking out words for all to hear. "And then, if by chance ya recover from today, I'm gonna come after ya again on Saturday, just as soon as detention's over. So ya just better hope that my stay is a short one, cuz for every hour of detention,

I'm gonna add an extra blow!"

Poor Cliff was squealing like a little five-yearold. "I didn't narc on you! It's not my fault Mr. Adams walked by!"

"Maybe not," DeWorken said with a big smile on his face, "but it *is* your fault for bein' so ugly."

The crowd laughed.

I hated bullies. They were all the same. They all made the same kinds of threats. They all humiliated people.

One of DeWorken's cronies chimed in. "Maybe when God handed out looks, he missed the bus."

Most of the gang laughed again, so DeWorken added more. "Yeah, or maybe he just got in the express line, nine features or less."

"At least he was in the line that gave out brains!"

Everyone looked the other way, toward Ben and me. Of course, you must know that Ben shouted the comment. I was hoping to get out of this jam with as little effort as possible.

DeWorken didn't look too happy. He had been on such a roll, and Ben was yanking the rug from under his feet. "Whaddaya want, Robinson?"

"Just came to see what the problem was."

"No problem."

I could see that DeWorken was trying to act cool, but it was obvious that he'd just as soon not get into a hassle with the captain of the basketball team. Still, DeWorken was pretty tough and gutsy. No telling where this could lead. They were really quite a sight, or quite a contrast, I should say: slender Ben, sharply dressed with neatly combed brown hair, next to husky DeWorken, with his sandy blond crew cut and an outfit which looked like he had little time in the morning to do much more than throw on some ragged jeans and a T-shirt.

Ben moved closer, practically in DeWorken's face. "No problem, huh? I hope not, DeWorken. I really hope not."

"None that you need ta worry about!"

DeWorken might not have wanted to fight Ben, but he wasn't backing down either. Why should he? He was bigger than Ben. That's probably why he played football and Ben played basketball.

"Oh, I'm not worried," Ben said. "But Cliff looks worried. Isn't he a little out of your league, DeWorken? Couldn't you take on something your own size, like a semitruck or something?"

A few gasps were heard from the crowd. This was gonna be good.

"You want me ta take on someone better, like you, Robinson?"

Another of DeWorken's friends interrupted. "Watch it, Doug. He knows martial arts."

DeWorken didn't look too happy with that bit of news. "Martial arts? What? Like karate?"

"No," the sidekick said. "It has a weird name."

"Judo?"

"Jujutsu, if you must know," Cliff said.

"Stay out of this, spaz! This don't concern you!"

It seemed odd, DeWorken telling Cliff to stay out of it when this whole mess was about Cliff. I wondered why Cliff had shouted out the word *jujutsu* instead of Ben. Then I remembered what Aunt Loureen had told me about Ben not needing to prove himself. I guess if you know how to fight, you don't have to tell people that you know how to fight. Ben had been taking jujutsu for three years — the Japanese kind, the kind that included actually throwing people. He asked me once if I wanted to take classes with him, but they were in the evenings, and to me it just seemed like more school, so I never did join him. But right now, I wished I had.

DeWorken was casing him out. "Jujutsu ... I never heard of that one."

"There's a surprise," Ben said.

"It's kind of like judo," DeWorken's friend added.

The smile was now gone from DeWorken's face. "What are ya ... a black belt or somethin'?"

Ben just stood there with a stone face. He actually *had* earned a colored belt ... not black. I forgot what it was, green or brown — something like that.

"This ain't fair," DeWorken said. "I'm not gonna fight a guy with a black belt."

"It's not a black belt," Ben answered.

"Well, what color is it?"

"You can take a guess when the fight is over."

A few people laughed, including Cliff. DeWorken turned toward Cliff, giving him a real dirty look. Cliff was acting stupid. He always did this: got real cocky when Ben was around, acted like a buried ostrich when Ben wasn't around.

"So, ya have a belt. Big deal."

"I'm not the one making a big deal out of it, DeWorken."

"Neither am I! I ain't scared of you, Robinson. Ya think I'm gonna shake just cuz you've taken a few martial arts classes?"

"Oh, you don't need to shake, DeWorken. You just need to lay off my friends."

"Ya always did keep drippy friends." DeWorken was looking at me now. Great … just what I needed.

"My friends are a package deal," Ben said. "You hassle them, you're hassling me."

"Well, I'm still gonna kill the spaz after school. What do ya say ta that?"

"I say we'll be waiting for you … Both of us. Come on, Cliff. It smells better on that side of the grass."

That afternoon, Ben and Cliff waited around from 2:30 to 4:00, long enough to see that DeWorken wasn't gonna show up. The next day, they learned that DeWorken had to get home early to start on his homework. That's why he wasn't there. His folks had threatened to ground him if he didn't come home and crack open the books. At least, that's what he told everyone. I had seen DeWorken around campus over a year now, and I don't think I ever once saw him "crack open a book." But anyway, he was gonna come after Cliff "some other time." He didn't say when, just "some other time." That was his excuse. Nobody believed it, but who wanted to tell Doug DeWorken that you didn't believe his excuse? Only Ben might have been willing to tell him, if he cared. But he didn't care because DeWorken always kept his distance from Ben after that day.

Anyway, this was my inspiration. This was my idea, an idea for a story. I decided to write about a hero like Ben who would stand up to the DeWorkens of the world and rescue the Cliffs of the world. At first I thought about the story just for kicks. I wasn't even sure I would ever actually write it down, but I kept thinking about it, and finally I made the story into a book — or well, more like a comic book. I had always liked stories, all kinds of stories, whether from comic books, regular books, TV or movies. And I had always thought about writing a story of my own, but between school and messing around with my friends, I somehow never made the time. Once, long ago, in the sixth grade, I had written about some stuff, mostly because Aunt Loureen said I should. I enjoyed doing it, but it wasn't a made-up story. It was more like a personal diary, and I never showed it to anyone because my friends would have thought I was weird to keep a diary the way girls do. When sixth grade was over, I put the diary away and stopped writing for years. Well, I mean I stopped writing on my own. There were still school assignments. I wrote essays for my English classes, and once in a while, the teacher would assign fiction writing. I usually got nailed for my grammar, but I also got good comments about my imagination. Still, it wasn't the same as sitting down and really writing about something that interested me. Yet, now I was serious. I wanted to write so badly. I had always heard that good writers wrote about things they had actually experienced or at least things they felt strongly about. Even if they were writing fiction, they based part of it on something they had really gone through, and this business with Cliff, this whole business about feeling too scared to stick up for him — well, it was causing so many deep feelings I finally figured I might be able to make a good story out of it.

In my new, hand-made comic, I changed the setting. It didn't take place in high school, and I didn't call the hero "Ben." I called him "Arch-Ranger." Arch-Ranger was kind of a Robin Hood-like character. He lived in the olden days, and he was good with a bow and arrow, but instead of stealing from the rich people, Arch-Ranger just traveled around the countryside helping anyone who was in trouble, whether they were rich or poor. Also, Arch-Ranger lived in another world. I got that idea from my sister, Shelly's, book, *The Magic Ornament of Lumis*. Even though I never read about a man named Arch-Ranger in the story, I decided that since the book was about a far-off place, I would also have Arch-Ranger live in a far-off place. I made Arch-Ranger a very brave man, mostly because I wanted to be brave myself, and if I couldn't be that way, I could at least make up somebody who was.

Arch-Ranger was kind of like a superhero, except that he didn't have any powers, so I guess he would have to be called "a hero" not a "superhero." Some of my friends told me that if a guy wasn't a superhero, he didn't belong in the comics, but I told them that comics could be about anybody. Besides, Batman didn't have any powers, just a costume and a lot of gadgets. Anyway, once they read *Arch-Ranger*, they really liked him, and they stopped complaining that he wasn't a superhero.

You're probably wondering how many high schoolers actually read comics. Well, a lot more than you'd think. Some of my friends thought that comics were "only for babies," but I had never gotten tired of them. Still, I was always careful not to let too many people know. I never carried comics with me at school, and I only talked about them with friends whom I knew also read them. Cliff loved comics — at least the ones that were science fiction. Ben thought they were stupid.

Anyway, back to Arch-Ranger. At first I was just gonna call him "Archer" since that's what he was: a guy who was good with a bow and arrow. But Archer was such a common name already that I hesitated using it. For one thing, I heard it a lot as a last name, like Mark Archer, a guy I had known in elementary school. But it was also a common name in fantasy stories. I still liked the name, but I also wanted to be original, so I kind of combined it with another word that we see a lot in fantasy stories, *ranger*. I don't mean *forest ranger*. What I mean is that I had read a lot of stories and seen a lot of movies about special heroes called "rangers." Usually, they were guys who went on important, unique missions, either because they were hired by some king, or just on their own because there was something special they were trying to accomplish. And so, my character's special mission would be traveling the world defending people who were in trouble. Anyway, two common names, *archer* and *ranger* were turned into the name *Arch-Ranger*. I know … that's still not the most original name in the world, but I didn't want to go too far in the other direction with something so fancy that nobody would know what I was talking about.

I first got into the habit of drawing Arch-Ranger during my more boring classes, because if I hadn't drawn something, I'd have gone out of my mind.

Each time I sketched him, he looked a little bit better, especially one time in social studies. Mrs. Pumpernickel was trying desperately to get us interested in the average annual production from Finland … something like that.

"Mr. Owen, are you taking notes like the rest of the class?"

Uh-oh. She caught me. "Yeah," I lied. "I'm taking notes."

"Are you? Bring them up here so I can see them."

Great! Just what I needed. "I meant I was *about* to take notes."

The class laughed.

"Oh, I see," she said, moving toward my desk. "And this is how you prepare?" She snatched up the picture of Arch-Ranger. It was drawn only in pencil, and like I already told you, it looked kind of like Robin Hood. "Look here, class," Mrs. Pumpernickel said, waving my picture around the room for all to see. "Look how Mr. Owen prepares to take notes!"

There was a lot more laughter until Jack Kilpatrick blurted out, "Hey, that's pretty rad!"

This changed the mood of the others, and a few more made remarks like, "Wow! Good drawing!"

People really were like sheep at times. They changed their opinions awfully fast, especially in a group setting. Still, I was glad Kilpatrick's comment got things going for me.

Mrs. Pumpernickel was looking a little bit embarrassed now. She'd meant to humiliate me in front of the class for not concentrating on my work, but the plan seemed to be backfiring.

After taking a more careful look, she mumbled, "Well, yes, it *is* a well-drawn picture. But this isn't art class. This is social studies."

Boy, is it ever, I said to myself.

"Mr. Owen, why don't I just hold on to this until after class? Without the distraction, perhaps you can travel to Finland with the rest of us."

When class was over, I waited until everyone else filed out. Then I slowly approached Mrs. Pumpernickel's desk.

"Yes, Mr. Owen?"

"I just came to pick up my picture."

"Tomorrow, Mr. Owen."

"But you said I could get it after class."

"I decided to hold on to it a little longer."

This was really weird. Why did she need to hold on to it? She didn't look angry either, just strange.

"How come I can't …?"

"I said you can get it tomorrow, Mr. Owen!"

I just stared at her, unable to say anything.

"You'd best be moving along. You'll be late for your next class."

The afternoon and evening seemed to go by slowly, probably because I was thinking so much about Mrs. Pumpernickel and about getting my picture back. In my mind I kept seeing two faces, Arch-Ranger and the large gray-haired Mrs. Pumpernickel. I had drawn other pictures of Arch-Ranger, so I guess it wouldn't have been that big of a deal if she never gave it back to me. But the weird way she acted when she refused to give it back — that's what I was so curious about.

Her lecture the next day seemed longer and more boring than ever. I wouldn't have been able to repeat a word of what I heard. Of course, that would probably have been true whether I was thinking about my picture or not.

When the bell finally rang and the class started leaving, Marla McIntire walked over to my desk and said, "No picture of Robin Hood today?"

She was smiling, obviously teasing me in a good-mannered way, so I made sure that I smiled back when I said, "Actually, it's not supposed to be Robin Hood."

"Well, you're the boss. It's your picture." Then she left my desk and walked out the door.

Wow! If I hadn't known better, I would have said that she was trying to get my attention, trying to flirt with me. Marla was a blond bombshell with light blue eyes and a cute voice. She'd been in my class all semester, but I couldn't remember her ever actually speaking to me before. I was starting to feel grateful that Mrs. Pumpernickel had snatched the picture out of my hand. Speaking of her, it was time to get this over with.

"Well, Mr. Owen," she said, looking up from her desk as I moved toward her, "I imagine you're here for your picture."

"Yes, ma'am."

She opened her desk drawer. "Here you are. Sorry to have held on to it for so long, but I *did* have my reasons. Sit down, Mr. Owen." There was a chair near the blackboard, and I pulled it up next to her desk. At last I was gonna find out what was going on.

"It's a handsomely drawn picture," she continued. "You have quite a talent."

"Thank you." This was going better than I'd expected.

"Of course, you understand why I took it away yesterday."

"Yeah. Cuz I should have been taking notes."

"Exactly. And I wanted you to think about that a little. So I postponed returning it to you."

Oh, brother! The stupid things adults did to teach us these "little lessons."

"However," she continued. "I did have another motive for holding on to your picture." Now she was making more sense. Sure. There had to be something going on other than that nutty reason she had just given.

"Mr. Owen, my son teaches art at West Hills Community College. He himself is a professional graphic designer, but he has an eye for all kinds of art. I wanted to show him your picture. I hope you don't mind."

"No. Not at all." This sure was a strange twist in the conversation.

"I know it was a bit presumptuous of me. I really was quite impressed with the drawing, but before telling you, I thought we should solicit an objective opinion, hear from a real, honest-to-goodness artist."

"Really? Well, what did he say?"

"He said you show a great deal of promise. He strongly encourages you to continue. May I ask what this is supposed to be?"

I was getting excited now. I told her my idea for the Arch-Ranger story. After I got going, I realized she might lose interest after hearing that it was meant to be part of a comic book. After all, teachers didn't usually like comics. They wanted their students to read "real literature."

But I was wrong. She still seemed interested. "And have you begun this comic?"

"Not yet."

"I suggest you begin as soon as possible. You have a gift. Don't let it go to waste. Don't procrastinate."

She was starting to sound like my Aunt Loureen now. Since Aunt Loureen was also a teacher, she used a lot of those same types of words, like *solicit* and *procrastinate*. But that wasn't the only similarity. Aunt Loureen was also a person who went out of her way to tell me how much she believed in me, even more than my parents did. Well, only a little more than my mom, but a lot more than my dad. I was starting to like Mrs. Pumpernickel. I could use another Aunt Loureen in my life, especially since I only saw her once in a while.

I still wasn't sure how good of a writer I would make because it didn't come naturally for me to use words like *solicit* and *procrastinate*. Oh sure, I knew what the words meant, but it never would have occurred to me to actually use them in a sentence. And yet, maybe in a comic book that wouldn't matter.

I decided to take Mrs. Pumpernickel's advice. Every day after school, before starting on my homework, I would draw a few panels of my Arch-Ranger story and fill in the talking bubbles with dialogue. Sometimes I got so excited about it that I even skipped a favorite TV show to draw an extra page.

The first person to see the comic was my dad, even though the story wasn't finished yet. He came into my room while I was at the desk, drawing.

"Son, I asked you two days ago to mow that front lawn after school."

"Sorry, Dad. I just forgot."

"That isn't an excuse, Son. We have an hour of daylight before the sun goes down. I want you to get out there right now."

"OK." I put my pencil down.

"What's that you're working on?"

"Aw … just a comic."

Dad picked up one of the pages. "You drew this yourself?"

"Yeah. I'm making a story out of it."

"Is this a school assignment?"

"No. I'm just messing around, just for fun." Dad was making me nervous. I had no idea how he was about to react.

"Not bad, Son. Not bad at all." I was relieved. It wasn't often that Dad complimented me. He continued. "I'm glad to see you developing a hobby. You know, I always thought you had a knack for writing."

Sometimes my teachers would show Mom and Dad my essays during open house. Mom usually said things like "How wonderful, Honey." Dad usually just grunted or nodded his head, so this was a treat, hearing him talk like he was proud of me.

"One of these days, you might just write a best-selling novel."

"I'm not ready for that," I said. "This is only a comic book."

"It's a start. Everyone starts somewhere. Your taste will change. Anyway, you better get cracking on that lawn."

"Sure, Dad."

A few years ago, Dad would have yelled at me for forgetting about the lawn. But he didn't yell much anymore, not since that weird day when Aunt Loureen had it out with him. And now he was complimenting me too. I sure was glad to see these kinds of changes in my dad. Most people just stay the way they are once they become adults. But hey, if my dad could change, anybody could, maybe even me. And somehow working on this comic was like a change since I'd never done anything like it before. It took discipline, and usually I was too lazy to do that kind of stuff. But it's strange. This project took more time and energy than any homework assignment, but I had so much fun, it didn't seem like work at all. I guess we only feel like we're working when people *make* us do things, like the lawn.

While I was in the garage getting the mower ready, I could hear Dad talking to Mom and my younger sister, Shelly, in the kitchen. He was telling them about my comic.

"I really was impressed. You should see it."

"Can I go get it?" Shelly asked in her obnoxious voice.

"Mike will let you read it when he's ready," Mom said gently.

"Well, Dad got to see it."

"That's enough, Shelly!" Dad said. Shelly was ten now, not as much of a brat as she used to be, but there were still times.

I finished the lawn as fast as I could, which wasn't too fast because whenever I did a sloppy job, Dad just sent me right back out to "do it right." I decided that someday when I had a house of my own, I would cut the lawn every other week instead of every week. I wouldn't want it to look so bad that the neighbors started complaining, but every other week was enough to keep it from looking horrible.

When I got back in my room, the comic pages were gone. Shelly! I darted into her room and burst the door open. There she was, reading it, the little creep.

"What's the big idea, stealing something from my room?"

"I wasn't stealing. I was just borrowing it."

"Give it back!"

"Can't I finish reading it first?"

"You can read it when I'm done with it."

"I wanna read it now!"

Annoying as Shelly could be, I suddenly realized that this was good news. The story was actually holding her interest. "You really like it?"

"I love it."

This surprised me because I figured that girls wouldn't care much for Arch-Ranger, especially at Shelly's age.

"It reminds me of my book about the Land of Lumis," she continued.

"Yeah, I did put it in a fantasy world, just to make it more interesting."

"But Lumis isn't make believe. It's a real place."

19

"I'm not so sure about that. But I'm glad you like the story so far. I'll let you read the rest when I'm done."

She was probably right about Lumis. In fact, deep down inside, I knew she was right. But it had been years since I had thought much about the ornament and that included thinking about the land it had supposedly come from. Yeah, I did think about her book a little to give me ideas for my own comic book fantasy world, but right now, make believe stories were a lot more exciting to me than true stories.

Two weeks later, the entire Arch-Ranger adventure was finished. It was meant to be the beginning of a series, so I didn't wrap up everything, but it was a start, the kind of story I would have loved reading if it had been written by someone else, a real author. And it was the kind of comic I would have pulled off a comic book store rack and bought. It had adventure, magic, and even a little romance. I figured if Shelly liked the adventure, other girls might like it also, but they would be guaranteed to like it if I added a love story plot. I didn't give the girlfriend to Arch-Ranger though; I gave it to one of Arch-Ranger's friends, a scared screw-up, like me. And I wrote romantic lines more easily than I thought I would, probably from rehearsing all those things I never had the guts to actually say to a girl.

The first person to read the completed version wasn't Shelly. It was Cliff. We were in my living room on a Saturday. It was two hours before the movie we were planning to see, and we had some extra time, so I took out the comic book and asked him to read it. I sat and watched him the whole time. He hardly ever looked up from the pages. Even when I offered him a snack, he just shook his head and continued reading. A few times he laughed. Part of it was meant to be funny, so I hoped he was laughing at the right part. It took him a half hour to read the whole story. When Cliff finally closed the last page, he stared at the cover without saying a word.

"Well?" I finally got the nerve to say. "What do you think?"

"I can't believe you wrote this, Mike. And I can't believe you drew it too."

"So you liked it?"

"It's one of the best comics I've ever read."

"You actually liked it?"

"Liked it? Mike, this is fantastic! You have to get this published. Send it to Marvel or DC. They'll take this in a minute."

I figured it probably wouldn't be that easy. Most publishing companies didn't even read your stuff unless it came through an agent. At least, that's what I'd heard. Besides, I was just a teenager. Who was gonna read something that a teenager wrote? But that wasn't important right now. He liked it! He honestly liked it! And from Cliff, that was no small praise. He was really picky about comics and movies. If he hated something, he went on and on. And he could tell you just exactly what was wrong with it.

"What was your favorite part?" I asked.

"Oh, gosh ... there were so many. Arch-Ranger himself is great. And that twist about the fountain of youth ... that was clever. I think my favorite character was Simon, the way he wanted to be brave like Arch-Ranger but couldn't." Suddenly Cliff sounded more serious. "Kind of like me."

"Kind of like me too." It was the first honest thing I had ever said. I guess writing honestly was causing me to speak honestly. Strange that such honesty could be part of a fantasy story since the first thing that comes to mind when you hear the word *fantasy* is *something untrue*.

"Mike, we need to get to a print shop and make about a hundred copies of this. Start showing it around at school. People will go nuts over it."

"You really think so?"

"Sure."

"A lot of high schoolers don't read comics."

"Yeah, people such as Ben don't like them. So what? I know about ten guys who will eat this up. And hey ... you need to get it copyrighted too."

"I don't know how to do that."

"Ask your folks or ask your social studies teacher. She'll know."

I was surprised that Cliff didn't know since he seemed to know just about everything else. Anyway, we didn't make a hundred copies, but we did make about fifteen. I gave the first one to Mrs. Pumpernickel, and Cliff handed out most of the others. A whole day went by before I heard from anybody. This made me anxious, but I knew I needed to give people time to actually sit down and read it. A lot of times, people say they're gonna read something, and it takes them forever to even get started. But as the days went by, the comments started coming in, and Cliff was right, a lot of guys really liked *Arch-Ranger*. Somehow it struck a chord, maybe because a lot of people think about courage and stuff like that. Even though Cliff wasn't popular, he knew a lot of the chess club and science club geeks. And each of them knew a few people who *weren't* geeks. Then there were the few copies I handed out myself, so in time, a pretty good variety of people actually got a hold of the comic. I didn't hear from any girls at first, probably because Cliff didn't know any girls to give it to, but the guys' comments were so good that I finally started to keep a list of them. They came from classmates, cross-country teammates, and a few casual friends.

"Hey, I didn't know you could draw!"

"Mike, your story was great!"

"Owen, where have you been keeping this hidden talent?"

"Owen, your story was rad!"

"Mike, way to go with *Arch-Ranger*!"

"Hey, Mike, got any more of those *Arch-Ranger* comics?"

"Come on, Owen, admit it. Somebody helped you. No way you made this thing up yourself."

"Hey, Owen! I heard about your comic, but every time I ask for one, that wheeler-dealer Cliff says that there are three guys waiting before me. Is he your agent or something? Can't you make more copies?"

"Mike, your story was sweet!" Everybody used that term *sweet* now. A few years ago it would have sounded like a strange description for a comic book. But now it was just the new term for *rad* even though people still used *rad* too.

But whatever the terms, the comments amounted to the same thing: *Arch-Ranger* was a hit, and not only from regular comic readers. Everybody seemed to like it, except Ben, and even Ben didn't hate it. With Ben, it just wasn't a big deal. With Ben, very little was ever a big deal.

It took a whole week for Mrs. Pumpernickel to talk to me, but she finally asked if I wanted to "chat about my artistic endeavors" one day after class.

I got the impression that she didn't like the story as much as my friends because she talked more about how well *written* it was than how well she *liked* it. But that was OK. The story was for kids, not adults, and she at least gave me some encouraging words. She started by telling me how to get it copyrighted. There wasn't much to it. All I had to do was fill out a two-sided form, send it into the Library of Congress with a twenty-dollar check, and that would be it. More importantly, she knew the name of a youth publisher who specialized in both novels and comics.

"Normally you would need an agent before they'd even consider looking at something like this," she said. "But it just so happens that I know a few people over there. You see, I'm a published author myself." She had a proud look on her face.

I was surprised. I always thought teachers did nothing but teach. It never occurred to me that they could do anything else.

"No fooling? What have you written?"

"Well, it wasn't much really. Nothing that made *The New York Times* best-seller list." She started chuckling and then stopped when she realized I wasn't laughing with her. I guess I should have laughed, just to be polite, but I didn't catch on that she was trying to be funny until it was too late.

Mrs. Pumpernickel continued. "But my novel *does* sell respectably. It's called *Precious Plains*: the story of a young lady who lives in the Midwest. It follows her through her first year at a new high school, her first dates, first slumber parties ..."

I tried really hard to act like I was interested, but I had never in my life heard of a more boring story.

"Well, anyway, Mr. Owen, they do know me there at Griffith Publications. Why don't I just make sure that a copy or two get to the right people?"

"That sure is nice of you, Mrs. Pumpernickel!"

"Now, now! It's my job ... inspiring our youth! After all, you are the future ... you and others like you ... In this world we have so many chances to make a difference. I must do my part as others around me ..."

She went on for a long time, and I stopped listening after a while, so I really can't tell you any more of what she said. But I did appreciate her.

The next day, I was waiting outside our homeroom door for the teacher to let us in. Ben was in the same homeroom, and he was waiting with me. Marla McIntire was not in my homeroom, so I was surprised to see her walk toward us, almost out of nowhere.

"Hi, Mike."

"Hey ..." I barely muttered. The expression on her face suggested that she had actually been looking for me, trying to hunt me down.

"I read your comic book. It was a lot of fun."

Fun? What did that mean? The book wasn't supposed to be fun. It was supposed to be ... Oh, who cared? Marla the Knockout was talking to me again. "Ah ... thanks. Glad you liked it."

"You know, Mike, while I was reading your story, I realized that we've been in the same social studies class all semester, and yet, I hardly know you."

"Yeah. I guess I don't know you too well either."

"Well, we should do something about that. You doing anything for lunch today?"

Ben answered for me when he saw I could hardly react. "He usually eats with me, but I think I can excuse him for the day." Ben looked like he was about to laugh.

Marla seemed to sense how shy I was. I had heard that sometimes certain girls got attracted to shy guys. Lucky for me, because I felt like an idiot being this shy and I didn't deserve a girl like Marla.

"Shall I meet you at the snack bar, Mike?"

"Sure, Marla ... Sure ... If I get in line first, I'll save you a place."

"Then it's a date." She giggled and walked away.

"Did you hear that, buddy? You may be about to have your first date. Don't screw it up for yourself. Try to talk to her."

"What do I talk about, Ben? You've been on dates. What do you say to girls?"

"Just talk about whatever interests you. Talk about your comic book."

"Yeah. She *does* seem to like it."

"Maybe. I think she just likes you. Girls are pretty good at pretending to like the things that guys do. She's trying to stroke your ego."

I wanted to believe that Marla liked my story. But when I really thought about it, it was actually a lot more exciting to think that she might just like me!

"Still," Ben said, "the comic is what got her attention."

"And you thought nothing would come of this comic," I kidded him.

"I never said that. I said I'm not into comics. But as far as comics go, yours is pretty good. It's at least drawn well."

Probably Ben didn't need stories about heroes because he *was* a hero. I guess it's hard to be impressed reading about something you can do yourself. Ben didn't use a bow or a sword like Archer, but he was certainly as brave as Archer. And he was brave enough to ask girls out. Ben already had a date for the school dance coming up.

"Hey, Ben! What was it like, the first time you asked a girl out? Were you scared?"

"Sure I was scared! Sometimes you just do things whether you're scared or not! Then it gets a little easier the next time. Try to ask her to the dance, Mike."

"Today? Ask her today?"

"Of course today! Why else do you think she's eating with you? She wants you to ask her to the dance, although with her, you never know. She might just ask you herself. But probably not. Girls like to be the ones asked. They don't like to do the asking."

"It sure would be easier if she did."

"Yeah? Well, that's probably not the way it's gonna come down, buddy."

"I don't know, Ben. I'm not ready to ask someone out."

"Come on, Mike. When will you ever be more ready? This one's being dumped on your lap. And she looks great. It could be worse. It could be some bowser asking you to have lunch with her. But this is Marla McIntire!"

"I don't have a license yet. I always figured my first date would be when I can drive."

"At the rate you're going, your first date will be shuffleboard at the retirement home. You can come with Jean and me. I'll drive the four of us. We'll double."

"But what if she says no?"

"Are you out of your mind? Didn't you see the way she was looking at you? Do you think she asked you to lunch because she needs help going over the menu? Hasn't she given you every signal on Earth? I mean, for Pete's sake, what are you waiting for? A tattoo with your name on it?"

"I guess she probably does like me."

"Probably?" Ben shook his head. "Yeah, probably a lot of girls like you, and probably you've been too stupid to notice. Remember that girl who always flirted with you back in sixth grade? The one you had a crush on, but you could barely even say two words to her?"

"Renee."

"Yeah! That's right! And when she moved away, you always wished you had said more."

"I know. You're right. I still think about her too, after all these years."

"OK. Well, do you also wanna be thinking about Marla five years from now, or do you wanna grow up this time and ask her out?"

I only got myself a soda from the snack bar because being around Marla made me feel too nervous to eat. Besides, I sometimes made a mess with food. And the last thing I wanted was to look like some slob.

We sat on a bench in the quad, near the open grass. Marla was eating a yogurt and some potato chips. She was dressed in black slacks and a red pullover sweater. I'd always thought Marla was pretty, but I hadn't actually spent more time thinking about her than any of the other hot-looking females. She sure had my attention now though, because unlike the others, this gorgeous thing was somehow interested in me!

It was easier to talk to her than I thought it would be, mostly because she did all the talking. In only a short time, I practically knew her life story — past, present, and future. She wanted to go to Stanford after graduation. She wanted to be a biochem major. She had two cousins, one in college, the other in junior high. Oh, yeah, and her folks were divorced.

"Has that been hard?" This may have been my first contribution toward the conversation — at least the first one I can remember.

"It's all fairly recent," Marla said. "Not enough time to tell. But it *has* been more peaceful since Dad moved out of the house. He was really strict."

I heard once that kids are strongly affected by their parents' divorces, whether they realize it or not. So I wondered if Marla was being honest with herself. But I had no idea since my parents seemed to be happy and I could never in a million years imagine them getting a divorce.

"Did your dad yell a lot?" I asked.

"No, not much. Just too many rules: curfews, dress codes, those sorts of things."

"My dad yells, but not as much as he used to."

"So," she said, changing the subject, "who are you taking to the dance next Friday?"

Wow! Ben was right! In fact, that idea of a tattoo with my name on it would have seemed more subtle. Why didn't she just ask me herself? She sure had no problem asking me to lunch. I guess lunch was a much different thing in Marla's mind than a dance. It was probably like Ben said: she wanted me to make the first move, even if she had to drag it out of me.

"Ah … well … I haven't asked anyone."

Marla had a sly look on her face …"You don't like dances?"

"Oh no, it's not that. I like them just fine … I guess … I haven't been to too many of them."

I had gone to a few dances before, stag. At each one, I spent the time with my fellow spineless friends, standing around the punch bowl, talking about football. All my friends but Ben, that is. Good ol' Ben was out there dancing and having a great time.

"Ah … are you going, Marla?"

"Of course," she smiled.

Suddenly I felt terrible. "Who's taking you?"

"I don't know yet."

That sounded better. "You haven't been asked?"

"Oh, I've been asked, by several …"

What a stupid question! Of course she'd been asked! I could think of a lot of girls who wouldn't be asked, but Marla sure wasn't one of them.

"So … I guess you're having trouble deciding, huh?"

"No. More like I'm waiting for the guy I'd really like to go with."

I could feel my adrenaline shooting around. We had talked about adrenaline in science class recently. I remember being bored hearing about body chemistry, but now I was feeling it! This was my chance. The door had been opened. Now or never! If I loused this up, I was gonna hate myself for the rest of the school year.

"Ah … well …" Great start! "Um … I was thinking …"

"Yes?" she said just as sweetly as she could.

"If, ah … I mean … We could … Or not … But maybe …"

"Yes, Mike?"

We were interrupted by the sound of laughter coming from the other side of the quad.

"Isn't that your friend over there?" Marla said.

Sure enough, poor Cliff was being bullied again. Couldn't they ever give that poor loser a break? This time it was Scott Pierce. Pierce kept tripping Cliff. Then, when Cliff stood up, Pierce tripped him again. Creative … Hmm … Maybe I could even help this time. Like I said before, Pierce wasn't one of the guys who scared me, and I'd always regretted not sticking up for Cliff that day in the locker room. But what if someone else came along to finish what Pierce was starting?

Enough people were gathering for this to become a big event. Anyway, Marla had asked me a question.

"Yeah. Poor guy. Not too many people seem to like him."

"Well, *you* like him, don't you?"

"Sure I do."

"Then go help him. He looks like he could use a friend about now."

I glanced around to see if I could find Ben. No luck this time. He'd probably finished his lunch early and gone to the library. What could I do? I really didn't wanna get involved, but if I didn't do something fast, Marla would see my cowardice, and she just might decide to accept one of her other dance offers. Why should she go to the dance with some meatball who can't even help his own friend? Was it worth the risk? Once you get into a fight, everything changes. People talk about it, and sooner or later somebody says, "I'll bet that Owen isn't so tough! I'll bet I could take him!" But I had to do it — not for Cliff, not really … for Marla!

Marla and I walked over together. *What would Arch-Ranger do?* I asked myself. *What would Arch-Ranger say?* Nothing! There *was* no Archer! OK, what would Ben say? There *was* a Ben. This *was* possible. I'd seen it! Others had done it! Others had shown courage! Time for me to do the same.

"Leave him alone, Pierce!" I was standing between them now. Cliff looked amazed. It probably took him a second or two to realize that this wasn't Ben. This was his other friend, the not-so-reliable one.

"Hey, get out of here, Owen!" Pierce said in a whiny voice which sounded a bit frightened. Already things were going well. I'd made the right decision.

"You don't have to be afraid of him, Cliff. He's mostly mouth, and he falls over as easily as you."

"Oh, look who's talking!" Pierce said. "The great artist! I didn't even like your stupid comic!"

"Yeah, well it helps if you learn how to read first."

Everyone laughed, and Pierce was looking embarrassed. I was proud of my snappy comeback. It was the kind of thing Ben would

29

have said, and I guess it came to me faster since these days I was in the habit of writing, which meant that I was thinking up clever words more than I used to.

"Why don't you mind your own business, Owen?" Pierce headed for Cliff again, probably to save face. I intercepted and tripped him. Everyone was laughing. Pierce just stood up silently.

"Oh! Oh! Is Cliff Reynolds in trouble again?" The familiar-sounding voice was coming from behind me. I turned and found myself staring straight at Doug DeWorken. Oh, man! That was it! My short-lived performance just had the life sucked out of it. I was gonna get creamed and right in front of Marla. My life was over.

"Hey, Reynolds! Don't ya ever get tired of people fighting your battles for ya?"

"Yeah," Pierce said. "And look who's defending him this time. Our school author!"

"Author?" DeWorken said, looking confused. "What are ya talkin' about?"

"Haven't you read that *Arch-Ranger* comic? Owen, here, is the author. He probably thinks he *is* Arch-Ranger! He probably thinks this is one of the big rescues."

Pierce had no idea how close he was to the truth. Not that truth was on his mind. It was meant only as a quick put-down. But he was on the right track, only kind of in reverse. Arch-Ranger was an idea born from a loathing of my own cowardice and my admiration of heroes like Ben. But at the moment, I *was* trying to act like Ben, only not for the purpose of being a real hero, rather to *look* like a hero. My whole motive was to impress a girl.

Anyway, because of Pierce's big mouth, DeWorken was no longer focused on Cliff. Instead, he moved closer to me. "I read that! You're the one who made up that story?"

"He sure is," Pierce said smugly.

It was hard to read DeWorken's face as he stared at me. He wasn't smiling and he wasn't angry. He didn't look like he wanted to cause trouble either. And he didn't look friendly. I guess he just didn't look any particular way at all. It seemed like hours were rushing by, even though only a half second or so had gone by. Finally, DeWorken spoke.

"I liked it!" DeWorken was extending his hand. "Good job, man! Good job!"

This was unbelievable. How could a day in high school possibly work out better than this?

A teacher came over to break up the commotion. The crowd slowly disappeared, and Cliff managed to get away peacefully without being hurt by Pierce or DeWorken. But Marla was still at my side.

"Well, Mike Owen, that was a wonderful thing you did."

"It wasn't so wonderful." I was acting modest, but I was also telling the truth. It wasn't wonderful at all. If DeWorken hadn't already read my story and somehow decided that he liked it, this would have been a whole different party. But Marla didn't know how I'd felt inside, and in her eyes, I was looking like quite the super-stud.

"It *was* wonderful," she said, reaching for my hand. "Now, then, are you going to ask me to that dance already?"

We both laughed, and all my shyness seemed to evaporate. "Say, Marla … I hear there's a dance next Friday."

"That's the rumor," she answered. "I'd love to."

Of course that day had gone as bad for poor Cliff as it had gone well for me. A few days later, after school, we were both in my bedroom cramming for an exam. The subject of Doug DeWorken came up. Evidently he was starting to hassle Cliff again, probably because he knew that the basketball team was having this week's pre-season game at another school tomorrow afternoon and Ben wouldn't be around.

"Ben isn't always going to be there to help me," Cliff said. "I need your help too."

Oh no! Just because I defended him one time, Cliff was maybe hoping I'd make a habit out of it. "Ah … well …"

"Relax, Mike. I'm not asking you to fight. I know you get just as scared as I do."

I didn't like hearing him say that, especially since I had called off Scott Pierce, but I couldn't really argue with him either. "What did you have in mind then?"

Cliff had an uncomfortable look in his eye. "Something drastic. But I've been thinking about it a lot lately."

31

"Thinking about what?"

"The ornament."

I felt a sudden sharp chill. Just hearing the word *ornament* yanked my mind back to a time I had tried hard to forget.

Cliff continued. "I thought I might just use that old Christmas ornament."

The ornament hadn't been used since seventh grade. I was scared then too because of all the stuff that had happened in sixth grade ... But Aunt Loureen said I should try it again since I was a year older. I did try and horrible things happened — things worse than my first adventure, things so terrible that I put the ornament away and never used it again. Someday I'll write about my second year with the ornament but not now because it has nothing to do with *this* story. Well, not much anyway.

For years, I had stopped thinking about the ornament. Sometimes it seemed like the whole thing had been a bad dream. Even Aunt Loureen finally begged off and quit bringing it up. In fact, I couldn't remember the last time she'd mentioned it. She must have been disappointed in me because she seemed to think that if the ornament was used "responsibly," I could learn a whole bunch of lessons from it. But Aunt Loureen had given up. She realized that I just couldn't handle that ornament anymore. The only one really good thing which had come from the whole ornament experience was a better relationship with my dad. I was grateful for that, but I figured I should quit while I was ahead. And like I already said, even when I borrowed ideas from *The Magic Ornament of Lumis* to use in my *Arch-Ranger* story, I was thinking of it only as a book, not focusing much on the belief that *The Magic Ornament of Lumis* might actually be a true story.

"Cliff, I haven't used the ornament in years."

"So? You still have it, don't you?"

"Yeah. But you remember all the trouble it's caused!"

"Not so much."

"Are you crazy? We all agreed to stop using it."

"That was mostly you and Ben who felt that way. I just went along with it."

"Have you forgotten all the messes we got into because of that thing? It's cursed!"

"It's not cursed. It sure helped you that time with Joe Blankenship."

"Yeah, it helps sometimes, but then something bad happens. You remember."

"The bad thing happens to someone else. And it has to be somebody nearby while you're making the wish."

More chills. Now he had me remembering all those stupid rules.

"You don't have to go with me," Cliff said. "So it won't affect you at all."

"I don't want it to affect *anybody*."

"Come on ..."

"Forget it, Cliff."

"When you used it on Joe Blankenship, the bad thing happened to him. It'll be the same for DeWorken."

"How do *you* know?"

"You told me! You said that if you made a wish against somebody, it counted as the good thing for you and the bad thing for him at the same time."

"Mostly, yeah. But there were also exceptions, stuff that took us by surprise. The ornament can't be trusted. It's too unpredictable. After Joe got hit by lightning, I was afraid he'd been killed. And I was lucky he didn't die."

"I'll make my wish carefully, just like you did. You wished that Joe would be hurt without dying, and that's why he didn't die."

"I know. But I'm telling you, that ornament is sneaky. It has an imagination, and it's full of tricks."

"I'm willing to take my chances."

"It isn't even Christmastime yet. The ornament won't work till it's Christmas."

"I saw some lights last night, right on my own street. Where do you think I got the idea from? Those lights reminded me of the ornament. Didn't you tell us the ornament considers it to be Christmas when the first light goes up on the first house?"

He was right. I hadn't noticed because it had been years since I'd paid much attention to early Christmas decorations or their relationship to the ornament. But he was right. It *was* November. Lights did start going up slowly in the month of November. Some people were so eager for Christmas, they couldn't even wait till after Thanksgiving.

"Come on, Mike. Be a pal. I'd do the same thing for you."

"Now don't start talking that way."

"I mean it. If the ornament were mine, I'd let you use it. I'd take turns. Is it still in your room?"

"Yeah. But it's hidden, and I'm not gonna give it to you."

It suddenly occurred to me that Cliff could make a wish right now if he wanted. The ornament was buried in my bottom dresser drawer, but you didn't have to see the ornament to make a wish. All you had to do was be in the same room. It was clear that Cliff had not yet thought of this, but I wished I hadn't admitted that the ornament was in my room. I had to get him out of there fast before he started getting ideas.

"Easy for you to say, Mike. You're not the one in trouble. You get to enjoy high school."

"I haven't enjoyed it all that much."

"Yeah? Well at least people like you."

"Not that many people."

"They do so! Especially with your Arch-Ranger comics. They've made you famous."

"What are you talking about? I haven't even heard from the publisher yet."

"I know. But the guys in school already like your book. You're already famous at school, and soon you'll be famous everywhere else."

"I wish that were true, Cliff, but I doubt it."

A strange expression came over Cliff's face. At first it looked like panic. Then he got happy and excited. Finally, he spoke slowly. "I don't doubt it, Mike. I don't doubt it at all. Because you just made a wish."

"Huh?"

"'I wish that were true.' Those were your exact words."

"Oh my God!" I sat down on the bed. How could I have been so stupid? Here we were again, after all those years of being careful. Even though I couldn't see it, and even though I only used the term *wish* as a figure of speech, the ornament could count that as an official wish if it wanted to. And I had just thought about the danger of wishing out loud in my room, just one second ago! I had been so worried about Cliff not saying anything that I forgot about my own big mouth!

"And what were you wishing to be true?" Cliff continued. "You were wishing to be famous, not only in high school, really famous!"

I just sat there, not saying a word.

"What are you worried about, Mike? Now you'll get your wish. Now you'll hear from the publisher."

I had wanted to hear from the publisher all on my own, because my comic book was good, not because of any magic.

"Let's just hope the ornament ignored me that time. It doesn't always grant the wish."

"Not always, but usually it does. Don't you want to be famous?"

"You're forgetting, Cliff, if I get my wish, something bad happens to you."

"Me?"

"Well, you're the only one in here with me!"

"Oh yeah!" All of a sudden, Cliff didn't look so happy anymore.

I shook my head. "It's starting all over again. I should have put this thing in the attic."

Most of the year, it was harmless keeping the ornament in my room, because most of the year it wasn't Christmastime. It used to be that I thought more about the ornament during Christmas and acted extra careful. But these last few years, I hardly remembered the ornament even at Christmas, and now I was wondering how many wishes I might have made by accident, how many things might have happened in my life that I wasn't relating to the ornament. Probably not too many because usually I was in my room by myself and I never talked to myself out loud. Even so, somebody would have needed to be in the room with me so that the bad thing could also happen. Still, I was really wondering now, especially since right now somebody *was* in the room with me: poor Cliff.

"Mike, you have to let me make a wish of my own."

"Why? So we can cause two problems instead of one?"

"Something bad is going to happen to me now. And I'll bet I know what it is. I'll bet DeWorken is planning on hassling me some more tomorrow."

"DeWorken would probably have hassled you anyway, ornament or not."

That didn't exactly cheer Cliff up.

"I need to make a wish more than ever now," he said. "I'm in trouble now, and only the ornament can get me out of it."

"Cliff, you don't understand. Even if it got you out of trouble, it would do it by causing *more* trouble. Why don't we continue this conversation outside?"

"Why? Afraid I'll make a wish?" Cliff had a sneaky look on his face. "I could make a wish right now if I want to, just like you did."

I didn't like the sound of this. "And then something bad will happen to *me*." I said. "Would you do that to a friend?"

"You just did it."

"Not on purpose."

Cliff sighed. "I know … I know."

I felt bad convincing him through friendship, especially since I had been such a lousy friend myself, but I could see that it worked. Cliff was thinking about what I said. Still, I'd be happier if he thought about it outside my bedroom door.

"Come on," I said, grabbing his arm. "Let's get out of this room before we really make a mess of things."

When we got into the living room, we saw Mom and Shelly giggling. Shelly looked up at me and tapped Mom on the shoulder. "Here he comes." Something was up.

"Mike," Mom said. "A letter came from a publisher. Come read it."

Oh, brother! This was happening awfully fast. It must have been the ornament, working already! Mrs. Pumpernickel had submitted my comic only a few days ago. Could they really have gotten to it so quickly? Didn't publishers have piles and piles of backed up manuscripts? Did they know Mrs. Pumpernickel so well that she talked them into putting my story ahead of the others? I was really nervous, the kind of nervous that I would have been even if I hadn't made the wish. I wanted my comic book published more than anything. I have to admit, I suddenly didn't care whether the ornament made me successful or not, just so long as this letter was an acceptance letter.

"You already read it, Mom?"

"I'm sorry. Normally I wouldn't think of opening your mail, but I was so excited ..."

"It's OK." I could tell it was good news. Otherwise they wouldn't be this happy.

Anyway, Shelly blurted it out before Mom even put the letter in my hand.

"They like your story! They wanna publish *Arch-Ranger*!"

"Shelly," Mom said. "I told you to let him read it for himself."

Good ol' Shelly! ... Oh well ... Who cared? They liked my book! They actually liked it!

"Read it out loud," Cliff said.

Sure enough, it was from Griffith Publications, the place Mrs. Pumpernickel had sent it to.

Dear Mr. Owen,

What fun it was to read the adventures of Arch-Ranger! Not only is the artwork handsome and original, we found the dialogue crisp and realistic. We would be honored to publish this piece in our comic book division. We want to offer you an advanced royalty check at the signing of our standard first-time contract ...

"How much?" Cliff asked before I could finish reading. "Do they say how much?"

"That's usually negotiated," Mom said. "Now, Michael, I hope you won't sign anything without first talking to our family attorney."

Attorney? Who cared about that right now? I was gonna be published. I was a writer! A real writer!

The rest of the letter gave me a phone number and e-mail so that I could contact the editor who had written me the letter and arrange an appointment. It also said something about how *Arch-Ranger* would be published as a one-time special story, but if it sold well, a whole comic series might be made out of the character. I could write some of the stories. Other people on their staff might write some too, but I would be paid a royalty every time Arch-Ranger was ever used, whether I wrote the story or not. This was too good to be true. Uh oh! That's right! It *was* too good to be true. And the timing ... I had already noticed how fishy the timing was. Now I *did* care again. I cared about whether this was the ornament or whether I did this on my own. Wait! Mom and Shelly had opened the mail right around the same time Cliff and I were in my room. They probably opened it before I made my wish, and even if they didn't, it took days for mail to come. Sure ... I had done this legitimately! Wait! What about all those times Aunt Loureen had explained how the ornament knew in advance what we would wish for and arranged stuff ahead of time? Now I was really confused. How could I ever know for sure? Hmm ... well maybe if Cliff got beat up by Doug DeWorken, that would tell me something. That, at least, would tell me if a bad thing followed a wish. No, even that wouldn't help because, like I already told Cliff, DeWorken was likely to beat him up anyway.

"Mike. I'm so proud of you," Mom said. "Wait till your father gets home! He'll probably want to take us all out to dinner tonight to celebrate."

I could just hear my dad going on and on about how I had gotten this because "I put my mind to it." I sure hoped that was how I got it.

"Can Dad take us to Burger King?" Shelly shouted out.

"I think a nicer restaurant is in order," Mom answered.

"The nicer restaurants don't taste as good as Burger King!"

"We'll let Mike decide, Honey. This is his night!"

***

Cliff looked frightened when it was finally time to go home to his own house. I walked him out the front door.

"Congratulations, Mike. I'm happy for you. Really, I am."

"You don't sound happy."

"Well, I'm just thinking about that bad thing. I have a feeling I'm going to be bumping into Doug DeWorken tomorrow at school."

"Maybe not. Some other bad thing might happen instead."

That didn't make him feel better either.

But anyway, now you know how I became famous at sixteen.

Cliff's Adventure with The Ornament

"Your taste will change."

That's what my dad had said about my writing the day he discovered my comic book. I found it hard to believe at the time. Of course, it must be obvious to you, the reader, that my dad was right: My taste *did* change over the years, and I eventually started writing real books, not just comic books. How could that not be obvious since you're reading Chapter Two of one of my books right now? Most of you are probably reading this one because you already read *The Dangerous Christmas Ornament*, the book I adapted from my sixth-grade diary.

Years later, in high school, after my comic book was published, I got so excited about writing that for the first time in years, I started keeping a diary again. That diary eventually became the book you're reading now.

Anyway, I'm bringing this up here in Chapter Two for an important reason. You may remember that in one of the chapters from *The Dangerous Christmas Ornament*, I wrote about some stuff that happened to Sonny and Shelly when they visited the old lady who still had her Christmas decorations up. I wasn't with them at the time, but I still put it in my book after talking to them and hearing about what had happened. I'm gonna be doing that kind of thing a lot more in *this* book. There'll be a lot of chapters from other people's points of view. To keep you from getting confused, everything that happens from the angle of my friends will be written in the third person, and whenever a chapter goes back to the first person, you can understand right away that it's me talking again. I'm probably breaking some kind of rule writing this way. I guess a book should either be written in the first person or the third, not both. But I figured I had to do it like that because so much goes on in this story, not only with me, but with a lot of my friends. Besides, it's my book, and I ought to be able to write it the way I want. I never cared much for stupid rules.

Obviously, before taking my personal diary notes and turning them into publishable text, I polished the wording a little. But I tried not to go overboard. As much as possible, I wanted to capture the way

I was talking while all the events of this story were actually happening, and I also wanted to reflect the way I was feeling inside. So I included such vernacular in the dialogue. I also used some in the narrative — not as much, but enough to make it still read a little bit like a diary, or at least the way my thoughts would have responded to things at the time I was keeping a diary. I did the same thing when sharing all the experiences from my friends' points of view. I tried to write their dialogue exactly as they talked, and I used similar informal narration to describe their train of thought. Again, I'm very aware that all of this seems to "turn literary etiquette on its head," as Aunt Loureen would put it. Maybe I'm being stubborn by writing this way. Sure, that's part of it. But also, once I got published, once I tasted a little success as a writer, it occurred to me that if my books became popular, the publishers would stick with me, rules or no rules. Besides, old rules were new rules at one time. So why feel an obligation toward them? After years of having to accept all those ornament rules, it was fun to create rules of my own, even if they only applied to my books.

But valid or not valid, that is the way this book will read. You'll see all kinds of slang and common vernacular, even in the narrative, except for those times when I'm writing about somebody who usually spoke with perfect grammar, like Cliff.

I'll be doing most of the third person writing much later in the story, but I want to begin doing just a little bit right now for two reasons: First, it will give you a chance to start getting used to it. But mostly, some stuff was going on with Cliff that I didn't know about at the time. Even when I was with him, unusual thoughts were going on in his head that he didn't share with me. It happened right after I got my letter of acceptance from Griffith Publishers. And so, it's time to make a switch and let you see things from Cliff's point of view:

***

Cliff looked through his sack lunch. He hated the food his mother packed, but there was no use complaining. If he complained, he heard a lecture about how taking your lunch is cheaper than using the cafeteria or the snack bar. Well, it did taste cheaper. That was certain! Today's entrée: a ham sandwich on bland wheat bread, a granola bar, and a messy orange that squirted out whenever he tried to peel it. Cliff looked across the quad to see if DeWorken was around. Mike had made his accidental ornament wish yesterday, and Cliff was expecting trouble, so much trouble he almost considered staying home. He finally decided to just bite the bullet and come to school. After all, if the ornament still had its old powers, something bad was bound to happen, and there would be no escaping it. The magical charm would get him whether he stayed home, went to school, or went someplace else. So he might as well go about his regular routine.

"Just my luck," Cliff said to himself. "The ornament makes things better for Mike and worse for me. I must be the world's worst jinx!"

"Hey!" It was Mike, arriving with his hamburger and Coke from the snack bar. Mike had it all: fame, a new girlfriend, even parents who let him eat the types of snacks he liked.

"Glad to see you're still willing to dine with us common people," Cliff joked. He meant for it to sound like harmless sarcasm, but Mike didn't seem to take it that way.

"Knock it off!"

"Touchy, touchy! You must feel good after Nichols' homeroom announcement."

Principal Nichols had spoken over the school intercom, telling all the students and faculty that Mike Owen had just received an acceptance letter from a publisher. Cliff was surprised to hear that the news had traveled about so fast.

"Valley View High is very proud today," the principal's message had loudly blasted over the speaker, "for one of our own students has pushed himself and excelled beautifully!"

"What did you do?" Cliff asked Mike, "Go to the principal's office first thing in the morning and brag?"

"Hey, I thought you said you were happy for me!"

"I am."

"Yeah? Well, it's starting to sound like sour grapes!"

"I'm only asking a question, for crying out loud!"

"Fine," Mike said, looking suspicious. "Fine. It's just a question. OK. Here's the answer. No, I did not go into the office bragging. I did tell Mrs. Pumpernickel during second period. She was very excited, and I think she must have told Mr. Nichols before homeroom period."

Cliff was feeling bad. At first he had honestly loved the *Arch-Ranger* comic, but after seeing how popular it made Mike, he *did* get jealous. He would never admit it to Mike, but he could admit it to himself. His jealousy was raging! Cliff wouldn't have felt so bad if he had a few things going for him the way they seemed to be going for everybody else. It's difficult to be happy for another when your own life is miserable. Ben was already a popular friend, and that was also a blow to his ego. Cliff *did* appreciate Ben, but he was also envious of Ben. At least Mike had been a more average friend, but now that was starting to change too. Mike had a date for the dance: Marla, one of the cutest, most stunning looking girls at school. Girls seldom paid any attention to Cliff unless they were laughing at him while some smart-mouthed guy insulted him or pushed him around. True, one of the girls in the chess club seemed to like him, but Cliff thought she was homely, so her admiration wasn't much of a compliment. As for the ones he *did* find attractive, they never gave him the time of day. Cliff had taken some solace in the fact that girls never seemed to pay attention to Mike either. All that changed after he circulated his *Arch-Ranger* comic. And when Cliff thought about how Mike had really accomplished this "special feat of hearing from a publisher" ... Well, it had to be the ornament — the ornament Mike wouldn't even share! Some friend! Cliff wasn't just jealous. He was angry ... angry and scared ... scared of what the ornament had cooked up for him!

And speaking of that ... Here he came, just as expected, the dreadful Doug DeWorken. The ornament seemed to be punctual as ever. Oh well! Maybe it was better this way. At least now he could get it over with. Sometimes worrying about a problem all day was worse than when the incident finally happened.

Much to Cliff's surprise, DeWorken ignored him and approached Mike instead. "How's it goin', Owen?"

Cliff could see that Mike was frightened, even though he tried not to let it show. "Hey, Doug!"

"Here's what I like ta see," DeWorken said in a jovial manner. "A man who knows how ta get in good with the principal."

Mike just grinned and shrugged his shoulders. DeWorken continued. "That Arch-Ranger dude is a wild idea! As good as any comic I've ever read!

"Thanks!"

Wow! Even the bullies liked him now! That comic had literally given Mike a whole new life. But then Cliff was hit with a more positive thought. He started wondering if Mike's new life might just spill over his way a little. After all, he was the one who had first helped Mike out by spreading copies of the comic all over school. And DeWorken liked the comic. Was it possible that he and DeWorken could actually share a common interest? If so, there might also be a chance of them getting along.

"It really is a great comic, isn't it?" Cliff said.

"I wasn't talkin' ta you, spaz! I'm tallkin' ta Owen."

Oh well. Nice try. The hope was gone almost as fast as it had come. Too bad. Too bad the *Arch-Ranger* story, with all of its charm and all of its lessons about caring for others, hadn't made a genuine impact upon DeWorken. Evidently, he liked the adventure without embracing the themes from the story. Instead, this was just another moment for Mike to feel great and for Cliff to feel humiliated.

"Hey, how come we don't see ya around more, Owen? Lots of us party together in the evenings. Ya should join us sometime."

"That would be great."

"Good. In fact, ya don't have ta wait for a party. Why don't ya come join us now for lunch?"

"Thanks, but I'm waiting for Marla."

"Marla McIntire?"

"Yeah."

DeWorken whistled. "Nice … real nice! Well, bring her with ya when she gets here. You're both welcome."

"Sure, Doug … thanks! Thanks a lot."

"Only ya might have ta find a babysitter for Reynolds. I don't think he would quite fit in. Know what I mean?" DeWorken laughed.

Mike smiled but didn't actually laugh. Cliff figured he was trying to look good for DeWorken without turning on his friend. That may have been what Mike was attempting, but in Cliff's mind, he failed miserably. A real friend wouldn't have even smiled. A real friend would have said something like "If Cliff isn't invited, then I'm not interested either." But Cliff should have known better than to expect that from Mike. Mike just didn't have those kinds of guts. He was good at writing about guts and courage, but he didn't seem to actually have any himself.

DeWorken returned to his social club. Mike was staring at the ground, probably ashamed of his behavior.

"So," Cliff said, "you're going to join them? You're actually going to do it?"

"Why shouldn't I?" Mike said defensively.

"I thought you didn't like DeWorken."

"I never said that. I don't even know him!"

"Well, you know he doesn't like me!"

"And that's *my* fault?"

"Oh sure," Cliff said. "Right … things have changed. You're a member of high society now!"

"Shut up, Cliff! He invited me, and I didn't wanna be rude. That's all! Quit making a big deal out of it!"

"I won't make a big deal out of it," Cliff said, standing up. "In fact, why don't I make it really easy for you? You won't have to leave me behind because I won't be eating with you anyway." He stood up and stormed off.

"Hey, Cliff, come on!" Mike shouted after him.

Cliff didn't look back. It wasn't as if this were the first time Mike had let him down, but it *was* the first time Cliff had ever complained, and he wasn't happy with himself. Why hadn't he just acted like a good sport the way he always used to? Probably because too many things were changing around him, changing quickly, and it was all due to that ornament.

Sitting by himself on a bench near the library, eating the last few bites of his dull lunch, Cliff eventually realized that the horrible conversation at least hinted at one ray of hope. DeWorken had failed to say anything about beating him up. Of course, DeWorken may not have felt the need to say anything, but that seemed unlikely. DeWorken enjoyed threatening people as much, if not more than, the actual fight itself. A better explanation was that DeWorken chose not to bully him in front of Mike since he seemed to respect Mike and wanted him as a new friend. Yes, probably DeWorken would still come after him, just as soon as they were alone, after school maybe. Of course, DeWorken never actually said it would be today. It could be anytime. But Cliff was assuming it would be today. For one thing, today was the day Ben would be gone. Also, the ornament usually made the "bad thing" happen rather quickly. Was it always within twenty-four hours of the wish? Cliff couldn't seem to remember. Most of the ornament's adventures had happened to Mike, not him. Cliff didn't recall off hand if Mike had ever mentioned a twenty-four-hour rule. He did remember that Mike's cat, Caligula, had been taken to the pound a few weeks after Mike's corresponding wish, but Caligula had *heard* that he was going to the pound long before it actually happened. So the bad news, at least, happened fast. But Cliff still couldn't remember if the bad news came one day after the wish or several days after the wish. It was all so long ago. Hmm ... this whole business about Mike joining a new click of friends — this was also bad news, similar to Caligula's bad news. Perhaps that was all the ornament was planning for today! Possibly that alone was the "bad thing"!

Anyway, for now, Cliff decided to finish out the lunch hour in the chess room. He decided that it might help to make him feel better.

***

"Wilson," Cliff said. "You're about to be checkmated. Just four more moves, I estimate."

Wilson shook his head. "I hate it when you do that. Can't you just beat me without announcing it all the time?"

"Sorry." But Cliff wasn't sorry. He desperately needed to prove his superiority to somebody. Here, in this room, he got a little respect. True, the chess club people were considered geeks and nerds, just like the science club people. But Cliff still enjoyed being a part of both groups. In this little refuge from the rest of the world, he could be himself. He was a brain, and around other brains it was OK to be a brain. Science, math, logic ... Cliff excelled at all of them ... better than that delinquent DeWorken ... better even than Ben, and Ben held a 3.7 average. And of course, he was much better than his former friend Mike.

His vocabulary was also superior, even though the increased vocabulary consisted primarily of science-related words. When the subject was something other than science, Cliff tried not to sound quite as sophisticated. Image was everything, and the many educated words made him sound more like a nerd. Even if he *was* one, he had no desire to contribute toward the stereotype, so he only talked intelligently when he was around other intelligent people, such as his math and science club peers. Yes, Cliff's words were kept under tight control. He decided when to use the big ones and when not to, with the exception of fearful situations. In such cases, all control went out the window, and he was at a complete loss for words — simple, fancy, or otherwise. This was a feature he seemed to share with Mike, being tongue-tied in the face of adversity. Still, Mike had found a way to let his gifts shine through his shyness, and now Cliff needed to discover a way of doing the same thing.

Thinking over his high school experiences to this point, Cliff wondered why he hadn't pursued closer friendships with his fellow nerds. Was it pride? A vain hope that he could climb above them? Or was it just habit, staying by the side of the two friends he had grown up with?

All at once, Cliff had an idea. It was a horrible idea, but a necessary idea. He figured out a way to get his hands on the ornament, or at least a possible way. If it worked, he could return to school tomorrow, ornament in hand, tucked away like a hidden weapon. But everything counted on his getting home fast. Ben couldn't drive him home today, and DeWorken might find him if he went and waited by the bus.

"Hey, Wilson, you have a car, don't you?"

Wilson looked up from the chess board and pushed the greasy, jelled, dark bangs away from his forehead. "You bet I do. A 1997 Honda."

A chess geek with a car. Who would have thought? Naturally, Cliff would never use the word *geek* out loud. He had no desire to hurt Wilson's feelings, even though other peers failed to show him the same courtesy.

"I was wondering if you could give me a ride home today."

"I thought Ben always drove you home."

"He has a basketball game this afternoon, so he can't."

"Sure. I'll give you a ride. Where are you during last period?"

"I have history with Peterson. Room 223."

"OK. Should I just come by and meet you there?"

"That would be perfect, Wilson. I certainly do appreciate it."

The ringing of the last period bell was a terrifying sound today because it might just signal a showdown with DeWorken. Everything depended on connecting with Wilson and getting off campus as fast as possible. If he pulled this off, he could meet DeWorken tomorrow instead, and they would be meeting on slightly different terms — terms DeWorken couldn't possibly imagine.

It worked. Wilson was waiting for him outside the classroom door just as he had promised. The parking lot wasn't far away, and DeWorken didn't seem to be around.

Cliff lived only a few blocks from Mike. Wilson dropped him off in front of his own house. Cliff made it look like he was going in, but as soon as Wilson drove off, Cliff moved away from the front porch. His mother was inside, and he didn't want her to know that he had been home. Time to commence with Operation Ornament. Time to take a casual stroll over to Mike's house.

Mrs. Owen opened the front door after Cliff rang it twice. She wasn't bad looking for a woman of her age. Cliff had noticed that for years.

"Good afternoon, Mrs. Owen."

"Well, hello there, Cliff," she said with a warm, friendly smile. "How are you?"

"Fine, ma'am."

"I'm afraid Mike isn't home yet. He's still at cross-country practice."

"Yes, I know. But he said I could use his computer." Cliff was lying through his teeth. He hadn't even seen Mike since lunchtime when they had that blowout. "You see, my own computer is busted."

"Busted?"

"Ah … well … my hard drive crashed."

It hadn't crashed. It was fine. And even if there *had* been a problem, Cliff was a wiz with computers. He would probably get a job as a computer programmer someday, and his personal computer was always in better shape than Mike's, upgraded with the latest software. But this was the best excuse Cliff could think of to get into Mike's room, and since he already knew that Mike was at cross-country (without Mike's mother needing to tell him), Cliff counted on a few good hours, far more time than he needed to get the job done. Cliff continued with his computer story. "I'll get it up and running again, but meanwhile, I've got a lot of homework to do. So Mike said I could use his computer."

Mrs. Owen looked a bit startled. This was the first time Cliff had ever come to the house without being certain that Mike was home. Cliff was uncomfortable around adults. If this had been anyone other than Mrs. Owen, he probably would have been too intimidated to try such a scheme. Mrs. Owen was a safe risk because Cliff knew she would be kind and welcoming.

"Well, of course, Cliff. Come right in."

Cliff followed her into the living room. So far, so good. If it had been *Mr.* Owen at the door instead of *Mrs.* Owen, Cliff wouldn't have tried it in a million years. Mike's dad was a real no-nonsense kind of man. He would have looked Cliff over suspiciously, and he would have asked obvious questions, such as "Doesn't the school library have computers?" or "Did my son actually give out his computer passwords? Is he that careless?" Yes, that was exactly what Mike's dad would have done. Luckily, he wasn't here. Luckily, he worked at an office all day.

"How about a snack before you get started?" Mrs. Owen said. "You must be hungry."

Yes, this visit was well-timed all right. Mr. Owen wouldn't have been offering a snack. Not that Cliff was about to take the snack. It's just that it was easier to pull off this caper in a friendly environment. "No, thank you. I'd better go ahead and get right to work."

"Are you sure? We have cookies and plenty to drink: juice, milk, Coke."

"That's all right. Thank you anyway."

Actually, Cliff was starving, especially after that miserable excuse for a lunch his mother had packed. But he already felt so guilty over what he was about to do that it didn't seem right to accept the snack. It would feel like he was stealing some food, along with the ornament.

Cliff knew this was a long shot. He knew that if Mike had half a brain, he'd have taken the ornament out of his room last night and hidden it somewhere else. On the other hand, Mike seemed pretty distracted over the publication news, and understandably so. Perhaps he was too busy feeling like a celebrity, and perhaps this made him forget about the ornament. Cliff was counting on it. Otherwise his chances of ever acquiring the ornament were next to nothing. He calculated the odds to be at least ninety-five to one.

Meanwhile, even if the ornament was still in the room, Mike had not told him *where* in the room. Of course, according to Cliff's understanding of the rules, he wouldn't have to actually find the ornament to make a wish. All he would have to do was be in the same room. But that would only work if somebody else was in the room with him, or in the same vicinity if they were outdoors. There always needed to be two people, and Cliff was counting on DeWorken being the second tomorrow at school so that the residue of his wish would somehow curse his nemesis.

He looked around … Lots of items. It could be anywhere. There were endless boxes piled in the closet. There was a desk with three small drawers and a dresser with three large drawers. And the bed was big too. Could Mike have hidden it under the bed? Not very likely. His mom would find it whenever she wanted to vacuum. Mothers usually did a thorough job with cleaning.

What about the drawers? They seemed like the last place Mike would hide the ornament because they were such easy, obvious places. On the other hand, they were also the easiest first places to check, and since Cliff had given himself enough time to check everything, he figured he might as well start with the easiest.

Nothing in the top drawer. Cliff checked the other two. *Well what do you know?* he said to himself, almost out loud, after opening the bottom drawer. *I don't believe this. He actually left it in his room after all. No wonder that dummy has so much trouble with the ornament. He's sloppy and he makes mistakes!*

There it was, under a pile of slacks and old sweaters. Cliff hadn't laid eyes on the ornament in years. He'd forgotten how beautiful this mysterious antique was, a genuine work of art, with a strangely shaped pink castle surrounded by a blue moat and white snow, all enclosed in a thick ornament-shaped glass which enabled it to function as both an ornament and a snow globe. Hard to believe that such a small, harmless-looking item could be filled with unspeakable power.

Cliff stuffed the ornament in his pocket. He had never expected to find it so quickly. If he left now, Mrs. Owen would realize that he hadn't really done any homework. Of course, he would be caught eventually anyway, just as soon as Mike looked for the ornament or as soon as his mom said something like "That was nice of you to let Cliff borrow your computer." That would sound very puzzling to Mike. Not only had he not made such a promise, but their last conversation had ended with bitterness. Mike would smell a rat and go to his drawer right away to see if the ornament was still there. Then he would come after him and ask what had happened to the ornament. Sure, Cliff knew he would get caught eventually. But that was all right. All he actually needed right now was time. So, for now, he should just do what he could to not look suspicious. He should actually sit down and use the computer. If he actually used it for at least an hour, he could probably go home, and probably things would stay calm for the rest of the day. Mike would come home, tired from cross-country practice, thinking about his new book or thinking about Marla. He wasn't going to think about Cliff and the ornament. Why should he? Why should he care?

Mike's computer was on. The screen saver showed the nine planets of the solar system. Mike was fascinated with outer space, but his interest was ignited only by science fiction. He knew very little about "science fact." Cliff moved the mouse across the pad. As the screen saver vanished, he stared at the different screen icons. Cliff really did need to do some homework, but it involved going on the Internet, and he did not have Mike's password. If Cliff wanted to, he could break the password. It would be a snap, but why add another trespass? Instead, he just used the word processor to get an early start on this week's English essay. When he was finished, he would put the file on a flash drive that he always carried on his keychain and then delete the file from Mike's hard drive.

One hour later, with the ornament stuffed away in his backpack,

Cliff walked out of the room. Caligula, the family cat, was standing outside the door, and Cliff was met with a very piercing stare. Cats always had haunting looks, but this one seemed especially chilling.

"Hello, Caligula!" Cliff reached down to pet him, but Caligula arched his back, hissed, and moved a few feet away.

The cat was some thirteen years old now. Cliff had been surprised to see him live that long, even though he had heard of cats who lived even longer, some of them up to twenty years!

Back when Cliff was in sixth grade, Mr. Owen decided he'd had enough of cats, and Cliff had been part of a vain attempt to spring Caligula from the pound. Later, Mike's Aunt Loureen talked Mr. Owen into changing his mind, so Caligula was rescued after all.

Mike had told him and Ben that Caligula could actually talk. This was evidently due to some ornament wish, but Mike was the only one who could hear him. From what Cliff recalled, Caligula did not especially enjoy talking to Mike, and Mike had promised not to instigate discussions any more.

Aside from parrots or cockatoos, Cliff wasn't sure he believed in talking animals, and those particular species weren't really talking anyway. They were trained to mimic certain tones and inflections, much the way a dog is trained to fetch a bone or roll over. This was not the same as an animal having any true conversation, and it was difficult for a science-minded person to imagine such a thing. But then, Cliff had certainly witnessed a lot of unexplained phenomena at the hands of the ornament, so he needed to keep an open mind. And right now, with Caligula staring him down, it did seem as if something intelligent was behind all that black and white fluff. Cliff had an unsettling suspicion that Caligula knew just exactly what he was up to. Oh well. He was still only a cat. What was there to be afraid of?

Cliff turned away from Caligula and went back into the living room to thank Mrs. Owen for her hospitality. She said he was welcome anytime and walked him to the front door. Cliff quickly headed home. Soon he would be safe. So far, so good!

***

Cliff opened his front door with a house key. No sooner had the door slammed shut behind him than he heard his mother's loud, mega-voice bellowing out from the kitchen. Cliff often wondered how such a small person could have such a large voice box. It seemed as though Mom had been born with nine-speaker Dolby Digital surround sound.

"Clifford! Where have you been?"

"At Mike's house!"

She walked out of the kitchen to meet him, her gray hair pulled back in a bun and an apron tied around her petite frame. Mom's aprons were always so clean that Cliff couldn't figure out why she even bothered wearing them. Obviously she never spilled things. In fact, she was clean to a fault. She even wiped the phone off every time somebody was done using it. Once, their phone had been off the hook all night until Cliff realized that Mom had dusted it off, accidentally leaving the rag on the receiver.

"I was worried," she said. "You should have told me where you were."

Cliff walked past her and threw his books down on the family room coffee table. "What were you worried about? I go to Mike's house a lot after school."

"Not since he started cross-country."

The older Cliff got, the more he was counting the days before he could graduate high school and flee to college. His mother annoyed him to no end. Cliff knew she cared about him, but that didn't make her seem any less intrusive. Mom sat down next to him on the sofa. He could see she wasn't about to drop this matter.

"Didn't Mike have cross-country practice today?"

Cliff almost said no just to shut her up, but he decided it would be better not to compound the lie.

"Yeah, he had it, but I needed to use his computer."

"What's wrong with *your* computer?"

"Nothing."

"Then why did you need to use Mike's computer?"

Always twenty questions with her. Oh well. Now he would need to compound the lie after all. "I was working on Mike's computer as a favor for him. I was installing a new program."

This was a different story than the one he had given Mike's

mother. Inconsistent lying was a bad idea because the people you lied to could always compare notes later. But what else could he do? Unlike Mrs. Owen, Mom lived here. Cliff had worked on his own computer until late last night, and Mom knew it wasn't broken. So he would still lie, but it had to be a variation of the lie.

"You were there while Mike wasn't home? How did you get in?"

"His mom let me in." Cliff reached for some butterscotch candy from a glass dish on the coffee table.

"Put that down! You'll spoil your dinner! How *is* Mrs. Owen? I haven't seen her in a while."

"She's fine."

"And how's little Shelly?"

"Fine."

"You saw her there?"

"No. She wasn't home."

"Then how do you know she's fine?"

"She just is. Mom, I need to get started on my homework."

Safe behind the walls of his room, Cliff took out the ornament, held it up, and started talking in a low voice so that his mother wouldn't overhear anything. "Hi, Ornament."

Cliff put the ornament down. This was ridiculous! What a way to start, saying hello to a Christmas ornament. If only those magic adventures hadn't taken place so long ago, if only they had been more recent, he might have found it easier to maintain his belief. Interesting how the passage of time makes it more difficult to trust that supernatural events were truly witnessed. But Cliff knew he hadn't hallucinated. The events had indeed taken place — long ago, perhaps, but definite happenstances nevertheless. And so, he needed to communicate his wish, and he wanted to do it in as polite a manner as possible. This entity inside, whatever it was, could be quite crafty. No sense getting on its bad side.

"Oh well. Let me start again. Greetings! Merry Christmas, Ornament, or whoever it is that lives inside. I don't know if you remember me. I'm Cliff. You know … Mike's friend. He told me once that you weren't just an object, that you actually think and hear. That's why I'm talking to you … or both of you. I guess there's really two of you inside … two angels … and you're trapped. Right? You can't get out. And one of you is good, and one of you is evil. Umm … well … to the bad one, I mean no disrespect. I hope you won't feel like you have to do something menacing to me just because I called you evil. Actually, if I'm recalling correctly, Mike said something about how it's really only one person now. You *were* two, but your personalities merged into one … Something like that. It's rather confusing because I don't remember everything Mike told me. It was a long time ago. The only thing I remember for sure is that it sounded confusing even when it was explained. I'm fairly skilled at following scientific explanations, but Mike didn't offer one. He just told me some sort of a backstory. I do know this: I know I need to be careful before I make a wish. So … all right … here goes … My wish … I mean … I realize I can't make it right now. I know I have to be with another person, but I thought it might be best to place my request at this juncture. That way, you'll have some time to think it over. Do you remember how you assisted Mike against a classmate named Joe Blankenship back in sixth grade? I'd be grateful if you could produce a similar situation for me, and I'd appreciate it if you could do it to Doug DeWorken. I imagine you already know him because you're an angel … Or you were once an angel. But just in case you don't know him, he's a bad sort. He bullies people. And he's a great deal bigger than me. I'm not much of a fighter. I've always been more into studying than sports or any other physical workouts. So I really need some type of advantage. I'm sure you understand. I'm not suggesting that you have to hit him with lightning as you did with Joe. That only got Mike into trouble anyway. And I don't want DeWorken dead … Well, sometimes I do, just to be perfectly honest. But I realize that would be wrong. Just … well … Could you think of some way to get him off my back so that he never bothers me again? But he should stay healthy. Please refrain from making him ill or blind or deaf or crippled. I know … I know I'm placing kind of a tall order. But you *do* have until tomorrow to come up with something because tomorrow I'm taking you to school with me. I'll keep you hidden in my pocket just as Mike used to do, or perhaps my backpack would work better. If you could do this favor for me, you would have my gratitude. I might even be able to think of a way to get you out of that glass trap. I'm fairly skilled at solving problems. Well … I suppose if you're an angel, or two angels, my feeble abilities wouldn't mean much. Just wanted to make the offer anyway."

***

Cliff's mom made better dinners than lunches. There were lamb chops, baked potatoes with butter and sour cream, and tossed green salad.

His mom always sat directly across the table, where she could interrogate him better. "Clifford, have some milk."

"The water is fine."

"Milk is good for you."

They'd had this conversation for the last fifteen years, or at least ten that Cliff could remember. And although he couldn't recall the toddler years, there was little doubt that Mom had told him all about milk being good for him. Even as a newborn infant, he had probably heard about the nutritional value of milk, despite the fact that, in those days, milk was all he could consume anyway. And tonight, Mom still seemed to think that they were discussing milk for the very first time!

Mom was lonely. Dad had moved out when Cliff was in the seventh grade. He wasn't too happy to see them split up, but Dad was always so quiet anyway, what difference did it make? Of course, Cliff could hardly blame his dad for not talking. Around Mom, who could get a word in edgewise? Cliff himself had long since learned to simply shut down while she talked, offering only minimal words, grunts, and gestures to pretend he was interested.

"The water is fine," Cliff said a second time, or at least, the second time that night.

"Uncle Fred called today before you got home. He said to tell you 'hi' and that he was sorry he missed you."

"Hmm."

"Your shirt is torn. Leave it in my sowing room before you go to bed."

"All right."

"How was school today?"

"Fine."

"Are you going to that dance?"

"No."

"Why not?"

"I don't like dances."

"Oh, they're lots of fun. And I'm sure there are many young ladies who would be delighted to go with you."

"Right."

"Of course they would. You're a very handsome young man, Cliff. You should get out more."

I would if I had some place to go, Cliff said to himself. But he would never say a thing like that out loud.

"Did you hear about that Texas flood in the news?"

"No."

"It's been in all the papers and all the TV news shows ... and on the radio."

"Hmm."

"Of course, I listen to the radio less than I used to. Jake Dolan's talk show used to be entertaining, but the man has turned so crass!"

"Uh huh."

"Of course, Dr. Elwood does an informative show."

"Yeah."

"I had lunch with Fran today."

"Hmm."

"Her last doctor visit wasn't good."

"Oh ... that's too bad."

"It might be her gallbladder this time."

"Hmm."

The kitchen phone rang, and Mom darted out of her chair to get it. Cliff wished she would just let the answering machine catch the phone once in a while, but Mom was not about to miss a chance to have a conversation, not even with solicitors. She never bought anything. Instead, she went on and on about how she couldn't afford whatever they wanted to sell her, and she seemed to enjoy every minute of it.

But this time, it wasn't a solicitor. "Cliff … Mike wants to talk to you." The kitchen phone, unlike the living room phone, was a remote. She handed it to Cliff.

Oh, boy! Either an apology about lunchtime or the third degree about being at his house, in his room. Cliff walked into the living room, but he knew his mother could still hear him.

"Hello."

"All right, what did you do with it?"

"I don't know what you're talking about."

"You know what I'm talking about, all right! What did you do with the ornament?"

"What's wrong? You lose it or something?"

"Look, Cliff, who do you think you're talking to?"

"Somebody who used to be a friend."

"Stop changing the subject and stop feeling sorry for yourself! I want that ornament!"

"Hey don't blame me just because you lose things!"

"I know you were at my house. And what was this big lie you told my mom about needing to use my computer? I never said you could use it. I never said you could use anything! And you didn't need to use it! My computer is a Fred Flintstone computer compared to yours. Now level with me! You were scrounging around for the ornament, weren't you?"

Cliff had no choice but to keep lying, at least until tomorrow — at least until he could take care of Doug DeWorken. "I made up the part about using your computer because I was angry about what happened during lunch hour. I was planning to remove that RTS game I gave you for your birthday. But I changed my mind and decided not to, and I went back home. That's all."

"Just how stupid do you think I am?"

"If I took the time to answer that, I'd run up a big phone bill!"

"Yesterday you asked for permission to use the ornament, and you knew it was in my room."

"I didn't know that at all. I figured you would have hidden it somewhere else by now."

"You have it."

"No, I don't, and you can't prove it!"

"How about if I drop by your house?"

"Mike, even if I did take the ornament, don't you think I would be smart enough to hide it in a place nobody could find? And I didn't take it anyway, so come on over if you wish. I assure you, it's a waste of time."

"Now you listen to me, Cliff … If you try anything with that ornament, anything at all …"

"Mike, I don't think this conversation is getting us anyplace. Goodbye!"

Cliff returned to the dinner table.

"What was that all about, Clifford?"

"Nothing, Mom."

"Are you and Mike having a problem?"

"No, Mom."

"Then what?"

"Nothing, Mom. Everything's fine, Mom."

***

First period was over, and Cliff was on his way to chemistry. He had taken the bus to school. Usually Ben came by the house to pick him up and drive him over, but Cliff knew Mike would be with him, so he pretended he wasn't ready yet, stayed in his room, and had his mother tell them he was taking the bus.

The ornament was in his backpack, and Mike would search him for sure just as soon as they bumped into each other. Cliff was beginning to think that he might need to take care of DeWorken earlier than he had intended. Originally, he was planning on catching DeWorken alone for a minute after school. He didn't want a big commotion, such as the one Mike had with Joe Blankenship. On that day, practically the entire sixth grade had known about the fight and gathered around to watch. Facing DeWorken would be terrifying enough without having to face him in front of a crowd. But the situation with Mike was complicating matters. He couldn't risk Mike getting the ornament away from him before confronting DeWorken.

Oh no! Too late! Mike had spotted him! Strange turn of events. Never in his life would Cliff have predicted a desire to run into DeWorken before running into his own friend. Mike moved closer. They were standing by some bushes along the sidewalk.

"Thanks for hanging up on me last night."

"Thanks for the attitude you've been sporting lately."

"Where is it? In your backpack?"

"No."

"No? OK, let's have a look. Hand me your backpack."

"Since when do I take orders from you?"

"Let me have it, Cliff!"

"Or what? Are you going to beat up on me too, Mike? Are you going start acting like all the others?"

Mike seemed to be taken aback by the remark. His voice softened. "I just want my ornament."

"I said it isn't here."

"Then you won't mind me looking through your backpack, will you?" Mike started pulling on the backpack.

Cliff pushed him away, taking Mike by surprise. "I may be afraid of a lot of people, but I'm sure not afraid of you!"

Mike stood silently. He didn't look scared, just ashamed. Mike hated bullies as much as Cliff did, and Cliff could see that he didn't want to behave like one.

"Cliff, I'm not trying to start a fight."

"That's smart of you, Mike. How will it look if the author of Arch-Ranger the Hero starts picking on his nerd friend?"

Mike seemed lost in thought. Finally, he said, "Promise me you'll return the ornament when you're finished."

Cliff started to respond, but Mike interrupted. "Don't lie anymore! I'm not buying it for a second! We both know what's going on here. When you're done with DeWorken, return the ornament to me. … OK? "

Cliff slowly nodded his head.

***

PE was over. Cliff hated PE, but today they just played volleyball, and he wasn't quite as terrible at volleyball as he was with other games. DeWorken didn't take PE because he was on the football team, but he did always come by the locker room around this time. A few of his friends were in Cliff's PE class, and lunch hour followed, so DeWorken would wander over to the gym locker room to meet his pals. The first few times it happened, he would also take a moment to slam Cliff into a locker. That unpleasant little ritual didn't occur anymore because every day Cliff showered and dressed as fast as possible, then scooted out of the locker room before DeWorken arrived.

But today he was waiting for DeWorken. DeWorken would be coming for his friends, and he would be coming alone. Cliff was all dressed and cleaned up from PE. He sat on an outdoor bench close to the locker room entrance and waited for DeWorken to wander by.

There he was, off in the distance, and he didn't see Cliff yet. The ornament was still in his backpack. Cliff realized that the ornament could exercise its option to not grant a wish. But if this worked for Mike, why wouldn't it work for him? Of course, not everything worked for Mike. It hadn't worked when they tried to get Caligula out of the pound. He got out eventually, but no thanks to the ornament.

"OK, Ornament, this is my wish. I wish for you to recall everything I said to you yesterday up in my room. Please grant me my wish about Doug DeWorken and please hurry."

Cliff felt he had to come up with a way to lure DeWorken over. Maybe he wouldn't need to. Maybe DeWorken would just come over on his own to hit Cliff quickly, one for the road. But in case he was in a hurry to find his friends and grab his lunch, Cliff needed a backup plan. Cliff was under the impression that the ornament would only grant his wish if he and DeWorken were in the middle of an actual conflict. After all, there were many people outside right now, although nobody was paying attention to him. Why would DeWorken be the recipient of the ornament's "bad thing" if he wasn't the closest one to Cliff at the time? Cliff knew this didn't *necessarily* need to happen, as that particular situation had never been articulated as an actual ornament rule. Perhaps the ornament would grant his wish the moment DeWorken even looked at him, but in Cliff's mind, Mike's wish against Joe Blankenship served as a type of template. In their case, Mike and Joe were actually in the middle of a conflict when the ornament's power kicked in. As for the present moment, Cliff's wish had already been spoken, and nothing had yet happened. Cliff wanted to cover all the bases, so if something didn't happen fast, he would operate on his template theory and provoke DeWorken. This would not be easy. It would be out of character, although occasionally, when Ben was around, Cliff did feel free to act a little braver.

Here he came. It was now or never.

"Hey, DeWorken!"

DeWorken stopped short, looking around.

"Over here!" Cliff shouted.

They were facing each other now. DeWorken formed a devious smile and moved toward the bench. Other people were walking by, but nobody seemed to be paying attention, probably because they were all anxious to hit the snack bar. Cliff had planned this well.

"You talkin' ta me, Reynolds?"

Nothing was happening. Time to provoke him. Time to get cocky!

"Where were you yesterday, DeWorken? I was waiting for you after school."

DeWorken's jaw seemed to drop open. "*You* were waitin' for *me*? Could I be hard of hearing? *You* were waitin' for *me*?"

Cliff nodded his head.

"Sure ya were. And I'm the King of all England."

"King of England? England is ruled by a queen, and I'll bet you couldn't even locate England on a map, you big, stupid oaf!"

DeWorken's face turned cold and stony. His voice lowered. "What did ya say?"

"Why didn't you show up, DeWorken? You bragged the day before about it. You chicken or something?"

DeWorken took another step forward. "Now, Reynolds, ya must know that I have to kill ya now. Ya must know that. And gee, it looks like your bodyguard ain't around today." DeWorken grabbed him by the collar. "Time to go huntin'. It's spaz season. Say it again, spaz! Say it again, how I'm chicken!"

Nothing was happening. The ornament was deserting him. But Cliff still felt good for some crazy reason. It was liberating to speak up once in a while.

"Say it again, Reynolds. Say it again, ya four-eyed, freckled-faced freak!"

And then it happened. DeWorken instantly vanished from his sight as Cliff felt the pressure released from his neck. It happened without any lightning. In fact, it happened without any sounds at all, without any fanfare at all. But it happened just the same.

"Hey! Hey, what's goin' on here!"

The voice was DeWorken's, but Cliff couldn't see him. And the voice had an unusual quality, a different kind of tone and volume, almost as though it were coming from somebody's Walkman radio. Where had he gone? Cliff started to look around.

"What did ya do? Hey, what did ya do?"

Could DeWorken have turned invisible? No, if that were all that had happened, he would still have his hand on Cliff's collar. Cliff was excited and relieved at the same time. *So,* he said to himself, *my bodyguard wasn't with me? If you only knew. I had the best bodyguard money can buy!*

"Reynolds! Hey, Reynolds!"

Where was he? Something had happened to him. But what? This was eerie!

"Reynolds!"

That voice. Where was the voice? And then he saw him. DeWorken hadn't gone anywhere after all. He was still standing in front of Cliff, only he had shrunk. Cliff was looking down upon a miniature Doug DeWorken, no more than six inches tall, if even that high. Aside from the leprechaun-type size, he looked exactly the same, and he even wore the same clothes, shrunken proportionately. Cliff was about to burst out laughing, but he didn't want to draw attention to himself, especially since DeWorken's buds would be coming out of the locker room at any time.

"Ya spaz! What did ya do? I'll kill ya! I'll kill ya!"

Oddly enough, those still sounded like menacing words, despite the obvious irony of the situation. Probably the words were just triggering a familiar reaction. He might be a small DeWorken, but he was still DeWorken. Maybe DeWorken was using his usual threatening lingo because he was in shock. Maybe he was so confused he wasn't quite fathoming the situation. Cliff picked him up.

"Put me down, ya little creep!"

"*I'm* the little creep?" Cliff chuckled. "*I* am?"

"I don't know what ya did, but I'm gonna kill ya for it. Ya hear me? I'm gonna kill ya!"

"You sure talk tough."

"What did ya do? Huh? Tell me! Oh, man, you're in trouble! You're in so much trouble!"

"You know something, DeWorken? I have a feeling that from now on, you and I are going get along just fine."

Amidst many miniature shouts and protests, Cliff stuffed DeWorken in his backpack, making sure to put him in a separate pouch from the ornament and also making sure that that the pouch was located in a spot where the tiny voice would not carry. DeWorken was so small now that hopefully the pouch itself would count as a separate room and he would not be able to accidentally make a wish.

After putting him inside, Cliff realized he needed to unzip the pouch ever so slightly to avoid any suffocation. Then Cliff moved away from the gymnasium before DeWorken's friends came outside and headed for the main quad. For once, he would enjoy his lunch. DeWorken and his friends were not going to be eating together today.

Chapter Three

Hints from the Other World

"Mr. Owen. They're ready to see you now."

It was the first time I'd ever been called "Mr. Owen" by anyone other than a teacher or school principal. She was a pretty secretary, sitting in a plush office, the office of Griffith Publications.

My dad had driven me over, but I asked if he would mind waiting down in the car. It seemed more grown up to be in here without my dad. Dad said he understood, but he still warned me that they might try to take advantage of a teen and that if he were with me, I could probably get a better deal. I said I still wanted to go by myself, so Dad just warned me again to ask lots of questions about money and agents and not to quickly sign anything. But I wanted to sign everything. I wanted to get this over with fast and come out of the office saying to myself *I'm a published writer!*

My folks had offered to get our family attorney to go with me, but he wasn't available for a few weeks, and I was really too excited to let things drag out. My mom kept trying to talk me into waiting, but Dad finally said to her, "He's old enough to make his own decisions."

The secretary took me into the editor's office. Three people were inside: a younger woman dressed in a light blue matching dress suit and two middle-aged men in dark business suits. The larger man, a bald guy with a mustache, sat behind a desk, holding a burning pipe. He put the pipe down, stood up with a warm smile, and moved from behind the desk. "Well, well, Mike Owen. What a pleasure to meet you face to face." He shook my hand with a tight grip. "I'm Brad Jensen, editor of Griffith Publications, and these are my two assistant editors, Phil Madison and Lisa Mason."

"Hi," I said.

"Folks, I want you to take a good look at this young man. Because I think he's going places. Indeed, I do! There's talent coming out of his ears!"

I shook hands with the two assistants, and they invited me to sit down in a comfortable leather seat. There were all kinds of pictures on the walls, blown-up covers of popular novels. There was also a lot of weird sculpture in the room and figurines of certain comic book super heroes.

Mr. Jensen went back behind his desk and picked up the pipe again. His desk looked like it was made of polished redwood. "*Arch-Ranger*," he said. "A simple but extremely profound tale. Well-written, well-drawn. It needs very little work, and I don't usually say that to a writer."

"No, he doesn't," the lady added. "I can vouch for that."

They all laughed. I laughed along with them because it seemed like a good idea, not because I particularly found the remark funny. I didn't wanna repeat the mistake I'd made when Mrs. Pumpernickel made her little stab at humor.

Mr. Jensen continued. "Well, Mike, you read the letter we sent you, and that pretty much covers it all. I have here on my desk a contract for you to look over. You can read through it right now or take it home and bring it back."

I wasn't about to take it home. If I did, my parents would find something wrong with it and spoil the whole thing. I wasn't sure what they would find, but they would definitely find something, some little clause that didn't sit well with them. I had zero doubt.

"I think you'll find it a pretty standard contract," Mr. Jensen continued. "We'd like to publish *Arch-Ranger* immediately, get it out long before Christmas. Since you already did all the drawings and layout, this can be done quite easily. We're offering you an advance royalty of one thousand dollars and, after that, ten percent of all sales. What do you say?"

The thousand dollars sounded great. The rest of it didn't sound so hot. "Just ten percent?"

"Ten percent is standard for a first-time writer."

"I see." That sounded fishy to me. I should have asked Mrs. Pumpernickel ahead of time how much to expect. Why hadn't I thought of that? Maybe ten percent *was* standard. I didn't know. It seemed kind of chintzy, but how should I know?

"Can I ask a few questions first? Is that OK?"

"Of course," Mr. Jensen said, still sounding very friendly. "We want you to feel comfortable. Ask away!"

"Ah ... OK ... Well ... ah ... first of all, ten percent doesn't sound like a lot of money."

Everyone in the room nodded their heads as though they were expecting me to continue pursuing this.

"I understand, Mike. I entirely understand. On a first glance, it does seem slim. But look at it this way. We're the ones taking all the financial risk. Although I absolutely love your story and don't have the slightest doubt that it will sell, nothing is ever certain. Supposing the comic didn't make money? You wouldn't be out a dime, but we would lose our shirts. You did provide the creativity, and that *is* the most important part, but all the risk is ours. That's why the primary profit is ours too. Now, if this first comic is a success, then we all go back to the table and perhaps next time we give you more — like, say ... fifty percent. But for now, ten is more than appropriate."

"I guess that makes sense."

"Well, it was a fair question, Mike, a very fair question. But you understand where I'm coming from, don't you?"

"Yeah. Sure."

"Great! Good enough. Other questions?"

I was a little more nervous asking this next one. "Um ... yeah ... A lot of people keep telling me that I shouldn't sign anything without an agent."

Jensen grinned at his associates. I was starting to feel weird for bringing this up.

"You can get an agent if you prefer. But let me tell you something. This is a good contract we're offering you. If you like, bring in an agent. He can wheel and deal all he wants, but you know what our final offer will still be? Ten percent! And then you'll have to give your agent fifteen percent of the ten we gave you."

"I see ... I guess there isn't much point in having an agent then."

"Well, some people still prefer to use them. But if you ask me, no, there isn't much of a point. Not really. But the choice is yours."

I wasn't sure how much I trusted these guys. I don't mean that I thought they were outright crooks. They had a legitimate business. This much I knew. Griffith Publications had been putting out comic books and best-selling novels for years. I would be crazy not to sign with them! Probably an agent *could* get me a better contract. At least, that's what my instincts told me. That's the part they weren't being straight about. But I wasn't sure I cared that much about the money anyway. I was really asking those questions to get Dad off my back, just so I could tell him I asked. And I knew I didn't wanna delay this. The sooner I signed the contract, the sooner my story would get published.

"OK. I'm ready to sign."

Mr. Jensen got up out of his chair and shook my hand again. "Wonderful, Mike. Wonderful. I don't believe you'll be sorry."

***

I was so excited; I could hardly eat any dinner that evening. I wanted to call Cliff and tell him about my time with the publisher, but he was acting so weird lately I figured he wouldn't wanna hear. Oh well … There were plenty of other friends who *would* be interested, new ones as well as old.

"Can I have a free copy?" Shelly asked from across the dinner table.

"They *did* say that I would get a few complimentary copies," I answered. "So, why not?"

"I wish you'd waited for our attorney," Mom said.

How lucky that the ornament wasn't in my pocket when she said that. I might have been whisked back through time, unable to sign the contract until Marvin, the family lawyer, had a free moment.

"It's a standard contract, Mom."

"So they say."

"I'll ask Mrs. Pumpernickel at school tomorrow. She'll know."

"She may know. But you already signed it."

"I'm sure she'll agree with what they told me. She knows them. She's the one who showed them my book in the first place."

The doorbell rang. Mom got up to answer it.

"Pesky, miserable solicitors," Dad mumbled. "They never leave you alone, not even at dinnertime."

"Mike, it's for you! Cliff is here!"

I was actually glad to hear this, glad Cliff was still speaking to me. I moseyed on over to the front door as Mom returned to the table.

"Hey," I said.

Cliff pulled the ornament out of his pocket and handed it to me. "Merry Christmas."

"Thanks … Ah … well … here. Come on in."

"I don't have time. I need to get home."

"So what happened?"

"Nothing happened."

"Come on, Cliff! What did you do? What did the ornament do to DeWorken?"

"Nothing. It didn't work."

"What do you mean, it didn't work?"

"That's the ornament for you. Sometimes it works. Sometimes it doesn't."

"And this time nothing happened? You didn't get your wish?"

"Nope!"

"Are you telling me the truth?"

"Why should I lie?"

"I don't know. I guess you just don't sound very convincing."

"I have to go." He turned and started walking off.

"Hey, Cliff! Wait!" Cliff turned around. I moved closer to him. "We're still friends, aren't we?"

"Sure," Cliff said. "Why not?" And then he continued walking off.

Just what I needed! My great day was being ruined. Cliff was still acting strange, and I didn't believe him about the ornament. True, the ornament didn't always work, but Cliff was acting like there was something he didn't want me to know. Besides, I'd already caught him in several lies yesterday. What could have happened? The ornament was so sneaky and so spooky. I just couldn't imagine what kind of shape DeWorken might be in right now. Oh well … Time would tell. Since DeWorken went to my school, I would find out soon enough. But then, this wasn't only about DeWorken. Cliff had had possession of the ornament for a whole day. What else might he have used it for? Hopefully he was smart enough to just make one wish and not use it again. But if he was dumb enough to use it once, he just might be dumb enough to use it two or three times. Cliff had known about all the trouble the ornament caused before, and he still used it. Somebody with an attitude like that would be tempted to use it more than once.

I decided to put the ornament away in the attic later on at night when everyone else was asleep. I still hated the attic, but I needed to quit while I was ahead and put the ornament in a place where it wouldn't be around for me to accidentally make wishes.

Hmm … Even the attic wasn't good enough. I really needed to get rid of the ornament permanently, but how? I thought about just taking out a hammer and busting it to pieces, but I was too scared to try. Anyway, that probably wouldn't work on a magic charm. Then I thought of something I should have thought of years ago. Why not just ask Aunt Loureen to come and take it back? Why was this the first time I came up with the idea? Probably because Aunt Loureen had given it to our whole family as a gift, and it would have been rude to return it. Also, she was looking toward the day when I would be brave enough to try using the ornament again, and I didn't wanna disappoint her. And then, over the years, I had pretty much forgotten about the ornament, so I had no reason to think about returning it or doing anything else with it. But anyway, it was back in my life now, and I really didn't wanna get involved with any more magic adventures. I just wanted to continue being a writer and date girls like Marla and get on with my life.

I decided to call Aunt Loureen after my folks went to bed. I had to be careful because this was a long-distance call, and if one of them suspected I was using the phone, they could pick up the other phone in their bedroom and hear part of my conversation. I didn't have my own cell phone yet. Lots of my friends had them now, and my parents really didn't object to my having one if I wanted to get a job and pay for it myself. I didn't want a job, and I usually didn't talk much on the phone anyway, even though Marla said she wanted to start calling me at home, so maybe it was something to think about. But for now, I needed to use our home phone.

After just two rings, Aunt Loureen's answering machine clicked on. "This is Loureen. I'm so sorry to have missed your call. Leave a message, and I promise to get back to you just as soon as possible. Have a meaningful day!"

Leave it to Aunt Loureen to say something like "Have a meaningful day" instead of just leaving a normal message like everyone else.

I waited for the beep and then talked softly into the phone. "Hi, Aunt Loureen. This is Mike. I hope you're doing all right. We're looking forward to seeing you at Christmas. Anyway, I need to talk to you. Could you call me back when you have a chance? I have some questions about the ornament."

That was enough. That would do it. Aunt Loureen would be intrigued that I was using the ornament again and call me back right away. I couldn't wait to hear from her. Not only was I gonna ask her to take it back, but I could also ask her some other stuff since she had become a sort of ornament expert. She could probably tell me whether I got my book published on my own or because of the magic.

Wait! Hold on! Hold everything! There was somebody else who could answer these same questions, and he'd been here all along! Caligula! He could tell me what I wanted to know. He'd hate me for it, but he would tell me just the same.

A long time ago, I promised Caligula that I wouldn't make him talk to me anymore. It wasn't hard keeping the promise because I really didn't enjoy our conversations either. At first it was fun seeing a cat talk, but he was such a grouch I'd just as soon not listen to him. Sometimes I heard him anyway when he was meowing at others in my family, asking for his breakfast or something. That couldn't be helped. The ornament had answered my wish in such a way that even when Caligula was involved in pure cat language, the language translated itself in my mind so that it sounded to me just like he was speaking English. He was aware of this, so he did his best not to meow in my presence. Once in a while over the years, he was so hungry I heard him anyway. But it had been a long time, and this helped me to forget about him being a talking cat. It also helped me to forget about the ornament itself, like I told you already.

There he was, asleep on the couch as usual. The lazy, worthless, good for nothing … Oh well. I really needed to learn a few things, and it was probably too late for Aunt Loureen to call me back tonight.

"Caligula."

He didn't move. But that didn't mean anything. Lots of times before, he had pretended not to hear me. Because of the ornament, he had to eventually get up and talk, but he was so stubborn he seemed to be able to somehow fight the forces of the ornament for a second or two.

"Come on, Caligula! Hey! You have to answer me. Remember that wish I made? You have to answer my questions."

Slowly his eyes opened and his head turned. "Oh, for crying out loud!"

"Well, well," I said. "It's been a long time."

"Not long enough! I thought you weren't going to bother me anymore."

"And I didn't. I haven't spoken to you in years. But I need to talk to you tonight. I don't really want to, Caligula, but I have to."

"No you don't."

"Yes, I do. Just a few questions and I'll leave you alone again, I promise."

"You promise? Sure. And your promises are so reliable … solid as gold."

"Just a few questions."

"Don't tell me … Something about the ornament."

"Well … yeah…kind of."

"You're a real piece of work, you know that?"

"Hey, you said we could talk again someday. You *did* say that."

"Yeah. I said maybe in about fifteen years."

"So? I still waited a number of years. I waited four years."

"You promised fifteen years, and you gave me four. Do me a favor, Kid. Don't major in math when you get to college."

"Let's just get this over with, and you can go back to bed."

"Fine. It's not as if I have any choice in the matter."

"Cliff stole my ornament yesterday."

"Yeah … I saw him come out of your room. And I had a feeling he was stealing the ornament, although I didn't know for sure."

"You didn't know? But you would have *had* to know. You know all about the ornament because of that wish I made years ago. Remember? I wished that you would know all about the rules and all about when it's working or not working."

"Yes, I remember. I've tried to forget, but I do remember. What you seem to have forgotten, however, is that when you made this wish about my knowledge, you made it with yourself in mind. You wished out of concern for your own usage of the charm. I know nothing about what happens when others are using the ornament. General rules certainly, but nothing about what they are specifically wishing for."

"So you can't help me? You can't tell me whether Cliff used it or not?"

"What difference does it make? As long as you weren't around at the time, his wishes won't affect you."

"That's true. OK. Well … I still need to ask you something else about the ornament."

"Oh … joy!"

"It'll only take a minute!"

"It never takes a minute. You should have burned it, Kid. You should have melted it down or thrown it in the sea or flushed it down the toilet. Instead, you used it again like an imbecile. And you're gonna start another one of those chain reactions that are impossible to stop."

He called me "Kid" as if that was my name, kind of like the way Aunt Loureen called me "Nephew" as if *that* was my name and the way Dad called me "Son."

"I didn't use it on purpose," I explained. "It was an accident."

"You wanna have an accident? Why don't you accidentally drop the ornament down the garbage disposal? That would be a productive accident."

"Well, I guess you must know what I'm about to ask. You see, I just finished making my own comic book."

"I know. It's all I've heard about in this house for the last couple of weeks. So much commotion for a stack of paper with drawings on it! You'd think somebody had discovered uranium!"

"Then you also heard about how a publisher sent me a letter on the same day I made my accidental wish."

"Yes. You accidentally wished because you were stupid enough to keep that hunk of glass in your dresser drawer. Real safe place! Good one, Kid!"

"All right. You obviously know everything about what's been going on ... So?"

"So what?"

"So, sometimes the ornament grants a wish, and sometimes it doesn't. Which was it this time? Did I sell the comic myself, or did the ornament do it with some magic?"

Caligula just shook his head, obviously not wanting to have this conversation or any conversation at all. He was a very stubborn cat, but we both knew that sooner or later he had to answer my question.

"Just tell me, Caligula! I need to know. This is important to me. Did my book get sold because of the ornament?"

Caligula cocked his head for a moment and glared into my eyes. "OF COURSE IT WAS BECAUSE OF THE ORNAMENT!!!"

This was painful to hear ... sharp and biting, right to the point. And Caligula seemed to enjoy giving me this horrible news, not because the news made him happy, but because he didn't like being pestered and this was his way of getting back at me.

He went on. "Did you really think a publisher would be interested in that tripe? A man with a bow and arrow who travels the world, fighting for truth and justice ... Give me a break!"

"It's not such a bad idea!"

"It's a stupid idea! I could make up a better story with my eyes closed. The fact that somebody went for such a juvenile plot should have been your first clue that magic convinced the publisher ... I mean, what else did you think convinced him? His taste? His critical sense? His love for the arts?"

"Yeah? Well, maybe it *wasn't* magic! Maybe you're lying to me."

"Cats don't lie!"

"Oh sure! Cats are the sneakiest creatures alive! Pretending that you can't talk, pretending that you aren't intelligent … just so that people won't put you to work! I'd call that deception all right!"

"There's a difference between being a liar and knowing how to keep a secret. Just because we don't gab, gossip, and cluck away like a bunch of busybody humans! Anyway, you reminded me yourself about your wish from years ago that I have to answer questions about the ornament, even against my own will. So, naturally, my answers would be truthful."

He had a point. He was telling the truth, and I knew it. I just didn't wanna admit it. I was doing what people called "denial." Aunt Loureen had confronted me about denial from time to time when I was younger and didn't wanna face up to stuff.

Caligula settled down a little and started to clean himself. "Aw, don't let it get to you, Kid. So you didn't sell the story honestly. Nobody knows but us! You made a wish, and you got your wish. What else did you expect? If you don't like using the ornament, get rid of it! You should have gotten rid of it long ago anyway. I did warn you. But if you wanna keep it, fine. Just quit your whining! And quit bugging me! I have more important things to do with my time."

"Yeah. That was an important nap you were in the middle of."

"Again with the nap? You always ridicule my naps. What's wrong with a good nap? Did you know that napping reduces stress? Why, there are whole countries in Europe where people close their businesses down for a couple of hours in the middle of the day, just to take naps. And these countries have lower crime rates because the citizens are better rested, more peaceful …"

"I don't care about naps! I'm trying to talk about the ornament right now!"

"Fine. So if you don't wanna talk about naps, quit bringing up the subject. Besides, this wasn't really a nap anyway. It's evening. This is bedtime. And speaking of bedtime, why don't you think about signing off yourself. That way we can both get a good night's sleep."

I didn't understand cats. They were so smart. They knew things about Europe and the rest of the world that even some people didn't know. And yet, for all that knowledge, the only thing Caligula ever wanted to do was lay around the house. Talk about a wasted life! What was the purpose of these strange animals? What did they accomplish? They were lazy, cranky, and finicky! Sure, he could have written that story with his eyes closed. He did practically everything with his eyes closed. The way my dad once put it, "Cats have no redeeming virtues." And he was right! At least, there was no virtue that I could see. I was beginning to wish I had just left him alone. I was so happy before, pretending in my mind that the story had sold on its own merit. Now all the excitement was gone. Still, since the truth was out, I had to keep probing. I had to understand as much as possible.

"So, where did the ornament get the idea from? If I didn't make up the story, it must have come from somewhere."

"I never said the ornament made up the story. I said the ornament answered your wish about being famous."

I felt a little better now. "So, I still could have made up the story?"

"A trained chimpanzee could have made up that story."

"Oh yeah? What's wrong with it?"

"Well, for one thing, it's a rip off of Robin Hood!"

"No, it isn't! He just looks like Robin Hood. That's all. But my story is different. Robin Hood robbed men in Sherwood Forest. Arch-Ranger travels the world …"

"Travels the world helping people … I know… I know … That's the part you made up, and that's the stupidest part."

"Why?"

"It's a hokey premise. That's why!"

"I don't think the idea of a man who wants to help people is hokey."

"If you say so."

"It could happen!"

"It could happen in another world, not this one. In *this* world, people don't behave that way."

"Says who? There are people like Ben who sometimes help …" I stopped short because something in Caligula's last sentence caught up with me in a kind of delayed reaction. "Wait a minute." I got up out of my chair and sat down right next to the cat. "Are you telling me that in some other world, this is a true story?"

"I'm not telling you anything."

"You have to answer my questions! Those are the rules of the wish!"

"Only if I know the answers!"

"It's about *my* wish this time, not Cliff's."

"That doesn't mean I can explain how the ornament accomplishes its purposes. The metaphysics are beyond me."

"But you know something else. You know something about the Arch-Ranger story."

"Yeah! I know the story stinks! But I didn't need the ornament to figure that out."

"There's something you're not telling me."

"Look, Kid, it's very late, and I'd like to turn in."

"You like to turn it whether it's late or not."

"If I knew any more, I would have told you by now — only by compulsion, but I would have told you nevertheless."

"Maybe. But you at least have some opinion. Share that."

"I don't have to share opinions. I only have to share knowledge and rules!"

"Yeah, but you still have to speak when I speak to you. If you don't wanna tell me what's on your mind, I'll keep you up all night talking about other things. One way or the other, you're gonna talk, so you might as well talk about what I wanna hear."

"Why, you spoiled, snippy, brat of a kid! You actually enjoy tormenting me, don't you? Can I help it if you're a lousy writer? Don't take it out on me! Learn another trade! Learn leather craft or something!"

"What about it, Caligula? What about Arch-Ranger? Is he real? Is there a real Arch-Ranger somewhere?"

Caligula gave an annoying sigh. "Just a suspicion, Kid. Well, think about it. *Arch-Ranger* takes place in another world, and the ornament comes from another world. So maybe what you think of as fiction is really a true event."

"Then you *do* know!"

"Are you paying attention? I said I *do not* know! I said it was a suspicion."

"But you know for sure that the story got published on account of the ornament."

"Yes, for the ninety-nine thousand, four hundred and twenty-first time! That much I know for sure. Now, you aren't gonna make me talk about this stuff every day, are you? Because nothing would depress me more. Maybe you miss these little heart-to-heart talks, but you've got to believe me ... I don't!"

I finally left Caligula alone. In no time at all, he curled up on the couch and went back to sleep. I was actually starting to envy him, being able to sleep like that, because I couldn't sleep at all. I kept tossing and turning in bed, thinking about my story. So many people had complimented it: all my friends at school, even my social studies teacher, and even my dad. They complimented my writing and my drawings. Had the ornament caused all that to happen? Was none of it real? Of course, these compliments happened before I had made the wish, but again, that was no honest comfort because the ornament could have prepared things ahead of time, knowing that I *would* make the wish. And I *had* been thinking about the "other world" when I made up the story of Arch-Ranger. I did borrow some ideas from *The Magic Ornament of Lumis* — nothing about Arch himself, just the idea of placing the story in another world. I kept batting the question back and forth. Was it my idea or wasn't it? I needed to talk with Aunt Loureen. Why couldn't she have been home tonight? She would have explained things, and she would have seen to it that I still felt good about myself regardless of what the ornament had or hadn't done. This was a gift Caligula didn't seem to have. It was a mistake talking to him. Oh well. Hopefully, Aunt Loureen would call me back tomorrow. For now, I needed to sleep. I needed to at least try. Funny, it seems that the harder a person tries to sleep, the less it's likely to happen. Sleep is just one of those things that either hits you or doesn't, kind of like ideas. They hit you or they don't. And when they hit you, what causes it to happen? Where did ideas come from anyway? Even without an ornament, where did ideas come from?

***

The next evening was the night of the big school dance. I was able to shave now, but I really only needed to do it once a week. Still, I quickly used the razor and then splashed a bunch of aftershave on my face. Then I put on a sports jacket, slacks, and a necktie. This wasn't a formal dance like a prom, so I didn't wanna overdo it.

Ben was gonna be picking me up. Then we'd head off and get the girls. I came out to the living room to wait for him.

"Oh, Mike, you look so nice and handsome," Mom said. "Doesn't he look nice, Jim?"

"Not bad," Dad said. "Not bad at all."

"Here, Mike." Mom handed me a corsage.

"This isn't that formal of a dance, Mom. She isn't gonna have an evening gown on."

"I know. But I guarantee some of the girls will still have corsages."

Ben tooted his horn like he usually did, without bothering to come to the door. I headed out quickly and hopped in the front seat.

"Nice threads, buddy," he said. "You're looking real sharp."

"Thanks."

"So … finally! Your first date. Nervous?"

"Yeah. Real nervous."

"I was too my first time. But your gonna have fun. I promise."

I believed him. But I was still nervous.

We followed the directions Marla had given me over the phone. They led us to a nice-looking two-story house. I hadn't met her parents, but since they were divorced, I figured I'd only see her mom, which suited me just fine. I was scared enough without having to deal with a protective father.

I was right. Her mom opened the door, and I have to say, she really looked an awful lot like her daughter.

"You must be Mike," she said warmly. "Come on in. Marla will be down in a moment."

A large brown dog started barking and jumping all over me.

"Down, Rex! Down!" Mrs. McIntire shouted.

He was wagging his tail, so I knew he wouldn't bite or anything, but he was still huge and smelly. He was also getting dog hair all over my nice clothes. It actually made me appreciate Caligula. Caligula might have been a pill, but he never jumped on you.

"Sorry! He's just a little eager to meet new people. Come on, Rex, let's go outside … Come on … Good boy, Rex! Good boy!" She put him out on the patio and then came back in.

This happened a lot over the years when I visited friends or family with big dogs. Sooner or later they put the dog out, but only after he jumped all over their guests. I always wondered why the dogs weren't just left in the backyard right off the bat before the guests arrived.

"Well, Mike, I've heard a lot about you," Mrs. McIntire said casually as if nothing had happened with the dog at all. "I understand you've become a famous author."

"Aw … I'm far from famous. I just signed the contract last night."

"You did? How exciting!"

Marla came down the stairs, wearing a bright pink dress. Her hair was beautifully refashioned. I'd describe it, but I'm terrible at describing hairstyles. All I can say is that whatever reaction she wanted her hair to give me, it worked.

"Hi, Mike."

"Hi. Ah … this is for you." I handed her the corsage.

"Thank you. It's lovely."

I felt weird pinning it on her in front of her mother, but my mom had said that was just exactly how it was done, "The man pins the corsage." I kind of bumbled through it, but I don't think I stabbed her or anything. At least, if I did, she acted like I didn't.

After we picked up Ben's date, we headed for the dance. Marla talked the entire way over — only to me, not to Ben and Jean. They were sitting in the front seat, caught up in their own conversation, but in the backseat, Marla talked about anything and everything. I was usually bored to death around chatty people, but for some reason, every word out of Marla's mouth fascinated me. She loved the little things about life, much like my Aunt Loureen. This seemed especially true when she mentioned some of her future plans.

"Someday I'm going to live in a beach house. I've always dreamed of a house by the sea ... a house with a fireplace where I can listen to the waves crashing all night. The ocean is my favorite location. It has a real mystical quality, especially at dawn when the water has a crispness about it. But I love it any time of the day. I love it at night with the stars and the fog. I love it in the summer when I can just put on my bathing suit, lay on the towel, and sunbathe."

Suddenly, I had a picture of the beach in my mind too.

"I love swimming in it, and I love just looking at it. What's your favorite place, Mike?"

Next to you, I said to myself. But to her I just said, "I don't know. I'd have to think about it."

The gym was decorated with lots of confetti. It was actually fun to see so many of my friends and classmates all dressed up. The band wasn't bad either. There was no reason not to have a good time, but until that first uncomfortable moment when I finally asked Marla to dance, it would be hard to relax. I did finally ask her, even though Ben and Jean had already danced through one whole number before I got up the nerve. It would have been pretty stupid to get all dressed up, bring a date to the gym, and not dance. And I knew that if I didn't make the first move, Marla would. So I finally said, "Well, shall we?"

She nodded, and we headed for the dance floor. The first dance was a fast one. I was horrible at dancing. I felt like a real klutz! But nobody seemed to be looking at me, and Marla was smiling with delight. She sure was full of energy! When the dance was over, I asked Marla if she wanted some punch.

"Such a gentleman," she said. "I'd love some."

One of the men at the punch bowl table was giving me a strange look as he stuck the glass dipper into the large red bowl and poured liquid into a couple of paper cups. I had never seen this guy before. I knew most of the teachers by face at least, even if I wasn't in their classes. And I didn't think he was a teacher. Sometimes parents came to the dances to act as chaperones. He must have been a parent. He was tall, with silver hair and a dark, neatly trimmed beard. He was also wearing a dark suit. Leave it to an adult to overdress for a casual dance.

"Nice girl!"

I figured he must be talking to someone else, and I was hoping he was talking to someone else, so I ignored the comment. But then he repeated himself. "I said, nice girl."

"You mean the girl I'm with?"

"Yes, of course! Marla!"

"Ah ... sure. She's nice."

"Congratulations on your new Arch-Ranger story. I hear it's quite good."

"Ah ... thanks. Thanks a lot."

I was getting a weird vibe from this character, but the news about *Arch-Ranger had* been spreading quickly around school, so I guess some of the parents knew too. Now the man was just staring at me again — not smiling, not frowning, just a stare. But the stare was giving me the willies. I needed to say something. The silence was killing me.

"Whose kid is yours?" It seemed like an awkward question, but if I didn't break the silence and ask him something, I would have gone crazy.

"Oh, I don't have a kid. I'm only a volunteer."

Hmm. No kid. Then how did he know Marla? And how did he know me? And how did he know about *Arch-Ranger*?

"So, Mike, what's the latest with science? Will you pass?"

This was too much. Who could know about my science class? I did hate science, and I was struggling to get a C, but I never talked to anyone about that. Only Mr. Finch, my instructor, knew.

"Ah ... it'll be OK ... I guess."

"Good. Good. Because bad grades can get you kicked off the cross-country team. In the height of your publishing glory, we wouldn't want you to ignore your studies now, would we?"

"Um ... I guess not."

"Sometimes you need to hit the books, whether you feel like it or not."

"Yeah. Yeah, sure. Well, nice talking to you."

"Nice talking to *you*, Mike. Say hello to your father for me."

"You know my dad?"

"Are you kidding? Jim and I go way back. Does he still get irritated with gifts such as ornaments?"

Now I was completely spooked. This man knew about the ornament. Wait. Hmm … Dad could have told some of his friends about it back when Aunt Loureen had given us the present, but the ornament never seemed to be very important to him, hardly a conversation piece at the office. Besides, that was so long ago. Why bring it up now of all times? And any talk about the ornament made me suspicious that ornament activity was going on. Who was this clown?

"He still gets irritated," I said, trying to sound lighthearted. "But not as much as he used to."

"Yes, Jim always did have quite a temper. I guess his sister, Loureen, talked some sense into him."

This was the last straw. I wanted to grab him good, shake him by the collar, and say, "Just who in the world are you?"

But instead, I excused myself and went back to Marla.

When I returned with the punch, a few other kids were standing around in a semicircle talking to her.

"And nobody has seen him?" Marla was asking.

"Not even his parents," one of the girls said. "I think they actually called the police. Hi, Mike."

"Hi."

I didn't know her either, but she, at least, was someone I'd seen around campus. She was a brunette, not as pretty as Marla, but pretty enough.

"I'm Jill."

"Nice to meet you, Jill." We shook hands, and Jill would not let go of my hand.

"I love your *Arch-Ranger* comic," she said in a very flirtatious way.

I just couldn't get enough of this. I was eating it up with a spoon. Marla separated our hands.

"He's taken, Jill." Marla spoke as though she were making a good-natured joke, but I had a feeling she wasn't really smiling inside.

"Don't be silly," Jill laughed. "I was only complimenting his comic."

"Of course, Jill."

I handed Marla her punch, and she started sipping. Jill waved goodbye and walked off with her friends.

"Catty little thing, isn't she?" Marla said to me.

"Huh? Oh … I thought she was just being polite."

"Michael Owen! You have absolutely no idea how attractive you are to the ladies, do you?"

Until very recently I'd been completely clueless, but I sure loved hearing about it. Still, I had to act like none of this was a big deal, so I quickly changed the subject. "What were they talking about before I got here? Did I hear something about the police?"

"It's Doug DeWorken. He's missing."

Oh, boy! He *had* lied, that jerk, Cliff. He had lied all along! What had he done? I tried not to look too concerned. "Missing? What do you mean?"

"Well, he didn't show up for school. And when his parents didn't call to excuse him for the day, the office called his house. His parents haven't seen him since yesterday. And some of his friends who were going to spend time with him yesterday only saw him on campus for about half a day."

"I see. And his folks called the police?"

"Yes. Sounds like it. I sure hope everything is all right. You hear about girls getting abducted, but who would mess with a huge guy like Doug?"

If you only knew, I said to myself.

Cliff wasn't at the dance. I'd have to wait till tomorrow to find out what had happened. That is, if I wanted to know. If the police were involved, maybe it would be better to just stay away from Cliff for a while.

Marla finished her punch and gave me a mischievous glance. "We've only danced once, Mr. Owen. Aren't you going to ask me again?"

"Ah … yeah … sure."

It was a slow dance this time, and it was the very first time I ever held Marla in my arms. Not a bad way to start. If we'd been at a movie or something I would have been too scared to try putting my arm around her. But at a dance, it was expected. Marla seemed to like being held. They were playing a slow version of a faster-paced hit song. I couldn't remember what it was called. I'd heard it on the radio a lot, without taking much notice, but I knew I needed to find out the title, because for the rest of my life, this would now be my favorite song.

Marla whispered in my ear. "You're a very special person, you know that?"

I wasn't sure how she could find me so special when she hardly knew me, but I wasn't about to argue the point. Her face was now against mine. Without even thinking, I kissed her cheek. If you had asked me earlier in the day, I would have told you that there was no way I'd dare try a kiss on a first date. But somehow, it just all seemed so natural. I got caught up in the moment without thinking. Marla looked up at me and stopped dancing. Her face had literally turned red! She moved away. "I … I think I need some fresh air."

This was the first time I had ever seen her nervous or frightened. I honestly didn't think she'd mind the kiss. After all, she'd been so forward in every other way. Women! Who could figure them out? Not me, and I didn't wanna figure them out. I wanted to turn back the clock and keep myself from giving her that stupid kiss. What a nitwit! Now I'd ruined everything!

I sat down on a chair. As if matters weren't bad enough, that man by the punch bowl saw me by myself and started walking over. Great! Just great! I needed him like a headache needs a symphony!

"Lost your girl, eh?"

Enough already. I wasn't in the mood for any more of this. "Look, I don't even know who you are!"

"How careless of me," he said politely, as though I had not even snapped at him. "My name is Charles."

I shook his hand, not really knowing what else to do. "If I may, Mike, allow me to give you a word of advice. When a lady runs off, it's always a good idea to follow her."

"Look, mister ..."

"Please, call me Charles."

"Look, Charles ... this is none of your business." I'd never talked to an adult like that in my life.

"Perhaps it isn't any of my business. Nevertheless, what I said is still true. A lady who runs off wants to be followed."

I just sat there, staring at the ground. Charles slapped me on the shoulder. "Well, think about it." He walked back to the punch table.

I knew nothing about this Charles other than the fact that I already hated him. Still, he might be right. I would have thought that Marla never wanted to see me again, but I knew nothing at all about women, and Charles, whoever he was, seemed to somehow know everything.

I walked outside and found her sitting on a bench.

"I'm sorry, Marla. I guess I shouldn't have done that."

She was teary-eyed. "You didn't do anything wrong, Mike. I wanted you to kiss me."

Now I was more confused than ever. I sat down next to her. "Then why did you run off like that?"

"It's hard to explain."

Strange! On the way over in the car, she'd talked about everything under the sun. Why should anything be hard for her to explain?

"Will you do me a favor?" she asked.

"Sure. Yeah ... of course."

"Will you hold me? I like being in your arms."

Maybe the evening wouldn't be a wash after all. I reached for her, and she practically melted into my arms. Something else must have been bothering her. It obviously couldn't be me.

"You asked me once about my dad," she said softly, almost in a whisper. "Remember? You asked how I felt about his moving out?"

"Yeah. I remember."

"I try not to think much about my dad. For some reason, he and I never got along too well."

"How come?"

"I'm not sure. He and Mom were always fighting. Dad started hating her so much he decided to move out. I always wondered if he hated me too."

"I'm sure he doesn't. A father wouldn't hate his own daughter."

"Maybe not. I know he never told me he loved me. Not once in my life can I remember hearing him say that."

"Wow ... I'm sorry, Marla. Really, I am."

She ran her hand through my hair. "I think you're wonderful. And not just because you're cute. Anyway, I *am* a lot like my mom. I look like her. I act like her. I have all her faults. So if Dad hates her, why wouldn't he hate me?"

"It's not the same. I don't think those faults bother him when he sees them in you. I have other friends whose parents are divorced. The parents still love their kids. At least, I've never met any who don't."

"You're probably right. But it still feels like he hates me, you know?"

"Can I ask you a question?"

"Yes."

"If you wanted me to kiss you, how come you ran off when I did?"

"I was scared."

"That's OK. I was scared tonight too, being my first date and all."

"Oh, I've dated before. Many times. And I've been kissed before. It never freaked me out. It never even meant that much. But it was different with you. You're the first boy I've ever really cared about. So it frightened me. That probably doesn't make any sense, does it?"

"I understand." I didn't understand one word of it. But I figured it was better to say that I did understand.

"My dad kissed me once," she continued. "Just once. Well, once that I can remember. The day he moved out, with his bags packed, sitting by the door. He leaned over and kissed me on the cheek. I couldn't remember him ever doing that before. He showed the kind of affection a girl wants from her father. And ..." she started choking up, "he showed it the day he left me. And when you kissed me, I started thinking about you leaving me."

I squeezed her hand tightly. "Hey, I'm not going anywhere."

"I know. And we hardly know each other. This really makes no sense. But when you kissed me, it just reminded me of Dad for some reason. That's all."

"Come here," I said, talking braver and more sure of myself than I'd ever been in my life. She leaned in again, and I whispered into her ear. "I'm gonna kiss you again. And you just watch me. I won't leave. I'll stay right here. You're stuck with me."

She laughed. And then we kissed, a long kiss on the lips. It was the most wonderful feeling I'd ever had.

***

Ben dropped Jean off first because she had a strict curfew. Marla was next. I walked her to the door, and we kissed good night.

"We barely know each other," she said, beaming. "But writers put so much of themselves into their work. And I felt like I was getting to know you by reading your story. Of course, I only know a few things. But I look forward to learning more."

"Me too."

She opened the door, turned back once more, and blew me another kiss. Then she shut the door.

"Congratulations," Ben said to me when I got back in the car. "I didn't think you had it in you."

"I didn't think I had it in me either." We both laughed out loud. For some reason, Ben and I seemed closer. I guess we had something new in common: girlfriends! I loved high school now. I loved being sixteen!

***

It was after midnight when Ben finally dropped me off at home.

90

The rest of my family was asleep, but I was too wired to go to bed. I went into the kitchen to find a snack, and then I figured I would watch a little TV before turning in. I had always heard that TV was a useless waste of time. But it actually did accomplish one important thing. It helped to put me to sleep … not when I worried about things. Nothing helped when I worried. But when I'd had a great day and I was still full of energy, the TV helped.

Mom had baked a cherry pie the night before, and hopefully there would still be a piece or two in the fridge, if Shelly had kept her mitts off of it.

There was a note on the fridge from Mom. "Mike, Aunt Loureen called. She says she's going to be up late tonight and you can call her back at any time."

Wow! I sure did love that Aunt Loureen! She knew I needed to talk to her at a time when everyone else was asleep. My feelings for Marla had helped to get my mind off the ornament. But there were still some burning questions in my mind, so I decided I might as well call my aunt while I had the chance.

I still wanted to eat something first, and luckily there was one piece of pie left. Sure enough, there it was, looking delicious as ever. Mom had evidently caught Shelly in time, before she scarfed it down. It was the best piece of pie I'd ever had, because this was the best night I'd ever had. When life goes well, food just naturally tastes better.

After listening to Aunt Loureen go on and on about how "wonderful it was to hear my precious voice," I finally told her what was happening. She already knew about my *Arch-Ranger* story because I'd sent her some e-mails and even a rough draft of the comic. Aunt Loureen hardly ever checked her e-mail, which is why I had contacted her by phone the other night, but that time, I did get a rare e-mail response from her about the comic. Like everyone else, she'd told me how impressed she was. But she didn't know anything about the recent ornament wish. I explained everything over the phone, including my conversation with Caligula. I also complained about how bummed I was to learn that I hadn't sold the story on my own merit. As I expected, she lifted my spirits right away.

"So what if the ornament gave you an advantage with the publisher? Publishing is a difficult industry to break into. People usually need a special contact of some sort, like your teacher. You told me she had a friend over at Griffith Publications, right? That was certainly an advantage. But it didn't bother you, did it?"

"No. I guess I just wanna believe they really liked my story."

"Of course they really liked it! But publishers often reject things they like for financial reasons, or uncertainty over how to market a certain story, or an unwillingness to take a risk on something original. In this case, the ornament probably just gave them an extra push, an extra incentive to stretch themselves with something fresh and new."

"But Caligula says the story stinks."

"Oh, goose burgers! What does he know? After all, he's only a cat!"

"But he knows stuff about the ornament."

"Yes. He knew that the ornament influenced the publisher, but he's adding his own interpretation, and remember, that gloomy puss loves to put the most negative spin on things."

"So, you're sure they honestly liked it, Aunt Loureen?"

"I can't say for certain, but there's no reason not to assume the best. For what it's worth, I do know literature. I'm a teacher myself, remember, and I can assure you, it's a wonderful story. And that's just based on reading the rough draft you sent me."

I felt better now about the publication, but I was still concerned about the source of the story itself, so I told Aunt Loureen about Caligula's guess that Arch-Ranger was actually a real person who lives in another world.

There was a pause over the phone before she answered me. "I'm inclined to say yes. At least, that's what my instincts tell me. I've learned to trust my instincts, Nephew, as you should learn to trust yours."

She was saying exactly what I didn't wanna hear.

"So," I continued, "let me see if I'm getting this. When I made my wish about getting the book published, the ornament not only influenced the publisher, but also influenced the story itself?"

"Something like that. Remember, the ornament knew ..."

"Yeah, you told me before. The ornament knew what I was gonna wish for before I even made the wish."

"You sound upset, Michael."

"I thought I made that story up myself. I thought I came up with an original idea."

"Nephew, there's no such thing as a completely original idea. Ideas are always combinations between inspiration and creativity. That's as true for you as it was for Charles Dickens." Dickens was Aunt Loureen's favorite author since he had written so many stories about Christmas. She continued. "Didn't you tell me in one of your e-mails that you modeled Arch-Ranger after your friend Ben? Wasn't Ben an inspiration?"

"Yeah, I guess he was … kind of … but Arch-Ranger is still a lot different."

"Absolutely he is! You added your own talent to the mix."

"Wait! Now you're saying my imagination *was* involved?"

"Of course, Nephew! But think! Your imagination was still inspired by your friend. Is that really so different from the inspiration which may have also come from the ornament? Everyone is inspired. Sometimes we're conscious of the inspiration. Sometimes it's a mystery. The most classic works of literature are deemed 'inspiration' by literary critics. There's no reason whatsoever to not feel good about your success."

She was cheering me up again. I sure was glad I had called her. "So even though there may be a real Arch-Ranger in some other world, I may have still made up his adventures myself?"

"Exactly!"

"Do you know anything about this *real* Arch-Ranger?"

"No. I'm only going by instincts, as I said. But I believe he *does* live in the other world."

"You mean the world where the ornament comes from?"

"Yes."

"And those angels inside the ornament … since they know this Arch-Ranger, they planted the idea in my mind?"

"Your comic book may have been inspired by beings familiar with a real Arch-Ranger. On the other hand, the real Arch-Ranger may have been inspired by your comic book."

"Huh? What are you talking about?"

"Well, Nephew, there may be two different worlds involved with this puzzle, but there's only one Creator. Throughout time, God has inspired people, and He's allowed people to inspire each other. We're made in His image, don't forget. He creates, and He delights in seeing us create. And remember, God isn't limited by time. He sees everything in one glance. He saw you write about Arch-Ranger on the same day He breathed life into Arch-Ranger, even if Arch-Ranger was born twenty to thirty years ago. Often times, God will create and nurture a person who's destined to become a great hero, the kind of hero people dream about or write about."

I wasn't following a word she said. Listening to her sometimes made my head hurt. "Aunt Loureen, you're confusing me! Is Arch-Ranger real or not? Did I make him up, or didn't I?"

"It's probably a little bit of both."

I should have known she'd say something like that. It was a typical Aunt Loureen answer, clear as mud. Hardly ever did she just answer a straight yes or no question.

"OK," I said. "Let me ask you a different question. Are your instincts telling you anything else about the ornament?"

"Should they be?"

"I mean, something about Cliff?"

"Cliff ... your friend?"

"Yeah, my friend. He stole the ornament out of my room. He used it to defend himself against some bully."

"Oh dear."

"He says it didn't work, but I don't believe him."

"I see ... Then this isn't about my instincts so much as yours. You must find out what happened, Nephew. This could upset the whole plan."

"Plan?"

Aunt Loureen's voice suddenly changed, sounding real urgent.

"There's a lot I haven't told you over the years, Nephew. I honored the fact that discussion about the ornament was disturbing to you. I don't have time right now to go into everything, and there are some facts I'm not allowed to share anyway, but over the last five years, I've acquired some information about this other world."

"What information?"

"Are you really ready for this, Nephew? Are you ready to come to grips with the ornament instead of viewing it as a thing to be feared?"

"I don't know." That was as honest as I could be. I usually hated the ornament until a talk with Aunt Loureen made me feel better. And when she was done talking, it somehow seemed that the ornament was part of my destiny. At this moment, I *was* curious about some of the stuff she said. I mean, who wouldn't be? But for the most part, I still just wanted to enjoy high school since I had never enjoyed it before.

"Well, you don't have to decide now. But things are happening in the other world. Important events! History is being made! And in some slight but significant ways, the two worlds are connecting."

"What do you mean, connecting?" It was silent. "Aunt Loureen? Aunt Loureen, are you still there?"

"I mean that some people from the other world are coming here. And some people from here are soon going into the other world."

"Who? Who's going into the other world?"

Whoever it was, I sure hoped it wasn't me. That's all I knew.

"Nephew, tell me something. Have you met anyone unusual lately?"

"Unusual in what way?"

"In any way. Have you met any strange people? Now think. Use your instincts for a moment."

But I didn't need instincts. I suddenly remembered the man at the dance, and I described him to Aunt Loureen.

"Hmm …" she said. "Very interesting. Very interesting indeed."

"Aunt Loureen, what's going on?"

"I can't tell you."

"Do you know this man?"

"No. But I'll bet dollars to donuts that he's from the other world."

I felt another rush of that adrenaline stuff. How come every time I had a good day, it had to be spoiled with talk about the ornament and the other world? Why had I called her back? Couldn't I have waited a day or two so that I could just go to bed after a great day?

"What's he doing here?" I asked.

But Aunt Loureen was lost in thought. Ignoring my question, she said, "So, it's starting, and we need to act fast."

"We? Come on, Aunt Loureen, I don't wanna get mixed up in this again."

"You don't have to. Not necessarily. Not if you don't want to. But I do need you to do me one favor. Do you have a pen and paper?"

"Yeah ... sure." I reached for a pad.

"I'm giving you an address ... the address of a store. You must go there tomorrow."

"Why would I go to a store?"

"Why would anyone go to a store, Nephew? To shop! You're going to purchase something!"

"I don't get much allowance, Aunt Loureen. Is this gonna be expensive?"

"I don't know. Probably not too expensive, but I'll pay you back either way. Bring it home and hide it until I can come out to your neck of the woods and collect it from you."

"Where *is* this store? Down at the mall?"

"No. A much smaller store ... a little antique shop ... the same store where I purchased the ornament."

"But I always thought it was a store near where *you* lived."

"No. I picked it up on my way to your house that Christmas when I gave you the ornament as a gift."

This was reminding me that I'd decided to have her to take the "gift" back. Maybe things would work out fine. When she arrived, I would give her both items at the same time. But what was this other object she wanted me to buy?

"Am I looking for another ornament?"

"No."

"Well, what then?"

"I'm not sure. You'll know when you see it."

"How? If *you* don't know what it is, how am *I* supposed to know?"

"I keep telling you, Nephew, you must learn to trust your instincts. In this store, you'll find one other item from the other world — not an ornament, a key."

"Oh. So I'm looking for a key."

"No, not a key in the conventional sense. It will be an object of some sort. Maybe a figurine. Maybe a paperweight. Maybe a box or a shell. Some kind of souvenir-type knickknack."

"Wait! I get it! And this object will also be a magic charm?"

"Exactly! But not like the ornament. A different kind of charm. It will serve as a kind of key."

"A key to what?"

"A key to a doorway ... a doorway into the other world. Nephew, I'm taking a trip into the other world. I was going to wait until after Christmas, but it seems matters are getting urgent. I need to go right away, and you need to help me."

Chapter Four

The Carnival

After finishing a breakfast of bacon and waffles, Cliff brushed his teeth, returned to his bedroom, and pulled a shoe box off of the closet rack. There was a jovial smile on his face as he opened the lid and peeked inside. "Good morning, DeWorken. How did you sleep?"

DeWorken was sitting in the box corner, curled up, almost in the fetal position. "Very funny! How would *you* sleep if ya had ta spend the night inside a box?"

"Well, I must admit, it's not exactly the Hyatt Regency, is it?"

DeWorken stood up and walked closer toward Cliff. "All right, Reynolds, you've had your fun. The joke's over. Now I want ya ta let me outta here."

Cliff picked DeWorken up out of the box, set him down on his desk top, and then sat in his desk chair, enabling a more even face-to-face conversation. "Where would you go? You're only six inches tall, DeWorken. It's a pretty dangerous world out there for somebody your size. What if you got stepped on? What if a hawk swooped down and scooped you up? What if you got trapped in a spider web?"

"Yeah! And ya sound real glad about that stuff! I never seen ya happier!"

"Well you *have* been kind of a thorn in my side for a long time, DeWorken. Can you really blame me?"

"So, what are your plans? Ya gonna keep me boxed up for the rest of my life?"

"No. Truthfully, I've been trying to figure out just exactly *what* to do with you. And it's proving to be quite a challenging dilemma. It really *would* be dangerous for me to simply turn you loose."

"Ya know what I'm talkin' about, Reynolds! I'm not askin' ta be emptied out on the floor! I mean change me back ta normal size! That's how ya let me outta here!"

"We went through all this yesterday. The ornament cannot reverse one of its own wishes. I already explained."

"Oh, yeah? Well ya can take your fairy tales and shove them up your …"

"Now, now. What happened to your manners? Let's not start talking crass."

"Look, I know all about you science geeks. This was some kinda experiment, wasn't it?"

"Hmm. An experiment with the molecular makeup of a human being. That *would* be a fascinating project. But I'm afraid I can't take any such credit."

"Listen, you warthog, I'm not spendin' the rest of my life in this box!"

"Relax. It was never my intention to keep you here permanently. But I had to hide you from my mom. Think about it, DeWorken. Would you want her to discover you and return you home? You really want all your family and friends to see you like this?"

DeWorken bowed his head in shame, not saying a word. Finally, he muttered, "All right. So what's gonna happen, then?"

"Well, for starters, I *have* prepared better accommodations for you." He picked DeWorken up and headed toward the room's back shelf. "Here you go. It used to be my hamster cage, but the hamster died." He opened the wire door and set DeWorken down inside. "Of course, when I'm not in the room, I'll have to put a cover over it and stuff it way back in the closet, out of Mom's range."

DeWorken started kicking the cage's sawdust floor. "Are ya nuts or somethin'? I ain't stayin' in no hamster cage!"

"Oh, stop being such a baby. I fixed it up with all the comforts of home. If you're hungry, hit this lever and food falls in. A nutritious mix. See?" Cliff demonstrated.

"If ya think you're gonna turn me into some kinda pet, ya better think again! What is that stuff? It looks like more than grain. And it smells! Is that some kinda animal food?"

"Picky, picky, DeWorken. OK. I'll put something else in there. Maybe M&M's. You like plain or peanut?"

"You're really gettin' a kick out of all this, ain't ya?"

"I could even put Skittles in there. Now, if you're thirsty, you suck from this bottle on the side. It only has water right now, but if you behave, I'll fill it with Coke. Just pray that my mother never discovers you, or she'll fill it with milk."

"Oh, man, when I get outta here ..."

"Heard it! Oh, and you'll probably want to work out, being that you're an important jock and all. So here's a little treadwheel for you. My hamster had hours of fun on it. In fact, one time I think he was almost smiling. Well, I'm off to school, but it's still early. No reason you shouldn't turn in again and catch some extra z's. How about a bedtime lullaby, DeWorken? You like the song 'Thumbelina'?"

"Ya think you're really tough stuff right now, don't ya?"

"I never cared much for the song before. It always seemed rather childish. But somehow, right now, this charming little tune seems strangely appropriate."

Cliff started singing:

"Thumbelina, Thumbelina, tiny little thing

Thumbelina, dance, Thumbelina sing"

"GET OUT!!!!"

***

Mr. Bennett was going through the element chart. Most of the kids looked bored. Cliff loved natural science and would normally have been a more enthusiastic student, but today he was having trouble concentrating. For two days and two nights, he'd managed to keep DeWorken hidden in his room. From the very first moment DeWorken shrunk, Cliff had been at a loss to figure out what to do with him. Keeping him hidden at home seemed like a natural first step, a fair plan until he could catch his breath and find a new course of action. He'd considered taking DeWorken back to his own parents' home. He even thought it would be fun to drop him in the mailbox, wrapped in a red ribbon. That would be hilarious all right, but then what? Although nobody would ever be able to explain his size, and DeWorken himself would offer no comprehension whatsoever, the one thing he *could* say is that Cliff was somehow responsible. Being interrogated by teachers, parents, and maybe even policemen was something Cliff would just as soon pass on. So he was keeping DeWorken for now, and so far he was getting away with it. He *did* enjoy tormenting DeWorken, but he also knew that, eventually, the novelty would wear off. When that time came, he would have to unload the scoundrel, get him off his back once and for all. But where? How?

Cliff had his lunch in the chess room as he'd done the last few days. He was avoiding Mike because he didn't care to be bothered about the ornament. Mike still believed he used it, and he wasn't about to let up. Cliff had considered confiding in Mike but decided against it. He was still angry at his friend and not yet ready to be forgiving.

Wilson moved his bishop closer to Cliff's king. "Hey, Cliff, were you planning on going to that carnival that's in town? I hear it's got a lot of cool stuff."

"I really hadn't thought much about it," Cliff said, moving his queen in such a way that Wilson would have to return his bishop to its original square.

"Well, my family's going this weekend, Friday or Saturday. Wanna come along? My folks would go their own way and leave us alone. We could mess around by ourselves the whole time."

Even though Cliff and Wilson had never been too close, Wilson was being a little clingy ever since Cliff had asked for a ride home four days ago. That ride request undoubtedly filled Wilson's head with ideas. He was a nerd, desperate for a new friend. Cliff hated himself for feeling so snobbish, especially since everyone considered *him* to be a nerd too. Cliff didn't feel like accepting the invitation, but if he didn't, was he really any better than Mike?

"All right, Wilson. That sounds like fun. How much does it cost?"

"Aw, forget about the money," Wilson said, looking chipper and grateful. "It'll be on me."

On his way to trigonometry, Cliff saw a few guys huddled together. He recognized most of them as DeWorken's friends, but he didn't know any of the names except for Scott Pierce. Undoubtedly, they were talking about DeWorken at that very moment. Everyone was discussing DeWorken today, both in and out of class. Some of the teachers even asked their students to pray for him, although a few qualified the request and suggested that they pray at home because of "separation between church and state."

And then it happened: Pierce saw Cliff and pointed his finger at him. "If you ask me, the police are looking in the wrong places!"

Cliff was used to ignoring such remarks and walking away, but this one looked too important, and Pierce didn't seem quite as scary anymore. After all, if Mike could take him on, anybody could take him on. So Cliff stopped. "What are you talking about, Pierce?"

"I'll bet you know what we're talking about."

"Our friend Doug," one of the others said. "Haven't you heard?"

"Yes, I've heard."

"It's so weird," another one said. "What do you guys think might have happened to him?"

"Who knows?" Pierce answered. "But if you ask me, the fellow they oughta be questioning is right here!"

Cliff could feel himself starting to sweat. "You think I did something to DeWorken? You're crazy."

"Am I?"

This was uncanny! How could this be happening? How could they suspect him of all people? He was guilty, of course, but why on earth should they suspect him? If ever there were a student who came across as unthreatening to a husky monster like DeWorken, it was him. Oh well, nothing to do now but continue the act.

"What could I have done to him? He's twice my size!" Later, when the pressure subsided, Cliff would have to take a private moment to laugh at the irony of that remark.

"There's a lot of things you could have done," Pierce said. "You could have shot him with a gun."

"Naw," said one of the others. "Any guy that can't throw a softball probably can't shoot straight either!"

They all laughed.

"Who says he has to shoot straight?" Pierce continued. "All he has to do is hold the gun up close."

Cliff shook his head. "You're imagining things, Pierce."

"Oh yeah? You sure you didn't just wig out on him because you got tired of him picking on you?"

"I said I don't know anything about it!!!"

Pierce laughed. "Look how defensive he's getting. That just proves he has something ta hide!"

But the others didn't seem to agree. "You're nuts, Pierce. Reynolds wouldn't have the spine to own a gun. He's too geeky!"

"What's the matter with you?" Pierce countered. "Don't you listen to the news? Whenever there's a school shooting, it *always* turns out to be some nerd who was being picked on!"

Wonderful, Cliff said to himself. *It's not enough that people like me get picked on. Now we're automatic suspects too. Our victimhood proves our guilt.*

"Maybe it wasn't a gun at all," another one said. "Maybe his friend did it … that Robinson guy."

"Ben Robinson?"

"Maybe. He was hassling DeWorken. Remember? And martial arts can kill people!"

This was even worse. Now his little stunt with the ornament was getting Ben in trouble too.

"Naw," said Pierce. "It wasn't Ben. He had no motive. You gotta have a motive ta kill. Ben wasn't worried about DeWorken."

Cliff felt better.

"But Reynolds was!"

Cliff felt worse.

That was it. That was the last straw. Cliff got right in Pierce's face, standing up to him for the very first time. "You watch what you're saying!"

"Or what?"

"Or you'll have your own trouble with the law! There's such a thing as *slander*, you know."

Pierce started imitating him in a high shrill voice. "'There's such a thing as slander, you know.'"

Cliff turned and walked away. Not the bravest confrontation in the world, but certainly not the worst. He almost felt like he could have socked him without worrying about the consequences. But this would be a bad day to show first-time violence. It might just add credibility to the accusations, make him look like a "tormented soul" who was finally starting to snap.

Pierce shouted after him. "Yeah, go on Reynolds! Go hide the body in a better place!"

Cliff didn't look back, but he *did* hear one of the others say, "Better be careful, Pierce. Nobody knows for sure that Doug is dead. If you keep talking like you know he's dead, somebody might start looking at *you* with suspicion!"

By the time trigonometry was over, Cliff had a chance to replay the conversation in his mind. He felt much better. It really wouldn't be a problem. Pierce was notorious for spouting off, and apparently the others weren't taking him too seriously.

***

"Clifford, what is that?" she said, pointing to a bag in his hand. "What did you buy?"

As always, the third degree from Mom the minute he got home from school. And it always happened within moments of coming through the front door. She was punctual as a well-managed train station, and she seemed to have some secret radar that informed her of his arrival the moment he approached the porch. If Mom ever stopped greeting him at the door to grill him about his day before he even had a chance to sit down, it would mean something was fatally wrong with the universe.

"It's just a bag of trail mix," Cliff said, heading for the stairwell.

"Trail mix?" She followed him to the stairs.

"Yeah. Remember? Dad always bought it when he took us camping."

"What do you need trail mix for?"

"I like it."

"What's in it?"

"Just a mixture of things."

"What things?"

105

"Peanuts, M&M's, raisins … That kind of stuff."

"Where did you buy it?"

She was never going to leave him alone. "I bought it at the 7-Eleven around the corner."

"So, you didn't take the bus home?"

"I did, but I got off at the corner and walked the rest of the way so I could stop at the store. I have a lot of homework, Mom." He started heading up the stairs. She followed.

"You bought it with your allowance?"

"Yeah."

"Don't you get enough to eat around here that you need to buy some kind of trail mix?"

"It's just a snack, Mom." Cliff closed his bedroom door behind him.

"Have an apple if you need a snack!" she shouted from outside the door.

Cliff shouted back, "Today I'm not having an apple! Today I'm having trail mix, OK?"

"Well, don't eat too much! It'll spoil your dinner!"

A few minutes later, Cliff was filling the dispenser in DeWorken's cage with trail mix.

"I think you'll enjoy it, DeWorken. At least it gives you some variety. We need to provide you with a balanced diet."

"Havin' fun, Reynolds?"

"Yes! Yes, I suppose I am."

"Hey, ya can't keep doin' this! Ya have ta turn me loose!"

"Who says so?"

"The law says so! I got rights!"

"Call a lawyer!"

"You're gonna be in a lot of trouble, Reynolds. Ya can't hide me forever. Sooner or later, I'm gonna be discovered."

"Not if I vacuum you up and throw you in the trash. Now,

pipe down, DeWorken! So far, I'd say I'm treating you fairly well, considering the fact that I don't even like you."

"Yeah? Well, the feeling is neutral!"

"I think you meant to say that the feeling is *mutual*, you stupid clod!"

"Ooh! The talkin' dictionary!" For a moment it got quiet. Then DeWorken started in again. "I suppose ya know I'm missin' the big game against Lincoln High!"

"Oh, that's right! Our team will have to play without its star quarterback! Tough times for the world of sports."

"We could lose the game all on account of you, Reynolds!"

"DeWorken, you're moving me close to tears. Let me tell you how I feel about these precious little sporting events. I hate sports. In fact, I hate all sports."

"Yeah? So, how come? What did sports ever do ta ya?"

"Never mind!"

All at once, Cliff realized that he might just want to talk about it after all. Perhaps it would be enjoyable to get a thing like this off his chest. When would he ever get another chance to let loose his feelings in the presence of a bully? So he went on a tirade, releasing emotions he'd bottled up for years.

"What have sports done to me? What have sports done to me? I'll tell you what they've done! Because of mandatory PE classes, people like me are humiliated by people like you! That's what sports have done to me!"

"You weaklings humiliate yourselves! Maybe if ya practiced a little! Maybe if ya worked out once in a while and kept yourself in shape!"

"Oh? Well, that should be my own choice, shouldn't it? Just what business is it of yours? I don't need some brainless jock setting up my workout schedule!"

Cliff started to cover up the cage.

"Wait!" DeWorken said. "Where are ya goin'?"

"I have to get started on my homework."

"I'm bored. Isn't there anything ta do around here?"

"You actually want to do something with *me*, DeWorken?"

"No. But anything's better than sittin' here by myself."

"Hmm … you like chess?"

"Chess?"

"Never mind. Dumb question. Besides, you're not much bigger than the pieces."

DeWorken got defensive. "I could play chess if I wanted to! I just don't like it! That's all! It's a game for nerds!"

"Well, then, I guess I can't help you, DeWorken. All of my games take brains. I don't own a copy of *Candy Land.*"

"Shut up, Reynolds! Just shut your trap!"

"You know, for a little pip-squeak, you certainly have a big mouth."

"This is cruel, leavin' someone alone all day without any company!"

"Oh, you're really one to talk about cruelty! Just between you and me, DeWorken, I think you would have ended up behind bars sooner or later anyway."

"Couldn't ya at least turn on some music?"

"I'll think about it. In the meantime, if you're lonely for a friend, I could try to find you a Barbie Doll."

"Very funny! I'll bet ya actually have one. I'll bet ya play with dolls!"

"No … I don't have dolls, DeWorken, but I'll tell you what I *do* have. I have a snake. Maybe you'd like to go into *his* cage for a while." DeWorken looked petrified. Cliff continued. "We keep it in the backyard. Mom won't let me bring him into the house. She says it's too slimy and slithery. But maybe you'll like him more than my mom does."

"Reynolds, ya wouldn't really do that, would ya?"

"His name is Sidney. How would you like to spend an afternoon with Sidney the Snake?"

"Come on, Reynolds."

"He really isn't that big. Oh yes. I forgot. To you, everything is big."

"Look, Reynolds, I know I've teased ya a lot, but I don't deserve this. I know ya ain't a murderer!"

"I'm not a murderer. That's true. But you start showing me a little respect, DeWorken. Understand?"

"Yeah. Yeah sure."

"For starters, you can try using my first name, Cliff. You see, I don't care much for the usage of last names. They're too impersonal. And at school, my last name has turned into nothing more than a signal for some ugly thug like you to start shoving me around. Of course, I'll still call you DeWorken. In fact, I'll do whatever I want."

"OK, Cliff. OK! Just no more talk about snakes!"

Cliff really did own a snake. He would never dream of putting DeWorken into the cage. That would be cold-blooded homicide. But he had to admit, it was awfully fun scaring him a little. This small taste of power was exhilarating!

***

The newfound enjoyment came to a sharp and sudden halt the following evening.

"Clifford! Could you come down here for a minute?"

Not in a hurry to hear today's scolding over some cup that he forgot to put in the sink after he finished using it or some jacket that he might have left on the living room floor, Cliff continued typing his history essay.

"Clifford? Clifford? CLIFFORD, GET DOWN HERE NOW!!!"

Cliff let out a sigh and slowly started down the stairs. All at once he realized that his mother wasn't alone, for he heard her say to someone, "He's a good boy. I'm sure he'll be glad to tell you anything he knows."

Oh, brother! Something was up, something bad, and Cliff didn't like the smell of it. He bolted down the rest of the stairs and found his mother sitting in the living room with two middle-aged men dressed in suits and ties. One of them was heavy but muscular. The other, rather thin and wiry.

"Clifford, these men are police detectives."

Cliff felt as though his stomach had just dropped out. "Police detectives?" He tried to form a casual, innocent-looking composure.

"Hi there, Cliff," the heavier one said. "I'm Detective Anderson. This is Detective Burns. Sorry to interrupt your homework."

They all shook hands. Anderson was definitely the friendlier of the two. He spoke congenially and smiled, but his partner, Burns, kept a suspicious frown on his face.

"How would you gentlemen like something to eat while we talk? I have a delicious strawberry-rhubarb pie in the kitchen."

"No, thank you, ma'am," Burns said. "We're a bit preoccupied right now."

"You're not the only one she asked," said Anderson. "*I'd* like a piece of pie."

Looking excited, Mrs. Reynolds got up and headed for the kitchen. Cliff was dying inside. Only his mother could think of ordinary hospitalities at a time like this. Why be concerned about the fact that two policemen wanted to talk to her son? As long as she could offer some of her famous rhubarb pie, life was ecstasy!

"What's going on?" he asked the detectives, knowing full well what was going on.

"Cliff," Anderson said, "would you by any chance happen to know a boy at school by the name of Doug DeWorken?"

"Sure … everybody knows him. Ah … I hear from some of my teachers that he's been missing."

"Yes, he has!" Burns said in a slightly sharper tone.

Anderson made a gesture with his hand and Burns, looking as though he had more to say, instead yielded the floor to his partner. Actually, the whole routine seemed rather rehearsed to Cliff.

"He's been missing more than three days," Anderson explained. "Now, Cliff, please understand, these are only standard questions that we're asking *many* people from your school."

"I understand."

Anderson continued. "Do you have any idea where Doug might

have gone? Do you remember him talking or maybe even bragging about taking a trip someplace? Someplace without his parent's consent?"

"No. But then, he wouldn't tell me a thing like that anyway. I'm not really a friend of his. I hardly know him."

"That's not what we hear!"

"Easy, Ed. Cliff, all Detective Burns means is that we did speak to a few students who said Doug has a habit of picking on you."

Wonderful. Just wonderful. He was in big trouble now, courtesy of Scott Pierce.

"Is that true, Clifford? You never told me you were being picked on!" Mom was still in the kitchen, but she could hear every word.

"There was nothing you could have done, Mom."

"Nothing I could have done?" She walked back into the room, handing Anderson his plate of rhubarb pie smothered in whipped cream. "There most certainly was! I could have called the school!"

"That wouldn't have stopped him, Mom."

"Oh?" said Burns. "Well, what *did* stop him? Did you find a way to stop this bully yourself?"

Burns' question was evidently the first wake-up call for Cliff's mom, the first clue that this might be more than a routine visit. "Excuse me, just what are you implying? How dare you speak to my son that way?"

Anderson stepped in again as the peacemaker. "Take it easy, Mrs. Reynolds. Nobody's implying anything. Ed, cool it! You're scaring the boy! He can't help it if he was bullied. Besides, he seems very cooperative so far. He'll tell us what he knows, won't you, Cliff?"

"Yes ... ah ... of course."

Responding to an inviting gesture from his mom, Anderson situated himself on a living room chair. The other detective remained standing.

"That's all we ask," Anderson said pleasantly. "The dessert looks fantastic, Mrs. Reynolds. Thank you." He took a bite. "Mm ... mm."

Cliff recognized this well-orchestrated performance. He'd seen it on television police shows dozens of times. The procedure was known as "good cop/bad cop." One tries to frighten you, while the other one comes to your defense. The resulting varieties of emotion were designed to eventually wear a man down and get him to confess something. And if they were going out of their way to try this charade on him, then he was a suspect all right. That was for certain.

Anderson continued. "Cliff, we don't mean to alarm you. But I'm sure you'll agree that it's unusual for a big fellow like Doug DeWorken to simply disappear off the face of the earth, especially before his important football game."

Again with the football. Was anything ever more important to people than football? It wouldn't have surprised Cliff if concern for the championship turned out to be the driving force behind finding DeWorken. "Yes. That *is* unusual. But I really have no idea what happened to him."

"I see," Anderson said with sincerity, or at least in a manner meant to *sound* sincere.

Then, like clockwork, right on schedule, Burns chimed in. "Still, you didn't like being picked on, did you Cliff?"

"Oh, this is so ridiculous," his mom said. "What child likes being picked on?"

Cliff's mom had seated herself on another chair. Only Cliff and Burns were still up. Cliff surmised that sitting might make him look a little more confident, a little less nervous, and a little less suspicious.

"Besides," he said while seating himself, "DeWorken is a lot stronger than me. What could I do to a guy like him anyway?"

"Probably nothing," Anderson said.

"Unless you had some help," Burns grunted.

Cliff slowly made eye contact with Burns. "Help?"

"With a weapon of some sort. Do you own a weapon, Cliff?"

Now Mom stood up. This was becoming a game of musical chairs. She walked closer to the detective. "Excuse me again, Mr. Burns …"

But Burns ignored her and just kept going. "Any kind of weapon? A gun, a knife, a club?"

"Now just a minute, Mr. Burns. You're not implying for one second that my son is a suspect …"

"Of course not," Anderson said. "Right now, *nobody* is a suspect."

"Well, I'm certainly glad to hear that! Because Clifford would never hurt anybody. He's gentle as a lamb. He's a good boy! And he's a wonderful, straight-A student!"

"I'm sure he is," Anderson said reassuringly. "But we *do* need to ask questions."

Cliff felt mixed emotions now. He was glad to see his mom finally wake up, and it felt good to be defended, at first. But this was the second time she had called him a "good boy," and that phrase was troublesome. Often, on the news, when they interviewed the mother of some convicted thug, the first tearful words out of her mouth were, "He's a good boy! He's always been a good boy!" And hearing Mom say that again and again just might suggest to the detectives that perhaps he *wasn't* a good boy. As for being a good student, Cliff often wondered why society assumed that intelligent people couldn't possibly commit crimes. But maybe he should be glad people did feel that way. Maybe his grades would save his neck.

"I assure you, your son is not a suspect," Anderson said again.

"And yet," said Burns, "in a way, everybody is a suspect."

Anderson interjected. "That is, we accuse no one, but we watch everyone. That's the only way to find this poor missing kid."

Cliff had thought of DeWorken in many ways, but never as a "poor kid."

"Well, then, you gentlemen had better make yourselves more clear. Because if you're going to talk to my son as a suspect, I'm ending the conversation right now! He doesn't have to speak to you without an attorney!"

Don't help me, Mom, Cliff said to himself. The more she talked, the more she put the noose around his neck.

Anderson got up out of his chair, put down his plate on the coffee table, and placed his hand on Cliff's shoulder. "Do you want an attorney, Cliff?"

This seemed like a double-edged question, and Cliff honestly didn't know which response would sound better. "Um … I'm not sure."

Anderson's countenance was still friendly. "You can have a lawyer if you like."

"That is, if you think you need one," Burns said.

"He didn't say he needs one! You're trying to trick him!"

Burns grinned for the first time, and it was a sly grin. "Trick him into what, ma'am?"

"I think you should leave."

"Mom, it's OK. I'll talk to them."

"You'll do nothing of the sort, Clifford. I know you're innocent, but they can still twist your words and use them against you."

"Mrs. Reynolds," Anderson said, "we're not here to twist anything."

"He's a minor and I'm his mother!"

"Of course, Mrs. Reynolds."

"And he is not going to waive the right of an attorney!"

She was out of her chair again, pacing back and forth.

Burns walked over to her. "Answering a few questions right now doesn't waive his right to an attorney later on. Attorney privilege during questioning can only be waived if Cliff refuses one *after* he's arrested."

"Or rather, *if* he's arrested," Anderson said. "Unlikely as that would be."

"It's OK," Cliff said. "I'll talk to you."

Anderson smiled warmly. "Would you, Cliff? Would you talk to us for a while, at least long enough for me to finish my pie?"

"He will not! Good day, gentlemen!"

"OK," Anderson said. "We'll leave if we're making you uncomfortable."

"Mom, I said I'd talk to them."

"It's not your decision to make, Clifford!"

"Well," Burns said, "how about if we just have a look around instead? Cliff, would you mind if we searched your room?"

"I already told you he has no weapons!"

"Of course," Anderson said. "And all we want to do is establish his innocence sooner. One quick look in the room and we'll be gone."

"You'll be gone now! And don't come back unless you have a search warrant!"

Burns took a few steps and spoke to her face to face. "We'll get one if we have to, ma'am. Make no mistake about that."

Anderson got in the middle of them. "Now, Ed. I'm sure it won't be necessary. Nobody here is acting like they have anything to hide. Sorry to have troubled you, Mrs. Reynolds. And we hope we haven't worried you, Cliff."

"No ... um ... no problem."

"I'll show you gentlemen to the door!"

Burns walked out first, followed by Anderson. Before his mom closed the door behind them, Anderson turned around one last time.

"Say, Cliff, you like this town you live in, don't you?"

Cliff shrugged his shoulders. "I guess I like it."

"Good. Then since you like the town, don't leave town."

***

Cliff decided not to say anything to DeWorken about their visit. All night long, he tossed and turned in bed, sometimes drifting to sleep for twenty minutes or so, but always waking back up. Never in his life had he felt so frightened. If every bully in school combined their efforts, it couldn't even come close to the terror these police detectives invoked. They'd be back. They'd be back for sure, with a search warrant. No, they wouldn't find a weapon but they *would* find DeWorken! True, nobody would be able to explain how he got into the dwarfed condition he was in, so it was unlikely that they could blame Cliff for a thing like that. There would be astonished looks and double takes. There would be reporters and scientists. But after the frenzy died down, there would also be the undeniable fact that DeWorken, however he got that way, had been Cliff's prisoner! He had to get rid of him, and he had to get rid of him fast. Killing him wasn't an option. It was starting to look tempting, but Cliff knew it was something he could never bring himself to do. But if he didn't kill him, he still needed to dispose of him. How? Where? And how much time did he have? How long before they returned with the warrant? Probably a few days to a week. They were a little suspicious, but there wasn't yet a whole lot for them to go on. And if they were snooping around school, they would have learned by now that DeWorken had picked on many people, not just him. Besides, he'd been willing to cooperate and answer questions. His mother came across as the more agitated one, but perhaps they would chalk that up to a mother's natural protective instinct. They probably talked to mothers like her all the time. They were used to it. Yes, probably a few days of grace to count on, but Cliff would need to spend every second of these days coming up with a solution. And then, after he got rid of DeWorken, he would also dispose of the hamster cage and clean his room really well, hopefully removing all possible traces of DNA. Even a small DeWorken had the same DNA structure, and they would be looking for it.

Why hadn't he listened to Mike? Mike warned him over and over not to use the ornament. True, the "bad thing" did happen to DeWorken, as expected. But Mike had tried to caution him about the ornament's sneakiness, about how the ornament had a tendency to solve one problem only by creating other problems which you could only get out of with another wish. And Cliff had no more wishes because he'd already returned the ornament. Hmm ... if he had it again, would he be tempted to use it again to get out of trouble? Probably, even though two seconds ago he was kicking himself for using it in the first place. There was something very obsessive about that ornament. In any event, wishing wasn't likely to help. Cliff seemed to remember from past experience years ago that a new wish couldn't undo the effects of an old wish. A new wish might help him in some other manner. He might, for instance, wish that the police stop suspecting him, but he would not be able to wish DeWorken back to his original size. At least, those were the ornament rules as best as Cliff could recall. In any event, the likelihood that Mike would give him the ornament again was zero times zero. Mike would have it hidden away in a better spot by now as well. There was no way that mistake would be repeated. And so, all things considered, Cliff realized it would be best to forget about the ornament and try to come up with some other idea.

The next evening, Cliff considered canceling his trip to the carnival, but he finally decided to keep the engagement in the hopes that it would take his mind off of things. He'd spent the whole day trying to think of a way out of his nightmare, and his mind was turning to mush. Perhaps a chance to unwind would rest his tangled thoughts and clear a passage for a fresh idea. That kind of result occasionally occurred in the past when Cliff was thinking too hard about a science project or essay topic. A little break, a small delay, and suddenly ideas started pouring through his head again. Hopefully the same thing would happen tonight.

Predictably, his mother tried to talk him out of going because she was worried about the policemen following him around, but Cliff just told her that he hadn't seen them at all since they'd been to the house, and if by chance they *did* run into him at the carnival, having a good time, it would only help matters because it might serve to make him look less suspicious.

His mother finally calmed down a bit after talking to an attorney who assured her that she had nothing to worry about and that the police did not yet have probable cause to obtain a search warrant. He also promised her that if she heard from the detectives again, she could call him, and he would drive out to the house immediately.

They arrived at the carnival around 4:00 in the afternoon, and it took forever to find a parking place. Wilson's parents did let them go their own way, as promised. The traveling carnival had been in town one week already, and Cliff had never visited it before, not even in previous years. He immediately noticed that it wasn't as big or as nice as the county fair, but there were still a lot of interesting attractions, and even without the livestock and other farm-related exhibits, this carnival *was* similar to a fair in many ways.

There were more snack stands than Cliff could count, offering everything from popcorn to cotton candy to hot dogs to Polish sausage to pizza. And the rides were all familiar; the usual assortment: roller coasters, bumper cars, a Ferris wheel, and a whole series of spinning rides designed to make a person dizzy. The roller coasters were the only rides that really interested Cliff. Wilson suggested that they also try the bumper cars after doing the roller coasters four to five times.

In addition to rides, there was a haunted house and a "fun house" with mirrors that distorted one's appearance, making him look fatter, skinnier, or shorter. There were also a couple of outdoor stage shows — one with acrobats, the other with some has-been rock singer from the eighties. They decided not to attend either show because the roller coaster lines were very long, and if they wanted multiple rides, they were going to have to cut down on other things.

The first roller coaster (also known as the Big Dipper) was so much fun that they decided to ignore the other smaller-looking coasters and stick to this one alone. Three times in a row seemed enough for a while, so after the rides, Cliff and Wilson walked up and down the outdoor game section, the kinds of games where you threw a ping pong ball into a goldfish bowl or won an automated horse race by playing pinball better than your opponents. Most of the prizes were stuffed animals or jewelry, things you would win for your sweetheart. It made Cliff wish he was here with a girl instead of Wilson, but even so, it was doubtful to Cliff that he could win anything anyway. It was even more doubtful that he would ever be here or anywhere else with a girl, even though his heart longed for such a situation, despite his attempts to minimize his feelings when his mother pressed him about going to dances.

Cliff and Wilson continued making the rounds. Whenever they walked too close to a game or stood still even for a second to watch, a barker would approach them instantly. "Try your luck, gentlemen! Throw a ball in the hoop and choose your own prize! It's just that simple! Only one dollar a ticket! Each ticket buys you five balls, five tries! You could probably do it in one try! But we're giving you, five, count them, five tries!"

Cliff hated the way those carnival barkers got in your face. Couldn't they just let a person browse the games and decide for himself what he wanted to play? Cliff was terrible at throwing or aiming. Hopefully he would find a game that didn't require such skills. If not, he'd go back and attempt that horse race pinball game. It was hard to mess up with a pinball, even for him. Still, it would be even nicer if he could find a game that didn't require any physical skill at all, but he wasn't holding his breath. Intellectual contests were fleeting at carnivals.

Toward the last row of games, Cliff noticed a larger green canvas, the kind of tent that might enclose a small circus. People were filing in, probably because some show was about to start. "Hey, Wilson, what's that over there?"

"I don't know."

"Let's go have a look."

Next to the tent was a marquee. The sign said: The Amazing Tinker Bell in giant colorful letters. Underneath the title was a cartoon-like drawing of a tiny female with light, petite, transparent wings and a leotard. Glancing at the smaller letters, Cliff read out loud, "Do you believe in fairies? You will, after you meet Tinker Bell, a woman so small, she can be held in the palm of your hand! Watch her dance! Watch her sing! Watch her do other amazing feats! You'll wonder how it's done, but you'll never figure it out!"

Under ordinary circumstances, Cliff would have assumed that this was some sort of children's marionette show and walked away. But the notion of a "tiny female" naturally made him think about another tiny person at home: a prisoner in his hamster cage, probably cussing him out this very minute under his breath and dreaming of what he would do to Cliff if he was ever restored to normal size again. Cliff knew this exhibit was bound to be a coincidence. After all, freak shows were just par for the course at carnivals. But he still felt compelled to investigate. Mike *had* warned him about the unusual, unexpected things that can accompany just one wish with the ornament.

"Care to see the show, Wilson?"

"Naw! It's a separate admission."

"True. But it's only five bucks apiece. I'll spring for it since you paid for everything else."

"You really wanna see this?" Wilson took a closer look at the sign, causing Cliff to wonder if he had really been paying that much attention when he read the advertisement aloud. "Tinker Bell? You mean the Tinker Bell from *Peter Pan*? I don't wanna see some kid's show! It's bad enough that my little sister always has those *Veggie Tales* on at home."

"You're missing the point, Wilson. This 'Tinker Bell' is supposed to be only a few inches tall!"

"Right! Like that's gonna look realistic!"

"Who knows? Maybe it will."

"Aw ... let's just ride the roller coaster again."

"Where's your scientific curiosity? Don't you want to see how they pull it off? Sure, she might look fake. But it *could* be a challenging illusion! Come on! It says on the sign that the whole show only lasts thirty minutes. That'll leave us plenty of time for more rides."

Wilson shrugged his shoulders. "All right ... I guess it's no big deal."

The usher escorted them into a horseshoe-shaped amphitheater where a large platform was surrounded by the audience on three sides. Recorded music was playing "There's No Business Like Show Business." They heard this repetitiously as people kept filing in.

"Thirty minutes?" Wilson said. "It's gonna take them thirty minutes to just start!"

Finally, a loud drumroll started as the lights dimmed on the audience and the platform lit up. An emcee with a large green top hat and a matching green suit with coattails ran out on stage. He looked as though he was dressed for a St. Patrick's Day party.

"Ladies and gentlemen! They say great things come in small packages! I think you'll agree when you meet tonight's star attraction! I'm about to introduce a special young lady! She's beautiful! But others are beautiful! She sings like a lark! But others have sweet voices as well! She's a skilled dancer! But there are many dancers! So why is she special? Why is she here at our carnival? Because she's one of a kind! And I promise, you've never met anyone like her before! Ladies and gentlemen, the one ... the only, Tinker Bell!"

All of a sudden, a miniature stage with a red curtain was lowered by wire on top of the larger platform where the emcee stood. Smaller lights shined down upon the junior stage. It looked like a model for a future, proposed theater. The curtains opened, and a small woman with bright yellow hair came out dressed in a green leotard that somewhat (although not entirely) resembled the outfit Tinker Bell wore in Disney's animated version of *Peter Pan*. She didn't have wings like the drawing on the marquee, but still, Cliff could scarcely believe his eyes ... Another miniature person, only six inches or so, just like DeWorken!

"Wow," Wilson whispered. "She actually looks real. How do you think they did that? A hologram of some sort?"

"Yes, probably." But even as he spoke, Cliff honestly doubted that it could be a hologram. He was very familiar with the latest advances in technology, and he subscribed to three different science journals. Holograms were a marvel all right, but no hologram could look so authentic. This became especially apparent when the emcee picked Tinker Bell up and had her dance on his hand. To do that with a hologram without some kind of light distortion would be absolutely impossible! Technology would undoubtedly get there sometime in the future, but not today.

The show lasted about thirty minutes. As promised, the so-called "Tinker Bell" turned out to be a splendid performer. Because of the normal-size microphone placed next to her stage, nobody had any trouble hearing her. Interestingly enough, her name and appearance were the only things in common with the Peter Pan story. Nothing else from that children's fantasy affected the theme of her performance. Instead, it was more reminiscent of Broadway or even Vegas. She sang a few classics, such as "My Funny Valentine" and "I Left My Heart In San Francisco." Cliff recognized everything. Although science was his favorite pursuit, he was considerably versed in the arts, history, and a whole host of other subjects.

In time, "Tinker Bell" switched her style and did some rocking oldies, like "Baby Love" and "Great Balls of Fire."

If Cliff had heard these songs on the radio, he would have had no suspicion whatsoever that they were being sung by a woman only inches tall. "Tinker Bell's" dances were also entertaining. They included elegant ballet-type moves and a more modern jazz dance. She did gymnastics as well: all kinds of backflips and even a trapeze act, on a very small trapeze, of course. Cliff would have been impressed even if the woman were normal size.

Later on, while waiting in line for cotton candy, Cliff explained to Wilson why the hologram theory was out.

"Yeah, I guess you're right," Wilson said. "Well, then they did it with mirrors."

"Mirrors? How could a mirror do all those things?"

"I don't know! Look at the stuff David Copperfield does, and he uses mirrors."

As they continued touring the exhibits, Cliff tried his hardest to analyze the situation. He didn't blame Wilson for assuming it was some kind of illusion. After all, that should always be the first guess of a logical mind when confronted with the paranormal. But of course, Wilson knew nothing about the ornament, and Wilson hadn't witnessed a genuinely shrunken person as Cliff had.

Could this carnival have somehow gotten its hands on another ornament? Had they reduced and enslaved some poor girl? On the other hand, if this had nothing to do with the ornament, could there be a whole hidden community of miniature people somewhere? People who were exploited by carnival barkers?

Of course, slavery was against the law. But since the average person would react like Wilson and assume it wasn't a real girl, the barker could actually get away with it! Who would ever suspect anything? Who would call the authorities? No one!

Maybe he was mistaken to assume that "Tinker Bell" was a slave. After all, she *could* be working for the carnival out of personal choice. All at once, it hit Cliff. The only reason slavery popped into his mind was because DeWorken had become *his* slave for all intents and purposes. Without ever thinking of it in those terms, Cliff had actually enslaved another human being! How could he do that? How could he practice such an evil enterprise, something he'd been taught to condemn his entire life?

Cliff tried to console himself. Slavery had never been his original objective. All he had requested of the ornament was some protection. He never expected the ornament to answer his wish in such an unusual manner. Technically, it wasn't slavery anyway since DeWorken wasn't being subjected to any forced labor. Nevertheless, Cliff was holding him captive. Technicalities notwithstanding, it was still slavery for all intents and purposes.

Unfortunately, once the idea of slavery hit him, it was all Cliff could think about. This carnival was suggesting a possible solution to the DeWorken question. There might just be a way to get rid of him. But the solution was likely to involve more slavery, and it made Cliff feel very guilty. Still, if Cliff could stop being the slave owner himself, if somebody else could take over, that would make him feel at least a little bit better. It would also remove DeWorken from his premises in case those detectives returned with a warrant to search his room.

It was dinnertime, and Wilson was off by himself looking for a hamburger stand. Cliff had told Wilson that he wasn't hungry and instead of eating he wanted to talk to the guy in charge of the Tinker Bell show to see if he would tell him how he did the trick. Wilson said he was more interested in eating than learning about the trick, so they agreed to meet back at the bumper cars in an hour.

"Going in to see the show again?" the ticket taker asked in a friendly voice, obviously recognizing Cliff from the previous performance.

"No," Cliff said. "Actually, I was wondering ... who's in charge of this exhibit?"

"You wanna see the manager?"

"Yes. The manager, if I may."

"What about?"

"I just have a question to ask him."

The ticket taker started looking him over in a suspicious way. "Tell me your question first."

"I'd rather ask the manager directly."

The man hesitated. Finally, he said, "Just a minute." Then he shouted over to the other ticket taker across the aisle. "Stuart! Take over for a second! I need to see Mr. Blake!"

Cliff was both happy and surprised that the guy had been so quickly agreeable. Such a reaction seemed to confirm his suspicion about something "under the table" going on. Evidently, Cliff's insistence on seeing the manager made this gentleman think they were in trouble. One only thinks he's in trouble if he's actually doing something wrong. It creates the habit of being extra cautious and looking over your shoulder. Unfortunately, Cliff was getting all too acquainted with that feeling.

A few minutes later, Cliff was led into a modest trailer office where a husky man with a shaved head and a tattooed arm sat behind his desk, writing in a ledger.

"Here he is, Mr. Blake," the ticket taker said before turning around and vacating the office.

"You have exactly two minutes," Mr. Blake muttered without even looking up from his work. "What can I do for you?"

The man was intimidating, but Cliff was onto an idea, and he needed to see it through. If he asked carefully plotted questions, he might be able to fool Mr. Blake into admitting the truth about his "world-famous performer."

Cliff's rapport with DeWorken seemed to be unleashing a more devious side to his personality, a side Cliff never realized he had. True, his cockiness around DeWorken was based on the helplessness of DeWorken. Nevertheless, squaring off with a person whose very shadow used to scare him was uniquely therapeutic. It allowed a whole new Cliff to break out of his shell.

And this new Cliff moved closer to Mr. Blake's desk. "Ah ... I just saw your show."

Mr. Blake looked up from his ledger. "Go on. You saw my show, and ..."

"Tinker Bell is very impressive."

"Glad you liked it, son."

Cliff sat down next to the desk. "I do a lot of science projects at school. I don't suppose you'd be willing to tell me how you did the trick."

The man had a sly look on his face. "Trick?"

"It must be some trick. I can't even figure you how you do it."

"Who says it's a trick? Maybe she's real."

"That would be impossible, Mr. Blake. It would mean that you discovered a woman only a few inches tall."

"Stranger things have happened."

"Not that strange. And I've read every volume of *Ripley's Believe It or Not*."

"I'll bet you have. Look, kid, I'm kind of busy."

But Cliff just continued. "The furthest my thinking takes me is that it must be done with mirrors."

"Whatever you say, son."

"It would mean a lot to me if you told me, mister."

"Magicians don't reveal their secrets."

"Then there *is* some secret trick."

"I'm not saying one way or the other. Your two minutes have expired."

Cliff stood up, ready to take the plunge and play his trump card. "The reason I know it has to be a trick is that if she was a real girl, it would mean you were keeping a living human being as a slave."

The man's face almost turned red. "All right, now I've had just about enough of this. Are you gonna get out of here, or do I have to throw you out?"

This was the reaction Cliff had hoped for. His comment obviously struck Mr. Blake in a vulnerable spot.

"There's no reason to get so upset, Mr. Blake. I just thought you might want to increase your act. I thought you might want a male version of Tinker Bell."

Mr. Blake looked as though he had suddenly been smacked in the head. "What did you say?"

"A male ... You know ... a friend for your little actress."

Blake's expression indicated partial concern and partial astonishment. His next question was laced with a cautious tone. "You actually think she's real, don't you, kid? You don't believe it's a trick."

"Maybe it is and maybe it isn't. Either way, I have the *genuine* article. I could sell you a man only six inches tall, and I assure you, it's no trick!"

Chapter Five

The Comic Book and the Girlfriend

It finally arrived. I didn't think the day would ever come, but it did. The postman rang the doorbell and had me sign for a light brown package addressed to "Mr. Michael Owen."

Inside were ten copies of the recently published *Arch-Ranger* comic, hot off the press, brand spanking new and colorful as ever.

I was so excited I almost tripped on my way back into the living room. Nobody was around to share the excitement with. My parents were away on a trip to England. They were gonna be gone two weeks, and I had the place to myself since Shelly was staying with another family. The parents of her best friend, Katie, had agreed to watch her so that Mom and Dad could have a kind of second honeymoon. They figured that between cross-country and all my upcoming book tours, I'd be too busy to watch my sister. Little did they know, I wouldn't have agreed to watch the little snip even if I had nothing to do but lay around on the couch all day like Caligula, but anyway, as it happened, I never had to push the matter.

Aunt Loureen had promised this trip to Mom and Dad for years as a kind of Christmas present. Mom loved the idea, but my dad always found some excuse for not going, like not being able to leave his job or needing extra time to build an extension to the house.

"A man who's always busy is too busy," Aunt Loureen loved to tell her brother.

But this time, Aunt Loureen was more insistent because she was using the trip as an excuse to get my parents out of the house. The story was that she would come and look after the place while my folks were away, but the real idea was that Aunt Loureen and I had a lot of ornament-related stuff to talk about, and she wanted to give us the privacy we needed.

Aunt Loureen had arranged a "leave of absence" from the school she taught at, but her schedule was gonna delay her, so I still ended up at the house by myself for a couple of days before she could arrive. My mom didn't like this idea. I reminded her that I was sixteen years old, and I didn't need a babysitter. I also reminded her of the many times she and Dad had gone away for a weekend, leaving me to watch Shelly.

"I know," she said. "But this is different. We'll be gone two whole weeks."

"Yeah, but for most of that time Aunt Loureen will be here. I'll only be by myself a few days."

Finally, Dad told her to stop fretting so much. He reminded her that I was "becoming a young man" and that "responsibility like this" was good for me. Anyway, that's why I was by myself when the package arrived.

Right before the postman had arrived with my *Arch-Ranger* comics, I'd been thinking about how Aunt Loureen would be here in a couple of days. There were still two things I needed to get out of the way before she came.

First, I had to go to that antique shop and find this special object she wanted. I had put that off. I usually did put off stuff I wasn't looking forward to doing.

My other "Aunt Loureen order" was to grill Cliff until he admitted what had happened with DeWorken and the ornament. I didn't wanna touch that one with a ten-foot pole because everyone at school was talking about how the police had been questioning Cliff, and I was afraid that if I found out what happened, I might get in trouble with the police too.

But Aunt Loureen was a hard one to say no to. I was starting to think of these favors as homework assignments, and now I was feeling guilty. She'd be here soon, and I had not done my homework. Leave it to Aunt Loureen to act like a teacher even around her nephew.

Oh well. I'd deal with the antique shop tomorrow right after school, and then I'd take on Cliff the next day. Today I was gonna just be happy about being a published author. I was gonna call Marla and talk about how my comic had arrived. Then tomorrow night, after I went to the shop, Marla's mom had promised to drive me down to the local TV station, where I would have my first television interview about *Arch-Ranger*. Griffith Publications arranged this for me, and it was only the beginning. In the next two weeks, I would be on national TV three different times!

"Hello?" Marla said

"Hey, it's me."

"Hi there!"

Her voice always turned cheerful the minute she knew I was on the other end of the phone.

"It's here!"

"What's here?"

"Some copies of *Arch-Ranger*."

"You mean you already saw it?"

"Several. The publisher promised to send me some advanced copies. And Marla, they really did a great job with the printing and layout!"

"Well, you're coming right over to show me, aren't you?"

"Sure. And I also wanted to remind your mom about tomorrow night. Marla? Hey! Are you there?"

I could hear her talking to her mom. She did this a lot, breaking off into some other conversations when I was on the phone.

"No, it's already arrived," she was saying. But I only heard her voice, not her mom's. "That's right! Can he? Thanks! Mike? Mom wants you to stay for dinner. She's fixing something special so that we can all celebrate."

A published comic and a girlfriend whose mother already liked me. Life just didn't get much better than this.

Chapter Six

The Gift

I enjoyed the antique shop more than I thought I would. It was filled with so much stuff that anyone was bound to see something he liked. There were old-fashioned chess sets, some shaped like Civil War soldiers, others like ancient Roman warriors. There were old coins and polished seashells. There were ships in bottles and any kind of timepiece you could possibly imagine: watches, grandfather clocks, anniversary clocks, cuckoo clocks, and lot's more. I got a strange feeling when I glanced at a large brass hourglass. I always thought hourglasses were cool, but this feeling was different. It was the kind of thing I can't explain, and I wondered if I was experiencing the intuition Aunt Loureen had mentioned. I picked the hourglass up. Hmm. Was this really it? How could an hourglass send her into another world? What a stupid question! How could a small Christmas ornament have done the incredible things I'd witnessed? I decided to stop analyzing the situation and just look at the price.

Five hundred dollars? I almost said out loud. No way! No way a simple object could be so expensive! Maybe it was some old, valuable antique, handmade by a famous count or something. Well, whatever the reason, it was not gonna be purchased today. I would just report the find to Aunt Loureen, and she could come get it herself if she needed it so badly.

I walked down the aisle, heading for the door. Enough of this. I needed to get home and shower before my interview. The station manager said that Marla could stay in the studio and watch. Afterwards, her mom was taking us out for a steak and lobster dinner! That would be two dinners in a row for me: one to celebrate the publication, the other to celebrate my first interview.

"Unique little store, isn't it, Mike?"

Oh, for crying out loud! Here he was again! That spooky man! That Charles guy who got under my skin at the school dance! And this will really sound weird: He was wearing the exact same suit!

"Splendid little antique shop … humble, quaint. I believe this store offers everything but the kitchen sink."

I was speechless, and my tongue almost dropped out of my mouth like it was numb or something. I just couldn't figure this character out, and I had no idea what to say to him. He was so annoying, but then, Aunt Loureen had seemed sure Charles had come from the other world, and I knew she wouldn't want me to brush him off. I knew she wouldn't want me to "be afraid of my destiny." So I figured I should try to talk to him even if I hated every second of it.

"Yeah ... ah ... Charles, wasn't it?"

"Yes, indeed. What are you buying today, Mike?"

"Nothing special. Just looking around. How about you?"

"Oh, I'm here for a more definite reason."

We were standing next to some small medieval-type figures, so I said, "Looking for a decoration?"

"Oh, no. Nothing like that."

Of course it was nothing like that! He was here only because I was here! Don't ask me how I knew, but I knew, and I was really getting fed up! What would happen if I just ignored him, turned around and stormed out of the place? What would happen if I decided I didn't care about letting Aunt Loureen down? I'd had enough of her little adventures!

"May I offer a suggestion, Mike?"

"Huh?"

"May I offer a suggestion? Regarding your purchase?"

"Who says I'm gonna purchase anything? I told you, I'm just looking around."

"Unusual place for a high schooler to be looking around. Generally, boys of your age are in the sporting goods store or the video games store. It's rare to find a sophomore who likes to go antiquing."

"Mister, I'm not antiquing. For the last time, I'm just messing around!" I didn't mean to snap at him or let him see how annoyed I was, but I almost couldn't help it.

"I see ... Just messing around ... Understood ... Well, while you 'mess around,' you might take a gander at that hourglass over there."

Man oh man! Something out in the cosmos was pulling my strings! That was for sure! Something or someone didn't trust me to go with my intuition, and now that same something was giving me a big shove! How could I back away now? There was no more doubt. The hourglass was meant for Aunt Loureen.

"Um … yeah … I do like it, but it's kind of expensive."

"It *is* a bit steep at that. Supposing I give you the money?"

"No, thanks, mister."

"Charles."

"No, thanks, Charles."

"Why not?"

"I'll tell you what you can do instead. You can tell me what's going on here."

"Just a gesture of friendship. After all, Christmas is right around the corner, and I do believe that hourglass would make an enchanting gift for your Aunt Loureen."

This was the final straw. "All right, now that's it. That's enough."

"Shh!"

I didn't realize how loud I was getting. Three people were now staring at us.

Charles lowered his voice. "I'm happy to do this for you, Mike."

"No, thanks. I don't take money from strangers."

"We can call it a loan instead of a gift if that would make you feel better."

"It wouldn't make me feel better. That thing costs five hundred dollars. I could never pay you back."

"Maybe you can pay me back some other way. Money isn't everything, after all. Just remember that I did you a favor. Someday you can do *me* a favor too."

This guy was starting to remind me of a loan shark … No … Worse than a loan shark … He was reminding me of the devil. Not that I'd ever met the devil, and not that I was even sure I believed in the devil, but I'd seen a lot of movies about people who met strangers like Charles, strangers who knew all sorts of things about them and did stuff for them. And every time, at the end of the movie, the poor sap realized he'd just sold his soul to the devil.

"Forget it, mister. No chance. I don't wanna owe you anything. Not even a favor."

"All right then. We'll forget about the favor. Now we're back where we started. We're back at square one. The offer, once again, is a gift: a free, unconditional gift."

I just shook my head.

"Now, Mike, why be so stubborn? We both know your Aunt Loureen wants you to get the hourglass for her. She sent you to the store for this very purpose."

"That's all, brother."

"Better keep your voice down. People are starting to look again. Say, why don't we step outside for a minute? We can talk more privately out there."

It actually sounded like a good idea. I was ready. This man might have been scary, but I was ready to have it out with him.

Once outside, he said, "Now, then, Mike. What exactly is the problem?"

"I think you know, mister."

"Charles."

"OK! OK! Charles. I know your name, but I know nothing about you! Who are you?"

"Well, I'm not the devil, if that's what you're worried about."

"See? See? I was just thinking that and you read my mind!"

"No," he laughed. "I don't read minds."

"Yeah? Well, you did something! You know everything about me, and I know nothing about you. Who are you? And don't say, 'Charles.'"

"But I *am* Charles."

"I don't care what your name is! I wanna know who you *truly* are!"

He formed a slow, eerie smile. "Haven't you figured it out yet?"

"Why should I have to figure it out? Why can't you just tell me?!"

"Because it would be so much more fun if you figured it out for yourself."

"Look, are you gonna tell me or aren't you?"

"Now, now, my boy, no impudence."

I lowered my voice. "Sorry, mister."

"Charles."

"Would you stop …? All right … all right … I'm sorry, Charles."

I was telling the truth when I said I was sorry. I'd always been taught to respect my elders, and I did feel bad about the way I was talking to him, even though he probably had it coming.

"Mike, don't I seem the slightest bit familiar to you?"

"No. You seem weird, but you don't seem familiar."

"Think … think!"

"You only seemed familiar when I thought about the devil."

"Well, I'm not the devil."

"You already told me. So who are you?"

"Somebody once said that the best lessons in life are the ones we discover for ourselves."

"OK. OK. Now I know who you remind me of. Aunt Loureen! I mean, you don't look like her or anything, but that stuff you just said about life's lessons … Aunt Loureen loves to make those kinds of remarks."

"Relax, Mike. I'm not your Aunt Loureen."

"I already know that, mister. I'm just trying to think about it, like you said."

"I understand. Like your aunt, I do enjoy a good mystery. That's what sounded familiar. But there's more, so much more. Never mind. I see it isn't going to happen just yet. Why don't you wait here while I go inside and purchase the hourglass? No more arguments, Mike. You may not know who I am, but you do know that you were meant to bump into me today, and you also know that Loureen needs the hourglass. Now I won't take no for an answer. I'm afraid I'm going to have to insist. Stay here and wait for me."

It almost sounded like a command. But I did as he told me. I waited. I didn't know what else to do, and this Charles guy was starting to freak me out. I was beginning to think that getting on his bad side might not be such a good idea.

Before I knew it, Charles returned with two white plastic bags instead of the one bag I was expecting. "Here," he said, handing me the larger bag with a red box inside. "This one is the hourglass. It's right inside the box. Give it to your aunt as soon as she arrives. The other one is for you."

"Huh?"

"Well, aren't you going to open it?"

"How come you got *me* a gift?"

"You're an impossible person to shop for, you know that?"

"I don't get it, mister."

"Mike, just open the package."

Inside the bag was a smaller box, a blue box. I popped it open. It was a gold key chain attached to a tiny gold sword, probably from that medieval section of the store.

"Do you like it?"

Actually, I *did* like it. Normally, I would just view it as a cool little knick-knack and thank whoever gave it to me. "Yeah, it's nice. It's just ..."

"Just what?"

"Well, I don't understand."

"You never understand, Mike. So what else is new?"

"What's it for?"

Charles sighed. "What's it for? You put your keys on it. That's what it's for."

"I mean, what's it *really* for?"

"Well, you'll just have to find out. But let me give you some advice. Keep it with you wherever you go. This device will protect you."

"Protect me? From what?"

"From some future danger down the road. You have a long and perilous journey ahead of you."

I didn't like the sound of that. I knew Aunt Loureen was planning a journey into the other world, but I sure as heck wasn't. "What are you talking about? I'm not going on any journey."

"Oh sure you are, Mike. You don't think you are, but you are. And when you pack, remember to bring the key chain along. I know it isn't as big as a *real* sword. But it'll protect you just the same in ways you can't even begin to imagine."

But I *could* imagine. I could imagine a lot of things, especially if this was another charm like the ornament.

Chapter Seven

Fame and Friendship

"Sports and weather in a moment. But first, in our Cultural Corner, Patricia Freiberg has a special guest. Take it away, Patricia."

"Thanks, Don. I'm here this evening with Michael Owen, one of Oak Hill City's own. And in my hand is a brand-new comic book that advanced reviewers are already calling a small classic. *Arch-Ranger* is the name, written and drawn by a sophomore at Valley View High. Welcome, Mike!"

"Thanks. Ah ... good to be here."

I'd been nervous while they were putting my makeup on and testing my wireless mic. Marla kept smiling at me, and occasionally she whispered from across the room, "I'm proud of you." That helped, but I was still nervous. I'd watched all kinds of shows on this station, and my dad watched the local news all the time, so I was surrounded by faces that I'd only seen on television, and my heart was racing. Still, after the interview actually got started and I had a chance to tell some of the Arch-Ranger story, I felt more relaxed.

"Sounds captivating, Mike. Where do you get your inspiration from?"

Like I told you at the beginning of the book, I actually had a good answer for that question, but I left out the details. "Well, from all kinds of things. From school and friends."

"I suppose high school provides a lot of experiences that call for courage. Now, let's see ... You're on the cross-country team, aren't you, Mike? Are we having a good season?"

"Yeah, so far. We've won six meets and only lost one."

"That must make you feel good."

"Sure. I mean ... the team should feel good. As a team, it's an awesome year. But I'm not really placing too well myself. I come in around fourth or fifth each time."

"Yes, but about thirty run at once, don't they?"

"Something like that."

"Well, fifth out of thirty is impressive. And I have a feeling your new book is going to be first!"

I loved this. I loved every minute of it.

***

There he was! It was lunchtime, and Cliff was on a bench by himself. We hadn't talked for ages. He was frowning, and the frown didn't leave his face when he saw me.

"Hey," I said.

"Hey."

"Mind if I join you?"

"It's a free country."

I sat down.

"Nice job on your interview last night," he said. "My mom and I both watched you on TV."

"Thanks. Next week will be even bigger. The major networks!"

"Yeah, I heard. A lot of the guys are talking about it. You seem to have it made."

"Cliff, we're still friends aren't we?"

"Why do you keep asking me that? I already said we were."

"Well, it seems like you've been avoiding me lately. Look, Cliff, I've been hearing a lot of rumors. I'm not sure what it all means, but it sounds like you're in a lot of trouble."

"I'm fine."

"Come on. If we're still friends, then talk to me like a friend. You look like you need someone to talk to."

Cliff's eyes were sad, and they seemed to be pleading with me to keep probing. I had heard once that the eye was the "lamp of the body," that no matter how much a person lied, their eyes always told the truth.

"Come on, Cliff, level with me. What's going on?"

"Nothing."

"Nothing? One day after you use the ornament, Doug DeWorken

disappears and nobody can find him. Some coincidence. The ornament *did* work that day, didn't it, Cliff? You lied when you said it didn't work."

All of a sudden, tears started streaming down his face. "Oh, Mike ..."

I put my hand on his shoulder. "I'm here, man. I'm here."

"Mike, I've done something terrible. The most terrible kind of a thing a person can do."

Chapter Eight

The Day Aunt Loureen Called Me Persnickety

It was always good seeing Aunt Loureen again. Even though I was starting to hate all this stuff about magic and far-off worlds, she had been my favorite relative ever since I was a little kid, and I couldn't help enjoying her company, no matter what we were talking about.

She arrived early in the evening and insisted on freshening up before we talked, even though I told her that I had some real important news. A few hours later, I gave her the hourglass, and she looked so fascinated that she could hardly take her eyes off of it. When I was done filling her in on my chance meeting with Charles, I started in with the "Cliff update," but she insisted that she wanted to make some hot ginger tea first.

Twenty minutes had gone by. Aunt Loureen was sitting on a chair near the fireplace, sipping her tea and enjoying it. She smiled, nodded, and sometimes even chuckled as I passed on the information Cliff shared with me. Only when I got to the part about the carnival and Tinker Bell did she suddenly look concerned. And then, when I reached the end and told her that Cliff had actually sold his small enemy, the way people used to sell slaves, Aunt Loureen had a look on her face like I had never seen before. In all the years we had been together, I don't think I had ever seen her worried.

"The problem is that the carnival has left town," I said to her. "Cliff did an Internet search and found its latest stop, a little town called Wendover. That's pretty far away! We even tried using the ornament, even though I was scared about what bad thing might happen. We asked it to just bring DeWorken back … just make him disappear from the carnival and reappear back at Cliff's house. But it didn't work. I guess the ornament decided not to answer the wish."

"I could have told you that it wouldn't work."

"You already knew, Aunt Loureen?"

"No. *You* knew. You knew you were going on a journey because this Charles fellow predicted it. I knew only after you told me. That is how DeWorken will be rescued. You're going on a journey."

I had forgotten about Charles' prediction. Originally I just assumed he had been referring to a journey into the other world, the same kind of journey Aunt Loureen was talking about. That's why it bothered me so much. Thinking about it now, I was relieved that he probably just meant some other kind of trip to bring DeWorken back. "Destiny" was not gonna force me into another dimension after all. Still, I really didn't wanna take *any* kind of trip just now. Too many good things were happening in my life, and I wasn't about to louse it up.

"Who says I'm going on a journey?"

"I do. "

"Now just a minute …"

"Hush! Sit yourself down and listen for once!" I sat across from her on the living room sofa. "Nephew, I already knew things were getting serious. But now we're beyond serious. The matter is desperate. Therefore, fast, desperate countermeasures must be taken … immediately! Your friend Cliff has 'upped the ante' so to speak."

She was scaring the snot out of me. "Well, what can Cliff do now?"

"Very little by himself. You need to help him, Nephew. The two of you need to get DeWorken back."

"Why does it take two of us? He can get him back without me."

"Don't you understand? Somehow this carnival barker has found a way into the other world!"

"You think Tinker Bell's from the other world?"

"My instincts tell me that. So do yours if you care to look at them honestly. And now, the two worlds are overlapping. DeWorken must be removed from that man's clutches. It's not just about Cliff being in trouble … It's not just about DeWorken being in trouble …"

"Well, then, what's it about? I don't really understand any of this junk about the two worlds coming together. I mean, what do you think is gonna happen? Are they gonna blow up or something?"

"Nephew, sometimes people detect danger in the wind, even if the details are not so obvious."

"Huh?"

"Just trust me. DeWorken's imprisonment at the carnival provides a precarious conduit to another mysterious world, a world he cannot possibly handle, not if he behaves the way you've described him. Get him out of there! Rescue him!"

"How?"

"I don't know how. Work with your friends. Work as a team. Ask Ben to go with you."

"He won't wanna come."

"Convince him. He's brave and reliable. Also, my intuition ..."

"Don't tell me. Your intuition says I should bring him."

She nodded. "Take the ornament too. I know you're afraid of it, but if you run up against too many obstacles, it may just come in handy, especially if you make your wish with care and forethought."

"It's risky to let Cliff near the ornament. He keeps getting tempted to wish for stupid things."

"Then you must convince him to refrain until it's absolutely necessary."

"Why don't you go with us? With your help, we won't make a mess of things like we usually do."

"I promised your parents I'd watch the house. I also need to acquaint myself with the hourglass and figure out how it works. I have a journey of my own coming up soon, remember."

I didn't like being reminded that Aunt Loureen was going away into that other world. "When are you going?"

"Could be weeks. Could be months. But soon. You don't need me for this little trip. Take the cat instead."

"Caligula? On a car trip? Oh yeah! Sure! That would be the day!"

"Your parents have a pet carrier for his visits to the vet."

"Yeah, and he hates it! He hates the cage and he hates the car and he hates me!"

"He may hate like the dickens, but if you put him in the caged-up

145

pet taxi, he can't do anything about it. You'll need him. He can answer questions about the ornament from time to time."

"This whole thing is nuts. I don't even see the point of it. What happens after we rescue DeWorken? … *If* we rescue him."

"Just bring him back. That's what you tried to do anyway with the ornament. Cliff is feeling painful guilt, so bring him back."

"But he'll still be only six inches tall. And the ornament never reverses a wish. So Cliff will be right back where he started. What's he supposed to do with him?"

"Take one step at a time. Don't fret about further obstacles down the road until you get there. The crucial thing is to remove Doug from that carnival barker. Now I suggest you call your friends and arrange to leave this weekend before they make other plans."

"*This* weekend?"

"Well, you can't miss school. I'd be willing to write you a note for a day or two, but your friends' parents won't understand what's going on. You'll need to make up an excuse for them, and that excuse will go over better with their folks if it's over the weekend."

Aunt Loureen was the only adult I knew who could help me make up lies for other adults to swallow.

"I can't go *this* weekend, Aunt Loureen."

"Why not?"

"Cuz on Monday morning I'm gonna be on TV. A big network this time. And they're flying me out on Sunday so that I can be there early the next morning. Mom and Dad gave their permission before they went to England. Marla's mom is driving me to the airport. Everything is all set. This is for my comic book."

"I already guessed as much. But you just had an interview. How many TV programs do you need to be on?"

"My publisher says I should be on as many as possible. It's a whole book tour."

"I don't begrudge the marketing strategy. But if you had to miss one or reschedule another, I'm sure he'd understand."

"But the next one is important. This is *Good Morning USA*! And they're national!"

Aunt Loureen sat next to me and took my hand, speaking gently. "Nephew, I realize how exciting that sounds. I also realize that you can postpone it for another time."

"You can't postpone an important show like *Good Morning USA*! Don't you see what a lucky break this is for me? I have to go on when they tell me to go on!"

"How do you know? If they're that eager, they'll reschedule."

"I don't wanna reschedule!"

"I see. Then *you* are the problem. Not them."

"I'm not gonna give up an opportunity like *Good Morning USA*!"

"Opportunity, eh? You're going to let your good friend Cliff go through this torture all by himself just so that you can have an opportunity?"

"It's his own stupid fault!"

"He's still your friend. Friends stand by each other!"

"Well, what's the big rush? You can't even tell me what to do with DeWorken after we get him back. So a few more weeks won't make any difference."

"A few more weeks of slavery won't make any difference?"

"I didn't make him a slave."

"And that means you can't help him? You should read your own story, Nephew. Or don't the virtues of Arch-Ranger mean anything other than a guest appearance on *Good Morning USA*?"

"Oh, come on! Can't a guy enjoy a little success without everybody getting on his case?"

"Oh, you're enjoying it all right … enjoying it to the point of forgetting the people who stood by you before you became so incredibly important!"

"That's ridiculous! DeWorken was never even my friend, and Cliff just needed all the friends he could get."

"My oh my! You've certainly turned persnickety!"

It was the funniest word I'd ever heard. Aunt Loureen always did have a knack for unusual-sounding words or phrases, and she made a lot of them up herself, like *goose burgers*. I would have burst out laughing except that I knew Aunt Loureen was upset, and she would have lectured me for laughing at a word instead of grasping the important stuff she was trying to jam down my throat. Strange, just recently around Mrs. Pumpernickel and the book editors, I had pretended to laugh at their jokes, even when I didn't think they were funny. Now, when another adult was being dead serious, I could hardly keep myself from cracking up. Why couldn't I ever match my feelings with the moment?

"Persnickety?" I said, trying to keep the smirk off my face. "What does that mean?"

"Don't you know, Nephew? I should think that a famous writer like yourself would have a better vocabulary."

I'd never seen her so mad. I was used to being complimented by Aunt Loureen. Oh sure. She scolded me a lot when I was younger, the way one would scold any kid, but this was different. This time, she was deliberately trying to take me down a peg or two.

"I think you made that word up."

"Oh? Well, then, your arrogance is matched only by your ignorance!"

Boy, she sure knew how to slice and dice her speech. I was not gonna win this argument.

"Yeah? Well, what does it mean then?"

"A persnickety person is a fussy person. You are acting very fussy right now over something that isn't important. And ironically, that leads to another part of the word's definition. A persnickety person is also one who focuses too much on trivial details or minor details. Put it all together, and we have somebody who makes a fuss over unimportant matters. You are whining and fussing over nothing."

"I am not! This isn't about nothing. I'm not talking about anything unimportant. This is a very important conversation."

"Well, certainly the *conversation* is important. But only in the sense that your attitude about the unimportant is being challenged."

"I can't understand a word you're saying!"

"*Can't* understand or *won't* understand?"

"I guess I understood part of it. I know I'm being a little fussy."

"A little fussy?"

"Come on, Aunt Loureen! Stop throwing my words back at me!

"Ok, Nephew ... I'll skip the formal definition and instead illustrate how the word applies to you specifically."

I was ready to throw something. She was finally about to translate all this formal dictionary mumbo jumbo into plain language, but not before talking all eloquent one last time."

"Just tell me what the word means! What does it mean to me?"

"What it means, Nephew, is that you're behaving like a snob!"

"Snob?"

"Yes, as in 'swelled head.' Or to put it in teenage lingo, you're getting stuck up!"

"I am not!"

"Keep telling yourself that, Nephew. Sooner or later, you'll start to believe it."

"What makes you think I'm stuck up?"

"Because important things are going on in your life. People you know are in trouble, and earth-shattering events are also taking place behind the scenes from two different worlds. But instead of caring about the important, you are fussing over the *unimportant*."

"I think my comic *is* important. You said yourself you were proud of me. Now you act like it doesn't matter."

"It's a matter of perspective, Nephew. Yes, you have a wonderful talent. I'm glad you published the comic. I *am* happy for your success. I truly am. You have much to be proud of. But the comic has arrived now. Its publication is a fait accompli."

"A what?" Only my dear aunt could finally get to the point and throw in one last fancy phrase at the same time.

"*Fait accompli*. It means the project is a done deal. The comic is being circulated now."

"I still wanna draw more of them and write more of them. And I still like talking about the comic on TV. Is there anything wrong with that?"

"Of course not. Enjoying your fame and your moment in the sun is fine, so far as it goes. But we must measure its importance against these other twists and turns in your life. Frankly, missing a few television interviews would not be the end of the world. But ignoring your ultimate destiny *could* be the end of the world!"

I knew she was right but I didn't wanna admit it and I didn't wanna be a loyal friend and I didn't wanna take a trip to some hick little dirt town to chase after a carnival. I just wanted to be on *Good Morning USA*.

"Isn't there a way for me to do both?"

"You just don't get it. You really have no clue as to what's going on, do you? Even after all that the ornament's done! Even after your encounter with Charles! Something catastrophic is happening. Danger is brewing in the other world."

"I just wanna live my own life, Aunt Loureen. I know you think that other world is important, but I wanna live my life in *this* world!"

She just stared at me, looking disappointed and ashamed. I was feeling too guilty to keep it up.

Finally, I caved. "OK. I'll see what I can do. I'll try to talk the guys into going ... But promise me that this is it, Aunt Loureen. I don't wanna go where you're planning to go."

"I can promise no such thing, neither can I reveal the future as your friend Charles apparently can. But I'll say this ... If you're meant to go into the other world as I am, nothing can stop it from happening. Let's not fret about that right now. Let's just concentrate on the moment, and for the moment our only task is to rescue poor Doug DeWorken."

Chapter Nine

The Plan

Two nights later, I called a special meeting at my house. Aunt Loureen had gone out to see a movie so that I could talk to my friends alone. Cliff complained when I insisted we meet in my bedroom instead of the family room. There wasn't much space in my room, but I wanted to keep us out of Caligula's hearing range. Since part of the plan would include taking that miserable creature along, it seemed like a good idea to put off the news and keep him in the dark as long as possible. I already hated the idea of taking this trip, and listening to Caligula grumble for days on end before we even left seemed unnecessary. Cliff sat at my desk. I sat on the bed. Ben was standing near the window. It reminded me of that time we gathered in Ben's room back in sixth grade. The plan then had been getting Caligula out of the pound, and now that whole mess seemed easy compared to what we were gonna try to pull off this time.

"OK," Ben said to me. "We're here. What's up?"

It took a very long time to fill Ben in on the all the little mishaps Cliff and I had gone through recently with the ornament. Ben listened patiently and was quiet most of the time. Once in a while he asked a question, and occasionally, Cliff moved the story along to explain some of his own involvement, but mostly I did the talking. When we were up to the part about selling DeWorken at the carnival, Cliff held his head down, not wanting to look Ben in the eye.

Ben finally let loose. "He did what?"

"He sold him to the owner of the Tinker Bell show," I said.

"I don't get you guys. I mean, I really don't get you guys. I thought we all agreed to stop using that ornament! I thought we agreed to that a long time ago! I mean, it's been years. I didn't even know the thing was around anymore."

"I never agreed to stop using it," Cliff said.

"Yeah? Well, you should have! Look at all the trouble it's caused."

"That's what I told him, Ben. I warned him not to use the ornament."

"Did you?" Ben said. "Well, you're no better. You used it too."

"By accident. Only by accident."

"And this trip? This little plan to get DeWorken back? Is this an accident too? Is it an accident that you're bringing the ornament along?"

"I don't wanna bring it, Ben. I don't wanna take the trip either. But like I told you, my Aunt Loureen says it's important."

"Oh, Aunt Loureen says it's important! What is it with her and that ornament? Why doesn't she just keep it herself if she likes it so much? Why does she hassle you with it?"

"I don't know. I really don't. Sometimes Aunt Loureen seems as weird as the ornament itself. But I did try to give it back to her. Instead, she just went on and on about me needing to take this trip with Cliff."

"Then take it with Cliff and leave me out of it."

"She thought it would be a good idea if you came too."

"Oh? And she also thought it would be a good idea for us to all try using it again in the seventh grade. You remember what happened then! That's why we all agreed to put it away for good."

"You and Mike agreed to put it away. Not me."

Ben walked over to the desk and grabbed Cliff by the collar. "If you say that one more time, I'll jam the ornament down your throat."

"Take it easy, Ben," I said. "You don't have to go. I'm just inviting you. That's all."

Ben had never hit Cliff before, and I was sure that he wouldn't do it this time either. He got annoyed with him once in a while, because nobody could hang out with Cliff without being annoyed once in a while. But I think this was the first time I ever saw him actually grab Cliff by the collar. I had seen Ben in good moods and bad moods, but I had never seen a conversation bug him as much as this one. Oh sure, he'd always detested the ornament. For some reason, it didn't amaze him the way it amazed Cliff and me, but this wasn't just about the ornament. Now he was acting like we'd committed some kind of crime. But actually, come to think of it, if slavery wasn't a crime, what was? That must have been what set him off, the whole slavery thing. Like I said already, Ben was a very good person, and maybe he was shocked to see his friends connected to something that looked evil to him.

Ben let up on Cliff and went back to the window, staring outside, not even facing us. "Why does your aunt think it's so important for me to come along?"

"Probably because you know martial arts," Cliff said.

"I'm asking Mike!"

"She admires you," I answered. "But mostly, when Aunt Loureen gives reasons, she just goes on and on about destiny. Look, Ben, I know you don't like that ornament. Believe me, neither do I. I'd just as soon get rid of it. But I can't deny all the stuff it's done either. And if something dangerous has started which needs to be stopped …"

"You mean this dangerously stupid thing that Cliff did?"

"Yeah."

Ben walked over to him again. "Let me get this straight. You shrunk Doug DeWorken? All this time, the whole school has been wondering what happened to him, and that's the story? You shrunk him?"

"Not me. The ornament shrunk him. I didn't know how it would answer the wish. I just needed some protection."

"OK. The ornament made him that way, but you held him captive. You kept him hidden the whole time."

"What else could I do? What would *you* have done?"

"I'd have done nothing. I wouldn't have used the magic in the first place."

Cliff was getting teary-eyed. "Well, you have a lot of things going for you, Ben. You don't need any help, magic or otherwise. It isn't so easy for people like Mike and me."

"Now don't start feeling sorry for yourself."

"I was scared. And then the police were questioning me."

"You should have told them the truth."

"The truth? That DeWorken had turned six inches tall?"

"All you had to do was show them. They couldn't deny their own eyes."

153

"But then I'd still get blamed. Nobody would believe in a magic ornament! All they would know was that I'd done something horrible to a fellow high school student. They wouldn't know *how* I did it, and they wouldn't *care* how I did it. They would know I was guilty. That's all they would need to know. It would make the news! It would be on TV. Every high-profile lawyer in the country would be salivating to take the case and file some lawsuit against me."

"So you solved the problem by selling him to a circus?"

"Carnival."

"So help me I'm gonna hit you right in the mouth! Who cares what it's called! We're talking about slavery, Cliff!"

"I didn't know what else to do! The police were on my back. Besides, I'm doing the right thing now. I'm willing to go get him out of there."

"How exactly?"

"I don't know, Ben. That's why I need help."

Ben sat on the floor and calmed down a little. "OK. Assuming we find him, and assuming we steal him back, then what? Do you take him back home? Do you just turn him loose? Do you hide him somewhere else? What?"

Cliff shrugged his shoulders, so Ben glared at me instead.

"We haven't thought that far ahead," I said. "I mean … I did ask Aunt Loureen. She said we should just take one step at a time and let our intuition tell us what to do next."

"Excuse me? Say that again?"

I knew that intuition stuff wouldn't cut it with Ben.

***

It was later in the evening now. We'd talked for hours, and I had just finished making us some hamburgers in the frying pan. Caligula liked to go out at night, so we were free to talk around the dining room table. As I expected, Ben did finally agree to go along. He hemmed and hawed a lot, but in the end, Ben always did the right thing.

Just as I told Aunt Loureen, I explained to Ben that an Internet search had located the carnival at the small town of Wendover, some

200 miles away. Over dinner we tried to come up with a plan of action. The food seemed to lift everyone's spirits. There were burgers, jalapeno-flavored potato chips, and soda pop.

For all of Ben's resisting, he was actually the first one to lay out a workable caper. Ben's parents owned a beach house. He was gonna ask his mom if the three of us could borrow the family van and drive up to the coast for the weekend. Then, instead of going to the beach house, we would head east instead, the opposite direction, until we hit Wendover. Ben's folks trusted him, and the ruse would be pretty easy to pull off. And of course, my parents were away in England, thanks to Aunt Loureen. But Cliff's mom was a problem. He figured he could talk her into letting him go to the beach house only if Ben's mom or dad were there with us.

"Sorry," he said. "She still treats me like a baby."

Ben reached for some ketchup. "So tell her my mom will be there too. What's the big deal?"

"The big deal is that she'll want a phone number, and she'll keep calling to check up on me. How do we avoid that?"

"It's easy," Ben said. "We give her my cell phone number, and we tell her it's the number to the beach house. When she calls, we put you on the phone, and you tell her that her 'little Cliffy' is just fine. It won't matter where we really are. She'll think you're at the beach house, where you said you'd be."

"That's not a bad idea," I added. "You told me before your mom hasn't made the switch-over to cell phones."

"True enough," Cliff nodded. "She's used to landlines."

"Exactly," I said. "So it probably won't even occur to her that she's connected to a cell."

Cliff was not reassured. "Supposing she calls and wants to talk to Ben's mom?"

"No big deal," Ben said. "We just tell her my mom stepped out."

"That buys us an hour. Maybe an hour and a half. No more."

Ben grabbed his second soda can and opened it up. "You're getting paranoid, Cliff."

"You know my mother. She'll ask when your mom is returning."

Ben was pouring the soda on top of his ice-filled glass. "Quit being such a worrywart!"

"She'll ask, I tell you. She'll want to know exactly where she went and exactly what time she'll be back."

Ben sighed. "I suppose I could copy our house answering machine message and transfer it to my cell phone voice mail. Then we leave the cell phone off. Every time she calls, it goes directly to voice mail, or better yet, we time it to ring a few times, and then it goes to voice mail. She calls and she hears my mom's voice. She thinks my mom put that message on from the beach house phone."

Cliff shook his head. "All that does is convince her that your mom has a phone at the beach house. How will that make her believe she's actually there at the same time as us?"

Ben looked like he was ready to keel over with exhaustion. "Is she that suspicious, Cliff? I thought you've been well-behaved all these years … well-behaved when you're not using the ornament, that is."

"I haven't given her reason to be suspicious, Ben. She's just neurotic. That's all. Well, you guys know her! You see her all the time! Do you really think I'm off base? In fact, this whole discussion is academic anyway. Mom would insist on talking to your mother first, before she even gave me permission to go. And she'd ask a thousand questions about how safe I would be." Cliff started mimicking his mother. "How warm is the house? How far does the ocean tide come up?"

Ben was frustrated. "Geez! OK, if she's that nutty, I give up. If anyone has a better idea, go for it!"

"Maybe we could get one of the girls to give her a call," I suggested. "Either Jean or Marla. You know … they could beat her to the punch … pretend to be Ben's mom and reassure her ahead of time … get all the questions over and done with."

By now, Cliff was so nervous he actually got up from the table and sat on top of the kitchen's breakfast bar. "She already knows what Ben's mom sounds like. It's not like they haven't met before. No high school girl is going to do a convincing impersonation."

I was as ready as Ben to give up. But Aunt Loureen had been awfully adamant about the need for this trip, and there would be no trip without first convincing Cliff that he could leave for the weekend without his mom thinking she needed to call out the National Guard.

"Yeah," I said. "She knows Ben's mom. But mostly from personal visits. People sound different over the phone."

"She's talked to Ben's mom on the phone too."

"You're wasting your time, Mike. No matter what we suggest, he's gonna shoot it down."

"Wait!" I said. "I have an even better idea, and he can't shoot this one down! Instead of the girls, we get my Aunt Loureen to help us. She's in on the whole thing anyway. That's why she got my parents out of town: to go over ornament business with me. And now this trip is a part of that business. She wants us to go. Since the idea is really hers, how can she refuse to help?"

"Not bad," Ben said. "That way we don't need to involve the girls at all. I wasn't too keen on that anyway. And as an adult, your aunt will sound more authentic over the phone."

Cliff just shook his head. "Nice try, but it won't work."

"Of course not," Ben muttered.

"Look, I'm just trying to bring some realism into this. By playing the devil's advocate, we can plug up the holes ahead of time."

"Fine," I said, sounding annoyed and feeling annoyed. "So what's the hole this time?"

"Well, for starters, I must point out once again that she has talked to Ben's mom on the phone before."

"Not that often," I argued. "And there are many times when I get a call from somebody I know and it takes a while to recognize their voice. Different phone connections can make a voice sound hard to recognize. Besides, we can coach Aunt Loureen a little and get her to sound like Ben's mom."

"That I'd like to see."

"OK," I persisted. "Aunt Loureen can explain over the phone that she has a bad cold."

"Wild guess ..." Ben said with his mouth partly full, swallowing a bite of hamburger. "Cliff doesn't like this idea either."

"Cut it out, Ben! I'm just trying to cover the bases."

Ben shook his head. "You've covered the bases all right. And the batting cage, and the bleachers. All of left field too."

"OK, Ben. OK! So let's say Mike's aunt can be made to sound convincing. Let's say that actually works. My mom will still call Ben's mom a few more times before we go because she'll continue to remember new concerns she wants to address. There's no way a single conversation could ever satisfy that lady!"

Ben took a long sip of soda. "So we start the whole thing off by telling her that my mom has already gone up to the beach house by herself ahead of time. You know … just to have a few days to herself before we get there. That way, your mom doesn't drop by my house for a chat. We give your mom my cell phone number, telling her it's the beach house number. Then we have Mike's aunt call her the first time to disarm as much worry as possible. After that, every time she calls back, she'll get my voice mail, thinking it's my mom's answering machine."

"You would have to stop answering your own phone whenever it rings."

"What are you talking about? I have your number programmed in, Cliff."

"That's true. You can see right on your phone screen who's calling and let your voice mail catch it if it happens to be Mom." Cliff was looking embarrassed. Probably because *he* was the tech whiz, and he didn't like being reminded about the special features of caller ID on a device as simple as a cell phone.

"All right then," Ben said. "After we listen to your mom's voice message, we talk to Aunt Loureen and get her to call back to answer whatever harebrained questions she has."

Cliff seemed deep in thought. "Maybe. Just maybe. That'll work *before* we leave for the trip. What about *after* we leave?"

Ben looked like he was ready to pull his own hair out. "*Now* what's the problem?"

"Mike's aunt isn't going on the trip with us. She has to stay and watch the house for his folks."

"No problem," I said. "Whenever your mom calls, I'll call Aunt Loureen, and Aunt Loureen will call her back. And don't tell me your mom will compare the phone numbers. I've seen that old phone at your house. It does not have caller ID, and I doubt your mom has ever even heard of caller ID. Anything else? I dare you to come up with another problem."

Cliff hesitated. "I can't think of anything at the moment, but if I come up with something, would that really be so bad? Better to work out the pitfalls ahead of time, isn't it?"

I just frowned at him. "Yeah, Cliff. Anything you say."

Well, anyway, that's how we finally agreed on a plan. I had no idea what to expect, other than the fact that we would probably be using Ben's cell phone about every fifteen minutes or so. I found myself hoping that he had a cheap monthly rate, but I decided not to bring it up.

Chapter Ten

DeWorken Talks Tough Once Again

Doug DeWorken woke up and stretched. At first he couldn't remember where he was. Then he thought about Cliff Reynolds and wondered if it had all been a dream. He *was* in a comfortable bed. Was he back home? Back in his own room? No. It suddenly all snapped together in his mind. He'd been put inside another cage, a better one than Reynolds' hamster cage — bigger, more comfortable, and with a real bed his own size, probably from some doll's house. Comfortable or not, it was still a cage, and Doug didn't understand all that had happened. He only knew that yesterday afternoon Reynolds walked into his room and suddenly, out of the blue, snatched him up in his hand and put him in that horrible shoe box again. Reynolds did all of this without saying a word. At first Doug kept yelling at Reynolds, demanding to be told what was going on. Reynolds got tired of hearing it and finally put tape over his mouth to shut him up. Then he bound his hands with more tape. After that, Doug kept quiet cuz there was nothing else he could do. From the sound and the motion, Doug knew that Reynolds had walked for over an hour until he finally heard him call a taxi. Reynolds didn't drive yet, so if he was calling a taxi, it must have been his only way to get rid of Doug and take him far away. Doug wondered at first if Reynolds was just gonna take him home, but after lots of time went by, he knew something was up and that he might never go home again. That wouldn't have bothered him if he was normal size again. But the way things were? Doug was pretty scared.

Later on, Reynolds picked up the shoe box and left the taxi. Doug heard lots of people, and he heard music that sounded like carnival music. A lot more time went by. Then he heard Reynolds talking to somebody, but he couldn't make out what they were saying because they were talking in low voices, and from inside the box, Doug couldn't hear too well. Then it happened. Some other guy, an older, bald man, reached his hand into the shoe box, pulled Doug out, and put him into this new, bigger cage. He opened a small compartment in the cage, a tiny room with a tiny bed, and stuck Doug inside. Then he pulled the tape off of Doug's mouth and hands. Doug cried out, but the man ignored him and walked away. Doug got up, opened the compartment door, and walked around the outer part of the cage. On the other side, he saw a compartment that looked just like his. He thought about opening it but then got scared because he remembered how Reynolds had threatened him with a snake, and it seemed safer to not open up any strange doors in cages unless he knew for sure what was on the other side. Outside the cage, Doug saw a giant-looking desk, chair, stove, and sink. Hours went by and nobody returned. Finally, Doug went back to his compartment, crawled in the bed, and fell asleep. Now he was awake again. It was morning.

What would happen today? How much longer would this nightmare go on? Doug actually wished he was back at home, even though he and his old man never got along. The old geyser had always liked Doug's younger half-brother more than him. Brother Randy did everything right, and Doug did everything wrong. Brother Randy meant everything to dear old Dad, and Doug knew why: because Randy came from another marriage, a better wife. Doug hadn't seen his real mom since he was five years old. She ditched Dad one day, just leaving a note on the dining room table. And nobody ever heard from her again. Two years later, Dad got married for the second time, so Doug got a new stepmom, but he hated her. Once he told his old man how much he hated her, and he got hit across the mouth. That was Doug's family. He thought of his friends at school as his real family. But today, anyplace would be better, even home.

Doug thought he heard a knock. He stood up. Then he heard a woman's voice.

"Hello?" the voice said.

"Who is it?"

"Just a visitor."

Doug could feel his heart pumping faster than ever. He opened the door.

"Hi. How are you today?"

Those were the words of the most beautiful woman Doug had ever seen. And she didn't look much older than him. But her beauty was only part of the surprise. The main thing was that she wasn't gigantic. In fact, she was at least one foot shorter than Doug. Had Doug turned normal size again? Was he out of the small cage and in a bigger place?

Had somebody rescued him?

"I was told you were coming," she said. "I'm very glad to meet you."

Doug just stood there with his mouth open. She continued talking. "I hope you don't mind me knocking on your door. We're in the same cage actually, but it was turned into two separate quarters. That way, we each get a little privacy." Doug still said nothing. She went on. "There's a larger area in the cage also — a mutual place, so to speak. Would you care to take a walk?"

So, this was still the cage after all, which meant Doug was still tiny, which meant she must be tiny too.

"Who are you?" Doug finally said.

"Oh. Of course. Forgive me for being so rude. Actually, they call me 'Tinker Bell.' I suppose you'd best call me by the same name."

"Tinker Bell? Ain't that from some make-believe story?"

"Yes. One of your Earth stories, I was told. They dressed me up to look like her too. And who do I have the pleasure of meeting?"

"Huh? Oh. I'm Doug. Doug DeWorken."

"I'm very pleased to meet you, Doug. It's been years since I've had company like you. Please, come outside and walk with me. It's still a cage, but at least there's more room and we can be together."

Doug followed her out. "What's your real name? It can't really be Tinker Bell."

"I'm afraid you wouldn't be able to pronounce my real name. And even if you could, my master prefers everyone to call me Tinker Bell."

"Master?"

She turned away, not wanting to look him in the eye. Then, almost as a whisper, she said, "Yes, *master*."

"Well, I ain't callin' ya Tinker Bell."

"I think you *are*, Doug. Because that's the way our master wants it."

"I ain't got no master. What's your real name?"

"Very well. If you insist. My name is Yzeipzxmnrtuowquzat."

163

"Huh?"

"I told you you wouldn't be able to pronounce it. Better stick with Tinker Bell."

"I guess … Whatever … How did ya get here?"

"Similar to the way you got here, I imagine."

"Naw … Couldn't have been the same way."

"Well, I realize we come from different places. What country are you from?"

"Country? America. What other country would I be from? Ain't that where you're from?"

"Oh, no. In fact, I didn't even speak English until the master taught me."

"What language do you speak?"

"Perusean."

"I never heard of that. Is it in Europe somewhere?"

"Oh, no, Doug. Not at all. In fact, Perusea isn't even in your world."

"*My* world? There's only one world. What are you talkin' about?"

"There are many worlds. But I keep forgetting that people around here know of only one."

"I know a lot of them. I ain't stupid."

"I didn't mean to imply that you are. I'm sorry."

"We only *live* on one world. That's what I meant. That's the only place we *can* live until they start livin' on Mars or someplace like that."

"But I *am* from another world. And my world has separate countries, just as yours does. I know we're in America, but you seem to be from a different country, a country similar to Perusea."

"Girlie, like I said … I ain't never even heard of no Perusea."

"Of course you haven't. I'm just wondering if there's another country where people *look* Perusean. I'm confusing you. I'm so sorry. What I mean, Doug, is I know I can't go home, but if there's another country here on Earth where everyone looks like we do, well, that's hope — at least, the first hope I've had in years."

"Like *we* do? Ya mean our size?"

"Of course. What else would I mean?"

"Wait a minute here ... Are ya sayin' ya come from a whole country of tiny people?"

"We don't call ourselves tiny. And I'm surprised that *you* do. But yes, everyone in my country is my size or at least close to my size."

Doug wasn't sure what to make of all this. It sounded crazy ... even more crazy when he remembered that the girl telling him the story called herself "Tinker Bell."

"You're the same size I am," she said. "So why be so surprised to hear of another country where people are the same size as you?"

She was right about that. She *was* his size, and she was standing right in front of him. A lot of nutty things had been happening lately, and this was just one more.

"Man ... Man oh man! How do ya all defend yourselves? Wouldn't it be easy for other countries to push ya around and conquer ya and stuff like that?"

"Naturally. Hasn't your country had the same problem?"

"America ain't never been conquered!"

"That's right. You're an American. You *did* say that. But America is divided into smaller countries, is it not? 'States' I believe they're called. So one of your states is like Perusea?"

"Naw. None of our states have been conquered either, unless ya count the Civil War. A bunch of states in the South was conquered by the North. But we ain't never lost a war with another country."

"We have, I'm afraid. We were conquered long ago. Most of my people are slaves now. They know about Perusea only through the stories handed down by our ancestors."

"Huh? Ya mean big people hold little people as slaves?"

"Exactly. Somewhat like you and me. We're slaves too."

"I ain't no slave!"

"I wish that were true."

"It *is* true. I ain't gonna be no slave. I'll escape. This cage don't

165

look so hard ta get out of. I'll escape, and when I do, I'll take ya with me … That is … if ya wanna go."

"I don't believe it's possible, Doug. But it's very kind of you to offer to take me along. I haven't heard a kind word in a long time."

Nobody had ever called Doug "kind" before. He had a lot of friends who looked up to him or feared him but none of them ever called him "kind."

"So this guy who's got us locked up is from *your* world?"

"No, my master is from *your* world. I don't know how he found us exactly. He never explained it to me … Doug … he's coming."

Doug heard a loud pounding. It sounded almost like thunder, kind of the way Reynolds always sounded when he was returning to his room, only much louder. Doug looked up and saw that huge man, the man Tinker Bell had been calling "master," the man who had yanked him out of the shoebox and stuck him in this new cage.

He sat down on a big chair next to the cage. "I see the two of you have been getting acquainted. Good. I like my employees to feel close."

"Employee? I ain't your employee!"

"In a manner of speaking, you are."

"Wrong, mister! I didn't apply for no job, and I ain't workin' for ya! Just who are ya anyway?"

"I'm Blake."

"Blake who?"

"Blake is my last name."

"Yeah? Well, what's your first name? Cuz I'm gonna give your whole name ta the police!"

"My full name to you will be 'Mr. Blake.'"

"Ha! In your dreams, pal!"

Blake was acting very calm. "Hmm. Tough guy."

"Tougher than you!"

The look on Blake's face changed. "Son, you wouldn't be tougher than me even if you were seven feet tall. And since you aren't even seven *inches* tall, how about showing a little more respect and a little less lip?"

The guy talked polite all right, but Doug still didn't trust him. Why should he? Why should he trust a man who kept slaves? "If ya don't wanna hear no lip, then let me go!"

"I used to talk tough like you. See this?" Blake held up his right arm, showing a large, dragon-shaped tattoo. The dragon was green-, red-, and gold-colored. It looked very slimy.

"So you got a tattoo! Big deal!"

"It's from a gang … a gang I belonged to when I was your age. What are you? Sixteen? Seventeen? Something like that?"

"None of your business!"

"I'd say at least seventeen. Yes, I thought I was pretty tough stuff at your age — that is, until somebody almost killed me. I had to join a gang just to stay alive. The gang protected me. This tattoo was our insignia."

"Who cares? I ain't scared of you!"

"Oh, I think you're scared enough. But it doesn't matter. I'm not asking you to be scared. All I ask is that we get along."

"I ain't never gettin' along with you, mister!"

Blake laughed.

"Did I say somethin' funny, mister?"

"It's just that you remind me so much of myself. That is, before I learned some manners. You see, son …"

"I ain't your son!"

Blake just ignored the remark and kept going. "You see, son, when you're part of a gang, when you belong to a reckless group that kills people, you don't need to talk tough anymore because you've gone farther than tough talk could ever take you. You're as bad as bad can be, and loud bags of wind just make you yawn."

"You won't be yawnin' for long!"

"Tell you what, Doug. I'm going to leave the room for a few minutes because you've been shooting off your mouth without thinking. When I return, we'll try again. We'll reacquaint ourselves and you'll be polite."

"Or what?"

167

"Now, Doug, I'm giving you a second chance. Don't be stupid. Just be polite when I return."

Blake slowly walked out of the room.

Doug gripped the cage bars tightly. Tinker Bell walked up behind him and squeezed his shoulder. "You should be more careful, Doug. Mr. Blake may talk a lot about manners, but he can actually get quite angry. You don't want to experience his wrath."

"Ah … he's nothin' ta worry about."

"Doug, I wouldn't want you to get hurt."

Doug turned around and took her hand. "Hey, don't worry none about me. I'll be all right."

They both sat down. She stared at him for a second or two. "Tell me something, Doug …"

"Sure …"

"It's what I was trying to find out before. Is there a whole country of people like mine nearby? Is that how Mr. Blake caught you?"

"Blake didn't catch me. He bought me. I didn't realize it till just now. He must have bought me. And I never seen anyone else this size till I met you. Ya see … I wasn't always this way. I've only been small for a couple of days. I used ta be normal size. I've been normal size all my life, and when I turn normal size again, first thing I'm gonna do is pay that Mr. Blake a little visit! What's wrong?" Doug could see that he had hurt her feelings somehow. "Why are ya looking so unhappy all of a sudden?"

"I'm sorry. It's just that expression, 'normal size.'" Where I come from, this *is* the normal size."

Doug felt bad. Strange, he never felt bad when he put someone down in school. It was fun, and he didn't give a hang how it made the other person feel. But he *did* feel bad now.

"Hey, I didn't mean nothin' by that. I guess where you come from, people like Blake are the ones who don't look normal."

"We call them 'giants.'"

"Yeah. I guess ya would."

"And you were a giant yourself? I've never heard of a giant turning into the size of a Perusean before. At least, not in my lifetime. There are legends from the past with such occurrences. How did it happen?"

"I'll tell ya how it happened. This weasel of a kid, this weakling who nobody liked … He did it to me."

Tinker Bell looked very curious. "How?"

"Search me! One minute we was talkin'. Next thing I knew, I was lookin' up at him … Reynolds was his name. And ya know what I'm gonna do when I turn giant size again? I'm gonna kill him! First I'll kill Blake. Then I'll kill *him*!"

"Did he explain himself? Did he explain how you were made to look Perusean?"

"Naw … He just made up some stupid fairy tale. He was tryin' ta mess with my head."

"Fairy tale?"

"Yeah. He said somethin' about a magic ornament."

Tinker Bell stood up. "Say that again, Doug?"

"Huh? Why are ya lookin' at me weird all of a sudden? It was just a lie."

"A lie about an ornament? He claimed that an ornament made you this size?"

"Well … yeah … I mean … not at first. I kept askin' what he had done ta me and how he had done it. For a couple of days, he didn't explain nothin'. But I kept askin' every time he opened up my cage. Finally, he said some stuff about an ornament. But I didn't believe him."

"Why not?"

"Cuz I ain't stupid! That's why!"

"Doug, please listen to me carefully. Did he just talk, or did he actually show you the ornament?"

"Naw. He never showed me nothin'."

For a minute, it looked like Tinker Bell was almost talking to herself. "Of course not. By showing you the ornament, he would be risking a chance for you to make a wish of your own." Suddenly she got very excited. "It's here … It's here in this world! The Magic Ornament of Lumis!"

"Huh? The what?"

"It's something ancient, thousands of years old … a legend to my people. The Magic Ornament of Lumis! The lost ornament! And with this ornament, wishes can be made. That's how you got small. This person made a wish."

"Yeah, he said that. Reynolds said he made a wish."

"And you chose not to believe him?"

"Nobody believes in magic wishes. Not unless they're little kids."

"I suppose you're right. If the people of your world believed in magic, they wouldn't be so astonished to see me. And they wouldn't pay money."

"Are ya sayin' *you* can do magic?" Doug could hardly believe his own words. Up till now, he'd thought very little about Reynold's' ornament story because he was sure the story was made up. He figured Reynolds was just messing with his head to amuse himself. But Tinker Bell didn't look like the kind of person who made things up. Besides, *something* had turned him small, and something had made her small too!

"Do magic myself?" Tinker Bell said. "No, I can't do magic myself. If I could, I would have escaped long ago. But I come from a place where magic is real and everyone believes in it — well, almost everyone."

"Where is this place?"

"It's far from here. So far, I gave up long ago on ever getting home. As I said before, it's another whole world."

"When ya say 'world,' ya mean like another planet?"

"I don't know anything about planets. And I don't know where it is in relation to *your* world. All I know is that people here call your world 'Earth' and my world — not my country, but the entire world I come from — is called 'Telios.' Aside from Mr. Blake, nobody from Earth seems to have heard of Telios. At least, I never hear them mention it."

This was the craziest talk Doug ever had. But he was getting interested. "Anybody from Telios ever mention Earth?"

"Some. It's whispered only in dark corners. I'd heard the name only once before Mr. Blake caught me."

"What did ya know about Earth?"

"Barely a thing. All I really knew was that, through the use of magic, some people could travel from my world into yours."

"Magic like that ornament?"

"That's one magic charm. But there are other charms and other ways to connect the worlds."

"Is that how Blake found ya? Does he have an ornament of his own?"

"No. He found another way. He found a way to get into Telios and steal Peruseans. He's done it for years. He steals us and brings us back to be part of his show."

"There are others? Ya have some friends around here?"

Tinker Bell looked upset. "I did," she whispered. "They're all dead now."

"He killed them?"

"No. They got sick. I think ... I think they just didn't want to live anymore." Doug put his arm around her, and she seemed to like it. Doug liked it too. She continued. "When Mr. Blake purchased you, he must have assumed that this Reynolds person had found you in the other world, although I'm sure Reynolds eventually explained otherwise because Mr. Blake didn't seem startled to hear you speak English."

"How does he do it? How does he get in ta your world?"

"I don't know. I was trapped inside some kind of container when he brought me across. But evidently he discovered a pathway of some sort."

"A path? An actual path?"

"Exactly."

"But that makes no sense. Ya have ta have a spaceship ta travel from one planet to another."

"I have no idea how he did it. All I know is that it involved nothing but walking."

"But …"

"That's all I can tell you, Doug. I'm sorry. I wish I knew more."

He decided to stop focusing on planet travel. It seemed to be upsetting her, and upsetting this gorgeous lady was the last thing Doug wanted to do. "It's OK. Just tell me more about yourself then. In your world, Peru— What did ya call them?"

"Peruseans."

"Yeah. In your world, Peruseans are slaves?"

"All except the few who can hide."

"Why would somebody keep a tiny person as a slave? What could ya do for Blake that he couldn't do for himself?"

"Well, in the case of my master in this world, I'm just an oddity. He has me do performances. Most people from around here don't see a person my size every day, and they come from miles around to see me perform. But back in the other world, we do work."

"What kinda work? We used ta have slaves in America, but everyone was the same size. So those that didn't wanna work bought slaves ta work for them. Slaves did the farmin' or chopped wood or cooked or somethin'. What could a tiny person like you do for a giant?"

"Now I understand what you're asking. And you're right, we don't really do anything that they couldn't do for themselves. Sometimes people just enjoy the *idea* of slavery. They ask us to fetch them small objects, such as ink pens or eating utensils. They ask us to announce them before they walk into a room when guests are gathered for a party or banquet. Sometimes they ask us to climb on their heads and straighten out their hats."

"That's stupid! That don't make no sense at all!"

"No … It doesn't. But the institution of slavery had gone on for nearly a hundred years, ever since Perusea was discovered and conquered. I wasn't raised as a slave. I was born free and belonged to a group of refugees who hid from the giants. The hiding place is within the borders of my country, the one undiscovered portion of my country. And none of the giants from Telios had ever been able to find us there."

"But Mr. Blake did?"

"Yes, somehow."

"Listen ta me, Tinker Bell, or whoever ya really are. Everything is gonna be fine now cuz I'm gonna take care of ya. I mean that. Back where I come from, nobody messes with me!"

"Oh no … He's returning. Please, Doug, be more polite this time."

"He don't scare me." But Doug knew he was only showing off. The man *was* scary. And not just cuz he was big enough to squash him with his hand. There was something else scary about him. But Doug had been talking tough for years, and he didn't know any other way to talk. Besides, why look chicken in front of a beautiful girl? The guy wouldn't hurt him. He'd paid good money. He wasn't about to kill something he'd just bought. And however he got into this other world, it must be hard, otherwise there would be tons of tiny people in the carnival act. Either they were hard to find or it was hard to get into the other world to look for them. So, Doug was valuable to Blake. Yeah. He could talk tough all he wanted. What was the sap gonna do to him?

The loud vibration seemed to be getting closer. Doug looked up. Sure enough, it was Mr. Blake!

Blake sat down next to the cage. "Ready to try it again, Doug? Ready to face your situation with a little reality this time?"

"Just wait till people find out what you're doin'!"

"What I'm doing? They already know what I'm doing. What I'm doing is putting on a show. Crowds of people watch the show every day, Doug. All they do is laugh, applaud, and buy tickets for the next show."

"Yeah? Well they wouldn't do that if they knew she was a slave! Wait till the UCLA hears about you!"

"UCLA?" At first Blake looked confused, but then suddenly he grinned. "I think you mean the ACLU. UCLA is a …"

"I know what UCLA is! I said it by mistake! I'm not stupid just cuz I'm small! UCLA is a football team!"

Blake seemed to be enjoying this. "Actually, UCLA is a university. The university happens to have a football team."

"I already know that! I'm a football player myself!"

Blake got a sly look on his face. "Are you? Are you now?" Blake leaned down closer to Doug. "Well, yes, you *are* built like a football player — at that, a small football player, but the muscles and proportions seem to be there. I did notice how strong you looked when I bought you, but I didn't actually think about football at the time. Hmm ... and what else can you do?"

"Huh?"

"I said what else can you do? ... Don't look so clueless, Doug. I'm asking you a question. What else can you do?"

"I don't know what you're talkin' about, mister!"

"No? Well, Tinker Bell can sing and dance. What can *you* do? My audience isn't likely to pay for a one-man football player. A whole team? That might be interesting. But one player? Who would you tackle? Who would you throw the ball to? So, I'll ask you again, Doug. What can you do?"

"I ain't doin' nothin' for you accept callin' the police!"

"The police, eh?" Blake chuckled. "Where's your phone?"

"I'll find a phone! Don't you worry! I'll find one all right! I'll find it after I break outta here!"

"Hmm ... you sure do have big plans. I suppose Tinker Bell could teach you a simple dance at least. Maybe the waltz."

"Waltz? I don't do stuffed-up freak dances like that!"

Blake ignored him and went right on. "It isn't too difficult to learn. She could do the rest of the act by herself, but it would still look good to have a tiny pair for at least part of the show. Could you do that, Tinker Bell? Could you teach him to waltz?"

"As you wish, sir."

"See? She even talks like a slave! Well, I ain't' gonna be no slave, and I ain't gonna do no waltz!"

"Oh, no? What kinds of dances *do* you like?"

"None of your business!"

Blake let out a big sigh. Then he stood up. "I can see that I'm not making much of an impression on you, Doug. So maybe it's time to put it another way."

Blake reached into the cage, pulled Doug out, and held him upside down by his small feet.

"I'll kill ya!" Doug shouted out. "I'll kill ya!"

"You kids make a brave noise these days. I must admit, if I were your size, I'd be more interested in learning some manners instead of popping off at the mouth. But since you never bothered to learn any manners, supposing I just go ahead and teach you some right now?"

Blake pulled a silver lighter out of his pocket and lit the flame next to Doug's upside down face.

"Ahhhhh! Stop! What are ya doin'?"

"Feel the heat? I could just as easily submerge your head in the flame and cook the rest of you like a *shish kebab*."

"Drop dead!"

Blake lowered the back of Doug's head into the flame, and his hair instantly caught fire. This time Doug cried out like an infant. "Ahhhh!!!!! Cut it out!!!! Stop!!! Stop!!!"

"Say 'please.'"

"OK! OK! Please!!! Please stop!!! Please!!!"

Blake turned the lighter off and quickly put out the scalp fire by smothering the flame with his finger. Then he rushed to the sink and stuck Doug under the running faucet. Doug was drenched from head to toe, feeling like he was under a waterfall, but at least it felt better than the fire.

Blake yanked him out of the sink and held him up next to his giant-looking eyes. "That's better. You'll find that manners go a long way with me. So, while we're on the subject, let me lay down some rules. First, you'll speak only when spoken to. I don't care to hear any more threats. I don't care to hear any more brave talk. It only makes you sound like a fool, and it annoys me ... makes me want to reach for my lighter again. Catching on? So you'll keep your little mouth shut, and you'll do everything you're told ... and I do mean *everything*! If I tell you to dance, you dance. If I tell you to sing, you sing. If I tell you to jump, you ask, 'How high?' If I tell you to sweep up your cage, you say, 'Yes, sir!' Questions?"

Doug was silent.

"Good. I'm glad we had a chance to straighten things out. It'll help us get along better in the days to come, and you *are* going to be with me for a very long time, so you'd might as well get used to it. That's all for today. Get some rest. Dance lessons start tomorrow. Tinker Bell, loan him one of your towels. I'll get him his own towels later."

Blake left the room. Doug sat against the cage wall and stared at the floor. He was dripping wet, but he didn't care. The burn stung badly. Without even looking up, he felt the top of his head to see how much hair he'd lost. It felt like only a little was gone, but without a back mirror, he had no idea what it looked like. It could have been worse. He was lucky. Tinker Bell had run to her own compartment to find him a towel. She came over and handed it to him.

"There was nothing you could have done, Doug. The man's a giant. What choice did you have?"

"Just leave me alone," Doug muttered without even looking up.

But Tinker Bell didn't leave him alone. Instead, she sat down next to him and put her hand on Doug's shoulder. Doug quickly jerked himself away from her.

"Don't feel bad," she said again in her soft voice. "You showed a lot of courage. It takes courage to stand up to a giant. Especially an evil one like Mr. Blake."

"Courage? I acted like a little baby!"

"You cried out in pain like anybody else would have. But most people would have given in long before you did."

"I already told ya, I wanna be left alone! Go on back to your own part of the cage!"

Tinker Bell looked hurt. "As you wish."

"Stop sayin' that! Stop sayin' 'As you wish!' I ain't your master, and you ain't my slave!"

Tinker Bell looked like she was about to cry. "All right, Doug." She got up to leave.

"Wait! I'm sorry. I know you was just tryin' ta help. I just … I don't feel like talkin' anymore today. Maybe tomorrow."

"It's all right, Doug. I understand. I'll see you tomorrow then."

"Yeah … yeah … tomorrow."

Chapter Eleven

The Day Marla Was Left Behind

"Why not? Why can't I go along?"

It was a nice, clear day in the park — cold but sunny, with a blue sky that was rare for the fall. Marla had come to think of this park as hers alone, a place where she could have Mike all to herself, without parents being around and without friends being around. Usually they were the only ones there, and they visited the park almost every day on their way home from Mike's cross-country practice, enjoying the green grass and the small clustered area of pine and maple trees. Occasionally, a mother or two could be seen in the distance pushing her toddlers on the swing, but for all intents and purposes, the park belonged just to Marla and Mike. They walked hand in hand, and occasionally, Mike would stop on an impulse, pull her close, and kiss her. Marla could think of nothing she enjoyed more than these daily walks.

Only today she didn't like the park. Today, Mike was ruining their park experience by telling her some bad news about the weekend. Not only was he canceling their date for Saturday night, but he was going away as well.

"Answer me, Mike. Why can't I go with you?"

"I already told you, Marla. It's just a guy thing. Ben isn't bringing Jean either."

"So you'd rather spend a weekend with your friends than with me?"

Marla couldn't believe such childish words were coming out of her mouth. She felt like hitting herself. He was just a new boyfriend, for heaven's sake. She could have any boy she wanted. Boys were crazy about her! They drooled over her! Just who was this Michael Owen anyway, and why did he seem to have such a hold over her? Marla had scolded many of her own friends for acting too immature around boys, and now she was doing the very thing she detested.

Mike reached for her hand. Marla pulled back and turned away from Mike with a pouting gesture.

"Marla, you know I'd rather be with you. But I promised the guys. I can't go back on a promise."

"I don't understand. Why do you need to take this trip? It's awfully sudden!"

"It's not so sudden. Ben and Cliff have been talking about it for a long time."

"You never said anything up till now. Why is that?"

Mike shrugged. "Because I forgot, I guess. I mean, it was never any big deal to me. I hadn't really thought much about it one way or the other. And then yesterday, when they reminded me … well, the whole thing just kind of snuck up."

Mike seemed to be lying. Marla wasn't sure. She'd only known him for a short time, so she hadn't had an opportunity to compare contrasting patterns of behavior. But everything about this conversation seemed odd. He *was* lying. He had to be. And Mike didn't strike her as a liar by nature. If he had, she never would have been interested in him. Something unusual was going on.

"Mike, this doesn't make any sense. How can you give up *Good Morning USA*?"

"I already told you. I'm not giving it up. They've rescheduled."

"Why? Why did you ask them to reschedule? Wasn't your interview more important than a silly beach trip?"

"It's no big deal, Marla. I'm still doing the interview. I'm just doing it in a couple of weeks instead."

Marla was about to say something else. Instead, she paused and offered an embarrassed-looking smile. "I'm sorry. I was just thinking of your writing career. You could have a great future, Mike. I'd hate to see you throw it all away."

"I'm not gonna throw it away. I promise."

Marla felt so foolish. At first, she'd complained because she couldn't go along. When that didn't work, she tried to make it sound like she was only thinking of Mike, as though she were unselfishly helping his career. But at least Mike was being patient with her, patient and gentle, something she never received from a guy before. Marla thought for a second about Barry Kaufman, whom she'd dated as a freshman. Barry was on the debating team, and this made it impossible for Marla to ever win an argument with him. Had she just pulled this stunt on Barry Kaufman, he would have accused her of "altering the premise of the argument." She finally decided to stop seeing Barry, and she was grateful that Mike didn't treat her that way. He was every bit as smart as Barry and probably did notice her switching arguments midstream, but he let it go. He didn't pounce all over it the way Barry would have done. Marla's feelings always seemed to matter to Mike, and he looked genuinely bothered right now. Marla could tell that he didn't enjoy hurting her. But she *was* hurt. If only she didn't care so much about this guy. If only she could take him in stride as she did her previous boyfriends.

Actually, both objections were equally valid. She honestly didn't want him to take this trip. She honestly preferred to see him think of his future. After all, his future might be hers as well. Still, if he was determined to go, she really wanted to go with him. She couldn't bear the thought of being alone over the weekend.

Why? Why did she need to go? Couldn't she handle him being gone for just two days? Some of the feeling was natural. Marla always turned to mush during the early stages of a romance. At first, the new boyfriend consumed all of her time, and she tended to shine off all of her girlfriends. But sooner or later, the newness would wear off, and Marla would no longer feel like she had to be with him every waking moment. She'd been dating Mike for close to a month. By now, Marla had expected the passions to wane a little, but they never did. If anything, they were stronger than ever. All she had to do was look at Mike and her heart felt like it was about to break in pieces. He was so cute, so innocent. And he was decent, the first decent guy she'd ever dated. She wanted to spend the rest of her life with him. It made no sense since they hardly knew each other, but this didn't change the way she felt. Mike was her future. Marla knew that, as sure as she knew anything else.

And she knew something troublesome was going on right now, something bigger than her own petty jealousies.

"Mike, are you in some kind of trouble?"

"Of course not."

"But Cliff is in trouble. Isn't this a strange time for him to be

179

taking a road trip? With the police watching him?

"The police are talking to lots of people. Not just Cliff. They always do that when somebody is missing."

"But you've heard the same rumors as me. You know Cliff is an actual suspect."

"Just gossip."

"Mike, if Cliff is in trouble, wouldn't it be better to keep your distance? I wouldn't want them to view you as an accomplice."

"Accomplice to what? Cliff hasn't done anything. But he's my friend, and if they do suspect him, then he needs me as his friend now more than ever."

He was right, of course. Ever since that first day when Mike defended Cliff from Scott Pierce during lunch hour, she could see that this was no ordinary guy. He did more than draw comic book heroes. He *was* a hero. Marla had encouraged the rescue herself, suggesting that Cliff could use a friend. Could she ask any less of Mike now, even though the trouble might be more dangerous? But what kind of trouble? Was the alleged Cliff/DeWorken incident related in any way to the forthcoming trip? Marla wanted answers, and she could see that she wasn't going to get any from Mike.

***

It was 8:00 in the morning. Marla usually slept in on Saturdays, but she'd promised her dad that they could have breakfast together, and he would be picking her up in half an hour. Marla stared at herself in the mirror. She didn't like her face or her body. Everybody always told her how attractive she was. In fact, her closest girlfriends envied her. So Marla accepted her good looks by faith. She figured her friends must be right. Why would anyone make up a thing like that? But she still didn't see it. In her opinion, there wasn't one single feature that couldn't stand some improvement.

At times, she talked with her Mom about her looks. Her mom said that all people at her age felt awkward about their appearance and that she would outgrow it. Marla wasn't so sure. There were many things about her self-image that seemed below average even though she was popular. Some of her friends saw therapists, and Marla often wondered if seeing one herself might not be such a bad idea. But whenever she thought about a therapist, she quickly put the idea out of her mind. For one thing, neither Mom nor Dad would be willing to pay for it since they wouldn't want to admit that their daughter could possibly be having a "psychological problem." And then, even if they *did* allow her to go, Marla had no idea what she would say. The therapist would ask why she had come, and Marla would shrug her shoulders. Marla tended to keep deep, personal feelings inside. Never had she opened up with her girlfriends, or even her parents — at least, not in any serious way. She had always heard how unhealthy that was, burying one's true sentiments. So perhaps it would be best to see a therapist, but once again, the very idea caused some timidity. Marla's grandmother had been good at getting her to open up, but the dear woman passed away a while back. The only other person she'd ever confided in was Mike, that night at the dance. Mike's tender, compassionate response completely stole her heart.

***

The restaurant seemed busy. Dad was enjoying a hearty breakfast of bacon, eggs, and pancakes. Marla often wondered how he remained so skinny over the years because he always had a big appetite. Marla herself was having a modest breakfast: strawberry yogurt and an English muffin.

These Saturday morning times with Dad made her very uncomfortable. The two of them had absolutely nothing in common and nothing to talk about. Dad always asked for an update but never seemed to listen while she was giving it. No sooner did she talk about something that interested her than he would change the subject to ask about grades. Never mind her dreams or her friends or her plans … Grades … that was the main thing … So long as Daddy's little girl was getting good grades, nothing else mattered.

They were finally finished with grades. Dad had grudgingly conceded that a B+ average was not the worst academic performance in the world, even though he was absolutely positive she could do even better. When she promised to take his advice on how to "turn that into an A average, where she belonged," he finally let up. They'd had this conversation about grades her entire life, and Marla was surprised he let it go so quickly this time. But the reason became immediately clear when he introduced a new topic. Something else had been on his mind that concerned him more.

"So, Marla, where would you like to go this summer?"

"This summer?"

"Don't tell me you've forgotten our trip."

She *had* forgotten. She'd wanted to forget. Even though Mom had custody, Dad was given certain visiting privileges, and they included keeping Marla for two weeks over the summer. Dad had said before that they could use the time to take a vacation to Hawaii or someplace similar. Marla could think of nothing more boring or depressing — not the idea of being in Hawaii, the idea of being there with him.

"Well, I think I might do summer school this year, Dad."

"Summer school doesn't take up the entire summer."

He was too smart for her. "True, but in the little time left over, I might need to get ready for fall."

She thought the relationship between summer school and even better grades might make her response to his invitation sound a little better. It wasn't working. He didn't go for it.

"Don't you want to take this trip with me?"

"Of course I do."

"Because if you don't, you don't have to. It's perfectly all right with me."

Perfectly all right with him. Of course! Perfectly all right with him! No, she didn't have to go. He would be wounded and devastated. He would assume for the rest of his life that she hated him, and he would do everything he possibly could to let her know he was feeling that way and to make her life miserable, but no, she didn't have to go. It was perfectly all right with him.

"I'll go, Dad. Of course I'll go. It'll be fun."

He seemed to cheer up a bit. Strange, in all the years Dad lived at home, he never showed a hint of interest in spending even one *day* with her, let alone two whole weeks. But now that he was out of the house, well, his parental rights were carved in gold, and nothing would get in the way. Marla often wondered if these custody courts really had the children's best interests at heart. Right now, she felt like property, not a person.

"So," Dad said, changing the subject again, "when were you planning to tell me about this new boyfriend? Your mother says you've been seeing quite a bit of each other."

Thanks, Mom, Marla said to herself. Then she started to tell him about Mike: how they met, how Mike had drawn his own comic and sold it to a publisher. It would be nice if he and Dad could get along, and she was hoping that she could make Mike sound interesting and responsible. But she could see that Dad wasn't really paying attention. He was just waiting for her to finish as always. Then he would say what he had already been planning to say.

"Be careful of these young men. They want only one thing from a pretty girl."

"That's not true, Dad. Mike isn't like that."

"All guys are like that!"

"Dad ..."

"I'm just warning you for your own good. Be on your guard. Never assume anything where guys are concerned."

"OK, Dad." It was pointless to argue.

"You realize I only say this because I care."

"I know, Dad. It's all right."

***

"Marla, your friends are here."

It was Mom calling through her bedroom door. Dad had returned her to the house at 10:00. It was closer to 11:00 now, and Mike had promised to stop off at the house to say goodbye. As Marla walked out the front door, she could hear Ben and Cliff arguing back in the van. Ben was still at the steering wheel. Cliff was halfway out the passenger side, swinging the door back and forth. Mike was at the front porch, waiting for Marla.

"I can't believe Ben's parents gave him the van for the whole weekend," Marla said.

"Yeah ... say ... we're running kind of late ..."

"I know ... I know ... I'll walk you to the car."

"Hi, Marla," Cliff said as they got closer.

"How are you, Cliff?"

"Pretty good, I guess."

"What's that? What's in the cage?" Marla leaned inside and her eyes met a very angry-looking Caligula. "You're bringing your cat?"

Mike nodded.

"Why are you bringing your cat?"

"Aw, just for the heck of it," he said.

Marla found this very unusual, and she could tell that Mike understood how weird it looked. He said a little more, looking very uneasy. "You know ... the rest of my family is gone, except for Aunt Loureen. The cat is kind of attached to me."

"So? Your aunt can feed him, can't she?"

"Sure. But ... you know ... he'll be lonesome for the rest of the family. He hardly knows Aunt Loureen."

Marla couldn't seem to recall hearing a whole lot about the cat up until now, and she had her suspicions that this attachment to a mere cat was another lie. But why lie about a cat? With every bit of new information, this weekend trip looked more and more mysterious.

"He might miss you, Mike, but that doesn't mean you take a cat on vacation the way you would take a dog. Cats don't like trips. Believe me, we used to own a cat."

"We'll be at the beach. It'll give Caligula a chance to run around a little."

"Michael, what are you talking about? Dogs may like the beach, but cats hate places like that. Water scares them to death."

"Maybe not. We'll see."

"Well, he looks miserable in that cage."

"I know. It's the only way you can travel with a cat."

"Cats are territorial, Mike. He'd be much more comfortable if you just left him at home."

"Yeah ... ah ... well ... yeah ... probably ... maybe ... but I'm still gonna bring him, just for the heck of it."

"Michael Owen, what's going on?"

"What do you mean?"

"Don't give me that! You know very well what I mean."

"Come on, Mike. We'd better hit the road."

"Just a sec, Ben." He pulled Marla against his chest and kissed her on the cheek. Marla was starting to cry, but she tried not to show it.

"I'll see you tomorrow night," Mike said. "And next weekend, I won't be with anyone but you. I promise."

***

Marla's mother was at the store, so she answered the doorbell herself. Looking through the eyehole, she saw a well-dressed man in a black suit, holding a briefcase. Probably just a solicitor, but he seemed harmless enough, so she opened the door.

"Excuse me," the man said in a very polite voice, "but if I could have just a moment of your time."

"Yes? What can I do for you?"

"I'm with the Big Brain Encyclopedia Company."

"Oh, I don't think we need any new encyclopedias, thank you."

"I understand. A fair response indeed. After all, encyclopedias do seem rather obsolete these days, especially with the convenience of the Internet. But I'm sure you're aware of the statistics."

"Statistics?"

"About the unreliability of most Web pages. And those few Web sites with credibility usually are connected to a reputable company like Big Brain Encyclopedia."

Marla had never heard of the Big Brain Encyclopedia Company. The name sounded rather silly. Was this some kind of joke? Were some of her friends playing a prank? No, that didn't make sense. If this were a high schooler at her door telling her about the Big Brain Encyclopedia, that would be one thing. But this salesperson was forty years old if he was a day. What would he be doing joining her friends for fun? No cameras seemed to be around either, so Marla also dismissed the notion of some reality TV show. In either event, Marla was beginning to wish she'd never opened the door.

"Well, it would be up to my mother, and she isn't home right now."

"Would you like me to leave a sample volume with you?" He opened up his briefcase and took out a thick hardcover book with black binding.

"That won't be necessary, sir."

"Just to browse? Why not? If you like it, if your mother sees how much you like it, you can always give me a call, and we'll conduct a transaction. Meanwhile, the book is complimentary."

All at once, Marla realized she'd seen this man before, but she couldn't quite place him.

"This is an interesting volume," he continued while thumbing through the pages. "It deals with sociological data, particularly gender-related studies. It might even help you to explain some of your boyfriend's recent bizarre behavior."

Marla felt as though a bolt of lightning had suddenly struck her. "Excuse me?"

"I'm sorry. That was a bit presumptuous of me. I merely assumed that an attractive young lady such as yourself must have a boyfriend."

"Sir, I think you'd better be on your way. You can come back some other time when my mother is here."

"You sure you don't want to take just this one volume?"

"Mister …"

"Charles."

"All right, Charles. I already told you, I do not need an encyclopedia."

"I can see why you would think that, Marla. After all, you do have a B+ average. But why be complacent? With the Big Brain Encyclopedia, we might just bring that up to an A."

Marla was frightened now. She put her foot by the door just in case he tried to move into the house.

"How do you know all this? How do you know my name?"

"Take it easy, Marla. I'm a friend."

"How can you be my friend if we've never met before? I'm only going to say this one more time. Leave now, or I'll call 911!"

"OK, Marla. I'll leave if that's really what you want. Sorry to have bothered you. And I'm even more sorry to have frightened you. Please, forget I was here and enjoy your weekend." He turned to leave. As Marla started closing the door, Charles looked back over his shoulders. "You know, it's a shame Mike and his friends can't take you along."

"What?" Marla was starting to feel as though she were part of a dream.

Charles walked back toward the door. "If you ask me, your presence would have provided a valuable asset."

"You know everything about me. How is that? How do you know all these things? Have you been stalking me?"

Charles laughed. "No, my child, I haven't been stalking. But you have every right to believe so. I don't blame you. I *have* been exhibiting suspicious behavior. In any event, I can fix it for you."

"Fix what for me?"

"I can fix it so that you join Mike, Cliff, and Ben."

"They already left."

"I know. We can catch up with them."

"Catch up with them? What are you talking about?"

"Wouldn't it be fun to catch up with them?"

"I don't know what to say to you, sir."

"You *would* like to catch up to them, wouldn't you?"

"How?" Marla was surprised to see herself respond this way. She didn't trust this man any more than she could throw, and yet he was still managing to entice her with promises about being with Mike.

"Let me worry about the 'how.' What do you say?"

"Mike doesn't want me along anyway. He wants to be with his friends this weekend."

"Actually, that's not true. Mike would very much prefer it if you joined him."

"I don't think so. Besides, they'll be back tomorrow."

"No, they won't."

Marla was getting frightened again. "But they will. This is just a weekend trip."

"So they think. They think it's only a weekend trip. But the trip is going to last much longer, and I do believe Mike would enjoy your company."

"All right. I've had enough. Thanks for the offer, but no, thanks. Good luck with your encyclopedias."

"If you change your mind, Marla, let me know. Here … my card." The card said CHARLES in bold blue letters, and that was all it said.

"What is this? There's no phone number and no last name."

"You don't need a phone number or a last name. If you change your mind, just call me."

"Call you? How?""

"You have a fireplace, don't you?"

"A fireplace? Yes."

"Take this card, burn it in your fireplace. No sooner will the ashes go up the chimney than I'll be here. You don't believe me. I understand. You don't know what to make of me. You've never met anyone like me before, and you don't trust me, even though I seem to know all about you. None of that matters. What matters is this: If you change your mind, if you decide to join Mike and his friends, do what I instructed with the card. Do no more and do no less."

Chapter Twelve

On The Road

Ben had to do all the driving since he was the only one with a license, but he enjoyed driving, so he didn't really mind. Cliff sat next to him in the front passenger seat, and I sat in the second row from the back, next to poor caged-up Caligula.

I'd managed keep the trip a secret from him until the last minute. He was in the middle of a nap when I suddenly picked him up and placed him in the cat carrier. I didn't wanna interrupt his nap because I knew how much that would irritate him, but since sleeping was practically the only thing he did, it was pretty much impossible to interrupt Caligula's day without interrupting Caligula's nap. Besides, I knew that once he found out where he was going, he'd get irritated anyway, whether I disturbed his sleep or not.

"Hey, what's the meaning of this?" he had shouted as I snatched him off of Mom's comfortable loveseat. Then, as I crammed him in the cage, he hissed at me and tried to scratch me. After that, he continued by cussing while I carried him out to the car.

When we got to the car, I finally explained what was going on. He reacted by calling me a bunch of names. Some of them I had never heard before, but by the way he was saying them, I could pretty much guess what they meant.

He settled down a little and sulked quietly on the way to Marla's house. After we said goodbye to Marla and got on the freeway, I looked into the part of the cage that wasn't covered up and saw Caligula's fluffy face glaring at me. It was actually kind of scary. His eyes almost looked like they had fire inside.

Eventually, he tried to sleep, but now and then, some noise or bump on the road would make him wake up, and he would start in on me again. "You're a real piece of work. You know that? How dare you kidnap me against my will?"

Of course, Ben and Cliff only heard meowing. Whenever Caligula talked to me in English, everyone else heard cat sounds because their minds were converting the speech. I'm not sure how, probably some

189

kind of telepathy. And like I already mentioned before, the reverse was also true. When he actually *was* speaking in cat sounds, *my* mind would translate it into English.

"What's with the cat?" Ben asked.

"Nothing," I said. "He's fine."

"I am not fine! Speak for yourself!"

"Why is he meowing so much?" Ben asked again.

Ignoring Ben, I said to Caligula, "Look, you know this isn't a kidnapping. At least not a real kidnapping."

"What do you call it then, Kid? And don't say something clever like 'cat napping'!"

I almost told him that I had *interrupted* a cat napping. But I kept the little joke to myself. Not only would Caligula not appreciate it, but he would have gone out of his way to tell me how stupid it was and that I should never work as a comedian in a nightclub or something equally sarcastic.

"Look, I explained the situation to you. You know why we're bringing you along. If it were a kidnapping, we would be holding you for ransom."

"What are you talking about?" Ben said.

Cliff turned to Ben and gave him a reminder. "He's talking to the cat. We hear Mike in English, but we hear Caligula in cat sounds."

Ben just nodded his head, looking unimpressed.

***

The drive was pretty for about an hour, but when we got into the desert, the scenery was dull and boring. I never liked the desert, even though Aunt Loureen used to tell me to appreciate it.

"The desert has its own unique beauty," she used to say.

Aunt Loureen sure was hard to figure out. How could somebody who loved colorful Christmas lights also love ugly-looking rocks and sagebrush? Besides, if she had to go out of her way to call the desert a "unique beauty," wasn't she already admitting that it didn't have a regular, normal beauty? If I had to *look* for the beauty, wouldn't that mean it wasn't really there?

Actually, it would have been nice to see things through Aunt Loureen's eyes. Since our destination, Wendover, was also in the desert, desert scenery would be the only scenery for the rest of the trip.

I missed Marla already. It was hard leaving her behind. She sure could make a guy feel bad, but it was my own fault for keeping her in the dark. I didn't blame her for feeling rejected, and I hoped I would never have to make her feel that way again. The thought of hurting her or breaking her heart caused a real miserable feeling inside of me. But how could I tell her the truth? How could I talk about ornaments and magic wishes? It would sound like I had lost my mind! This relationship was the best thing that ever happened to me, and I wasn't about to ruin it by scaring her away. And yet, was this any better? Lying through my teeth? I was a terrible liar even though I'd gotten used to lying since the ornament came into my life. Marla definitely knew something weird was going on, with a sudden trip from out of nowhere and my clumsy, bumbling explanation about why I was bringing the cat along. Oh, brother! I'd be lucky if she ever spoke to me again.

I thought about asking Ben if I could borrow his cell phone so I could call her and tell her how much I missed her. But I really didn't wanna talk to her in front of the others. Anyway, saying goodbye a second time probably wouldn't do much more than make us both feel bad again, like the first time.

I glanced at my watch … Almost three hours to go, or maybe more since Cliff kept asking us to stop. First he wanted a milkshake from an old Foster's Freeze that was advertised on a billboard. Later, he remembered that he accidentally left his allergy tablets at home, so we had to get off the freeway again and look for a convenience store. The third time, he just had to go to the bathroom. I could see that he was driving Ben nuts. I wasn't too thrilled with him either. Cliff could be such a pain at times.

Speaking of cell phones, Cliff's prediction at our planning meeting turned out to be right on target. Exactly one hour and five minutes into the trip, his mother called, thinking Ben's cell was the phone at his parents' beach house and figuring we must have arrived at the beach house by then. The first time, when Ben saw on his phone screen who was ringing, he let his voice mail pick it up, and Mrs. Reynolds heard the voice of Aunt Loureen, pretending to be Ben's mom.

We had decided late in the game to use a recording of Aunt

Loureen instead of hijacking Mrs. Robinson's real voice off of their home machine since Aunt Loureen had already phoned Mrs. Reynolds to reassure her about the trip and Mrs. Reynolds was now used to Aunt Loureen's voice. Aunt Loureen never ended up using the ruse I suggested, claiming to explain a different-sounding voice with a cold. Instead she reminded me of her many years of reading children's literature aloud to her elementary school students, changing her voice for each character.

"I'm quite certain an old thespian such as myself can mimic the rich tone and texture of Ben's mother."

I had never heard the word *thespian* before. Aunt Loureen explained that it was another word for *actress* and said that as a new and budding author, I should consider taking time to broaden my vocabulary.

I reminded her that I was only a sophomore and that I only wrote comic books, not literature, and I didn't need fancy words like *thespian*. I guess I don't have to tell you that it was a pointless response since nobody — not me, not my dad, not any person on the planet — was capable of winning an argument against Aunt Loureen.

But anyway, whatever she wanted to call her voice, it actually worked. She kept trying one tone after another with Ben. Ben actually seemed very impressed, and for Ben to be impressed was no small feat.

"That's pretty good," he would say and then add, "Maybe raise the pitch just a little ... No. That's too much."

After that, Aunt Loureen asked about certain expressions his mother was fond of using.

All to say that it worked. My aunt did a very convincing job when she called Mrs. Reynolds. Still, we were all aware that, close as the voices sounded, they were not an exact match. We decided not to take a chance on Mrs. Reynolds comparing the authentic voice on the answering machine with real-time conversations with Aunt Loureen, especially since most of the time we were gonna let Mrs. Reynolds' many calls go to voice mail, which meant that most of the time she was gonna hear the machine, or what she thought was the machine. So we finally just decided to make a fresh message for Ben's cell phone voice mail.

Now, here we were on the road experiencing "the fruit of our labor," as Aunt Loureen would have described it.

"You should have picked it up," Cliff said. "Obviously she's assuming we're at the beach house by now."

"So?" Ben answered. "She'll think we got there late."

"You don't want her thinking we're late. She'll worry and keep calling."

"Chill out," Ben grumbled.

Ten minutes later, she called back. Ben took the call this time. "Hello? ... Sure, Mrs. Reynolds. He's right here." Then Ben teased Cliff by raising his voice. "Clifford? Is there a Clifford in the house? Somebody wants to speak to a Clifford!"

Cliff grabbed the phone out of Ben's hand. "Very funny ... Hello? Hi, Mom ... Yes, I'm fine. No, it's not too cold ...I don't know. We might swim later on ... Of course I brought a towel with me ... Who? Oh ... ah ... she's not here. She went shopping ... I don't know! How should I know? ... Why do you need to talk to her? Didn't you talk to her before we left? All right ... all right! Hey, Ben," he said loudly so his mom could hear. "When's your mother returning from the store?"

"Oh, I don't know," Ben said playfully. "A year ... two years."

"He says an hour or so. All right ... all right. Mom, I've gotta go ... Because I haven't even had a chance to unpack yet ... Right ... Sure.... OK ... All right ... All right!!!" He finally managed to hang up.

Ben reached for his cell phone. "Geez, Cliff! It's a wonder she lets you out of the house every day for school!"

"Yeah," I added. "I'll bet the first time she dropped you off at nursery school she probably went into cardiac arrest."

"Funny! You're a couple of funny guys! You better call your Aunt Loureen and have her phone my mom in a hurry."

I dialed Aunt Loureen, but I only got our house answering machine, so I left a message and told Cliff to be patient.

An hour later, Mrs. Reynolds called again, and Ben let the voice mail pick it up for the second time. Twenty minutes later, she called again, and Cliff talked to her. I heard him say about fifteen times that Ben's mom was still at the store.

When she called back for the fifth time, Cliff asked Ben to get it. "Tell her I'm out taking a walk or something. She won't keep you on the phone as much as me."

Ben frowned and picked up his phone. "Yes, Mrs. Reynolds ... No, not yet ... Well, yeah, Cliff told you an hour, but we were really only guessing. When my mom goes shopping, she can take all day ... Sure ... Oh sure, just as soon as he gets in ... No, he's not here. He's out taking a walk. I don't know. He just wanted to hit the beach by himself. Oh, he's not actually swimming, Mrs. Reynolds, so I don't think you have to worry about sharks ... Well, Mike and I wanted to gather some firewood ... Oh, I'm not sure. You know Cliff. He likes to study things. He's probably checking the seashells for fossilization." I could see Cliff shaking his head back and forth with annoyance as Ben tried to wrap up the conversation. "I will ... I will ... Yup ... OK ... Bye." Ben turned off the phone. "Mike, could you call your Aunt again and have her call Mrs. Reynolds? I'm ready to toss this cell phone out the window."

I dialed Aunt Loureen again. This time she was home.

"Well, hello there, Nephew. How's everything going so far?"

"OK, I guess. Say, Aunt Loureen, have you had a chance to call Cliff's mom yet? She's phoned about five times."

"Sorry. I've been occupied, trying to figure out that hourglass. I'll call her right away. Let's see ... The story at this point is that you all arrived safely at the beach house, right?"

"Yeah. But you need to also act like you just got back from the store. Tell her you're watching us carefully and tell her Cliff's fine and try to get her to stop worrying so much."

"I'll take care of it, Nephew. Keep your focus on the mission."

"I wish I wasn't on any mission, Aunt Loureen."

"Nephew! You're being careless!"

"Huh?"

"Be careful how you throw around the word *wish*."

"Oh yeah. Sorry. I guess it didn't make any difference. I'm still here."

"Fortunately for all of us, that ornament has a mind of its own."

Yeah, lucky me, I said to myself. But to Aunt Loureen I just said, "Goodbye."

I had almost forgotten about Caligula, but as soon as I handed the phone back to Ben, Caligula started in on me again. Without even seeing his face, I could hear his loud voice from behind the cage. "Are you all gonna be yacking on that portable noise machine all day long? Can't a cat get any sleep around here?"

"Don't look at me. I can't help it if Cliff's mom keeps calling."

"Haven't you idiots ever heard of an off button? She can call till she's blue in the face, and we won't have to hear a thing … Phones … What a nuisance. An infernal, intrusive device if you ask me."

"Look," I said. "Why don't you just sit still and be quiet? You hate talking anyway, so don't talk, cuz I'm tired of hearing it."

"Now you listen to me, Bullwinkle … I have every right to complain because this fun little outing was *your* stupid idea."

"It wasn't my idea. Aunt Loureen told me to do this."

"Aunt Loureen is always telling you to do things. Can't you think for yourself? Does Aunt Loureen tell you when to blow your nose too?"

"Hey, Aunt Loureen saved your life, Caligula! She's the only one who was able to talk Dad into bringing you home from the pound! You oughta be more grateful."

"Oh really? Well, precious Aunt Loureen also endangered my life by giving you that pesky ornament in the first place!"

"You always have an answer for everything! You're such a grouch!"

"Grouch, am I? Kid, when have I ever gone out of my way to complain, aside from those times when you make me talk against my will or drag me into another one of your brainless ornament adventures?"

"Look, like I said, right now, nobody's making you talk! Believe me, I'd have been happy to leave you behind. But we need you. You know how to answer questions about the ornament."

"Kid, I tried to tell you before, but you wouldn't listen. You were too busy packing up the van."

"What are you talking about?"

"I'm talking about my knowledge of the ornament. If that's the only reason I'm here, then there *is* no reason. I don't know how to break this to you, Kid, but that ornament doesn't work anymore."

"Huh? What?"

"You heard me. I said it doesn't work anymore." Then he turned his head away from me and muttered, "At least, I don't think it does."

"Cut it out, Caligula. I'm not buying it. This is just a trick so that I'll let you out of that cage."

"Kid, you aren't paying attention. I said, *it doesn't work*!"

"Sure it works! It has to work! It's still Christmas time!"

"I know what time of the year it is, imbecile! But something has happened."

"What? What's happened?"

"I'm not sure. Something caused the magic to stop. Well, think about it. When's the last time the ornament granted a wish?"

"It's granted plenty of wishes! That's our whole problem! That's why we're taking the trip, because of what the ornament did to DeWorken!"

"That wish happened weeks ago. How many wishes have you witnessed since then?"

"Well, we've been trying not to use it."

"Oh sure you have. Give me a break, Kid. You and that pinhead, Cliff, are always trying to use it. I mean, who are we kidding? Just recently, you tried to bring DeWorken back home magically, right? I was laying down in the den, resting, when you tried. I heard everything. And it didn't work, did it?"

"So? Sometimes the ornament just doesn't give us our wish. You know that. Doesn't mean it's stopped working completely."

"I think it does. Because I also tried to use it. Do you think I'd still be sitting in this cage right now if the ornament were working? You've been right here with me in the same van with the ornament tucked away in your suitcase. Don't you think I'd have used it by now?"

He was right. If he wanted to, he could wish something horrible for me right this very minute. I almost started shaking inside. How could I keep making these blunders? How could I keep forgetting these basic ornament rules? I knew the rules, but I constantly failed to stop and think about them. I tried to make myself feel better by remembering that Aunt Loureen didn't think of it either, and she was the one who told me to take Caligula along. But then, she probably just assumed I'd be smart enough to keep the ornament in the trunk, out of Caligula's "wish range." After that, I told myself that I was just out of practice on account of it being years since I used the ornament, but the truth is, I kept making mistakes back then too. I wasn't sure which was worse, the thought of Caligula making an evil wish or the thought of the ornament completely losing its power and not being able to help us rescue DeWorken.

I said to Caligula, "Maybe the ornament is refusing your wish because it knows we need you on this trip."

"Or maybe you're in denial. I'm telling you, Kid, something happened. All the magic has been drained out of that thing!"

I'd heard enough. I got out of my seat and moved to the third and final row toward the very back of the van. I stared out the window silently. Was it possible? Could he be right? Could the ornament have somehow lost its power? I suddenly remembered the accidental wish I made over the cell phone while talking with Aunt Loureen. How many times in the past had I made accidental wishes, and every time the ornament granted the wish. True, the ornament sometimes chose not to grant *planned* wishes. But the ornament was sly and sneaky, and it did seem to enjoy granting the accidental ones. Only this time it didn't!

When we stopped for gas, I offered to pump it since Ben was doing all the driving. I also chipped in for one-third of the cost with some saved-up allowance money. Ben thanked me for the money and went inside the station's mini-mart to buy us each a soda. Cliff stayed with me while I pumped the gas.

"Mike, may I speak with you for a moment?"

"Sure." I removed the gas cap and jammed the pump nozzle into the slot. "What's up?"

"It's about the cat."

"What about him?"

"When you talk to him and we don't hear him talking back …

well … it looks kind of weird."

I stopped pumping the gas manually and clicked the lever which pumped it automatically. Then I turned to Cliff. "I already explained to both of you why you can't hear him. It's because of the way I accidentally worded things when I first made that ornament wish."

"I know! You explained it years ago. You don't have to go through it again. I haven't forgotten."

"OK. Then what's the problem?"

"The problem is it still looks weird. Maybe you should talk to the cat when Ben and I aren't around."

"Now just a minute … Am I all of a sudden supposed to worry about looking weird in front of my friends?"

"There's no need to get defensive, Mike. This is only a word to the wise."

"What are you talking about? If you already understand what's going on with the cat, then why should it look weird?"

"Well, with Ben, he only half-believes all this ornament stuff anyway. I accept all of it, of course, but I still get an unsettling feeling when I see my friend acting so peculiar."

This was the last straw. He was really pushing my buttons. "Is that so, Cliff? Well, you really are one to talk about looking peculiar. You're the weirdest person at Valley View High, and I've never said anything about it."

Cliff looked hurt. He stared at the ground, barely muttering. "You did just now."

"Don't start feeling sorry for yourself again! You play that wild card every time I confront you about something, and I'm getting sick and tired of it! You know, I put a lot on the line to help you this weekend. Believe me, there were plenty of other things I could have been doing. And all I get for my trouble is a lecture on looking weird? Well, you can shove it, Cliff! Just shove it!"

"All right. I'm sorry. I shouldn't have brought it up." He lowered his voice, sounding more sincere. "I do appreciate you taking this trip with me, Mike. I really do, and I meant no offense."

"OK then."

Chapter Thirteen

Little Town, Big Trouble

When we finally reached Wendover, the sun was down. It was a dinky little town, and we saw no sign of a carnival, but we were so hungry we agreed to grab a bite to eat and hunt for the carnival afterwards.

We decided on a rustic-looking bar and grill with a big statue of a cow on the outside roof. Only a handful of customers were inside, so we figured we might get served right away. Only two waitresses seemed to be working, a younger one and one in her forties maybe. The older waitress greeted us with a warm smile, brought us over to a fairly large table, and handed us some menus. I looked around. The place had a lot of atmosphere. There were actually a few moose heads on the wooden, cabin-like walls.

The waitress didn't look bad for a middle-aged woman, but I think her hair was dyed. The color was brown, but it just didn't look that natural to me for some reason, so I'm pretty sure she dyed it.

"I'm Maple. I'll be your waitress this evening. Can I start you off with drinks?"

Ben and I ordered Cokes. Cliff ordered iced tea.

"I'll be back in a flash," she said.

"Can you tell us how to get to the carnival?" Cliff asked.

"Carnival?"

"Yes," Cliff said. "We don't know where it is because we don't live around here."

"I already knew that, honey. Who could live in this town without knowing everyone else who lives here? Now then, I take it you're referring to Heartland Carnival?"

"That's right," Cliff said.

"Twenty miles east on 88."

"Oh?" Cliff said. "We thought it was in Wendover."

"No, honey. It's on the outskirts of Wendover, but not actually in town."

"I see."

"Well, let me get your drinks, and then I'll take your orders."

"Did you hear that?" Ben said as Maple walked away. "She called you 'honey.'"

"Cut it out, Ben."

"I think she likes you," Ben teased. "After all, she didn't call me 'honey.'"

"Waitresses call everyone 'honey.' Besides, she's twice my age."

I looked at my watch. "It'll be 8:00 by the time we eat and drive another twenty miles."

"Yeah," Ben said. "But the darkness might be an advantage since we have to steal DeWorken back and then make a run for it."

"Do you think our plan will work?" Cliff asked.

"Search me," Ben said. "It's a harebrained scheme no matter what plan we try. I guess one is as good as the other."

Maple returned with our beverages. "Have you decided?"

"Yeah," I said. "I'll just have a burger and fries."

"The bacon burger or the regular burger?"

"Oh … the regular, I guess."

"Maple." An old man with gray hair and a scraggly, half-shaven face was standing behind her, calling her name. His clothes were kind of ragged, and I wondered if he was homeless.

"I'll be with you in a minute, Andy."

"But I need a refill."

"Just as soon as I'm done taking these orders, Andy."

But Andy didn't move. He kept staring at her. His eyes looked lost and hazy.

"Andy, please go back to your table."

Andy returned to his seat which was about six or seven down from ours.

"Sorry," Maple said under her breath. "He's kind of a permanent fixture around here."

"You mean he's homeless?" I asked.

"That's the least of it. Andy has been the town character for years. If you ask me, the government made a big mistake when they let all these people out of the nuthouse."

I was very curious. "You mean he's crazy?"

"Well, you tell me, sugar. The man always talks about some magic which takes people into another world."

I almost fell out of my chair. "Another world, you say? What kind of world?"

"You'll have to ask him, sugar. I'm just a waitress, not an astronaut."

"Meanwhile," Ben said. "I'm ready to order."

"Oh, I'm sorry." Maple moved over to Ben's side of the table. "What will it be?"

"I think I'll go with the steak sandwich."

"How would you like your steak cooked?"

"Medium is fine."

"It comes with a choice of baked potato or French fries."

"Hmm ... I'll go with the fries."

"Got it." Maple finished writing and glanced at Cliff.

"If I order the shrimp," Cliff said, "do I really get a lot of shrimp?"

"Well, just what would you consider a lot, hon?"

"I don't know. How many to a plate?"

"Seven or so."

"Only seven?"

"The plate also comes with carrots and peas."

"Could I substitute the carrots and peas for more shrimp?"

Ben buried his face in his hands.

"Sorry. We don't do substitutions."

201

"OK." Cliff picked up the menu again. "Does the chicken Caesar salad have a lot of chicken?"

Ben was moaning. "Geez, Cliff."

"Yes it does."

"More than the amount of shrimp?"

"Yes, honey. You won't be disappointed."

"What size plate does it come on?"

Maple held up her hands. "About like this."

"Hmm ... all right. I'll have the chicken Caesar salad."

***

My burger was tasty, and the others seemed to be enjoying their food too, even Cliff, although I half expected him to take out a ruler and measure the size of his salad.

I chose not to discuss Maple's comment about the other world. My friends were so tired they obviously hadn't made the connection, and I didn't wanna do anything to talk Ben out of this trip. Sure, they knew that Aunt Loureen had told me about some other world, but all that stuff about me maybe going there if it was my destiny ... Well, why say anything to change Ben's mind about the mission?

"Are we really driving home tonight?" Cliff asked.

Ben nodded his head. "If we can get DeWorken fast enough, why not?"

"That's a lot of driving for you," I said.

"I don't mind."

Cliff looked concerned. "But I can't go back home late tonight. My mom thinks we're away for the whole weekend."

Ben smiled. "I'm sure she'll be ecstatic to have her little Clifford home early. But if you're worried, maybe we can spend the night at Mike's."

"Sure," I said. "No problem."

Suddenly, we heard a bunch of loud motors and looked out the window. A group of six young men were parking their motorcycles.

Cliff put down his fork. "Oh no. This could be trouble."

"Trouble?" I said. "Why? Just because they ride motorcycles?"

"No, it's not just the bikes. See those jackets? They all match."

Each of the dudes wore a thick black leather jacket with some kind of red, diamond-shaped insignia on the back. I asked Ben if he thought they were a gang.

"Yeah, probably."

But as always, Ben didn't look too concerned. As for me, I was awfully glad we'd talked Ben into coming along.

They burst in like they owned the place. Without even waiting to be seated, they plopped into a large booth close to the door and across the aisle from the old man whom the waitress had called "Andy." Both waitresses looked concerned. They also looked like they'd waited on these creeps before.

Two of the bikers were huge, but even the skinnier ones looked meaner than bulldogs.

One of them shouted at the top of his lungs, "Hey, when do we get some service around here?"

"Great," Ben said. "A bunch of rowdy, loud mouths. So much for eating in peace."

I nodded my head. A dumpy bar and grill in a small, quiet town was the last place I'd expect to find these bully types. No, they hadn't bullied anyone yet, but a bunch of wild, nasty-looking guys? It would happen. It would happen just as sure as there was a nose on my face. Lately it seemed like I couldn't get away from conflict. It was as if something was forcing me into these little adventures. I started thinking about the day I helped Cliff against Scott Pierce. That *totally* seemed forced. I had no choice, no choice at all, because I had to impress Marla or be a coward in front of Marla. And then there was this whole trip, or "mission," as Aunt Loureen liked to call it. Wasn't the mission forced upon me? Didn't that Charles character tell me I was going on a journey even though I thought I wasn't? Didn't Cliff force the trip on me by stealing the ornament out of my room and making a stupid wish that got him and DeWorken into trouble? Didn't Aunt Loureen also force me by making me feel guilty about not wanting to help them? I started thinking again about destiny. I had a horrible feeling deep in the gut that destiny was forcing me into this place at this moment. The bully types would never go away until I learned to deal with them, really deal with them, not just put on a show in front of a girl by taking on some punk who never really scared me in the first place. That wasn't courage. That was just an act — a good act, but an act. And now, today, I was gonna learn how to handle people who *really* frightened me.

The ornament was back in the van, locked. I had locked it in the trunk when we stopped to get gas. I really hadn't expected trouble at a simple restaurant, and I didn't wanna carry it in my pocket like I used to do since it looked kind of dorky. And Caligula had already tried unsuccessfully to make a wish, so there was no danger leaving it in the van, even if the entire automobile counted as one room despite the ornament being separated in the trunk. Anyway, if Caligula was right (and he usually was), the ornament wouldn't work, and even if it did, how would I know if I was supposed to use it or instead learn some courage all on my own? Just because courage was part of my destiny, that didn't mean I was meant to gain it with magic. Would I really want to find my courage and then spend a lot of sleepless nights wondering if the ornament changed my personality or if I changed it myself? That would just be a lot of confusion like the kind I felt when I got my letter of acceptance from Griffith Publications.

Still, those guys were scarier than any high school jock or gang member. They were long out of high school, probably in their mid-twenties, and they looked like they could tear up the whole town if they wanted to. Maybe it would be a good idea after all to go out to the van and fetch the ornament. It was Aunt Loureen who told me to bring the ornament on the journey, so it *had* to work. Why would Caligula know it wasn't working if Aunt Loureen didn't know? Both of them had special ornament knowledge. As a matter of fact, why hadn't Aunt Loureen thought about Caligula using the ornament to make a wish? I was the careless, forgetful one, not her. Then I remembered that I had already asked myself that question early while we were driving and assumed she thought I'd keep it in the trunk. But then, she had never said anything about a trunk, and Aunt Loureen was the type who gave those kinds of reminders. But anyway, to grab the ornament now, I'd have to go out the front door of the restaurant, and that would mean passing the bikers' table. So far, they hadn't noticed us. They hadn't even noticed Cliff, the bully magnet. Wouldn't it be foolish to bring attention to ourselves?

It was then that I remembered the sword-shaped key chain from Charles. I did have that with me, but how was it to be used? Charles never explained how it worked. It would be awfully dumb to assume this key chain granted wishes like the ornament did. Still, Charles said it would protect me on my journey, and the journey had started, or at least, this was the only journey I knew of so far. What did the key chain actually do? If it were a real sword, that would be one thing, but an inch-long, sword-shaped key chain? Either it had some kind of magic charm or it couldn't do jack! I reached into my pocket and pulled the key chain out, staring at it in my hand. There wasn't much to lose by making a wish. Either it would work or it wouldn't. Why not just try? But I'd have to talk to myself out loud in front of other people. Even if I whispered the wish, I would look stupid and one of the bikers would point me out to the others, saying something like, "Hey, look at the geek who talks to himself!"

Maybe I could just leave the table, go into the bathroom, and make the wish there. But if I was alone in the bathroom, it wouldn't work. Other people had to be in the room while I wished, or at least that was the case if it obeyed the same rules as the ornament. Oh well. Probably a different charm meant different rules, so why not just go into the bathroom and try it? Maybe Charles knew that the ornament had lost its power, and maybe that was why he gave me this new device. For that matter, maybe I didn't need to wish at all. Maybe the key chain just gave me good luck.

But a moment later, I got so distracted, I never ended up leaving the table to study the key chain. This was because we could hear every word from the bikers' table as Maple the waitress came to take their order. I could tell by the way she spoke that she knew them well. They probably came in here a lot, and Maple had gotten used to putting up with them. "Can I start you off with something to drink?"

One of them whistled. "You can start me off all right, babe. You sure can start me off."

Maple gave a polite but annoyed grin. "I'm not in the mood tonight, guys. Drinks. What would you like to drink?"

Another one said. "Beers all around. You got Coors?"

"Sure. We have Coors." As she turned to leave, one of them slapped her in the rear.

"Do that again and you can find another place to eat and drink!" Maple snapped.

"OOOOH ..." several of them said together as the others laughed and grinned. Maple left to get their beers.

Cliff looked worried. "Aren't there laws against slapping a girl's behind?"

"Yeah," Ben said, "if she wanted to press a case. But it looks like she can take care of herself. Waitresses are used to dealing with all kinds of people."

"I don't know," Cliff said. "They look like they're in the mood for trouble. What if they actually assault her or pick a fight with someone else in the restaurant?"

Ben just sighed. "Quit getting paranoid, Cliff."

Cliff took a sip of his iced tea and washed down another allergy tablet. "You don't ever get scared of anything, do you, Ben?"

"Sure I do. Everyone gets scared."

"Oh? Well, I've never seen you frightened. What are *you* scared of? I'll bet those guys don't scare you at all."

"Well, no. *They* don't scare me because I learned years ago how to defend myself."

"Yes," Cliff said. "Sometimes I wish my dad would have forced me to take karate or something."

Ben started pouring a bottle of ketchup over his fries. "It wouldn't have been a bad idea. If you had, you'd be enjoying high school."

Cliff turned to me. "How about you, Mike? Did you ever learn any self-defense?"

"No ... not really ... Well ... I did take some judo when I was a kid, but I never stayed with it."

"Did you learn any throws before you quit?" Cliff asked.

"Three ... that's all."

Cliff looked very interested. "So, did you ever use it on anybody?"

"Once ... just once ... in third grade. A fourth-grader was picking on me during recess. He was twice my size, but I threw him and he hit the ground. It was the first time I ever tried any judo outside the gym."

"Wow!" said Cliff. "Then what happened?"

"Well, I never really learned what to do after throwing somebody. He stood up, madder than a hornet, ticked off that a little third-grader had thrown him like that …"

"Yes? And?"

"Then he came over and practically tore my face off."

Ben started laughing. Cliff followed, and finally I laughed myself. After all the years, it did seem kind of funny, looking back, but I sure wasn't laughing much on the day it actually happened.

Maple returned to the bikers' table with a tray of filled beer mugs.

"I think I'm in love," one of the bikers said.

After distributing the drinks, Maple pulled out her order pad. "What can I get you?"

The biggest guy grabbed a menu and started stroking his black, scraggly beard. "Let's see. What kind of pies do you have tonight?"

"Almost any kind you want."

"Yeah? Well, listen, tootsie … Why don't you list the fruit pies?"

Maple sighed. Then she rattled them off very quickly from memory. "Apple, raspberry, blackberry, boysenberry, strawberry, and peach."

"Hmm … you got any cream pies?"

"Chocolate cream, banana cream, coconut cream, butterscotch, and lemon meringue."

Another one of the goons joined in. "Could you list those fruit pies again?"

An irritated Maple repeated them. "Apple, raspberry, blackberry, boysenberry, strawberry, and peach!"

"Thanks, babe," the big one said. "But I think we're gonna go with just the beers tonight."

Maple stormed off as they laughed their heads off.

"You were great, Butch," one of them said to the big guy who seemed to be their leader.

"They actually think they're funny," Ben said.

"Yes," Cliff added. "But who wants to tell them the truth? I sure don't."

Now Butch had his eye on the old man. "Hey, Grandpa! Hey, Gramps! Yeah. That's right! I'm talking to *you*! What are you drinking tonight?"

"Just coffee." The old man looked scared.

"Coffee? Shouldn't you lay off the caffeine? A man your age needs a healthy diet." The gang busted up again.

"I think that Andy fellow is gonna need some help," Ben said.

Cliff put his drink down. "They aren't hurting him."

"Not yet," Ben said. "But the name calling is usually just the beginning. You oughta know that, Cliff. That's what happens to you at school. It starts with name calling, and eventually somebody starts to get physical. And this old guy isn't a spunky personality like Maple. This is the kind of man people take advantage of."

"True," Cliff said. "But would they actually get rough?"

"I don't get you, Cliff," I said. "A moment ago you were very concerned about them getting rough."

"Yes, I was ... but ... here's the thing ... This isn't school. It's a restaurant, a public place."

Ben leaned in closer to Cliff, almost whispering. "They're a gang. Gangs do what they want, especially in these small towns."

"You could probably take on all of them at one time," I said to Ben. "I mean, with your jujutsu and all."

"Who do you think I am? Superman?"

"I thought with martial arts you could take on more than one guy at a time," Cliff added.

"Not that many. There are six of them."

"I'll bet you could still make a good account of yourself."

"You've been watching too many movies, Cliff."

Butch walked over to the old man's table. "Hey, old timer! How about if we buy you a drink?"

The man spoke softly without changing one expression on his face. "No, thanks."

"Aw, come on! We insist!" With that, he poured his mug of beer on top of the poor guy's head. I glanced around the restaurant. People were just staring, like a bunch of cowardly crumbs. But then, I wasn't doing anything either, and like I said, I had never made that trip into the bathroom to figure out if my key chain could be of help.

I couldn't see Maple, but the other waitress ran into the kitchen, hopefully to find the manager.

"That's it," Ben said. "Guys, we need to go help him. We can't just sit back and watch something like this."

Cliff sighed. "We aren't fighters, Ben. We don't know martial arts like you do."

"I know, Cliff, but there are too many of them. I might be able to take on a few with the jujutsu but not all six!"

"OK, Ben," I said. "I'll help you." But I said it only because I didn't wanna look chicken.

Ben turned to Cliff. "Are you in?"

"I don't know, Ben. It could distract us from our primary purpose. We came to find DeWorken, not to get ourselves into even *more* trouble."

"There isn't time to argue. I need your help now."

"Ben," I said. "Could you at least give us a few pointers?"

"Pointers? What are you talking about?"

"You know … some tips. Some fighting tips."

"Now? You want a lesson now? We need to get over there before they hurt him good."

After wiping his head with a napkin, the old man tried to get out of his seat and leave, but Butch pushed him back down before he was even halfway up.

"How about another drink, old timer? I think you spilled your last one."

"I'm heading over there," Ben said, "with or without you two."

"There must be something you can teach us," Cliff said.

"You guys are something else, you know that? Look … if your opponent is good at boxing, wrestle him. If he's good at wrestling, box him."

"That's it?" Cliff whined.

"What do you expect? A one-second course? I offered to take both of you to jujutsu classes with me. I've offered for years. You were never interested. Well, this is where it comes in handy, but chances are, these dopes don't know martial arts anyway, so fight them the best you can. Now, are we ready?"

One of Butch's gorillas poured another beer on the old man. This made me so mad I think I actually felt more anger than fear, and that was good! It helped me find the nerve to get out of my chair.

Cliff stayed behind. I was disappointed in him. I was also concerned about it making the odds worse. I had to hope Ben's jujutsu was as good as everyone thought it was. I never saw him actually use it before. All I ever saw was people staying away from him because they *knew* about the jujutsu.

"Hey!" Ben shouted at Butch. "How would you like to try that with me?"

Butch quieted down for a sec. Silently, he looked Ben over. Then he glanced at me. The other five got up from their table. I could feel my heart beating a mile a minute.

"Well, looky here," Butch said. "One of our schools must be on a field trip today."

Ben stepped closer to Butch. "I'm only gonna say this once, so I hope you're paying attention. Go back to your own table, sit down, and shut up, and nobody will get hurt."

But unlike DeWorken, Butch didn't back off. Instead, he lunged for Ben. I can't even describe what Ben did to him. It involved twisting Butch's arm, picking him up, and suspending him over the shoulder. Then, within seconds, Butch was on the floor.

Someone in the restaurant screamed. The two waitresses came out of the kitchen but without any manager.

Two of the other bikers stood in front of Ben and three stood behind him. They seemed to be ignoring me. In the twinkling of an eye, the first two were down, thanks to more of that marvelous jujutsu. Then, one of the remaining three pulled a chain out of his large jacket pocket. He was about to hit Ben from behind.

I had to think fast, and I believe it was the first time in my life that I *did* think so fast. The guy with the chain was almost as big as Butch. I wouldn't stand a chance face to face. Ben's hasty tip rang in my head. "If your opponent is good at boxing, wrestle him." I didn't know if he was good at boxing, and I didn't wanna find out. I figured he would be good with a chain, and even though I didn't know how to wrestle either, it seemed that something closer to wrestling was in order. I dove down quickly and tackled him by his knee caps. Since he was facing Ben, I caught him off guard. Before I could catch a breath, he rolled us over and stayed on top of me. I could hear the last two goons going after Ben. I hoped he would cream them as fast as he creamed the others, and I hoped he'd still be in good enough shape to give me a hand.

The guy on top of me spit in my face. "You made a mistake, choir boy. A big mistake!"

One of my arms was pinned down more than the other. With the better arm, I reached for his chain, which had fallen next to me on the floor. The anger was swelling, and with this anger, I mustered up as much strength as I possibly could. One thing was certain: No magic charm was helping me. All my thoughts and moves were coming from me alone. At least, that's what my instincts were telling me, and Aunt Loureen said I should pay attention to instincts. In my face-off with Joe Blankenship, I'd made some clever remarks which obviously came from the ornament because I normally wasn't that amusing. But no unusual thoughts or words or ideas were coming to my mind right now. This was all done naturally. This was all just me. And it felt good. Or, at least it *would* feel good if I could get out of it alive. But I knew what I had to do. I had to get even more angry. I had to let the anger eat up the fear. Suddenly, he wasn't a biker anymore. He was every bully and every evil person I had ever known. He was that fourth-grader who massacred my face. He was Joe Blankenship hassling me after school in sixth grade. He was Doug DeWorken picking on Cliff. He was Hitler, Genghis Khan, and Saddam Hussein all rolled into one.

I forced my arm completely free and walloped him in the head with his own chain. He started punching me in the stomach, but I managed to loop the chain around his neck and catch him in a good stranglehold.

"Stop! You're choking me!"

Since his arms were now trying to pull off the chain, I broke free from under him, stood up, and pulled the remaining chain slack.

"Let me go! Let me go!"

"Are you gonna leave my friend alone? Are you?"

"Yes!"

"Are you gonna get on your bike right now and ride away?"

"All right!"

"Ease up, buddy." It was Ben. I noticed for the first time that the last two bikers were now also down with the others.

"Come on, buddy … ease up."

"I hate these kinds of people, Ben! I hate them!"

"I know. It's over now. It's over."

Cliff and Maple moved toward us.

The old man got out of his chair. "Thank you," he said. "Both of you. I'm forever in your gratitude."

"Forget it," Ben said.

Five of the bikers were getting up, moaning and limping out the door.

"Hold it," Maple shouted after them. "First you pay for the beer!"

"I never had time to drink no beer," one of them said.

Ben approached him. "What was that?"

Immediately, they pulled out their wallets and slapped bills on the counter.

"Put in a little extra for pie," Ben said.

"We didn't eat no pie!"

"I know. Put in some extra anyway."

"What for?"

"For making her list them twice when you had no intention of buying them. And for thinking that you were funny just because you were acting like a jackass. And for ruining everyone else's dinner because we had to listen to you whether we wanted to or not. And for …"

"OK, OK!"

"Hey!" one of them said. "Butch is still down!"

Sure enough, Butch was laying on the floor. I couldn't see any blood, but he was laying still just the same.

"Somebody call a doctor!" one of the customers shouted.

The younger waitress picked up a phone and dialed 911.

Maple pulled us to the side. "That was brave, boys. But you chose the wrong people to tangle with. Do yourselves a favor. Leave immediately."

"We haven't finished our dinner," Cliff said.

"Never mind the dinner! Never mind paying for the dinner. The ambulance is on its way, and the sheriff won't be far behind!"

"I need to stay," Ben said. "He may have some kind of concussion."

Maple shook her head. "There's nothing you can do. It's up to the doctors."

"I can't leave until I know he's all right."

"Sweetie, there's only one thing you need to know about Butch. He's the sheriff's son."

"The sheriff?" I said.

Cliff tugged at Ben's arm. "Let's get out of here."

"I'm willing to talk to the sheriff," Ben said. "This was self-defense. If we run, it will look like we had something to hide."

Now Maple was getting teary-eyed. "Are you listening to me? He's the sheriff's son! That means it wasn't self-defense!"

"What are you talking about?" I said. "We have a dozen witnesses!"

"You also have a sheriff who won't care. This isn't the first time Butch has been in trouble. A sheriff looks bad when he's embarrassed by his own son. So the sheriff decided a long time ago that, no matter what Butch does, it was not Butch's fault. That means it's *your* fault! Are you catching on?"

Chapter Fourteen

The Cave

"I sure appreciate you boys," Andy said. "I'm glad you were willing to pick me up and take me along like this. It gives us a chance to get to know each other better."

Sure, Andy was glad to be in the van. He was glad, and he was the only one who was glad! In a way, it was Ben's decision to bring him, but in another way, Andy kind of invited himself.

It had all happened in the restaurant parking lot. We were in a hurry to get out of there because of Maple's warning. Andy had followed us out to the van without any of us noticing, and Ben almost hit him backing out of the parking space, but he caught a glimpse of Andy through the rearview mirror just in time.

"Geez!" Ben said, jamming his foot hard on the brake. "What's the old guy doing?"

"He must have followed us out," Cliff said. "He probably wants to hang with us now, since we protected him."

"*We* did not protect him," Ben said. "Mike and I protected him."

Andy walked out from behind the van, moved to the driver's window, and made a gesture for Ben to roll it down.

"He wants to tag along," Cliff whispered to me. "Like the old saying goes, 'Once you feed a cat, you never lose it.'"

Caligula didn't speak words this time, but he looked up at Cliff from his cage as if to say "Drop dead!"

"Hey," Andy said to Ben after the window was rolled down. "You young ones are going to need a place to hide. If you want, I could take you to a little spot where they'll never find you. Not the sheriff, not the police ... nobody!"

"No, thanks," Ben said.

Cliff leaned forward. "Maybe we should listen to him. I'm already in trouble with the police back home. I don't need any more trouble."

"You don't have any more," Ben said. "Every person in the

restaurant can testify that you just sat there keeping our table warm."

Boy, Ben sure was giving him a pounding. I guess he was disappointed in Cliff. He probably figured that after all those years of protecting him, he had a right to expect more out of his friend. Instead, Cliff had let Ben down when he really needed him. But it didn't bother me. I was just thankful that for once *I* had done the right thing. Later on, I would have more time to think about it. But for now, I was hoping we could get out of here fast before the happy memory of my newfound courage was ruined.

"I'm still part of the group," Cliff said to Ben. "I could be considered an accomplice, especially since we're all riding off together."

"He's right," Andy grunted. "None of you are safe right now. Better let me hide you."

"What kind of place are we talking about?" Ben asked.

"A cave."

"Cave?" I said. "There's a cave around here?"

"There is. A big and beautiful cave. But it's not a public tourist attraction. It's out of the way, miles off the road, and the entrance is hidden, well-blended with the rest of the desert. You'll never find it by yourselves at night. It would be difficult to find in the daytime also. Better let me come along. I'll act as your guide."

Ben shook his head. "I don't know, mister. We have things to do."

"Well, you won't be doing them if you don't get out of here fast."

"Then tell us fast where the cave is," Cliff said in one of his cockier tones.

And that's how the whole deal started. Andy didn't pay much attention to Cliff, but because we were in such a hurry, Ben finally agreed to let him ride with us while we figured out what we wanted to do. After a while, Ben softened like he always did sooner or later and gave Andy permission to go ahead and lead us to this unusual hiding place. Like I keep saying, Ben was a person of high conscience, and I think he finally figured that old Andy was as interested in hiding himself as hiding us. After all, that restaurant fight had started on account of him. Not that it was his fault, but it was starting to look like we were in a town that didn't much care who was really at fault.

So anyway, now we were on the road again, and Andy hadn't stopped talking since we brought him aboard. He never seemed that outgoing in the restaurant. Maybe it was because people thought he was a weirdo and nobody ever talked to him. But he sure was talking now. He talked by rambling from one topic to the next. If the ride had been long enough, I don't think he would have missed a single subject.

"Cave formations have always fascinated me. Geology is so interesting."

For a second, Cliff looked like he was about to respond. He liked geology too, along with all science subjects. But before Cliff could open his mouth, Andy had moved on to a new topic. "Now *spelling*. That was my best skill. When I was in grade school, I won the annual spelling bee three years in a row ..."

Even Caligula finally perked up. "Great," he said under his breath. "Where on earth did you find this meatball?"

All Andy heard was a meow, and it made him notice the cat carrier for the first time. "Well, how about that! You have a cat with you. Look at the nice kitty. My oh my! He's a big one!"

Caligula just grumbled again. "What are you people running around here? A Salvation Army? Just what I need! Another cleaver along for the ride!"

"Nice kitty. Nice, pretty kitty."

Caligula finally realized that his meows were only bringing attention to himself, so he piped down, and Andy continued with his drivel.

"It's been a long time since anybody has helped me as you boys helped me in the restaurant. Yep, a long time. A very long time. A long, long time."

The only long time I could think of right now was the long time he'd been talking.

"Most folks my age have children to look after them. My kids never come to see me. Of course, there's no house for them to visit. I lost my home when I lost my job. Used to run a hardware store in town, you know ... Did great business for years until the new mall opened. I lost my business, and then the bank foreclosed on my house."

I felt sorry for the old man, but I still wished he'd quiet down for a while. He was really depressing me.

"Yup … I've become obsolete, like so many other parts of our historic little town. But I like the town. Lived here thirty years, you know. Seen plenty of changes, but town hall is still the same. We used to have town meetings every Wednesday night. Old Mayor Broomfield was around then. Hmm … Broomfield … Now *there* was a mayor! Oh, he had his vices, mind you. All men have vices. What was it Abe Lincoln once said? 'I don't trust a man who has no vices.' And I agree. I've seen lots of vices and lots of places. And not just from this little town. I traveled all over the states before I settled here. Couldn't do that now at my age, mind you, but years ago, yes indeed, I was a traveling man! You know, I remember once back in Raleigh …"

"Shut him up!" Caligula said. "Shut him up!"

Andy leaned closer to Caligula's cage. "Aw … The poor kitty is meowing. Maybe he wants a bowl of milk."

"He's fine," I said. "We just fed him."

"Oh? Then he only wants some attention, don't you, pussycat? Maybe if I took him out and pet him."

It didn't matter to me whether he pet the cat or not, but I knew Caligula would hate it. Oh well. I really couldn't think of a reason to not let him do it — at least, not a reason that would have sounded like it was making any sense. "Ah … yeah … sure … go ahead."

Andy popped the cage door open and reached his hand in. Caligula hissed and tried to bite him.

"There, there," Andy said, pulling him out and placing him on his lap. "Let's be nice. Let's not be a naughty pussycat."

"Serve it on toast, you old fossil!"

Once again, everyone else in the van heard cat sounds while I was "treated" to Caligula's irritated thoughts. By now, Caligula was pinned down on Andy's lap.

"Nice boy. Yes, he's a good boy. He's a good pussycat. I had a cat of my own once, black and white, just like you. We called him 'Sneakers.'"

Caligula's whiskers twitched. "Sneakers? Wow! How terribly

original! I never heard of a name like 'Sneakers' for a black and white cat. You should send the idea in to *Reader's Digest*."

I have to admit, sometimes I got a kick out of Caligula's snappy comebacks.

Andy continued. "Yup! Ol' Sneakers and I got along great."

"Sure! I'll bet you were the high point of his life."

Andy was on a roll, lost in thought. Now he was talking to all of us again. "And the cat wasn't my only pet. We had many animals. I grew up on a farm, you know. We had pigs, sheep, chickens …"

"He's never, EVER going to stop," Caligula said. "NEVER!!!"

"Geese, goats, horses. We had them all. Our farm produced everything: oats, barley, corn, potatoes …"

"Please make him go away," Caligula pleaded.

"Harvest time … Now that was something else …"

"This guy's as interesting as a public access channel."

Andy ended up talking all the way to the cave. His speech eventually focused on one topic, something about a special discovery that he was eager to show us. It made me wonder if this was really about a hiding place or about Andy just wanting us here for some other reason. His directions were excellent. Not once did he steer us the wrong way, and I could tell that this must be a place that he visited often. I wondered why. But I didn't worry too much about it because I knew that older people always seemed to like being around younger people and always seemed to have one thing or another to show them. They were fascinated with the most boring, ordinary stuff.

Andy was right about the cave being well-hidden. After telling Ben to veer off the freeway at a certain point, we drove for a few miles across raw desert — I mean, without a road or anything. It was nighttime, so we couldn't see much, but we could see enough to tell that the ground was flat and dull. Then, almost from out of nowhere, a cluster of small hills popped up, and Andy had Ben make a sharp curve, which brought us right to a large, open cave entrance.

"You probably don't want to drive in any farther," Andy said. "The terrain is rough, full of rocks and holes. But we're already well inside and well out of sight."

"It sure is dark in here," Cliff said to Ben. "You sure about those flashlights?"

"Of course I'm sure. They're part of the emergency kit."

"OK. I just hope your parents didn't forget to keep their emergency kit in the trunk."

"They never forget things like that," Ben said. "Besides, I checked everything before we left. The flashlights are in the kit, and they're fully charged."

"How did you guess we would need flashlights?" Cliff asked him.

"I didn't. I always check on everything before a trip."

"Great," Andy said. "You get those flashlights, and I'll take you to the back of the cave. Believe me, you're about to see something amazing."

We all got out of the van as Ben opened the trunk and handed one flashlight to Andy. He kept the other one for himself. Both lights gave a strong beam. They seemed especially bright since everything around us was so pitch black.

Ben moved his beam around to see the cave formations on the surrounding walls. "Interesting place," he said.

"Not as interesting as what I'm about to show you," Andy smiled.

"OK," Ben said. "Show us already. Lead on."

"Hey, wait!" Caligula called out from inside the van.

"Your cat wants you," Cliff said. "He's meowing his head off."

I wasn't in the mood for Caligula right now. "Just leave him. He'll be fine."

"Aw," Andy said. "The poor pussycat wants to come with us."

"He's not coming with us!" Ben snapped.

"Hey, Kid! Kid! This is important!"

If he hadn't used the word *important*, I would have just kept on moving.

"Wait up, guys," I said. "The cat sounds urgent."

"I'm not standing around listening to you and that cat," Ben grumbled. "Just catch up with us."

220

I really didn't like the idea of catching up later, but I knew how much Caligula hated talking, and for him to actually speak first, something had to be up. True, he had already talked a lot on this trip without me forcing him, but that was mostly to complain about being kidnapped, and the kidnapping put him in such a horrible mood that he continued to complain about other things, like the cell phone or like Andy. But right now, it didn't sound like a complaint. Right now, he just sounded honestly concerned. Of course, when I finished talking to him and I wanted to rejoin my friends, it would mean hiking through a spooky cave by myself. Oh well ... another chance to learn some bravery, a different kind of bravery. I asked Ben to leave me one of the two flashlights. Then I got back in the van as the others disappeared in the dark.

"All right. I'm here. What do you want?"

"I want you to let me out of here. I'd like to see this cave!"

"You?" I said. "*You* wanna see the cave?"

"Why shouldn't I?"

"You're actually interested in something?"

"Spare me all the mouth, Kid!"

"I didn't mean that as a put-down. It's just that you never seem interested in stuff."

"Oh really? You've never heard of a cat being curious before?"

"Sure I've heard of it. I know cats are supposed to get curious. But you haven't been that way since you were a kitten."

"Is that so? Well, for your information, curiosity is still a strong trait of mine, whether you observe it or not. And you're not exactly Columbus when it comes to making discoveries, are you? Now are you gonna let me out of here?"

"How do I know you won't just run off?"

"Run off to where, Columbus?"

"Stop calling me Columbus!"

"Where am I supposed to run off to? We're in the middle of the desert! You think I wanna walk back home instead of riding in the van with the rest of you? Or maybe I could hitchhike! Think, Kid. Think!

Just try it for once. It'll be a whole new experience for you."

"Why should I let you out when you're always insulting me?"

"Because it's wrong to keep me locked up, that's why!"

"Well, you stop being rude, or I'll let Andy hold you and pet you all he wants."

"Total, total idiot," he said under his breath. Then he shouted it out. "TOTAL, TOTAL IDIOT!!!!!"

"Oh yeah? You may think of me as an idiot, but I'm smart enough to know that something is up. Even if you *are* curious, you hate being around me and the others. I know you'd rather stay in the car and have some peace and quiet without listening to Andy talk about what a nice pussycat you are. I know that, all right? I just know that! Now tell me what's really going on!"

"I already told you. I want to get out of this disgusting portable prison! And who said anything about joining you and the other goobers? I can explore the cave just fine by myself."

"You're not allowed to lie, Caligula! If this has anything to do with the ornament, you have to …"

"Oh, here we go again! You're gonna quote ornament rules for the fiftieth time! I said all I needed to say about the ornament. I said it doesn't work anymore! It's finished! It's gone. And I'm finished having to talk about it! Understand? Capeesh? Comprende?"

Interesting … Not only did he speak English, he seemed to know some foreign words too. I wondered if he actually spoke those languages or if he just picked them up by overhearing some casual clichés. I almost asked him, but he probably would have told me to mind my own business, and besides, the cave conversation was more important. There was something eerie about Caligula and this cave. I needed to find out what was going on.

"You said before you only *thought* the ornament stopped working. You didn't know for sure."

"I'm almost ninety-nine percent sure! Juries have hung people with lower percentages than that!"

"Well, even if the ornament doesn't work anymore, you could still know stuff about it."

"What is there to know if it doesn't work anymore?"

"Plenty. For starters, you can tell me something about that other world, that world where the ornament comes from."

"I don't know anything about the other world except that it exists."

"Do you know anything about this cave?"

Caligula turned his head away, and I could see that I was on to something. Suddenly, all the different events of the day started to fall in place.

"That's it," I said. "Isn't it? You know something about the cave, don't you? I mean, Andy is already known all over town as a man who talks about another world, and this same Andy brought us to the cave, and this same Andy knows about something mysterious in the cave."

"Don't start acting like a detective. The part doesn't suit you ... unless the part is Inspector Clouseau."

"Caligula, I've had enough of this! Quit stalling and tell me what you know about the cave!"

"All right! Fine! You wanna know about the cave? It's dangerous! We shouldn't have come here! It's just one more stop on the road of serious blunders that you three stooges keep bumping into!"

"Dangerous in what way? Does it lead to the other world?"

"How should I know? It's just dangerous, that's all."

"You and Aunt Loureen drive me crazy, you know that? All I get from you are feelings or impressions. Just once, can't you give an actual detail? Do you have to feel everything? Don't you ever actually *know* anything?"

"I know you're a pathetic fool. No guesses or impressions there. Just facts!"

"OK, Caligula, if the cave is dangerous, then you'd be better off locked safely inside the car. Why would you want to explore it?"

"Oh, for crying out loud! I don't know *why* the cave is dangerous. It just is! But something is going to happen, and when it does, I'd prefer to be out and about and free to run if I have to. Now what's so hard about that to understand?"

"Well, we should leave then."

"You think? Yeah, we should leave all right. We should leave fast! If you're smart, you'll go fetch your two friends, Moe and Curly, and tell them it was a mistake to come here. Only why not arrange to accidentally leave Rip Van Winkle behind?"

"Why didn't you warn us before we got here?"

"I didn't sense anything until after we arrived. That's why."

"Well, why didn't you speak up as soon as you *did* sense it instead of giving me some dopey story about being curious?"

"You wanna argue with me, or you wanna get out of here? Just get them now! Move!"

"All right!" I started to leave.

"Wait! Let me out first."

"What for? All I'm gonna do is get them and come right back to the car."

"In the unlikely, unprecedented event that you might actually mess things up and fail to accomplish what you set out to do, I want to be free and mobile, as I just said. NOW LET ME OUT OF HERE!"

He was an impossible cat to argue with, and he was wearing me out. Besides, I believed him when he said he wouldn't run off. He kind of made sense when he reminded me that riding with the rest of us was his only way back home.

"All right," I said, flipping the cage open and letting him out of the van. "Now come with me."

Caligula ignored me and started cleaning himself.

"If you're not gonna stay in the car, you might as well come along in case any of this is related to the ornament."

"Buzz off!"

"Come with me, or I'm putting you right back in the cage!"

"Why would I come with you? What possible reason would I have for doing such a stupid thing? I just told you how dangerous the cave is. Do you know what the word *danger* means?"

"You're already in the cave. It could be just as dangerous staying here."

"I don't think so. Somehow I get the feeling that avoiding danger means avoiding you. Someday your name will be in the dictionary as the definition of danger."

"Now hold on ... You made all that fuss about getting out of your cage just to sit next to the van by yourself?"

Caligula rolled his eyes. "I'll explain it to you one more time. Just one more time ... As long as I'm not locked inside ... as long as I can move around if something menacing suddenly comes my way, I'll be fine."

"Caligula, I'm not gonna debate you! You come with me or I put you back in the car! That's your choice!"

"Kid, you know what I like about you?"

"What?"

"I'll let you know if I ever think of anything."

We finally got going. Caligula kept up with me, sulking the entire way. The flashlight Ben gave me was pretty good, so it wasn't too hard to see the cave around us. The strange formations looked kind of weird, almost like huge icicles dripping down from above. I thought it might be cool to come back and see this cave sometime in the daylight. Then I remembered there wouldn't really be any more light in the daytime anyway since caves were always dark.

"I want you to answer my question now, Caligula. Why didn't you warn us to leave right away?"

"What good would it have done? You always ignore my warnings, and your pumpkin head friends are having trouble believing I can talk anyway. Since nobody was gonna pay attention, I figured I'd spare us another of those long, delightful conversations."

"Well, we ended up having a long conversation anyway."

"Only because you have a big mouth which quickly sucks the energy out of your BB-size brain."

I decided it was pointless to complain about his insults. So I ignored the comment and continued with my questions. "Your feelings and intuitions are on account of my ornament wish. That means the stuff you know or feel has to do with the ornament. So this cave must

225

have something to do with the ornament. Right?"

"Wow, Kid. You're amazing."

"Go ahead and be sarcastic. I don't care. If the cave is connected to the ornament, then the cave must lead to where the ornament comes from … the other world … right?"

"Maybe. Or maybe the cave is the result of some other wish made with the ornament years ago from some other stupid kid."

"Never mind."

***

At first it seemed like the cave went on forever, but when I looked at my watch, I realized that we had only been walking for about ten minutes. Finally, off in the distance, I could hear their voices. Ben and Cliff seemed to be arguing with Andy about something. I could hear Andy saying things like "I know what I'm talking about, boys. I'm not one to make up tall tales."

Then Ben said something back to him. I couldn't make out his words, but he was definitely arguing with the old guy. I started walking faster, shining my beam until their three figures came into my sight. They were at the end of the cave, standing in front of a stone wall where the path came to a dead stop.

"Glad I caught up with you guys," I said. "I think we need to split. This place is dangerous."

Cliff frowned. "Who says so?"

"Caligula."

Andy looked puzzled. "Caligula? Who's that?"

"His cat," Ben said with the same kind of irritated voice he always had when my cat was the subject of conversation.

"You talk to your cat?"

"I don't have time to explain right now, Andy. I know it sounds crazy."

"There, there …You'll never catch *me* calling another man crazy. Who knows what crazy is anyway? Everyone in town calls *me* crazy. But I'm not crazy. I know what I've seen, and I know what I've experienced, and so must you, young fellow. Never doubt yourself. Never doubt for a moment."

Just what we needed. Andy was starting in on another monologue.

"So you call the cat 'Caligula'! Interesting name. I used to study the Roman Caesars in high school, but I dare say, he doesn't look quite like a *Caligula*. *Antoninus Pious*. Now *there's* an emperor's name. Perfect title for a cat."

At the first brief pause, I jumped in. "Andy, I'm sorry to cut you off, but it's important. We need to get out of here."

"And go where?" Cliff said. "We'll get in trouble if we leave the cave."

"Maybe. But there could be even more trouble if we stay."

It was clear that Cliff was not about to leave this new hiding place. "Mike, is it possible the cat just doesn't like it here, that he made up a story to trick us into leaving?"

"No, that's not it. He says the place is dangerous for all of us. And I think we should listen to him. Besides, Aunt Loureen didn't send us here to hide. She sent us here to rescue DeWorken."

"I think that mission is off for now," Cliff said. "At least until things die down."

Andy wasn't listening to either one of us. Instead, he had reached down to scratch Caligula under the chin. "Come here, pussycat. Come to Uncle Andy." Andy picked him up and cradled him like a baby. "Nice pussycat. Yes, he loves his Uncle Andy. Doesn't he? So, you talk, eh? Well, let me hear you. Say something for Uncle Andy."

Instead, Caligula scratched "Uncle Andy" in the eye. Andy was so startled he dropped him, and the cat instantly ran out of sight.

"You OK?" I said to Andy.

"Oh sure. A little cat scratch isn't going to hurt anyone. Believe me, life has dealt worse blows than that."

"You might have to stop picking him up," I said. "He really hates that sort of thing."

"Aw, nonsense. I never met a cat yet who didn't love his Uncle Andy."

Andy asked Ben if he could borrow his flashlight, and he aimed it at the back cave wall. "Here, kitty! Here, kitty, kitty, kitty …"

"Hey!" Cliff exclaimed. "Where did he go?"

"Uh oh," Andy answered. "I hope he didn't go too far."

"Too far?" Cliff said with concern. "If you mean what I think you mean …"

I didn't like the sound of this. Suddenly I had a creepy feeling in the pit of my stomach.

"What are you talking about, Cliff?"

I couldn't tell if Cliff had heard me or not. He quickly grabbed the flashlight out of Andy's hand. "Here, let me try."

"Cliff," I said again. "What's going on?"

Cliff kept combing back and forth with the flashlight. "Well, Mike, before you got here, Andy was telling us about the cave wall. He said it leads to an alternative dimension of some sort."

I felt another one of those adrenaline rushes. It came on me instantly like some kind of fountain bursting from the inside. So … I was finally here. We had finally arrived. Without even hearing the details, I knew. Without even asking for an explanation, I knew. Despite all I had done to avoid it, the same destiny that forced me to fight in the diner was now gonna force all of us into the other world. From the moment the ornament came back into our lives, we had been on a road without any turns.

But I still went through the motions of denial. "How can a stone cave wall lead to another world?"

I knew it was a stupid question. We were dealing with the supernatural. Magic was magic. Nobody could explain it, and nobody could stop it, not even Caligula. Caligula had tried even harder than me to avoid all this. Oh sure, he was a *mean* cat, but he was also a *smart* cat. What's more, the ornament had given him knowledge about the ornament and feelings about the ornament. And that obviously included feelings about the ornament's magical world. From the moment we got here, Caligula felt something strange, and he knew there was something spooky about the cave. Still, none of that caution was able to save him. All it did was backfire. The whole reason he asked to be let out of the van was to avoid danger, but he never knew what the danger actually was. He didn't understand the details. And it seemed now that he'd have been better off to just stay in the van after all.

"Here," Andy said. "I'll prove it to you. Here, Cliff, shine your flashlight against the cave wall."

The wall was lit well now. It looked ordinary to me, jagged rock with green moss. I saw no signs of any magic.

"Now, boys ... watch carefully ... Watch my hand."

At first it looked like a magician's trick. Andy was actually sliding his hand in and out of the wall as if the wall were nothing but thin air, as if it only appeared to be solid but was really some kind of projected image.

"Now do you see? Do you see where the cat went? He ran this direction quickly, out of instinct. It was dark and he didn't watch where he was going."

"But cats can see in the dark," I said.

"Well, he didn't see this. Maybe his eyesight is so fine-tuned that it bypassed the shadowy image of a solid wall since, at that moment, the wall was not really solid. Maybe he kept running because he saw the passage continuing. And the passage *does* continue. In any event, now he's on the other side of the wall, and on the other side of the wall is another world, another whole world!"

Chapter Fifteen

The Adjusted Plan

"Incredible," Cliff said. "If I didn't see it with my own eyes, I never would have believed it."

Andy was smiling like a man who had just won a sporting event. "How about you, Ben? You seemed to be doubting my story. You believe your own eyes, don't you?"

Ben didn't say anything, but he slowly moved toward the wall and put his own hand through. Finally, he spoke. "That's so weird."

"Now you see for yourself, young man. Now you see why my story confounded the whole town. This is the place, a gateway into another land."

"I don't know about another land," Ben said. "I know something mysterious is going on, and I know the cat is missing, but another land?"

"You can find out for yourself," Andy said. "The rest of your body can go through as easily as the hand."

"No, thanks. Who knows what this thing might do?" And with that, Ben quickly pulled his hand out of the wall. Then Cliff started sticking his own hand in and out of the phantom-like stone.

I was still in shock, even though I should have expected all this. But shock or no shock, I was finally ready to ask a few questions. "You've been on the other side, Andy?"

"Several times, young fellow, and long ago. But like a fool, I told people about it. I should have known better. I should have known they would think I was nuts."

"Well, sure," I said. "Anyone would doubt you at first. But all you had to do was bring them in here, and they could see for themselves."

"I *did* bring people to the cave … a lot of people."

"Yeah? So what happened?"

"Nothing happened. The wall was solid again, and it looked as though I had either made up the whole incident or lost my mind.

Word got around fast, and before long, I was known as the town character. Anybody got a watch?"

"I do," Cliff said.

"Tell us the time, Cliff."

Cliff glanced at the fluorescent watch on his left hand. His right hand was still inside the wall. "About ten after nine."

"Take your hand out of the wall, Cliff."

"What for?"

"No time to discuss it! The wall is about to change again! If you don't remove your hand, it will be caught inside solid rock!"

Cliff instantly pulled his hand out of the wall and backed up a few spaces. Ben looked at Andy suspiciously. "Maybe you should explain to us what's going on."

"Explain? There's nothing to explain. I don't even think a scientist could explain. What I can do instead is share an observation. Every hour on the hour, this wall changes into some kind of incorporeal state and opens up a pathway into another world. The portal stays open for exactly ten minutes, no more, no less. Then it closes again until another hour passes, or another fifty minutes, to be perfectly exact."

Ben was shaking his head in disbelief, but Cliff looked excited in a happy way. "We'll find out for sure," he said, staring at the second hand on his watch. "Fifty-eight, fifty-nine ... and now!" Cliff rushed to the wall and placed his hand back on the surface. "It's solid," he said with amazement. "Just as Andy said it would be."

Ben followed him over and touched the rocky surface with his own hand. "Hold on," he said. "Are you actually telling us that this wall disappears at exactly the same time every single hour of the day?"

"Indeed it does, young fellow."

"And yet, you can't explain it."

"Not everything in life can be explained," Andy said.

"Most things can."

"I believe you're mistaken, young man. Nature itself is a mystery."

But Ben wasn't buying it. "Come on, mister ... This isn't nature. There's nothing in nature that makes stone disappear and reappear."

"Of course there is," Andy laughed. "You just witnessed it."

"Yeah," Ben said. "I witnessed it. But how can you call something like this 'nature'?"

"The same way we label other fascinating things," Andy said. "Who can explain how a bear knows when it is time to hibernate or how a swallow navigates as it flies south for the winter? Who can explain a salmon swimming upstream to find the exact place it was born before laying eggs? It's all part of nature, and it's all unexplained."

"But it *is* explained," Ben insisted. "Those things all happen by instinct."

"Yes, instinct, but can anyone explain where the instinct comes from or exactly what makes it work?"

"Scientists can."

"Not really," Cliff interjected. "Scientists or zoologists study animal behavior and catalogue their behavior. They may also talk about certain traits emanating from a species' DNA, but that is not the same as *explaining* the behavior."

"Maybe not," Ben grumbled. "But we aren't talking about animals anyway."

"No, we aren't," Cliff continued like a professor anxious to bore his class with a lecture. "We're talking about geology and physics."

Ben sighed, realizing that he had accidentally given Cliff an opening to show off some of his science knowledge. "Cliff, even you can't explain this one."

"Not at the moment, but what Andy said makes sense. And there *are* geothermal precedents in nature."

"Oh yeah?" Ben challenged. "Name one."

"Old Faithful."

"What?"

"Old Faithful. You know, Ben. Old Faithful at Yellowstone. Yellowstone National Park."

"A geyser? You're comparing this to a geyser?"

"Old Faithful erupts on a regular basis."

"It's not the same thing. And it doesn't happen at exact intervals."

"It comes considerably close, Ben. The intervals are predictable, ranging from 35 to 120 minutes. And 90 percent of the time, the next eruption can be forecasted somewhat meticulously, with a plus or minus factor of merely 10 minutes."

"All right, spare us the encyclopedia. None of that matters because people can still explain Old Faithful. They can explain the heat changes and the formation of the springs. They can tell you exactly why it happens."

"They can *now*," Cliff said. "But history tells us that when Old Faithful was first discovered, it looked as fantastic to them as this does to us."

Andy was smiling and nodding. "Interesting observation, young man."

"That isn't much of a parallel," Ben said. "Old Faithful doesn't disappear and re-appear. And it isn't connected to another world."

But Cliff seemed to be enjoying this new twist of adventure, and nothing Ben said was gonna change his mood. Cliff turned to Andy again. "So the reason nobody believed you was because you didn't know about the wall transposing only once every hour?"

"Exactly. I just stood there in front of the small crowd who had followed me into the cave to humor me or make sport of me. And when all I was able to show them was an ordinary cave wall, I went silent, shrugging my shoulders and wondering if the Almighty was playing some sort of practical joke on ol' Andy."

Not only was Cliff taking in every word, but he seemed one step ahead of the story. "And before you brought them to the cave, before you even told anyone about it, you had already journeyed to the other side? The other world?"

"Yes, I did go exploring. But the first trip was brief. I didn't stay for a very long time."

"What's it like over there?" Cliff asked. "If we waited for an hour and then walked through the portal, what would we find?"

"You're not really thinking of going inside," Ben said.

"I don't know. It might actually be fun."

"Fun? Where do you think we are, Cliff? At Disneyland?"

It was interesting to see Cliff a little more carefree. Usually he was the scared one of the group. But I'm not saying Ben was scared. Ben got cautious a lot. Yeah … he was real cautious about stuff, but that's because he always thought ahead of time before he made decisions. He wasn't impulsive. Still, a conversation where Cliff seemed less worried than Ben was kind of unusual.

"I don't know *where* we are," Cliff continued. "But Andy does."

"I don't know much more than you," Andy said. "When you step into the wall, the first thing you see is a cave just like this one. You look behind you and there's another cave wall, the wall you stepped out of. And you come back the way you came in."

"Through the wall again?"

"That's right, Cliff."

"But how did you get back?" I asked. "If the portal closes after ten minutes and the wall hardens, how did you get back through?"

"He probably stayed less than ten minutes," Cliff said. "So the passage was still open."

"It *was* a brief visit the first time. I was too scared to stay for an extended period. But I didn't time myself either, so I'm not sure how long I was on the other side, and remember, I didn't know yet about any ten-minute rule."

"How could you have gotten back then?" I asked. "You would have had to stay less than ten minutes or more than an hour."

"Actually, it was neither. As I said, I wasn't paying attention to my watch. That is, I wasn't paying attention until I returned. But I know it was less than an hour and more than ten minutes. Nevertheless, when I was ready to come back, I could."

"How? The wall should have been solid by then."

"Well, Mike, it doesn't work quite the same way on the other side. On the other side, you can step back in at any time. When I returned and saw a discrepancy between my car clock and my watch, I estimated the amount of minutes it had taken to leave my car in the front part of the cave and hike to the back. After that, I figured the time it took to walk back to my car after returning from the other land, and I realized that I must have stepped back into this world at the exact same moment I had left."

"Huh?"

Cliff answered me before Andy even had a chance. "He means this portal not only travels through space but travels through time as well."

"That's right," Andy said, looking amazed. "But I'm surprised to see you accept the explanation so quickly, Cliff. Doesn't time travel sound rather far-fetched to you? It does to most people."

"Well, time travel is a legitimate theory today in the field of quantum physics. And there *is* a definite relationship between space and time. Of course, it would involve traveling faster than the speed of light, but for all we know, that happened somehow when you stepped into this other dimension."

"You're a bright young man. I don't know as much as you do about physics. I did take physics in school. I had a teacher named Mr. Laredo who ..."

"Let's get back to the portal," I said, trying to prevent another series of Andy's "good ol' stories."

"Yes, of course. Well, when I returned to *our* world, to *this* cave, no time had passed. I decided to go into town and tell as many people as I possibly could. It was all too fantastic to keep to myself, and I was a little too frightened to venture farther than the connecting cave and explore another whole world without a companion or two. This cave is so well-hidden that very few people have ever seen it over the years, and that's probably why no one had ever documented the shifting wall."

"You discovered this cave yourself?" Ben asked.

"Well, yes, I did discover it myself, but I'm not the first. Afterwards, I looked in the county records and saw that the cave was mapped and documented. But evidently, I am one of the few who have been here in a long time. Surprising, since I would think that such a beautiful cave would have been turned into a national monument long ago. It may be that a good number of the previous explorers got lost in the other world and never returned to tell the story. Or it may be that it's just too out of the way, and previous settlers didn't care to cultivate the desert around it. Funny place, the desert. It's barren–looking, and yet ..."

"So, you brought them to the cave," I said quickly to get him back on track. "And when you did, the wall was solid?"

"Yes. I couldn't explain why. Needless to say, a man doesn't forget about a phenomenon like this. At the first opportunity, I returned again and studied the wall long enough to observe its routine procedure. I timed it again and again. Without fail, the change comes every hour on the hour and lasts exactly ten minutes. But this newfound explanation did nothing to rehabilitate me in the eyes of the villagers. To them, it sounded like a lot of prime poppycock. Only one man was curious enough to come back with me for a second look, and he doesn't even live in town."

"Doesn't live in town?" Cliff said suspiciously. "Where does he live then?"

"Well, I suppose you *could* say he lives in this town, but only once a year. Actually the man has no regular home at all. He travels constantly, year-round, I believe. He's the owner of some freak attractions, and he exhibits them with that carnival which comes through annually."

"Oh, brother," Cliff said. "I'll bet I know who he is: a certain Mr. Blake."

Andy was so taken aback by Cliff's words he almost fell over. "Yes … Why yes … That's exactly who he was. Young man, you keep guessing the rest of my story. Are you clairvoyant by any chance?"

"No, sir. It's just that Mr. Blake and I have met before."

Andy nodded his head. "Well, then you know firsthand what a cold-blooded customer he is. Just my misfortune, that of all the people around, he alone would give me a second chance. As a carnival man, he was always looking for unusual things. And it worked. This time, the portal opened up right on schedule because, this time, I knew the schedule and I timed it all perfectly. Mr. Blake was plenty amazed. The supernatural cave wall went beyond his wildest dreams."

"Did the two of you venture into the other world?" Cliff asked.

"Oh yes, into the second cave and out beyond the cave. A beautiful world with the most unusually shaped trees and hills you've ever seen. But dangerous over there. Very dangerous. You mentioned Disneyland. It's not Disneyland."

Ben looked concerned again. "If it's so dangerous, then why did you bring us here?"

"I brought you here so that you could hide in the cave. That decision had nothing to do with the time portal. It was years ago when I brought some of the villagers here. Most of them don't live in the area anymore. As for the other few, they barely remember where it is and never even think about it. Oh sure, rumors continued to get passed around about me being psycho and talking about another world, but nobody is around anymore who actually remembers the cave itself."

"Except for Mr. Blake."

Andy sighed. "That's right, Cliff. But it's the law you're running from, not Mr. Blake."

Soon we'll be running from the law and Mr. Blake, I said to myself, but I didn't say it out loud because we hadn't yet figured out what to do with Andy when it was time to finally try the rescue, and I didn't wanna bring it up without checking with the others. Of course, Cliff was kind of bringing it up anyway by talking about Mr. Blake, but I still wanted to huddle a little before letting Andy know any more.

"It was never my intention to take you into the other world," Andy continued.

"Oh really," Ben challenged. "Then why did you bring us straight to this back wall? Why did we come here immediately?"

"Because I know Maple the waitress said something to you about me. I overheard her. Couldn't make all if it out, but it sounded like she was talking about the 'crazy old man and his tall tales.'"

"You just didn't want us to think you were some kind of mental case," I said.

Andy nodded. I started feeling sorry for him again. "I understand. I guess I can't blame you for wanting us to think the best of you."

Cliff didn't seem to care one way or the other about Andy's motives. He just wanted to get back to the explanation, back to Basic Time Portal Theory 105. "Aside from the hills and trees, what else did you and Mr. Blake discover?"

"Well, it's a backward world, centuries behind ours. In many ways, it reminded me of the way Europe would have been in, say, medieval times. We saw riders with swords. We saw small castles with towers, and every place we ventured to, the people seemed unfriendly. Of course that may have been because of the unusual way we were dressed — unusual to them, I mean. But whatever the reason, we didn't have much of a chance to find out because we couldn't understand anyone's language. Mr. Blake seemed intrigued, and he acted like he loved every minute of it."

Andy and Cliff kept talking while Ben and I mostly sat and listened. Cliff finally told Andy all about DeWorken and Tinker Bell and even the ornament. I was ticked that he blurted it all out without checking with Ben and me first. But it probably had to come out sooner or later anyway, and Andy didn't seem to have much trouble believing it. I guess anyone who travels through time by walking inside a wall will believe anything else he hears. But Andy didn't know anything about the tiny people, even though we had all figured out by now that Blake must have stolen Tinker Bell from the other world. According to Andy, the other world scared him too much, so he had stopped taking journeys. As for Blake, well, Andy knew nothing about what *he* did in the other world, only that he *did* go there a lot, as often as possible, whenever the carnival was in town. Andy didn't trust Blake and didn't wanna associate with him. That's why he stayed away from the carnival and didn't even know about the Tinker Bell show.

Anyway, once we learned from Andy everything he knew about the other world (which really wasn't much) I finally reminded everyone that Caligula was over there right now.

My reminder seemed to sadden Andy. "I'm afraid something may have happened to your poor kitty."

"What makes you say that?"

"Because he hasn't returned."

"So? He's probably just confused right now."

"That's not what Andy means," Cliff said to me. "Since Caligula traveled through time, he can stay in the other world as long has he wants ... a day ... a week or a year. But however long it is, once he figures out how to return, he should return at the exact moment he left, which means he'd be back by now, which means from our point of view, it would look like he had never left at all."

"Well, maybe he's trapped somewhere," I said. "And we're meant to bring him back."

"Interesting hypothesis," Cliff said. "And an interesting paradox. If he can't get back without us, and if we *are* successful in rescuing him, then would he return at the same moment we step through or the same moment *he* stepped through?"

I hated all this time travel talk. Aunt Loureen had tried to explain time travel to me back in the sixth grade. The more she explained, the more confused I got.

"Look," I said. "All I know is that if he's in trouble, we should help him."

Ben hadn't taken much interest in our discussion till now. Finally, he spoke. "Let's be clear about something. I'm not going into some bizarre dimension I know nothing about. I wouldn't do that for anybody or anything. And I especially wouldn't do it for a cat."

"You tried to help Caligula before," I said. "We all did, that time he went to the pound."

"We were younger then. Younger and stupider. It's just a cat, Mike."

"I know. But I kinda feel responsible for him. It's kinda my own fault that he's over there. Besides, I have a feeling I'm meant to go into that other world anyway."

"I wouldn't advise it. It's up to you, but you need to understand, buddy, I've gone about as far as I can with all this. If you go into this other world, you go without me."

The thought of going without Ben was not a pleasant one. "What if we were *all* meant to go? What if it's our destiny?"

"I decide my own destiny. Besides, all this destiny talk keeps changing."

I found his words curious. "What do you mean, Ben?"

"I mean the only reason we took this trip in the first place was because of your so-called destiny, because your aunt said it was important to rescue DeWorken, and, well ... OK ... I agreed to help. So the *rescue* was the destiny, not traipsing around some new world to chase down a stray cat."

I nodded my head and sat down. "You're right, Ben. You're right. Aunt Loureen never knew for sure if I was meant to go into the other world. All she knew was that we needed to keep *DeWorken* from going into the other world."

"Well, there you have it. So let's get back to the original plan."

"OK ... sure ... that makes sense ... I guess ... It's just ... all this stuff with DeWorken had something to do with the safety of the other world ... the safety of both worlds actually. So it doesn't seem like a coincidence that we stumbled into meeting Andy and he brought us here."

Andy was watching us with obvious interest. It seemed odd that he wasn't jumping in to join the conversation, but I think the reason he stayed quiet was because he was thinking hard about what we were saying. I kinda got the feeling he enjoyed being described as part of our destiny. It probably made him feel important. I had heard once that old people usually don't feel important anymore, and even if I hadn't heard that, Andy sure acted like somebody who wanted to feel important.

Anyway, even though Andy didn't interrupt us, Cliff did. "Quite true. None of this seems like a coincidence at all. Frankly, when you think about it, this other world may not be so bad. In fact, I'll go you one better. It may be a superior world, a preferable world."

"Excuse me?" Ben said.

"I don't really care much for our own world," Cliff continued. "What has it ever done for me? A new world might also mean a new start."

Ben moved closer to Cliff, looking him in the eye. "Do you know what you're saying?"

"I know all too well. Look at the opportunity we have here. Just think about it for a minute! When the next hour is up, the portal will open again. We have a chance to travel as far as far can be. And yet, by some fantastic miracle, this far-off place is only inches away!"

Ben walked over to the wall and put his hand over it again. "The new world could be worse. And if it's like Andy said, all medieval, how would you ever survive, Cliff? You can't even take care of yourself in your own time. So what do you think you're gonna do? You think you're gonna go back in the past and joust some knights?"

"Just because it's backward technologically, that doesn't mean we have to joust knights or joust anybody. And thanks for having so much faith in me."

"Look, Cliff," Ben continued. "When it comes to science, you're brilliant. But this looks like a world that doesn't yet have much of a place for scientists."

"I couldn't disagree more," Cliff countered. "What *is* magic anyway? Is it something unscientific, or is it actually a science itself, a science we don't yet understand?"

"Well, *you* don't understand it," Ben said. "Your clumsiness with the ornament created the whole mess we're in."

"I wasn't trying to be clumsy! I was trying to defend myself!"

"All right. Calm down."

"There isn't much lately to calm down about, Ben. I have two police detectives who suspect me of a crime, and you have a sheriff after you for beating up his son. In light of all that, give me one reason why we wouldn't be better off in the other world."

"Because we came here to rescue DeWorken," I said. "Ben's right. We need to stop all this talk about the other world and get back to our mission."

"Maybe I'm not interested in the mission anymore. Maybe I'm more interested in survival."

"That's the cowardly way out, Cliff."

"Oh sure, Mike. You have plenty of room to talk. Plenty of room! How do you like this guy? He gets into one fight, and suddenly he thinks he's a mercenary."

"I didn't say that."

"Good! Because if Ben hadn't been with you, it would have been a different event. So don't kid yourself!"

"At least he stood with me," Ben said. "He fought the best he knew how, and he actually helped me big time! What did *you* do, Cliff?"

"All right, I'm a coward! Is that what you want to hear me say? Fine, you're both a couple of heroes, and I'm just a gutless wonder!"

Andy placed his hand on Cliff's shoulder. "Easy, young fellow."

"Leave me alone! All of you! Just leave me alone! OK, Ben. You're in charge of your own destiny? Fine! Well, I'm in charge of mine! When the clock turns to the ten-minute interval, I'm going through the portal."

Cliff headed for the stone wall, and Ben intercepted him. "You're not doing anything of the sort!"

"Who says so?"

"I do! We came here to rescue DeWorken."

"So who's stopping you? I'm the cowardly one, remember? Apparently you'll get him a lot easier without me."

"No, I won't. We came up with a plan, and the plan involves you."

"Then come up with another one that doesn't involve me."

"You're going with us, Cliff. After we fetch DeWorken, you can do whatever you want. You wanna go sightseeing for castles in some backward land? Be my guest. *But first we rescue DeWorken.* Understand?"

"No, I don't understand. Supposing I could think up a second plan, one that didn't require my presence? In such a case, why should I have to go along?"

"BECAUSE YOU SOLD HIM INTO SLAVERY!!!" It looked like Ben was gonna yell some more, but instead, he panted a little and lowered his voice. "That's why ... Now you're going with us if I have to pick you up and carry you."

Ben seemed unhappy with himself for having shouted so loud. But I think it made an impression on Cliff, and it was definitely something he needed to hear.

***

We ended up spending the night in the van because when we had finally finished talking and arguing about the mission and the time portal and Caligula and everything else, it ended up being too late to hit the carnival. We would have gotten there after closing time.

I didn't sleep very well. The backseat did fold out, but there were too many of us to lay down comfortably, so I volunteered to just sleep in the front seat. Even though I would have to sleep propped up instead of laying down, I figured it would be better than being kicked all night by one of the others.

Andy was the first one to nod off, and he snored louder than an ocean at high tide. I kept waking up throughout the night, and I also dreamed a lot. When I woke up for good in the morning, I couldn't remember any of the dreams except one: I was back in the diner fighting that biker dude, only this time I wasn't doing so well, and then I was suddenly in another place. You know how dreams can be. They keep changing, and it never seems weird at the time, only later on after you wake up and try to make sense of it all. Anyway, the other place was with Marla. We were in our favorite park, and she was trying to tell me something, but I never heard what it was.

We were all hungry for breakfast but of course there was no way we were gonna hit another restaurant. We didn't wanna be seen right now, and also, we didn't have very fond memories of restaurants at the moment.

Ben pulled some granola bars out of his emergency kit and passed them out while I tried to call Aunt Loureen from Ben's cell phone. I wanted to tell her about the time portal and about how Caligula had gone to the other side. Aunt Loureen had been very concerned about this other world, and maybe she would tell us what to do next if I got a hold of her, but I never did get a hold of her on account of the signal being too weak from inside the cave.

Anyway, now it was time to get on with the plan. We'd worked the plan out before even leaving for the trip. But for all the different ideas and all the debating and all the changes and all the new adjustments, it was really a pretty simple plan we had ended up with: Cliff would take us to the carnival and arrange another appointment with Mr. Blake. He would then offer to sell him some more miniature people. It would be a lie, but since Blake had no idea where DeWorken truly came from, Cliff might be able to convince him that he'd gone into the other world to steal him and that now he had stolen a few others. Cliff had deduced that this race of small people was hard to find, and that even when Blake went into the other world, he really wasn't sure where to search. The way Cliff phrased it, "that handicap might sweeten our offer." But the condition for selling more miniatures would be to first check on DeWorken's health and well-being. Cliff would insist that he see DeWorken first. Then, with DeWorken in our grasp, Cliff would say that he had a change of heart and give Blake his money back and demand that DeWorken be set free to return home with us. Blake would refuse, of course, but since Ben would be with us, maybe we could get away with it. A lot of the plan hinged on Ben, maybe too much, but anyway, that was the plan.

Cliff suggested that we wait until evening again. "The van won't be as noticeable at night, plus it delays things by a whole day, and by that time, the sheriff will probably assume we left town. He certainly won't be expecting us to hang around for a carnival."

"No, he won't" Ben said. "Which means he especially won't expect us to be at the carnival in broad daylight. We've had enough delays. Let's just get this over with once and for all. We can't keep postponing the inevitable."

"Wait a minute," Cliff said. "If Blake knows where this cave is and comes here often to go searching in the other world for new tiny people, then we don't even need to go to the carnival. Sooner or later, Mr. Blake will come to us."

"Probably," I said. "But DeWorken won't be with him. I mean, why would he bring DeWorken along?"

"You may be right," Cliff said. "On the other hand, if he comes here once a year to look for more miniatures, it makes sense that he might bring along the ones he already has — you know, to act as a kind of guide."

I laughed slightly. "Once DeWorken says two or three words, Blake will know that he's from our world, not Tinker Bell's world."

"True enough, assuming DeWorken has been talking to him. But consider this: Your Aunt was concerned about DeWorken going into the other world, so Blake bringing him along is certainly a possibility."

"Her concern wasn't so specific."

"That's what you said before."

"I know. I did say that. But since then, I've been going over Aunt Loureen's conversation in my mind. It wasn't necessarily about DeWorken traveling into the other world. I mean, sure, I guess that could happen. But it was mostly about him being connected or being a *conduit*. That was the word she used ... And he's already connected by being with Tinker Bell. And Blake is connected. I guess they're all connected."

But Cliff never gave up easily. "OK, let's say Blake comes alone. Even so, maybe Ben could hassle him a little and scare him into just fetching DeWorken for us."

Ben shook his head. "I didn't come along to beat people up. We're in enough trouble already."

"And I'm trying to spare us from even more trouble," Cliff said. "That sheriff could have your license plate number."

"I doubt it. We left in a hurry."

But Cliff showed no sign of giving up on this debate. "Well, he has your description, at least."

"Maybe not. That waitress, Maple, seemed interested in helping us."

"She also seemed scared of the sheriff. And she wasn't the only witness. Anybody in the restaurant could describe us, especially the bikers who hate us now. At the very least, they'll remember we were in a van."

"There's lots of vans on the road," Ben said. "Besides, I have an idea. We can minimize the risk by splitting up a little. If you don't mind, Andy, we're gonna leave you here for a while so that you can stay out of sight and stay hidden." Andy looked disappointed. "It's nothing personal," Ben said. "But everyone in town knows what you look like, and probably someone saw you go off with us in the van."

"That's true," Andy said. "I stick out like a sore thumb. I'm being a burden to all of you. So sorry."

"Don't worry about it," Ben said gently. "It's cool." Then he turned to me. "And maybe you should also stay, buddy."

"Huh? Me? What for?"

"Because we can't all go. If that sheriff *is* looking for us, he's looking for three kids, not two. I'm trying to imagine ways to blend in with the crowd better."

"Now just a minute, Ben. I was meant to be a part of this plan."

"I know, buddy. But a lot of new wrinkles have developed."

"Yeah ... they have. But maybe I should still come along, and we can just leave Andy for now. That way we continue with the original scheme, all three of us going after DeWorken."

Ben shook his head. "Not good enough. Like I said, even without Andy, that sheriff will be looking for three teenagers, not two."

"But you're the one who was most noticeable," I said, "since you did most of the fighting and you're the one who hurt the sheriff's son, so if anyone should stay hidden, it should be you."

"That is not an option," Cliff said. "I'm not interested in this plan at all anymore, but if I *am* going, I am going with Ben. Mr. Blake is one scary guy."

"That he is," Andy agreed.

"But if Ben ..."

"Mike, you're talking foolishly! Ben can handle Blake! You can't! That's all there is to it! You got lucky in the diner. That doesn't mean you can ..."

"Give it a rest, Cliff! You keep acting like I've got a new swelled head over that fight! Well, I don't! I never claimed to be able to take on Blake or anyone else! I'm just offering to go. That's all. I'm just trying to do the right thing. OK?"

"The discussion is pointless," Ben said. "Since I'm the only one here with a driver's license, I am going one way or the other."

"I had a license," Andy said. "But I haven't renewed it because it's been years since I've had a car."

"That's fine, Andy. Now I think everything is settled. Cliff and I will head for the carnival and get DeWorken. Andy and Mike will stay here. Then, after the rescue, we'll return to the cave, maybe stay hidden another day or two until the heat is likely to be off. Then we'll drive home. Better draw me a good map, Andy. Otherwise I might not be able to find this place again."

"Got some paper in your car?"

"A small pad in the glove compartment. I'll get it."

Cliff was staring off in the other direction, probably too embarrassed to look me in the eye. But Andy was looking at me. He was looking right at me with an ear-to-ear smile. "It won't be so bad, young fellow. We can take advantage of this extra time and get to know each other better."

"Yeah ... ah ... sure, Andy ... Sure ... that'll be great."

A few moments ago, I'd had mixed feelings, part of me wanting to go on the adventure and part of me so grateful for a chance to stay hidden that I decided not to protest more than once or twice. But now my feelings were suddenly clearing up, and it occurred to me that I'd be willing to face all the danger in the world just to avoid listening to Andy, who would surely speak nonstop for just as many hours as the mission took. In my mind, I prayed for a very short mission, but I didn't have much faith. Nothing so far had gone the way we'd planned, and I figured I'd be in this cave listening to good ol' Uncle Andy for a very long time.

Chapter Sixteen

The Rescue

"You've been awfully hard on me lately, Ben. How come?"

"Sorry about that, Cliff. It's just that this has been a dangerous trip, and well, I guess I'm thinking we wouldn't have had to take the trip if it hadn't been for you."

They'd been driving for a while without saying a word. They would be at the carnival soon, and Cliff wanted to get things squared with Ben before all the new commotion started.

He'd been miserable on this journey. At first, it was almost enjoyable, hopping in a van and heading off with his two best friends. It was tough keeping the whole DeWorken incident a secret, and Cliff was relieved to have the problem out in the open. He was also grateful for two friends who would stand by him like this and put their own lives in jeopardy. So, between the gratitude and the prospect of a fun adventure, the trip had started out OK.

But any pleasant feeling at the beginning of the trip quickly vanished during the restaurant fight. As usual, Cliff had behaved cowardly, and that cowardice seemed especially potent when contrasted to Mike's newfound courage. No longer could Cliff console himself by assuming that, with the exception of special people like Ben, his own personal fears were somewhat normal and understandable. No longer could Cliff tell himself that others, like Mike, would have done the same thing. Mike was changing. Mike was working on himself and making progress. Maybe it was because of the ornament. Maybe it was because he had a new girlfriend and that boosted his self-esteem. Maybe it was because the fictional character Arch-Ranger was rubbing off on the author. Whatever the reason, Cliff was raging with jealousy. He hated Mike now — yes, Mike, one of his two best friends, and Cliff actually hated him.

It bothered him that he felt this way about Mike, but it wouldn't bother him as much if he could at least regain *Ben's* respect. "Hey, Ben?"

"Yeah?"

"Maybe when we return home, you can teach me some of that jujutsu."

At first Ben didn't say anything. Maybe because back in the cave Cliff had made it quite clear he had no intention of ever returning home, and therefore, any discussion predicated on the notion of still being a part of Ben's life sounded disingenuous. But Cliff knew there was a good chance Ben wasn't taking all that talk about living in the other world seriously. Cliff actually *was* serious, but who knew for sure what lay ahead? At the moment, his friend was sore at him, and he wanted to make it right somehow. Cliff also knew how busy Ben was in high school between basketball, studying, and balancing a social life, so there was also the question of whether he even had the time anyway. Cliff hoped Ben would be glad to see his friend interested in learning how to fight instead of annoyed at the prospect of an additional slot taken up on his calendar.

"Sure, Cliff," Ben said in a consoling way, without much enthusiasm. "Sure, I'll teach you, if that's what you want."

***

"Hey, Doug. Come on out!" DeWorken had grown to hate this voice. It was Blake. No mistaking that thundering sound. "Right now, Doug. Get out here! I want to talk to you."

Doug walked outside of Tinker Bell's compartment and looked upward at his master. "Here I am, sir."

"Two days ago, you and I had a little discussion about the show. You remember what I said?"

"Yeah. Ya said I needed ta smile more while I was dancin'."

"That is correct. Now I watched you carefully last night, and still there was no smile on your face. You need to look like you're enjoying yourself up there, Doug."

"Yes, sir. I'll try ta do better today, sir."

"That's all I ask. All right. Go finish your breakfast."

Doug sat back down at Tinker Bell's table to continue eating. Blake had filled their plates with crushed cereal and bacon bits. There were also tiny glasses of orange juice.

"You're getting much better, Doug. I enjoy dancing with you."

"I like dancin' with you too," Doug said.

"Do you? Do you honestly?"

"Ya know how I feel about ya."

"I suppose. It's just that you never look happy when we dance. The master is right about that. You *could* stand to smile more."

"I would be if we was dancin' just for ourselves ... just ta make ourselves happy. But doin' it for that big ogre Blake ... I just can't stomach it."

"I know, Doug. I understand. But he keeps asking you to smile, and you really haven't done so yet. I get nervous when I see you disobeying our master."

"I'm doin' the best I can. At least I talk polite ta him now."

"You do. Yes, you do."

"But I gotta tell ya, sometimes I feel like if I disobeyed him and he got so mad that he killed me, maybe it wouldn't be so bad. At least then I'd be free of him."

Tinker Bell held her head down. "I know you hate being here, but I'd be dishonest if I didn't admit how nice it is to have company. I was so lonely before you came along."

Doug leaned over and kissed her on the cheek. "Ya won't never have ta be lonely again. I promise."

That seemed to cheer her up. "Then you'll do as you're told? For me, if not for anyone else?"

"I'd do anything for you."

***

"An accident?"

"Yes, Sheriff ... an accident."

Usually Maple enjoyed her morning break. Waitressing was hectic and stressful, and the breaks helped to take some of the bite out of her dreary days, but right now, she was hating the break because Sheriff Watson had wandered into the restaurant requesting to talk to her just as soon as possible.

She'd already given him a report last night, but she'd kept it vague. Sheriff Watson didn't press for much at the time because he was worried about his son and needing to get to the hospital as quickly as possible.

Today, he had returned for all of the gritty details. They were in the back, out of sight, borrowing the office of the restaurant manager. The manager wasn't here. It was just her and the sheriff. Watson was a large man, and he looked out of place sitting on a small table chair.

The last thing Maple wanted to do was get those brave boys in trouble. But she knew there might not be a choice. This was Sheriff Watson, after all, a persistent man, a towering figure, and the most powerful person in Wendover.

"What I think you mean," Watson said, "is that Butch accidentally got hurt as bad as he did. But the fight itself was *not* an accident. Somebody started the fight."

"That's right, sir. The boys were only trying to protect Andy."

"Andy? Oh, the old coot. Somebody was bothering him?"

"Yes, sir ... Butch."

Watson slowly leaned forward, glaring at Maple from across the table. "You're saying that *Butch* started the fight? *My* Butch?"

"Well, sir ..."

"Did you know he's still in the hospital? He had a concussion for seven hours straight. He finally came to, but it was a close call. That's for sure."

"I'm glad to hear he's all right, sir."

"I know you are, Maple. You're a sweet lady. You always *have* been. Butch says he can't remember what happened. After listening to the doctor describe his concussion, I can understand why he's having trouble remembering that or anything else. I spoke to Butch's friends and several other people who were in the diner last night. They all seem to agree. They say these kids who blew into town were real troublemakers."

"I don't know who said that, Sheriff, or why they said it. Some people may be afraid to admit that your son was involved."

"Why would they be afraid to admit that? I'm the law. That's all. People need to speak truthfully to the law."

"I agree, sir. But maybe you can understand how hard it would be to admit that Butch ..." She stopped short, frightened to death and wondering what to do next.

"Go on ... It would be hard to admit *what* about Butch?"

"Um ... well, it all happened so fast. Maybe people from different angles had a different view of who ..."

"Hold it right there. Now, Maple Jean, we've known each other for years. Your daddy and me have been friends for the longest time. I was there for your baptism and your very first birthday party. Now, I'm gonna ask you again, Maple Jean, because I'm sure I must have heard you wrong the first time. It sounded for a minute like you were blaming all this tarnation on my son, Butch. I don't think that was what you really meant to say, was it?"

Maple felt as if a loud, glaring alarm had gone off inside of her. "No, Sheriff. I meant to say that ..."

"Yes?"

"I ... I just meant to say things got out of hand."

"Yes, things do get out of hand at times. But Butch didn't start the fight, did he Maple Jean?"

"I don't know who started it. I was in the kitchen when it started."

"The kitchen? Really? You didn't mention that the first time. That's very interesting. So for all you know, it may have been those other boys ... the strangers ... They could have started the fight."

"Maybe."

"So why did you say before that Butch started it?"

"I was going by what I heard."

"Heard from who?"

"A customer."

"Which customer?"

"Somebody who was just driving through. I didn't get a name."

"Maple, I'll ask you one more time. Who started the fight?"

"I just don't know who started it, Sheriff."

Of course Maple did know, and she felt bad about lying, but she'd never work in this town again if she crossed the sheriff. She knew that, and he knew that she knew. But if she was going to lie, she would still lie in such a way as to not accuse the innocent.

"All right, Maple Jean. I can accept that. The important thing is, nobody saw *Butch* start it." Maple nodded her head. The sheriff continued. "You know, Maple Jean, it suddenly occurs to me ... The last time I was in here, I left you a poor tip. I'd like to make it up to you."

"You've always been a generous tipper, Sheriff."

"Well, I try to be. I do try. After all, you waitresses work hard, and you're not paid nearly enough, with all the freaks and weirdoes who pull off the freeway and drop into your diner. No, girlie girl, you are not paid even half of what you're worth. Why, if we cashed every one of your paychecks and stacked every month of salary, one on top of another, I don't think we'd even have a pile the size of an ant hill! That's why I usually leave generous tips. But once in a blue moon, I get a call, an emergency call. Heck, when those calls buzz through, I can't even finish up a cup of coffee, let alone breakfast. And I skipped your tip last time."

"Sheriff ..."

"No, no ... I did. So I'm gonna make it up to you today." He opened up his wallet and pulled out a fifty-dollar bill. "Here's for the tip I missed ... Oh ... and I'm sure there are others that I missed, that I never remembered to make up. In fact, while we're at it, why don't I take care of future times too? I'm sure there'll be other interruptions, other police calls. No matter how often I come in here, I'll still be the sheriff."

By now, there was a small stack of bills in front of Maple, most of them hundreds and fifties, none of them smaller than a twenty.

"Really, Sheriff, this is so unnecessary."

"Unnecessary my eye! You go out and buy yourself something really nice now, you hear? Something you've always wanted."

***

The carnival smells of hot dogs, popcorn, and cotton candy were distracting but not really enticing. Cliff would be more in the mood for eating once this whole mess was over. What a concept: the mess being over. Cliff could scarcely remember what it had been like to not be in trouble. It was probably wishful thinking to believe that today all his problems would be over, but for the moment, it was a comforting thought, and he needed a comforting thought to get him through.

They hadn't brought the ornament with them. Cliff had wanted to, but Ben refused. In any event, Mike had insisted that the ornament wasn't working anymore. His source for this depressing information was Caligula, and Cliff wasn't sure they should believe a cat. He tried not to think about his own failed attempt to release the angels inside. He had made the promise, so he had made the attempt, but nothing happened, or more correctly put, *apparently* nothing happened, at least nothing that he personally witnessed. It had been weeks ago and Cliff hardly ever thought about it, being much more distracted over the whole DeWorken caper. So presumably the ornament was still working, but either way, they did not have the ornament with them. They were on their own.

"This way," Cliff said to Ben. "We need to veer left."

"You sure are familiar with the place. It's as though you've been here before."

"I *have* been here before, Ben. Not in this location. But the layout is the same. Every piece of this carnival is situated exactly as it was in *our* town. There! You see? See that sign off in the distance? The Amazing Tinker Bell ... That's it."

The ticket takers looked familiar, and the amphitheater was identical. The pre-show music was also the same, as were the announcer and the announcer's green, leprechaun-type outfit. When Tinker Bell finally came out, she came out alone. There was no sign of DeWorken. Cliff had forgotten how awesome her act had been. He watched Ben carefully to see if the dancing, singing, or acrobatics were making an impression on him, but nothing ever seemed to make an impression on Ben.

"What do you think?" Cliff said.

"What do I think about what?"

"The show. She's something else, isn't she?"

"Yeah, I guess. I would have figured this was all some kind of trick if I didn't know better. So where's DeWorken? Isn't he supposed to be in the show too?"

"That's what I thought."

After the fifth number or so, the emcee started talking about some raffle while Tinker Bell disappeared behind the stage curtain. She came out again a few minutes later, dressed in a white formal evening gown.

"Ladies and gentlemen," the emcee bellowed, "for our final number, I take pride and pleasure to introduce Tinker Bell's brand-new partner … Say hello to Tom Thumb!"

Tom Thumb? Oh no! Could it be? It sure was. DeWorken walked out dressed in a black tuxedo.

"Oh my God," Ben said, smiling for the first time. "This is unreal."

"Look at him," Cliff laughed. "He's such a clod."

"Yeah," Ben agreed. "He looks like some kid dressed up against his will and dragged in front of a children's play for the PTA."

A classical waltz started playing over the loudspeaker. Cliff recognized it as a piece by Johann Strauss Junior, but he couldn't recall the name of the composition. The dance was actually quite eloquent, and DeWorken managed to move with relative grace.

"So, now what?" Ben asked.

"When the show's over, we'll head straight for one of the ushers and ask to see Mr. Blake."

"What if they say he isn't available?"

"They *will* say that. They always say that. But after I mention my name and they tell Blake who it is, he'll see me. Otherwise he'll be too scared that I might go to the police."

Everything took place on schedule, just as Cliff predicted: the denial that Mr. Blake had time and the subsequent, "Well, OK. He'll see you, but only for a minute."

Cliff was back in Blake's RV office. There he was, just like the first time, sitting at his desk, writing in his ledger.

Cliff cleared his throat. "Do you remember me?"

Blake slowly lifted his head, but he didn't say anything, not one word. His stone face gave no hint of emotion, positive or negative.

Cliff was even more frightened than he thought he'd be. But the milk had been spilt. There was no backing off now. "Mister Blake? Do you …?"

"Yeah, I remember you. But I don't remember agreeing to a second meeting. What do you want?"

"Not much. Not much at all. Just wondering how my friend Doug is working out."

Blake raised his eyebrow. "Your friend, eh? You have a lot of brass, junior. I didn't think I'd ever see you again." Blake pulled out a cigarette from his shirt pocket and stuck it in his mouth. Then he opened his top desk drawer, whisked out a lighter, and started smoking, as if he didn't have a care in the world. "He's working out OK. At least, he is now. You didn't tell me that your little friend had such a big mouth."

Cliff chuckled. "I guess it never came up. I hope he hasn't been too much trouble."

"Like I said, we worked it out eventually. Doug has learned a few manners since he's been under my care." Blake was focusing on Ben now, and Cliff found it curious that he hadn't yet asked anything about him, such as who he was or what he was doing here. Ben's presence must have made it obvious that at least one more person knew the carnival act was not an illusion and was instead done with real people. But if Blake was worried, he certainly didn't display any evidence to that effect. "Now, I'm a busy man. If you're *that* interested in your little friend, go watch the show."

"Oh, we saw the show already. Very entertaining. I never knew Doug had it in him. You know, Mr. Blake, I've seen that show twice now, the first time being Tinker Bell's solo performance. I believe it was a lot more fun the second time. I enjoyed watching Tinker Bell dance with a partner."

"Glad you approve. But you didn't really come here to write a review. So maybe you'd better get to the point."

"The point … All right … the point … If two miniatures were better than one, just imagine what your show would be like with a whole ensemble." Blake shrugged his shoulders, looking unimpressed. Cliff was starting to perspire. "Well, just in case you're interested, I have more."

"More?"

"Yes, sir. More. More miniatures … Plenty more … As many as you want."

Blake rubbed his chin as if stroking an imaginary beard. "Just where are you finding all these people, son?"

"The same place you found Tinker Bell, I imagine."

"Nice try. Now how about the truth? Doug did *not* come from the same place. As a matter of fact, he keeps telling me some story about how he was a normal person once upon a time, and he says you shrunk him somehow."

Cliff offered a fake laugh. "Doug tends to exaggerate."

"You better hope so. Part of his story included a plan to come after you." Blake was acting amused now. "Of course that's only after he turns tall again and first kills me."

Cliff found it amazing that DeWorken would be bragging and threatening despite his size. Maybe that was the only thing he knew how to do. Later, when Cliff had more time to think about this, he would recall an article he'd once read on the power of hope. It talked about how hope, more than anything, kept people alive, even in the most precarious of situations. Of course, DeWorken would be too stupid to understand the profound implications of hope. In his mind, it would all be about revenge, but underneath, hope was the driving force whether he was aware of it or not.

"Well, Mr. Blake, however I find these people, I *do* find them."

"Really? How?"

"It's a secret."

Blake formed sly grin. "Let *me* in on your secret, son."

Cliff knew it was time to take the plunge, time to gamble that old Andy was telling the truth. Andy had been accurate about the shifting cave wall. Hopefully the rest of his story would also check out. "Very well, Mr. Blake. These people live in another dimension, and there's a portal to this new world on the back wall of a cave not far from here."

Blake's mouth dropped open so wide it almost looked like a cave entrance in its own right. His eyes were almost just as wide, and Cliff knew immediately that Andy had been dead-on accurate. Andy's "other world" was indeed familiar to Mr. Blake. It was undoubtedly the same world Tinker Bell came from and the same world Mike's Aunt Loureen spoke of.

Blake got out of his chair and moved toward Cliff, squaring off, face to face. "Maybe we *are* on the same page here. But something isn't quite right."

"Why not?"

"I already told you, son. Doug didn't come from Tinker Bell's world."

"So he says."

"Why do you keep trying to lie? Tinker Bell couldn't even speak English until I taught her. Doug not only claims to be from our world, he speaks and acts like he's from our world."

"That's only because he's been with me for so long."

Blake smiled again. "Now why don't I believe you?"

"All right, Mr. Blake. If Doug didn't come from the other world, how did he get so small?"

"Search me. All I know is that he keeps insisting *you* made him that way."

"How exactly?"

Cliff was acting pompous, but he wasn't really feeling that way inside. He could see that Blake didn't appreciate being spoken to in this manner. Apparently, Blake was a man seldom confronted by those around him.

With a colder expression, Blake responded, "He said it had to do with magic."

Cliff mustered up another fake laugh. "And you believed him?"

"I didn't say that! But *something* fishy is going on. That's for sure. And you watch your manners. This is my office, so you just watch your manners."

Cliff had mixed feelings. Naturally, he was frightened. Who wouldn't be? Blake would be an intimidating presence in any situation. But Blake was also on the defensive, and Cliff knew that the best strategy was to act like he was holding all the cards. Besides, Ben was with him. Ben would protect him if things got out of hand.

"OK, Mr. Blake. You go ahead and listen to DeWorken if you want." Cliff turned to Ben. "Let's go. I know plenty of other interested parties."

Blake reached out his hand, pulling Cliff back. "So, you're a big important dealer with 'other interested parties'?' I think you're bluffing. And you don't do it very well. Besides, what makes you think I need your business? I can go to the cave myself and travel into this mystery land anytime I want."

"True," Cliff said. "But don't forget, you still have to find the miniature people. Since Tinker Bell was the only one you had before I came along and since you were chomping at the bit to buy DeWorken, I'm guessing that not all of your expeditions have been particularly successful. I, on the other hand, know exactly where they all live, and since the carnival only comes into this town once a year, I'm assuming you don't have opportunities to travel into the other world very often."

Blake sighed. "Have a seat. Both of you." Cliff sat in the chair across Blake's desk. Ben took a seat closer to the RV wall, but it was such a small space that he really wasn't too far away, which suited Cliff just fine. Blake remained standing but leaned against the front of his desk. "What did you have in mind? How much money do you want this time?"

"We can talk about that later, Mr. Blake. First, I'd like to see Doug."

"You wanna see him?"

"That's right."

"What for?"

"Just to make sure he's all right. Before I sell you any more, I need to be certain you're treating him properly."

Blake's voice was laced with obvious suspicion. "Hmm ... proper treatment, eh? A very noble gesture. Somehow you don't strike me as the sentimental type. You didn't seem to care before whether or not Doug had a nice home. In fact, you acted only like you were anxious to get rid of him."

"Well, now I'm acting like I want to see him."

"If you saw the show, then you know he's all right. Sickly people couldn't move around on stage the way he does."

"I still want to see him offstage, and I want to talk with him."

"You're in no position to make demands!"

"Do you want me to help you find more miniatures, or don't you? Because if you do, I suggest you bring me to Doug right now."

It was silent for a moment, but it was the longest moment Cliff had ever experienced.

"All right ... he's in the back room. But your friend stays here."

"Why?"

"Because I said so. That's why."

"Actually, Mr. Blake, I think I'd be a lot more comfortable if my friend came along."

"Now you listen to me ..."

"No, *you* listen! I want Ben with me. And the very fact that you don't want him along makes me even more sure that I *do* want him along."

***

"Hey, Doug!"" Blake shouted. ""Doug! Come on out!"

"What for?" His voice came from the other side of the tiny door.

"I have a surprise for you."

"Ya said I could rest between shows."

"I won't ask you a second time, Doug."

The small door from the cage compartment quickly opened and DeWorken popped his head out.

"Look who's here," Blake said.

At first DeWorken seemed uninterested. Suddenly he recognized Cliff, and his subdued face changed to a much more alerted look. "Reynolds ..." Then his eye caught hold of Ben. "And Robinson too. I shoulda known. I shoulda known ya were both in on this!"

Ben didn't say a word. Cliff finally offered a friendly remark. "Hey, DeWorken ... How's it going?"

261

"Ya already know how it's goin', ya miserable, ugly-lookin' freakazoid!"

Blake chuckled. "Now, Doug. Where are your manners? These boys came to check on your welfare. The least you can do is talk civilly."

But DeWorken ignored Blake and continued. "You're dead, Reynolds! You're a walkin' corpse!"

Cliff was starting to regret this rescue attempt. Back in the cave, he'd suggested abandoning the plan only because of fear and safety concerns. But right now, at this crucial moment, he wasn't actually worried about the plan failing. He was worried about it succeeding. If he succeeded, he was stuck with DeWorken again, stuck with his foul mouth, stuck with the same dilemma as to what to do with him, and stuck with those two suspicious police detectives.

Cliff remembered how good it had felt to unload DeWorken on Mr. Blake. Certainly he'd felt guilty, but he'd also felt free, and maybe in time the guilt would have dissipated. This new plan to rescue DeWorken included no ideas about what to do with him after the rescue. All this work, all this scheming, and all this danger … for what? To be right back where he started? It didn't seem worth it, not even for the sake of treating a guilty conscience.

Blake opened the cage, took DeWorken out, held him up for a moment so Cliff could get a better look, then set him down on the table outside of the cage.

The other compartment door opened, and Tinker Bell also walked out, wearing an outfit different from what she had on during the stage show — a long, pink, cotton dress.

"Take a good look at these guys," DeWorken said to her. "These are the creeps who double-crossed me."

Tinker Bell looked upward at Cliff and Ben. Her eyes were inquisitive, but there was no sign of scorn or hostility, nor did such traits seem imaginable from a gentle woman like her.

"All right," Blake said to Cliff. "You wanted to see Doug. So, now you've seen him, and you can see that he's in perfect health. I don't mean to spoil the tearful reunion, but the longer this goes on, the more we'll have to listen to Doug's healthy mouth. So I believe it's time for you gentlemen to be on your way."

This was the moment Cliff had dreaded. The very notion of crossing a man like Mr. Blake seemed like insanity, and for all Cliff knew, even Ben might not be able to stop a person like him.

"Here, Mr. Blake." Cliff opened up his wallet, took out a wad of bills, and slapped them in Blake's hand.

"I beg your pardon?" Blake said.

"This is for you."

"I don't want your money." Blake stuffed the bills back in Cliff's hand.

Cliff set the money down on the dining table. "Then I'll just leave it here."

"What's going on?" Blake demanded. "What's this all about?"

"That's everything you paid me for DeWorken, plus fifteen percent more for all your trouble. I'm buying him back."

"Buying him back?"

"Yes, sir."

"Who says so?"

"I do. I've had a change of heart. I don't like the idea of trafficking in the slave market. It isn't right."

Blake raised his eyebrow again, this time in a much more provocative manner. "Not right, eh? Too bad, son. Too bad you didn't develop a case of the scruples before you sold him to me. But you *did* sell him. Doug is mine now, and he's not for sale, not to you or to anyone else."

"I'm afraid I can't take no for an answer, Mr. Blake. Ben and me, we're bringing DeWorken back home with us."

Blake glanced back and forth from Ben to Cliff. DeWorken had a look of disbelief in his eyes. Cliff figured he was finding it hard to imagine anyone caring enough about him to return and wage a rescue.

Blake's voice was still calm. "Let me see if I'm understanding this. You plan to take something that belongs to me and simply walk away? How exactly are you going to pull that off?"

Cliff glanced at Ben as if to say, "I've done all I can. It's your turn. Take over, please."

Ben was the wild card to be played at the last possible moment.

And Ben was faithful to the task, speaking to Blake for the very first time. "Look, mister, he offered to give you your money back. Considering that DeWorken is a human being and not a used car, I'd say you're getting a pretty good deal. People can get in trouble running the kind of business you run. So why don't you just take the money? We'll leave with DeWorken, and you won't have to see us again."

For a second, Blake just stared at him. Suddenly, he broke into laughter. "You're serious, aren't you? You little punks actually think you're going to order me around."

"Pick him up, Cliff," Ben said.

Cliff reached for DeWorken and tucked him in the palm of his hand.

"Wait!" DeWorken shouted. "Take Tinker Bell too!"

"Let's not push it," Cliff said. "We're rescuing you. That's all."

"Tinker Bell too."

Cliff shook his head. "Just you, DeWorken."

"I ain't goin' nowhere without Tinker Bell!"

"Actually, Doug," Mr. Blake chimed in, "you're not going anywhere at all. I've been patient with your friends, but my patience is wearing thin."

DeWorken ignored his master and kept on like a broken record. "Either Tinker Bell goes with us or I stay."

Cliff erupted. "Oh, shut up, DeWorken! You've been more trouble to me than you're worth! We're rescuing you whether you like it or not!"

Tinker Bell was teary-eyed. "I'll be all right, Doug. The important thing is for you to save yourself."

Ben sighed. "Pick up the girl, Cliff."

"Are you crazy?"

"I don't feel right about leaving her behind. Pick her up."

"What are we going to do with her?"

"I don't know. Just pick her up."

"I wouldn't do that," Blake said. "It'll only make me twice as angry."

Cliff hesitated.

"Ignore him," Ben said. "Take the girl."

"Yeah, Reynolds. Show some spine for once in your life!"

Cliff held the miniature nemesis up to his eyes. "So help me, DeWorken! One more word out of you, and I'll flush you down the toilet!"

"CLIFF, QUIT BANTERING WITH DEWORKEN AND PICK UP THE GIRL!!!"

Finally, Cliff fetched her. She felt lighter than a feather in his hand. Uncertain what to do next, he just stood there, facing Mr. Blake, DeWorken in his right hand, Tinker Bell in his left. Blake made no attempt yet to stop him, but Cliff knew that didn't mean anything. At the moment, these were merely "still waters."

"Good," Ben said. "You have your money, and we have what we want. So we'll leave now. Take it easy, Mr. Blake."

Blake clapped his hands. "Wonderful performance. I wish I could put all of you in the show. But the show's over now. What shall we say? The count of three? Sure ... the count of three. That's how long you have to put them back down and leave this complex. Oh ... almost forgot. You're never to return again. *Do* remember that part."

Ben stood between Blake and Cliff.

"You're making a mistake, son. The count starts now. One ... two ... three."

Cliff headed for the door. Blake tried to follow him, but Ben intercepted. Blake lunged toward Ben and immediately found himself suspended in thin air. Ben tossed him on the floor, a little more gently than usual. Cliff could see that he was restraining himself so as not to hurt him as badly as Butch the Biker.

Blake slowly stood up, looking quite astonished but not too concerned, and this worried Cliff.

"Very good. I'm impressed. Really, I am. You know something? There's only one thing wrong with flaunting the martial arts. Sooner or later, you run into somebody else who knows them. For instance, I may

265

not be able to copy those fun maneuvers you just pulled, but I happen to know another humble technique called 'karate.' I wish I could demonstrate on you, but you see, karate kills. It kills in just one fatal blow. So let me demonstrate another way." And then, with a mighty thrust, he slammed his hand on top of the desk, literally ripping the entire desk in half with a single swipe! Books and pencils rolled on the floor, and a glass paperweight shattered. "That desk could just as easily have been your head. Since they don't arrest people for murdering desks, it seemed like the better way for me to showcase my talent. Now then, Cliff, be a reasonable fellow and hand me back the two cast members of my show."

"Don't do it, Reynolds!"

Cliff ignored DeWorken and glanced at Ben.

"Just stay where you are," Ben said. "Let me handle this."

Blake moved closer to his opponent. "You're not going to handle anything, son. You're going to play it smart and leave."

Ben walked right up to the man, looking fearless and brave. "If we leave without our friends, we go straight to the police. I'm sure they'll be interested to know that you hold people as slaves, especially since they're already looking for DeWorken."

"That will put your friend Cliff in equally as much trouble. If I end up talking to the police, I'll have to tell them who sold Doug to me in the first place. Yes, I'll have to tell them all about it."

But Ben didn't back down. "We're willing to take that risk, mister. Are you?"

Blake had a defiant look in his eyes. "Yes … Yes, I am."

"Move toward the tent exit, Cliff. I'll follow."

"You're not walking out of here with my property!"

"You can't stop both of us at once," Ben said.

"Oh, no? Just watch me."

"Go, Cliff. Start moving."

"Stay where you are!"

Cliff froze, dead in his tracks. Blake turned to Ben again. "You caught me off guard a moment ago. It won't happen twice. Compared to karate, your fighting skill reminds me more of ballet."

Cliff was feeling horrified, but Ben kept his composure. "Call it what you want, mister. Even if I end up in the hospital, Cliff will get away and you'll go to jail. And that's just for starters. Because afterwards, I'll retire off the settlement of a very expensive lawsuit against you, and life as you've known it will be over."

Blake hesitated. Cliff could see that Ben had obviously called his bluff. Karate or not, this man was not prepared to get in trouble with the law — at least, not tonight.

"All right. Take them. Take both of them. But know this. The only other people who ever defied me are dead now. I won't bore you by bragging about the details because that would make me sound like Doug. So you won't hear me talk anymore about killing. Instead, I'll simply do it. I'm coming after you, at a moment when you least expect it. And I won't get in trouble with the police because it won't be a public place. It'll be a place of my own choosing. Your bodies will be buried and never found. Questions? Good. Feel free to leave now, gentlemen. Until next time."

***

"Where are ya takin' us?" DeWorken demanded.

"Back home," Cliff said. "Back to Oak Hill. Where did you think we were taking you?"

They'd been back on the road for ten minutes. So far, so good. No sign of the sheriff or any other police. In another fifteen minutes, they'd hit the turn off to that old dirt desert road, and then on to the cave.

DeWorken and Tinker Bell were sitting on top of the front dashboard. "I don't get this, Reynolds. Why did ya come back for me?"

"You already heard my reason. It's like I said to Mr. Blake. I started feeling bad about what I did."

"Not as bad as you're gonna feel when I turn tall again."

"Give it a rest, DeWorken."

"I'll give you a rest, Reynolds ... a permanent rest."

"You oughta be grateful we came back for you," Ben said.

"Oh yeah? Well, I ain't grateful ta no one!"

Tinker Bell took his hand. "They *did* rescue us, Doug. Couldn't you be a little nicer to them?"

"So they rescued us! So what! They were the whole reason I needed ta get rescued in the first place."

"Get them off the dashboard," Ben quickly said.

Cliff turned to Ben. "What's going on?"

"Get them off of there, fast! There's a flashing red light behind us. It looks like the sheriff's car."

Chapter Seventeen

Marla Meets Aunt Loureen

"Honey, you have to stop moping."

Marla had been sitting in the living room for over an hour, holding a magazine on her lap, barely glancing at even one word. Mom had been pretty patient with Marla up to now, but she was getting concerned, and it was one of the few times her motherly concern didn't seem exaggerated or overdone.

"I know you're crazy about Mike, but believe me, men aren't the only things in life. It's important to remember that." Mom smiled and changed her tone to take away the tenseness of the moment with a lighter comment. "Otherwise, you'll set women's lib back three hundred years."

Marla believed in women's lib, at least the sensible part. Some feminists seemed less interested in equality and more interested in teaching that all men were pigs. Marla had no use for that kind of anti-male agenda. But neither did she like the other extreme: She had far too many friends who gained all of their self-esteem from their boyfriends. Every time she ran into an old acquaintance and they got together for lunch or something, the first words out of her mouth were, "OK, let me tell you about this new guy I met."

Marla had been proud of herself for gaining self-esteem in a wide variety of ways, not simply from her boyfriends. Still, as she'd reluctantly admitted to herself several times now, Mike was different. Maybe this wasn't about self-esteem as much as loneliness. As for Mom, was this mother/daughter talk really motivated out of feminism, or was it instead some kind of sour grapes? After all, Mom was certainly lonely herself these days, and she had seemed *very* attached to Dad before he surprised her with the news that he wanted a divorce.

"Was it like that with you and Dad early on? Did you find yourself unhappy when you couldn't be around him, even if it was only for a short time?"

Mom looked a bit taken aback, probably surprised to hear her daughter pursue this kind of topic. "Hmm … it's hard to remember anymore how I felt back then. It was such a long time ago."

"I know you met Dad at college, but you never told me anything about it."

"Such as?"

"Oh, I don't know. How did he ask you out for the first time?"

A nicer, more peaceful look formed on Mom's face. "I was at a campus coffee shop, by myself, studying for a midterm. I was so focused on my books that I never even noticed him walking over to my table. I looked up to see a charming man sitting across from me, charming and a bit older. He was a grad student."

"I never knew any of this, Mom. What did he say?"

"I can quote him word for word because it was the kind of introduction a girl never forgets. He said, 'I know this is going to sound like a line, but you are the most beautiful, the most breathtaking woman I have ever seen in my entire life.'"

It was the most romantic thing Marla had ever heard, and it seemed impossible that such conversation could have transpired between her father and her mother. "So what did you say back to him?"

"I said, 'Of course it sounds like a line because it *is* a line.'"

Marla giggled. "Nice comeback. Good for you, Mom. Then what happened?"

Mom smiled. "That look of fascination on your face. It reminds me of when you were a little girl. I would tell you bedtime stories, and your eyes would be wide open with wonder, hanging on every word. Remember when we'd continue a story from night to night and you would whine and fuss because you didn't want to wait for the next chapter?"

"I still don't like it," Marla said with a dry smile. "So ..."

Her mom laughed. "All right. He admitted that it *was* a line, and he admitted that he'd used the line before on other women. But in my case, every word happened to be true. At least, that's what he said."

"Did you believe him?"

"Of course not. But I admired his daring manner, and as a matter of fact, it just so happened that *he* was the handsomest, most breathtaking man *I* had ever seen."

Marla had never known Mike to act suave or self-confident. Of course, Dad and Mom were in college at the time, much older and more mature than a high school sophomore. Nevertheless, Mike didn't seem to have that kind of personality anyway. But it didn't matter. Marla still loved him to pieces.

After dinner, Mom went shopping with a friend. She offered to take Marla with her. Marla said she should get some homework done instead. Mom just stared at her lovingly, knowing that she would never be able to concentrate on homework and would instead be waiting by the phone, hoping Mike would call.

Actually, Marla did manage to read a little of her biology book, but very little, and she finally needed to put the textbook down. She preferred not to sit by the phone like a fool. She thought she'd distract herself by watching some television. Marla flipped through the eighty-some channels: five shopping networks, six all-news channels, eight sports channels ... Amazing ... So many channels but not a thing on. Finally, she keyed in on one of the shopping networks. The show was specializing in a special line of ladies' shoes. After watching for about five minutes, Marla turned the TV off.

Marla found herself worrying again about Mike. All at once, she remembered! Mike's delay had actually been predicted. That unusual gentleman with the encyclopedias had told her that Mike only *believed* he was going on a short trip. Marla really hadn't thought much about that peculiar stranger. Certainly he had the attention of her thoughts for an hour or two after he left. But as the weekend moved on, the thoughts faded. The conversation had been so bizarre it just seemed easier to put the whole thing out of her mind. Now it was all coming back to her: some kind of promise that she could be with Mike again soon if she really wanted to. This man who called himself "Charles" would help her, but she would first have to summon him. And then, that unusual method of calling him, taking his business card and burning it in the fireplace ...Would she really be willing to try this? Was she actually contemplating taking the plunge and conducting the grand experiment? No, how could she? How could she even consider such lunacy? And yet, Charles had already done the impossible, spoken of matters he couldn't possibly have known about in any natural, ordinary way. It wasn't a very cold evening. If Marla built a fire, she would have to explain herself when Mom returned from the store. But what else was there to do? She was *not* going to sit around by the phone all evening. That would be ridiculous. If she was unable to do anything besides miss Mike, she'd might as well do something about it, even if that something made absolutely no sense.

Marla took the card out of her purse and headed for the fireplace. On her way, she glanced at the card again, only to find that she was somehow holding the wrong card. This one didn't say "CHARLES." It said "LOUREEN."

"What the …?"

Marla sat down on the couch and stared at the card for a solid minute. "But …"

Was it possible that Charles had given her two cards by mistake? She rummaged through her purse. If he *had* given her two cards, where was the other? She found nothing else. Could her eyes have been playing tricks? No. Not possible. That card had said "CHARLES" in big, bold print! Who could forget a card like that, a card that had only one word: a name, without an address, without an e-mail, and without a phone number? Besides, Charles had talked about the card. He had acknowledged that his name alone was on it. Her hearing and eyesight couldn't both be wrong.

It didn't take her long to figure out who LOUREEN was. This had to be a reference to Mike's aunt, the very same aunt who was house-sitting while the family was away. What did this mean? What was going on? Marla had never been into the supernatural. She did go to church, and she accepted the idea of miracles, at least the miracles which went on in biblical times. But Marla had never anticipated actually encountering miracles herself. Still, now it seemed unavoidable. Someone or something was trying to relay a message, and somehow this message involved Mike's Aunt Loureen. It would be a few good hours before Mom returned, so why not? Why not pay Aunt Loureen a visit?

Thirty minutes later, Marla was on Mike's front porch, feeling very nervous. She'd finally met Mike's parents before they left for England, and they really seemed to like her, but Mike talked about his Aunt Loureen a lot more than he talked about his parents, so this would be a truer test of acceptance.

The door opened and a friendly, pleasant-looking woman said,

"Yes, may I help you?"

"Hi. Um … you don't know me, ma'am, but … Well … are you Mike's aunt? Is your name Loureen?"

"Indeed it is. And who do I have the pleasure of meeting?"

"I'm Marla, Mike's girlfriend."

Loureen's face formed a large, warm smile. "Oh my goodness! Yes, of course! Mike speaks of you often and very enthusiastically, if I dare say. Please, come in."

Marla instantly felt relieved. This woman had a way of putting people at ease. Walking into the living room, Marla was reminded of some family pictures on the wall, and she went out of her way to look at them a second time, including some of Mike when he was in grade school. There was also one baby picture and two of him when he was a toddler. The pictures were cute, but they made her miss Mike even more.

"Can I get you anything? I was just about to fix myself some ginger tea."

"No, thank you."

"Mike has told me so much about you. I feel as if we've already met. Please, have a seat. Make yourself at home."

"Aunt Loureen, have you heard from Mike since he left for the weekend?"

"I did have one brief conversation, early yesterday. Why do you ask?"

"Oh … I don't know. It's just that I thought he'd be back by now. Mike said they were planning to get back early Sunday."

"You know what happens when boys go off on an outing. These trips always take longer than the original estimated time." Loureen could immediately see that something was wrong. "What else is on your mind, child?"

"Well, the trip was all so sudden, and from the beginning, I've had the strangest feeling about it."

"I do want to hear everything you have to say, my dear, but first, if you'd be kind enough to give me some assistance, I'd like to build a fire."

"A fire? But it's not that cold."

"I know. I just thought a fire would be nice. I'm doing it for the atmosphere." Loureen pointed to a small wooden cabinet next to the fireplace. "Kindling is in there, along with some old newspapers. I'll get the larger pieces from our woodshed out back."

Marla found it extremely unusual that Aunt Loureen was wanting to build a fire. After all, if not for the changing card print, Marla would have built a fire of her own by now.

A few minutes later, the fire was blazing and heating up a room that had been fairly heated already.

"Now then," Loureen said, seated comfortably and sipping her tea, "you were telling me how concerned you are about this trip."

"I guess I shouldn't be. Mike seems to know what he's doing."

"I can see by looking at you that your attraction to my nephew is no casual infatuation."

"Oh, no, ma'am."

"Please, call me Loureen."

"Thank you, Loureen. No, Mike is in a class by himself. It's almost as if there's a strange light about him."

"That's very perceptive of you, child. To tell you the truth, I've always believed my nephew was destined for greatness — greatness far beyond this current, insignificant, comic book fame. I see it so clearly, but he doesn't see it yet. He underestimates himself."

"To me he's already wonderful. Mike is unlike any boy I've ever known."

"I'm glad you feel that way about him. I think you'll be good for Mike. You may be just the inspiration he needs to make the right choices in life."

"Oh, but he already makes the right choices. The very first time we had lunch together, I watched him stand up for his friend Cliff."

"Yes, he does do the right thing eventually, but only after he's been bulldozed into the situation against his will." Loureen stopped herself. "I'm sorry. I shouldn't be bursting your bubble like that. In essence, we

274

agree. My nephew is definitely on the right road. That much is certain." Marla still looked confused, so Loureen said even more. "I think the world of my nephew, and I wouldn't want you to believe otherwise. Mike's life is about integrity. And by that, I'm referring to more than his mere potential. He's already a young man to be proud of. But back to your concern over the trip. Perhaps you're just missing him."

"I do miss him." Tears started rolling down Marla's cheek. "I feel like such a baby lately. I can't even think about Mike without feeling hurt. I don't mean that he's done anything to hurt me. I just mean it hurts thinking about him. This must not make any sense."

"Oh, dear one," Aunt Loureen reached out her hand and placed it gently on Marla's hand. "My dear, sweet child. Of course it doesn't make sense. You're in love. Falling in love is something we can't explain. Believe me, wiser heads have tried. Nobody has ever figured it out."

Marla burst into tears, and Loureen held the sobbing girl in her arms.

"I love him so much. I wish I didn't. I don't want to feel so helpless, but I do."

"It's all right, child. Just go ahead and let it all out."

A few minutes later, Marla was drying her eyes with some tissues Aunt Loureen had given her. Marla had planned to take some out of her purse until she remembered that she had chosen not to bring the purse with her since the walk to Mike's house was not very far.

"Here," Loureen said with a sympathetic smile. "Put a few extra in your jeans pocket. I have a feeling you'll be crying some more for a while."

"I guess I'll get over this. But right now, I can't imagine going through even one day where I don't wish he was with me."

"I entirely understand, Marla."

All at once, Marla sat up, looking very startled. "What's that?"

"What's what, my dear?"

"Over there."

"Oh, just an old antique. Do you like hourglasses?"

"Yes, very much. But what kind is it? How come it glows like that?"

"I beg your pardon?" Loureen got up and moved toward the coffee table. "Glowing, you said? Did you mean something inside was glowing or the entire apparatus?"

"The whole hourglass. It had an orange, blinking light. But it's gone now."

Loureen carefully reached for the hourglass and picked it up. "I've had this for days. So far I've seen nothing out of the ordinary. An orange glow?"

"Yes, ma'am. Almost as if it was blinking on and off. Look … There it goes again!"

This time, Loureen saw it too, and she became very concerned. "Child, I think it might be a best if you returned home."

"What? I don't understand."

"It's this object, child. It may not be safe."

Marla was feeling frightened. Aunt Loureen had been so warm and congenial … comforting too. And now, in the twinkling of an eye, all those traits had vanished, and she was acting eerie. It was as if someone had pulled a switch, turning off one Aunt Loureen and turning on another.

"I'm sorry to be so abrupt about this," Loureen said.

"Aunt Loureen, from the moment Mike told me about this trip, nothing has seemed quite right. There was something about the trip that Mike didn't want to talk about. Please, Aunt Loureen, I really care about Mike, and I need to know what's going on."

"Poor child. This has all been so hard on you."

"You won't send me away, will you, Aunt Loureen?"

Loureen sighed. "It does seem that you were meant to be here."

"Does it? Do you really think so? Because I think I agree. In a way, I was sent to you."

"Sent? Whatever do you mean?"

Marla took out her card and placed it on the coffee table.

"What's this?" Loureen picked up the card. "Unusual. Where did you get this? It looks like the kind of item someone would print up at a novelty store."

Marla told her everything: her visit from Charles, Charles' detailed knowledge about her personal life, and finally, the card with his name that now had Loureen's name printed instead.

"Hmm … Can you describe this Charles for me?"

"Do you know him?"

"If it's the same Charles I'm thinking of, Mike has encountered him several times. Silver hair, dark beard, dark suit?"

"Yes, that's him. That's him exactly! He seemed like such a nut. Normally I would have just ignored him, but then he told me all this stuff about Mike and me."

"Hmm … I think it's time I met this Charles. I have a matter to discuss with him."

"How will you find him?"

"Just the way he instructed you. He asked you to burn the card. Let's do it. Let's burn that infernal card and see what happens. I thought I'd built this fire for atmosphere, and that's true enough. I love fires. But it seems there was another reason as well. We're obviously being guided by forces out of our control. So we'd probably be wise to cooperate."

"But the card doesn't have his name on it anymore."

"Oh, no?"

And there it was! The original print was restored, exactly as it had been before, saying "CHARLES" in the same bold letters. This time, Marla wasn't as surprised. Given the events of the past few days, very little would surprise her from here on out.

"Evidently you are not the only one who's meant to summon this character," Loureen explained. "He directed you here first. Interesting how much communication can take place from a single, simple business card. Here. Hand it to me."

After taking the card out of Marla's hand, Loureen threw it over the top burning log, watching it disappear instantly in a whiff of dark blue smoke. Before they even had a chance to talk about such unusually colored smoke, they were interrupted by a cheerful voice.

"Good evening, ladies." They turned around to see Charles standing only three feet behind them with his usual smile and attire.

Marla was quite jittery inside, but Loureen kept her composure. Marla could see that very little frightened this woman.

Loureen grunted. "Sir, how fortunate for you that I already believe in magic. Otherwise you would look like an intruder, and I'd be forced to call the police."

"Police? How worthless would they be right now?" Charles laughed.

"All right. You wanted our attention and you got it. So it's time to let us in on what's going on. Who are you exactly?"

"Now, now, Loureen. Marla already told you my name. So did Mike. My name is Charles, of course."

"You know what I mean, sir. An explanation as to your true identity."

Charles ignored her. "Something far more urgent is running through Marla's' mind. Don't worry, Marla, he's fine. No harm has come to Mike, and you'll see him soon. In fact, you'll see him much sooner than you think."

"I will? When is he coming back?"

"Oh, I didn't say anything about him coming back. What I said is that you'll see him soon. Consider it a reward for the faith you showed today."

"Faith?"

"Faith in me. By burning that card, you showed some trust, an ability to take a person at his word."

"I didn't burn the card. Mike's Aunt Loureen did."

"Semantics. You were about to burn the card until the name change which led you here. No difference to your faith. You trusted against all facts and sensibilities. I appreciate you."

Charles lifted his hands in the air, like a magician on stage who was about to perform a spectacular trick. "Have courage, Marla. It will be frightening at first, but all is under control. Always remember that."

"I don't understand."

The same blue smoke that had consumed the business card was now surrounding Marla. She screamed and Loureen ran toward her, only to find that Marla had vanished. It was as if the smoke had sucked her up and consumed her. The smoke funneled out and poured itself into the hourglass, swiftly penetrating the glass exterior and disappearing in the sand within. Seconds later, not even one trace of smoke could be seen, just as though nothing had happened. But something had happened because Marla was nowhere in sight.

"What have you done? What happened to her?"

"She was suffering, in agony over Mike, strangled with worry and all kinds of other troublesome feelings. Now she'll be at peace. Now she'll be with her young boyfriend."

"You sent her into the other world."

"Very good, Loureen."

"So that's where my nephew is? He went into the other world after all?"

"Not yet. But he'll be there soon, and now shortly after he arrives, he can be joined by Marla."

"What's happened to my nephew? He's all right, you say?"

"He's fine."

"Then why would he need to go into the other world? Mike has no interest in that other world. He would never enter it unless he was backed into a corner."

"Hmm. Backed into a corner. Interesting description. Couldn't have said it better myself. Yes, Mike is backed into a corner. But I'm sure that comes as no surprise. Your nephew's relationship with trouble can be likened to a magnet and a pin. Actually, I was just on my way to Wendover. Relax, Loureen. Mike and company may be in a jam, but I'll get them out."

"OK. I've had just about enough of this! Now, I demand that you reveal yourself!"

"Loureen, I'm surprised at you. It's one thing for Mike not to figure out my identity. After all, Mike never figures out anything. But you? With all your wisdom? And all your insight? Well, what can I say? I'm disappointed, truly disappointed. I would expect Mike to be hating riddles and demanding answers. But you always seemed to love a good mystery and the challenge of personally solving it."

"You'll excuse me, sir, if my interest in mystery wanes where the safety of my nephew is concerned."

"You know better than that Loureen. Mike can have his rendezvous with the mysterious and remain safe at the same time. It all depends on … I believe the word you like to use is *destiny*."

As he spoke, his words seemed to awaken something deep inside. Suddenly Loureen felt as if the obvious were being made more obvious. "Wait! Oh my word … I *do* know. I *do* know who you are!"

Chapter Eighteen

The Attorney

"Quick," Ben said to DeWorken. "You and your friend get under the seat."

"What's goin' on?"

"We're being stopped by police."

"What for?"

"No time to explain. But Cliff and me might be on our way to jail. So get under the seat. No telling what they'd do if they saw you two."

DeWorken and Tinker Bell scampered under the front passenger seat. Cliff could hear DeWorken cussing under his breath while they moved.

Ben pulled the car over to the side of the road. A squad car drove up close behind him, and a large man wearing a sheriff's hat and dark sunglasses got out of his car. There was also a slender deputy by his side.

Cliff's nerves felt like a sack of jumping beans hitting every side of his stomach. "We're in for it now," he said.

Ben put his hand on Cliff's shoulder. "Just chill. And don't say anything. Let me do the talking."

The sheriff was banging on the window now, so Ben rolled it down.

"May I see your driver's license please?"

"Was I speeding, officer?"

"I'll ask the questions, Wild Bill. Just show me your driver's license." Ben opened his wallet. "Take it out of the wallet please. And then I'll need your vehicle registration too."

Ben opened the glove compartment and grabbed the registration. The sheriff barely glanced at the slip of paper as Ben placed it in his hand.

"Are you the owner of this van?"

"No, sir. It belongs to my parents. Their names are here on the registration."

"You're a ways from home, junior. Do your folks know you're in Wendover today with their van?"

"Yes, sir. You can call them if you like."

Although Ben's parents would have been surprised to hear that they had gone to Wendover instead of going to the coast, Cliff understood why Ben had offered to call them. Maple the waitress had warned them about this man. The sheriff was less likely to hassle them and less likely to take the law into his own hands if some parents were alerted. But the sheriff ignored Ben's offer and instead turned to Cliff. "How about you, boy? You got some identification?"

"Only a Student Body Card. I don't have my driver's license yet."

"Well, fish that card out and make it snappy."

"Do you mind telling us what this is all about?" Ben asked.

"We had some trouble at the diner last night. A lot of people were hurt, including my son. Were you boys at the Open Flame Bar and Grille last night?"

Cliff wondered if Ben would deny it, but he wasn't surprised when Ben immediately told the truth. The sheriff had obviously been given a good description of the vehicle, and lying would only have made matters worse.

"Yes, we were, officer, and we didn't start the fight."

The sheriff removed his sunglasses. "Well, well. So we finally caught up with you."

"There's nothing to catch up with. We did *not* start that fight."

"Didn't start it, eh? Then why did you leave in such a sure fire hurry?"

"We just did."

"You just did … Good answer. OK, you boys sit tight for a minute. I'll be right back."

The sheriff and his deputy returned to the squad car and got on the radio.

"Hey!" DeWorken shouted from the floor. "What if they start

checkin' under the car seats?"

"Just keep moving around quietly," Cliff said. "They won't be removing the seats. They'll just be feeling around with their hands. If you move quickly enough, you should remain undetected."

"Easy for you ta say, Reynolds."

"Shh!" Ben said. "They're coming back."

"Well, boys, it seems there's an APB on one of you."

"A what?" Ben said.

"APB," the sheriff repeated. "Do you know what APB means?"

"It means All Points Bulletin," Cliff said.

The sheriff nodded his head. "Bingo! And you seem to fit the description."

"Whose description?" Cliff said.

"The description of two police detectives who talked with you once before. A certain Detective Anderson and a certain Detective Burns. I have the report right here … Skinny … redheaded … freckled … same name as on your Student Body Card. Your name is Clifford Reynolds, isn't it?"

"Yes."

"Well, then, you're the man of the hour. Apparently they asked you not to leave town, and you left anyway. They'll be here soon to ask you some questions. In the meantime, why don't you boys hop in the squad car and come back to the police station with us? We have a few questions of our own."

"Let my friend go," Cliff said. "Those detectives aren't looking for him." Cliff didn't think that would matter, but he said it anyway, hoping Ben would view it as a courageous gesture. Cliff was very anxious to redeem himself in Ben's sight. Still, he was relieved when the sheriff said, "No, we want both of you. The detectives might not be interested in your friend, but *I* am."

"If there's anything you want to ask us, you can ask us right here," Ben said.

"That's where you're wrong, junior. Both of you are under arrest. Now we can do this peaceful-like or I can slap some handcuffs on you.

Which will it be?"

Ben and Cliff got out of the van and into the backseat of the squad car without any more protests. Never before had Cliff been inside a police car, and being there now did not exactly feel like the high point of his life.

"What about my van?" Ben said.

"It'll be towed to the station. Once we clear this mess up, you'll get it back. You boys cooperate, and we'll get you out of here fast as lightning. But you give me any trouble, and you'll be getting real familiar with my jail, every bar on the cell, every crack in the ceiling. Understand?"

"'Yes, sir," Ben said.

"Now before we head for the station, there were three of you at the restaurant. Where's your friend?"

"We left him at the carnival," Cliff lied.

"The carnival? Why is he there while the two of you are driving around?"

"He liked it more than we did."

"What's your friend's name?"

"Harold," Cliff lied again.

"Harold what?"

"Harold Hoopengarten."

Cliff could tell by the look on Ben's face that this new lie was not going very well. It would have been better if he'd offered a more natural-sounding last name, such as *Williams*. But it was all happening too fast to think.

"Harold Hoopengarten. You just made that name up, didn't you?"

"No, sir. It's his real name. At least, that's what he told us. You see, we never knew him before. We picked him up hitchhiking. That's why we left him at the carnival. He's not from our hometown anyway."

"OK, boy. For now, we won't worry about your friend. But we can run a check on that stupid-sounding name real easy-like. If you're lying, I'll find out, and I won't be very happy to know that you lied to me. Understand?"

"Yes, sir."

"All right. Buckle up, boys."

The sheriff's station was only ten miles away, but to Cliff, it seemed like hours, hours of horrible anticipation. Cliff had no idea how to get out of this one. He even doubted that Ben would be much help, not against a crooked sheriff protected by the law and all its powers.

They finally arrived. The deputy escorted them inside a modest, rustic-looking building. There was an older woman behind a desk, using a typewriter of all things. There wasn't one computer in the room. Could the little town of Wendover possibly be more backward? Other than the typing secretary, the place seemed empty.

The sheriff confiscated everything: their wallets, watches, keys, even Ben's cell phone. All items were placed in a small plastic bag, and the bag was set on a shelf. Cliff was surprised that they didn't take any fingerprints. Instead, the sheriff simply said, "All right, boys, just follow me."

Then he and the deputy led them down a gloomy corridor to a section that had three separate cells. They were all empty. The deputy opened up the center cell with his key and made a gesture for Ben and Cliff to get in.

"Here you go, boys," the deputy said. "We have a nice little place for you to stay."

Ben got inside but Cliff stood at the entrance.

"Aren't you supposed to book us and process us before locking us up?"

The sheriff's patience was waning thin. "You trying to tell me how to do my job?"

"No, sir."

"Then keep quiet and get inside."

"What about our phone call?"

"Phone call?"

"We're supposed to get a phone call."

"Where do you think you are, boy? At summer camp? You think you're gonna call Mommy and tell her you don't like it here? You think she's gonna fetch you and bring you home?"

"We're entitled to one phone call," Cliff repeated.

"You wanna talk to someone? You can talk to me. Yeah, we'll have a nice long chat, you and I."

"Cliff," Ben said. "Just get in the cell like he told you."

"Hear that?" the sheriff said. "Your friend seems to have his head set squarely on his shoulders. Maybe you should follow his example."

Cliff finally got into the cell, and the deputy locked the door behind him.

"Sorry we ain't got no video games," the deputy said.

"Now you just relax," the sheriff added. "Just relax for a few minutes. We'll be back in a jiffy to ask you some questions."

Both men continued talking as they headed back out to the front office. Cliff couldn't make out what they were saying, but it didn't sound good.

"How are we going to get out of here, Ben? This sheriff is a loose cannon."

"I don't know. Something will work itself out. Only don't lie anymore. Let's just do as he says and answer his questions."

"I always thought of sheriffs as good people," Cliff said. "But now I might just hate them the rest of my life."

"No need to feel that way," Ben said. "Don't let one rotten apple spoil your view of the law. Usually the law works."

"Well, we're not exactly in Main Street, USA."

"No. That's for sure."

Cliff was disappointed that Ben hadn't said anything about his "courageous offer." He figured Ben had probably just been caught up in the moment. He decided to revisit the subject and give Ben another chance.

"I was hoping they'd let you go when I pointed out that the police detectives were only interested in me."

"Not a chance," Ben said. "He cares more about what happened at the diner. Your own trouble back home is just something extra to him."

Still no response. What was the point of acting brave if it went unnoticed or unappreciated? All at once, Cliff felt especially guilty. He should be doing the right thing simply because it was right, without any thought of reward. He started wondering if this was the kind of reflection Mike had gone through before he found *his* courage. Thinking of Mike right now, he envied him once again. Not only was Mike gaining more courage, he had also been spared the arrest, which would have tested his courage once again.

"What do you suppose Mike is doing right now?" Cliff said to Ben.

"Sitting in the cave, waiting for us to return, and pretending to be interested in whatever stories old Andy is telling."

"Hey, wait a minute, Ben! I just thought of something. They have to read us our rights."

"I don't think they care much about our rights, Cliff."

"No, you don't understand. If they didn't read us our rights, they have to let us go."

"Are you out of your mind? You think that sheriff is gonna let us go?"

"He has to, Ben. It's the law."

"Cliff, you need to return to reality."

"I'm telling you, we caught him in a legal loophole. He can get into big trouble for not reading us our rights. He'll have to let us go."

"That'll be the day."

"I'm serious."

"So am I, Cliff. Now you just keep your mouth shut and don't be making things worse. In case you haven't noticed, the sheriff doesn't like it when you remind him of the proper procedure."

"But Ben ..."

"I'm telling you, THIS sheriff isn't letting anyone go."

"He'll have to."

"Forget it, Cliff. Just put it out of your mind. You said yourself he's a loose cannon. So let's just cooperate, and who knows? Maybe they'll let us out of here quickly like he promised."

"That promise didn't exactly make me feel better. I don't think this man can be trusted."

"You're probably right. But what choice do we have? Let's try the path of least resistance. Besides, if he can't be trusted, then he can't be trusted to care about your legal loopholes either."

Thirty minutes later, the sheriff and deputy returned to the cell, opened the door, pulled up some chairs, and sat down next to the boys.

"OK, boys. Let's take it from the top. Describe what happened last night, from the moment you entered the diner to the moment you left."

"Excuse me, Sheriff," Cliff said. "But I know something about our rights, and we don't have to answer any questions."

The sheriff suddenly turned silent, as if Cliff's words had pulled a plug. His raised eyes had a look of mischief. He slowly moved closer to Cliff. "You a lawyer?"

"I've studied civics in high school."

"Oh really? Well how about that? Ain't that nice? You getting all this, Ed? He's studied civics in high school. He knows all about the law." The sheriff leaned in closer. "Know this, you smart-mouthed little guttersnipe ... The only thing you need to know about the law today is that *I am* the law! The only law you're gonna find in *this* town. You're a far cry from the big city. The sooner you boys catch on to this important little detail, the better off you'll be."

"The law is the same no matter where we are, and we don't have to talk to you without an attorney. In fact, you didn't even read us our rights. That means you have to let us go."

Ben started shaking his head back and forth. Cliff wasn't surprised, since he was doing just exactly what Ben had asked him not to do.

The sheriff pressed his face against Cliff's. "What did you say? We have to do what?"

Cliff responded timidly and with less certainty. "You have to let us ... um ... you have to let us go."

The deputy was laughing, and the sheriff had a big smile pasted on his face. "Let you go, eh? Why do we have to let you go? Please explain it to us."

"Because you never read us our rights. According to the Miranda law, that means you have to release us."

"Miranda? Ed, do you know anything about a Miranda?"

"Gee, I never met her, and I thought I'd dated every pretty girl in town."

"You were supposed to read us our rights. And you were supposed to tell us that we're entitled to an attorney."

"Ed, did you hear me read them their rights?"

"Sure did, Sheriff."

"Whew ... that's a relief. So you can be my eyewitness then?"

"Sure will, Sheriff. I'll even swear it in court."

"And Ed, did you hear them say they didn't want a lawyer?"

"Sure did, Sheriff."

"I thought so. I thought we heard this kid say he knew so much about civics and all that he didn't even need a lawyer."

"Yeppers ... that's what he said, all right."

"There you are, boys. Now who do you think they're gonna believe? Two high school delinquents out on the prowl or two respectful law officers who are only trying to keep the peace, who have dedicated their entire lives to fighting crime and injustice?"

The utter injustice of the situation was melting Cliff's remaining timidity. "This is an outrage!" he shouted.

The sheriff slapped him hard against the jaw. Cliff keeled over. Ben got out of his chair, took a few steps toward the sheriff, and then stopped.

"You look like you wanna come after me," the sheriff said to Ben. "You also look smart enough not to. Why get yourself in even more trouble than you're already in?"

But Ben spoke bravely. "When it comes out, mister — when all of this comes out in the open — you're the one who will be in trouble."

"In trouble for what? Because the kid attacked me and I had to stop him?"

"OK, mister, we'll see. We'll just see about that." He helped Cliff up. "You all right?"

Cliff nodded. He was bothered that Ben didn't go after the sheriff the way he would have gone after any other bully, but he knew it would have been pointless for Ben to challenge the law like that. It would only get them both into more trouble … if such a thing were possible … if more trouble than this actually existed.

"OK," the sheriff said, "let's go back to the office to get fingerprinted."

Cliff found the delayed fingerprinting very odd at first since the sheriff hadn't been too concerned about doing things by the book up until now, but it suddenly made sense. Cliff had gotten to him. Sure. That was the only explanation. Even though his lying deputy would help him in court, Cliff had still scared the sheriff, at least a little. He was going to book them properly now and clean up the informalities as much as possible, especially with two city police detectives on their way who would have an agenda of their own and not care about the diner incident.

Walking down the corridor and getting closer to the front office, Cliff could overhear the secretary talking to some man.

"I'm sure the sheriff will be happy to let you see them. Please have a seat."

"Thank you, ma'am."

Stepping into the office, Cliff saw a middle-aged gentleman with a dark suit and briefcase seated comfortably with a peaceful look on his face, as if to suggest that he didn't have a care in the world.

The man smiled warmly when he saw the boys. "There you are. Having a bit of trouble today, are you?"

"Do we know you, mister?" Ben asked.

"Let's just say I was sent by a mutual friend." He stood up to extend his hand toward the sheriff. "Sheriff Watson, I presume."

The sheriff did not take his hand. "Who are you? And what do you want? We're busy right now."

"Yes, I'm sure you are, Sheriff. I represent these two kids. I'm their legal counsel."

Cliff could see that the sheriff was quite astonished. Why shouldn't he be? He knew full well nobody had called an attorney, which made this whole thing a mystery — a welcomed mystery, but a mystery.

"Allow me to introduce myself," the stranger said. "Charles C. Troubleshooter, Attorney-at-Law."

The sheriff frowned. "Charles C. Troubleshooter? What the Sam Hill kind of name is that?"

"Oh, our firm goes way back. 'Lewis, Brooster, and Troubleshooter.' You honestly haven't heard of us?"

"I heard of you," said Deputy Ed.

The sheriff shot a dirty look at his deputy.

"Well, I *have*," the deputy insisted. "I heard of them."

"Sheriff," Charles continued in as pleasant and congenial a voice as one could imagine, "if we could step into your private office, the five of us … I'm sure your secretary has a lot of work to do, and I believe you'll want to have this conversation in private."

The sheriff looked like he was about to protest. Instead, he stopped himself and said, "All right. Sure. Why not? Let's all step into my office."

There were only a few chairs in the smaller office. The attorney sat down beside Ben and Cliff. The sheriff sat across from them while his deputy remained standing.

"Can I get you some coffee?" the sheriff asked Charles.

"That's very kind of you, but I'll decline. Well, Sheriff, we seem to have a problem on our hands, but I've come with great news. I know a way out of this little dilemma that will be mutually beneficial to everybody."

"*We* do not have a problem," the sheriff said. "*Your clients* have a problem."

"Now, don't be so modest, Sheriff. You know you have a problem of your own."

"Do I? How's that?"

"Well, for starters, you arrested two innocent people."

"Hmm … a lawyer who says his clients are innocent. There's

something new. Who else says so besides you?"

"Who else says so? How about every single eyewitness of the fight? It seems your son, Butch, was bothering an old man, and these brave boys stepped in to stop him. Now, Sheriff, I'm sure you raised young Butch better than that. Surely he knows other ways to prove his manhood besides picking on weak, helpless old men. In fact, if I might be so bold, if you could indulge me long enough to entertain a suggestion ... It might just do Butch a world of good to start taking responsibility for himself."

The sheriff reacted with coolness. "Just keep on talking, Mr. Troubleshooter. Just keep on talking, because talk is all you're gonna accomplish around here. You see, I read it differently. I already spoke with every customer in the restaurant."

"So did I. And I was so inspired by what they said, I decided to commit it to writing. I obtained sworn affidavits from each and every one of them." He opened his briefcase and handed a stack of legal-looking documents to the sheriff.

Cliff didn't understand what was happening, but he loved every minute of it. This Troubleshooter fellow was some kind of miracle worker.

"Hmm ..." the sheriff said, looking through the documents hastily. "Yeah ... hmm ... Well, this don't square with what they told me. And what they told me is already on the record. I think we'll just let Judge Carson decide."

"Yes, I've heard of Judge Carson. And I know the two of you get along great. Indeed, you go way back — kindergarten buddies, if I'm not mistaken. But even your good friend Judge Carson might have to throw this case out when he hears you never read them their rights."

The unordinary, yet wonderful, conversation was not letting up. Cliff was even more surprised at this strange, fantastic twist regarding their Miranda rights, but not so surprised that he failed to give Ben a look which said, "I told you so."

"Who says I never read them their rights? I did so read them, didn't I, Ed?"

"Sure did, Sheriff."

"Good acting," Charles said. "Oscar-caliber. But my voice recorder contradicts you, and recorders don't lie."

"Recorder? Nobody around here had no tape recorder! What are you trying to pull?"

"Easy, Sheriff, I'm happy to explain. You see, Ben called me from his cell phone the moment you pulled him over."

Ben and Cliff exchanged a quick glance, each knowing full well that no such call had taken place.

Charles continued. "He got my voice mail and subsequently forgot to turn off his phone, so all exchanges were accidentally recorded."

"Bull!" the sheriff said, looking worried for the first time. "That'll never hold up in court. Recordings are not admissible evidence! Judge Carson will throw it right out!"

"Yes, your friend the judge does a lot of things for you, doesn't he? But he won't throw this one out, not when I tell him I have proof he's been fixing the mayor's traffic tickets. That would be about as embarrassing to him as all the other items I have on you."

"What other items?"

"What other items? Oh, Sheriff, where do I begin? How about looking the other way at Miss Margaret's bordello? How about the five hundred a month to ignore those closed blackjack games? Oh, and the kickback from that drug cartel. Now, Sheriff, you don't really want me to bring all these things up in a court of law, do you? After all, once we get into court, you run the risk of bumping into a few jury members who aren't afraid of you. In fact, if I can obtain a change of venue, and I think I can, given your special relationship with fellow golfer Judge Carson, then not one of the jury members will even know you. We might even find a few old-fashioned ones — you know, the kind who think a sheriff should be upholding the law instead of breaking the law and making a mockery out of it. Now, Sheriff, do you really want to face all of this? Especially when it's so unnecessary? Wouldn't it be easier to just admit that Butch isn't quite the Good Samaritan you make him out to be? He isn't exactly a candidate for the Nobel Peace Prize, is he? I mean, who you do you think you're kidding? Butch's nature is already apparent to everyone. The only reason nobody tells you to your face is that they don't want to wind up in jail. But they see Butch for what he is. 'By their fruits you shall know them,' as the old saying goes. And so, why not let Butch deal with his own basket of fruit while you protect yours? It might end up being the best thing for him. He might just turn over a new leaf and stop riding his motorcycle with that pack of hyenas. You could end up getting a whole new son, just in time for the holidays. So, what's it going to be, Sheriff? A new son or a new job?"

Fifteen minutes later, Charles was walking Ben and Cliff out to their van.

"Now, you got off easy this time, kids. Next time, it won't be so easy."

"Where did you come from?" Cliff asked. "I mean, you're amazing, but where did you come from? Did Mike's aunt send you?"

"Loureen? No. She's a friend. I do know her, but she didn't send me."

"Then how did you know we were in trouble? And how did you find us?"

"I wouldn't worry about that right now, Cliff. I'd just get out of here while the getting's good. I put the sheriff in a quick, confused stupor. It hit him so fast he hasn't had a chance to regain his bearings. But that doesn't mean he can't bounce back. He's a stubborn man, so you better scoot before he changes his mind or before those police detectives arrive. They don't have a dishonest record like the sheriff, and I can assure you, they won't scare nearly as easily."

Ben extended his hand. "Well, mister, however it happened, we sure are grateful."

"I know you are, Ben," Charles said warmly.

"Wait," Cliff said. "How did you know about him not reading us our rights? Ben never called you from his cell phone, and I never saw any recording device."

Charles sighed and shook his head. "It's a gift, Cliff. Just accept it and don't worry about recorders."

"The recorder is only one of my curiosities. How did you gather those affidavits so quickly? And how did you talk the people into signing them? It seemed to me that everyone in this town would be afraid to testify against the sheriff's son. And the sheriff's history …

How did you know all that?"

"Cliff, my young friend, you think too much. Why analyze it? Why not just appreciate that I got you out?"

"I'm only curious, Mr. Troubleshooter. If that's really your true name."

"Cliff," Ben said. "Shut up."

"Oh, come on, Ben. Are you telling me you aren't even the slightest bit curious?"

"I'm more interested in getting out of here."

Charles shook Cliff's hand. "It was nice to associate with you again, Cliff."

"Again? But we never met before."

"That's where you're mistaken."

"Now just a minute … You're saying I've seen you before?"

"No. I didn't say that you've *seen* me. I said we've met."

"How could I meet someone I've never seen? I don't remember talking to you on the phone, and I don't chat over the Internet at all."

"Sounds like you have everything all figured out, Cliff. OK, we never met. Feel better now?"

"I don't mean to sound unappreciative. I'm very grateful for what you did."

"No problem. Only I won't always be there for you, so try to be careful from here on out. Lately I've done a lot for you and your friends."

"You have?"

"Yes. Far more than you realize. But my abilities are limited. This is the last thing I'm going to be able to do, at least for a while, although I did give Mike a present that has some power, if he uses it properly."

"You know Mike?"

"Of course I know Mike. He's waiting for you back at the cave. In fact, I have a message for him. Tell Mike not to forget the gift I gave him. It's about to come in very handy. But he has to use it properly. He can't mess things up."

"Mike *always* messes things up," Cliff said.

"Yes, I suppose he does. Well, he can't make mistakes this time. You tell him that. You tell him firmly. Because this time, your lives are in danger."

Chapter Nineteen

The Inevitable

Everything about their story was pretty astounding. It seemed to me like Cliff and Ben had been gone for days, not hours, especially with Andy as company to pass the time.

As I listened to them explain all about how they had dealt with Mr. Blake, I found myself thinking not only about what they reported, but our entire trip so far, with all the strange things that had happened in the short time we had been away from home.

Our journey had started off simple enough: just me, Ben, and Cliff, with Caligula sitting in the cat carrier. Now Caligula was gone, lost in some other world on the other side of the cave wall, which reached into another dimension or something like that, which Cliff could explain better than me, or at least he thought he could explain it.

In the cat's place were two miniature people, DeWorken and this woman everyone called Tinker Bell. She was very pretty, and she actually looked a little bit like the Tinker Bell in the movies, blond hair and all. It was hard to concentrate on her beauty, though, since the amazing thing about her was her size more than her face and features. Normally I would have been sure my eyes were playing tricks on me. I guess my history with the ornament and its magic had kind of made me used to anything.

But even more amazing than Tinker Bell was DeWorken. He's the one I couldn't get over, mostly on account of the contrast. The last time I had seen him, Cliff and I were eating lunch in the school yard. DeWorken was inviting me to have lunch with him and all his rough, tough buddies. He was being nice to me because he liked my comic book, and he was being mean to Cliff at the same time. Now, here he was, that popular high school jock Doug DeWorken, no bigger than a slide ruler, sitting on the ground next to Tinker Bell, looking up at the rest of us.

So we had two more in our party now, three if you counted Andy, and who could forget Andy since he never stopped talking?

But anyway, right now, the only ones talking were Ben and Cliff.

Here they were, having had quite the adventure. Naturally, the part that jumped out for me personally was all this business about Charles rescuing them from the sheriff. I should have known something like that would happen. It sounded like a very typical Charles incident, popping into the scene from out of nowhere.

"So, Charles claimed you had met before?" I asked. "Is that true? Do you know who he is? Because if you do, please tell me. That guy has been driving me bonkers. He seems to know all about me, and I haven't the foggiest clue who he is."

"I felt the same way," Cliff said. "That is, I felt that way at first. But on our way back to the cave, everything came together for me. Yes, I know who Charles is. He's one of the two angels."

"What?"

"From the ornament, Mike. One of the two angels from inside the castle in the glass. The good angel … Well, think about it. According to Shelly's book, the good angel's name is Char. Char … Charles. The biggest clue was staring us in the face this entire time."

I had to sit down. It all made perfect sense. And yet it was also so hard to believe. That ornament had been in my possession since sixth grade. And now, in high school, one of the angels inside had found a way out. I had met him and talked to him. He even bought me a gift. And somehow he was responsible, or at least partly responsible, for sending me on this unusual journey. "But he said *you* had met him before, Cliff."

"Well, I *had*, in a manner of speaking, when I made that wish to be protected from DeWorken. By talking to the ornament, I was actually talking to Charles without realizing it."

Things sounded like they were finally falling in place as far as Charles was concerned, but it still took me a second to respond. Finally, I spoke again. "I see. But I'm still kind of lost. How did he get out? He was supposed to be trapped inside. And not just trapped. He was with another angel, and somehow the two of them had merged into one being. Are they now two separate angels again? And if they are, is that evil angel on the loose too?"

"Good questions," Cliff said. "I'm not entirely certain. I can only make an educated guess. Yes, I believe they separated. Yes, I believe they have both been released."

"How?" I asked.

"As a result of my second wish, that's how."

Oh boy! Now things were really getting weird. What on Earth was he talking about? I walked closer to Cliff, almost afraid to ask. "Second wish?"

"Yes. Well, let's go back a few days so I can fill you in. There are a couple of things I haven't told you."

"That's for sure," Ben said with scorn.

"When I first made my wish, I wasn't at all confident it would be granted. After all, you told me the ornament had a mind of its own. But I tried to remember all that mythology we had read in your sister's book. I vaguely recalled the story of the two angels, and I realized that it was *their* mind, not the mind of some inanimate ornament that I was addressing. I tried to make a deal with them. I offered to free them if they would grant my wish."

Now I was more confused than ever. "Free them? How could you possibly free them?"

"I wasn't sure. In any event, it's irrelevant, because as it turned out, I never figured out how anyway. But I did make the gesture. I promised to at least try. Meanwhile, as you all know, they *did* grant my wish. DeWorken is the proof."

DeWorken was staring the other way now, not even looking in our direction at all. Who could blame him? This conversation couldn't be much fun for the poor guy.

Cliff continued. "At first I was happy with the situation. I loved seeing DeWorken no bigger than a small stalk of celery. For the first time in my life, I felt in control. But after a while, I got pretty scared. I realized I had no idea what to do with DeWorken, and I was afraid of getting in trouble. Even before those police detectives arrived, I was afraid. So, I went back and tried to reverse the wish."

"You can't reverse a wish," I reminded him.

"I know. You've told me a million times. But I was desperate, so I tried anyway. Then, when it didn't work, I remembered the deal I had made with the angels about trying to get them out of the ornament. I had been naïve to think I'd come up with some scientific explanation. This ornament represents a science light-years ahead of where we are. It would take decades, maybe even millenniums, just to comprehend even the most elementary principles. But still, I did not want the ornament being mad at me for backing off of a bargain. So instead, I put science aside, and I just made an unselfish wish. I wished for the angels to be released from the ornament."

I stood up. "You did what?"

"I was ignoring the obvious. So busy trying to come up with complex ideas, I had forgotten to try the simple."

"It couldn't be that simple," I said.

"Why not?"

"Because," I said, "if somebody could merely wish him out of the ornament, wouldn't they have done so long ago?"

"How many people would even know about Charles in the first place?" Cliff retorted. "Throughout history, those who came in possession of the ornament discovered it had power, but they probably didn't understand where the power came from. Neither did they care. And even if they figured out that some kind of entity was trapped inside, who's to say that would even have mattered to some selfish individual concerned only with getting his own wish granted?"

"I guess that kind of makes sense," I said.

"So I made the wish. I wished for the angels inside to come out."

Wow! Had this been a movie, I would have been on the edge of my seat. "And what happened?"

"Nothing happened," Cliff said. "Or so I thought."

"And now you're convinced Charles is Char, just because their names sound similar?"

"That's not the only reason. How about all the mysterious things Charles has done? Trust me, Mike, there is no human explanation for the way he rescued us from the sheriff. And from what you've told me, he's done a lot you can't explain either."

I nodded, "You're right about that."

"And when he told me we'd met before, well, that just clinched it.

This must be him. When he said we had met before, he meant that I had talked to whoever was inside of the ornament, granting wishes."

"It *would* explain why the ornament doesn't work anymore," I added. "There's no one inside to make it work."

"Exactly."

"Wait a minute," Ben said. "I thought that whenever the ornament grants a wish, something bad happens to somebody in the same room. If Charles being released was the good thing, what was the bad thing, and who did it happen to?"

Ben took me by surprise for two reasons. First, he brought up an ornament rule that I'd forgotten about while trying to figure things out with Cliff. Second, it was unusual for Ben to take interest in the ornament at all, and I never would have guessed that he'd remember *any* of its rules.

"Well," Cliff said carefully, "I thought about the bad thing, and I kind of covered it in my wish. I'm not sure if it worked exactly as I wanted, but I'm guessing that it did. According to Shelly's book, those two angels eventually became one angel with two natures: a good nature and an evil nature. I wished for the angels to become separated again, and I also wished for the evil one to be destroyed."

"Impossible," I said. "It couldn't have happened that way."

"Why not?"

"Because, as you just put it so well, the ornament does not really have a mind of its own. At least not the ornament itself. It is the two creatures inside of the ornament who think and feel and grant wishes. So when you made your wish, only *they* could have granted it. Why would the evil angel have agreed to be destroyed? What did he do? Kill himself?"

"Once again, the two angels had become one. My wish had to do with the separation."

"Same problem. So they separate. So what? Now there's two of them again. What made the bad one choose to disappear?"

"Maybe the bad one did nothing. A bad thing does not have to come from the bad angel. Maybe my wish merely gave Charles the strength he needed to destroy his opponent, and therefore, even though the evil angel is evil, something bad happened to him — personally bad for him, good for the rest of us because now he's gone."

"I don't think that can happen," I said. "Angels are immortal. They can't die."

"Oh?" said Cliff. "And just exactly how do you know that? Did you read it in some rule book? What do we know about angels? I'm telling you, this one *did* die. I'm sure of it."

"Wow," I said. "Pretty dangerous wish. If it didn't work, you now have some evil creature very mad at you."

"Mad at all of us," Ben added. "Guilt by association."

"Well, it *did* work," Cliff insisted.

"Says who?" Ben snapped.

But Cliff did not look shaken. "Obviously it worked, Ben, because Charles is out and about."

Ben wasn't convinced. "So you've said. Maybe Charles is the *bad* angel. Did you ever think of that?"

"That's ridiculous," Cliff said. "Why would the bad angel have helped us?"

"Who knows?" Ben said. "Who knows why half of this stuff happens? He could have had a sinister motive. Maybe it's all part of some trick and we're falling for it."

"No," Cliff continued. "For *any* angel to be out of that ornament, for *either one of them* to have escaped, it would mean that my wish was granted. And my wish included something bad happening to the evil angel. So he must be dead, with Charles, the good one, remaining."

"How can you be so sure?" I said. "If there's one thing I've learned about the ornament, it's that it grants wishes in very surprising ways. Maybe your wish just let them both out. Maybe both of them being released is the good thing and the bad thing at the same time."

Cliff looked like a man stopped dead in his tracks. "Hmm … I never thought of it that way."

"You haven't been thinking much at all lately," Ben said.

"Wait!" Cliff exclaimed suddenly.

Ben sighed. "Here he goes. Only half a second and he figures out an answer. Now Cliff will explain how he's still right and we're all wrong."

"Give me a break, Ben! The exact words of my wish were for the bad angel to die. So if my wish was granted, he's dead."

"But if angels can't die," I said, "then your wish might have been granted some other way. Maybe to an angel, destruction means something different than what we think of as dying. I know that's true of the angels we read about in the Bible. They end up in hell, but they don't die."

"And there's one more thing," Ben added. "You both just said no new wish can undo an old wish. According to your sister's book, wasn't it a wish that put those two angels into the ornament in the first place?"

"Wow!" I said. "You're right, Ben. At least, I think you're right. I think that's what I read in the book. It was so long ago, I'm not sure."

Even Cliff didn't have an answer for that one. "Look, all I know is that Charles is out and about. And he's trying to help us. He even sent you a message, Mike. He wanted me to remind you of that other magic charm he gave you."

"You mean the key chain?"

"Yes, do you still have that thing? He asked you to be very careful with it."

"Yeah, I'm being careful, for all the good it's doing me. Charles never bothered to explain how it works."

"Well, he still warned you to watch it carefully because it *does* work."

"OK. So it works. What difference does it make if I don't know how?"

"Charles gave me a clue."

"Just a minute," Ben said. "Charles gave *you* a clue about *Mike's* charm? When did this happen? I don't remember him saying anything."

"It was said quickly, right before he left. You were making sure DeWorken and Tinker Bell were still hidden inside the van before we took off from the sheriff's station."

"OK," I said. "So just what is this big clue?"

"Charles said the magic key chain will work only one time. You're to watch for a unique opportunity, an incident that will accomplish poetic justice."

"Poetic justice?" I said. "What the heck does that mean?"

"Haven't you ever heard of the term *poetic justice*?'"

Actually, I had. Aunt Loureen explained it to me once, and it popped up from time to time in some of my English lit classes. I figured I'd better assure Cliff quickly that I knew or we'd be in for another lecture.

"I know, Cliff. It means somebody gets what he deserves."

"Partially correct."

Great. Just great. "Partially correct" meant Cliff was gonna explain the rest.

"It means this person who gets what he deserves gets it in an ironic way."

"What do ya mean 'ironic'?" DeWorken said.

Cliff smiled. "I'm glad you asked."

"I'm not," Ben grumbled.

Cliff continued. "Actually, DeWorken, you serve as the perfect example of irony. You always used to pick on people smaller than you. Now, you're smaller than anyone, Tinker Bell excepted. See the irony?"

DeWorken stared at the ground, wanting to say something but looking too humiliated.

"It's ironic," Cliff continued. "It's also poetic justice, in the sense that you're getting just exactly what you deserve."

"I ain't got nothin' ta do with poetry," DeWorken said. "I don't even like poems. But girly guys like you probably love them."

I guess that was the best comeback DeWorken could think of on the spot — not very good, and he knew it, the poor guy.

Cliff shook his head. "I'm not talking about that kind of poem, you stupid ignoramus."

"I'm remembering all of these insults, Reynolds. You're gonna pay for every word someday. Count on it."

Cliff moved toward his shrunken enemy. "If I were you, DeWorken, I'd keep my mouth shut."

"Or what?"

"Oh, it's not a question of *what*. It's only a question of *how*."

Ben stood in front of Cliff, blocking his path to Doug. "Leave him alone."

"See?" Cliff said. "Another irony. Ben used to protect me from DeWorken. Now he protects DeWorken from me."

Ben looked disgusted. "Put a lid on it, Cliff. You're not exactly proving your manhood by picking on a guy six inches tall."

"I don't need no protecting," DeWorken said.

Tinker Bell took DeWorken gently by the hand. "Doug, please. I don't want you to get hurt. This is how you kept getting in trouble with Mr. Blake."

"Cliff's not really going to hurt him," I said.

Cliff smiled mischievously. "Oh? And just how do *you* know?"

"Because," I said, "you're not that kind of person. Besides, look at all the trouble you went through to rescue DeWorken. You didn't go through all that only to then turn around and kill him."

"Yeah? Well, his gratitude is somewhat less than overwhelming."

"You didn't do squat, Reynolds. It was Ben who rescued me."

"With my help!"

"Like I already told ya, Reynolds … If not for you, I wouldn't have needed no rescuin'. So I ain't grateful for nothin'!"

"Fine," Cliff said. "But an unthankful, squeaking little mouse may just make me forget my decency. Be on notice, DeWorken: every time you open that garbage mouth of yours, it makes me think about walking over and stepping on you. I could do it as easily as squashing a butterfly. In fact, I'm just salivating at the thought."

"All right, knock it off!" Ben shouted.

Cliff laughed. "I'm just playing around. Anyway, that's one example of poetic justice. Incidentally, DeWorken, *poetic* does not have to be a poem. It can also refer to the unusual twists and turns of fate, like a gangster who spends his life killing others and ends up getting rubbed out himself, or a man who invents a special computer program and then gets fired because the very computer he created is now able to do *his* job."

"Spare us," Ben said.

"No, think about it," Cliff continued. "The guy works his way out of a job. It's like a riddle. If he succeeds, he fails. If he fails, he succeeds."

"Your examples don't help me, Cliff," I said.

"Why not?"

"Because nothing changes the fact that I'm holding an unusual magic charm, and I still don't understand how it works."

"But now you have a clue."

"Some clue: poetic justice."

"It'll come to you."

"How?"

"Through your intuition."

"Now you sound like Aunt Loureen. My intuition never worked very well."

"I think Charles meant that you would know how to use the charm at that exact moment when you *need* to use the charm."

"My suggestion," Ben said, "is that we not even allow ourselves to get into a position where we need the charm or any other help from Charles. We finished our mission. DeWorken has been rescued. We've accomplished everything we came out here for. So let's all pile back in the van and head for home. Andy, you're welcome to come with us."

Andy nodded his head in gratitude.

Looking up at Ben, DeWorken shouted off a question, "What about Tinker Bell?"

Ben answered him kindly. "Of course, DeWorken. Tinker Bell too. Everybody. Let's get in the van."

"But what happens when we get back home?" DeWorken said. "Where do I go? What do I do?"

"I'm not sure," Ben said with compassion. "But it's a long drive back, so we have some time to figure it out."

"We can't leave," Cliff said.

Ben frowned, as if expecting Cliff to raise some objection. "Oh, no? Why not?"

"Because it still isn't safe. Have you forgotten Mr. Blake?"

"Let me worry about Blake."

"He vowed to get even, Ben. He vowed to come after us."

"So what?" Ben said. "He has to find us first."

"He doesn't need to find us. He figures we got DeWorken and Tinker Bell from the other world, and he's quite familiar with the other world, including the entrance to the other world: this cave wall, this very cave wall where we're standing right now. It's the first place he'll look."

"All the more reason to get out of here before he arrives," I said.

Ben put his hand on my shoulder. "Don't waste time trying to argue with him. Cliff's just getting paranoid again."

"No, I'm not. I think we need to go through the cave wall at the next dimensional shift. I think we need to go inside and then make tracks, get as far from Blake as possible."

Ben shook his head. "Why would we want to do that when we can just as easily head home?"

"I already told you why. He wants to kill us."

"Once again," Ben said, "he has to find us first."

"I'm telling you, he knows we're familiar with this cave, and he knows where the cave is, and he's coming after us."

"So?" I said. "If he knows about the cave, he also knows about the other world. He'll just go in after us. So how are we better off in the other world?"

Like I said before, I pretty much knew by now that I was gonna end up in this other world no matter what. But I was stubborn and grasping for any straw I could think of to keep us out of it. Whereas before I had given in to the situation, figuring I needed to go fetch Caligula, at this moment I was thinking it wasn't worth it for a mere cat — a mean, sarcastic one at that.

But Cliff had other reasons for wanting this other world, and they had nothing to do with Caligula.

"Yes, it's true Mr. Blake could just as easily follow us into the portal, but it's a whole new world in there … probably a big world. Chances are, he'll never find us."

"Well, there's also another whole great big world *outside* the cave," Ben said. "Now that we've completed our mission, it's time we went back home where we belong. The coast is clear. The sheriff isn't after us anymore."

"But Blake is!"

Ben wasn't giving in. "So he said he would come after us. So what? Nobody knows when that will be."

"He sounded like he wanted to get even as soon as possible," Cliff argued.

"He said, 'someday,'" Ben reminded him. "That doesn't mean today."

"But it doesn't *not* mean today either," Cliff replied. "I think we should go into the other world before it's too late. For all we know, he's headed to the cave right now to stop us before we have a chance to get to the van and drive away."

"This isn't about Blake," I said. "What's going on, Cliff?"

"I'll tell you what's going on," Ben interjected. "The same thing that was going on before we rescued DeWorken. DeWorken may be OK now, but Cliff realizes there's no way to explain his size back home. And back home there are two other policemen, and these guys *are* still looking for him."

"That's right," Cliff said. "I'm concerned about the policemen. And they're not back home. They were on their way to the sheriff's jail, remember? The sheriff will give them a good description of your van."

"That was before Charles got us out of there," Ben said. "Sheriff Watson probably radioed the detectives and told them not to bother coming out."

"Doesn't matter. They still know where I live. And yes, I'm also concerned about DeWorken. Do you really think we're going to figure

308

out how to explain him in one drive back home?"

"It's still home," Ben said. "It's where we belong."

For the first time, Cliff sounded very sad and much more honest. "Maybe the rest of you belong there, but not me. I never belonged. I can't think of one thing worth going back to. I hated school. For that matter, school hated me."

"And you honestly believe this other world is somehow going to be better?" Ben asked.

"It couldn't be any worse."

"Sure it could," I said. "It could be a lot worse."

"I'll take my chances." Cliff stood up and headed for the wall.

Ben blocked him. "You're not going anywhere."

"Let him go," DeWorken said. "Who needs him? I say good riddance."

"I'll miss you too, DeWorken. Get out of my way, Ben."

"Cliff, you can't solve your problems by running from them."

"That's easy for you to say, Ben. You have everything going for you. I don't. Maybe it'll be different in the other world."

"The other world won't solve anything, Cliff. Sooner or later, you're gonna wise up and realize that wherever you go, you have to take yourself with you."

Ben was sounding kind of profound. That was the sort of comment Aunt Loureen would make, not that she had ever made that particular comment, but she said those *kinds* of things.

"Interesting philosophy," Cliff said to Ben. "Now stand aside."

"For what it's worth," Andy offered, "if he *is* going to leave, he needs to do it quickly. We're very close to 2:00 here."

Cliff looked down at his watch. "He's right. It'll be 2:00 in thirty seconds or so. I was waiting for the next shift, the 3:00 one, so that I could have time to talk the rest of you into going with me. But I see that's not going to happen, so I may as well just go now. I'll go with or without the rest of you."

"Just go already!" DeWorken shouted.

"You're in my way, Ben."

Ben continued blocking him. "Cliff …"

"I've made my decision."

"Well, it's a stupid decision and a hasty decision. Think about it some more."

"I won't let anybody stop me, Ben. Not even you."

Ben got right in his face. "Sit down, Cliff!"

All at once, Cliff punched Ben in the jaw. I never thought I'd live to see such a thing, even if I turned as old as Andy. It was a hard punch too, one Ben didn't expect, and he fell over on the ground. Cliff ran for the wall. I chased after him and tackled him right as he reached his destination. Ben got up immediately and followed after us. I managed to get a hold of Cliff's foot.

"Let me go," Cliff shouted as his arm disappeared behind the changing stone.

"Hold on to him," Ben said, catching up with me and grabbing Cliff's other foot.

And then the ground started shaking.

"It's an earthquake!" Andy yelled in fear.

"You guys need to let me through," Cliff said. "This portal is where the two worlds meet, and by preventing me from going through, you're causing instability in both worlds."

"You're full of it!" Ben said.

"Oh, yeah? Well, how else do you explain an earthquake at the exact moment of our struggle?"

"He may be right, Ben," I said.

"Never mind! Just hold on to him."

"That rock boulder looks like it's coming down on top of us," Andy said. "We better go inside. All of us!"

"Are you out of your mind?" Ben shouted.

"It's either that or we die," Andy said. "We're about to be buried alive."

The ground shook harder. Even Ben looked concerned now. "All right, move!" he said. "DeWorken, Tinker Bell. Over here ... quickly!"

And that was it. That was how careless wishes, lectures about destiny, a stranger at strange moments, Cliff's stubbornness, dimensional shifts, two connected, unstable worlds, and a desperate fear for our lives finally forced me into a land I had never been to before.

Part Two: The Other World

Chapter Twenty

A New Course of Action

I've never been very good at description. In my comics, I didn't need to write any. I just drew the background instead of talking about what it looked like. The only actual writing I did in my Arch-Ranger comic was mostly dialogue. I'm telling you this now because I wish I could do a better job of describing how the new world looked. It was like nothing I had ever seen before, and I could tell immediately that the others all felt the same way. We were in some kind of forest with weird-shaped mountains in the background that looked mostly pink with a little bit of purple thrown in. The trees were something else altogether, jagged and uneven, almost the kind of plants you would see in a Dr. Seuss book. They *were* green. That was really the only thing about them that looked normal. Even so, it was a shade of green I had never seen before, or if I had, I'd forgotten.

"Fantastic!" Cliff said. "Have you ever seen such an incredible place in your life?"

"No, I haven't," Ben panted under his breath. "Neither did I want to. We're here only because of you."

"Why don't ya slug him?" DeWorken said. "He punched ya in the jaw. Ya owe him. And *you* can take Reynolds with one hand."

Ben had a strange look on his face. I think for a moment he'd forgotten about the punch. It was an easy thing to forget. Here we were, in a whole new world. Ben had other things on his mind. All of us did. But DeWorken did a good job of reminding him, and Ben looked tempted.

Cliff stepped away. "I didn't mean to hurt you, Ben, and I *am* sorry. It's just that I really needed to come to this place, and you were doing everything you could to stop me."

"Never mind the mealy-mouthed apology," DeWorken said. "Let him have it, Ben! Slug him! Slug his ugly face right off."

"Please, boys," Andy interjected. "Hasn't there been enough violence for one day?"

"I agree," Tinker Bell said.

I walked over to Ben. "So what do we do now?"

"No big deal," Ben answered reassuringly. "Andy, didn't you tell us you've traveled back and forth between the two worlds?"

"Indeed I have."

"Well, all right then. If that's true, then the cave portal should work from this side too. All we have to do is wait for an hour before the next shift, and we'll go back in the way we came."

"We don't have to wait," Andy explained. "As I said before, time is different in this world. We can step back through whenever we want." He demonstrated by pulling his hand in and out of the cave wall. "See?"

"Even better," Ben said. "Cliff, you do what you want. You want to stay in this godforsaken place, go right ahead. The rest of us are returning."

"I wouldn't try it," Cliff said.

That might have been the last straw. Now Ben looked like he was ready to kill. He grabbed Cliff by the collar. "Oh, *you* wouldn't try it? Why wouldn't you?"

"Because of the earthquake and cave-in. It's filled with dirt and boulders on the other side. If we walk through that wall, we'll materialize inside solid rock."

It turned silent for a moment as all of us took in Cliff's words. Ben slowly released his collar.

"Terrific," Ben said. "Absolutely terrific. You did a fine job of screwing things up for all of us, didn't you, Cliff? DeWorken is right. I ought to pound your face into the ground for punching me, but I'm saving it. You know why? Because if anything happens while we're here, if one single member of our party gets injured, even so much as a scratch, I'm holding you responsible."

"Nobody forced you to come with me, Ben. All you had to do was let me alone and that earthquake never would have happened."

"Oh, so now you're a seismologist along with everything else?"

"It doesn't take a seismologist to understand what went on.

314

By holding on to me when I was already partway into the other dimension, both worlds became unstable. That's what caused the cave-in."

"I think your brain has caved in," DeWorken said.

Cliff looked down at his nemesis, "I wouldn't try thinking, DeWorken. It really doesn't suit you. You'll find thinking to be a difficult, unfamiliar experience."

"Shut up!"

"And since what you're thinking about is *brains*," Cliff continued. "Well … do you really want to go there? Do *you* of all people really wish to start discussing the condition of *brains*?"

"I said shut up!!!"

"Make me."

"That's enough!" Ben shouted. "OK, Cliff, for a while longer, I'm stuck in here with you. All of us are. But if that's the case, we'd better get a few things straight. You stay away from DeWorken. Understand?"

Cliff had a dry, confident look on his face. "Sure, Ben. Anything you say."

Funny, now that I was actually in the other world, all my worries were gone. I guess that's an easy thing to explain. There wasn't much point in worrying that something might happen when it already had. Now, instead of worrying about ending up here, I could look forward to getting home. Aunt Loureen described this sort of thing to me once before. She called it the difference between fear and hope. I'd been living in fear. Now I would live with hope. It was like how I used to dread getting homework. And then one day, Aunt Loureen said something that made a big difference. She said, "Thinking about the work is harder than actually doing it."

That made so much sense. Now that I was in the other world, things weren't so bad. At least I was here with my best friends, and at least I'd learned some courage in that restaurant fight before entering. That was probably meant to prepare me for the adventures ahead. Yes, my attitude was quite different ever since I stood up to those motorcycle guys. I hadn't thought I had it in me, but I came through.

Of course, feeling more comfortable than I had expected was not the same as wanting to stay in some foreign land the rest of my life. I was still anxious to get out of here and continue my book tour on shows like *Good Morning USA*. I knew that was a long shot. According to Aunt Loureen, I was here for some purpose. Destiny had brought me to this other dimension, or whatever the heck it was, and that same destiny would not allow me to return home until I had accomplished whatever it was I was meant to accomplish. As for what this fate would be, I had no idea, none at all, so in the meantime, I figured I should do what I could to contribute toward the group effort of getting home, even though such plans were probably a waste of time.

"So if we can't go back through the cave wall," I said, "how *do* we get out of here?"

"Shouldn't be impossible," Cliff said. "Undoubtedly there are other time portals. This can't be the only one."

Ben's eyes were full of fire. "Just exactly how would you know that, Cliff?"

"All right. I'm not absolutely certain, but doesn't that make sense?"

Ben looked over at Tinker Bell. "This is your world. Any thoughts?"

"Yes," she answered timidly. "Yes, it's my world, but not my country."

"And we should get her back ta her country," DeWorken said in a very protective-sounding voice.

"First things first," Ben replied. "But after we figure out a group plan, I don't mind dropping her off. Do you know the way back home, Tinker Bell?"

"I'm afraid not. I was kidnapped, after all. Besides, it takes more than me finding my country. My country has been conquered. I still use the word 'country' because I still think of it as my country, but what I'm actually talking about is a hiding place on the outskirts of my country — a sanctuary for my people, refugees, safe in a camouflaged area that giants have never discovered."

"Giants?" I said.

"She means anyone your size," DeWorken explained.

"I see," Ben said. Then he turned to Andy. "You've been here

316

before. Do you know of any other ways back to our own world?"

"Sorry, boys. No can do. This cave is the only way I ever went in or out, and the only way for Mr. Blake as well."

"That's good news," I said. "Well, kind of. At least we know now that Blake won't be able to follow us."

"He could dig the rocks and dirt away," DeWorken said.

"True," Cliff added. "But then, if he does so, we'll know the passage home is clear for us as well. Or at least clear for all of you since I plan on staying."

"Great," Ben said. "So the only hope of getting back home is to encounter that psychopath Blake."

And then we heard the gentle voice of Tinker Bell once again. "If it's all the same to you, gentlemen, I'd prefer not to wait around for Mr. Blake to find us. The thought of becoming his slave again is most unpleasant."

"What other choice do we have?" Ben asked her.

"Blake isn't the only one who's entered our world from your world," she explained. "Many others have done the same over the years, namely my own people, stolen for the purpose of becoming slaves. But some escaped and returned. I've heard stories about all kinds of connecting portals. Cliff is right. This is not the only one. Unfortunately, it's the only one I went through. Before Blake kidnapped me, I had never left home, but if we return to my home, I have many friends and family who would be only too happy to help us out. Somebody could draw us a map."

"Well, what are we waiting for?" I said with excitement. "Show us the way back to your home."

"I'm afraid that's easier said than done," Tinker Bell answered with a warm, sympathetic smile.

"Right," Cliff added. "Aren't you paying attention? She just told us a moment ago that she doesn't know the way back home."

Tinker Bell continued. "Blake had me in a box when he brought me through. So naturally, I have no inkling of the way back from here."

"Well, look around," Ben said. "I mean ... this is the best lead we've had so far. Does anything look familiar to you? Are there any landmarks at all?"

"I'm afraid not, Ben."

"Let's tackle this from another direction," Cliff said. "How much time passed between your kidnapping and coming into the other world?"

"A few hours at least, I believe. That's the way it felt, and of course, Mr. Blake had made many trips back and forth, so it couldn't have required too much traveling."

"Good," Ben said. "Now, we're getting somewhere. And Andy, you did some exploring with Blake?"

"Very little."

"Well, anything would help. Could you at least get us started in some general direction?"

"Yes, I suppose." Andy began looking around.

"Uh oh!" DeWorken suddenly said. "We ain't alone. They have animals here too."

Ben glanced in DeWorken's direction. "What are you talking about?"

"Look over there. It's a cat climbing down the tree. A big black and white cat!"

Chapter Twenty-One

Caligula's Zingers

"So you finally arrive," Caligula said to me. "Do you have any idea how much trouble we're in now?"

"Hey, I didn't ask you to go running into the time portal."

"And just how was I supposed to know it was a time portal? I only meant to get away from Grandpa Andy before he could 'pick up the pretty kitty' again."

"Well, I'll be," Cliff said with amazement.

All at once it hit me. Cliff had been listening in on the ten-second conversation. So had everyone else! I had been so relieved to find Caligula and to see that he was all right, I rushed over to the tree and stood there waiting for him to finish climbing down. I never even noticed the others following. Then, after Caligula started ripping into me in his usual style, things between us were so familiar I almost forgot about the others completely. But now, after Cliff's response, I turned around to see them. They each looked astonished. Andy's mouth was wide open. DeWorken and Tinker Bell were staring up from the ground like little kids at a circus, which was kind of weird since they themselves had come from a place very much like a circus — a *carnival* — and at the carnival, *they* were the star attraction. But now a new attraction was in town: my talking cat, my whinny, irritable, pain-in-the-neck, talking cat. Even Ben looked shaken, and for Ben to be shaken is no small thing.

"So now you see it for yourselves," I said.

"See and hear," Cliff answered. He approached me, extending his hand. "Mike, I'm sorry. I'm sorry I doubted you."

"It's OK, Cliff." I shook hands with him and turned back to the cat. "Anyway, Caligula, however we all got here, since you did get here first, can you tell us what you've seen or learned so far?"

But Caligula had gone silent. He just looked at me with his spooky eyes, and as always, it felt like those eyes were staring right through me. I sensed the cat's contempt, but sensing was all I could do because his talking had stopped. The moment Cliff acknowledged our conversation, the moment it became apparent that I was not the only one who heard Caligula, he stopped talking. It was almost as if somebody had suddenly pulled the battery out of an animated toy.

"What's wrong with the kitty?" Andy said. "How come he stopped talking?"

"Did we really hear a cat talk?" DeWorken asked.

"You sure did," I answered. Then I turned to the cat again. "OK, Caligula, I know you don't like to talk, and I have no idea why everyone else can hear you now too, but you still need to help us. We all need to work together."

Silence.

"Look," I continued. "Don't make me force you. Because of my ornament wish, I can make you talk if I have to. I'd rather you did it willingly."

"This is trippy," DeWorken said. "Can ya really force him ta talk, Owen? Go on! Make him talk again. I never heard nothin' like that before. It was funny."

Caligula looked down at DeWorken the way a cat stalks a timid rodent. It occurred to me that DeWorken might not be very safe if we weren't careful.

I stood between DeWorken and the cat. "All right, Caligula, that's enough. You leave me no choice. I command you to talk."

Caligula glanced at me one last time, then turned his head, pulled his paw over his face, and started cleaning himself. It was as if he was telling me to buzz off, just like he had done back in the cave, only without using words this time.

"I don't get it," I said to the others. "He never likes to talk, but up till now, so long as I commanded him, he *had* to talk. Something strange is going on. First, all of you heard him, which wasn't supposed to happen, and now *nobody* hears him, not even me. That isn't supposed to happen either. This isn't the way it's meant to be. This breaks the rules. This isn't the way the ornament arranged things."

"I suppose we could have imagined it," Ben said. "A lot of weird things have been going on today. Maybe our ears are playing tricks on us."

"All at the same time?" Cliff challenged. "Not a chance! I know what I heard, and the rest of you heard the exact same thing."

"I guess you have it figured out, as always," Ben said. "The man with all the answers."

"I'm telling you, that cat talked! Didn't he, Mike?"

"You're asking me? I've been telling you forever that the cat talks. None of you wanted to believe me."

"I believe you now," Cliff said.

"Well ... OK ... Good ... I'm glad. A guy likes to have his friends believe him."

"But up until now," Cliff said, "you were the only one who heard Caligula. How come the rest of us hear him now?"

"I'm not sure, Cliff. That's what I was just saying. Something has changed, and it doesn't look like he's going to explain. Caligula hates talking. He always has. Or at least he hates talking to human beings. The only reason he ever talked to *me* was because the ornament forced him when I made a wish. And then, even when he just meowed and stuff, like a cat is supposed to, it always translated into English around me, but *just me*. Nobody else heard him. But he always hated it. He hated that I knew his thoughts."

"If all this is true," Ben said, "why would we be hearing him now? I thought the rules of the ornament couldn't be broken."

"They can't," I answered. "Unless ..." A thought suddenly hit me.

"Go on," Cliff said.

"Well ... hmm ... OK ... ah ... well, it's just that one of the things Caligula *did* say to me recently is that the ornament has stopped working. Remember? He wasn't absolutely sure, but he was pretty sure. So maybe all the wishes have reversed themselves."

Cliff shook his head. "Not possible."

"Why isn't it possible?" I said. "You yourself backed up Caligula's story by telling us about how you might have been the one responsible for the ornament not working. You said you made some kind of wish that might have released the angels inside. Empty ornament ...

powerless ornament."

"Yes, that is what I think happened," Cliff said. "I do agree that the ornament has lost its power. But that doesn't mean the wishes previously made have reversed themselves."

"Why not?" I asked.

"Because," Cliff explained, "if the wishes had reversed themselves, DeWorken would be tall again."

"Lucky for you, Reynolds. Cuz as soon as I do turn tall ..."

"Spare us," Cliff snapped back quickly. "We're trying to figure something out right now. Hey, Mike, maybe it has nothing to do with the ornament not working. Maybe instead, things just work differently in the new world. Maybe in this new dimension, the cat is talking because it's simply natural for cats to talk. Tinker Bell, have you ever heard an animal talk before?"

"Not in my own land. But we have heard of such stories from other lands in this world."

Cliff looked at Ben as if to say, "There you go. I was right again."

"Well, all I know, guys, is that Caligula talked to me before because the ornament forced him to as part of the wish. Aunt Loureen explained to me that cats could talk anyway ... anytime they want ... even in our own world. And anyone could hear them if the cats wanted to be heard. That part had changed because of my wish. As a result of the wish, only I had been able to hear Caligula. The ornament kind of forced the words out of him. And then, as the ornament usually does, there were other things about the wish coming true that I hadn't expected. Now, even when Caligula only intended to meow, others heard the cat sounds, but for me, the sounds translated into English."

"So you heard him on two counts," Cliff said. "The English he already knew, but never spoke until the ornament compelled him against his will, and the traditional cat dialect, which the ornament somehow translated for you, perhaps by some type of telepathy which converted the message in your brain."

"Whatever ..." I said, "something like that, I guess." It was good to see that Cliff was finally on board and not thinking I was crazy for talking to an animal. Still, he looked like he was about to try explaining talking cats the same way he suddenly acted like an authority on cave wall time portals. Only Cliff could learn about something new and speak like an expert mere seconds after the lesson.

Ben interjected. "But going back to the first possible explanation … Mike's idea … If ornament wishes are now cancelled …"

"Then it's back to the old way," I added, finishing Ben's sentence. "Which means he will talk only if he darn well feels like it. And believe me, this cat *never* feels like it."

"Well, he sure seemed to feel like it a moment ago," Cliff reminded us.

"Yeah," I said. "Maybe it just kind of slipped out because he was happy to see us."

"He doesn't look happy," Andy said.

"If he was here all by himself," I said, "not sure how to get back home, he might have been glad for some company. But cats are stubborn. They never like to admit stuff like being happy or needing people."

"True," Andy added. "But the good Lord outsmarted them by creating the purr."

"He's right," Cliff said, as if making an amazing discovery. "The purr function gives forth an involuntary signal."

Caligula stopped cleaning himself, turned his head in my direction, and rolled his eyes. I could recognize that aggravated look anywhere. I figured he wanted to talk and tell us just exactly how annoyed he was, but he held it back because if he talked, that would make him the focus of our discussion, and he would hate that even more. But then, right now, he *was* the focus of our discussion anyway.

I turned back toward the others. "Look, if he doesn't wanna talk, he isn't gonna talk. It's just that simple, so we may as well go back to the plan of finding our way out of here. We were about to figure out the correct direction toward Tinker Bell's country."

"Wait!" DeWorken said. "I'm confused."

Cliff looked like he was about to tease Doug again, but before he could open his mouth, Ben raised his hand as a stop gesture for Cliff and gave Cliff a forbidding glance, as if to say, "Don't even think about it."

Probably Cliff was gonna make another smart-mouthed comment, something along the lines that naturally a dumb person like DeWorken would be confused.

Instead, Ben, after preventing Cliff's comment, spoke gently to DeWorken. "What are you confused about?"

"Well, you guys keep talkin' about the ornament's wishes reversing themselves. Then why am I still small?"

"For that," Ben said, "you'd have to ask Mike. He's the ornament expert. Cliff *thinks* he's the ornament expert, but only because he thinks he's the expert about everything. Mike is the one who has owned that contraption for years, and it's Mike's aunt who told him all about its finicky rules."

"Well, not just my aunt. Caligula also knows."

Now *everybody* looked confused.

"Don't you remember, Cliff? … Ben? I told you. That's why Aunt Loureen wanted me to bring him on this journey. Years ago, right after Aunt Loureen gave me the ornament and returned home, nobody was around anymore to explain ornament rules. So I made a second wish about the cat: that *he* would understand all ornament rules."

"In that case," Cliff said, "the cat can tell us himself why everyone is now able to hear him talk."

"Which only brings us back to where we started," I said. "He *won't* talk. He doesn't wanna talk. Cats never like to talk. And if I can't make him talk, that means something about the ornament's wishes no longer apply, even though Doug is still tiny."

"But he did talk a moment ago," Cliff said.

"Only because, at that moment, he must have felt like it for some reason. His will was involved. But before, back in our own world, my ornament wish was making him talk even when he didn't want to. If the ornament wishes are reversed, that will no longer happen. So now, he'll talk if he wants to, but if he doesn't, wild horses can't drag the words out of him."

Ben sighed. It was obvious he was getting tired of the conversation. I couldn't really blame him. We kept going round and round. A mystery was taking place, and instead of just admitting the mystery, we kept trying out one opinion after another. I used to see this kind of stuff on TV news panel shows. My dad, sitting on the couch next to me, would always get angry watching the news, and he called the panelists "talking heads."

There would be some big event, a lost plane or something. Each talking head started by saying, "Well, first, let's be clear; right now, there isn't enough information." Then he'd go on and on anyway with his opinions about what *must* have happened. I had always thought the whole thing was kind of stupid, and yet, here we were with a mystery of our own, doing the exact same thing.

Andy placed his hand on my shoulder. "Mike, maybe he would talk if we gave him more of a chance."

"Don't count on it, Andy."

Andy ignored me and kneeled on the ground facing Caligula. Then he made a motion with his hand. "Here, kitty. Here, kitty, kitty, kitty …"

I sighed. "Just leave him be, Andy."

But Andy wouldn't let up. "Maybe the poor kitty's just frightened."

And then it happened. Caligula cut loose. Not only did he talk, he talked loudly and directly at Andy. I guess Andy's comment was the "straw that broke the camel's back." At least, that's what Aunt Loureen would have called it.

"Oh, I'm frightened all right, old man. Frightened that you might start talking again. You already sucked up all the oxygen from our own world. Are we really going to have to listen to you in *this* world as well?"

There they were again, all of my companions with mouths hanging open like before. Only this time, each person was smiling, except Ben. Ben was just as astonished, but he wasn't smiling. I guess he didn't like cats whether they talked or not. Andy seemed to be smiling more than anyone, even though Caligula had just taken quite a shot at the poor guy. I actually liked what he said, and probably everyone else felt the same way about Andy never shutting up, but the bigger thing right now was a talking cat. I don't think anybody much cared about what *kinds* of words were coming out of his mouth, just that he was talking, period.

And Caligula wasn't finished yet either. Next he turned toward DeWorken.

"So this is DeWorken. This is the great DeWorken! The topic of conversation for the last three miserable days! You locked me in a cage and risked your lives for this little pip-squeak of an imbecile?"

I was wondering if DeWorken would be offended. I guess not, because now he was laughing harder than ever. Probably the idea of a cat talking was so funny to him that he hadn't stopped to think about what Caligula was *actually saying*. I wondered how long this could keep up. Sooner or later, DeWorken would react to Caligula the same way as anyone else who dared to hassle him.

"Talkin' cats," he said. "What a trip!"

Caligula looked down at Doug more intensely. "I'm glad you're having such a good time, DeWorken. As for me, I haven't eaten all day, but I do know how to catch and digest small, bothersome critters. I've crunched up mice bigger than you. So maybe you should think seriously about just shutting your ridiculously stupid-looking pie hole."

Well, that one did it. Suddenly the smile left DeWorken's face. "Hey, I ain't scared of you. Ya think I'm gonna shake just cuz ya know how ta talk? Ya ain't nothin' but a mangy cat."

"Oh really? You figured that out all by yourself? Say, you're good! How long did it take you to distinguish me from a kangaroo?"

Now Cliff was laughing.

"Shut up, Reynolds!" DeWorken popped back.

"Sorry, DeWorken. It's just that the cat seems to have sized you up, no pun intended."

Ben shook his head, obviously irritated with Cliff's dumb little joke and probably just as bothered over the exchange between DeWorken and Caligula. But DeWorken was only focused on the cat.

"Now look here, ya fat blob of fur, I don't take that kinda talk from nobody, especially some ugly, dorky-lookin' animal. For your information, I used ta throw rotten eggs at cats on Halloween!"

"Oh, was that you, DeWorken? Not a very good aim, are you? And they put you on a football team?"

"Who decided to bring this cat along? Huh? Who?"

Just like DeWorken. Instead of toning things down, he couldn't seem to drop the matter. I was starting to understand why that Blake guy had gotten all riled up. When he had purchased DeWorken from Cliff, he'd gotten more than he had bargained for.

On the other hand, when it came to an exchange of words, Caligula was far more than *DeWorken* bargained for.

Caligula let out a deliberate yawn, patting his mouth with his paw, almost as if to mock the yawn of a human and jab DeWorken a little more. "Mike decided to bring me, DeWorken, and I can assure you it was not my idea. Had he asked my permission, I would have told him that instead of rescuing you, I could think of about thirty-seven thousand other things I'd rather do."

"Nobody asked for your help, cat! And nobody asked for your opinion of football. What would ya know about sports anyway? And what would ya know about throwin' stuff? Besides, whenever I tossed eggs at cats, I hit them. I *never* missed."

This was insane. Doug DeWorken, the well-known high school jock, defending himself against a pet I had owned since being a little kid. Never in a million years would I have dreamed of such a conversation. Since Caligula hated talking to humans, I wondered why he didn't let up. He actually seemed to be enjoying himself. It was kind of like a word contest. Maybe after all these days of being silent and holding it in, Caligula felt like getting stuff off his chest.

Either way, he let poor Doug have another helping: "You may be right, DeWorken. I suppose that might not have been you on Halloween. Perhaps I'm confusing you for some other ugly, single-cell-brained Neanderthal. You must feel lucky, not having to buy a mask for Halloween."

Cliff started laughing so hard he keeled over on the floor, needing to stretch his stomach muscles.

"Knock it off," Ben shouted at Cliff. Then he turned to me. "Mike, can't you keep your cat under control?"

"Nobody keeps a cat under control," I said. "But I do apologize, DeWorken. Caligula is being rude."

DeWorken calmed down a bit. "OK, Owen ... OK ... But why

did ya bring him?"

"Good question. At the time, it seemed like a good idea."

I had brought him because Aunt Loureen told me to. I had even said that out loud moments ago in this same conversation. Obviously DeWorken missed it because he was lost in thought or just slow, as Cliff gleefully enjoyed pointing out. I could have reminded him that I had just explained, but right now didn't seem the time to press the matter. What was the point? The poor guy didn't need another reason to feel bad about himself. And anyway, for some reason, DeWorken was still being kind to me. There wasn't much point in causing him to change his mind about me.

"I guess there's nothin' ya can do about it, Owen. Dogs obey. Cats don't."

I felt so unusual, hearing these more or less friendly words from a bully whom I used to fear, even though he had never gotten around to picking on me personally. But it felt even stranger realizing that I pitied the poor guy.

Caligula moved closer to DeWorken. "If you're distinguishing me from a dog, you couldn't possibly be paying me a higher compliment. Do cats bark every time a mailman walks on a porch or a Girl Scout rings the doorbell? For that matter, do we bark every time a leaf falls from a tree?"

I picked Caligula up and moved him farther away from Doug. "That's enough!" I said. "We don't need to get into a discussion about dogs."

"Oh yeah?" Caligula retorted. "Well, it's no wonder that a stupid jock would like stupid dogs. Two peas on a pod."

Cliff was still howling like a hyena, and there was no sign of him winding it down.

Unfortunately, DeWorken wasn't about to stop either. "Ya know nothin' about football, cat! I bet ya don't even understand the game."

"What's to understand? You throw a ball and you run around the field tackling people. It's not exactly like comprehending astrophysics."

Now Cliff was sounding hysterical. I don't think I'd ever seen him enjoying himself so much, probably because he was terrible at sports, and Caligula (without realizing it) was helping Cliff to feel better about being so uncoordinated with his body yet intelligent with his mind. Making Cliff or any person happy would have been the farthest thing from Caligula's mind, but it was still having that effect.

Like an unthinking punching bag, DeWorken set himself up for even more blows. "Football takes skill."

Caligula yawned again. "If you say so, DeWorken."

"I *am* sayin' so, cat! What do *you* do all day? Ya clean yourself! Big talent!"

"Considering that foul odor coming from your direction, DeWorken, might I suggest it's a talent you'd do well to master?"

"I haven't had a chance ta take no bath!"

"Apparently not for at least a year or two."

"So cats are clean! Big freakin' deal! Have ya ever done anything useful?"

"You mean more useful than *your* contribution to society? You spend hours a day practicing, for what exactly? So people can pay good money to sit in the bleachers and watch you play ball?"

"It takes skill ta play ball! And jocks do all kinds of important stuff after they finish school. Who do ya think fights for their country? It ain't the science geeks!"

"Oh?" Andy said, looking interested. "Are you planning on enlisting in some branch of military service? That's very commendable."

"You bet I am! Just as soon as I graduate!"

Caligula's eyes widened. "Graduate? Don't you first have to learn how to pass at least one class? Don't you need to learn the difference between an eraser and a piece of chalk?"

Still laughing, Cliff sat up and joined in. "I believe the Army is looking for somebody just a tad bit taller, DeWorken."

"I ain't gonna be this size forever!"

"Please, Doug," Tinker Bell said. "They're only trying to make you upset. Don't take the bait."

"Well put," Ben added.

But DeWorken either didn't hear or didn't want to hear. I figured this poor guy had spent his entire life defending himself and he just didn't know how to stop, no matter who crossed him. To Doug, the situation was the same whether it was a dangerous man like Mr. Blake or a weakling "science geek" like Cliff or a wise-cracking cat who wasn't even a fellow human being anyway and probably not worth the bother, although I had to admit, considering DeWorken's size and Caligula's threat to eat him like a mouse, DeWorken had to be admired for not backing down.

"When I turn normal size and finish high school, I *will* defend my country. Just you wait and see!"

"I didn't qualify for military service," Andy offered. "I was 4-F due to flat feet."

Caligula slowly turned his head in Andy's direction. "When I tell you how much that fascinating piece of information brightens my day, I really want you to believe me."

Now, *I* had to control myself from laughing. Sure, I felt sorry for DeWorken, but Andy was a bag of wind, and I was happy to see Caligula head him off at the pass, sparing us another story.

Cliff chimed in. "The Army looks for people with values and character, DeWorken. If you ever possessed those traits, your high school career has certainly failed to demonstrate it."

Wow! Between Cliff and Caligula, poor Doug was really taking a pounding. Both Cliff and the cat were starting to sound very similar as insults bounced back and forth from one mouth to another. I guess I'd never noticed before that my pet and my good friend had something in common: a lack of respect for people who weren't as smart as *they* were. For a brief second, I considered saying something about how it's wrong to look down on people. But I stopped myself. Why give one of them an excuse to make another joke at DeWorken's expense, something like "How can we help but look down on him?" I wasn't sure which one would have said it first, but one of them would have, maybe even both of them at the same time. They were quick, and if even I thought of that one myself, there's no way *they* would have missed it.

"I don't need ta demonstrate nothin' ta nobody, Reynolds! And for your information, I'm not joinin' the Army. I'm joinin' the Navy!"

"As what?" Caligula asked. "An anchor?"

Cliff lost it again. There he went, back on the ground, shrieking with delight and rolling around.

"OK, Caligula," I said. "Since you don't seem to mind talking right now, how about putting the talk to good use? In case you've forgotten, we're all lost in a new world."

"Are we? And just whose fault is that?"

"I suppose you're gonna blame it on me!"

"Bingo!"

"Oh, come on," I shouted back. "You must have known something would happen! You said yourself you had a bad feeling about the cave."

"A bad feeling? Yes! A cave wall that suddenly isn't a cave wall? No! I thought it was just another passageway. As I ran away from that walking, talking mop head," he continued, pointing his paw at Andy, "it looked like nothing was ahead of me."

"Really?" I said. "I thought cats could see well in the dark."

"Can we now? You should have become a zoologist!"

I hated it when Caligula talked like that. If he was shouting at Cliff, it would be another matter. Cliff really did think he was a zoologist, and a geologist, and a physicist … You name it. All I wanted to do was figure out what was happening and get out of here. But then I realized Caligula was just being sarcastic. This wasn't his way of calling me boastful or stuck up. This was his way of calling me stupid. That didn't make me feel much better, but at least he wasn't putting me in the same category as know-it-all Cliff.

"Yes, we can see in the dark," he continued, "and far more than you conceited humans have ever discovered, which means that when the cave transformed itself, the rest of you thought you were seeing solid rock. But since I have cat eyes and since at that moment the solid rock was no longer there, to me it looked like just another passageway. Catching on?"

"Well, you seem to know all about it now. So you must have known then."

"Hey, genius, just because you got here thirty minutes ago, that doesn't mean I did. I've been here for days. We traveled through time, don't forget. And I've had some time to go back to the cave and study it. So yes, I finally figured out what was happening, but I didn't know before."

"All right! All right! So you didn't know before! So I thought you did! Quit busting my chops! I thought you knew all about this stuff. You knew all about the ornament, so I thought you knew about this too."

"This has nothing to do with the ornament, idiot!"

"Stop calling me names!"

"Yeah!" DeWorken chimed in. "Stop callin' him names!"

"And it does so have to do with the ornament," I continued. "This is the world the ornament comes from, and you already know stuff about the ornament."

"The ornament, yes, and how the ornament related to you, yes! But nothing else and certainly nothing about this new dump!"

"Well, if *you* didn't know with all your ornament facts, how on Earth was I supposed to know?"

"You're not *on* Earth anymore, Columbus. You've discovered a whole new world. And like Columbus, you discovered it accidentally."

"You mean this is another planet?" Cliff asked.

"What?" Caligula said, glancing at Cliff and looking as if he had just remembered that there were a few more people in our group he hadn't cut into yet.

"Well," Cliff said, "I realize we're in another world so to speak, but I wasn't thinking of this as some other planet in a separate solar system or another galaxy. To me, it seems more like another dimension."

Caligula approached Cliff and looked up at him. I have to admit, Cliff had been so annoying on this trip that a part of me was actually looking forward to what the cat might say.

"Oh, is that the way it seems to you Copernicus? Well, putting aside the fact that I could care less whether this world is another dimension or another galaxy or a cesspool on Pluto, you just heard me tell your idiot friend Mike that I know nothing about this place. Just what part of the phrase 'I don't know' are you failing to understand?"

"Well, you knew it was another world," Cliff said.

"And your first words to me were that we are in trouble," I added.

"Obviously we're in some other kind of world," Caligula said with a big sigh and a bigger frown. "Nobody walks through a cave and sees landscape like this without realizing he's in another world. And obviously an unknown world is bound to mean unknown danger. But, believe me, I'm as clueless as the rest of you, and considering the premium on bright ideas around here, that's saying quite a mouthful!"

But Cliff was not one to give up easily. "Oh, come on! There must be something you can tell us. This place looks so fascinating."

"Fascinating eh?"

"Come on, cat. What do you know about this world?"

"You want my appraisal of this world? Do you? OK: It sucks raw eggs!"

"Details!" Cliff insisted. "We need details!"

"It sucks them with two straws! Happy now?"

For the first time on our trip, Cliff was at a loss for words. Clearly he'd met his match in Caligula. He walked over to a fairly large-size boulder and sat down, quietly reflecting on the situation.

I approached the cat. "Take it easy, Caligula. If you don't know, you don't know. It's fine. But you must know at least something. You said you studied the cave for days. *There's* something we can talk about. The cave! Why didn't you just cross back into our world after you figured out what was going on?"

"Because my cat vision saw the other side, and it was blocked with rocks and rubble."

"But if you were here for days …"

"It's the time difference," Cliff said, as if welcoming a chance to participate again by talking about a subject he understood well. "However many days he was here, the pathway back evidently connected to sometime *after* the cave-in."

"But if it had already caved in," I said, "then that would mean we had already transported to this side since we ran through in time to avoid the cave-in."

"Not necessarily," Cliff said. "Caligula could have been sitting in front of the cave wall prior to our arrival, nevertheless looking back at our world and seeing the view hours after we went through, or years after we went through, for that matter. And when we entered this world we apparently entered *after* Caligula was studying the wall and looking back in time."

"This is confusing," I said.

"It sure is," DeWorken added.

"It's like I tried to tell you boys earlier," Andy said. "Time passes at a different rate in each world."

"Although," Cliff said, pacing, scratching his chin, and talking like he was lecturing a classroom of students far more fascinated with the topic then we were, "in your case, Andy, you always returned at the exact moment you left. Clearly this would not have been the situation with Caligula had he walked back through. So something shifted. We're dealing with an additional variable, a random element, possibly the instability caused by the attempt on Ben's part to keep me from entering the portal, the same instability which created the very cave-in we're discussing."

I was never gonna understand the time stuff, and I didn't wanna try anymore. I decided to get back to the subject of Caligula's speech. That would be easier for me to follow, provided he supplied some information. "OK. So you saw that you couldn't go back through. Why can the others hear you now? And why are you able to decide when to talk, without my commands making a difference?"

For a moment, Caligula almost looked happy, and such looks on the face of this particular cat were rare. "Yes, we do seem to have a new situation, don't we? Sorry, Kid. Can't help you. Don't get me wrong, I'm quite pleased with the arrangement. Now I don't have to talk if I don't want to, but since we're not on Earth, the mutual worldwide cat pact no longer applies either."

He was talking about the pact Aunt Loureen had explained to me back in the sixth grade when she first gave me the ornament for a present. She said all cats are intelligent and speak the language of people, but there was a sacred understanding amongst them to never let the secret out of the bag. The idea was that if pet owners knew how intelligent cats really were, they might put them to work, and cats wouldn't be free to do nothing but eat and sleep all day.

Caligula continued. "So I'll talk when I want, which still won't be often, but you and your clodhopper friends are so reckless and so annoying that from time to time I may need to speak up and say *something*. But *I* will decide when! Understand, Kid? Now *I* decide. Not you."

"And this is because the ornament has stopped working?" I asked. "You had a feeling it had stopped working."

"Yes, I have a feeling it's stopped working. More correctly put, it stopped working the way it did before."

"So that's why you can talk or not talk at will?"

"No, that's not what I just said. How many times are we going to go over this? The new situation with my talking is unrelated to the change in the ornament. If so, DeWorken would be his normal size again. That much you and your genius companions already surmised, although I'm surprised you managed to pull enough electricity out of your brains to figure it out. It was very out of character."

I decided I'd better ignore each insult, or I'd never get through the conversation. He didn't have to talk to me anymore if he didn't want, but at the moment, for whatever reason, he *was* talking, so I figured I should take advantage of the situation and at least get any information that he might have, even if he knew nothing about the new world.

"OK, OK ... So it isn't because of the ornament. Why is it then?"

"Search me."

"Wait! But if you know the ornament has nothing to do with your talking, then you must know what the real reason is."

"Oh, I must know, eh? Says who? For a person who shows interest in learning rules, you certainly don't hesitate to make up your own rules as you go along. It doesn't work that way, Kid. Since I was given ornament knowledge, I would know if the ornament had something to do with my talking. And that much I can tell you. The change in the ornament has nothing to do with my talking. But just because I know what *didn't* cause the change, that doesn't mean I know what *did* cause it. Catching on?"

"Well, what about our other idea?" I asked. "That maybe in this world it's just natural for cats to talk, so you kind of changed after going through the portal."

"It's as if the shift into this dimension acclimated you to fit your surroundings," Cliff said. "And for that matter, since it's natural in this world for certain people to be tiny, that could mean that DeWorken is now in a natural state as well."

"Shut up, spaz! This ain't my natural state!"

"Actually," Caligula said to Cliff while ignoring DeWorken, "you may be on to something. I don't know. I seriously don't know, but for what it's worth, it may be just as you're guessing."

"OK," I said. "Well, thanks for telling us that much at least. I mean, I know you don't have to talk. So what now? Are you gonna stay with us or take off on your own?"

"Me? Explore this hellhole on my own? Are you out of your mind? No, much as I hate to admit it, there is safety in numbers, so I'll stay with you, but for crying out loud, try to shut Andy up once in a while, and DeWorken too. For that matter, I don't really care to hear any more of Cliff's brilliant lectures either. Ben is not so bad. Neither is Tinker Bell. But the truth is, if all of you gave your mouths a vacation once in a while, I'd be very grateful."

"OK," Cliff said. "That's all we're going to know for now about your voice. So let's get back to that other comment you just made about the ornament."

"Didn't take him long, did it?" Caligula said with a frustrated grumble. "No sooner do I make my request to be left out of the fascinating conversation than Professor Plumb starts right in with a new subject."

This time DeWorken laughed. It was as if everyone was taking turns having a round with Caligula, as previous victims of his wit got a time-out and were treated to the amusement of watching him take on somebody else.

"What I mean," Cliff said, "is that I'm of the opinion you were right about the ornament not working anymore, and I know why. As I was telling these guys, I made a deal with the angels that I'd wish for them to be set free from the ornament if they granted my wish. So that's why the ornament doesn't work anymore. There's nobody in there to make it work."

Caligula merely stared at Cliff as if there was nothing at all about his idea that was of any interest to him.

This was making Cliff uncomfortable, but he decided to continue. "Anyway, I never saw them come out with my own eyes, but I'm pretty sure that's what happened. So am I right?"

Caligula still stayed silent.

"He doesn't know," I said.

"But this is about ornament stuff. And didn't he tell you that the ornament stopped working?"

Ben interjected. "Mike said he doesn't know. We're not going to get any more information from that cat. And just in case nobody else has noticed, the sun is starting to go down."

"Or some sun," Cliff said. "This could be another planet circling a star in a solar system thousands of light-years from Earth."

Ben was getting very frustrated. "I didn't point out the sunset to hear an astronomy lesson. It's getting dusky. We need to find someplace to make a camp or something for the night."

Cliff didn't seem to care. "Well, I'm still in the middle of something here, Ben."

"Fine. Talk to the cat. Talk all you want. I'm going to look for some firewood."

"Need help?" Andy asked.

"Yes," Ben said. "From everybody."

Ben gave Cliff a cross stare, and it was clear that "everybody" really meant Cliff since Ben probably figured that the rest of us would all volunteer like Andy just had, although there wasn't much DeWorken and Tinkerbell could do, except maybe find a few twigs that to them would be the size of logs.

"I'll help with the wood," Cliff promised, "but I want to settle this other matter first. Because if Caligula is sure the ornament isn't working anymore, then this is a corroboration of my theory regarding Charles. He is one of the angels, and both of them were set free."

This time Caligula *did* answer. "I told your friend Mike that

I *thought* the ornament stopped working. The kid's wish gave me a lot of knowledge about the ornament, but I never knew absolutely everything, and I never claimed to know absolutely everything."

"That's right," I added. "He did say that before. He doesn't know everything."

"Sometimes it was feelings and impressions."

"That makes no sense," Cliff said.

Caligula almost hissed. "Look, braniac, I don't make the rules. Take it up with the complaint department if you can find one in this real-life nightmare."

"Thanks for nothing," Cliff said.

"Actually, Cliff, he's telling the truth. Aunt Loureen says the ornament answers a wish only within reason. That's the way she put it."

"Aunt Loureen," Caligula mumbled, almost to himself. "The day she decided to trust you with something as dangerous as the ornament, her brains must have been out for pizza."

"Yeah, well at least when she's around, she tries a little harder to answer my questions."

"Don't you think I'm trying?" Caligula said. "Don't you think I'd tell you everything I could if it were at all possible."

"No," said Cliff. "I don't. You don't seem to like us very much."

"Really? What gave it away? No, I don't care much for people. There's very little about them that interests me unless they're putting something in my food dish, and even then, I lose interest if it isn't exactly the right brand. And I especially don't like being whisked off a nice, comfortable sofa, kidnapped, stuffed inside a cat carrier, and forced into another world because some crotchety old coot escaped the rest home, went on a field trip to a cave, and decided to 'pet the pretty kitty,' creating a situation where running accidentally into a time portal was the only way I could dodge the miserable old buzzard. Still, if I *could* tell you more, I would, because maybe then you'd all shut up and leave me alone."

"You don't have to talk to us anymore if you don't want to," I reminded him.

"True, but I still have to listen, and if I don't answer, you go on and on. At first I only had to deal with *you*. Now there's a whole peanut gallery listening in. Oh, happy days are here again!"

"All right," I said. "Forget it. We won't bother you anymore. But can you a least give us a break and not be so rude just because we wanted a little information? Was it really such a wild thought? You got here first. We thought you might know something."

"Look, Kid. If you want to find out about this new world, I suggest you ask somebody who actually lives here."

"We already asked Tinker Bell. She's being as helpful as possible, but even *she* doesn't know how to get home."

"Who said anything about asking Tinker Bell? Ask him!"

"What? Ask who?"

"Him!"

Caligula was lifting his paw, as if pointing out something behind me.

I turned around. Sure enough, in the distance, we could see the silhouette of a tall, thin man holding on to some kind of staff, like the kind shepherds use. It was hard to make out his features in the dusk.

"How long has he been there?" Cliff said quietly, almost under his breath.

Ben moved in. "If he's been watching the two of you spar with that cat, he might have been listening for a long time."

"Who do you think he is?" I said to Ben.

Ben lowered his voice. "Nobody panic. Just keep your nerves about you."

It was eerie, knowing this could be our first encounter with an alien of the new world. Sure, we'd already met Tinker Bell, but that didn't seem as unusual since we were still in our own world when we met her.

The stranger seemed to be wearing a robe and a long beard, but I could just barely see because, like I said, it was getting dark and we were really only viewing a silhouette.

"Caligula," I said. "Is he really from this world?"

"Looks that way to me, Kid. Anyway, I hope so. If he *is*, you won't be busting *my* chops anymore."

Whoever the man was, he started moving toward us. The staff was higher than his head, and it kept touching the ground as he slowly approached, one quiet step at a time.

Our group started huddling closer together, out of instinct I guess, or fear. I sure felt afraid. It was easy for Ben to tell us not to lose our nerve. I could no sooner do that than I could stop breathing, and I heard myself breathing pretty heavily. I was surprised to see myself feeling this way. After that fight with the bikers, I thought I'd learned courage. Maybe courage was the kind of thing that needed to grow slowly. I wasn't sure. All I knew was that I was afraid. There was only one of him and four of us, not counting the cat and the little people. Four of us, and I was still terrified. My journey had already taken so many twists and turns. But now I was in the thick of it, a meeting of the two worlds. This was what had concerned Aunt Loureen, and now we were about to find out why!

Chapter Twenty-Two

The Prophet

We could finally see the color of his robe, only it didn't really have much color. Just gray. His beard was very white and very long, much different-looking than Andy's beard, kind of like one of those department store Santa Clauses, except that the guy was real thin, and nobody would ever confuse him for Jolly Old St. Nick.

At first, all he did was stare. I'm not sure how much time went by, but the guy kept looking us over one at a time: first me, then Cliff, then Ben. Then he repeated himself, looking at the three of us a few more times before finally turning to the others. He glanced at Andy only once, as if nothing at all about Andy was interesting to him, which I found kind of funny since nothing about Andy was interesting to me either. For a sec, he looked down at Tinker Bell and DeWorken. He looked at Caligula a little longer. Caligula arched his back and hissed. I wondered if this meant the guy was dangerous since cats can sort of sense danger. They always hiss when they're frightened or at least when they're bothered, but then I remembered that Caligula did that routine with his back and hissing constantly and at practically anything: other cats in the yard, Mom's vacuum cleaner, even me when I tried to rub his belly and he wasn't in the mood.

Anyway, this silence was awfully weird. I could see that everyone else was bothered too, but like me, they were afraid to say anything. All except Ben. He looked like he'd had enough and finally broke the silence.

"Is there something we can do for you, mister?"

The man turned out to be very kind and friendly, which was a relief to all of us. "No, lad. There is nothing at all that you can do for me, but I believe there is much I can do for you."

The fellow almost talked Irish or Scottish, the way he called Ben "lad." In a way, he even seemed to have that same kind of accent, but not exactly Scottish and not really Irish either. Just kind of similar. I figured he couldn't be one of those nationalities anyway since this was a different world. Then again, he did speak English. It sounded so natural, at first I didn't even think about it, but then it hit me: a person from a different world should not be speaking the language of our world. True, Tinkerbell spoke English, but only because Mr. Blake taught her. English was not her natural language. Also, Andy had already told us that when he visited this world before with Mr. Blake, the few people they encountered spoke unfamiliar languages. That's what made the English so amazing and confusing at the same time. I wanted to ask about the English, but at the moment, it just seemed better to let Ben do all the talking.

"You can help us?" Ben said. "How? You don't even know who we are. For all you know, we may not need any help."

"That's where you're mistaken, lad. I know exactly who you are … I also know that you're lost."

"Can you help us get home?" I asked him.

"Yes, Mike; I can. When you are ready to get home, that is, which will not be for a while. But when the time comes … yes, I can help … And in the interim, I must help you in other ways."

He reminded me of Charles on account of his knowing my name and knowing that we were trying to get home. But his personality was different from Charles. Charles was much cheerier and over the top. This current fellow, although friendly enough, spoke with a much lower voice and also very carefully … slow … like he was constantly trying to think of what to say next. He also seemed less jovial than Charles and more serious about things. And since I could see wrinkles on his face (the little bit of face that was not covered with a beard), he was obviously a lot older than Charles too.

Cliff took over the conversation. I kind of expected this. Ben was always the brave one who tested the situation. Once the coast was clear, Cliff liked being in charge. But anyway, this time I was glad because Cliff started asking questions that were going on in my mind too.

"How is it that you speak our language?" Cliff asked.

"I know all about your language … and all about your world."

Cliff nodded and scratched his lower chin as if he was back in the school science lab doing some kind of experiment. "And you know *all* of our names, I assume? Not just Mike's?"

"Yes, Cliff, I know your name. I know Ben's name as well. And this is Andy ... Doug, a woman whom you call Tinker Bell but who really has a different name ... and finally ..." He stopped short while looking at Caligula. Immediately the smile went away from his face. "And *this* is Mike's cat."

I wondered why he didn't call Caligula by his name. He must have known the name since he knew everything else. I was also glad to see him call poor DeWorken by his first name, Doug. First names are so much more personal. I remember Cliff and I had had a conversation about that once before, and we were both in agreement that we didn't like being called by our last names. In school, my friends all called me "Mike," but in gym class, where guys do a bunch of showing off, they always called me "Owen." Everyone else went by their last names too, whether the names were Reynolds, Robinson, DeWorken, or anything else. Anyway, I was feeling so sorry for DeWorken that I myself had been calling him "Doug" because a first name just sounds nicer, and if this man was doing the same thing, it probably meant that he was nice too. He already *talked* friendly, but maybe by going out of his way to call DeWorken "Doug," he was showing a genuine kindness inside.

"So," Cliff continued, "you know our names and our language. And yet ..."

"And yet this is a whole new world," the man said, finishing Cliff's thought. "Therefore, you wonder how a man from outside your world could know so much about you. I believe Mike could help explain."

"Me?"

"Yes, Mike ... Before embarking upon this journey ... your aunt told you a little about a different world, did she not?"

"How do you know all this, mister?"

"How do I know?" he repeated. Then he looked up toward the sky, almost as if he was searching for an answer to my question. Finally, he lowered his head in a very mysterious way and said very slowly, "I know because I'm a prophet."

"Profit?" DeWorken shouted from the ground. "Ya mean you're like them carnival men? Out ta make a quick buck?"

Cliff looked delighted by DeWorken's comment. "Not profit for money, you nitwit. He means *prophet*, as in a person who knows the future."

"You're partially right," the stranger said. "But prophets are not merely about the future. We are every bit as interested in the past and present. And so," he said, turning to me again, "you were about to share with us what your aunt already told you about this world."

"Only that she was afraid of the worlds getting too connected," I said.

The stranger nodded in agreement. "A legitimate fear ... But your aunt was only sensing clouded images. Actually, this world has already been connected to your own world since the beginning of time."

"The beginning of time?" Cliff said with astonishment.

"Yes, Cliff ... Only let me state that more correctly: since the beginning of *time distortion*. I thought you might appreciate such a distinction since, within this present company, you apparently understand time and space better than the others."

Cliff seemed to like that comment, and I could tell that he was already thinking he'd made the right decision about wanting to live in this new world. Why not? The first person we met gave him a compliment. But I was also glad we had met this guy. After all, in a new world, we could have met anybody at all. We could have met bandits, deadly beasts, soldiers with swords ... Instead we met a man who knew our names and our language and who offered to help us. It seemed like a lucky break that this guy was our first encounter, but then I suddenly remembered what Aunt Loureen always told me. There is no such thing as luck, at least not "random luck," as she would put it. This was more of that destiny stuff, and since this older gentleman was talking enough like Aunt Loureen and Charles to know about our reason for being here, it suddenly hit me that just because the guy was friendly, it didn't mean there weren't rough times ahead. It just meant that *whatever* was ahead, I was meant to go through it.

"Time distortion," Cliff repeated.

"I'll explain, but not here. Let us change the venue, lads. My cottage is not far off. Right around the bend, as a matter of fact. Please, come join me. All of you. I can offer food and drink. You also need to rest. The whole lot of you must be exhausted."

"Um ... thanks," I said uncomfortably. "I guess we could go with you. Sounds good."

Ben hesitated, probably because the idea of finding a friendly human being in another world so quickly seemed too good to be true. But finally, even Ben agreed.

"I don't believe I caught *your* name," Cliff said to the stranger.

"My name is Cephalithos."

"Cepha ... lithos?" Andy repeated.

"Exactly. Cephalithos."

Andy offered his hand in friendship. "That's a very unusual name."

"Not so unusual," Cliff said. "Those are two words from our own world. The Aramaic word for *rock*, or at least close to that word, *cephas*, and the Greek word for *stone, lithos*."

"You'll have to pardon him," Ben said to the stranger. "Cliff thinks he knows everything, and the rest of us have been trying to figure out how to break it to him that there are still one or two facts he hasn't acquired yet."

The stranger gave Ben an unusual look, almost like he knew Ben was being sarcastic and he was wondering whether or not to laugh. Instead of laughing, he formed a faint smile. "Well, Ben, you are correct. There are many things Cliff does not yet understand, and our world will be a rude awakening for him. However, in this particular moment, he figured it out right away. That *is* the meaning of my name — a compound word and both of them represent the same thing more or less ... rock or stone."

"Why would your name be based on words from our world?" Ben asked. "Why not words from your own world?"

"It has to do with the cave ..." he said very slowly, just like he was saying everything else. "The cave that brought you here." Then, looking like he was happy for a chance to elaborate on his point, the stranger asked us a question — not the kind of question he needed an answer to, more like what Aunt Loureen would have called a rhetorical question. "What is the cave made out of for the most part?"

"Rock!" Cliff shouted back, looking very pleased with himself.

"Exactly," Cephalithos said. "I realize this takes a bit of explanation, but there is plenty of time for that. Come, lads. Follow me to the cottage. Let me offer you a well-deserved rest and refreshment."

Ben offered to pick up DeWorken and Tinker Bell since we would be walking behind somebody else rather than going at our own pace. He figured it might be hard for them to keep up. I could tell that Doug didn't wanna be carried, but so many weird things were going on, he probably just felt overwhelmed by it all, so a second or two after Ben offered to carry them, Doug slowly nodded his head.

"Thank you," Tinker Bell said to Ben. "It's very considerate of you."

When we reached the bend, there weren't as many trees. Instead, there was a kind of green meadow, and off in the distance, we saw the man's cottage. It was made out of stone, kind of like his name, and it was much bigger than I had expected. I guess when I hear the word *cottage*, I think of a small house. But this place looked huge, with three different stories and even a couple of towers. If the prophet hadn't called it his home and if it had a few soldiers guarding it, I would have thought this was more of a castle than a cottage.

We reached a wooden door with a very rustic-looking doorknob, the kind that you saw in movies that took place in the olden days, mostly the Middle Ages.

Cephalithos took out his key, then stopped and turned back toward us. "The cat will have to remain outside."

"How come?" I asked.

"Who cares?" Ben said. "It's his house. If he doesn't want the cat inside, that's his own business."

"I do not mind telling you," the prophet said very matter-of-factly. "Cats are evil creatures."

"Evil?" I said. "What do you mean?"

"I'd be happy to explain, lad. But later. Not in front of the feline. Do make sure he stays out, but as for the rest of you, welcome. Please, make yourselves at home."

With that, he opened the door, took a step inside, and gestured with his hand that we could all follow him in.

It felt kind of weird making Caligula stay outside.

"Do you mind?" I asked him.

"It doesn't matter if *he* minds," the prophet said. "I mind."

Caligula looked up at the stranger with a snarl. "Don't worry about it, Mr. Holy Roller. I have about as much interest in your hospitality as having a canker sore removed."

All at once, everything about the prophet changed. His posture got tighter, his eyes got brighter, almost like we could see a strange flicker of light in his eyes, and also (I might not be remembering right on account of it all happening so fast), his face seemed to almost turn red as he moved toward Caligula.

"Be gone, you infernal beast!"

Caligula coiled in fear, then turned around and ran across the meadow, back into the woods, just as fast as he could. In all the years we'd owned that cat, I had never seen him move so quickly. Mostly while I was growing up, the cat ate, slept, and moved as slow as he could from the couch to his food dish, just barely dragging that fat, fluffy belly as he changed locations. But now he was moving faster than lightning! I never imagined he could do such a thing! Sure, there were times in the past when Caligula had shown speed, like when he was chasing a bird in the backyard or when Dad was about to swat him with a newspaper for scratching the living room drapes. Still, those times were nothing compared to this!

I think this was the first time in my life I actually felt bad for the cat, seeing him so scared and all. I had worried about him before, like years ago when Dad sent him to the pound and it took Aunt Loureen to talk Dad into bringing him back, and also just recently when he disappeared behind the cave wall, coming into this new world ahead of us. But that was different. Right now, it was not about me being worried. It was more like I had never seen Caligula so caught off guard, and I had never actually felt so sorry for him.

"Gee, mister," I said. "Was that really necessary, scaring him that way?"

"It was," the prophet said, with his posture changing back to the way it was before and his voice returning to its lower, unemotional tone. "Almost as necessary as casting out a demon."

"Demon?"

"Fear not, lad. Your cat is not quite as bad as a demon. Close, perhaps, but not quite as bad. Then again, cats have no redeeming

347

virtues either. They are motivated one-hundred percent out of selfishness."

"Some cats are friendly," I replied. "At least some of them *seem* friendly."

"Quit arguing with him," Ben said. "Let's just do as he asks and go inside."

The prophet ignored Ben and continued talking to me. "Some cats friendly? Yes, there are always exceptions. Is your cat an exception? Is he among the friendlier ones?"

I could tell he wasn't really expecting an answer. This was another one of those "rhetorical" things. Since we all knew the obvious answer to that question, I just decided not to say anything else.

The prophet placed his hand on my shoulder. "Don't worry, lad. I know he's your pet, and you needn't be concerned. Even though he ran off, he did not go far."

"Will he be back?" I asked.

"He's a cat," Cliff said. "Cats always come back."

"Unfortunately," Ben added.

The prophet nodded. "Your friends are correct. He'll be back, but for now, there are far more important matters to discuss. Please lad, enter my home." Then he turned to the others. "All of you! Come in! And welcome!"

Each of the chairs inside was made of wood. There were also some wooden-framed sofas with comfortable-looking, blue-colored cushions. Everything else was stone, from the floor to the walls to the ceiling. His dining room table was also made of stone. He invited us to sit down around the table, and it felt good to be on an actual chair for the first time in days. Much to my surprise, he also opened a cupboard and found two miniature chairs like you would see in a doll's house, only they were exact replicas of the big chairs. He placed them on top of the table, one for Tinker Bell and one for DeWorken. It was as if he had been expecting them and had made provisions ahead of time.

"We'll start with some bhrem," Cephalithos said, opening up what looked like some sort of ice box. Then he realized that, for the first time, we probably *were* hearing a word from this current world, because none of us had any idea what he meant by "bhrem." Even Cliff looked clueless.

"Bhrem?" Andy said.

"Sorry," the prophet smiled. "Bhrem is a beverage similar to drinks from your own world, somewhat of a cross between soda and ale. I also have plenty of meat in storage. What do you lads prefer? Venison? Antelope?"

"Those are the same animals we have in our world," I said.

"Yes, lad. You will find many similarities between the two worlds. Many differences as well, but with two or three exceptions, the animals are the same. How about venison tonight?"

"Venison?" DeWorken said.

"He means deer," Cliff said, happy for another chance to show how stupid DeWorken was. It bugged me when Cliff acted this way. If I had a camera, I would have taken a picture of Cliff's confused face one moment ago, trying to figure out what bhrem was. Then I would have made it a permanent picture in my wallet so I could whip it out every time he acted like a know-it-all.

The meat was the best I'd ever had in my life, probably because it was our first good meal in days. But whatever the reason, the meat was fantastic-tasting. So were the potatoes he served. And that drink wasn't bad either. He also gave us something for dessert that seemed like a combination of Jell-O and strawberry ice cream, but it was neither. I forgot what he called it, some name that I probably wouldn't have been able to pronounce right anyway.

Cliff kept wanting to ask more questions over dinner, but the prophet wouldn't let him.

"Patience, lad," he kept saying. "There will be time for a nice discussion. For now, we are eating. Dinner is sacred too. Eat hearty. You will all need your strength for the days ahead."

I didn't wanna hear about needing anything for the days ahead, whether that meant needing strength or anything else. If he had to describe it like that, it meant that there was gonna be stuff in the days ahead that I wouldn't like. But I wasn't gonna let it spoil this great meal, and whatever the future might bring, the guy was right about one thing: We were all tired and drained from our adventure so far. We did need extra strength.

After dinner, we sat in the prophet's parlor on comfortable chairs. Everything in the room was still made out of stone or wood.

His fireplace was really awesome-looking, the kind of fireplace Aunt Loureen would have called "magnificent, with a ferocious blaze." The fire was started just in time. Up till now, I hadn't paid much attention to the weather or climate, but right around the time when it started getting darker and colder, the prophet lit some cool-looking green candles and started up his fireplace.

Once the room was set up and everyone was comfortable, Cephalithos finally offered some much-needed information. "To begin with lads, you are on a planet that exists on the other side of your galaxy. Even if your people should design a space craft that travels faster than the speed of light, they would never find this world. *You*, on the other hand, arrived by taking a shortcut."

"Shortcut?" Cliff said. "That's the understatement of the century. So that cave had the effect of a wormhole? How can that be? Wormholes only exist in space."

"The cave is not a wormhole," the prophet said gently.

I didn't understand anything about space or wormholes, and I didn't much care. What I cared about was that, however it happened, we somehow did get here, and I just wanted to know *where* we were. I had accepted the idea of being on another world. I had no choice but to accept it since the idea was introduced by Aunt Loureen long before we arrived, and also by Andy and his stories, Tinker Bell too. Still, to actually hear a native of the world describe our location as being on the other side of the galaxy was almost too fantastic to swallow. This was something right out of a science fiction movie.

"What's the name of this world?" I asked.

"The planet is called Telios."

"*Telios*," Cliff said. "That's the Greek word for *perfection*."

Ben didn't say anything, but he looked over at Cliff as if to suggest that if Cliff offered one more vocabulary lesson, he was gonna get slugged.

"Correct once again, lad."

"How come there are so many similar things?" Cliff asked. "You have the same animals, and you call your animals by the same names. And you yourself are a human being just as we are, or at least you *appear* that way. You also speak English, and you have a name for yourself and your planet taken from another Earth language, Greek."

"It's because our worlds are specially connected, lad. They may exist light-years apart from each other, but the caves connect these worlds nevertheless, not only in space but in time."

"It just seems strange," Cliff went on, "that the first person we find in this new world is somebody who already knows all about us."

"That *does* seem like quite a coincidence," I added.

"Nothing is a coincidence, lad. All events are watched over and influenced to some degree by the Author of Life."

"Author of Life ..." Andy said. "Would you by any chance be referring to God?"

"Yes, as you would call him in your world: God."

"So you're a prophet of God?" I asked, remembering Bible stories about God using prophets.

"In a manner of speaking," he answered.

"OK," Cliff said, as if he was racing against the clock on a game show, needing to figure everything out quickly so that he could win a prize or something. "So the reason you were waiting for us is that some kind of higher being spoke to you and told you we were coming?"

I remembered that Cliff liked using phrases like *higher being* more than the actual word *God*.

Cephalithos continued. "The Author of Life does speak at times, yes, but the situation is a bit more involved, lad. I am not merely a prophet. I belong to a very specific order of prophets called 'Chronos Protectors.'"

"*Chronos* ..." Cliff began.

"Is the Greek word for *time*," Cephalithos continued, finishing Cliff's sentence and making the rest of us feel grateful that we were spared another uninvited lecture from our friend, although in my case, I really didn't realize at first what *chronos* or any of those other Greek words had meant, and I didn't mind learning about them if somebody other than Cliff was explaining. For or a second, it occurred to me that *chronos* must be where the English word "chronology" came from, especially if it was just another term for "time." I almost said something to show Cliff he wasn't the only smart one in our group, but it would have been rude to interrupt the old man's explanation, and also I didn't care as much as Cliff did about showing off my brain. My only reason for sharing my discovery would have been to make him feel bad, and somehow that didn't seem like a valid reason. I'm pretty sure Aunt Loureen would agree. And even if I didn't care about living up to Aunt Loureen's ideals, my comment probably wouldn't have even made much of a difference. Cliff would have said something to the effect that I was only partially correct and would have explained some additional information about the relationship between Greek and English words. I'm sure of it.

Anyway, after that little hiccup about the meaning of the title "Chronos Protector," Cephalithos continued. "The reason you met me so quickly after coming through that cave is that I guard this time/space entrance. When people from your world cross into ours, it affects our world, sometimes in good ways, other times, not so good. I am here to minimize the damage, so to speak."

"Wow, mister!" I said. "The more you explain, the more confusing it sounds."

"I sympathize, lad. Let me back up a bit. I'll begin by filling you in a little on how our worlds became connected. You see, the most major event in the history of the United States never *made* history in the United States."

The mysteries were starting to annoy me. I got up out of my chair and helped myself to more of that drink. "Another riddle? I've been getting nothing but riddles these past few weeks."

"No, lad. No riddle. At least not yet. I actually do have a riddle to share, or rather, a prophecy told in the form of a riddle, but that very serious warning must be postponed until I first relay other matters. At the moment, I am not offering a riddle; I am instead offering an explanation. In the year 1990 of your world, a university professor experimented with a time machine."

"Time experimentation ..." Cliff said sounding kind of amazed and kind of skeptical. "How come I never heard about this?"

"Because," Ben said, "maybe there are one or two things that go on in the world without people checking with you first."

Cephalithos continued. "The inventor was not one to sensationalize his work. He took the importance of time very seriously."

"Well, sure," Cliff said. "Maybe he didn't want to go on television. But this would have at least made scientific journals."

"Just let the guy finish what he's telling us," Ben snapped.

Cephalithos got up out of his chair and paced back and forth a bit. "As I said, this never made history, which means it was never written about or reported anywhere."

"Then how do *you* know about it?" Cliff asked. "What was the guy's name?"

Ben kicked Cliff in the shins. "Shut up!"

"Easy, lad. He's just curious. Nothing wrong with that. The inventor's name is not important, Cliff. His *invention* is. Although the professor himself was cautious and responsible, he had a friend who did not respect the boundaries of time and space. His friend, desperate to change an event in the past, broke into the lab by night and took a journey back through time."

"Where did he go?" I asked.

"That's not important," the prophet said.

Of course, I said to myself while I continued to listen. *God forbid that anybody should ever give me a complete explanation about anything.* In my own way, I was just as impatient as Cliff, but for totally different reasons. I wanted to know what we were doing here and how to get out of here. Cliff just wanted to understand the science behind it all, and I couldn't give a hang about the science.

Cephalithos went on. "What's important is that this usage of time was unauthorized."

"Unauthorized?" Andy said. "Unauthorized by whom?"

"The Author of Life."

For some reason, Andy's face seemed to light up every time Cephalithos talked about that Author deity. "And once again," Andy said, "when you use that phrase, you mean God?"

"Yes. God put the worlds and galaxies and dimensions on full alert because of this unauthorized interaction with the boundaries of eternity: one careless, thoughtless trip through time by a man who did not know what he was doing, who had no right to tamper with history. The result was disastrous. It opened up time portals, connecting events in your Earth's history, from ancient times to the farthest future of modern man's innovativeness. And yet, time and space are not limited to planet Earth. Not only was the history of your human race connected to other times on Earth, it was also connected to other times and locations throughout the universe. Earth and Telios have a special rapport because, for reasons I won't go into right now, there has been much back-and-forth traffic over the centuries between these particular worlds. But the truth is, all worlds are connected now by these time portals. That is why the Author of Life placed time protectors in front of each portal."

This was an incredible story which I normally wouldn't have believed, but my experience with magic over the years forced me to accept every word the guy was saying, even though I found myself wishing none of it was true.

"So are you really some kind of angel?" I asked. "In my world, we met a man named Charles. It turned out that he wasn't really a man. He was an angel. I mean … that's what we all think now. We never saw any wings."

"Yes, I know of Charles."

"You've met?" I asked.

"We have not met. But I know *of* him. And you are correct. Charles is an angel."

"Would you be an angel as well?" Andy asked.

"No, Andy. I am mortal like yourself. But once again, my order of prophets has been given the assignment of watching these time caves."

"What happened to the watcher on our side?" Cliff asked. "He obviously didn't do a very good job."

"That person has long since perished."

Cliff was about to say more. The prophet raised his hand, as if to suggest Cliff stop probing and listen instead. "I know what you are going to ask, lad. Why wasn't he replaced? There are many questions and many good answers. But our time for today's divine encounter is limited."

"You promised over dinner that you would explain what's going on," Cliff whined like a little kid. "Well, all right. We've had our dinner, and we're very grateful. Now I would like some explanations."

"He *is* explaining!" Ben said.

"But I cannot explain everything, lads. Yes, I have some very important information to share, and that is what we are doing now, sharing, but that does not mean I can explain everything."

"Well, how about at least explaining *some* things?" Cliff said. "This is very difficult to swallow. I *am* familiar with Einstein's theory of relativity. I accept his premises about matter and energy. But to travel into the future or past as some have theorized, wouldn't we need a spaceship going faster than the speed of light?"

"In other words," Ben chimed in, "if Cliff can't explain how it happened, it never happened."

This time, Cliff snapped back. "Cut it out, Ben! Need I remind you that nobody up until now has doubted all of the magic and miracles more than you?"

"Yes, I had doubts," Ben said. "Any sane person would have had doubts. But we're here! Even I can't deny my own senses, and we seem to have gotten here without you needing to understand everything."

"Of course we're here!" Cliff shouted. "Have I once suggested this isn't happening? Have I even insinuated that this was an illusion? I accept all that has happened. I just want to see how it fits with science as I've known science. What's wrong with that?"

"What's wrong with it?" Ben replied with rage. "What's wrong with it? You're driving us crazy! That's what's wrong with it."

The prophet's gentle voice brought us all back on track. "I'll tell you what, lads … Let us simply accept that there is another kind of science which not all people have learned to harness. Perhaps Cliff can take me at my word that the relationship between energy, mass, and dimensional shifting exists not only in *outer* space, but *inner* space as well."

"What?" Cliff said.

"He means *shut up!*" Ben said. "It's just that he's too polite to say it that way."

"For now," the prophet continued, "what's important is that I do indeed know how you got here, and I need to help you."

"And you also said you could help us get home,"" I reminded him.

"Yes, lad."

"How?" Cliff asked. "Forgive me, Ben, and calm down, Ben. But I have a right to ask how. The cave is blocked on the other side unless we can go back to that moment before the earthquake. And even if we did that, I assume we would run into ourselves in the past, standing at the cave portal before the earthquake! And while we're on the subject, if this is a cave that connects time as well as space, how come we didn't arrive the exact same second Mike's cat arrived?"

"A fair question," Cephalithos said. "Even though this portal brings people to the same general time, if they leave your world at different moments, they arrive at staggered intervals in my world too. Otherwise we time watchers would never be able to keep track of them all. God may live outside of time and see everything in a glance, but we don't."

"I think I get the time travel stuff," I said.

Actually I barely got a word of it, at least none of the stuff about how it all worked: matter and energy or whatever. But I at least understood what was important to our journey. I understood that this strange old prophet was watching those who came in from other worlds. That meant us. That meant me. He said he could get us home, and I wanted to hear how. So I said I understood in the hopes that we could press ahead and talk about our return trip.

"If I don't understand it all," Cliff said to me, "how could *you* possibly understand?"

I was about to tell Cliff to dry up, but the prophet answered him before I got a chance.

"He merely means it's time to move on. And I heartily agree. You lads are welcome to spend the night. In the morning, I'll send you on your way."

"Send us on our way to where?" Ben asked.

"Another good question," the prophet answered. "A very good question. Actually, there are two different destinations. There's the destination you desire, and then there's the other destination."

"What do you mean by 'other destination'?" Ben said carefully.

"Well, lad, I realize your purpose is to get home. And you *will* get home, at least some of you will."

"Some of us?" I said.

The prophet ignored my obvious concern and kept on talking. "You're looking for another time cave. You were planning on going to Tinker Bell's country to find it."

"Yes," Tinker Bell said.

"But only because we don't know where else to look for another time cave," Ben quickly added. "And she thinks some of her people could show us the way. If you know of a different cave, mister, or a closer cave, and if we could just go directly there, bypassing the need to find some country first, well, I vote for *that* plan."

"Not fair!" DeWorken chimed in. "Tinker Bell has a right ta go home first."

"In any event," Cliff said, "I am not interested in going home anyway."

"Cliff thinks he's staying in your world," Ben explained to the prophet.

The prophet turned to Cliff. "My suggestion, lad, is that first you help your friends get home. You owe them that. After all, they wouldn't be here if not for you. Once they are safely home, if you really think you're made of the kind of savvy and material that can navigate in my world, I'll help you. First, you help your friends, understood?"

Cliff lowered his head in shame and slowly nodded.

Cephalithos turned away from Cliff and spoke to the rest of us. "As for the nearest time cave … As it happens, Tinker Bell's country is on the way, not far off the path, so your original plan might work. I can draw you a map. Then you can drop her off before returning home."

This was starting to sound too good to be true, especially since I kept remembering how Charles told me I was going on a special, important journey, and Aunt Loureen had lectured me over and over about destiny. Was I really meant to travel into a whole new world, only to find a way out so quickly and easily? And even if I had misunderstood Charles and Aunt Loureen, Cephalithos just got through talking about our *true* destination as opposed to our *intended* destination. What the heck did that mean? I was almost afraid to ask because I really didn't wanna hear his answer.

Anyway, before I had a chance to ask, DeWorken spoke up. "Mister, since ya seem ta know all about these strange powers, can ya do anything for me? Can ya turn me ta normal size?"

Tinker Bell looked like she was about to cry. DeWorken put his arm around her. I never knew Doug could be so tender. "I didn't mean that," he said to Tinker Bell. "I know, where you come from, this *is* the normal size. I respect that. I just meant ... normal for me."

"I know what you meant, Doug," she said. "And it's all right. I only thought ..."

"What?"

"Well, happy as I am to finally be going home, I've grown accustomed to you being with me. I thought perhaps that you might find a way to accept your size and maybe come live with me. In my country, everybody is like us. You won't stick out. You won't look like a miniature man. You'll merely look like Doug."

I could see that DeWorken was moved by her words. "I've been so eager ta help ya get home, I hadn't really thought about losin' ya."

"In any event, lad, there is nothing I can do for you, not about your size anyway."

"I thought ya knew magic."

"There is no such thing as magic. Not technically. True, you'll find the word used on Telios, but it's not magic as you would understand it in your world. We have no magic in the form of an isolated power source. What we witness, what some might call 'magic,' are abilities from the Author, from his angels, and from the descendants of those angels who fell away: demons. Certain people and certain devices sometimes channel these abilities, but the word *magic* is not appropriate."

"I thought you was some kinda guy who has power from God," DeWorken said.

"Yes, lad, but I can only do what my Maker enables. Yes, sometimes He shares power with me, and there is much I can do to help you lads, but not that. I cannot restore your size."

Cephalithos headed for the corner of the room while he continued to talk and opened up an old storage closet. He started rummaging around the shelves inside, as if looking for something. "What I *can* offer are some gifts that will assist your journey. First of all, you will need *this*. Michael, I believe this belongs to you."

It was the first time he called me Michael instead of Mike. But that wasn't the reason for my jolting response. He was holding another Christmas ornament, an exact duplicate of the one Aunt Loureen gave me!

"Is that another wishing ornament?" I asked.

"Not another one. The *only* one. This is the Ornament of Lumis."

"Impossible," I said. "How can you have it when I …"

All at once, it hit me. Never in my life had I felt so incredibly stupid! With all our talk about the ornament, with all our arguing about whether it still worked, I had never once stopped to notice that I never even brought it with me into this new world. We got here by accident, and I had put the ornament away in the trunk of the car long before we arrived in the town of Wendover. Since Caligula had insisted it didn't work anymore, I kind of forgot about the ornament until we had that big discussion about angels being released and ended up on this side of the cave wall, where we talked some more about the angels. But with all that talk, I was kind of imagining the ornament still being in our possession, and I forgot that I had left it in the trunk. Like I said, this was just about the stupidest, most absentminded thing I had ever done.

"How did you get that?" I asked. "The last time I saw that ornament, it was packed in Ben's van."

"He's right," Cliff said. "We never brought it along."

"No matter," Cephalithos explained. "It was sent ahead of you."

"By who?" Ben asked.

Cephalithos shook his head. "Charles, the angel, I imagine. All I know is that yesterday I looked in my cupboard for a different item, only to find the ornament staring at me."

"I thought you didn't know Charles."

"I don't. But, as I said, I know *of* him. Everybody in my prophetic order knows Charles, or more properly, we know him by his true name, Char."

"But until recently," I said, "Char was trapped inside the ornament with an evil angel."

"Yes, lad. You need not explain. Everyone in the world of Telios knows the story. Some think the event is only mythology, others accept it as history. But everyone knows about the Magic Ornament of Lumis."

DeWorken was frowning. "I thought ya said there was really no such thing as magic."

"That's merely it's conventional title, lad. The alleged magic was the work of angels trapped within. Many centuries ago, an earlier prophet, one of the forefathers of my order, gave a prophecy. He predicted that the angels would someday be separated."

"I remember reading that in my little sister's book back home!" I said.

The prophet smiled at me. "Anyway, this is your property, so I am returning it."

"But if the angels are now gone," Cliff said, "what good is the ornament?"

"That, I cannot tell you. I only know that this ornament still has a connection to those angels."

"Even in this world?" I exclaimed.

"Lad, they *come* from this world. They hail from this world. Yes, even in this world."

"So Charles is here on this planet?"

"Yes, Michael."

"Wait," Cliff said. "If Charles and the other angel are both here, then the evil angel could hurt us."

"He could," Cephalithos said. "And Charles could protect you from him. More importantly, the Author of Life will protect you."

"Well, if the angels are out and about," I said, "then how does the thing work?"

"You'll have to wait and see, lad. But take some advice from a new friend: Don't fixate yourself upon one mere charm. There are other charms, other tools."

I started thinking about the little sword key chain Charles had given me. I still had it in my pocket. That one I'd managed to hold on to.

And then, right while I was remembering the key chain, Cephalithos handed me something else. "This will be of great value."

"A rock," Cliff said.

"Not merely a rock, lad — more like a polished stone."

Everything about this guy seemed to have something to do with stones. The stone was oval-shaped, about half the size of the palm of my hand. It did look all smoothed and polished with a kind of off-white color.

"What does it do?" Andy wanted to know.

"Well," the prophet began, "to put this in words familiar to your own world, you could call this a navigation device. It will warn you away from danger. As you set out to take Tinker Bell home, watch this stone carefully. When it turns slightly red, there is danger on the horizon. When it turns bright red, the danger is imminent. On the other hand, when it turns blue, something pleasant is ahead. White, the current color, is merely neutral."

"Thanks," I said. "This should come in handy."

"Who says he was giving it to you?" Cliff complained.

"It's for all of you, lads. It matters not who holds it."

"Well, then," Cliff said, "since Mike already has the ornament, maybe I can be the one who watches over this stone."

"Be my guest," I said to Cliff, handing him the stone and feeling quite annoyed.

"Is that our only method of warning?" Cliff wanted to know.

"As a tool for the journey, yes, lad. But there are other ways of looking ahead. I have one more device to consult."

He returned to the storage closet. This time, he came back with an hourglass, the same one I had bought for Aunt Loureen in the souvenir shop, or anyway, the one Charles had purchased for me.

"Did that also come into this world ahead of us?" I asked. "That belongs to my Aunt Loureen."

"This is not the same hourglass," he answered. "Your Aunt still has hers. What you guessed *incorrectly* about the ornament is *true* in this case. My hourglass is a duplicate of the one your aunt has in the other world."

"What does it do?" Andy asked.

"Well, as the shape of a timepiece might suggest," the prophet explained, "with this hourglass, I can look across time and space to any era, any world."

"You mean a kind of crystal ball?" Andy exclaimed.

"No! Prophets do not use crystal balls. Not true prophets anyway. Crystal balls are deceptive. Those who use crystal balls think they harness great power, but actually all they plug into are demons telling them what they want to hear. Stay away from crystal balls."

"My aunt was planning to take a trip into this world," I said. "Is that how she plans to get in, by first looking through and finding the right spot?"

"Hold on," Cliff said. "I thought a person had to go through one of those cave walls to travel from one world into another."

"That's one way, lad. Those time portals opened up because of the unauthorized time experiment. But there are many other ways to travel through time which the Author of Life previously allowed, only by responsible beings."

"Well, if that hourglass is a way," Ben said, "then why don't we use it to go home right now?"

"I'm afraid it's not that simple, lad. Only with the help of an angel can one travel through the hourglass. In the hands of a mere mortal, all we can do is look through the glass … Oh … this is interesting. Michael, I believe I see her. I believe I see your Aunt Loureen."

I walked closer to the hourglass. "I don't see anything."

"No, you will not see anything," the prophet explained. "Or hear anything. It takes skill and training to look through an hourglass. But I see her and she sees us. There she is right now, looking at us from the other side."

I put my hands on the hour glass. "Other side?"

"The other world. Your world … Earth … and your home. The actual house you live in, where she is staying as a guest. She's looking at us through her own hourglass."

"Wow! At this very second, she just happens to be doing the same thing you're doing?"

"He's a Time Protector,'" Cliff said. "He knows how to time things."

I still had my doubts, so I asked Cephalithos to describe Aunt Loureen, and he did. He described her to a T and even described her purple dress that she wore a lot.

"Is she all right?" I asked.

"Concerned. Very concerned about you, but in no actual danger."

"That's good."

"At least, not yet … Wait. She just saw you, Michael. She's smiling. She's smiling because she knows you're all right."

"Really? So that means we'll all be safe in this world, right?

"My son, she knows you're all right because she sees you, not because she's a prophet who predicts the future."

"OK. OK … But *you* can predict the future, so I'll ask *you*. Am I in any danger? All of us … I mean … are we in any danger?"

"No. You are quite safe …"

"That's good."

"For now."

I knew he would add that last part. I just knew it!

"Come on, mister," I said. "There must be more. What else are you getting from that hourglass? Are you still seeing Aunt Loureen?"

"No," he answered solemnly. "She's gone. But she left you a message. Your lady friend has vacated her own home and ventured into our world."

"Who? What? Lady friend?"

"*Marla* is your lady friend's name?"

"My girlfriend, yes. I don't call her a lady. Marla is coming here?"

"Yes."

"How?"

"Your aunt saw her vanish into the hourglass."

Those last words were like a bolt of electricity. I had to sit down. I wasn't sure whether I felt excited that I would soon see Marla again or worried about her being in danger. All I knew was that I could feel my adrenaline flowing like Niagara Falls. "I thought you said mortals couldn't travel through the hourglass."

"She didn't lad, at least not through her own effort. Charles moved her through."

"So where is she?"

"I don't know," he said with a grave expression.

I stood up and grabbed the prophet by the collar of his robe. "What do you mean, you don't know?"

"Take it easy," Ben said.

"He just told me Marla took a trip through the hourglass, and now he says he knows nothing about it."

"Come on, buddy," Ben said as he gently pulled my hand off of the prophet. I was grateful Ben showed more patience with me than with Cliff.

"I only know what your aunt said, lad. Now her image is gone. It faded away before she could tell me anything further."

"Well, look again! Maybe you'll see something else."

"I'm seeing many things, Michael. Not all of them are related to your lady friend, but all are important. You must be careful. Someday you will be caught in a large, blazing fire."

"Excuse me?"

Great! Just great! The day was getting better and better! One minute, the guy sees my aunt. The next minute, he tells me my girlfriend is on her way. Then, he talks about me burning up. I was

364

getting so sick of all this.

"That's quite a dire prophecy," Andy said.

"Perhaps," Cephalithos said. "But remember: All of this is a warning. The purpose in a warning is to *avoid* danger."

"Anything else?" I said sarcastically and in the worst possible mood.

"Only one more, lad. Just one more prophecy. And this prophecy is the riddle I told you about earlier. It came to me last night in a vision from the Author of Life — not through an hour-glass or a time cave, from the Author Himself. So listen, all of you, not merely Michael. This warning is for each person in the room. You must take heed."

It turned cold and silent. Finally, Cliff told him to go ahead. Ben nodded slowly.

"All right, lads. Listen carefully. These are the exact words I received on your behalf:

'Tempted by wickedness,

All of you will,

Two turn to evil,

The others hold still,

One turns again,

So his soul can be crowned,

The other stays lost,

And can never be found.'"

For a few minutes we all just sat there, not knowing what to say. Finally, DeWorken broke the silence.

"What a bunch of mumbo jumbo!' It don't mean nothin'."

"Yes, it does," I said. Unlike all that talk about time and space, this one I understood very well. It kind of jumped right out at me. "It means two of us are gonna turn evil."

"And then one will turn back," Cliff added. "But the other stays evil."

Ben walked right up to the prophet and looked him in the eye. "Who? Who are you talking about?"

"Who specifically? That I cannot say, lad. They are not my words, after all. They are from above, loaned to me, in the trust that I would be a good steward and share them with you."

"Why us?" Ben asked.

"Because it applies to you. Two people in this very room will turn evil. I'm sorry. I know this is not pleasant news. But it had to be said."

Chapter Twenty-Three

Around The Campfire

The old prophet woke us up early. The sun was still rising, or whatever that ball of red in the sky really was. I guessed it was the sun or some other name they gave to this star our strange planet was orbiting. Anyway, it felt good to sleep, and I didn't quite get why Cephalithos thought he had to wake us up and send us on our way so darned early. He said something about it being important, but after my first night on a good, comfortable bed, it seemed like a few more hours wouldn't have made much difference. There were enough rooms and beds for each of us to have our own. And since the prophet's map showed Tinker Bell's country at least a couple of days' journey from the cottage, we obviously were gonna be camping — all the more reason to sleep in for a few good extra hours on a real bed before leaving. But anyway, we didn't sleep in.

There were eggs and milk for breakfast, along with more venison. The old prophet also packed some knapsacks for us, loading them with bread and a dried meat that reminded me an awful lot of beef jerky. He also had water bottles for us which looked like those wineskins that mountain climbers use.

Tinker Bell asked the prophet why he thought her country was a few weeks away when she remembered being kidnapped and brought into our world after what seemed to be only a few hours passing.

"I am sending you to the northern tip of the land that was once your country before its conquest," he explained. "That area is closest to the next time cave. That was the original plan, after all. If you stopped at your own area and asked directions to the cave, they would only send you up north anyway. By taking this diagonal route over a very small mountain range, your friends can spare themselves an extra whole day. Once you arrive at the cave, you can all go your separate ways. Doug can escort you home. Cliff can find someplace to live in this world, should he so desire, and the others can return to Earth."

Cliff figured he had just one more chance to ask again for more of a detailed scientific explanation about time and space and cave walls before we left. But when he started in, the prophet told Cliff he didn't need to know any more for now.

I asked for more information about Marla, and about the fire I was supposed to avoid, and about how long I would be in this new world before going home. The prophet told me the same thing he had told Cliff: that I didn't need to know any more for now.

Before we left, Ben borrowed some tools from Cephalithos and made a couple of small seats for Tinker Bell and DeWorken. He attached them to his backpack by tying them down really good with rope. He did this because there was no way the two of them could keep up with us otherwise, and we couldn't keep on carrying them in our hands.

After wishing us a pleasant journey and blessing us in the name of the Author of Life, Cephalithos bid us farewell. I could have done with a quick goodbye and a skipping of all the fancy talk.

"When I go back inside my cottage," the prophet said, "feel free to call your cat."

"How do you know he's still around?"

"I assure you, Michael, he's still around. Be safe, lads."

Cephalithos stepped into the house, and Andy wasted no time calling for Caligula.

"Here, kitty, kitty, kitty."

"Andy," I said. "Don't call him like that,"

"Why not?"

"Because he hates it! That kind of call guarantees that he *will not* come!"

"Let's just get going," Ben said. "If the cat follows us, he follows us. If not ... Oh well."

I had gotten used to Ben not liking Caligula. But as it happened, he was probably right. All we had to do was start walking, and that lazy blob of fur was sure to come prancing after us.

Ten minutes went by, or something close to ten minutes.

"Here he comes," Cliff said.

Sure enough, from behind a tree, Caligula finally made his appearance.

"Are you all right?" I asked him

"Eat my hairballs!"

I took that to mean that he was all right.

***

The scenery was beautiful, mostly more of those unusually shaped trees and also some odd-colored mountains. Like I already said, I'm terrible at describing scenery. Instead, I sketched some of it. The prophet had given me some paper, an old parchment kind of paper. He seemed to know about my comic book back home, and he told me that maybe someday I could draw a new comic based on our adventure in this new world. I had kind of a mixed feeling when he made that suggestion. I didn't like the idea of more adventure, but then, if the old prophet was assuming I would eventually get home to write and publish more comics, probably he saw it in my future, so that was pretty good news, I guess.

We walked most of the day, stopping for a snack of bread and dried beef. Before dinner, Ben led us in picking out a flat spot for camping. We didn't have any tents or sleeping bags, but the old prophet had given us lots of blankets and tarps, except that he called the tarps by some other name which I don't remember, and I didn't really care what they were called anyway.

Cephalithos had given us one ax to take along in case we needed to cut wood for a fire, but there were so many old, dead branches along the way which broke into pieces easily, along with smaller kindling, we didn't even need to use his ax for firewood that first night.

The fire got going in no time. Under Ben's direction, we found about nine large stones and put them in a circle to create a fire pit. Ben finally did use the ax, not for firewood, but to slice some tall, thin sticks for people to cook their own meat with. He also remembered DeWorken by tearing off a very small piece of meat and placing it on something the size of a toothpick.

"I'll barbecue it for you," he said. "I don't want you going too close to that fire."

"Fine with me," DeWorken said. "It looks like a whole forest fire from down here."

I started wondering how it might feel if the ornament had

369

turned me miniature like DeWorken. I could see how that small campfire *would* look like a whole forest fire if I were that size. Then I remembered the prophet's warning about being trapped in a fire someday in the future. What kind of fire would it be? What kind of size would I be when I faced it? Would I become like DeWorken and Tinker Bell? In this new magical world, anything could happen. Even though the prophet insisted there was no such thing as magic, whatever he called this stuff, it all seemed pretty magical to me and extremely dangerous. I missed home. I also missed Marla.

Not all of them were interested in dinner. Andy and Tinker Bell were asleep. So was Caligula, but I probably didn't need to tell you that.

Ben noticed that I wasn't doing much talking, so he sat down next to me. "You look worried, buddy."

"I guess I *am* kind of worried … about Marla mostly. She's supposed to be in this world now, but I have no idea where."

"Or when," Cliff added.

"What are you flapping about now?" Ben said to Cliff.

"Well, you heard the prophet. He said Marla went through that hourglass at Mike's house, the hourglass that belonged to his aunt. If that's true, Marla not only traveled through space, she also traveled through time, just like us."

"Yeah?" I said. "So?"

"So if she went through time, we have no idea when she is destined to arrive. She may not even be here yet. On the other hand, she may have arrived one hundred years ago. There's no way of knowing."

"You aren't exactly making me feel better, Cliff."

"Just ignore him," Ben said. "She'll turn up. I wouldn't worry. If your aunt wanted that prophet guy to know Marla was coming, that's probably because she also knows we're all going to connect."

That made sense and it helped a little. "I guess you're right, Ben. But it's hard to figure. Everything that old fellow said was so mysterious, especially the part about somebody turning evil. Who do you think he meant?"

"That's easy," Cliff said. "He was talking about DeWorken!"

"He was not, ya stupid spaz! So just keep your filthy trap shut!"

"See how he talks?" Cliff said, obviously enjoying himself. "I believe my point has been made."

But Ben shook his head. "It doesn't matter how he talks. Given DeWorken's size, I doubt that he could cause much harm to anyone."

"He might not stay that size," Cliff argued.

"Ya better hope not, spaz! Cuz if I'm ever made normal size again, you're dead!"

"Just keep on talking, DeWorken. Keep proving me right. There's our man, or should I say, 'There's our little elf'?"

"You watch it!"

"Oooooh! I'm shaking!"

"There's no way we can figure it out right now," I said. "Cephalithos was talking about the future. It could be any of us."

"I disagree," Cliff said with a smirk. "The evil member of this little expedition is fairly obvious."

Ben gave DeWorken a thorough stare, then turned again to Cliff. "You're forgetting, the prophecy talked about somebody *turning* evil. Not somebody who *already is* evil."

"And even so," DeWorken quickly added, "I ain't evil!"

"Well, maybe not completely evil," Ben said. "But then, you didn't exactly have a reputation for being the friendliest guy on campus either, did you, DeWorken?"

"Yeah? Well, if ya ask me, that prophet dude was talkin' about Reynolds! I sure seen *his* evil side!"

Cliff started laughing. "Can you believe this character?"

"I've known Cliff for years," Ben said. "He's been a pain on this expedition, but all in all, he's a decent guy."

"Not lately!" DeWorken argued. "He kept me prisoner! He sold me as a slave!"

"I already explained that," Cliff said defensively. "I had understandable reasons."

"Yeah, sure ya did. And did ya tell them how ya almost put me in

371

that snake cage?"

"What?" Ben said, looking very concerned.

"I was just having some fun, DeWorken. I would never have really done it."

"Oh, no? Sure, Reynolds … Sure ya wouldn't have done it."

"You're still here, aren't you? If I wanted you dead, you'd have been dead a long time ago!"

"You loved makin' all them threats! Admit it, Reynolds!"

"Just payback, DeWorken. You deserved it."

"I think we're all capable," I said, helping myself to another piece of meat. "That's probably what Cephalithos wanted to get across. If a person thinks he can't be tempted by evil, he's just setting himself up for a big fall."

I'd always considered cowardice to be on the "evil list," so I guess all the lessons I learned from the ornament about my own fears were responsible for my little speech.

"You might be right," Cliff said.

"In fact," I continued, "I'll admit right now that it could easily be me."

"Maybe," Cliff said.

I didn't like that he agreed so quickly.

"After all," Cliff went on, "the prophet said there are two who turn evil."

"But only one who *stays* evil," Ben added.

Cliff moved closer to the fire, warming himself. "Hey Ben, do you agree with Mike? Could it be any of us?"

"Not me," Ben said. "You'll never catch me turning into some sleazy criminal."

"Well, according to Mike, that very attitude itself could be your undoing."

"According to Mike. Not according to me."

Ben sounded very sure of himself. He was probably right. The idea of Ben turning evil seemed like an impossibility.

"Well, Ben," I said. "You're the best of us. That's for sure."

"I tend to agree," Cliff said. "He's certainly the most altruistic."

DeWorken had a puzzled look on his face. "Altruistic? What does that mean?"

Cliff seemed to glow with the chance of humiliating him again. "Oh, I'm sorry, DeWorken. I keep forgetting that you have a tiny brain."

"Shut up!"

"Of course, your brain was already tiny before. Maybe it's only fitting that your body finally caught up."

Ben intervened. "Knock it off, Cliff."

But Cliff was on another roll. "See? Ben cares about everyone, DeWorken. Even you! An altruistic person is a person who puts others ahead of himself."

"Anyway," I said. "There were two other people with us during the prophecy. It could be Andy."

"True," Cliff said. "We know so little about him. Or it could be Tinker Bell."

"It ain't Tinker Bell!"

"How do you know?" Cliff said to DeWorken. "Because you have the hots for her? That's no basis for drawing a conclusion."

"Now look, Reynolds, don't you be sayin' nothin' mean about Tinker Bell!"

"I'll say whatever I want! Who's going to stop me?"

Cliff was reminding me of an old story Aunt Loureen used to tell me as a kid. I think it was actually one of those Aesop's Fables. It was about a billy goat who was put up on top of a roof by his owner. I don't remember why, but whatever the reason, the goat spent the day on the roof looking down at things. Later that day, a wolf came along, and because the goat knew the wolf could never make the climb, he wasn't scared like he normally would have been. Instead, he hurled a bunch of insults at him. Boy, if DeWorken ever did turn normal size again, I sure wouldn't wanna be Cliff. It would be messy.

While thinking about Cliff and DeWorken, I started watching

Cliff with interest while he kept looking down at his miniature enemy, offering one jabbing insult after another. It was very unusual to see this kind of interaction between two people that were known up to now as a nerd and a bully. I figured it must be every nerd's dream to be able to say anything he wanted to a bully who used to pick on him.

In Cliff's hand was Cephalithos' magic stone, the one that was supposed to turn red when we faced danger. Cliff kind of liked being in charge of the stone, and nobody else seemed to care, so we just let him have it. Cliff also tended to take it out of his pocket, and sometimes without even thinking, he kind of bounced it around from hand to hand while talking, almost like a nervous habit.

I had thought the prophet meant that the stone would change color only while we were traveling, like if a lion or something was out of sight, about to pounce on us, but now I was noticing something really strange. The closer Cliff walked toward DeWorken, the redder the stone got. When Cliff walked away again toward the fire, the stone returned to its white color. The faint red could barely be seen, but when the color got more red, it also seemed to light up like a sky after sunset. Evidently the change in color had nothing to do with the way the stone felt in Cliff's hand. It was pretty obvious that Cliff never noticed anything about the rock because he was too focused on the stuff he wanted to keep blasting at DeWorken while he paced back and forth between DeWorken and the campfire. But I sure noticed! If this meant what I thought it meant, then the revenge which Doug DeWorken kept promising Cliff Reynolds was not a matter of if. It was only a matter of when.

Chapter Twenty-Four

A Warning for Cliff

The others were all asleep in their blankets, some close to the fire pit with its last few red cinders, protected by the large rocks of our homemade stone surrounding. Others were farther away. I was one of the farther away ones. I didn't wanna be too close to the fire pit. It had still been giving off smoke before I was ready to turn in, and I didn't like breathing the smoke or even breathing air close to the smoke. That would have been true even apart from that warning about fire from the old prophet.

But anyway, I was up now, and it was the middle of the night. I had been sleeping on my back and in my clothes. This wasn't very comfortable, but I wanted to keep the ornament in my pocket, and it was my intention to keep it in my pocket for as long as we were in this dangerous new land, or "this godforsaken hellhole," as I had heard Caligula put it the few times he spoke up. I figured so long as I didn't roll over in my sleep, the ornament wouldn't break. I had no idea how to use it now — now that its power had changed like the prophet told us — but whatever it was able to do, one thing was sure: we would never find out if I clumsily left it behind again like a forgetful jerk. That was one stupid mistake which would never be repeated.

I heard some kind of strange noise as soon as I woke up, but I don't think the noise was what woke me. I woke up because I mostly had too much on my mind, so all on my own, noise or no noise, I just couldn't sleep — at least, not much. I slept here and there, but I kept waking up, thinking about all the stuff Cephalithos had warned us about and even more about Marla. One time I even dreamed about her. She was off in the distance, calling me from across a dark field. Even though it was pitch black, I could see her all lit up, almost like a spotlight was shining on her, only I couldn't see the beam, just her, wearing her pretty plaid dress that I'd seen her in many times at school back when I used to notice her, but before she ever noticed me. Anyway, in this dream, Marla was calling my name. I couldn't tell if she was scared or happy to see me. Actually, it didn't seem much like either. It was just weird. Then I woke up. Minutes later, I was asleep again.

I dreamed all kinds of other stuff that night too but didn't remember anything except the Marla dream. I just knew I had been dreaming. I always found that strange, to dream like crazy and not remember anything other than the fact that I had dreamed about *something*.

And when I woke up, I lay under the stars, worrying. The stars … They were something else altogether … There were tons of them everywhere I looked. There didn't seem to be one inch of sky that wasn't filled with those tiny sparks of light. This reminded me of camping trips I took, both when I was little with my family and also when I was older with my friends. We always saw so many more stars up in the mountains than down in the suburbs, where I looked at stars out in the backyard. I loved it when lots of stars were out. Once, Aunt Loureen joined us for a camping trip when I was just a little kid. She always encouraged me to look up at the stars. She said it was a sign that life was an amazing mystery, and she liked to wonder out loud what was out there.

"Just look at that firmament, Nephew," she used to say. "Why, that sky is absolutely blanketed with stars."

Tonight's sky was blanketed with stars too. I figured they must be completely different stars than I had seen before if we were really stuck on some planet on the other side of the galaxy, as the old prophet had said. I couldn't recognize any constellations, but I was never too good at astronomy anyway, and unless it was something obvious like the Big Dipper, to me the stars were just stars. I really couldn't tell you one from another. Cliff could name every constellation when we camped with Ben. Yep, Cliff could name them, and he went out of his way to name them. Ben and me could care less. But tonight, I paid more attention. It was strange to think that I was looking at stars from a whole different world. For all I knew, one of those stars out there in the night sky could be our own sun that Earth orbits. I could be staring at home right now!

I heard the noise again. It wasn't a bad noise … nothing that made me worry, just something like a combination of wind and whistling, but it was very low and kept repeating itself almost like a rhythm.

I decided to get up and walk around. It felt good to stretch. Since I was up anyway, I figured I may as well track down the noise. It turned out to be DeWorken snoring. Since he was miniature, the snore wasn't as loud. I smiled to myself when I imagined what this big muscular jock probably sounded like sleeping at full size. Tinker Bell was next to him, and he was sleeping with his arms around her. She looked content in his arms. DeWorken seemed like a whole different person when he interacted with Tinker Bell. But whenever Cliff made one of his little comments, the old Doug DeWorken snapped back fast as could be. It was almost like Dr. Jekyll and Mr. Hyde.

Looking at DeWorken, I suddenly remembered another reason I couldn't sleep. I was also concerned about Cliff. Sooner or later, he was gonna shoot off his mouth one too many times. At the moment, I didn't see how DeWorken could hurt him since this was a miniature DeWorken, but in a magic world with magic charms, anything could happen, and it was a magic charm which had already given off a warning. The stone in Cliff's hand had turned red whenever he went near Doug. Cliff had not noticed. I had. So why didn't I say anything? I guess it was only one of many things on my mind, including Marla, the warning about fire, and all that guessing about who was gonna turn evil. That and the fact that I was tired kind of put the whole Cliff/DeWorken thing in the back of my mind, causing me to only half-notice the red rock, with casual concern.

But even though I was tired enough to wanna forget about the rock and go to bed, I kept waking up anyway with all kinds of fears haunting me.

Now, at this moment, staring at little DeWorken and Tinker Bell and being the only member of our party awake, I found myself more concerned for Cliff's safety. I thought maybe I should warn him and maybe now was a good time, with everyone else asleep.

***

"I think we're out of hearing range," Cliff said. "So what is it? Why did you wake me up?"

"OK," I said. "Here's the deal. While we were talking around the fire, you made some comment about how DeWorken could possibly turn to normal size again. Do you remember saying that?"

"Yes, I said it. Why are you bringing that up now? Is this why you awakened me?"

"Just listen," I said. "Do you really believe this? Do you believe it's possible for DeWorken to change back to his regular size?"

"Well, I haven't thought that much about it, but yes, I suppose so. Anything is possible. I mean, a few weeks ago, who would have thought that DeWorken could be reduced in the first place? But he was. And even though the ornament wasn't able to change him back, perhaps something else can. We *are* in a new world, after all."

"Exactly. And this world has all kinds of magic, not just magic from the ornament, right?"

"Yes, Mike. But all this is rather obvious. I still don't see why we are having such a discussion in the middle of the night."

"Because while you were popping off at DeWorken around the fire, that stone in your hand turned red."

"Turned red?"

"Whenever you were near DeWorken, it got red. When you walked away, it got white again. You never noticed it because you were on a roll insulting him, but I noticed."

Usually Cliff picked up on things really fast, but he didn't seem to be grasping this one. Maybe he was still too tired to think. I wasn't sure. But anyway, Cliff pulled the rock out of his pocket. I guess he must have had the same idea I had: sleep with your magic charm close by.

"It turned red, you say?"

"Every time you went near him."

"I thought this stone only warned us of danger ahead."

"That's right, Cliff. Danger ahead. And the danger ahead of you is DeWorken."

Cliff started showing concern as the point I was trying to make finally dawned on him. "But ... surely the prophet meant *geographical-*related danger, something along our path while we travel."

"That's what I thought too. But you know how these magic charms can be. They're full of surprises."

"So you're assuming it can also relay danger ahead in *time*, ahead in the *future*?"

"I guess. Why else would it turn red?"

Cliff looked very frightened. I think he was regretting mouthing off at DeWorken, probably for the very first time.

378

"But ... but what could DeWorken do to me in the condition he's in?"

"Nothing I can think of. That's why I wanted to remind you that he might not stay that size. You said it yourself. In this world, anything could happen."

"You're right, Mike. I've been very careless, haven't I?"

"Well, maybe if you toned it down just a little, Doug wouldn't be fuming and counting the seconds till he can get even."

"Yes, of course. I've been a fool. You must think I'm really out of my mind. I suppose there's no valid excuse. It's just that DeWorken picked on me for so many years, I wanted to ..."

"I know, Cliff. I understand. I've been picked on too. I know what it feels like. It felt good to get stuff off your chest. But you've had your fun. Maybe you should lay off for a while. Maybe that stone is warning you to lay off."

Cliff nodded. "Yes ... I think that might be the wisest course of action. For all I know, DeWorken might not even need the help of magic. Even a tiny Doug might be able to do something to me in my sleep."

"Probably not," I said. "But you never know. He hates you, Cliff. Back at school, he just picked on you to show off for his friends, like he picked on everybody else. But now he hates you, so please be careful."

"I will. Thanks, Mike. Thanks for warning me. You're a good friend."

I slapped him on the shoulder. "Who knows? Maybe if you started acting nice to him, he might even get to like you."

"I don't think that's going to happen."

"Well, anyway," I said. "I guess we should get back to sleep."

I started toward the camp, but Cliff wasn't following. I took a few steps back. "You coming, Cliff?"

He looked like he was trying to figure something out.

"Cliff?"

"Hey, Mike, I just thought of something. Maybe the stone is warning me so that I can take some kind of precautionary action."

Already I was regretting waking Cliff up. Now he was gonna keep me up all night trying to analyze the situation.

"We don't have to solve the problem now, Cliff. Just watch your back and try being nicer to DeWorken."

"That won't be enough, Mike. I may need to resort to other measures."

I knew I was gonna regret asking, but I asked him anyway. "What other measures?"

"Maybe we can use the ornament."

I couldn't believe my ears. Suddenly my mind flashed back to that dreadful day at my house when Cliff had the exact same idea.

"Cliff, you can't be serious."

"I'm very serious, Mike. I need protection. You just told me yourself that some kind of danger from DeWorken is lurking in the shadows. Obviously he can't do anything in the state he's in. At least, that's the lesser probability. This means that, in all likelihood, DeWorken will be helped by magic sometime in the near future. I need to shield myself ahead of time. I need the ornament."

"Have you forgotten that all your trouble with DeWorken began with the ornament?"

"No, my trouble with DeWorken did not start with the ornament. My trouble with DeWorken started with DeWorken."

"But Cliff, we practically had this exact same conversation before. You wanted the ornament to use as protection from DeWorken, and look at all the trouble it caused you. Things are worse — not only for you, for all of us!"

"But the ornament is different now. It can't trick us like before."

"Who says so?"

"The angels have been released, Mike. And I released them."

"You say that like you're proud of yourself."

"Maybe I *should* be. It was prophesied years ago that the angels would be separated and released from the ornament. And my wish made it happen. So I stumbled into my destiny. Maybe the angels will be grateful and help me out."

"That's up to them. And one of them is evil. You don't even wanna mess with that one."

Cliff shook his head in disagreement. "Charles isn't evil. He certainly did a number on that sheriff back in Wendover. And he did it for us. He got Ben and me out of jail."

"OK. So if he wants to help you again, he will. That's the way Charles works. He just kind of shows up when you least expect him. It has nothing to do with the ornament."

"It has everything to do with the ornament. Charles is in *this* world now. And somehow he's still connected to the ornament. Why else would the ornament have appeared in Cephalithos' cottage? And the same Cephalithos told us about Charles being here."

As usual, I started getting irritated with Cliff. He never gave up on an idea. He pestered and whined and argued till he got his way, and I could see he was planning to do the same thing again. I would never get back to sleep, not that I was sleeping all that well anyway, but I would rather lay awake gazing at the stars again than listen to all this. And it was too bad. I'd just had a nice moment with Cliff where he called me a good friend and all.

Cliff continued. "Isn't that what the prophet told us? Didn't he tell us Charles was still connected to the ornament?"

"Yeah, I guess."

"What do you mean you guess? He spoke about Charles at length, and you were asking questions."

"I know, Cliff. I did hear him talk about Charles, but he said so many other things also, it was hard to keep track of it all."

"Not so difficult. I think you were paying attention until he mentioned Marla. The mere sound of her name derailed you."

Cliff was annoying the snot out of me. "He mentioned that she came into this world, Cliff. And she's not here! At least we haven't seen her yet. I'm worried about her safety! So give me a break!"

"Hey, take it easy, will you? We're all worried."

"Yeah? Well, you don't act worried."

"I am, Mike. You're my friend. I care about you. But there are all kinds of dynamics associated with our predicament, not merely the situation with Marla. I'm trying to process a lot of things, and the ornament is perhaps the most obvious. After all, you did forget about it back in Ben's van, and yet it followed us into this world anyway. It appeared as if by magic in the prophet's closet. That means something."

"OK. So it means something. But I have no idea what it means, and neither do you, even though you think you know everything."

"You and Ben need to stop saying that. When have I ever claimed to know everything?"

"Forget it."

"No! I don't want to forget it! Let's get this settled once and for all. I know what's going on. You're thinking about our discussion around the campfire, aren't you? About one of us turning evil, and you think it's going to be me."

Actually I had only been thinking of that a little bit. Marla was my bigger concern, but probably concern about somebody turning evil was more important. Anyway, Cliff's words brought that back to the front of my mind again. I lowered my voice, feeling bad that I had snapped at him.

"I don't know what to think, Cliff. I'm more worried that it could be me."

"I know. I heard you before. But there will be two turning evil, and I'll bet you believe one of them is me, regardless of who the other one is."

"I never said that."

"Maybe *you* never said it, but DeWorken did, and nobody argued the point."

"Ben argued the point."

"Only until DeWorken told him about the snake cage."

"Well, you have to admit, Cliff, that was a pretty hairy thing to do."

"I never did it! I already told all of you. I never put DeWorken in any snake cage. I was just messing with him."

"Look, Cliff, I have no idea who will turn evil. Hopefully nobody will. Maybe the old guy was wrong."

"He can't be wrong. He's a prophet."

"OK. I'm tired, and I don't wanna argue any more. Can we go back to the camp now?"

"Mike, I need you to lend me the ornament."

"Are you crazy? After what happened last time? You are not putting your hands on the ornament. Understand? Besides, the prophet gave it to me and told me to watch over it."

"That doesn't mean you can't share it."

"You're the one who's reminding me of the prophet's words. You can't have it both ways, Cliff. If you believe the prophet when he says the ornament is important, then you need to also believe him when he says I'm the keeper of the ornament."

"Fair enough," Cliff said. "So as the keeper of the ornament, why don't you summon Charles yourself and make a wish on my behalf?"

"What kind of wish?"

"A wish that protects me from DeWorken, DeWorken in any form: large or small, magic or mortal."

"Who says the ornament is gonna have anything to do with wishes anymore? All we know is that it still has some kind of magic."

"Yes, but magic related to Charles. My guess is that you use the ornament to summon him."

"It could be that. It could be a hundred other things."

"Will it hurt to try?"

"OK, Cliff. Tomorrow I'll try something."

"No, Mike, it has to be tonight."

"Why tonight?"

"Because tomorrow may be too late. In broad daylight, we'll all be traveling together. How can we make wishes about DeWorken in front of DeWorken? We need time to experiment. We may as well do it right now while everyone else is asleep."

Suddenly I felt very jealous of everyone else and the sleep they were experiencing. If I lived to be a hundred, I was gonna regret waking Cliff up. It would never happen again. I remembered the old saying

"Let sleeping dogs lie." Growing up, those kinds of common phrases meant nothing to me. But I was learning. Sayings are created out of real situations. And I would give anything right now to get over this situation with Cliff.

"OK," I said, just to get him off my back. "Maybe tomorrow night while they're all asleep, we can sneak out of camp again and try to summon Charles."

"Why wait until tomorrow night? We're here now with the ornament. Now is as good a time as any."

Nothing I was gonna say would end this conversation. That was becoming very obvious. No word, no sigh, no gesture. Nothing.

I took the ornament out of my pocket. "What do you suggest we do? Before, all I did was make a wish, but if the angels aren't inside the ornament anymore, what exactly am I supposed to do now?"

"How should I know?" Cliff said.

"Well, you're the one who wants to try this! So give me an idea."

"Maybe you rub it like Aladdin's lamp."

I had no idea what to do, but if I was sure of one thing, this would not be like Aladdin's lamp. Aunt Loureen warned me way back when she had first given me the ornament as a Christmas present that I should forget about Hollywood, and in her mind, Aladdin was part of Hollywood, meaning that this would not be like any fantasy movie. And for that matter, she meant any story at all, not just from Hollywood. Any book, any fiction … I was supposed to forget about that stuff and learn the real rules of the ornament.

"All right," I said. "I'll hold it and try to summon Charles."

I took the ornament out of my pocket. But while staring at the thing, all I could do was think of all the trouble it had caused.

"Well?" Cliff said. "Don't just stand there. Go on."

"Charles, are you there?"

It all felt so stupid. And I wasn't surprised that my "summons" was met with silence.

"Say it again, Mike."

"What for? Nothing is happening."

"You called his name one measly time. And you're giving up already? Try it again."

"OK, OK ... I'll try it again. Charles ... Charles ... Are you there? Come in, Charles!"

"Oh, for Pete's sake, Mike, you're acting like Charles is on the other end of a walkie-talkie."

"You wanna try it?"

"I'd love to try it. Hand it over."

"Wait! No! Forget it. Cephalithos gave it to me."

"Then talk better."

"I don't even know what that means, Cliff. How do I talk better? If he doesn't answer, he doesn't answer."

"Hmm ..."

"What? What is it, Cliff?"

"Well, just going with your thought about how the prophet made you its custodian ... Maybe only one person at a time can use this device. Maybe the fact that both of us are here together is the problem. We're kind of both summoning Charles at the same time."

"Could be the problem," I said.

"It could be indeed ... OK. I'll tell you what, Mike. I'll leave you alone and go back to camp if you promise to try calling Charles on your own after I leave. What do you say?"

I would have said anything to get rid of him. "Sure, Cliff. Good idea. Let's try it like that. You go back to camp. I'll call out Charles' name again, and we'll see what happens."

When I was finally alone, I decided to just sit still on a large log, enjoying the peace and quiet. In fact, I hadn't even decided whether or not to try summoning Charles. Maybe I would just tell Cliff that I had tried and it didn't work.

But after a while, I figured it wouldn't hurt to give it another shot. For all I knew, Cliff might be right. Maybe this new ornament power could only work with one person at a time. That's the way it happened before. Only one person at a time could make wishes. Even with new ornament rules, that one particular rule might have stayed the same.

Besides, with all my other worries, like Marla and the prophecy about fire, it might be nice to get some help from Charles, not to mention some information from Charles.

"Charles, I don't know if you can hear me, but if Cliff is right … if you are now out and about and if you are still connected to the ornament like the prophet told us … and … well … and … if you're here to help us, I sure could use your help right now. Could you please make another appearance?"

All of a sudden, I heard a hissing noise. I turned around and saw a bunch of blue smoke, kind of like what happens in movies when a genie is about to appear, except that this blue smoke was not coming out of the ornament. It was just coming out of thin air. I had held the ornament tightly in my hands while calling Charles, but as far as I could tell, there didn't seem to be much connection between the ornament and what was now happening.

As the smoke faded away, I slowly made out Charles' figure standing straight ahead.

He was still wearing the dark suit which he had on when I saw him in my own hometown. That looked kind of strange in our new surroundings, and I wondered why he wasn't dressed the way people from his own world dressed — something from the olden days, like Cephalithos and that ancient-looking robe. But anyway, I guess it didn't matter. I was more interested in getting some important answers, and I figured how he dressed was his own business.

"Well, Mike," he said. "We've come a long way, you and I, haven't we? Welcome to my world. From this point on, you and I are going to have a completely different relationship."

Chapter Twenty-Five

The New Rules of the Ornament

Charles made fair-weather chit chat at first. He kept asking how everyone in the group was.

I finally lost my patience. "Don't you know all this? Come on, Charles! You already know how they are. You know better than they do! Aren't you following us around invisible or something, just watching us?"

He smiled, "Yes, something like that. Not actually invisible, but with the ability to observe from a parallel dimension. As for knowing everything, if only that were the case. It isn't. But yes, the Author of Life has found it in His purpose to include me in on a few important, crucial matters. He did this by bestowing special powers upon me long ago, and yes, Mike, I am watching you. I am watching all of you, at least most of the time."

"Well, if they're such crucial matters, I wish you'd answer a few questions for once so that I can know what's going on."

"Anything I can, Mike. But I must warn you right from the onset, the questions you are most curious about, I cannot answer."

"*Cannot* or *will* not?"

Charles smiled warmly. "It's a little bit of both."

"I'm mostly curious about my girlfriend, Marla."

"Lovely girl."

I wanted to slug him. If I hadn't been taught to respect my elders, and if he hadn't been an angel, and if I was the kind of guy who even went around slugging people anyway, I would have.

"I'm glad you think she's lovely, Charles. And you know that isn't what I wanna talk about. Aunt Loureen contacted this prophet guy …"

"I know."

"OK. So you know we were all told that you sent Marla into this world. Is that true?"

Charles nodded.

"What for?"

Charles continued smiling.

"Don't tell me," I said. "Forbidden information."

Again he nodded.

"OK ... Then never mind *why* you sent her. Just tell me where she is."

"She'll arrive in due time."

"She's not here yet?"

He could see that I was getting upset. "Calm down, Mike. Everything will be all right."

"Easy for you to say. Where is she?"

More silence.

I continued. "Cliff said something about how since she traveled through time, she could arrive at any moment at all and not be here yet."

"That is correct. She is not here yet."

"Why not? When will she get here?"

"It's complicated, Mike. It has to do with balancing the time/space displacement of these two worlds."

"Come on, Charles! Boy oh boy! Between you and that prophet ... Can't you guys ever just speak plain English?"

"You really should learn to relax, Mike."

I could see I wasn't gonna get anywhere with him. I sighed, "Can you at least tell me if she's safe?"

"Yes, Mike, she's safe because she's between time and between worlds right now."

I was getting so sick of all the time and space talk, but I asked another question anyway.

"This world seems kind of backward compared to Earth, or at least Earth in the twenty-first century. This place reminds me of the Middle Ages. So did the book I read about Lumis and the ornament years ago.

I know I'm on another planet, the same planet the ornament comes from. Am I also in *the past* on this other planet?"

"Planet histories develop at different speeds. And these two planets are on opposite sides of the galaxy anyway, which means that since time and space are related, it is irrelevant to describe where one planet's era is in relationship to another."

I should have known better. Ask a stupid question, get a smart answer that makes me feel even stupider. "OK ... There was a prediction ..."

"About a fire ... No, I can tell you nothing about it."

Three for three so far, not counting that explanation about planets and time, which wasn't much of an explanation anyway. But three strikes so far for anything I personally cared about: two questions about Marla and one about the fire. He would not tell me why he sent Marla to this world, neither would he tell me when she would arrive. He did at least tell me Marla was safe. I guess that was something. But I mostly wanted to know when I would see her again.

I knew it would make no difference, but I tried for one more question.

"There was another prophecy ..."

Once again, he jumped in before I could finish. "Those who turn evil must find out in due course. Nobody will be made privy to such information ahead of time."

I stared at the ground for a moment. He was driving me nuts, interrupting me before I could finish a question, or just staring at me when I did finish a question. When I was little, my parents used to talk about a TV show called *Candid Camera*. And I myself remembered a program kind of like it called *Bloopers and Practical Jokes*. Part of me wanted to believe this was all a joke, that some camera was following us around while Charles was messing with my head, and I was really on TV making an audience laugh.

I finally looked back up. "Is there anything at all you can tell me?"

"Plenty. You did make a wish that I would answer questions, and every question I am permitted to answer will be answered. I must start with the new rules of the ornament itself."

"Yeah, I guess that's something. But I have another favor to ask. Cliff also wanted protection from DeWorken."

"You only get one wish today, Mike, and you already made it. You wished for some answers."

"I didn't realize I was making a wish. I was just telling you how frustrated I am to be constantly left in the dark."

"Frustrated or not, the words 'I wish' were given once again. You do that often, Mike. You wish without thinking."

"Well, I didn't even know if wishes were still connected to the ornament anymore."

"Perhaps not, but it was a fair guess, and the very fact that you summoned me to ask favors demonstrates, at the very least, that you were considering this possibility. Try to be more careful. In any event, you wished for answers, so answers are all I can give you at this unique moment. I can do nothing for Cliff today."

"Well, you don't seem to be doing much about answering questions either. Seems like a wasted wish so far."

"Not wasted at all. What I *can* tell you today is the most important thing you need to know: How does the ornament work now? What does it mean to make wishes in our present situation when I, your friend Charles, and another angel, an evil angel, are both free?"

"Fine," I said. "I'd rather hear *something* at least. If that's all you can give me, then let me have it."

Of course I did wanna know all about the ornament rules. Who wouldn't? That was obvious, but I was still annoyed that Charles wouldn't explain more of the personal stuff, and I wanted him to know I was annoyed. Looking back, I feel bad that I behaved that way. It was kind of like throwing a temper tantrum, even though I wasn't really losing my temper and I wasn't actually throwing anything.

"All right, Mike, you may want to sit down for this."

He pointed to a couple of boulders. We each sat on one.

"Thanks to your friend Cliff, I am free from the ornament. But other incidents have happened since then. For this reason, I am tied to the ornament once again, but not quite like the first time. Before, I lived inside the castle in the glass, not by myself, but with the wicked angel, Hamartio. And you know the backstory. You read about it years ago in your sister's book."

"Yeah. You and Hamartio fought for so many years you eventually became one person."

"One entity, part good, part evil — like human beings, like you see in your own human nature which battles back and forth, part good and part evil — only I had once been completely good, and so that part of the entity who had once been known as Char the Angel longed for a separation, longed to be an individual who one-hundred percent obeys the Author of Life."

"That's where Cliff comes in," I said. "He made a wish, and now you are separated."

"Cliff's wish for our separation was granted, but only to a degree. Obviously, he couldn't destroy Hamartio because angels can't die."

"That's what I told him."

"Yes, you did tell him that. And you were uncharacteristically correct on that particular occasion. In any event, we were a single entity at the time. Cliff's wish separated us."

"How?"

"Since neither Hamartio nor myself wanted to be one being, the combined entity was only too happy to cooperate with Cliff's wish. We separated inside the ornament. Then, as individual beings, we escaped the ornament."

"But I thought you were trapped because of previous wishes. And I thought new wishes couldn't cancel old wishes."

"They couldn't in the original world we came from, Telios, this world that we are both inhabiting right now. But of course, the ornament had made its way into *your* world, planet Earth, where the rules changed."

I was surprised by his answer. "Wait. So if things changed, how come you never got out before?"

"Well, even though the old rules no longer applied, that didn't mean there were no rules at all. The ancient laws morphed into modern laws. Now a mere wish *could* supersede an old, but the wish still had to be made."

"So how come I was never able to undue a wish?"

"Simple, Mike …"

Then he started to explain. But even as he answered my question, I figured it wasn't really gonna sound all that simple. In fact, I didn't expect it to sound anything close to simple.

"In either world," Charles said, "mine or yours, the ornament had the same rules."

"Huh? You just said the rules changed."

"Not the rules themselves, but rather the *application* of the rules. That would have been a better way to describe it. I am talking about the residue of a wish already granted and whether that residue still lingered."

Charles could see that I looked more confused than ever.

"OK, Mike … Let me put it another way. Ornament rules only apply to the wishes in standing while the ornament stays in its respective world."

"What do you mean 'wishes in standing?'"

Charles seemed patient, and I was glad. I didn't get the feeling that I was frustrating him or anything like that. Instead, he sounded happy to explain and in no hurry, as if we had all the time in the world. Also, he didn't act all stuck up like when Cliff explained something in a way that made me feel stupid and made him look intelligent. Instead, Charles just wanted to help and had no desire to make me feel bad while he answered my questions. Even before, when he talked about how it had been "uncharacteristic for me to give a correct answer," I never felt like he was putting me down, just stating a fact about how all this magic stuff didn't come easily to me. But no matter what Charles said to me, he said it like a gentleman. Unfortunately, even his better manners weren't making much of a difference. I still didn't understand.

"'Wish in standing' refers to the effects of a wish already made. A wish in standing cannot be undone in the world where the wish was made, but it *can* be undone in another world. Once the ornament found its way into your world, wishes from the previous world could be undone, although for the most part, there was nobody on your side of the cave wall who had been in the other world making a wish. So who would have known about any wish in standing? Who would have even needed to undo anything? Meanwhile, anybody in your world who stumbled upon the ornament and used it had the same rules apply. Those new wishes could not be superseded. In other words, when a person makes a wish in *your* world, that wish cannot be undone. When a person makes a wish in *my* world, that wish cannot be undone either."

"But if a wish is made in one world," I said, "and after that, the ornament changes worlds, that wish could be undone by somebody from the new world?"

"Exactly, Mike. Couldn't have said it better myself."

I felt like I got it that time, finally. And he was right. He couldn't have said it better himself, because he tried saying it several times himself and confused me until, finally, I thought I was catching on and took a stab at explaining it back to him. But now, I still wanted to be absolutely sure.

"So the ornament's rules are the same in either world?" I said. "In either world, when somebody makes one wish, they can't undo it with another wish?"

"That is correct. But once the ornament goes into a new world, any wish from the previous world *can* be undone."

"Yeah, I think I got that. But … if a person from the new world makes a wish, then that wish will have the same rule? That new wish cannot be undone?"

"Yes, now you're catching on. So let's illustrate by applying it to Cliff. The ornament from my world, Telios, has traveled into Cliff's world, which is the same as your world, Earth. Hamartio and I are trapped in the ornament, due to a wish made in my world that cannot be undone in my world. But in Cliff's world, it *can* be undone. So Cliff makes a wish and the ornament complies."

"Wow! That's what Cliff suggested. You mean the only reason you never got out of that ornament before is because nobody ever wished it?"

"When human beings make wishes, they're thinking about themselves. They're not analyzing how the ornament works. When you were a kid and you first heard the story of Aladdin's lamp, did you ever once worry *how* the lamp worked, or did you instead think of what you would have wished for?"

"Yeah. You're right," I said. "OK ... So now the situation is kind of in reverse. I'm on *your* side. I'm on *your* planet. So now, if I wanted, I could make new wishes that would undo the old ones?"

"Yes, you could, or more correctly put, *you would have been able to* had Cliff not interfered and let us out. Now, it's a whole different ornament."

"It sure looks the same."

"If by that you mean the size and shape, certainly. It still looks like a Christmas ornament. It still *is* a Christmas ornament. In fact, physically speaking, it's the exact same one. But it no longer works the same way. That is what's different. Hamartio and I got out, and according to the former ornament rules, our escape ended up being the good thing and the bad thing at the same time: good thing, meaning I got out; bad thing, meaning Hamartio got out, now more dangerous than ever, with virtually unlimited power. But I had abilities too, and I intended to use the magic at my own disposal to banish Hamartio. Once we were out of the ornament, it was our own power working against each other back and forth, forging new rules, rules of compromise between what I wanted and what Hamartio wanted. And these rules were no longer bound by which world we were in."

"Then he's gone?"

"Not exactly. I banished him from your world, but he had to have a place to go. Guess where?"

I felt a sudden, sharp chill because I was sure of the answer. "This world?"

"Bingo! Yes, Hamartio is back on this planet, Telios."

"Wait ... I thought angels didn't live on planets. I thought you and Hamartio were originally from Heaven."

"That is technically correct. Both of us are heavenly, or both of us once *were*. Hamartio fell into sin, out of graces with the Author of Life. But we loyal angels exist to assist the Author as He looks after human beings. We each have certain assignments, various jurisdictions. My assignment originally was Telios, not Earth. Hamartio's assignment was also Telios, only his mission from the Master Enemy was to deceive and destroy. My mission was to protect and inspire. We ended up on your planet by mistake. First we got trapped inside the ornament. Then, many years later, or many years ago, from your point of view, a human being from Telios traveled through a time cave, carrying the ornament to Earth."

"So Cliff's wish got you out of the ornament, and then Hamartio came back to this world? This world that you keep calling Telios?"

"Yes.

"So why did you also return to Telios? You could have stayed where you were. You could have stayed back on Earth without ever having to face Hamartio again."

"Somebody has to keep an eye on you."

Much as I hated my situation, I had to admit, his words were touching. "You came back to this world just for me?"

"That's an important part of it. But Telios was also my original jurisdiction, don't forget, the world I belong in. True, there was a lure in staying on Earth, away from Hamartio. But as angels, we do not merely care about planets in the abstract. It is *people* whom the Author of Life wants us to look after. Whatever planet you come from, the Author loves you no less. You have a mission to accomplish. I was duty bound to assist."

I really didn't wanna hear about this mission, and since I was still curious about what had happened to both angels, I kind of ignored that remark and just continued with my questions. "But when Hamartio finds you again, won't the old rules apply since you're back in your old world?"

"No. Inasmuch as the ornament has bounced back and forth between space and time, the rules have been reset."

I knew it was too good to be true. For a moment, I was finally understanding him. Now I was getting lost again. None of this made sense to me. All the little details and loopholes seemed like a lot of legal *gobbledygook*. It made me wonder if Heaven had ten lawyers for every one angel. How else would they come up with so many rules and so much fine print to govern their powers? Why did magic even have to have rules at all? Who made up all these loopy laws? I decided to ask. Charles listened patiently, nodding as I talked, not saying anything till I finished.

"Mike, can you just imagine how chaotic the universe would be without law and order? There are laws of physics, laws of biology, laws of genetics, and laws for the supernatural."

"Wait. The laws of science were made by God."

"By the Author of Life, yes."

"So would that mean God made all these supernatural laws too?"

"That's exactly what it means."

"God alone? You sure it wasn't a bunch of lawyers?"

Charles laughed. "Lawyers. That's a good one, Mike."

"I'm serious! You actually rescued Cliff and Ben by pretending to be a lawyer."

"*Pretending* being the operative word. I am not a lawyer. I do not make these rules. They are made by the Author of Life, whom you call 'God.'"

"Seems like He could have made things less complicated."

"Yes, that's a common objection from mortals. Just remember, you don't see things the way God does."

"That's for sure. Hey wait! A minute ago, you said something about you and Hamartio forging new rules once you came out of the ornament. So how could you forge rules if all rules come from God?"

"Mike, I am very impressed with that question. It shows you are doing a better job of listening. God's general rules govern the universe. But God likes to create sentient beings, such as humans and angels. He gives us abilities too. Within the boundaries of the more general rules, we can make rules of our own. Your own country, the United States, serves as a perfect example. Your forefathers drafted a constitution, based upon the same laws of nature that God had already put in the human conscience, stamped right into the DNA of people: a sense of right and wrong. They believed human beings were, as they put it in the Declaration of Independence, 'endowed by their Creator with certain inalienable rights.' And yet, in the *application*, with the objective to establish very specific rules which govern a new nation, humans, made in the image of God, created your marvelous constitution with all its checks and balances. Now then, take this same idea and try to understand that supernatural rules come about in a comparable manner. We angels can contribute to specific rules, but those legalities are governed by the more general supernatural rules of God."

I nodded. I kind of understood. There were still some questions, but for now, I figured I was understanding about as much as I was going to.

And then it happened, a major shift in our conversation. A serious look came over Charles' face, different than I had ever seen before from him.

"OK. Now listen carefully. It's very important that you understand how the new rules work. In this world, Hamartio and I are connected to the ornament once again."

"You mean you still have to go back inside that thing and live in the small castle?"

"No. We're free to roam now, but from the moment we both entered this present world, we have had no power to assist you unless somebody holds the ornament and makes a wish."

"Wait! Before I only had to be in the same room as the ornament. I have to hold it now?"

"Yes. You have to hold it in both of your hands with the hands turned upright, inside the palms of the hands."

"Do I also have to rub it?"

"Did you rub it a moment ago when you summoned me?"

"No."

"All right then. This isn't the story of Aladdin."

Again with Aladdin. I sure was getting sick of the name *Aladdin* and I started hoping we could think of some other fable or story to illustrate ornament rules.

"Do I make the wish before you appear or after?"

"You tell me. When did you make the actual wish?"

"After."

"Exactly. So summoning me for the purpose of making a wish and actually wishing are two separate steps. However, you need to have the ornament in your hands for both experiences. Once again, that's both hands for both experiences. And in that vein, you forgot to ask this, but

I'll throw it in for free. I could have come earlier even when Cliff was still with you. It's true that only one person at a time can wish, but it doesn't matter if that person is accompanied by another."

"Then why didn't you appear when I first called you?"

"Because you were holding the ornament in one hand and not both."

This was starting to sound like a joke. I knew he was serious, but it sure sounded like a joke.

"You're kidding," I said.

"Not at all."

"Kind of a picky rule, don't you think?"

"Perhaps. But we've already established the importance of rules and the structure they bring to life."

"Yeah, but that rule seems lame and fussy."

"What it seems like to you doesn't matter, Mike. We aren't here to debate the merits of a particular rule. Just trust that it was laid out for a reason."

"But you're not gonna tell me the reason, right?"

"If you were to spend less time analyzing the purpose of the rules and more time simply memorizing them, it would be time better spent. Shall I continue?"

"Yeah, I guess."

"OK. After Cliff left, you were making less of a halfhearted attempt for the purpose of getting him off your back and more of a concentrated effort. Out of impulse, you held the ornament more tightly and more formally in both hands. And after I arrived, while making your wish about getting answers, you continued to hold the ornament in your hands. You did nothing else. You did not rub it. I must agree with your Aunt Loureen about how Hollywood distorts people's thinking when they encounter the truly supernatural. Honestly, that Aladdin story has led to more confusion."

In my mind, I quickly shifted from being tired of Aladdin to wishing things *were* as simple as the Aladdin story. Aladdin and his genie weren't confusing. Charles *was*.

"And so," he continued, "no more of this nonsense about wishing for a good thing and then worrying about a follow-up bad thing. Instead, we alternate."

"Alternate? What do you mean?"

"When you make a wish, I answer your wish every other time. Or, more correctly put, every other *day*."

"We can only wish once a day now?"

"Yes, so be careful and don't wish for frivolous situations. You're in a very dangerous world, and you need to save your wishes for when they can really count. I see what you are about to ask: No, you cannot wish yourself out of this world. You'll leave this world when you've completed your mission. Not a moment sooner."

"And you're still not gonna tell me what the mission is."

"Now you're catching on."

"So you answer my wish one day, and then what? Hamartio does it the next day?"

"Yes."

"But he wouldn't answer my wish."

"Left to his own devices, no, he would not. But now he has to. He has to obey the rules. Still, unlike me, he won't *want* to honor them. He'll be sneaky. He'll look for loopholes. He'll find ways to technically give you what you want, but in such a way that it hurts you. So be cautious. Make sure you phrase everything with specific, precise directions."

Once again, I kind of relayed stuff back to Charles to make sure I was getting it all. "OK. So we can wish once a day, and every other day, we get a different angel. One day it's you, the next day it's Hamartio."

"That's about the gist of it. Only let me offer a few more tips to give you a greater advantage. First of all, remember, just because you *can* wish every day, that doesn't mean you *have to* wish every day. If the wish is not absolutely necessary, skip the wish."

"What for?"

"You're asking an excellent question once again. So follow my answer and be sure to soak this in good. Supposing I grant you a wish on a Monday. The next day is Tuesday and you skip the wish. That means you also skipped Hamartio. So you wait until Wednesday. Now, it's my turn again. You denied Hamartio his turn."

I was impressed. "That's a pretty cool loophole, Charles."

"I had a good teacher: Hamartio. He's the prince of sneaky, crafty, loopholes. Why should evil horde all the craftiness? We have to be crafty too. Otherwise we will lose this great battle."

"So if I wish every other day, I never have to deal with Hamartio at all?"

"Exactly. And in a perfect world, that would take care of the problem. Only you aren't in a perfect world. Situations may arise so dangerous that you'll have to wish on Hamartio's day because there simply will be no other choice. If those days are few and far between and if you are very careful to word your wish properly, you'll be OK. And one more item: As you remember Hamartio's sneakiness, remember your own too. That charm I gave you for instance ..."

"Yeah when are you gonna explain that one?"

"I'm not permitted to explain it. But Cliff gave you one clue already."

"Something about poetic justice."

"Yes, and your other clue is that this charm will also work like a sneaky loophole."

"I'm still confused."

"Just think of it as a bonus prize, something to compensate for my limitations."

"OK, fine, I guess. But I still don't understand how you expect me to use that thing when I have no idea what it will do. Can't you give me a third clue?"

"No. I'm only permitted two. But perhaps I can tell you a little more about the device itself. You see, unlike the ornament which has unlimited power at its disposal, this key chain comes from a whole different line of magic charms. It's known in this world as a 'disposable riddle'"

"Disposable riddle? What are you talking about?"

"I mean a quick, emergency device — a temporary device with a limited purpose that only works once."

Charles sighed, seeing that I didn't understand. "Perhaps an analogy will help," he continued. "In your own world, tourists often buy temporary cameras made partly out of cardboard. They take a few pictures and then they throw it away. Think of this as a disposable camera, only instead of taking pictures, it works some magic for you. But it does the magic only one time. After that, it's disposable."

"Wow," I said. "Not as handy as the ornament."

"Handy enough, Mike. It will do its job."

"How? I still don't understand how."

"That's the whole key. Figuring out the riddle is the same as figuring out the power."

"But don't you see? I *can't* figure it out."

"That's only because you aren't meant to yet. When the time comes, when the hour of desperation arrives, then and only then will you be able to grasp its remarkable capabilities."

I answered Charles with nothing but a blank stare.

"Think of it like this," he said. "You'll be in a situation where magic is the only way out. You'll suddenly imagine how helpful that key chain might be if it could only perform this one function. And when you figure out the function, the key chain will work for you. Just remember what I said. It's a quick emergency device."

"You're saying it will only work if I first figure out *how* it works?"

"Exactly."

"And you're also saying I won't figure out how it works until the moment I need it to?"

"Spoken with eloquence and accuracy. You are starting to catch on far more easily."

"I don't think I'm catching on at all. Ever since I started on this trip, there have been all kinds of times when magic might have been helpful ... like right before that fight in the restaurant. I was hoping it would work then."

"Something better worked then, Mike. You found your courage."

These words excited me. In fact, they made me so happy, I suddenly didn't care about the magic charm. "You mean I did that all on my own? No help from the charm? No help from you?"

"All on your own, Mike. And let me add how proud I am of you."

"Thanks."

"As for other situations, you had not yet heard the riddle."

"And part of the riddle is what you told Cliff? This charm will bring about poetic justice?"

"Yes. And the other part of the riddle is what I told you. The poetic justice will work in a sneaky way. So don't let that charm out of your hand for a second. You are the custodian of the charm. Guard it with your life. The ornament too."

"Will the ornament work for anybody?"

"Yes, anybody who holds it in his hands, including people of lesser repute."

"You mean if some bad person made a wish, you'd still have to grant it?"

"I wouldn't want to, but yes, I would have to. I'd have no choice. I'll try to find more of those technicalities around the wording. I'll try to minimize the damage as much as possible. But we're still talking about a dangerous situation. So don't put me in that position, Mike. Hold on to the ornament. Because if it falls into evil hands, those hands have an evil angel only too happy to assist.

"Hamartio."

"Yes. And those same hands also have me, forced to assist."

"And you are forced because of new rules of magic that you and Hamartio somehow made together?"

"As a result of us battling back and forth after we were released from the ornament, yes. Any more questions before I leave?"

"Leave?"

"You made your wish about wanting answers. I gave you some very important answers. It's time now for me to go."

"So now we can't wish anymore tonight?"

"Not until tomorrow."

"Does it have to be a full twenty-four hours?"

"No. It merely has to be the next day."

"Oh. OK. So as soon as it turns morning?"

"It already *is* morning, Mike. It may be dark, but it is the middle of the night, or morning, properly. So sometime when the next shift of hours takes place, sometime after midnight this evening. And this world is governed by the same units of time — twenty-four hours, midnight to noon and then noon to midnight — so you won't have to concern yourself with any kind of conversion calculation."

That didn't make me feel much better. "OK. So anytime after midnight tonight."

"Yes."

"But that will mean that we can never make wishes in broad daylight."

"No, it will just mean that you have to wait until 12:00 midnight for the next day to begin. At midnight you might not need to make a wish yet, and if you don't need to make one until 7:00 in the morning or 3:00 in the afternoon, so be it."

"Oh yeah. I see. I guess I was still thinking about a regular twenty-four hours, even though you said that wasn't an issue. That cave wall was timed, so I got confused for a minute and thought about the ornament being timed."

"I see. Yes, the cave time portal is a whole different matter. Those are timed intervals. The ornament functions much differently. In any event, Mike, since the answering of questions was your first wish, I am giving you an opportunity to ask any others you have before I leave."

I couldn't think of any more, but I knew that the minute he left, then I would think of something, and it would be too late unless I wanted to wait till the day after tomorrow and make some other question my next wish. And we might be in some kind of jam that day which needed a better wish than just getting some kind of question answered, so I figured I should try to think of another one. "Wait ... Can you give me a minute?"

"Certainly. Take as much time as you need."

I finally thought of one: "The prophet Cephalithos said that all this power has nothing to do with magic. And yet, you keep calling it magic."

"What he means, Mike, is that back on your world, people think of magic in two ways: tricks, such as what you would see a magician do, where it looks like magic but really isn't, and then the second kind has to do with those who dabble in the occult — witchcraft, séances, and other practices where people think they are obtaining power but are really being deceived by demons. What Cephalithos was telling you, and what I confirm, is that the source of all power is either the Author of Life, whom you call God, or the Master Deceiver, whom you call Satan. But unlike Earth, the miracles of God and the power of Satan battle back and forth at times through the use of charms and other devices which funnel such power."

"Yeah ... Cephalithos said something just like that."

"Because you grew up on stories and fantasy movies and because what you see in this world will remind you of that, we have used the word *magic* to simply describe the supernatural. *Magic,* after all, is merely a word. So long as we define the word properly and do not confuse it for the black magic arts of Earth, there is no harm in using the word."

"I see. So we do have magic charms in this world, but ..."

"But know that each one is from God or from Satan, and in the case of the ornament, I'm afraid both powers are still doing battle. Any more questions?"

I was too tired and drained to think of any more. "I guess not. Thanks."

"Then I bid you farewell. I am with you always and often watching, even when you don't see me."

"Yeah? Then how come you appear in that blue smoke?"

"For the same reason I will leave that way. It serves as a very clear sign to you when our wish sessions are beginning and ending. Such as now. It is ending. You aren't a little kid anymore, Mike. You are becoming a young man. Act like a man. Be wise. Be cautious. And be extremely careful. Your choices are no longer merely about you. A whole world is at stake: my world. That is why I'm here to help you. By helping you, I am saving my own world."

Now I was suddenly filled with questions again. But it didn't matter. Charles disappeared just like he had come, in that same whiff of blue smoke.

Chapter Twenty-Six

The New Custodian of the Ornament

"Angels which take turns," Andy said. "In all my years, never could I have imagined anything so fascinating."

"Yeah," I responded, grabbing some fruit. It was morning. Our entire company was having breakfast together. Everyone ate except Cliff. He seemed more interested in "debriefing" my talk with Charles and made sure he asked the first round of questions. Actually, by "first round," I mean first round *that morning*. The night before, I had to explain to him that I had been unable to get anything done about DeWorken since Charles only granted one wish per visit and mine was a wish for information. I also told him that I was too tired to share all the information, that I would explain in the morning, and that I was going back to bed. After pouting a little, Cliff went back to bed himself.

At the break of dawn, Cliff started in again, practically demanding that I share every word that had transpired between Charles and me.

Then, after a while, Cliff let up on what seemed like a *60 Minutes* interview for CBS and started pacing back and forth. It almost looked like he was talking to himself.

Ben and Andy took over the grilling. The cat and the miniatures (as Tinker Bell said she preferred to be called instead of "tiny" or "small") just sat there taking everything in.

Ben wasn't quite as excited as Andy, but like I said before, Ben never got too excited about anything. Still, even though Andy was more interested, for some reason, my conversation with Charles did seem to interest Ben a little, or at least more than anything else we had encountered so far. I would think that anyone would find the whole situation gnarly. All our lives we had heard about guardian angels. Now we actually knew who they were, or at least who one of them was, and we even knew his name, Charles. I guess Hamartio shouldn't be called a guardian angel, more like a guardian demon or demon who messed with our lives instead of guarding our lives. But even he might have to guard us once in a while if we made the wish just right. I tried explaining all this to the group, and I tried to grab some breakfast at the same time since Ben wanted us to be soon on our way, "angels or no angels," as he put it.

I wasn't enjoying breakfast a whole lot. I was already tired of eating the same food. It would have been nice to have some eggs. I already mentioned that we *had been* served eggs that first morning before we left on our journey. The old prophet had a few eggs on his estate, which had been laid in the barn by some kind of bird that looked like a hen but actually wasn't a hen (I don't even remember what he called it), but anyway, we all knew it was impossible to pack eggs and take them along without breaking the shells, and Cephalithos hadn't had any of that powdered egg stuff like we used to store in our backpacks on camping trips. Dried meat, fruit, and nuts. That was about it.

But while both Ben and Andy questioned me, they each seemed interested in different kinds of things. Ben was after information — not scientific information like Cliff, more like the kind of stuff I wanted, facts about how to get home or how to stay out of trouble. Andy was different. He just liked the idea of a human talking to an angel. He called it "an awesome wonder," and he wanted to hear what that was like in as many details as I could offer. The actual words Charles shared with me were not as much of an issue to Andy as the fact that some fantastic angelic being was interacting with us, period! Andy wanted to know all about Charles' looks, mannerisms … even his expressions.

One expression *did* come back to me. "He always said, 'good question,' just like the prophet. But even though my questions might have been good, that didn't mean he answered all of them, and by not answering, he was also like the prophet, because *he* didn't answer half the stuff we asked either."

"So let me get this straight," Ben said. "Two angels, one good and one evil. They are no longer in the ornament, and they follow us around like a couple of ghosts?"

"I wouldn't call them ghosts," I said. "But yeah, they are invisible until we summon them. Actually, not invisible either. Charles said something about another dimension."

"And a wish can only be made every other day?" DeWorken asked to double-check my story.

I felt so sorry for poor DeWorken. This was his first question since I had given my report, and I'd been talking for a long time. There was only one thing on Doug's mind. When would he get his own chance to make a wish and become tall once again?

I sat next to him and spoke gently. "That's right, Doug. Well, I mean, every other day if we only wanna deal with Charles. It would be a mistake to ask anything from Hamartio."

"And tomorrow is Hamartio's turn?" Tinker Bell asked.

"Yes," I said. "And we're all agreed, aren't we? Nobody should use the ornament when it's Hamartio's turn?"

"Of course we agree," Ben said. "And you need to be careful with that ornament, buddy. Our friend Cliff already screwed things up by making that first wish, which shrunk DeWorken. We don't need his trigger-happy fingers on the ornament a second time. Hold on tight to that thing and never let it out of your sight."

I wondered at first why Cliff didn't take offense at Ben's comment, just as he hadn't stopped our conversation to explain exactly what it might mean to "live in another dimension," and then I realized he never actually heard those parts of the conversation. Instead, Cliff was still pacing and thinking about something else. Finally, he returned to the fire.

"That word sounds so familiar," Cliff said.

"What word?" Tinker Bell asked.

"Hamartio. The evil angel's name. Hamartio ... Hmm ... I knew that word once, but I can't seem to place it. I don't know why I can't remember."

I didn't know why he couldn't remember, either, since Cliff was usually so good at remembering things. All I knew was that I was kind of glad. Not that I didn't wanna figure out stuff about our situation. It's just that if Cliff were to start remembering, he'd go on and on about it. The information might be useful, but the long lecture going with it wouldn't seem worth the price.

Tinker Bell asked a third question. "So can a wish made to one angel do away with the effects of a wish made to a previous angel?"

Her words hit me like a ton of bricks. It was such an important question, and I had no answer.

"Um … ah … he didn't say."

"Well, didn't you ask him?" Cliff said sharply.

"I guess not."

Cliff shook his head, looking very aggravated and disappointed. "That would seem like a fairly obvious question."

Ben had a kind look on his face, unlike Cliff. "What's wrong buddy?" he said to me.

"He's right, Ben. Cliff's right. I can't believe Charles talked to me for so long, and I never asked if one wish could be undone by a previous wish."

Ben smiled a little and shrugged his shoulders. "Don't let it get you down. It sounds like you asked him a lot. And it sounds like you learned a lot too."

"Not as much as I should have."

"Not everybody can conduct a perfect interview the way Cliff would have done," Ben said in that strange kind of tone that was nice to one person and scolding to somebody else at the same time.

"Who said anything about being perfect?" Cliff shot back. "But I, at least, would have asked him about one wish being undone by another. Under the old ornament rules, a wish had permanent effects. You couldn't just reverse the process with your next wish."

"Well, I'm sure it must work the same way now," I said.

"You're sure?" Cliff said. "What makes you so sure?"

"Because that's the way it was before."

"Yeah? So? These are new rules. You just told us these are new rules."

Ben came to my defense again. "Quit hassling him. If he forgot to ask, he forgot to ask. That's all. When it's your turn, you can act like Clarence Darrow and get every last detail out of the angels. Mike did the best he could."

I appreciated Ben coming to my rescue, but I still felt really bad.

I turned to Cliff again. "I think he would have said something if that part had changed. Probably the rule about one wish not undoing another wish was assumed."

Cliff pointed his finger at me the way he always did when he was giving one of those lectures that adults called "patronizing." At least, that's what Aunt Loureen would have called it, "patronizing."

"Never assume," Cliff said.

"Sit down, Cliff!" The command came from Ben, so Cliff did as he was told.

"All right." Cliff said. "All right. Just curious. Well, OK then, how about our other mystery? According to Mike, all wishes made with the ornament back in our old world have been reset. So why is DeWorken still a miniature?"

"Yeah!" DeWorken said. "That's what I'd like ta know."

It was the first time on our trip that DeWorken and Cliff had been in agreement on anything, even if it only had to do with curiosity over the same question, each one hoping for a different answer. Cliff hoped nothing could change DeWorken back, and DeWorken dreamed of turning normal size so that he could use Cliff's face like a vacuum cleaner on the dirt path.

"Sorry, everyone," I said. "I don't have that information either."

Cliff sighed. "Geez, Mike. What did you guys talk about? The weather?"

"We talked plenty! And I did think about that reset question. That one I *did* think of, only I was too late. I thought about it after he disappeared — in fact, just a few minutes after. I was kicking myself since it was such a major question that we'd all been wondering about. I guess I should have remembered to ask. Probably I forgot because we talked about so many other things, it kinda slipped my mind."

"Maybe you can ask him next time," DeWorken said, looking like a little kid eager to get a break.

"Well, maybe Doug," I said. "But I'm not sure we wanna waste another wish by summoning him and asking, especially when we have to wait two days for his next wish. By that time, who knows what kind of trouble we might be in? We might need to rely on some other wish to get us out of a jam."

"There, there," Andy said. "Why be so gloomy? Who says we'll get in any trouble?"

I found that comment kind of funny coming from Andy, since if it hadn't been for him, we would never have come to the cave in the first place and gotten trapped in this world on the other side of the back cave wall. Ben was mostly blaming Cliff, and the prophet Cephalithos seemed to agree with Ben that this was Cliff's fault, and yeah, I agreed a little. Cliff did cause a lot of this problem, but I hadn't forgotten that we never would have learned about the time portal and would never have gone anywhere near it if not for Andy taking us there so that we could "hide in a safe place where nobody could find us."

Anyway, Andy started in on one of his monologues. I wasn't sure who was worse, Andy or Cliff. Cliff bored us with facts. Andy never bragged about knowledge the way Cliff did, but he bored us just as much with his "good ol' boy stories."

"When I was only a youth," Andy said, looking very interested in what he was about to tell us and looking like the only one interested. "Oh ... say ... seventeen ... I used to take a more pessimistic view of life ..."

I needed to do something fast, or he'd go on and on.

"But then," Andy continued, "I decided to 'grab the bull by the horns' as the old saying goes ... Hmm ... 'Bull by the horns' ... I always wondered where that expression came from."

It was just like Andy to start a story and then get off on some tangent just because he ended up using a familiar expression and now wanted to talk about where the expression came from instead of finishing his original thought.

I expected Cliff to speak up. I figured he knew just exactly where that saying about the bull and the horns came from and every other piece of information about every stupid saying that ever existed. But Cliff wasn't paying attention. Neither was anyone else. Nobody really paid attention to Andy anyway, but this time Cliff had already shut himself out of the conversation for a different reason. He was back to thinking again. I could always tell when Cliff was trying to figure something out. He got unusually quiet and had a look on his face like somebody trying to solve a crossword puzzle or something even brainier, like that Rubik's Cube. He was probably still trying to remember where he had heard the evil angel's name before.

"Yep," Andy continued. "Yes, sir ... Life has its curves. And they come when you least expect them. But I say, a hearty attitude is always the best remedy for ..."

I interrupted him quickly. "Great, Andy ... That's great. But to finish my point, I don't wanna waste another wish by asking about why DeWorken is still miniature. Besides, Caligula more or less told us already. DeWorken stayed that size because miniature people exist in this world naturally. And Caligula talks in this world for the same reason. He talks when he feels like it because, in this world, it is natural for cats to talk human language."

Caligula gave me his usual dirty look. I figured it meant that he hadn't actually said all that and I was misquoting him. He did say it was possible, but that's all, only a possibility. For that matter, I started thinking that if wishes from our world had been reset, any knowledge Caligula had about the ornament must also be erased since he knew stuff only as a result of a wish from me. But whatever he still knew or didn't know, he was annoyed that I remembered his words wrong, except I didn't remember them wrong. I knew it was just a guess and maybe that was all he could do now in the new world, guess. Still ... I liked the guess ... Only I wasn't phrasing it as a guess right now, so he was annoyed, but not so annoyed that he was gonna talk if he didn't feel like talking. Too bad Andy and Cliff couldn't learn from Caligula and turn off the mouth once in a while.

"Doug," Tinker Bell said, "when we get to my country you will be no smaller than anyone else. And you'll like it there. I promise."

All at once, it hit Cliff. "Hey, I remember now ... Sin!"

Ben was throwing dirt on the fire so that we could break camp soon and begin today's journey. He turned around. "What? Sin? What about sin? What are you talking about?"

Cliff looked very excited and happy with himself, just like he did every time he discovered some new fact or remembered a fact he had once forgotten. "The word *hamartio* ... It comes from the Greek word *hamartia*: sin!"

"So his name means *sin*," DeWorken said. "So what?"

Once again, Cliff seemed just delighted for a new opportunity to put DeWorken in his place.

"I can see where that word may have limited chilling effect upon you, DeWorken. Sin is such a natural part of your life, you are used to it, not unlike the man who is used to his own smell. But the rest of us do smell your sin. Make no mistake. And the smell is pungent."

"Knock it off!" Ben shouted.

"Ah, let him alone, Robinson. I don't need no help from you. He doesn't even come up with original stuff. The cat already made that same smart-mouth comment."

Caligula turned away, obviously not wanting to be part of the conversation, whether he thought DeWorken stunk or not.

"You think so?" Cliff said. "Well, I was only talking about your smell in an allegorical sense. Caligula meant it literally. That's because animals have a keen sense of smell. But in your case, that keen sense is not necessary. Even a person with a stuffed nose would smell you coming a mile away."

"Just keep talkin', weasel! One of these days, I'm gonna be normal size again, and you'll eat every word. It'll be like Burger King, only ya won't enjoy it, cuz I'll be the one feedin' ya."

DeWorken had a point about Cliff's big mouth. I had tried to talk to Cliff about this, but I might as well have been talking to my shoe. As I said to Cliff, I did understand why he liked being able to say anything at all to a guy who used to make him squirm, but the whole reason I even summoned Charles in the first place was because Cliff had asked me. Since Charles had not allowed me to wish on behalf of Cliff, the situation between him and Doug had not changed. He was just as worried as ever about what might happen should some new magic spell come our way and turn Miniature DeWorken into Terrifying DeWorken. Cliff was very concerned that this could change at any time, and yet here he was, still shooting off his mouth. I had already suggested he stop doing it, and Cliff seemed at the time to regret all of the DeWorken wisecracks. So why did he keep doing it again anyway? I didn't understand him. He'd been my friend for years, and after all this time, I still didn't understand Cliff. For a guy who loved facts and bragged so much about the things he learned, Cliff sure wasn't learning anything where DeWorken was concerned. Aunt Loureen talked to me once about people who were intelligent but still got into trouble for their own foolish choices. She called it "the difference between knowledge and wisdom."

But anyway, right now Cliff was more interested in showing off his knowledge. He continued explaining the word *hamartia*.

"It may not be significant to DeWorken but the word *sin* in association with an angel speaks volumes. We were already told that this being was evil. Evidently his very name backs that up. In fact, the literal name is a derivative, *hamartio* with an *o*. The word technically means *I sin*, so this is what Hamartio declares about himself."

"I guess we shouldn't be surprised," I said.

"In ancient times," Cliff continued, "people were named for character traits that parents desired of their offspring. When children grew older and changed their character, their names changed also. In the Bible, for instance, the name Jacob means 'cheat' because Jacob cheated his brother Esau out of his birthright. Later, Jacob stopped being a cheater, and his name was changed to Israel, meaning 'He struggles with God.'"

"Who cares?" DeWorken snapped.

For a second, it looked like Caligula was gonna say the same thing. Maybe DeWorken beat him to the punch.

But with or without anyone's interest, Cliff was bound to continue.

"I first heard the word *hamartio* from an old Sunday school teacher," he said. "Mr. Bianki."

The second he said that, I kind of remembered too. I never in a million years would have thought that a Greek name would be something I'd remember, nor a word from any other foreign language for that matter. But I have to admit, the moment Cliff said this, it sounded familiar. It's because Cliff and I went to the same church when we were younger and also the same Sunday school class. So Mr. Bianki was my teacher too. He'd always bored the class to death by going into definitions of Greek words.

When I was little, Sunday school had been fun. We heard about David killing the giant Goliath with a slingshot. We heard about Noah escaping the flood. We heard about the Red Sea parting for Moses. Those stories were cool.

But when we got older and went to church as middle schoolers, Sunday School turned boring. Mrs. Webber almost put us to sleep talking about the missionary journeys of the Apostle Paul. Mr. Bianki was even worse. He claimed it was important to not only know the "great doctrines and theologies of the Bible" but to also know some Greek since the New Testament had been originally written in Greek. I had no idea at the time that I would someday be brought into a new world where prophets and angels and even the planet itself were named after a bunch of Greek words. If I'd had any inkling, I might have paid better attention to Bianki.

Of course, Cliff *did* pay attention, but he would have paid attention even if the teacher was talking about the amount of legs on a centipede, the varieties of coffee beans in Colombia, or eighteen different species of fungi. Cliff was interested in anything. He didn't even believe in the Bible anymore when we were going to Bianki's class. He had accepted it on faith as a little kid, but in junior high, he stopped believing. When I asked him why, he said that a scientific mind could not take Scripture seriously. He kept going to church anyway, only because his mom made him.

My mom made me too. At first I just accepted the Bible miracles on account of my pastor and Sunday school teacher saying they were true. Dad never believed in them, but he didn't make much effort to keep Shelly and me from believing, probably because he didn't wanna make Mom unhappy or argue with Aunt Loureen, who would have gone on and on with him about it. Anyway, I mostly found Bible stories fun to listen to as a kid and accepted them without questioning them a whole lot.

In junior high, right around the time when Cliff started doubting, I had doubts too. But Aunt Loureen gave me a whole different way to look at God.

"Nephew," she used to say, "I have a great respect for science, but you must remember that most of the wonderful scientific discoveries over the years came from men who accepted a Creator. Thus they presumed an orderly universe, for the universe cannot have design without a designer. In their arrogance, many of today's scientists continue to study this design, and yet they have jettisoned the designer."

Cliff looked at it much differently. Although he didn't have too much problem with the idea of some kind of designer or "supreme being who set up the cosmos," as he put it, Bible miracles were a whole separate subject to him and gave him a totally different reaction. Even in junior high, he sounded like some intellectual on public television.

"The very idea of the Red Sea parting or somebody rising from the dead is ludicrous," he said. "Miracles make sane science stand on its head."

But Aunt Loureen had an interesting way of putting it. "Nephew, when the Bible says God does a miracle, it does not mean that God is some kind of magician who waves a magic wand or throws science out the window. There *is* a scientific explanation for everything. We simply do not yet know what all of them are. Human beings probably know less than 1 percent of the obtainable knowledge of the universe. God does His miracles with the 99.9 percent of the knowledge we don't have."

That made a lot of sense to me, and I often thought it would have been fun to watch Aunt Loureen debate Cliff, but it never happened. Cliff brought that kind of stuff up to me and never mentioned it in front of Aunt Loureen.

Anyway, since she was an adult and Cliff was just a kid, and since she was a school teacher, and since she always seemed very smart, I figured it was OK to believe in miracles.

Still, even though he no longer believed, Cliff liked learning about stuff, even the Bible, and if his mom was gonna force it on him, he was gonna make the best of the situation and learn as much as he could, even though he called those who accepted the Bible "naïve."

Cliff had been one of the few students who found Mr. Bianki's Greek side notes interesting. Unfortunately, other guys from the public school were also dragged to Sunday School, and seeing Cliff interested in something like Greek just made them view him even more as a nerd.

And while I personally understood that Cliff was simply taking in the Bible like he took in any other subject, everyone else in class was confused. They didn't know what to make of Cliff. He knew more about the Bible than most churchgoers, but he stopped believing in the Bible and they hadn't.

Even with all the ornament power that he first witnessed in sixth grade, it made no difference to Cliff. He called that "the unexplained," but he still didn't like the word *miracle*. It was kind of funny because when I listened carefully, it seemed to me that Aunt Loureen was defining a miracle exactly the same way, *something unexplained*. So maybe she and Cliff agreed on more than Cliff admitted.

But whatever he called it, Cliff absolutely observed the supernatural around the same time I did, back when Aunt Loureen first gave me the ornament. There was no denying this, and I just didn't see how anybody could believe in the supernatural if God didn't exist.

For that matter, how could Cliff believe in angels living inside the ornament? Or angels who had now escaped the ornament and live outside? How can you have angels without God? And back when we were in the cave, Ben was the one who had had the most trouble believing in that time portal. Cliff accepted it right off and tried to show Ben that there were similar things in nature, like Old Faithful, even though Ben thought that was a lame example and I kind of did too. So Cliff was accepting the supernatural right from the beginning of this mess we found ourselves in, a mess that he himself started by believing in the supernatural enough to steal my ornament, make one wish about DeWorken, and another one that freed the angels inside.

Focusing on all this, I realized that it had been a long time since I'd heard any of Cliff's doubts about miracles. Without even thinking much about it, I guess I just assumed that he must have come to accept them over the years. And even if it hadn't happened up till a couple of weeks ago, everything about this trip showed that he was at least accepting miracles *now*. I thought I even remembered hearing him use the word *miracle* once or twice on this current journey. And that's why I figured he must also be accepting God.

Then again, Cliff never had denied the existence of God anyway, not even back in junior high. He did seem to believe in *some* kind of God, or like I already said, some supreme being or some kind of something out there. It was just the God of the Bible he had trouble with. But even that must be different now as a result of being in this new world. How could he not believe in the God of the Bible with all we had been through, or at least a God who does miracles? Didn't we all hear the old prophet talk about God, even though he called God by a different name, the Author of Life?

By now, I wasn't even paying attention to Cliff's dumb lecture anymore. I sat there watching him flap his lips and continued thinking about all our beliefs. I played the whole thing over in my head one more time. Up till now, with one adventure after another, I had forgotten that Cliff declared himself a Bible skeptic long ago. Obviously, this could no longer be the case, but I had not thought to even ask. It never came up in my mind, just like the fact that I had left the ornament in Ben's car before going through the cave wall never entered my mind and just like those important questions I should have asked Charles never entered my mind. I was starting to wonder if there might not just be something wrong with my mind. I'd heard of old people getting forgetful. Aunt Loureen often talked about friends and family who had what she called "short-term memory." But my forgetfulness seemed even worse. It seemed *long term*, not *short term*. Was it just on account of me being careless, concentrating on the moment and forgetting big picture ideas? Or was there something really wrong with me? And if something was wrong with me, how come Charles and Cephalithos thought I was destined for some special mission? How can anybody that forgetful save a whole planet or whatever it was I was meant to do?

Anyway, I was thinking of bringing the subject of God up right now in the hopes that Cliff might let us in on his current beliefs. He was talking about Mr. Bianki anyway, so why not bring up a related question and ask how he felt these days about miracles after all the supernatural stuff we had experienced together lately? But first I would need a moment for him to stop talking and let me get a word in edgewise.

That moment was about to come, because Cliff seemed to be wrapping up his little lecture that nobody had requested. But no sooner did he stop than we realized that one member of our party was not as bored with Cliff as the rest of us, Andy. He seemed fascinated. I guess he liked listening to speeches as much as giving them.

"What about the name *Charles*?" Andy asked.

Every single eye, including Caligula's, quickly turned toward Andy, wishing he had left well enough alone.

"Great!" Caligula said. "Just great! He was about to wind things down, and you wound him up again."

But Andy didn't seem to even notice the cat this time, and Cliff didn't care either. We were all getting more used to Caligula chiming in once in a while, just like a regular human member of the group, and Cliff was always very grateful for a new question, *any* question.

"Well, the meaning of the name *Charles* is irrelevant," Cliff said. "That was a disguised nickname which somewhat camouflaged his true identity that Mike had read about in that ornament mythology book years ago. Charles may have appeared to Mike and to me in the form of a man, but he is really an angel, and this angel's name is *Char*."

Ben stood up. "I'm going to fill up my canteen with some water from the brook. I'll be back in a few minutes."

Cliff might have been an expert with languages, but the rest of us were better translators right now. We knew exactly how to translate Ben. Words like *water* and *canteen* meant, "I'm skipping the next lecture because if I hear one more word from Cliff, I'll throw up."

"So, young man," Andy said to Cliff as Ben walked away, "what does the name *Char* mean?"

Cliff's eyes beamed with delight. A kid opening a birthday present couldn't have looked happier. "That too, is a Greek word. *Char* is the Greek word for 'joy.'"

"Ah …" Andy said, stroking his chin. "Interesting … how interesting … One angel whose name means 'sin' and another whose name means 'joy.' They certainly are opposites, not only in their missions but in their personality traits, like you said … Fascinating … yes … very interesting … Char … what a marvelous name."

"Actually," Cliff said, "it's pronounced 'Kar.' We write it with a *ch* only in the English transliteration."

Now I was ready to lose it, "Oh, for crying out loud, Cliff, do you really think anybody cares?"

Suddenly Caligula surprised me by taking my side for once. "Oh yes! Well said, Kid! Tell that walking, talking encyclopedia to zip it! Good for you, Kid. I knew it could only be a matter of time before you finally made a constructive comment. Give a monkey a typewriter, sooner or later he types a word."

Just like Caligula. Even while offering me a compliment, he couldn't resist insulting me at the same time. Still, his comment had an effect on Cliff, because he just stopped talking all of a sudden. I'm not sure why Cliff was able to ignore Caligula's earlier comment and get tongue-tied after the second. Maybe he found the second interruption longer and more insulting.

And Cliff wasn't the only one who took more notice this time. Andy also reacted.

"Aw … the poor kitty. He probably isn't used to conversations like these."

Caligula cocked his head and glared at Andy as if he wanted to kill the old man.

"That may be," Cliff muttered in a lower voice, "but it's difficult to concentrate when you hear words coming from the mouth of a feline. English from the lips of a cat may be an interesting phenomenon, but I believe I liked it better when he wasn't talking at all and just behaving like an ordinary animal."

"Fine," Caligula said. "I'll make you a deal, Cliff. *I'll* stop talking if *you* do. In fact, how about if *everybody* gives it a rest? The hot air around this camp could fill a helium balloon and fly it around the world in eighty days. Can't a cat get any sleep around here?"

"Sleep?" I said. "It's morning."

"So? I like to sleep in. I was up all night!"

"Doing what?" I asked.

"He's a cat," Andy said. "Cats are night creatures."

"Yes," Cliff added. "They are nocturnal."

"Man oh man," Caligula said under his breath. "The way you two blather on! How about taking me at my word and minding your own business? *Why* I was up all night is my own affair. I don't need an interpretation based upon the mistaken opinion that human beings are experts on cats. First we hear from this living fossil who thinks he's the proprietor of the San Diego Zoo. Then our redheaded Isaac Newton has to say the exact same thing all over again by wording it just differently enough to sound like an intellectual. Bravo, Cliff, bravo! Yes, *nocturnal* is a more official-sounding description of night creatures. Everybody is impressed."

That was enough to make DeWorken laugh and add his own two cents. "Yeah, he thinks he knows everything."

Tinker Bell reached for his hand. "Doug, please. This is only going to get you all riled up again."

"I'm OK, honey,"

How strange to hear DeWorken call anybody "honey."

Ben was returning with his canteen. Cliff noticed him off in the distance and immediately moved closer to DeWorken, probably wanting to get in one more free shot before Ben stopped him.

Looking down at the two miniatures, Cliff said, "It's not that I think I know everything, DeWorken. It's just that compared to you, *anybody* would feel smart."

"Very funny!"

"Just ignore him," Tinker Bell said.

"Who can ignore this loudmouth? He thinks he's funny and he thinks he's smart, but he don't know nothin'."

"The correct phrase would be 'doesn't know anything,'" Cliff corrected. "Since you're so eager to turn large, you might as well start by growing your brain a little."

DeWorken was getting just as riled up as Tinker Bell had warned.

"Ya already told that one, Mr. Comedian!"

"Well, I'm telling it again!"

Ben was close enough now to hear. "He's right, Cliff. You need some new material."

"Or better yet," DeWorken said, "just shut up."

"Perhaps that would be best," Andy said to Cliff. "It isn't nice to be so insulting, young man. I would think that with angels watching us and God Himself, you would be more careful."

This was my opportunity. I could find out more about Cliff's current beliefs and stop the tiresome banter back and forth between him and DeWorken at the same time.

"Speaking of God," I said … "Tell me something, Cliff … With all we've seen and all that's happened, you must not feel anymore the way you did back in Mr. Bianki's class. You finally believe in miracles, right?"

Cliff looked confused. "Miracles?"

"You used to reject miracles and God and all of the Bible stories. You said that to me a long time ago. But a lot has happened to us since then."

"Oh," Cliff said, sitting down. "I see what you're getting at. Well, we are certainly experiencing the paranormal. But miracles? That might be a stretch."

"You're kidding!" I said. "We meet prophets of God! We meet angels! We travel through time! We go into another world! We listen to a talking cat! You make a wish and poor Doug shrinks! … Sorry, Doug, just making a point …"

Tinker Bell wrapped her arms around Doug with affection before he could say anything, and it looked like he decided to just let it go, probably because he preferred snuggling with Tinker Bell to arguing with Cliff.

"You see all this," I continued, "and you still don't believe?"

"One must always maintain a degree of healthy skepticism," Cliff said.

Ben wasn't buying it. "More like healthy stubbornness."

"Look who's talking!" Cliff said. "You've been the biggest skeptic of the group, Ben. For years, you only half-believed in the ornament, and on this trip, you raised doubts about everything."

"Like I told you before," Ben said, "I trust my eyes and ears more than hearsay. But by that same token, my eyes and ears are now giving me a different picture."

"And it's a picture we've all witnessed," Andy said to Cliff. "Surely, young man, you cannot doubt God's existence in the face of this enchanting new world."

"Hey, I never said I don't believe in God! Never said it! Not on this trip, not back in school, not even back in Mr. Bianki's class. I am *not* an atheist, and I never have been."

"Well, you don't seem to like using the actual word *God*," I said. "You keep calling Him a supreme being instead of calling Him 'God.'"

"Who cares what we call it?" Cliff said. "It's the same cereal. It's just a different box."

"Easy, young man. Let's not be referring to the Almighty as a mere bowl of cereal."

Cliff shook his head. "You just did the same thing, Andy. You called God by a different name. You called Him the Almighty. So, I used an alternative name as well. Almighty? Supreme being? We're mincing words and talking about the same thing."

"Hold on," I said. "It doesn't seem to me like we're talking about the same thing. When I talk about God, I mean the specific God described in the Bible."

"As do I," Andy said. "And the term 'Almighty' *is* found in the Bible as a matter of fact."

"Yes, that title is found in the Bible," Cliff explained. "Translated from the Hebrew, *El Shaddai!* We also have the name *Yahweh*, or the generic word for God in general, *Elohim*."

"Here we go again," DeWorken said. "He thinks he's really hot stuff with all these big, fancy words."

"I'm just saying I know what the Bible teaches. I know better than the rest of you, and since I'm the only one in this group who has actually studied Scripture, I feel free to dismiss it."

"Young man," Andy said, "I have studied Scripture as well, and it cannot be dismissed."

"Why not, Andy? Why do I have to believe in the Bible to believe in God?"

"Well, for one thing," I said, "the Bible talks about angels, and *you have met angels*."

But Cliff was not one to give up so easily. "Char may be using those terms merely because they are familiar to us, as conventional reference points."

"Then why all the Greek in this new world?" Andy asked. "You yourself reminded us moments ago that the New Testament was written in Greek."

I have to admit, that was the first good argument I had heard from ol' Andy.

Even Cliff seemed taken back a peg. But he finally came up with a response. "Cross traffic between the worlds. That's what Cephalithos said. Much cross traffic. That means similar languages and the sharing of similar myths."

"You're wasting your time, everybody," Ben said. "Cliff will never admit he's wrong. If he doesn't like the word, *God*, he will not use the word *God*. It's just that simple. So stop arguing with him. It isn't worth the effort. Cliff would wear a bathing suit in a snow storm if the snow contradicted his prediction that the weather was gonna be sunny and warm."

Cliff snapped at Ben. "You don't believe in the Bible either!"

"Since when?"

"Since always!" Cliff said. "I've heard you say again and again that you think the Bible stories are just fables."

"Maybe they are," Ben said. "But they have good morals, and the lessons in the stories could still be inspired by God."

"I don't know, Ben," I said. "If we're actually meeting angels and prophets, it makes me think the Bible must be a lot more than fables."

Andy nodded, "I agree."

I didn't really like being on the same side as Andy. He was a nice guy, but if we were on the same side, he'd keep talking to me, and I'd just as soon he talked to the others and leave me alone.

"Whatever," Ben said. "I guess it's all a moot point now. In this world, we *do* see the supernatural. That's all I can say. But the Bible doesn't apply to this world. It was apparently written for our world back home, so we can all go on thinking whatever we want about the Bible."

"True enough," I said. "But I have a book at home which does apply to this world, *The Magic Ornament of Lumis*. And in that book, the author talked about Christmas. Doesn't that tell us something right there? Christ is in the Bible, and Christmas is a celebration of Christ."

"Not originally," Cliff said. "Before the Catholic Church took over Rome, December 25 marked a celebration of the pagan festival of Saturnalia."

"See?" Ben said. "Saturnalia. Are you catching on, Mike? Quit arguing with him. He always has some new rabbit to pull out of his hat."

But I didn't wanna give up so soon.

"It doesn't matter what the holiday was originally called. That book used the word *Christmas*. That comes from Christ. Come on, Cliff, you're a word guy. Admit it. Christmas comes from Christ."

"Yes," Cliff agreed. "But once again, with all the cross traffic between the worlds, the custom of Christmas may have been brought over here without the meaning. That book never mentioned Jesus, did it?"

"Nope," Ben said sarcastically. "Never mentioned Jesus. Well, that's good enough for me. You win again, Cliff."

"Not so fast," I said. "Look, Cliff, in that same book, Hamartio had a superior angel, Lucifer. Lucifer is the same as Satan. That brings us back to the Bible for sure."

"Not really," Cliff said." "The name *Lucifer* is a mistranslation from Isaiah. The actual Hebrew words read as 'Day Star.' And Isaiah was not referring to a heavenly being in that chapter. He was talking about an Earthly king."

Ben stood up. He'd had enough. If I wasn't gonna take his advice and end the discussion, he was gonna end it his own way. "Let's make tracks people. Whatever the angels call themselves in this world and whatever God calls Himself in this world, I mean to get us *out* of this world. So pack up your gear, and let's start moving!"

***

The journey wasn't as interesting today. Mostly because we were surrounded by the same kind of scenery and terrain.

We did climb uphill a little more but not much and not over any mountain. Just more of an upward incline.

I thought it was real nice of Ben to be looking out for the miniatures by making those small seats which fit into his backpack, and today I volunteered to trade backpacks with Ben so that he could get a break and I would be the one to carry them.

Ben agreed, and as a result, I couldn't help but overhear some interesting exchanges between DeWorken and Tinker Bell while we were hiking, mostly stuff about how much DeWorken would like her country.

"You'll be looked up to and admired, a strong, handsome man like you."

"Do they have football games in your country?"

"Well, no, my love. Not football. But there are other athletic events. And you'll do well. You'll be a natural."

I wondered if she was just buttering him up so that no one would change their minds about bringing her back to her home country, especially since she had already told us that her country wasn't really a country anymore in so many words, that her country had been conquered and her people scattered. True, she said there were still gatherings in hiding places, but it was hard to imagine sporting events in hidden communities. Still, what did I know? Tinker Bell seemed very innocent and sincere, at least from my point of view, even though I hardly ever talked to her and really hadn't gotten to know her too well.

I also heard her tell DeWorken that she wished she could have been more helpful in our conversation about cross traffic between the two worlds. She grew up learning about the Magic Ornament of Lumis, and she did know that the people in Lumis celebrated a holiday called 'Christmas' many centuries ago, but she had never learned anything about Jesus until being kidnapped and brought to Earth, and she heard nothing about Lucifer while growing up either, apart from his role in the Lumis legend.

Maybe Cliff was right after all. Maybe people in this world knew of some Earth terms and Earth holidays, and that was all. Maybe the meaning had been lost to them, even if those customs and words originated with the Bible.

And as usual, it hadn't occurred to me to just stop in the middle of the conversation with Cliff and say "Wait! We have somebody from this world right here in our midst! Let's ask her!"

Chalk up another obvious question I had failed to ask. But at least in this case, I wasn't the only scatterbrain. Nobody else had thought of asking her either, not even Cliff.

Caligula was following us. At times I overheard him cussing under his breath, especially when Andy was speaking. Right now, Andy kept talking about the price of food when he was our age.

"Ten cents! That's what a hamburger used to cost. Ten cents! I could order two hamburgers, fries, and a chocolate shake and still get change back for my dollar!"

I wished he wouldn't talk about food, especially fast food. I loved burgers and almost any other kind of junk food, and I figured we wouldn't be finding anything like that in this new world. Listening to Andy was making me hungry, even though we had just finished breakfast.

I picked up my pace to get away from Andy and moved closer to Ben and Cliff, who were way ahead. They were arguing, something about how Cliff wished he had put his allergy pills into his pocket before going through the cave wall.

For myself, I didn't care about Cliff's pills, or Andy's fond hamburger memories, or what life would be like for DeWorken and Tinker Bell should they ever get to her home.

Instead, I kept thinking about our Bible discussion. It seemed that Andy and I were the only ones who really took the Bible seriously. Cliff was right when he reminded us that Ben used to view it as a mere book of fables. And the supernatural on our adventure wasn't making much of a difference to Ben since, like he said, we were in a different world where the Bible probably didn't apply. But I kept thinking about the fact that we were hearing a lot about God in this world. It made me wish that I had paid more attention in church growing up or that I had taken the time to study the Bible on my own. Even after my first experience with the ornament back in sixth grade, one would have thought I'd have been more interested in God and miracles and angels. The Bible would have been the perfect thing to study. Instead, I spent my time thinking about girls and sports and hanging with my friends.

I was feeling disappointed that we talked so little about the Bible before Ben changed the subject. And I was also bugged that Cliff seemed to (on one hand) accept the miraculous and, (on the other hand) still talk about the Bible as if it was nothing but a book of fairy tales.

I was looking at things quite differently, because if the Bible was really true, if the Bible was exactly what it claimed to be, the Word of God, then anything we knew about God from the Bible would also apply in this new world. It would be useful information. After all, if there was only one God, He must be the God of this world too, and that was how the book about Lumis started off, by saying this story was "in one of the other worlds God created." Come to think of it, the prophet told us the same thing, about how God set up time watchers over all of His worlds across the galaxies to work against the damage some Earth time traveler had caused. He never claimed it was the God of the Bible in so many words, so Cliff might still be able to doubt on a technicality. Still, for all these reasons, I was wishing I knew the Bible as well as Cliff, and yet, Cliff who knew the Bible inside and out, didn't care about the Bible. How ironic.

That night, after we made our new camp and had dinner, I asked Ben if I could talk to him alone. We walked a little way from the camp.

"What's up, buddy?"

"It's about the ornament. I think you should hold on to it."

"Me? What for?"

"Oh, I don't know. I guess I'm feeling concerned about all the stuff I keep forgetting. It's important not to lose this thing, and I already left it behind in your car. If not for that old prophet, we wouldn't even have the ornament right now."

"True," Ben said. "But you've done a good job of watching it since then."

"I know, Ben, but Cliff is just chomping at the bit to use the ornament and protect himself from DeWorken. There's no telling what he might do. I'm not even sure he's willing to wait another day for Charles."

"You think he'd go to that other angel? The evil one?"

"I don't know. But I've been seeing a whole different side of Cliff. It's kind of scary."

"Cliff has his issues, and I already said we should keep the ornament away from him, so with that, we are in full agreement, but I'd like to think he's too smart to go making wishes with an evil being."

"Maybe, but we've already been warned that one of us is gonna turn evil. I'm not saying it will be Cliff. I'm just saying, maybe we should be careful."

"You *have* been careful, Mike. You haven't let the ornament out of your sight since we got it back."

"I know, Ben. But you'd still be doing me a big favor by taking it. Look at the questions I forgot to ask Charles. I've been so forgetful and clumsy. You shouldn't trust me with the ornament."

"As a matter of fact, buddy, you are the one person in this camp whom I do trust. I see how hard you try to do the right thing and how fair you are to everybody, even DeWorken."

"That's nice of you to say, Ben, but … even if I was being careful, Cliff could try to steal it at night from me while I sleep, maybe even clunk me on the head or something."

"He's not gonna do that," Ben said reassuringly. "And even if he wanted to try such a stunt, who says he wouldn't do the same thing to me, knock me on the head while I sleep?"

"It's different with you. You're the only one around here that Cliff respects. I'm his friend too, but he's been jealous of me on account of me becoming more popular at school recently. We already know how he feels about DeWorken. He also hates the cat. He could care less about Tinker Bell … And Andy … well, Andy is Andy … The only authority Cliff respects is yours. That's why I'm sure he won't mess with you, even while you're asleep."

"You underestimate yourself," Ben said. "And you *overestimate* me."

"Maybe, Ben. I don't know. Maybe. But could you please do this for me anyway? Just take the ornament. Let's make you its official custodian. I would feel so much better if we did it that way."

It took a little longer to convince him, but finally Ben agreed. When Cliff asked me later where the ornament was, I could see he was disappointed and concerned that the ornament was now with Ben. This made me more suspicious than ever about Cliff and his intentions.

I slept better that night. No dreams about Marla. No nightmares. Probably I was feeling more at peace. Giving the ornament to Ben relieved me of a big burden. I suddenly remembered that Charles had referred to me as the "custodian of the ornament." I was also "custodian of the key chain." I hadn't given the key chain to Ben. Only the ornament. But I was supposed to be custodian of both. Had I shirked my responsibility with the ornament? No. Not possible. Charles might have viewed it like that had I given it to Cliff. But what better way to protect the ornament than giving it to Ben? That was probably the smartest thing a "custodian" could do. And so, even after thinking about Charles, I was still at peace. Also, I could now roll over without worrying about breaking the ornament, although I was starting to wonder if this device could ever really break anyway, and I seemed to remember that the book I read years ago said something about how it couldn't be destroyed, one more thing I had forgotten and was now starting to recall. I wished I would stop remembering stuff because all that happened was that, by remembering, I felt bad that I had forgotten in the first place.

My peaceful sleep was interrupted by a sharp, jarring shake. It was Cliff.

"Mike! Mike! Wake up! Come on. I need you up."

"Huh?" I was startled by the jolt and also very tired. "What's going on?"

"It's about Ben."

"Ben? What about him?"

"He's gone."

"What do you mean gone? You mean he's not sleeping in his blanket?"

"No. I mean he has disappeared. Ben is missing. He's gone, and I don't think he's coming back. The ornament too. The ornament disappeared with him."

Chapter Twenty-Seven

The Disappearance

When Cliff told Mike that Ben was missing along with the ornament, he was not being entirely honest. At its foundation, the story was accurate, but only partly, because Cliff supplied an erroneous detail, resulting in a story which relayed a half-truth.

The true half was that Ben was indeed missing, that Cliff had nothing to do with his disappearance, and honestly had no idea what happened to him. It was also true that he was with Ben shortly before Ben went off into the woods to investigate a strange noise, failing to return.

What wasn't true was Cliff's insistence that the ornament was also missing. With regard to the ornament, Cliff had lied. In fact, Cliff knew just exactly where the ornament was, and later today, he planned to find a private place away from the others and use it.

After awakening to the news about Ben, Mike seemed to be in panic mode. Cliff understood. Certainly Ben was the bravest and most stabilizing person in their party. Being without Ben was being without protection. Even with Charles the angel looking out for everybody, Ben was the person whom people depended on. Undoubtedly, Charles with all of his powers was a much greater asset, but the experience so far was to rely on Ben rather than the mysterious and only occasionally visible Charles. After all, Ben had been with them constantly. They could see him, hear him, and interact with him every single day. Ben was a calming influence. His reassuring voice had an almost tranquilizing effect. Ben's courage and ability to fight also helped people to feel less fearful about whomever or whatever they might encounter.

And so, Cliff did not blame Mike for being scared. Cliff was every bit as frightened and just as concerned about Ben's absence, even though it happened in a such a way that it turned out to be personally convenient. The result of Ben's disappearance left Cliff in possession of the ornament. It was hidden now, and only Cliff knew the location. Had Ben still been around, that would not be the case. Ben would be holding on to the magic charm as Mike had requested. Ben would be preventing Cliff from making the wish he desperately needed to make, that critical wish that would keep DeWorken off his back for good.

Mike was not taking the news well. He was very upset while asking Cliff what had happened, and he did not ask his questions quietly. With the high volume of their conversation, it was only a matter of time before the others awakened.

The evening was exceptionally chilly. Mike and Andy started a special middle-of-the-night fire. They didn't get it going as quickly as the previous fires Ben had built, but finally everyone was seated around the primitive stone fire ring, listening to Cliff as he tried to explain what happened.

"What do ya mean, he's gone?" DeWorken said.

"Gone," Cliff said. "As in *disappeared*."

"How so?" Andy asked. "Do you mean he just vanished into thin air right in front of your eyes?"

"No, I don't mean he disappeared as in some kind of magic act. He went out into the woods to check on a noise and failed to return."

Cliff noticed Mike watching him very suspiciously. Mike had already heard this part of the story while the others were still asleep, and he had since calmed down a little. The look of panic on his face was gone, replaced by a calmer expression, and yet, Mike's eyes showed distrust. He moved closer to Cliff.

"I keep thinking about this noise, and I still don't understand. Tell me again. What kind of noise?"

"Well, Ben thought it was coming from an animal."

"Huh?" DeWorken said.

"An animal noise," Cliff repeated with minor elaboration.

Mike shook his head. "That doesn't make any sense. Why would he go after an animal at night when he can barely see, especially unarmed?"

"I don't know," Cliff said. "To me it didn't sound like an animal anyway."

"Yeah? Then what did it sound like?"

"I'm not sure, Mike. More like electricity."

Mike only looked more confused. "Electricity? They don't have electricity in this backward place."

"Of course they do," Cliff explained. "They just haven't yet developed the technology to harness it. But electricity is everywhere."

"You know what I meant, Cliff."

Andy looked very puzzled. "How can two people listening to the same sound have such different interpretations of what it was? What kind of animal would sound the same as electricity?"

"What does electricity even sound like anyway?" Mike added.

"Like the sound of some kind of static," Cliff said. "Electric static. That's what I meant to say. Let me offer an example, not entirely accurate, but perhaps it will at least give you an idea. The sound can be likened to when you lose a signal on TV, that noise which comes with all the snow."

Mike walked up to within inches of Cliff's face. "That doesn't sound the same as an animal."

"I never said it did. Ben thought it sounded like an animal. Not me."

"So Ben decided to go check on a noise?" Andy asked for clarification.

"Yes."

"And he did this for no reason?" Mike asked, looking and sounding like Cliff's prosecutor, judge, and jury all rolled into one.

"I already told you the reason. He wanted to see where the noise was coming from."

Mike didn't seem to be buying it. This concerned Cliff because, so far, everything he had said was the exact truth. If Mike didn't accept the truth, how would he react when Cliff moved on to the second part of the story, the part he was going to make up, the part about the ornament also being gone?

"It seems to me," Mike said, "that Ben is too smart to go off into the woods unarmed. Why didn't he take the ax with him?"

"I don't know," Cliff said. "It happened fast. But it's not as if he was *really* unarmed. Remember, Ben had the ornament with him. Maybe that gave him reassurance."

"Ben has never used that ornament," Mike said. "He is the last one who would think of using it for protection. He was holding on to the ornament to keep it safe … so that nobody could swipe it and make a wish with the wrong angel!"

Cliff knew that last little insinuation was articulated for his benefit. It bothered him that Mike was so suspicious, even though in this particular case, his suspicions were well-founded.

Everything had happened so quickly. Cliff was the only person other than Ben who heard the strange noise in the woods. It woke up Ben, but nobody else. It didn't even wake up Cliff. Cliff was already up. He hadn't been able to get to sleep. Too many overwhelming thoughts were on his mind. That would have been happening anyway, simply because of the wondrous adventure they were all on.

But this evening, he'd had an extra dose to ponder: God. Cliff didn't like being lectured to about God by his friends, and he especially didn't like it when crotchety, meddlesome old strangers such as Andy joined in, jumping behind the podium with their own little self-righteous, sanctimonious sermons. Nevertheless, when a group of people talk about God and challenge you for not believing in Him or at least not making Him more central in your life, it's a difficult subject to simply ignore.

Of all the people in their company, Mike was making the biggest issue out of religion and the Bible. Cliff didn't understand why. This was a side of Mike he had never witnessed before. In the past, Mike expressed only a microscopic interest in the mysteries of science or metaphysics. Not even Mike's history with the ornament and its power had seemed to produce anything other than a fairly average middle schooler and high schooler. But Mike was not the same anymore, and Cliff could see that this was about more than that comic book going to his head. Maybe it had something to do with this sense of destiny he had obtained, first from his eccentric aunt, then later on from Charles and the prophet. This was the best theory to account for Mike's behavior. After all, Mike was intelligent — not an A student, but he did have enough going on upstairs to conclude that if there was really such a thing as destiny, then there must also be a God. Thinking about this gave Cliff a strange sensation, as if he was increasing his openness to God while feeling reluctant to do so. Cliff hated religion, but he despised those who ignored logic even more. Given the accuracy of a premise, certain conclusions must follow. In this case, the premise was destiny. If destiny existed, God existed. End of conversation. The alternative was that human life came about according to randomness and chance. Creatures who exist by mere accident have no destiny and no purpose. They can invent their own personal purpose to make life endurable, but without God, they would not exist according to any prior plan. They would simply live for a while and then die, clueless as to why they were even born at all, and without God, there would be no reason anyway. Without God, what *is* just *is*.

Cliff tried to block this private train of thought which seemed to bounce back and forth in his mind like a table tennis match. It was keeping him from falling asleep. In fact, the thoughts were so consuming, Cliff would no sooner try to turn them off than another emotionally laced idea would hit him and he would forget about sleep, reflecting once again upon God, life, and the order of the cosmos.

For most of his years, Cliff had no problem reconciling science with some kind of supreme force or spirit or eternal entity that formed the universe. Even Einstein himself, while remaining uninvolved in organized religion, had talked about a "manifest spirit at work in the universe" and suggested this as an obvious observation to any scientist who was honest or who had even a degree of humility.

And so, no problem with God, or at least, no problem with something very much *like* God. But in Cliff's mind, allowing design to have a designer was a far cry from the ludicrous, irrational beliefs held by Christians or those other pea brains involved with a wide assortment of group worship and espoused creeds. Why not just accept life as a mystery instead of trying to fill in the gaps with fanciful mythology? Besides, there was so much hypocrisy in the name of religion, from wars to bigotry to laughable rules which condemned dancing, card playing, and so many other harmless social gatherings. Even when they were activities Cliff didn't personally involve himself with, he found it amazing that people could be so restrictive or make such mountains out of molehills. Surely if there were a God, He would have nothing to do with this uncanny nonsense.

Even Cliff's parents served as bad examples. They dragged him to church when he was younger and listened to those superior morality lectures every week. Most of the time, their pastor talked about the importance of family values. So where had it all led? What was the eventual outcome of those hundreds upon hundreds of sermons? What was the summation of the church's influence? His parents were now divorced!

Of course, Cliff often wondered if that was less the fault of the church and more the fault of a henpecked father who got tired of listening to a wife who could probably power the entire state of California with the energy coming from her nonstop talking.

For a moment, Cliff found himself smiling at the thought of his mother meeting up with old Andy for some reason. What an interesting observation that would be! Cliff would enjoy watching that little performance more than a Broadway show! Who would end up talking more? It would be quite the contest. Gamblers in Vegas would have difficulty predicting the odds. The best money would be on a photo finish.

Then again, Cliff's friends often accused him of giving boring, uninvited lectures himself. Cliff was aware of his reputation, but he considered it unfair, viewing himself as a special case. Unlike Andy and his mother, when Cliff talked, he actually had something to say.

All of this was on Cliff's mind when he heard the strangest sound ever to vibrate an ear drum. Cliff threw off his blankets and stood up. Only Ben was out of bed, looking off in the direction of the sound. Everyone else was asleep, even the cat, which was strange because animals, as a general rule, tended to home in on unusual noises out of instinct.

The first thing Cliff did when he got out of bed was take the magic stone out of his pocket. It was still white, or as best as Cliff could make it out, it was still white. It was difficult to see at night, but he knew that if the stone were activated due to some good or bad circumstance, the color red or blue would be an illumination, so white must be the color, and it did look white as best as he could make out. Hopefully that meant the noise in the woods was nothing dangerous.

"What is that?" Cliff said to Ben.

"You got me."

"I've never heard a noise like that in my life."

Ben seemed mildly curious but not very concerned. "Probably some kind of animal."

438

"Animal? What makes you say that? It sounds nothing like an animal."

Ben was getting irritated again with Cliff, and Cliff could see it. He knew he wasn't in Ben's graces these days and that it would probably be a better idea to not argue with him, but curiosity was a stronger pull than manners right now.

"Oh, it sounds nothing like an animal?" Ben said mockingly. "OK, Mr. Expert, *you* tell *me*. What are we listening to?"

"I don't know, Ben. I've never heard a sound quite like it."

"Well, if you've never heard the sound before, then it can be anything, can't it? The sound comes from the woods. It's probably an animal."

"Just because it's in the woods, it comes from an animal?"

"Well, there aren't any cities with skyscrapers nearby, are there?"

"Have you ever heard an animal make a noise like that one?"

"No. But we're a far cry from home, Cliff. This could be some strange creature we've never seen before or learned about before."

"I suppose. Yes, that's possible, of course."

"Well, I'm curious," Ben said. "Let's go have a look."

"What? Are you crazy? I'm not going off into the woods unaware of what's out there."

"Is that the prophet's stone in your hand?"

"Yes."

"Looks white. Coast is clear."

"It's still white at the moment. But that doesn't mean anything. It could turn red when you get going after the noise."

"I don't think so. We already hear the noise. If it was dangerous, that stone would be bright red or at least a little red, at least warming up a bit."

"We know very little about these magic tools, Ben. I think it's a mistake to take a needless risk."

"OK. OK. Calm down. I'll go check myself."

"Check? With what? We don't even have any flashlights with us."

"So? I'll make a torch out of that piece of branch wood."

"I don't get it, Ben. Why go out there?"

"Why not?"

"It could be dangerous. That's why not."

"Doesn't sound dangerous to me. And no danger is showing up on that stone radar."

"Come on, Ben. I know you're a laid-back person, but even *you* have to admit that noise sounds ominous."

"Not to me. Mysterious? Sure. But it's not a growling sound or anything like that."

"You just said yourself you have no idea *what it is*. So why take the risk?"

"Because the noise is driving me crazy and I'm curious. I just wanna take a quick look."

"Don't do it, Ben."

"Relax."

"It would be different if you had a weapon on you."

"That old man prophet didn't give us any weapons. Probably because he figured we wouldn't need any. He thought the stone was all we needed, and the stone is giving a clean bill of health, so I won't worry."

Ben picked up the ax, fashioning his branch into the shape of a torch.

"Well, at least take the ornament with you. If push comes to shove, the angels will offer protection."

"Oh, I'll take the ornament, Cliff, but not to use it. To keep it away from you."

"Thanks a lot."

"Sorry, pal. Your track record with the ornament is not a good one. So I'll keep it with me. But I wouldn't think of using it, even for protection. If we use it now, we get that evil angel, according to Mike because it's after midnight and technically morning."

"All right ... all right, Ben ... Well, if you don't plan on using the ornament, maybe you should leave it behind."

"Leave it behind? Give me a little benefit, Cliff. What kind of fool do you think I am? Didn't you hear what I just said?"

"I heard you. Now hear *me*. Just hear me out. There are reasons for leaving it behind."

"What are you talking about?"

"Look, Ben, I don't want anything to happen to you, but you seem determined to go out there and investigate anyway. All right. Fine … fine … that's your choice. But if you put yourself in danger, you also risk losing the ornament. I know you're always thinking of the group, so think about us again right now … Leave the ornament behind. We need it. That ornament is our only link to Charles. Never mind Hamartio. I'm just thinking of Charles, the good angel. We need his protection. You lose that ornament and you lose our only link to Charles."

"Nice try, Cliff. I don't trust you with the ornament. It's just that simple. Come with me if you like. Stay here at camp if you don't wanna come along. But I'm going to check out the noise, and I'm taking the ornament with me. Understand?"

Cliff reluctantly nodded his head, and Ben disappeared in the night. Cliff knew he should have insisted that Ben also take the stone. He wasn't convinced that simply because the stone gave no warning here in camp, it wouldn't light up later. But Ben didn't ask for the stone, and Cliff really didn't want to part with it anyway. This was one magic charm that *had* been placed in his possession, and he intended to hang on to it.

Three minutes later, the noise stopped, and Cliff never heard it again. But Ben did not return. Thirty minutes went by, and he still didn't return. An hour went by, and he still didn't return.

Cliff sat in silence, trying to decide a course of action. On one hand, he was afraid to go out there. On the other hand, he felt guilty for being a coward once again and not joining Ben. This might have been his big opportunity to make up for what had happened with the bikers in the diner, but as usual, Cliff thought only of himself, and he was starting to literally hate himself. It seemed that self-preservation always overrode everything else, like the default setting on a computer.

Why was Ben able to rise above personal selfishness? And why couldn't Cliff be more like his friend? If there *were* a God and if Cliff ever met Him, that would be the very first question he would put to the Almighty. "God, why did you make me the way I am?"

Maybe it wasn't too late. Maybe he should go looking for him. But if Ben was in trouble, what could Cliff do? What could possibly happen to a person like Ben that a person like Cliff would be able to remedy? All at once, the simplicity of that question brought about some rather obvious answers to Cliff's mind, and he did start thinking of a few things. Ben could have tripped in the dark and fallen. Or maybe he was simply lost. Ben was a resourceful person and a brave person, but he was still a person, mortal and flawed as everyone else. There were endless possibilities. Cliff knew he needed to rise to the occasion and look for his friend. He made a torch of his own and headed off in the direction Ben had gone.

Since Cliff had counted about three minutes before the noise ceased, he decided to time himself and stop exactly three minutes into the woods, following the same direction Ben had been heading. True, Ben could have changed direction, but for only a three-minute duration. Cliff figured that timing himself while walking in Ben's starting direction was the most sensible way to begin.

Cliff was feeling mixed emotions — frightened certainly, but happy for once to be embarking upon a task with somebody else's safety in mind. Of course, his whole reason for staying with the group rather than just running off, hiding, and starting a new life for himself in this awesome new world was also an unselfish gesture, but Cliff might not have done it had Cephalithos not rebuked him in front of the group, shaming him into accompanying his friends. It had also been unselfish to go back with Ben and rescue DeWorken from the clutches of Mr. Blake, but that too he had done only because his friends had shamed him into it. Besides, DeWorken wouldn't have been with Mr. Blake in the first place if not for Cliff, so it was less of a rescue and more like cleaning up his own mess. Oh well, if people could guilt Cliff into doing things, at least that meant he still had a conscience. If he had a conscience, then he would not be one of the two people who were going to turn to evil, or at least there was a better chance of avoiding that horrific-sounding fate.

Cliff was standing still now, looking in all directions. The three minutes were up. What now? Suddenly he remembered the stone and took it out of his pocket. The stone was blue — only faintly blue, but blue. That was the good color, the safe color. So Ben must be nearby. Or maybe not. It could mean something else that was safe and good. Cliff experimented by walking a few paces in each direction and then returning to where he had first ended up after the three-minute count. If during any of those experimental moves, the color got brighter, that would be a rather major clue as to which direction he should continue walking.

He went back and forth a few times. The stone remained blue, but only with the same faint shade. The intensity had not changed. One more direction to try. This time, the blue got brighter and more luminous. Cliff was excited — still a little frightened, but not as much, not if this stone device could be trusted.

Off in the distance, Cliff noticed a shining object. It was the ornament! Ben had dropped the ornament! Or maybe not. Ben wouldn't be so careless. Cliff assumed he was imagining things, only thinking he saw the ornament because it was on his mind. But then, the blue stone indicated that he was on to something. Since the ornament was associated with protection, blue *should* be the color on the stone. Yes. And there it was! It was not a mirage. This was the ornament all right! So if the ornament was lying on the ground all by itself, what on Earth had happened to Ben? In fact, since they weren't on Earth anyway, what on Planet Telios could have happened to Ben? What in the whole galaxy had happened to Ben? What in all the infinite dimensions of the universe had happened to Ben? Anything could be going on right now.

Cliff picked the ornament up and waved his torch while he turned back and forth, hoping for better vision in various directions. Should he call out Ben's name? If he did, whatever had made that mysterious noise might find him as well. Better to stay silent.

The stone had turned back to white. Cliff repeated his same experiment, moving one direction, then another. No color. The blue did not return. Neither did the stone get red.

Without any further clues from the stone, Cliff decided to call off the search and for that reason, he never did find Ben.

Now, hours later, sitting with his companions around the

campfire, Cliff was into the false part of the story. He insisted that both Ben and the ornament were gone. He left out that one small detail about having found the ornament shortly after Ben vanished. He also left out his rather deep-rooted meditation regarding what to do with the ornament. He wanted to take advantage of this strange twist of fate which put the object back in his possession. He wanted to summon an angel and make a wish. But it wasn't that simple.

If Cliff made a wish this same evening, he would be doing so in the presence of the evil Hamartio. If he waited until the next day, skipping Hamartio's turn so that Charles could get a crack at granting the wish, Cliff would have to keep the ornament hidden. How? How would he do that if they continued on their journey toward Tinker Bell's home country? He could try to pack it away with other stuff in his knapsack or keep it in his pocket, but the ornament was bound to be discovered that way, especially with a suspicious Mike who might just decide to go rummaging through Cliff's things. In any event, Cliff had no idea how Ben's absence would affect their plans. Would they put off the journey by a day or so for the purpose of searching for Ben instead? Not being sure what to do, Cliff decided to bury the ornament and come back for it the next morning at dawn or perhaps a little earlier while it was still dark. Either way, he thought it best to buy himself some time and calmly go over a plan of action in his mind. He took a good, long look at one of the trees, studying its size and shape. This would be his landmark so that he could bury the ornament directly behind the tree and remember exactly where it was placed.

The questions continued from Mike, Andy, and DeWorken. Tinker Bell sat there in silence, and Caligula didn't seem to care if Ben was lost, found, dead, or resurrected. In fact, if a few others from the group also vanished, that would probably suit Caligula just fine.

Mike was wondering why Cliff hadn't volunteered to go with Ben, and he asked about it quite pointedly. Cliff responded by assuring Mike that Ben had seen no danger due to the stone remaining white. Cliff also pointed out that he at least went to look for him afterward. When Mike expressed doubt, Cliff showed him his torch with the charred tip. "Why would I have made this if I didn't intend to use it?"

"Well, there isn't much point in searching any more in the dark," Andy said. "Let's try to get some sleep. We can look for your friend in the morning with daylight."

Mike seemed impatient at the idea of waiting, but Andy finally convinced him that nothing more could be done at night.

Now, Cliff was lying in his blankets again, trying to figure out the scenario of the next day. He hoped they would find Ben or that Ben would simply turn up on his own. But if that happened, what would Ben say about the ornament? It all depended on what had happened to him, but supposing Ben had been chased by an animal after all? Wouldn't he remember roughly where the ornament had fallen out of his pocket? Probably not. If he were being chased, he would have been thinking about running and probably forgetting all about the ornament anyway. But perhaps not. Perhaps Ben put it down deliberately to keep the ornament away from whatever animal or person or supernatural force was attacking him. Maybe he remembered where he placed it and would go back looking for it. Maybe he would be suspicious of Cliff if he couldn't find it, especially since Cliff had just admitted that he made a torch of his own and went into the woods after him. Or maybe Ben would start snooping around and discover the ornament buried. This would not be too difficult a task since Cliff hadn't buried it far from the three-minute mark.

Finally, Cliff made a decision. He needed to bite the bullet and use the ornament tonight, before the others woke up again in the morning. This might be his only chance. He might get away with a wish without anyone else being the wiser. And even if his wish was discovered, it would be too late. Once a wish was granted, it could not be reversed. At least those were the rules before, and Cliff was gambling on this being a continuing clause, even in the new world.

Walking back into the woods with his torch lit again, Cliff thought about his plan. He didn't like the idea of depending upon Hamartio, but there was no other choice. It was Hamartio's turn. Hamartio was the angel du jour this dark morning. Charles had told Mike to skip Hamartio's turn whenever possible, but he had added an interesting amendment, that sometimes the dynamics of the situation would make it necessary. Well, it was certainly necessary for Cliff. He hated being so deceitful, but what were the alternatives?

Cliff stopped, looked up at the stars, and wondered if there really was a supreme being of some sort watching over him, a God, if you will, more powerful than the two angels, more powerful than anything or anybody.

"God, if you *do* exist ... If you are watching me, forgive me for what I'm about to do. I have no intention of turning evil. I promise I will not be one of the two in our group mentioned in the prophecy. But I must summon Hamartio and make my wish. I do intend to be careful. Please help me. Maybe you can meet me halfway? Maybe you can keep him from tricking me."

At first the prayer made Cliff feel silly. But then, he had felt just as silly that first time he spoke to the angels inside the ornament. Time had born witness to the fact that they really existed and really heard him.

On the other hand, if God did exist, what would He think of a guy who promises he will never go down the road of evil, all while planning to ask an evil entity for help? And what would God think of the fact that lately Cliff had been lying so much.

Cliff didn't like lying to his friend Mike, but once again, there didn't seem to be much of a choice. Just as he had hated stealing the ornament originally, back on that fateful day when he stole it out of Mike's room to use it on DeWorken at school, Cliff found himself burdened with the same mixed emotions and a very similar decision. That original theft had been necessary, and now Cliff needed to steal it again for the same reason, more or less. Under no circumstances could he allow DeWorken to return to his regular size. The day that happened would be Cliff's last day, or at least his last healthy day. DeWorken had made this abundantly clear, and Cliff believed him.

Probably DeWorken was exaggerating with words such as *kill*. Probably his threats meant nothing more than the fact that Cliff was merely going to get beaten up good. But that was not much of a consolation. Besides, Cliff didn't put it past DeWorken to actually follow through with that seemingly idle threat and truly kill him if push came to shove. That reckless jock could do anything. Maybe back at school he would refrain out of a fear of going to jail, but this was a whole different world, where DeWorken could perhaps end somebody's life and then head off into the woods to a strange land where nobody would ever be able to find him and punish him. For that matter, Cliff had no idea how the law worked in this new world, so who knew if eliminating an enemy out of revenge was even considered a violation of the law anyway? There was no way of being sure. But one thing was certain, when a man expresses evil intentions, he should be listened to.

Among other interests, Cliff was also a history buff. How many peace treaties had been made with evil dictators and tyrants, men who had no intention of following the treaties? While studying World War II, Cliff remembered his history teacher playing a recording of British Prime Minister Neville Chamberlain speaking to a crowd and proudly holding up a copy of a peace treaty that had just been signed by the Chancellor of Germany, Adolf Hitler. The crowd cheered with delight and applauded like a pack of mindless sheep. Hindsight is always 20/20. Now, in modern times, World War II history books point out what should have been obvious long ago to any thinking person: Hitler had never intended to honor that treaty or any other treaty. Cliff had read Hitler's *Mein Kampf.* He had also read many of Hitler's speeches. Anybody paying even half-attention to this maniac could have predicted with certainty that he was always planning to do just exactly what he finally ended up doing.

It always sounds good to negotiate, but if human nature offered one lesson, if one recurring theme threaded itself in the fabric of history, it was that if you listen to an evil person long enough, sooner or later he'll tell you just exactly what he plans to do.

Hitler was only one example, and of course Cliff wasn't so simpleminded as to think that DeWorken was as evil as a man like Hitler — not even close, not even in the same stratosphere. Then again, people like Doug DeWorken don't encounter the kinds of circumstances which put them in charge of an entire nation. Maybe if DeWorken had been born into a different situation, maybe if DeWorken had managed to obtain a greater influence, with unchecked power and control over the lives of his citizens ... Well ... who knows? Who was to say that he might not have become another Hitler or Mussolini or Genghis Khan?

As a matter of fact, Cliff had observed quite some time ago that high school life, with its designations such as *clique* or *nerd,* often seemed like the bigger world in microcosm. In school, there were certain people you didn't hang around with. You weren't allowed to like them — not if you wanted to be liked yourself, not if you wanted to be popular. It made no more sense than the kind of reputation Jews in Germany obtained, despite the fact that they were well-assimilated. In fact, many German Jews saw themselves as Germans first. Some even fought for Germany during the First World War. They were veterans and heroes, decorated by the kaiser himself. None of that made any difference once Hitler and his Nazi thugs got into power. The Jews were now a despised lot, scapegoats for all of Germany's problems. It made zero sense. Some German citizens believed the pack of lies because they were brainwashed. Others knew the truth but kept silent out of fear. Between cowardice and gullibility, human beings usually followed the crowd, and they were at their worst while doing so.

In high school, the crowd only got so big. In families, the numbers were even smaller, only a handful. But Cliff knew many students who came out of dysfunctional families, and he numbered his own family amongst them.

Some of his friends not only came from unhealthy domestic situations, but sad, frightful homes where their dads were absolute tyrants. Thankfully, Cliff's own father was passive, but many of his friends were not so fortunate. Their dads were physically abusive in some cases, emotionally destructive in other cases. The result was that they only ruined the lives of their children, but how many lives would be ruined if these heads of families had a chance to became heads of state?

In any event, Cliff had no way of knowing how bad DeWorken could become if given a chance. Perhaps he would find out. Perhaps that prophecy about somebody turning evil applied to DeWorken. But whatever DeWorken may or may not become, he was already bad enough and mad enough to get even with Cliff. That's what he kept saying, and Cliff knew the most sensible course of action was to simply take DeWorken at his word.

There it was! The tree! Cliff had been wise to pick one with a very unusual shape so as to make no mistake relocating it. He hadn't buried the ornament too far down. In no time at all, it was back in his hands. Cliff dusted off the dirt. Some of it was moist from the cool of the ground.

This would be tricky because, according to Charles' warning, as relayed through Mike, Hamartio was tricky himself. In fact, he was a master at deception. But Cliff had spent some time rehearsing the exact words of his wish, just as he had that day DeWorken was transformed. If he was careful, Hamartio would have to honor his request, regardless of any preferred evil agenda.

It still took Cliff a while to go through with it. Was he making a mistake? Should he be less concerned with DeWorken's evil and more concerned with his own?

The very fact that I'm concerned, Cliff said to himself, *the very fact that I'm aware, means that I will never turn evil. If I wanted to be evil, I could just pull DeWorken out of his tiny bed right now, crush him in my hand, drop him in the river, and make up a story about how he disappeared. But I'm not doing that because I would never dream of killing a fellow human being. Instead, I'm simply protecting myself. And I'll be careful. I wasn't the only person in that room when Cephalithos recited his riddle. The prophecy could be about anybody. Who says it will be me? I won't let that happen, but I have to do this.*

Cliff's ability to rationalize made him feel better, but only for a few seconds. The irony of the situation hit him on the head like a ton of bricks. He was making a personal vow to ward off evil temptations moments before summoning an evil angel to ask his help.

On an impulse, Cliff took the stone out of his pocket. It was red, and not just a shade of red, bright red.

The reason was clear. Red meant danger. But why would this magic stone view the ornament as dangerous now if it wasn't before? The stone had turned blue when he found the ornament earlier. Yes, blue because, as a general rule, the ornament is a good device which protects the group. It needed to be found, and the stone helped him find it. But the current situation was much different. Cliff was about to use the bad side of the ornament, so to speak. He was about to talk to Hamartio, and the stone was warning him not to do so.

Cliff wished he had not taken one last look at the stone. Sometimes ignorance is bliss. Now he was without excuse. He was being warned and not heeding the warning. Still, the human mind has ways of ignoring its conscience. Cliff wanted to use the ornament, and he was determined to do so with or without the stone's approval. But he couldn't make such a decision fully admitting to himself that he was being reckless. Instead, he spent some more time rationalizing.

Red means a warning, he said to himself a few times. *That's all. So yes, if I am not careful with Hamartio, it could be dangerous. But I'm planning on being careful ... extremely careful! So everything will be all right. Warning received. Warning properly heeded.*

Of course, Cliff was too intelligent to be fooled by a mere mind game, even his own. His brain had an uncanny ability to cherry-pick convenient excuses and ignore all the rest. But there was no turning back. Cliff held the ornament in his hands and stood up, ready to summon Hamartio. His course of action was set. For better or for worse, it was set.

Chapter Twenty-Eight

Cliff and His Preemptive Strike

He looked almost exactly like Charles, or at least the way Charles had appeared when he showed up at the sheriff's station masquerading as an attorney. Only one difference: This man's hair was white. Charles' hair was darkish gray. Charles also wore a dark suit. This fellow had a white suit that almost matched his hair. Cliff's initial thoughts took him to film and television stereotypes of the quintessential hero dressed in white. Of course, Hamartio was supposed to be the evil one, and Cliff wondered if this "role reversal" of clothing was intentional or merely a coincidence.

Cliff had not been sure what to expect by way of looks prior to the angel's materialization. He had merely stood up, holding the ornament in the palms of his hands, while repeating some words several times over until they became like a chant. "I need to talk to the angel. I summon the angel. I need to talk to the angel. I summon the angel."

Mike had not said anything about exact, precise wording. Wording, supposedly, was going to play a more prominent role while the actual wish was being made. To summon the angels, all one had to do was hold the ornament in his hands, or at least that was what Mike had said. Mike tended to get so many things wrong, Cliff decided to take no chances, and for some reason, reciting the same request formally and repeatedly seemed like the way supernatural transactions ought to be administered.

It worked. Whether he needed to do it that way or not, it worked. There it was, the same hissing sound Mike had described, followed by purple smoke. Cliff expected blue smoke since that was what Mike had seen, but he was OK with purple because he was relieved to see anything happening at all. Had the ornament failed to work after his much exerted effort and subversive behavior, what would he have done then?

But it did work, and if that meant purple smoke, all the power to it! At least it was purple and not red. Cliff had seen enough red for one day. He did not need a further color-coded reminder about the road he was embarking upon.

"Do you know who I am?" the human-looking being said with a friendly demeanor as the last wisp of smoke faded away.

Cliff tried not the shake, but he wasn't doing a very good job. "Um ... yes, I do ... At least ... I believe I do ... The angel, Hamartio?"

"Excellent."

"Ah ... um ... nice to meet you."

"Likewise ... You look worried, Cliff."

"I'm not worried."

"You're lying."

Cliff *was* lying. He was not only worried, he was absolutely petrified. He quickly decided it probably wasn't a good idea to lie to an angel, especially a dangerous one. Better to agree immediately if the angel was perceiving his true feelings.

"Well," Cliff barely choked out, "with all due respect, I *have* heard some things about you."

"Have you? Such as what? Go on, Cliff ... tell me. What have you heard?"

" I guess ... I guess I've heard that you're an evil angel."

"That's what I thought ... Who told you this? Charles, I imagine."

"Yes, sir."

"No need to be so formal, Cliff. You can call me by my name."

"OK. Yes. Your name ... Hamartio, then. Thank you, Hamartio."

Hamartio stepped closer to Cliff, his eye contact never once deviating. Cliff almost moved away but then thought better. He was determined not to do anything to provoke this unusual entity. That not only applied to his words, it applied to his actions as well.

"So Charles said I was the bad angel. Therefore, by a process of elimination, it must follow that Charles, presumably, is the good angel."

"Isn't he?"

"What *is* good? What is evil? Are they not mere titles, mere opinions invented by human beings to describe their own personal perspectives? And how much emotion and subjectivity goes into such designations? Your own Western philosophies have raised these questions for years with classes on situational ethics and moral relativism. Books and lectures have dominated the centuries of Earth history, settling nothing."

Cliff decided not to argue the point. He'd already flirted with enough trouble. Besides, the decision to call upon Hamartio was a done deal. All the back and forth mental gymnastics were over. A decision had been made, and there was nothing now but to see it through. Hamartio was here, staring at him. This was no longer an idea. This was no longer a secret, deceptive plan. This was an established fact. A wish was about to be offered, regardless of any opinion Cliff might have about the angel's lack of virtue.

"I suppose that's true," Cliff said. "I suppose philosophers do debate a lot about reality."

"Yes they do, Cliff. And you being in this new world is the clearest, most obvious example of a new reality in its own right, is it not? Shouldn't you be questioning everything you ever learned?"

Cliff wasn't about to second-guess everything he'd ever learned. He loved knowledge, and he was proud of the knowledge he'd acquired. And yet, Hamartio was certainly making a valid point. The experiences of these last few weeks had made previous assumptions about science, history, and ethics stand on their heads.

"So you're claiming not to be evil?"

"What I'm claiming," Hamartio said definitively, "is that I'm here to grant you a wish. Why would you have called upon me if you thought I was evil?"

This was a good question. Cliff decided he'd better answer at once and not look like a fool.

"Because I need my wish fast and because it's your turn."

Hamartio stared at Cliff for a long time. Cliff was afraid of what might happen next. The angel's piercing eyes felt eerie and menacing. This made Cliff think about the details of his wish back home, his fateful verbiage which resulted in a releasing of both entities from the ornament castle. His exact phraseology intended to divide them so that the one joined being could become two separate angels once again. But

Cliff had wished for more than a mere separation. He wanted the evil angel destroyed. Why was Hamartio being so friendly to a person who had tried to end his life? The danger of even being on the same planet with this potentially vengeful celestial creature was already precarious enough, but here Cliff was actually engaging the angel in conversation, a conversation where he was specifically asking for help.

Of course, the ludicrous nature of this situation had occurred to Cliff long before he summoned Hamartio. Cliff had decided to go ahead with his plan anyway, although at this particular moment, he found himself reviewing the reasons. Bravery was not his strong suit, so where did he muster up the nerve? There had been several considerations:

First of all, Mike had said something about Charles and Hamartio being forced to forge new rules together and that these latest spiritual laws included an obligation on the part of each angel to grant wishes, provided it fell within their purview and they actually had the capabilities. Both angels were compelled to honor even those wishes they disliked. Hopefully that rule protected Cliff right now. Hopefully any angel who existed for the purpose of fulfilling human requests could not just arbitrarily take it upon himself to end the life of one of these humans. Hopefully Hamartio wasn't pretending to be friendly to Cliff and stringing him along, only to later cut loose and destroy him at a time of his own choosing.

Also, when Cliff pronounced his potential death sentence, he really didn't know one angel from the other, and at that time, they weren't distinctly different angels anyway. They were a single being with two natures, a good nature and an evil nature. Cliff had not yet met Charles, nor had there been a Charles to meet. Neither had he met Hamartio. There was only that joined spirit inside the ornament. And so, Cliff hoped that in lieu of all this, Hamartio had nothing to take personally. In fact, if this current encounter was any barometer, his idea was being verified. After all, Hamartio seemed to be suggesting that Cliff had no way of really determining who was the good angel or who was the bad.

And finally, Cliff had decided he had nothing to lose by trying, regardless of the odds. He was consigned to the fact that this was a dangerous world, and he was willing to roll the dice, hoping his future would be better on Telios than on Earth. DeWorken served as a sobering reminder/representation of Cliff's former life in high school. There was no telling what Hamartio might do, but Cliff knew *exactly* what DeWorken would do if given a chance. Besides, if Hamartio was free to murder Cliff and hell-bent on doing so, it probably would have happened by now.

But all of these reasons, which seemed so solid hours ago, were melting away in the presence of Hamartio's penetrating stare.

Finally, Hamartio spoke. "Good, honest response. I find it very refreshing."

Cliff didn't remember anymore what his "honest, refreshing response" had been. He needed to find his bearings and think for a second. Oh yes … he had said, "Because I need my wish fast and because it's your turn."

"All right," Hamartio continued. "What's your wish?"

Cliff had hoped they could talk before diving in with a wish. He wanted to find out about Ben since there was a very good chance this unusual being knew just exactly what happened to Ben and perhaps was even responsible for his friend's disappearance. But Cliff also decided that such a hope would be realized only if Hamartio brought up the subject. Cliff would not instigate any discussion about Ben. He needed to be careful. When Mike asked direct questions of Charles, the answers counted as a granted wish. Of course, that only happened because Mike had clumsily used the word *wish* while asking his questions, but Cliff still decided to play it safe by bridling loose-lipped questions until he got his request about DeWorken out of the way. The only questions he might ask would be questions which prefaced his wish. Quite frankly, he was less interested in Ben's safety than his own. Earlier, it had been painful to admit such a thing, even to himself, but it was becoming easier.

"Well, first I need to review the rules again, if that's all right."

"Of course."

"Are they similar to the ornament procedures? I mean, back when you and Charles were inside the ornament? I can't get just anything?"

"That is correct. As before, the wish must be within reason."

"And you will decide all on your own if it is within reason? You don't need to check with anyone else?"

Hamartio started laughing. "Tell me you're not serious! No, I do not need to check with anyone else."

"OK. So how about if I asked for some special power that would protect me from all danger the rest of my life?"

"You're a bright, young lad, Cliff. I think you already know the answer to that question."

"Yes, I thought so. Too much. Well, no harm trying I suppose."

"Try all you want. Nothing ventured, nothing gained."

It seemed odd to hear an angel using such a common human expression.

Cliff was grateful to see that they were discussing ornament rules without it counting as a wish. Why not? Cliff was the careful one. By avoiding the actual word *wish* until he truly needed it, Cliff was gleaning all kinds of information. On a roll, he went for the bonus point, the one Mike failed to obtain.

"And before, one wish could not undo the effects of a previous wish. Is that still the case?"

Hamartio smiled. "Couldn't have said it better myself."

Cliff recognized that expression as something Charles had used during their brief interaction back at the police station when Charles was passing on more clues about the key chain he had given Mike. In fact, many of Hamartio's mannerisms were similar. Perhaps all those years as one entity caused them to retain portions of each other's personalities even after they separated.

Cliff continued his attempts at clarification. "And that application remains constant, regardless of which one of you granted the wish?"

"You have a nice way with words, Cliff."

"You can't undo anything from Charles, and he can't undo anything from you?"

"Correct again."

Cliff wondered if these answers could be trusted. Undoubtedly, an evil angel was also a lying angel. It might be different if he was answering in response to an official wish. In that case, the evil angel more than likely would have to speak the truth, but nothing was

456

compelling him if the word *wish* wasn't being used. Suddenly Cliff felt a little less reassured. Perhaps he had not been accomplishing nearly as much as he'd thought. Maybe he would have to wait for another day and get the straight scoop from Charles. For now, time to move on. Don't press the point. Don't go insinuating that the angel standing in front of you is a liar. That would not be the brightest move in the world.

Before continuing, Cliff decided to review one more rule. This one could be trusted because Mike had already heard about it from Charles, but Cliff wanted to double-check anyway.

"And yet, the rules relating to any wish made on Earth were reset when the ornament was brought into this new world."

Hamartio nodded. Cliff finished his statement. "So unless the wish was made here on Planet Telios, one *can* undo the effects of a previous wish."

"Not exactly, but you're close for all intents and purposes."

Cliff wanted to be more than close, but he went on anyway. "All right. Well, let me get to my wish then, and I do believe it is one you *can* grant. At least, I hope so."

"Be my guest."

"Well, it's about DeWorken."

Hamartio forged a light-hearted grin. "Ah ... I just thought it might have something to do with him."

"Yes, sir. Here's the thing: DeWorken is desperate to turn back to his normal size, and now he knows there's a way to make that happen. He can take a turn and make a wish with the ornament because, in his case, he was turned small on Earth and now, on Telios, that particular wish can be reversed."

"It doesn't work exactly that way, " Hamartio explained. "The reset normally would have changed DeWorken back to his original height the moment he came into this world, much as that cat can now talk or refuse to talk at will, Mike's previous cat wish having been undone. But since miniatures, such as Tinker Bell, are natural in this world, DeWorken's anatomical structure acclimated to his new surroundings and stayed small. And so, it would not be about *reversing* a wish. It would be about a miniature man simply wishing to bypass his natural state and become tall in the first place, keeping in mind that in this world, he has not yet been tall."

The technicalities were getting cumbersome to Cliff. "I understand. But however it works, DeWorken could still make a wish and turn back to his previous size. Right? Whatever the label, practically speaking, we're talking about the same thing."

"I'm sure DeWorken would love to do just exactly that," Hamartio said. "But I believe he will find it rather difficult. Ironically, the very size which concerns him would make his usage of the ornament impossible. How is he going to pick it up?"

"Oh, he might be able to pull it off. DeWorken is very strong. And even though he's now a miniature, his strength remains proportionately. He might just be able to wrap his arms wide around the ornament and lift that thing into the air a little."

"That would not be enough. The entire ornament must be held and suspended in a person's hands, just as you're doing right now."

Cliff felt a little better hearing this news. "I see."

Hamartio continued. "In any event, with you in possession of the device, your nemesis DeWorken would not even be able to get near the ornament unless somebody helps him."

"Yes, assuming I hide it again in the ground. But I can't keep doing that. I need to return it when I'm done talking with you. We can't continue this journey without the ornament, and I can't keep it hidden forever if I have it on me. After making this wish, I was planning on telling all the others that I found it."

"Were you now? Very resourceful."

"Yes ... So after I return the ornament, who's to say that DeWorken won't be helped? Mike seems very sympathetic to his plight, and the two of them get along really well. DeWorken respects Mike. And Mike feels sorry for him in this condition. For all we know, it may be only a matter of time before Mike submits a wish of his own on behalf of DeWorken that would make DeWorken normal size again. And Mike *can* hold the ornament in his hands. If that ever happens, DeWorken is going to come after me before doing anything else."

Hamartio's light-hearted smile looked devious now. "Will he? I just can't imagine why."

458

Cliff felt irritated and wanted to tell the angel to stop making sport of a serious situation. He stopped himself, remembering who he was talking to. Getting on the bad side of Hamartio would be a fate worse than twenty DeWorkens.

"Yes," Cliff said respectfully. "So we agree. Once DeWorken is his old self, I'm a dead man. He'll pound me good."

"You might just be right about that, Cliff."

"OK then. Here's my request. We need to make sure I *am* protected from DeWorken."

The angel was looking him over again, but the expression on his face was different this time. It was as if Cliff looked to him like an interesting study.

"What's wrong?" Cliff asked.

"Did I say anything was wrong?"

"Well, it seems like there's a problem."

"Just thinking."

"I didn't know angels needed to think."

"Excuse me?"

"I guess that didn't come out right," Cliff said with a careful, apology-laced tone. "I mean … Of course you think. Obviously you think. You're an intelligent being. You think all the time. I merely meant to say … Well … I thought that when people made wishes, you didn't need to think long about them."

"I *am* thinking long about it, Cliff. It may be a simple wish. And it's obviously a predictable wish, given your stellar relationship with DeWorken. I'm just figuring out the parameters."

"What parameters?"

"By 'parameters,' I mean the boundaries of the wish, the limitations of its effect. For example, am I protecting you from DeWorken in every conceivable way, or am I merely making it so that he is unable to return to his original size?"

"Do I have a choice? Because if I do, that 'every conceivable way' idea sounds great."

"It does sound great, doesn't it? Unfortunately, you do *not* have a choice. The choice is mine."

"OK, then, if you could just keep him from returning to his original size that will be enough."

Even as the words were coming out of his mouth, Cliff wondered if he was being wise. After all, DeWorken being small had only been a kick for the first day or two. After a while, DeWorken's disappearance had gotten him into trouble with the police and even after DeWorken was rescued from Mr. Blake, nobody, including Mike or Ben, had figured out how to explain DeWorken's miniature body if they were to ever return home. Then again, Cliff wasn't home right now. Neither was DeWorken or anybody else in their traveling band. And chances were, they would never get home again. Besides, even before venturing into this new world, Cliff had decided this was going to be his new home, for better or worse. He was planning no return trip through any cave portal. And so, all things considered, Cliff was ready to cut his losses and just make sure DeWorken never turned tall again.

"OK. I'll take what I can get. I want DeWorken to stay miniature and never return to his normal size, never again for the rest of his life."

"Aren't you forgetting something, Cliff?"

"I don't think so."

"You have to phrase it as a wish. The word *wish* must actually come out of your mouth."

The whole conversation was starting to sound trifling. Cliff felt like he was on the game show *Jeopardy*, forgetting to phrase his answer as a question. But whatever the rules, Cliff needed to cooperate.

"Yes, I wish it. I wish that DeWorken never turns normal size again, normal being defined as what was normal to him on Earth, not what is normal to Tinker Bell's people on Telios. May he never turn normal size again, never for the rest of his life, no matter what anybody else might wish."

"Well done. You phrased that with detail and precision, covering all possibilities and avoiding the pitfalls of generalized wording. Very impressive."

"Thank you."

"All right, Cliff. Fair enough. Let me see what I can do."

"That's it?"

"Is there a problem?"

"You're going to see what you can do? That's your answer to my wish? You're going to see what you can do?"

Hamartio's pleasant countenance disappeared as his left eyebrow raised slightly. Cliff got frightened again, afraid that his voice had been too casual and too confrontational. Up until now, Hamartio had been cordial ... jovial too. But if this angel was as evil as everybody said, the good mood was nothing more than still waters, waters that could be stirred and aroused at the slightest provocation.

"I mean," Cliff continued ... "With all due respect ... this is not quite what I was expecting."

Hamartio smiled again, and Cliff was relieved. "Yes, Cliff, I will see what I can do. Why the big surprise? If that's not what you expected, what exactly *were* you expecting?"

"Well," Cliff said carefully, like a person walking on egg shells so as not to offend, "I suppose I expected a yes, or I was at least hoping for one. Or maybe a no if that's your answer. But one way or the other, I had counted on finding out right away."

Hamartio nodded, looking sympathetic and understanding. "Yes, we all want things quickly, don't we? But hasn't a period of waiting time been your experience with the ornament up to now? You make a wish, and often, you wait a while to see what happens. The ornament always behaved that way. The only difference is that we workers of the magic are outside now to interact with people, rather than the prior situation when we were prisoners inside the castle in the glass."

"Not always," Cliff countered. "My wish that made DeWorken small happened right away."

"True. But with your other wish, the one where you released us from the ornament ... you did not see the effects immediately. In fact, the consequence of this wish made weeks ago has only recently been discovered."

"OK," Cliff agreed. "So it's happened both ways. But now that you and Charles are out of the ornament, I thought it might be different. The rules are different. So why can't you answer wishes more quickly now?"

"Cliff, I'm not sure you're paying attention. We could already answer them quickly before, and sometimes we did, as you so skillfully pointed out. It depends on the specific wish. That was the criteria before, and that is the case now as well. In any event, I heard you. I will take your request into consideration."

Hamartio extended his hand. Cliff shook hands, wondering if he was doing something likened to making a deal with the devil.

Hamartio vanished in a whiff of purple smoke. Cliff stood there by himself. The ornament was still in his hands, still looking beautiful. One would never have guessed that so much danger could come from a mere Christmas tree decoration. Cliff placed the ornament back in his pocket. Time to return to the others and pretend he found it without using it. But he would wait until tomorrow so that the "find" would not appear too quick and obvious.

As always, after dealing with the ornament, he realized he'd just made matters a whole lot better or a whole lot worse, probably worse since this had been the evil angel, despite all the good manners. But what choice did have? DeWorken had to be stopped. If he could only be stopped by evil, so be it.

Chapter Twenty-Nine

The Collaboration

Doug DeWorken had never felt so helpless. Sure, he was glad to be away from Mr. Blake, but it sounded like Blake could enter the cave wall and come into this new world anytime he wanted. All he'd have to do was clear the rocks and dirt that blocked the way on account of the earthquake. As for the new world itself, Doug hated this stinking place. He hated everything about it: all the talk about angels, all the warnings from the prophet. He even hated the scenery. Everyone else kept talking about how pretty all the trees and mountains were.

They should try looking at it from down here, Doug said to himself.

Most of all, Doug hated the company. Like everyone else, he was tired of listening to the old man. But unlike the others, Doug was counting the days until he could turn to his normal size and beat the everloving snot out of Cliff Reynolds. He hated Reynolds for putting him in this fix, and most of his time was spent trying to think of a way to get even. It wouldn't be easy unless he used that magic ornament … But then … Doug was tired of all the talk about the ornament too.

Once in a while, at brief times, he wasn't so angry. When he had a chance to settle down a little while resting or eating, Doug admitted to himself that he didn't actually hate the whole group. There were a few exceptions. He felt a little bit different about Mike Owen. Owen had been pretty decent to him. So had Ben Robinson, even though he still resented Robinson for embarrassing him at school that day he was picking on Reynolds.

So, yeah, he kind of had to be thankful for Robinson since the guy had sort of rescued him from Blake, but he still didn't like Robinson much.

Tinker Bell was different. Doug didn't count her as part of the group anyway since they had been alone together before the rescue. She was the only bright part of this whole crazy journey. Everything else was a nightmare.

Right now, everyone was talking to Reynolds. Nobody had broken camp yesterday. That had been the original plan, to break camp and move on like all the other days. But the others didn't wanna go anyplace right now. They were hoping Robinson might turn up. Nobody was gonna leave without him. Reynolds had gone off by himself to look for Robinson. Now he was back.

He'd been gone a couple of hours before coming back and claiming he found the ornament lying in the woods. Everyone was glad to have the ornament back. Doug was glad too. Sure, he hated the ornament cuz of what it had done to him, but that very same ornament was his only hope, and having the ornament again meant he might get a crack at one of those wishes and turn tall again.

But Doug was also suspicious of Reynolds. It seemed kind of strange that he found the ornament so fast after it had been lost. Reynolds may have been a brainy, weakling, geek back in school, but here in this crazy new land, the guy seemed to be changing. There was something very different about Reynolds, and Doug was wondering why the others so quickly accepted his story about finding the ornament. What if it had never really been lost? What if Reynolds had used it to make a wish? That would be bad news for Doug. The last time Reynolds made a wish, it ruined his life. A new wish from Reynolds would probably be something even worse … a real blow … something along the lines of never being able to turn ta normal size again.

But just in case Reynolds was telling the truth, just in case there was still a chance, Doug needed to get a hold of that ornament. How? He wasn't big enough to hold it in his hands and use it the way everyone said it needed to be used. Maybe Owen would help him. But that would take come convincing. Owen and Reynolds were friends. Doug had to get Owen to view him as a friend too.

***

It had still been dark when Cliff returned to camp very early in the morning with his story about finding the ornament, but now the sun was rising again. Old man Andy and Reynolds were off gathering wood for a breakfast fire. Doug and Tinker Bell were sitting together. Owen was sitting by himself holding the ornament. Doug decided to go talk to him.

Tinker Bell pulled him back by the hand. "Where are you off to?"

"I gotta speak ta Owen."

"It's about the ornament, isn't it? You're still determined as ever to be restored to your original size."

"Yeah? So?"

"You don't need for me to say it again, Doug. You already understand how that makes me feel."

"Come here," Doug said tenderly.

Tinker Bell rushed into his arms. She felt good in his arms, like this was where she belonged.

"Now listen," Doug said. "I ain't never leavin' ya. I already told ya that."

"Then what's the purpose of using the ornament? It's only necessary for you to turn back into a giant if you plan on returning to your own world."

Doug found it kind of funny to hear the word *giant* even though Tinker Bell had told him before that this was the name her people had for all those folks who were bigger, who used to bully her people and invade her country. But it was weird thinking of himself as having been a giant. In Doug's mind he had just been normal size, but he made sure not to say that anymore cuz he knew the word *normal* offended Tinker Bell.

"That's where my life is, honey. But ya can go with me."

"Back to Earth? Back to where people will look at me like an odd curiosity?"

"I won't let nobody call ya odd."

"Doug, I want to return to my own people, not merely for the purpose of obtaining information about the local cave portals, but to stay. It's where I live ... where *I* belong."

"But then they'll look at *me* as the odd freak."

"Not if you choose to stay this size."

"I know this is natural for you. I respect that. But it ain't natural for me."

"It *will* be when we get home. You'll look like everybody else."

"Yeah? But what happens when your people get picked on by giants again? That happens all the time. That's what ya told me. Maybe

465

if I turn back ta the way I belong, I can protect your people."

Tinker Bell's eyes widened. "You would do that? You would stay in my world with me?"

"I'm not sure what I'm gonna do with my future, except that I do know two things: I ain't never leavin' you. Ya can come live with me on Earth, or I'll stay here with you. We'll stay together no matter what. But right now I need ta concentrate on gettin' tall again. I can protect ya better that way. So that's the second thing: I gotta get tall again."

Tinker Bell still looked sad.

"What now?" Doug said. "That's good news I just gave ya."

"You say you'll stay with me regardless of the circumstances. But supposing Mike helps you with the ornament and wishes you back to your original composition? Will you be happy living with a miniature?"

"Sure I will. That won't matter none."

"But it does matter evidently. If size didn't matter, you wouldn't be so eager to change back."

"I already told ya. If I change back, I can protect ya better."

"Yes, that's very gallant of you, Doug, and I do love the way you protect me. But relationships are built upon more than mere chivalry."

"Huh?"

"Let me put the question to you in a more delicate manner. After your physique is proportionately restored, how will you relate to me …" She stopped for a sec, looking very shy … "How will you relate to me … physically?"

Doug understood what she meant. He hadn't thought about this before cuz, up till now, they had been the same size and he just looked at Tinker Bell as a pretty woman and thought about her as a pretty woman. She would still be pretty if she stayed tiny and he turned tall, but it would be hard to hug and make out and do all that other stuff that a couple would do if they ever decided ta marry. Doug would have to think about it later. Right now, he just wanted her to feel better. He tried hard to find the right words. Finally, something came to him.

"You mean more ta me than physical pleasure."

"I do?"

"Of course ya do. Look, we'll talk more, but I need ta get Owen's attention while he's alone."

"All right, Doug." She sounded happier, not much happier, but at least a little happier.

"Hey, Owen … Owen! Down Here!"

Mike looked down. He was kicking back on a kind of crude table that they'd made out of some flat wood with tall rocks as legs. The guy looked like he was just sitting by himself, thinking. Doug figured there was a lot on his mind with his friend Robinson missing. And he was probably also worried about his girlfriend, who was supposed to show up sometime in this world and hadn't showed up yet. But anyway, this was the perfect time to talk cuz lately nobody had much chance to be alone, traveling in a group, and now they did have a chance.

"Sorry, Doug," Mike said. "I didn't notice you down there. Here … let me help you to the top of the table."

Mike picked him up and set him down.

"Thanks, Owen. Hey, I was wonderin' … Can we go off and talk somewhere in private?"

"Sure … or why not right here? There's nobody else around."

"Yeah, but they'll be comin' back soon. I'd like ta keep this a secret. I kinda got a favor ta ask."

"Does it have to do with the ornament?"

"Well … yeah … sorta …"

Mike looked uncomfortable, but he still talked friendly.

"If it's about me wishing you back to your normal size, I'd like to help, Doug … I really would. But I'm afraid of what you might do to Cliff."

"Aww … I won't really do nothin'."

Mike didn't look like he believed him, and Doug knew that he shouldn't believe him cuz he was really lying.

"Doug … I do feel bad about what Cliff did to you."

"Then why not help me?"

"Because Cliff is my friend."

"I thought we was friends too, Owen."

"Sure we are … Sure … but …"

"Look … It's up ta you. Can't we just at least go off together and talk about it some? Maybe just hear me out and then make up your mind?"

Mike paused for a minute. "Sure, Doug. Of course. We should talk."

***

Doug sat on top of the table, waiting while Mike got his backpack ready by putting the ornament in one compartment and fastening the small chair-like contraption Ben had made so that he would not need to hold Doug in his hand while they ventured away from camp to talk privately.

But before Mike was finished, Reynolds came up to them, and Doug could see that he was on to something.

"Where are you two going?" Cliff asked.

"Just off for a walk," Mike said.

"All right if I go with you?"

"What for?" Doug said in a very unfriendly way.

"I was asking Mike. Not you."

"Doug and I are gonna talk in private," Mike explained.

"In private? How come?"

"We'd be happy ta explain," Doug said, "just as soon as it becomes any of your beeswax."

Cliff leaned down. "Watch your mouth, DeWorken!"

"Who's gonna make me?"

"Listen to this guy," Cliff said with a wicked smile. "You'd never think I could throw him on the ground, step on him, and scrape him off my shoe like a dead cockroach."

"Cut it out!" Mike shouted.

"Then tell me where you're going! And tell me why you need to take the ornament with you!"

Andy, Tinker Bell, and the cat came closer to see what all the fuss was about.

"Maybe I'm planning to make a wish," Mike yelled.

"If you're making a wish, the entire group should first be consulted."

"Like the way you consulted us?" Doug said. "Admit it, Reynolds, ya already made a wish all on your own."

"I did no such thing."

"Yeah? Well, I don't buy it. And I don't trust ya any farther than I can throw!"

Cliff started laughing. "Maybe not, DeWorken, but then, you can't really throw *anything* anymore, can you?"

"Shut up!"

"You can't throw footballs anymore. Heck, you'd barely be able to even climb on top of a football. So what are you going to throw? A kidney stone?"

DeWorken grabbed a handful of dirt. "I'll show ya what I can throw!"

"No, Doug!" Tinker Bell cried out.

But Doug wasn't listening, and he threw the dirt hard at Cliff's foot. He knew it wouldn't make any difference, but it still felt good.

Cliff looked amused. "Oh, that hurt, DeWorken! Ouch … That really hurt."

"Just wait!" DeWorken said. "Just you wait and see! One of these days, you and me are gonna look each other in the eye again, and when that day comes, it'll be your last look, cuz I'm gonna poke your eyes out. Both of them!"

All at once, Cliff swooped down his hand and pulled Doug up to the level of his face like one who moves a hand puppet.

Tinker Bell screamed.

"Cliff!" Mike shouted. "Put him down."

"Who put you in charge?" Cliff said to Mike. Then he faced DeWorken again. "You want eye-to-eye communication? You got it.

Now listen to me, you whiney little pip-squeak, and listen good! Your days of being a heroic jock are over."

"Please stop," Tinker Bell pleaded.

Doug wasn't feeling very scared. He knew maybe he should be, but Reynolds was a nerd — a big nerd, but still a nerd. It wasn't like when Mr. Blake had held him. Maybe this nerd was upset, but Doug was not gonna give him the satisfaction of acting scared, especially since he didn't really feel too scared anyway.

"All right," Andy said. "That's enough."

"Enough is right!" Cliff shouted. "And I'm the one who's had enough! I've been listening to this creep for years because I had no other choice. I've been ridiculed … humiliated … beaten up."

"Well, now you're doing it to him," Mike said. "Now *you're* being the bully."

"So what? He deserves it! So far, I've done nothing that can even remotely compare to what this sack of filth has put me through. I've been the butt of his jokes for years. I've been subject to his whims for the longest time, and I'll be damned to hell if I'm listening to him any longer! Maybe I had to listen to you before, DeWorken, but never again. I choose to censor your speech from here on out, and there's not a thing you can do about it. You hear me? Nothing you can do about it! And I'll tell you why! Because you're never turning back to your normal size again! Never! So you start getting used to our new arrangement. You start treating me with respect. As for myself, I'll treat you any way I want, and right now I feel like treating you as the miserable excuse for a human being you are."

Tinker Bell was sobbing and pulling on Cliff's pant leg dangling over the side of his shoe. "Please, Cliff. Please, I beg of you. Don't hurt him."

Doug could see that Reynolds was affected by Tinker Bell's words. For a second, the spineless piece of vermin actually looked like he felt bad.

"Maybe if he begged himself," Cliff said, lowering his voice and catching his breath from all the shouting and fast motion. "Go ahead, DeWorken. If you don't want your new girlfriend to beg for you, beg yourself."

"I ain't beggin for nothin!"

"Didn't think so. Then how about if I throw you to the bottom of my canteen?"

Now Doug *was* feeling scared. No denying it. He could tell that something in Reynolds had snapped, and he figured a guy who snapped like that was mad enough to throw him in a canteen or throw him in anything.

But Cliff never moved toward his canteen. Instead, Mike got into Cliff's face. "I won't allow that. Now I'm only saying it one more time, Cliff. Put him down!"

It didn't do any good. Doug could see that Cliff was feeling defiant and he didn't plan to back away from Owen the way he used to back down from Robinson. And speaking of Robinson, Cliff brought up his name as a way of making fun of Owen.

"Oh, look who suddenly thinks he's taken over Ben's role!"

"Maybe somebody has to," Mike said. "You never laid a finger on DeWorken when Ben was around. So now that he's missing, you feel like you can pick on somebody who isn't even one-tenth your size? Is that the way it works?"

"Don't talk to me about picking on people!" Cliff said, almost in tears. "Talk to him! He's been picking on people smaller than him his whole life. If he's now become even smaller, I say good! I say this is no different from the humiliations he put me through, only in reverse. As for Ben being gone, yes he's gone, and I don't recall any decision to make you the new leader of the group."

"Maybe not," Mike said. "But I'm not gonna stand here and watch you pick on a helpless human being, whether he used to do the same to you or not."

Doug didn't like hearing Owen describe him as a "helpless human being." But like it or not, Owen was coming to his rescue. With Ben gone, Owen was his only hope right now.

"Helpless, my foot," Cliff said. "Now if you want to stick up for your new friend, I suggest you talk him into apologizing. Because I put a lot on the line to rescue him from that carnival, and his gratitude has not exactly been overwhelming. I know! I know! Don't say it! If not for me, he wouldn't have needed to be rescued in the first place. I've heard it from all of you, and I don't need to hear it again. But I still rescued him. I rescued a person who didn't deserve to be rescued, and all I've received in return is a lot of mouth. It's going to stop, or so help me, I'll do it. I'll drop him into the bottom of my canteen. And then I'll throw the canteen into that river."

Mike stood between Cliff and the canteen. "You'll have to get by me first."

"Oh, look at the hero!" Cliff mocked. "Still cocky from your fight with the bikers? That fight where Ben creamed a bunch of them and you barely took on one?"

"That was one more than you took on," Mike said.

The next thing happened so fast, it caught Doug by surprise. Cliff quickly turned around cuz the old man had snuck up behind him while he faced off with Mike. Then the old man pulled Cliff's hair. Out of impulse, Cliff shrieked and put his hands up over his head to remove Andy's hand. When that happened, he had to let go of Doug for a sec and Doug jumped off. Mike caught him and set him on the ground next to Tinker Bell. Tinker Bell threw her arms around Doug, still sobbing.

"It's all right, honey," Doug said, holding her tightly. "I'm all right. Don't worry."

Cliff turned toward Andy and shoved him on the ground.

Mike grabbed Cliff by the collar. "Are you gonna pick on an old man now? Bothering a miniature isn't enough? Now you pick on old men?"

"He pulled my hair!"

Mike put his right foot behind Cliff's right leg and threw him down by pushing hard against his shoulder.

Cliff slowly got up off of the ground. "Is that an example of the judo you learned as a kid? Not much like Ben and his jujutsu, is it?"

"Never claimed it was," Mike said. "But whatever I'm able to do, I promise it will be worse if you ever touch DeWorken again!"

Cliff still stood his ground. "As I said, I don't recall electing a new leader."

"I'll vote right now," Andy said, standing up with difficulty and dusting himself off. "In Ben's absence, I believe the most mature and most capable member of our group is Mike. I vote for Mike to be our leader until Ben returns."

"So do I," Tinker Bell said.

"Me too," Doug added. "Maybe if I was normal size, I'd vote for myself. But as things are, Owen is the one I trust, not you, Reynolds."

Doug could see that Owen wasn't really interested in being a leader, only in doing the right thing. But maybe the fact that he didn't really wanna lead made him the best leader of all, a leader who wouldn't get all stuck up and full of himself.

"That's three for Mike," Andy said. "I guess that's a majority, unless the pussycat wants to add his vote and make it unanimous."

Doug knew that Mike's cat didn't really care much, even though his eyes had gone back and forth, following all the fuss and commotion.

"Right," the cat said. "As if I could give a cow's cud which one of you idiots leads this stupid expedition."

"Very well," Andy said. "That's one abstention and three in favor of Mike. You're outnumbered, Cliff."

Cliff stormed off.

Mike got down on the ground next to Doug and Tinker Bell. "You OK, Doug?"

"Yeah ... sure. Thanks, Owen. I guess I owe ya one."

Chapter Thirty

DeWorken and a Twist of Magic

It had been several hours since the incident with Cliff. Doug and I were off in the woods sitting on another large boulder, not as big as the others, but for the most part, these huge rocks offered the only way of sitting without being in the dirt or the leaves.

I wanted to help Doug. But it didn't seem right. Just the other day, I had summoned Charles for the purpose of making a wish on Cliff's behalf so that Doug could be prevented from any revenge. Instead, Charles had taken things a whole different direction, and I never accomplished what Cliff requested, but I had still made the attempt, partly for the sake of friendship and mostly to get him off my back. Now, in a complete about-face, I felt like a traitor just for even listening to Doug. The only way I could help him was to turn against my friend, although I had to admit, lately Cliff was seeming more dangerous than Doug, and not just because Doug was a miniature. Cliff had changed and was changing more every day. Today especially, when he came back to camp with the ornament, there was something different about him. And the way he went after Doug, threatening to drown him! I already knew Cliff hated Doug, but this was something different, something real scary. It made me wonder if that prophecy was starting to come true. Was Cliff going to be the first one of our party to turn evil? Was he turning evil right before our eyes? Doug was obviously wondering the same thing. While we talked, he suggested several times that maybe the ornament had never really been lost, that maybe Cliff had known where the ornament was all along and had only pretended to find it. I have to admit, the thought had also crossed my mind. It also crossed both of our minds that Cliff might have made a wish already with Hamartio. Of course Doug had already asked him about it, and Cliff had already insisted he never made a wish.

Anyway, Cliff wasn't around right now. It was just Doug and me. Doug kept making his case. He went on and on about how hard it was to be a miniature. He asked me several times how I would like being in his shoes. I told him I wouldn't like it and resisted making a joke, because between the two of us, Doug could honestly fit his entire body into *my* shoe. But I knew he was upset and probably didn't need another joke at his expense just because he had used a common expression.

"I'll tell you what, Doug. I'll make you a deal. If I summon Charles and make the wish, will you promise to leave Cliff alone?"

"Come on, Owen! The guy's been askin' for it!"

"No argument from me. But you talk like you plan to kill him."

"I'm not really gonna kill him. But he does deserve ta be roughed up a little. Now come on Owen, you gotta admit that."

"Yeah," I said. "Yeah, you're probably right. But I'll feel bad if anything happens to him. Anything at all. Even if you just rough him up, I'll feel responsible. I'll know that if it hadn't been for me, it wouldn't have happened."

"OK, Owen. Ya got a deal. Get me turned back ta normal size, and I'll lay off. I'll leave Cliff alone."

I knew he was agreeing too easily. I didn't believe him.

"Do I have your word?"

"Sure … sure … ya got my word."

"Doug, we don't know each other well. You seem like a nice enough guy. At least, you've been nice to me. But I'm not sure I know you well enough to believe you."

"Look, Owen. I'll be honest. I wanna give it ta Reynolds and give it ta him good. But if the only way ta turn back ta normal size is ta leave him alone, that's better than nothin'."

I wanted no part of this, but I knew I'd never hear the end of it otherwise. What would happen if Doug went back on his word? Would any of us be able to stop him? Had Ben still been around, I wouldn't have cared. Ben would never let Doug get near Cliff. But what would *I* be able to do? Doug was a huge, muscular football jock. He could make mincemeat out of me. I got lucky with that one biker. Cliff was right about that. It would be different with DeWorken. And if I wasn't able to stop DeWorken, old man Andy sure as heck wouldn't be any help. But again, I really didn't want him begging me for the rest of the trip. Besides, that was a pretty cruel thing Cliff had done, turning him small with the ornament. The whole reason we'd gone off on this journey in the first place was to rescue DeWorken. What kind of rescue would it be without him being restored to his original size?

"OK … I'll trust you, Doug."

Doug's face lit up like a lantern. "Thanks, Owen! You're a great friend! I mean that!"

"You won't let me down though, right Doug?"

"I promise. I won't let ya down."

***

I went through the whole routine again — holding the ornament, calling out for Charles, watching the blue smoke … Everything was the same.

Charles seemed happy to see us.

"Greetings, Mike. And hello to you as well, Doug. We've never met, at least not formally, but I feel as if I've known you for a long time."

I could tell Doug was uncomfortable, but he tried to be polite. I guess he figured any angel that could help him out was worth being polite to.

"Ah … hi … nice ta meet ya."

"What can I do for you, gentlemen?"

Doug quickly glanced my direction as if to remind me that the ball was in my court, so I decided to start right in.

"Well … you see … DeWorken needs something which only your power can provide."

"Very good, Mike."

"Huh?"

"I said, 'Very good.'"

"I heard what you said. What do you mean? What did I just do that was so good?"

"You broached the subject of your wish without immediately phrasing it as a wish."

"Oh … I see. … Yeah … I kind of learned from last time … when we talked before. Since I used the word 'wish' before asking questions, getting answers ended up being my whole wish."

"Exactly. Had you simply started in with your questions without prefacing them with the word *wish*, I could have answered those very same questions, and you still would have had a wish to spare."

"Yeah … it would have been nice to make a real magical wish, especially since you didn't answer too many of my questions anyway."

"I answered some, left you curious about others."

"Well, can I ask some more before we start? And notice I'm still not wishing … just asking."

"Certainly, Mike … Ask anything you want."

"And you'll answer every one of them this time?"

"Oh, I didn't say that," Charles replied with a dry smile.

I shook my head. He wasn't bugging me as much as last time. I knew this was simply Charles' way. Aunt Loureen used to tell me that most people will probably always stay the same and that I should learn to just accept my friends for who they were. The way she put it, "We tend to exert far too much effort, offering vain attempts to alter things that will ultimately remain grounded, despite all desires to the contrary." I was starting to see what she meant. Charles was Charles. He knew a lot of mysteries, and either he loved keeping me in suspense, or he had no choice but to keep me in suspense. Probably it was a little bit of both. In fact, he had said something to that effect the last time we spoke. Charles seemed to really care about me, and I figured he was helping as much as he could. But he also seemed to enjoy the guessing games and riddles. Whatever was driving him, one thing was sure: I wasn't gonna be able to change his nature, so I might as well stop trying. No sense getting myself all worked up over stuff I couldn't do anything about.

"OK. Here's my first question."

"Hold on!" DeWorken shouted out. "Can't we hold off the questions till later? I wanna make a wish!"

"I'm afraid the only one who can wish is Mike," Charles said sympathetically.

"I know," DeWorken said. "That's what I meant ta say. Mike will make the wish cuz only Mike is big enough ta hold the ornament in his hands. I got all that. But the whole reason we're here together is so that he can wish somethin' for *me*, and I wanna get started."

"Sorry, Doug," I said. "I know how anxious you are, but first we need to find out what happened to Ben."

"Ben?" Charles said, looking alarmed. "Something has happened to Ben?"

For the first time since I'd met Charles, he seemed taken aback. Up until now, Charles had always come across as being one or two steps ahead of the game, but this was an expression I had never seen on his face before. I didn't like this. It made me feel a rush of panic. A surprised look from Charles' face could hardly be a good sign.

"Shouldn't you know that already?" I said. "I assumed you knew what happened to him."

Charles shook his head with concern. "Not only do I not know *what* happened to him, I was not aware that *anything* had happened to him at all."

"That's impossible!" I said. "How can you not know? You know everything!"

"When did I ever tell you I know everything? You're ascribing abilities to me that I don't really possess, Mike."

I knew he was speaking the truth, not that I expected Charles to ever lie anyway, but even if I wanted to doubt his word, I could tell from his tone that something was terribly wrong. Obviously, this news was a shock to him. I found it alarming to see Charles so caught off guard. It seemed like our whole journey was unraveling. First, the bravest member of our group disappeared. Now, our supernatural protector had this look on his face like he might not be able to protect us as much as we had thought. He sure hadn't protected Ben, not if he hadn't any idea where Ben was.

I spent the next half hour going over every detail of Ben's disappearance that we had heard from Cliff. Charles listened keenly, barely uttering a word except to ask an occasional question. It was strange, *him* asking the questions for once. But I still had questions of my own. I mostly wanted to know what he was gonna do about Ben.

"Offhand, Mike ... I have no idea. None at all."

"But you're an angel," I said, hoping against hope that somehow I misunderstood him and that, after listening to the details, he might have figured out at least some kind of clue about Ben after all.

"Just because I'm an angel, that doesn't mean I know everything."

"Well, maybe not *know* everything. But don't you at least see all the stuff that happens to us? You said you were watching over us. You said you could see us from another dimension or something like that."

"Yes, Mike, I do watch over you as much as possible, but unlike the Author of Life, I am not omnipresent."

"Omni what?" DeWorken said. "What does that mean?"

"I think that means Charles can see us at times but not always. Is that what you meant to say, Charles?"

"Yes, Mike. At times I have other matters that need attention. It all relates to battling Hamartio, but I cannot always see my nemesis. Neither can I always see you or your friends."

"Great," I muttered. "Just great."

Charles continued. "However, I *was* under the impression that I'd been made privy to everything concerning *this* mission, even apart from watching constantly. I was unaware that anything crucial could be hidden from me. I thought I was only missing minor, small-talk conversations, and I had every reason to expect that I would be alerted at once to anything important or dangerous. But clearly that has not been the case."

"I still can't believe this," I said. "You know nothing about Ben's disappearance? There was nothing passed on to you from Heaven?"

Charles looked sad. "I'm afraid I haven't heard from Heaven in a long time. My own powers and instincts alert me to things, and yes, those come from Heaven, or at least originated from Heaven. Heaven is where I first obtained them, but I receive no direct messages anymore."

I was very puzzled, and Charles could see it in my eyes. He looked ashamed, or at least very unhappy with himself.

"You know the background of the ornament," Charles explained. "Remember? You read about it long ago in your sister's book about my world, *this* world. I never returned when the Author of Life commanded me to stop fighting Hamartio. I chose to be on my own, and that's where it left me … alone."

"But you're free from the ornament now."

"Not entirely free. As I explained, Hamartio and I are still connected to each other. We move about now, but there is a tie that cannot be severed."

I still found this hard to accept. "You got no prophecy about Ben? You didn't even have an inkling or warning or anything?"

"I did not. His disappearance is as much of a surprise to me as to you, which means that something is not right. Something is off-kilter."

"Could this be the work of Hamartio?" I asked.

"No. I can at least assure you of that. I do not see Hamartio constantly, and I have no idea what he's up to, but in our present state of affairs, he has no abilities to use the supernatural apart from my knowledge, due to the new rules he and I forged together while in battle."

I felt a little better hearing that Hamartio hadn't done anything to Ben. But then, I suddenly realized that if it wasn't Hamartio, then something even more mysterious had happened.

"Are you sure? I mean, if something bad happened to Ben, it just seems natural that it would be the bad angel."

"I'm sure, Mike. If Hamartio had been free to simply work whatever magic he wanted, anytime he wanted, trust me, he'd have done more than harm Ben. You yourself wouldn't be alive right now. Neither would your friends. But *something* is going on. Something happened to Ben, which means that things are out of alignment, so to speak. Mike, I need to leave and investigate this."

"Ya can't leave!" DeWorken pleaded. "What about me?"

Charles looked over at DeWorken but didn't say anything. It seemed to make DeWorken feel bad.

"I don't mean ta sound like I don't care," DeWorken started explaining to Charles. "Ben and I weren't friends, but he's treated me all right on this trip. And he did rescue me from the carnival. I wish he wasn't lost but it seems like there's nothin' we can do about it, and I still want my wish."

DeWorken was pretty brassy, talking to an angel like that and practically demanding his wish, although, by comparison to the way he talked to everyone else, he at least sounded a little bit respectful with Charles. Maybe Doug was learning that in this new world of magic, it was necessary to bow to authority. From what I knew about Doug, he never bowed to anyone — not teachers, not principals, not even that carnival barker, Mr. Blake, who had held him as a slave and could have killed him at any time. According to what I'd heard, Blake had to hurt Doug with fire before he finally agreed to perform with Tinker Bell. So respect didn't come easy to Doug, but if he was learning to at least show respect for a supernatural being, I guess that was something.

"Once again," Charles said to DeWorken, "the only one who can make a wish right now is Mike. And I'll let you do so, Mike. I have no option to resist since you summoned me with the ornament. But with this choice at your disposal, please consider an alternative. You could choose to forfeit your wish and instead allow me to use this time to look for Ben. Perhaps that would be the better course of action."

"No!" DeWorken snapped.

I guess his newfound respect didn't last too long.

"The choice is not yours," Charles said in a grave, almost monotone voice. "The choice is Mike's."

I wasn't sure what to do. I did wanna help Doug. I was tired of all the bantering between him and Cliff, and it seemed that if Doug was finally turned back to his normal size, none of us would have to listen to that anymore. But I wasn't just thinking of myself. If I was only thinking of myself and the kinds of conversations I didn't wanna hear anymore, I would skip the whole Cliff/DeWorken saga and wish instead that Andy was turned into a mute. So it wasn't only about me. Like I said before, I really did feel sorry for Doug.

"You'll still have plenty of time to look for Ben," I said to Charles. "The wish won't take long."

"It will if you take your time and wish carefully, which is just exactly what you should do. But because of our urgent situation, perhaps you should let me go, take even more time, continue to think about the wish, and summon me again the day after tomorrow."

"Please, Mike," DeWorken said. "Please don't make me wait no more."

It was funny, thinking now about DeWorken's lack of respect for people. It only seemed to include authority figures or people he couldn't stand, like Cliff. My case was different. Other than Tinker Bell, he treated me nicer than anyone else. And right now, he was begging me as if his entire life was in my hands. I didn't have the heart to refuse him.

"I promise to make this fast, Charles. I also promise to be careful."

Charles gave a slight shrug. "Very well."

DeWorken was relieved. "Thanks, Mike. So ya asked your question. Now for my wish."

"No, Doug. First there are two more questions."

"You gotta be kiddin'!"

"They won't take long."

"Whaddaya mean they won't take long? That last one took forever!"

"They won't take long if you stop interrupting me and let me get on with it!"

It seemed strange standing up to a school bully, even if the bully was smaller than a toy action figure. It still seemed strange. But Doug backed down. What else could he do? Charles and I were holding all the cards.

"All right. All right. Just stop takin' so long. We called him for a wish, and so far he don't even know what you're gonna wish for."

"Not so," Charles replied. "*That* I do know. I know exactly what you plan to wish for. I also know that there's a complication."

"What do ya mean, complication?"

"What I mean, Doug, is that your impatience could unravel everything. So perhaps it would be best to let Mike exhaust his questions before articulating a hastily worded wish."

"I don't care about no questions!"

"I understand that. But Mike is still learning how to make his requests with care, so the more he learns about our rules, the less dangerous things will be."

"Easy for you ta say! You get ta fly around as an angel all day! I'm stuck here on the ground, smaller than a toad."

"Come on, Doug," I said. "Chill out! We'll get to your wish. I promise. But Charles is right. I haven't been very careful up till now. If I don't wish exactly the right way, something even worse might happen. You don't want me to make a mistake, do you?"

DeWorken lowered his voice a bit. "I guess not."

Charles continued. "What were your further questions, Mike?"

"Just a couple of things I forgot about the last time we talked. Back home, the ornament only worked when it was Christmastime."

"That applied to *your* world, Earth. In this world, the ornament works only in the country of its origin, the Kingdom of Lumis, where they celebrated Christmas year round ... Or more correctly put, that was the rule before. All rules have been reset. The ornament presently works anytime according to the procedure we discussed."

"You mean about getting one wish a day and the days alternating between you and Hamartio?"

"Yes, Mike."

"OK ... So this next one is a question Cliff brought up right after I talked with you before. He pointed out something important I forgot to ask. Before, no new wish could undue an old wish."

"That rule remains the same."

"It does? OK. And it remains the same no matter which one of you granted our wish? If you give me my wish, Hamartio can't undo it?"

Charles was looking very concerned again. "Correct," he said. "But Cliff should know that answer by now."

"How would Cliff know? He didn't talk to you. I did!"

Charles shook his head. "Another wrinkle I did not anticipate. But also an informational reverse, because the parallel truth is something I *did* know but apparently *you* didn't."

"Huh?" DeWorken said.

I almost said it before he did.

"To put it more plainly," Charles continued, "I know something you don't know, and you knew something I didn't know. I was unaware that Cliff was continuing to keep his secret."

"Secret?" DeWorken said. "That skunk is keepin' a secret?"

I was just as concerned. "What secret?"

"Cliff has used the ornament. He spoke with Hamartio and already obtained an answer to this current question you are asking."

"The liar!" DeWorken shouted. "He said he didn't wish for nothin! I knew it! I just knew it! Didn't I tell ya this already, Owen? Well? Didn't I?"

I was very disappointed in Cliff but not all that surprised when I thought of how he had assaulted Doug earlier. This whole adventure was changing my friend. He had become sneaky, untrustworthy, and very dangerous.

I walked up closer to Charles, hoping he could say or do something to take away the cold chill I was feeling with this disturbing news. "I'm afraid to ask. What did Cliff wish for?"

"*That* I cannot tell you."

"Now wait!" I said. "Did you see this? Did you actually watch Cliff making his wish?"

"Yes, I saw it."

"Then you know more than you're letting on."

"Calm down, Mike. Think … You've heard me. What did I say about my knowledge? What have I told you precisely?"

I thought for a minute and then answered him. "You said there were some things you know and some things you don't know."

"Yes. And within those boundaries, I also told you about the subcategories."

He was driving me insane. As if there weren't enough rules, now the rules had "subcategories." To make things worse, he was acting like I should know every clause of his stupid angel contract by heart.

"I can't keep up with all this, Charles. How can I ever make a proper wish when you keep introducing newly added little features?"

"You're not paying attention, Mike. Focus! This is not new. It is merely a reminder. Some things I know. Some things I don't know. And under the heading of things I know, some I am allowed to reveal, others you must discover for yourself."

I was about to complain again, and then I remembered Aunt Loureen's advice. I should stop wasting time arguing about what I can't change. The rules were the rules. I needed to stop resisting them and just learn them better instead.

"OK ... What *can* you tell me?"

"I already did. Cliff made a wish with Hamartio."

"What did he wish?" I asked carefully, aware that I had already asked it.

"What kinda question is that?" DeWorken popped off. "We all know what he wished for! Any peabrain could figure it out! He wished for more protection against me! We don't need no angel to tell us that one."

"Is he right, Charles?"

"We just went through this, Mike. I'm afraid I cannot tell you what he wished for."

"Well, can you at least tell me if the wish was granted? The ornament does not always grant wishes."

"Old rules," Charles said. "Under our new, current rules, we are compelled to grant the wish if we possibly can. Angels don't have as much power as the Author of Life, but we have a lot, and if it is within our ability to grant the wish, we must grant it. There is no other choice."

"So whatever Cliff wished for, Hamartio would have had to give it to him."

"Yes. But you're forgetting the other stipulation."

"Come on, Charles! There are more stipulations than trees! Of course I forgot the stipulation, whatever it was."

Charles remained calm but still looked very serious. "Mike, the stipulation is that when we angels receive a wish that we don't care to grant yet are compelled to grant anyway, we look for a legal loophole."

"The loophole. Yeah ... right ... I do remember you telling me about the loophole. So that means Hamartio answered Cliff's wish but maybe tricked him somehow?"

"Yes. If, hypothetically, Cliff was not careful about his wording, the wish would come true literally, but not exactly the way Cliff intended."

"But you can't tell us what Cliff wished for?"

"No, Mike, I cannot. Believe me, I would if I were permitted."

"Are you permitted to offer any detail at all?"

"Only this. Hamartio lied to Cliff regarding his abilities. He told Cliff that he would consider the wish and think about it. Under the new rules, Hamartio has no such option. He must comply, unlike the old rules. Under the old arrangement, when we were a combined entity living inside of the ornament, we did not always grant wishes."

"Cliff is pretty smart," I said. "I'm surprised he didn't catch that."

Charles nodded. "Yes, Cliff is smart, but not nearly as smart as he thinks. Hamartio got away with the lie because he was describing a situation which, under the old rules, would have been true. Since Cliff was accustomed to the old rules, he failed to catch the subtle distinction, and he fell for the trick."

"Which means," I added, "that whatever Cliff wished for he will get."

"Yes. But it won't happen exactly the way Cliff wanted it to happen."

It was silent for a long time. Nobody said anything, but it was obvious what each person was thinking. Charles was hoping I would postpone my wish so that he could investigate Ben's disappearance and, more importantly, discover why he personally had been kept in the dark about the whole thing. Probably that part concerned him even more than Ben's safety, although I'm sure he also cared about Ben. And DeWorken, of course, with his one-track mind, was waiting for me to just get on with it and wish for him to be tall so that he could feel like himself again and make Cliff regret that he had ever heard the name *Doug DeWorken*. Despite his promise, I was still pretty sure of DeWorken's true plan. As for me, I didn't know what to do. It seemed like all my questions about the rules were answered, but there were so many. Was I keeping track of them all? And were there even more I was forgetting to ask about? If Cliff was here, he might remind me about something else to ask, but even Cliff didn't think of everything. Charles had just pointed that out.

Anyway, I couldn't think about rules all day and I wanted to make my wish, but then there was the other problem: Charles was clearly acting like the wish wasn't a very good idea, so I was caught between wanting to be cautious, but not so cautious that I stood there all day without doing anything.

"Here's a good question," I said. "And this should cover them all. Are there any rules about the ornament that I haven't asked or you haven't told me?"

"No," Charles said. "You have heard everything you need to hear. The issue is remembering."

"OK. So Cliff made some wish. You can't tell us what it is. I think it was about DeWorken, but you won't say."

"It's not that I *won't* say. I *can't* say."

"But you do know."

"I know."

"And you seem concerned about the wish I wanna make, and you do know the wish I'm about to make."

"Yes on both counts."

"Enough!" DeWorken cried out. "I could have made fifty wishes by now!"

"Shut up, Doug!"

That wasn't the smartest thing to say to a guy who might turn back to his normal size any moment, but I was getting as tired of his complaining as he was getting tired of the postponements.

"You are wise to be so slow and thoughtful," Charles said.

I decided it was time to go for it. "All right, I wish that my friend Doug would turn back to his normal size."

I added in that part about him being my friend so that, after the wish was granted and Doug was returned to his normal, strong, bully-ready size, he would be grateful and think of me as a friend instead of clobbering me for telling him to shut up. Since I was on a roll about being cautious, I figured that kind of caution wouldn't hurt either.

"I'm afraid the answer is no," Charles said.

DeWorken's eyes looked like they were about to explode.

I sighed. "What do you mean the answer is no?"

"I cannot grant your wish, Mike. It is forbidden."

"I knew it!" DeWorken said. "I just knew it. We spend an hour talkin' ta this bag of wind, and he still doesn't do nothin'!"

I was frustrated too. Not as much as DeWorken, obviously, since the wish was not about me. With a calmer tone, I approached Charles. "I know you didn't want me to make the wish so fast, but I was careful as I could be. Now you did say to us that, like it or not, you have to grant wishes. You said that! I know you said that! I know I heard you."

"Yes, if at all possible."

"But by 'possible' you meant within your abilities. Now, come on, Charles. If you and Hamartio had the ability to turn DeWorken small in the first place, it has to be within your abilities to turn him back."

"True, our ability is one stipulation within the realm of possibility. But there was another stipulation."

I just gave him a blank stare. Words no longer existed to express how sick and tired I was of the conversation.

Anyway, it didn't matter because Charles just continued talking anyway.

"The impossibility of this wish is not credited to any lack of abilities. It is because one wish cannot undo the effects of a previous wish. We just reviewed that rule. You brought it up yourself for clarification."

"So Cliff *did* make a wish about DeWorken."

"Yes. I was not permitted to reveal that before, but since you tried to make this very specific wish, a degree of information must unravel to explain why the wish is not granted. I am compelled now to inform you that Cliff pulled a protective maneuver, a preemptive strike, if you will."

"So he made a wish that DeWorken would never be able to turn tall?"

"I can't repeat his exact words, but you have the right idea. His wish was about DeWorken."

"Fine thing!" DeWorken cried out practically in tears. "Fine mess! So what am I supposed ta do now?"

"There are other ways I can help you," Charles said, looking very sorry and very helpless. "Size isn't everything."

"Easy for you ta say, angel!"

Instead of throwing a tantrum, I decided to find out about other possibilities. "OK, can you give us some ideas, Charles? I'd like to help Doug in any way I can, so if I can't wish for him to get tall, what *can* I wish for?"

"Ya really wanna help me, Owen?"

"Well, sure I do."

"Then make the wish again."

"Again? What's the point?"

"Just make it again."

"Aren't you listening? We can't."

"I don't believe this guy, and I don't trust him. He coulda told us a long time ago that we was wastin' our time. He knew what you was gonna wish for. He even *said* he knew."

"So?" I said. "That doesn't change the answer. The answer is still no."

"Well, don't accept that answer! If I was your size and I could hold the ornament in my hands, I would stand there and keep tryin', no matter what this sap says. Try it again."

"Don't listen to him, Mike."

"See?" DeWorken said. "See? I thought so."

"See what?"

"If he really can't answer the wish, he wouldn't be given ya no warnin'. The warnin' wouldn't be needed."

"Mr. DeWorken," Charles said firmly and formally, "you simply do not know what you are talking about."

"Yeah, I do! I know what I'm talkin' about all right. I'm tired of people thinkin' I don't know stuff. I might not be a good artist like Owen or a brain like his weasel friend Cliff, but I'm what they call 'street smart,' and I can smell a rat a mile away. Mister, you smell like a rat."

"Give it up," Charles said.

In my mind, I was actually wondering if Doug might not be on to something. Charles *was* acting sort of strange, and he did seem worried about me making a wish right from the very start. If he already knew the wish could not be granted, what was concerning him? What would have been the harm if I had made this same wish an hour ago? Probably he was afraid that if I reworded the wish, some bad twist might happen, but I still wasn't sure. I would need more information, and although normally Charles would chat with me as long as I wanted, he wasn't himself today. He was anxious to figure out the "Ben mystery." Between Charles not being himself and DeWorken being impossible to deal with, I needed to make a decision fast. Either make another wish or call off this session altogether.

"Look, Owen," Doug said. "I never asked nothin' from ya before, have I? I thought we was friends. Please try it again. Make the wish again."

"Charles already said it can't be done."

"I don't believe him."

"I do."

Even as I spoke those words I wasn't sure I really meant them. I knew Charles wouldn't lie, but Charles didn't exactly volunteer a whole lot of truth either. He was a master at withholding things.

"Please, Mike! Please! Maybe it had ta do with the way ya worded it the first time. Just word it differently. I wanna be my regular size again."

"That cannot happen," Charles said again. "Ever! So you may as well stop asking."

My resistance to Doug's plea was fading. "Charles, just in case it had something to do with the way I worded it, I *am* going to reword my wish."

Charles raised his hand in protest. "Mike, that is exactly what NOT to do."

"See?" DeWorken said. "See? If ya really wasn't allowed, he

wouldn't be tryin' ta stop ya."

"I agree. But if he's trying to stop me, he has a good reason."

"So? It's my life and my responsibility. If it ends up wrong, it won't hurt nobody but me. Right? You'll be fine. I'll take what comes. I'll take the chance. It's my dice ta roll, not yours. Please, Mike! Just one more time! One more time for a friend. If it doesn't work, I'll stop buggin' ya. I promise. One more time! Please!"

I'd had enough, and I wasn't gonna listen to any more. "OK, Doug. One more try ..."

Charles moved so close he was almost nose to nose. "Mike, you're making a mistake!"

"Then tell me why, Charles. Start offering some real information or stop telling me what to do."

"Way ta go, Owen!"

Charles looked like he was about to say something again, but he stopped himself. "Very well. Be my guest. Reword your wish."

Even though Charles was bugging me ... even though I enjoyed telling him off a little to pay him back for all the rules and fine print and extra annoying little provisions, I still wasn't so stupid as to ignore his warning. I had been careless with this ornament once too often. Charles may have been a pain, but he was still concerned that if I made some kind of wish that could actually be answered, the magic would backfire due to an interference from Cliff's wish. Only a fool would plow ahead and pretend he hadn't been warned. Cliff had beat us to the punch, and I was pretty sure what he'd wished for. I didn't know the details but I had a pretty good idea. He probably just wished that DeWorken could never turn tall again. That's exactly what I'd have wished for if I'd been in his place. I guess there was a chance it could be something else, something similar which accomplished the same thing. Maybe he just made a more general wish that Doug could never harm him no matter what size he was. But that seemed unlikely. A moment ago, Charles had told Doug that he was never going to return to his normal size again and he should just put it out of his mind. This could only be true if Cliff had made that exact request of Hamartio. I felt bad for Doug, but I was also a little relieved. If Doug could not turn tall again no matter what, then there couldn't be any harm in me wishing it again. The worst that could happen was that Charles would just refuse the wish one more time. So why even bother? Why even go through the motions? To get Doug off my back. This way, he would still think of me as a friend, but I wouldn't be risking more trouble. Sure, there were other ideas. I could try to make some different kind of wish. I could ask for Doug's protection in some other way, something along the lines of Cliff not being able to bother him anymore, even though he would remain a miniature. So why didn't I try it that way? Why make a wish I knew couldn't be answered instead of trying one that possibly could be answered? Because of the warning from Charles. He was very concerned that if I wasn't careful with my wording, something worse might happen. Better to not even take the risk. But what if later in our journey Doug turned back to normal size from some other kind of magic? It couldn't happen from the ornament, but we might meet up with other prophets, other magicians, maybe even other charms like the key chain and the magic rock. I had no idea, but if, by chance, DeWorken ever somehow became his normal size again, I wanted him to remember me as the guy who tried to help him, instead of the guy who refused. So the idea was to make it look like I was trying again but, in reality, play it safe by just making the same old wish that I knew Charles wouldn't answer.

On the other hand, I had to make it look like I was really trying and really hoping. I wouldn't be able to pull that off unless I reworded the wish like Doug had suggested. So how could I reword it, but in a way that amounted to the same wish? How could I find new words that would have no more effect than the old words?

I hesitated for a moment to review the way I had worded it before. I had said something about DeWorken turning "normal size." How could I say the same thing but leave out the words *normal size*?

It finally came to me.

"My wish is for Doug to be the *same* size as the rest of our group. I don't mean in actual feet … just that he will be one of us, able to talk face to face without being picked up, without having to climb anything."

That was as careful and specific as I knew how to be, but not exactly the same as the previous wish. It wouldn't work, but Doug had promised to get off my back for trying one last time, and that was my way of making it look like I was trying.

"Very well, Mike." Charles waved his hand in the air.

All of a sudden, everything got blurry, but it only lasted seconds. Then I could see clearly again. Doug was standing next to me, the same height he was when I first met him, a few inches taller than me.

How could this be? I had wished the exact same thing, only with different words. How could it work the second time if it hadn't worked the first time? Oh well. At least nothing bad happened. Here he was, Doug DeWorken, back to normal.

"It worked!" DeWorken shouted like a kid on his birthday. "It worked that time. Oh, Mike! How can I ever repay you?"

"Don't thank me. It was Charles' doing."

I turned toward Charles but was unable to see him. Instead I was facing what looked like a giant shoe and the bottom of a giant leg.

"Charles?"

"I'm here." His voice sounded loud as thunder.

I looked up. He *was* here. Charles hadn't gone anywhere. Neither had he turned DeWorken back to his normal size. Instead he changed *me*. Now *I* was a miniature.

"What have you done?" I shrieked in horror. "What have you done?"

"It's not a matter of what I did Mike. You did this. You failed to heed my warning, and you reworded your wish. Because of Cliff's preemptive request, I could not restore Doug to his former size, but your second request did not ask for that. You asked for Doug to be made the same size as the rest of you, and you were thinking about your traveling band of companions while you uttered the fateful words. So now all of you are the same size, but since Doug could not shoot up to your level, you shot down to his. Not only you, all of you — the entire band of companions. When you return to camp, you'll find the same situation with everyone else: Cliff, Andy, even the cat. Tinker Bell will be the same because she was already a miniature. Are you happy now, Mike? Are you proud of yourself for getting impatient and not listening? Are you glad you took Doug's advice, decided not to trust me, and shrugged off my warning? Now you're all miniatures, miniatures in a foreign land. This world was already going to be a challenge, but it just became a whole lot more dangerous, and your friends have you to thank, Mike. They have you to thank."

Chapter Thirty-One

Revenge at Last

"I said where is he?"

Doug was demanding to know Cliff's whereabouts. Andy was trying to calm him down. I was feeling helpless and guilty and just plain stupid. We were back at camp, even though it didn't look like camp with all the items being so huge, from the table to the fireplace to the ax to our blankets. It looked like another whole new world, but it was really our same camp seen through the eyes of two helpless miniatures, Doug and me ... and everyone else too for that matter. That is, everybody but Cliff. Oh, he had changed too, all right. I just mean that he wasn't at camp when we returned. The others were all here: Andy, Caligula, and Tinker Bell. Doug was waiting impatiently for one of them to help him find Cliff. All we knew so far was that he had also turned small like everybody else and had run off, knowing that Doug would probably be coming back looking for him.

And that is just exactly what happened. Obviously DeWorken had no intention whatsoever about keeping his promise to me, the one about not hurting Cliff if I wished on his behalf. And now a wish *had* been granted. It didn't turn out the way we expected (to make the understatement of the century), but it was good enough for the likes of Doug DeWorken. So long as he and Cliff were now the same size, regardless of how it had happened, DeWorken was still salivating for sweet revenge. Now he was gonna do what he'd been threatening to do on the whole trip: make Cliff pay for everything, from the snide comments to the jokes to the threats to the dreadful wish itself which had turned him tiny in the first place, and most of all, for having been sold into slavery. Doug meant to get even, and I saw no sign that he even remembered promising otherwise, let alone keeping the promise.

Doug and I hadn't talked about Cliff when we were first transformed. We were both shocked over the new nightmare we found ourselves in the middle of. Before returning to the others, we stayed out in the woods with Charles, listening to him explain in more detail exactly what had happened and why. Charles reminded us several times that he had urged caution. He also expressed, to put it in in his words, "the deepest, most profound regret that he was compelled to carry out my wish, even though he knew it was such an irresponsible, thoughtless wish."

I had tried at first to get Charles to reverse the wish. Naturally, Charles reminded me that wishes could not be reversed, that this was the whole problem in the first place, namely me wishing for DeWorken's size to change when Cliff had already sealed DeWorken's fate by wishing that could never happen. Charles reminded me that I already knew the rule and that I was wasting my time. I didn't need to be reminded. Yeah, I knew the rule. Boy, did I know! We were in this fix because of my own stupidity, and I felt horrible. But Charles still had magic abilities, and I hoped there might be some special exception rule. Why not? There were so many other clauses, and subclauses, and fine prints ... Maybe one or two of them would be a loophole to bail us out of this mess. I suggested my idea to Charles.

All he said was "You know better than that, Mike."

He sounded like a member of my own family, like the way Aunt Loureen would have sounded or maybe my dad, disappointed in me, but disappointed out of love, disappointed because he really cared about me. What made me feel sick to my stomach was that my idiotic, careless wish had done more than ruin things for *me*. It had ruined things for my friends too. And not just my friends. It also affected Charles. Charles may have worked the magic and directed it against me, but the experience depressed him every bit as much, if not more. This seemed to be like torture for poor Charles, torture because this rotten apple answer to my wish was granted by him. He *had* to grant it. He had no choice. But whatever the reason, *it was still him who actually performed the feat of magic.* He was the one who turned me into a miniature. Charles hated having to be the bad guy because he *wasn't* a bad guy. He was a man of principle, or an angel of principle. I guess that would be the way to put it, even though he always appeared as a man.

Charles had already been confused and concerned about not knowing Ben's current location. I had only made matters worse by ignoring his warning and wishing for DeWorken to turn big anyway. Aunt Loureen would have called it "pouring salt in his wounds."

And yet, from my point of view, I had been very careful. I mean, it didn't turn out to be careful, but it sure seemed that way at the time.

I hadn't just plunged in with my mouth wide open the way I had with earlier wishes. I had thought of every word and every possible angle. In fact, I thought it through until my brain was tired of thinking. And what did I get in return for being so careful? All that happened was a literal fulfillment to one of the dumbest, most dangerous wishes a human being could possibly make!

Doug wasn't as bothered as me. Oh sure, he would have preferred to turn back to his normal size, but at least things were a *little* better for him now. At least he was the same size as everyone else in our little party, thanks to the clumsy words which I still couldn't believe had come out of my own mouth.

At least now Doug didn't have to ride on anyone else's back while we were hiking, and most important of all, now he could get even with Cliff. I sensed immediately that he planned to do so, but like I said, we didn't talk about it at first because I was mostly trying to talk Charles into finding some special exception rule or new piece of magic to reverse the situation. I understood that it couldn't come from the ornament, but we were in a whole new world filled with all kinds of other magic charms or prophets or whatever. Surely there was something Charles could do or somebody Charles could introduce us to, and I wasn't shy about asking.

But Charles was not gonna be much help right now. This was clear, even though I hated to admit it. Unlike other times, Charles' explanation was brief, and he had no plans to hang around and explain further. Not only was he disappointed in me, he was *disgusted* with me and with himself too, because even though the rules of the ornament forced him to grant my jerk of a wish, it still happened by his hand. He even said something to that effect, how "having to do this to our group had injured him as well."

"I don't believe I'll ever be the same again after today," Charles said in such a painful way that I started feeling sorrier for him than for myself.

Anyway, Charles finally told me we needed to wrap up our conversation.

"You made your decision, Mike. You could have listened to me. You could have heeded my warning. Instead, you listened to your friend over there, and so you will simply have to accept the consequences."

"There must be something you can do!"

"You're in denial, Mike. You know there's nothing else."

It was so weird speaking with him in my new condition. Before, Charles and I were always able to talk to each other face to face. Now I had to look up at him. I felt like one of those little peewee characters in the Green Giant commercials, staring up at the Jolly Green Giant, except that Charles was anything but jolly. His voice was similar, but with a thunderous echo. Was this what the rest of us had looked like and sounded like to Doug all this time? No wonder the poor guy was desperate to change back to normal size! I thought I had already understood. Often, I imagined what it would be like to be in his place. That's what kept me nicer. That's why I treated him with kindness instead of the way Cliff treated him. But now, finally experiencing the exact same thing for myself, I realized that I'd had no idea … not really. Nobody could be prepared for a change like this.

I made one last attempt to get something out of Charles. I needed him to throw me some kind of bone or at least give us an inkling of hope.

"You said before to Doug that there were other ways of helping him."

"Yes," the megaphone voice of Charles answered from above. "And instead of pursuing that with me, you charged ahead like a bull in a china cabinet."

"I already told you how sorry I was."

I had apologized maybe ten times when we first talked, in those dreadful exchanges where Doug and I were trying to figure out what had happened. Even though I was the one who turned small and Charles remained his normal size, I was the one who kept apologizing, since, like I already said, I could see how bad he felt. But I wasn't gonna apologize any more.

"Being sorry won't help, Mike."

"OK. Being sorry won't help. But there are other ways you can help. That's what you told Doug."

"We'll explore those possibilities the next time we talk."

"The next time? You mean I have to wait another two days?"

"That is correct. It would involve another wish, not a wish that reverses anything, but perhaps a wish that protects your group in some other manner."

"But we need protection now! We can't wait two days!"

"You'll just have to try to hold on. Your wish for today is used up, and should you choose to utilize the ornament tomorrow, you'll only get Hamartio."

"Oh yeah? Well, there doesn't seem to be much of a difference! Cliff got Hamartio, and instead of tricking him in a sneaky way, Hamartio simply granted his wish! So what's the difference?"

"The difference is that I made an effort to slow you down, to get you to think about your exact wording so that you wouldn't be trapped by the casual carelessness of your literal words. Hamartio did no such thing with Cliff. Had he been concerned for Cliff's well-being, he too would have urged caution and reminded Cliff to go over his words carefully before making a wish. Now, mind you, he would not have been permitted to actually ghostwrite the words, but with a little coaching, Cliff might have figured out the need to express more detail. Instead of merely asking for Doug to remain the same size, he might have asked that Doug always remain miniature *compared to him*! See the difference? Hamartio was only too happy to take Cliff at his word and grant a wish that he knew would lead to catastrophe later on. I, on the other hand, made every attempt to slow you down, for all the good it did. But the attempt was still made, so to answer your question, THAT is the difference between Hamartio and myself!"

"OK! OK! It just seems that maybe there's something special you can do on your own to help us in the meantime. I'm not saying I deserve it, but you keep talking about serving God. Isn't God merciful? Doesn't God help people even when they don't deserve it, like in that Bible story where Cain was banished and God still put that mark of protection on him to keep him from danger?"

"I already included an act of mercy, Mike."

"You did?"

"Yes, even as you muttered those fateful words, even as the rules of the cosmos forced me to comply, I embedded some mercy in the granting of your wish."

"What mercy? I don't see any mercy."

"Well, it's there."

"Could have fooled me."

"Yes, well, it seems you get fooled very easily, Mike. And therein lies your whole problem. You don't think."

"Just tell me! What did you do?"

"Certainly, Mike. I'll tell you. It's right in front of your nose, but I'll tell you. Where is the ornament right now?"

"The ornament? I'm holding it. Where else would it be?"

"Yes. It is in your hand, which means you will still be able to make wishes. That is the act of mercy, assuming you learn to make your wishes responsibly."

I just continued staring up at him.

"What I'm saying, Mike, is that when your body was transformed to Doug's size, the ornament was reduced right along with you. Had this not happened, you would have a giant ornament in front of you, one that you would never be able to pick up again, one that would be impossible to make wishes with."

"Is that all? Is that your act of mercy?"

"You're welcome, Mike. And your appreciation seems a little on the light side."

"I don't get it! How's that mercy?"

"It's mercy because I did not leave you entirely unprotected. You still have usage of the ornament. You don't deserve this continued usage, but it's been granted anyway, ergo ... mercy."

"But the ornament would have shrunk with me anyway."

"Oh, it would have? Sure of that, are you?"

"Come on, Owen! Ya ain't gonna get no more outta him. He enjoys messin' with your head. Let's get outta here. Let's get back ta camp."

"No, wait, Doug, I need to understand this. Look, Charles, when Doug turned small, his clothes turned small with him. So I just assumed the ornament turned small for the same reason, because I was holding it in my hand at the time I made the wish."

"You assume too much."

"Well, that's the way it worked with Doug and his clothes."

"Yes, that is the way of the ornament, the natural outcome, the general progression of things. When the ornament is used to change a person's size, the range of the effect includes anything the person is wearing and anything the person is holding."

Charles was making it sound like Cliff and me had not been the first people to make those kinds of wishes. Considering how old and ancient this ornament was, I had to wonder how many other people had been magically reduced over the years. For all I knew, maybe Tinker Bell's whole country turned miniature as a result of some princess or witch or another evil person getting their hands on the ornament and its power.

But there would be time to ask about that later. Right now, I was still trying to understand my own situation.

"Well, if it was natural for the ornament to shrink with me, then how was that an act of mercy? It just happened."

"Things are natural for a reason, Mike. That applies to magic rules as well as the rules of nature. The ornament is not its own sentient being. Its properties are governed by the compromises Hamartio and I forced upon each other, him for the sake of destruction, me for the sake of mercy and deliverance. Therefore, the natural progression of magic reduction is only natural because my influence made it so. And I could retract that influence if I so desired. For example, when Cliff first made his wish about your friend Doug here, Doug would have shrunk right out of his clothes as a naked miniature had my own mercy not been part of the magic process. My influence offered damage control. I mitigated the effects of the wish and made them less severe for Doug. At that time, Hamartio and I were still inside the ornament, merged into one entity, but my side of the entity countered Hamartio's side with a merciful ingredient. And just now, had you been bargaining with Hamartio, he would have taken you so much at your literal word that the ornament would have stayed the same size. After all, you were wishing that Doug would be the same size as *the rest of you*, not the same size as the *ornament*. Yes, I was compelled to answer your wish, but I saw to it that the clothes and objects in your possession also reduced themselves proportionally. That was my mercy."

"Big deal!" DeWorken said. "We're still tiny, so thanks for nothin'!"

"Actually, " I said, "it *is* better than nothing. OK, Charles ... Well ... thanks ... I mean ... a real thanks ... from me at least ... Thanks ... I guess ... So now can you tell me ...?"

"No, Mike," Charles interrupted. "Today I can tell you nothing else. Today I can do nothing more for your company, except perhaps search for Ben. If I locate him, he at least will be his original size ... I presume ... depending on exactly what happened to him. If so, his role as a protector will take on a whole new dimension. OK, Mike and Doug, may the blessings and mercy of the Author of Life be upon you. Until next time."

And with that, he disappeared again in the blue smoke.

So anyway, that's why up till now, Doug and I hadn't talked about his promise not to hurt Cliff. We didn't talk about it on our way back to camp either because it took us a lot longer to get back to camp than it had taken to get to the spot in the woods where we had summoned Charles. I guess the reasons are obvious. Since Doug and me were both miniatures, we had a much farther distance to travel. It was also hard to figure out where we were going. The forest was the same, but it sure didn't look the same. Even Doug had seen it from higher up before since he had been in that knapsack seat up on my shoulders. That knapsack had shrunk with me and would no longer do Doug any good unless somebody screwed things up even worse and made a wish that he turned even tinier.

Since we spent our journey back to camp talking about familiar sights and figuring out where we were, Cliff never came up.

When, finally, we figured out the right directions and approached camp, we were greeted by Andy. He met up with us when we were almost back at camp but not quite. It was good to see him because it was the first familiar sight I had seen since our magical ornament encounter. But then it hit me that the only reason Andy looked so natural was that he too had shrunk, just as Charles said he would.

Anyway, Andy, asked us right away what had happened. I told

him the whole story. He just listened patiently, nodding his head once in a while, saying, "I see. Oh yes. Well, that explains a lot, doesn't it?"

I was just as curious to hear what had happened from their end, so I asked Andy if the group had gotten kind of freaked out turning miniature in the flash of a second.

"Well, of course it was quite startling," he said. "What helped is that we were all together at camp, so it didn't take us long to speak with each other and discover that the enlarged objects around us meant we were the victims of a new twist of magic. It was Cliff who first suggested that perhaps you and Doug were out in the woods making a wish, and that in all likelihood, the wish had backfired."

"It backfired all right," I said. "So is everyone mad at me?"

"Nobody knows for sure that you had anything to do with it, Mike. All they have to go by so far is Cliff's suggestion. As for me, I understand. You were only trying to help poor Doug."

"That's nice of you to say, Andy. I hope the others have the same attitude."

"Well, of course it doesn't affect Tinker Bell. As a matter of fact, it's now easier for her to interact with the others. Your cat is another story, mad as all tarnation, but the cat is never in a good mood anyway, so I wouldn't worry too much about him. As for Cliff, I suppose Cliff will be angry with you."

"Oh, will he?" Doug said. "I really do hope Cliff is angry. And I hope he tells us just exactly how angry. In fact, I'd like him ta explain it ta me personally."

Andy placed his hand on Doug's shoulder. Doug instantly shook his shoulder free, looking very annoyed. I could tell he didn't like being touched.

Andy still talked pleasantly. "Actually, Doug, this is why I came out to meet you myself. I assumed Cliff guessed correctly, and I assumed you'd be coming back our way fairly soon, so I intercepted."

"Intercepted? Don't go usin' football terms on me, old man. I know what you're gonna say. Do ya think I'm stupid or somethin'? Ya want me ta give Cliff a break and spare him."

"Would you?" Andy said, almost unaware that Doug looked like he wanted to hit him too. "Would you spare the poor fellow? That would be such a fine gesture, the gesture of a gentleman."

Whatever else DeWorken aspired to, I had a feeling being a gentleman was not high on his list. But Andy continued by talking about "how frightened the poor chap Cliff was feeling right now." Then he went on to say that "he was scared as a muskrat."

It didn't seem like this was having any influence over Doug. He still looked like a man salivating over a steak that was on the barbeque and almost ready to be served. "Yeah? Well, Cliff's *smaller* than a muskrat too. And that suits me just fine. That geeky pest is finally gonna get what he deserves."

"Hey, come on, Doug," I said. "You made a promise."

"What promise? I didn't promise nothin'."

This was exactly what I had been afraid of. I didn't want Doug to turn on me. I wanted to stay in his good graces, especially since he was no longer so small that I could hold him in the palm of my hand. He could beat me to a pulp if he wanted, but the group had elected me as their leader in Ben's absence, and I couldn't let them down, especially since I had already let them down with my birdbrain wish. I had to make things right. Before, I was protecting DeWorken from Cliff. Now, I had to do the same thing in reverse. I had to protect Cliff from DeWorken. But standing up to Cliff was easy. DeWorken was gonna be another story altogether!

"Yes, you did, Doug. You promised that if I made a wish to turn you back to normal size, you would not take revenge on Cliff."

Doug stopped for a second, looking me over. Would this be it? Would this be the moment he turned against me and put me on his enemy list? The list was already quite long. What would one more name be to Doug? And yet, I had stood up for him and protected him. I was hoping his memory and his gratitude would be stronger than his quick temper.

So far, so good. Doug didn't seem mad, but neither did he give in. "Yeah, I did promise that, Owen. But ya never came through with your part of the deal. Your wish never did turn me back ta my normal size, did it?"

I was starting to think that Cliff and Caligula would need to take back all their insults about how dumb DeWorken was. In their eyes, DeWorken was "not the sharpest tool in the shed," but if only they could see him now, talking like a lawyer who had read a contract more carefully than anyone else.

"Come on, Doug. It amounts to the same thing. You and Cliff are the same size."

"Doesn't matter. Ya never did your part."

"I tried to. I tried for *you*. And I screwed things up for everybody else by trying so hard. Isn't that worth anything to you?"

For a moment, Doug looked genuinely touched. "You've been a good friend, Mike. You're all right. I do appreciate ya." He extended his hand and we shook. "But I still have ta do this, Mike. I gotta get even."

"Be honest, Doug. You would have gone after Cliff even if the wish had been granted the way you had hoped, right?"

"We're wastin' time talkin'. Let's get back ta camp."

***

So, now, here we were, back in camp. Andy had failed to make any headway. Neither had I. When we first returned, Tinker Bell ran up to Doug, kissing him until he finally said, "OK, honey. It's OK."

"I was afraid I lost you," she whispered.

"Naw. You ain't never gonna lose me."

"Cliff still hasn't returned?" Andy asked Tinker Bell.

"Why should he?" Caligula chimed in. "Cliff may be the biggest pill this side of an aspirin bottle, but he's smart enough to know that he should get as far away from bulldozer DeWorken as possible."

"Hey, listen, cat! You ain't bigger than me no more. In fact, you're smaller now, just a regular cat. So watch your mouth!"

"Or what?" Caligula said in defiance.

"Or I'll kick the crud outta ya!"

Caligula started licking his chops. "Go ahead, DeWorken! Find out what a cat's claw feels like! Go on. Just try me."

DeWorken smiled. "One thing at a time. You're on my list, cat, but right now I wanna know what happened ta Reynolds."

"Caligula already told you," I said. "Cliff is hiding from you."

"Maybe you too," Caligula said looking at me. "You and that ornament are more dangerous than a kid who plays marbles with a rolled-up scorpion."

It seemed like Caligula had put some thought into that latest jab. I wondered how long it took him to come up with it. Probably it came to his mind shortly after turning small. For a while, before Doug and I returned to camp, the group would have been talking, and Caligula, as usual, would not have wanted to contribute much to the conversation. So, instead, he probably sat back silently, stewing over what had happened. He probably couldn't wait to tell me off. But being told off wasn't as bad a fate as what lay in store for poor Cliff. Anyway, we didn't have time to deal with the cat right now, so I ignored him and tried instead to get some kind of group plan in motion.

"OK," I said. "A lot has changed, so we need to put our heads together and figure out our next step."

"I already know MY next step," DeWorken said. "Which way did Cliff go?"

Nobody answered.

DeWorken tried again. "I said, where is he?"

"Doug, please," Tinker Bell pleaded. "There's been enough unhappiness for one day."

"Which direction, honey? Tell me."

Tinker Bell looked the other way. I couldn't be sure if she was trying to protect Cliff or just pouting because she was hoping DeWorken would become less violent and more romantic.

Anyway, whatever her purpose, romance was the last thing on DeWorken's mind. He walked back over to Andy. "OK, old man. Which way did Cliff go?"

Andy shook his head. "I won't help you, Doug. But I *will* say this. You're wasting your time going after him."

"Oh?" Doug said. "Why's that?"

"Cliff still has the navigation stone in his hand. When it started turning red, he surmised that the rock was warning him about you, that you and Mike were on your way back to camp. So he skedaddled out of here faster than greased lightning."

I had wondered about the magic stone while Doug and I were returning to the group. I figured the stone would be affected or unaffected just like the ornament. According to what Charles told us, if the stone had been out of Cliff's hand or out of Cliff's pocket, set aside on the ground, at the time of the magic transformation, it would have stayed its original size. Nobody would be able to pick the rock up any more, at least not easily, and we sure as heck couldn't put it in anybody's pocket to take it along on the journey.

Since Andy said Cliff had the rock in his hands when it turned red, that must have meant that he also had the rock in his hand when everything changed, or maybe in his pocket, which made sense since he always clung to that rock like a life preserver. And in this case, maybe it truly *was* a life preserver for him. The rock had "reduced proportionally," as Charles would put it, and for this reason, it acted for Cliff as a convenient DeWorken barometer.

"What are ya talkin' about?" DeWorken shouted at Andy.

"I'm talking about our warning device that the prophet provided and explained to everybody, including you. It turns red when there's danger, and in this case, Doug, YOU are the danger."

"I ain't a danger ta nobody but Cliff!"

"Maybe so," I said. "But that's enough of a danger for the rock to turn color. Shouldn't that tell you something, Doug? Don't forget, the stone warns us of evil. And there was a prophecy about two of us turning evil. You don't wanna be one of them, do you? Maybe you should call this whole thing off."

"Nice try, Owen. First of all, I ain't turnin' evil. There's nothin' evil about givin' that know-it-all freakazoid what he deserves. And that prophet dude never said nothin' about the rock turnin' cuz of evil, only cuz of danger. This may be a danger ta Reynolds. No argument there. But it's also justice."

I have to admit, up till now I wouldn't have imagined DeWorken using a word like *justice*. I'm sure he knew what the word meant. Like I said, I was already realizing that he was not quite as dumb as Cliff made him out to be, but it still didn't seem like a word in his vocabulary. *Justice* was the kind of word we got on civics or history tests. DeWorken sounded more like himself when he just talked about "giving Cliff what he had coming."

"How will you find him?" Andy asked. "How? Every time you come near, the rock in his hand will turn red, and he'll dart off the other direction. You could chase him all day like that and never get anywhere."

Andy was making an interesting point. It made me wonder what it might have been like when I was little, playing games like Hide and Seek or Kick the Can. That magic rock sure would have come in handy.

"All right," Doug said. "Never mind for now. No sense bustin' my bones over him. But Reynolds won't be gone long. Sooner or later he'll be too scared ta be out in the woods by himself. He'll need ta be around people again, and he'll come back. Just you wait! You'll see! He'll come back. And when he does, he'll wish he'd stayed in the woods!"

***

He did come back, about an hour and a half later — not exactly for the reason Doug had suggested, but Doug was fairly close.

We were having dinner, breaking up bigger pieces of meat and bread the best we could and trying to figure out ways to get water out of the now giant canteens. Fortunately, not all of the canteens were big. Andy still had a smaller one. His canteen and strap were slung around his shoulder when the transformation hit, so the canteen had shrunk right along with him. There had also been a canteen in my knapsack when Charles turned me into a miniature, so that made two. A larger canteen was propped open in a way that Andy could scoop his smaller canteen inside and fill it. I did the same. Then the two of us allowed everyone else to share sips.

While we were drinking, Cliff slowly approached, almost as if from out of nowhere.

"Well, speak of the devil," DeWorken said, looking like a prospector who had just seen some gold in his pan.

"Hello, Doug," Cliff said very politely. "I'm glad to see you're all right."

DeWorken let out the loudest, most hideous laugh I'd ever heard. "Glad ta see I'm all right? Are ya? Are ya really? Sure, Reynolds! I'm glad ta see you're all right too! Cuz if ya wasn't all right, it would mean somebody beat me ta the punch!"

"Look, I know you want to get even," Cliff said carefully, "but I'd suggest you hold off and listen to me first ... all of you. We're in danger!"

"Ya got that right, Reynolds. But only part right! You're the only one who's in danger."

"Just a minute," I said. "What kind of danger, Cliff?"

"I don't know. I was out in the woods hiding."

"I'll just bet ya were!"

"Yes, Doug," Cliff said while almost trembling. "Yes, I was hiding from you. When the stone turned red, I knew you were coming. When I got a little farther into the woods, the stone turned back to its regular white color. Then it started turning red again. At first I thought it meant you were after me, so I continued in the other direction, but the farther I got, the more the rock changed. Its color turned bright and luminous, redder than I had ever seen it. So I decided it would be wiser to turn back and get away from whatever was out there. I headed for camp, and as I got closer, the color faded until it turned white again."

"So now it's white?" I asked. "It's still white?"

"Well, no," Cliff said. "Now it's red again because I'm so close to DeWorken, but the color was much brighter back in the woods than it is now, so I thought I should come back and warn everybody. Clearly, whatever was out there in the forest is the greater danger."

"Aww ..." DeWorken said. "Poor little Cliffy! His little pet rock warns him of danger no matter which way he turns."

"I was just thinking of the group!" Cliff said again, more emphatically.

"How's that thinking of the group?" Caligula said. "All this means is that whatever's out there, you probably have it on your trail, and now it will threaten all of us. Good one, Cliff!"

"Now hold on," Cliff said. "I figured you'd all want to know of a danger that's only a short distance out in the woods."

"Ya came back cuz you're chicken!" DeWorken said. "No other reason! You're just chicken! Too chicken ta face things alone."

509

"Oh yeah?" Cliff said. "Fine, DeWorken! If you're so brave, why don't you go out in the woods and discover for yourself what's out there?"

"Maybe I will, Reynolds. Maybe I will. But first you and me got an appointment. I'm gonna remodel your face and rearrange that big mouth so ya can never talk again."

Tears were running down Cliff's cheeks, and I could see his knees shaking. "Please, Doug, I never meant you any harm."

Doug moved closer to Cliff. "Hear that everyone? He never meant no harm. None at all."

"I was just trying to protect myself. You said you were going to beat me up that day at school and for something I never even did. I never narced on you! Honestly I didn't! And I never asked the ornament to turn you into a miniature either. All I did was ask it to protect me ..."

"Yeah? And what about sellin' me ta the carnival?"

"I didn't know what else to do with you!"

"Well, I know what ta do with you!"

"I had no choice. I was getting in trouble with the police!"

"Not as much trouble as you're in now!"

I couldn't watch this anymore. Sure, Cliff deserved to be put back in his place, but he was still my friend, and it was hard watching him turn into a quivering bowl of Jell-O right before our eyes. I had no desire to stand up to Doug and no desire to lose Doug as a friend. Neither did I have any confidence that I could stop him anyway, but if I didn't at least try, I'd lose all the pride I'd earned after standing up to those bikers back in the diner. I'd be a coward once again. I only had seconds to make a decision because DeWorken was gonna do this thing to Cliff fast unless he was stopped. Andy was protesting and trying to reason with him again, but that had about as much influence over DeWorken as an artist trying to stop a grizzly bear with his paint brush.

In those seconds, my mind flashed back to the diner when Cliff and Ben and I were watching the bikers tease Maple the waitress, wondering if we were gonna need to step in and help her out. Cliff suggested that Ben never got scared of anything, and Ben corrected him right away by saying that everyone gets scared. He probably meant the same thing Aunt Loureen meant when I told her once that I didn't have any courage because I got scared so easily. "Nephew," she said, "only a fool is never afraid. True courage is doing the right thing despite your fears."

I always liked that definition of courage, especially since it was the only one that could ever be true of me. It helped me to not think of myself as a coward, even though I always still *felt* like a coward until that night with the bikers. But then, looking back, that biker incident actually proved Aunt Loureen's words. I had been afraid to join Ben when he went to rescue Andy, but I joined him anyway. And since then, Charles had told me that I did this all on my own, without any help from the ornament.

So this present situation really wasn't any different. Yeah, I was afraid to stand up to DeWorken, but I just needed to do the right thing anyway. The courage would be in my *actions*, not in my *feelings*.

I got between DeWorken and Cliff. "I know you're angry, Doug, and you have a right to be. But I can't let you do this."

Doug was taken aback for a split second, but he didn't need much time to decide what to do.

"I thought we was friends, Owen."

"We are," I said while listening to my own heart racing. "We *are* friends, but Cliff said he was sorry."

"And that's it? He casts a spell of magic on me, sells me as a slave, needles me the entire trip, and I'm suppose ta let it go cuz of one freakin' apology?"

"I *am* sorry!" Cliff whimpered. "I'm sorry, Doug!"

"Listen ta him whine like a baby! I'll give ya somethin' ta really cry about, Reynolds!"

DeWorken tried to move around me. I blocked his way.

"Now look, Owen. I don't wanna hurt ya. You've been a good guy up ta now, so don't make me do somethin' we'd both regret."

I stood my ground. "Leave him alone."

DeWorken moved forward. I put out my hands to stop him, and before I could even blink, he punched me hard in the gut. I keeled over. Tinker Bell screamed. My hands were on my stomach, and I was just barely standing. I saw nothing but dirt beneath me. DeWorken grabbed me by the shirt collar and shoved me hard on the ground.

"Sorry, Owen. But I been lookin' forward ta this for a long time, and nobody is gonna stop me ... not even you."

I probably don't need to tell you that Cliff offered zero help, even though I was now lying on the ground because of him.

But Tinker Bell did interfere. Now *she* was the person between DeWorken and Cliff.

"Please, Doug. You're better than this."

Her sweet, gentle voice did cause Doug to calm down a little, but he still wasn't about to stop.

"Honey, ya need to stand aside."

"The Doug I know would never do such a thing. The Doug I know is gentle."

"Gentle?" Caligula said. "He's about as gentle as a Florida hurricane."

I slowly started getting up. It annoyed me to hear the cat because I knew talking was all any of us could expect from him. Had he wanted to, Caligula could jump on DeWorken's back or claw him, as he had threatened a few minutes ago. But instead, he did what cats always do when there's danger ... He just watched with fixed eyes and a curious head that rotated back and forth depending on where the action was. Not like dogs. Dogs are loyal. Why did I have a cat for a pet and not a dog? Cats only protect themselves. Dogs protect their masters.

Tinker Bell threw her arms around DeWorken and continued pleading with him.

But DeWorken wasn't buying it. "Stop, honey," he said. "Ya need ta stop. You're a nice person, so ya don't wanna see nobody hurt. I get that. But this guy ain't worth it, and I'm gonna do what I promised. I gotta do this, so ya might just as well sit over there. If ya don't wanna watch, turn around."

"No, Doug. I'm not leaving. You'll have to hurt me to get to him."

"Hey, that's not fair! You know I would never hurt ya!"

"Yes, I know. So if the only way to keep you from hurting somebody else is to assert myself, so be it. The man I love will not commit this terrible act."

"I already told ya before. I ain't gonna kill him. I'm just gonna rough him up."

"Then you'll have to rough me up too."

DeWorken stopped talking for a minute. I was up on my feet again, but my stomach felt like it had a hole inside.

"OK," Doug said to Tinker Bell. "OK. I won't do nothin' to him. Ya satisfied?"

"Don't be angry with me, Doug."

Doug kissed her lightly on the cheek. "I ain't mad. Who could get mad at someone like you?"

"Do I have your promise?"

"Yeah. I promise."

I started thinking about the reliability of DeWorken's promises. Was he lying, even to his own girlfriend? Probably.

"Thanks, Doug," Cliff said, sounding very relieved.

"OK, Reynolds. Consider yourself lucky. The lady just saved ya. Honey, how about some water from the canteen?"

"Of course, Doug. You look flushed. I'll get the water."

The moment Tinker Bell severed herself from DeWorken, he charged after Cliff and tackled him to the ground harder and faster than he would have brought down a rival football player in the big school game he had recently missed.

I started running over to see if there was anything at all I could do, but the pain in my stomach turned so sharp I lost my balance and fell over again.

"No!" Tinker Bell cried out. "No, Doug! You promised! You promised!"

But DeWorken wasn't even listening to her anymore. He was sitting on top of poor Cliff's chest looking down at him.

"Tell me again how stupid I am, Reynolds!" He slapped him

hard on the face. "Go on! Tell me!" Then he grabbed Cliff by the hair, pulling him up for another round. "Let me hear one of your science lectures! Let me hear one of your threats!"

This time he punched Cliff's face, and I wondered if the blow didn't knock him unconscious.

DeWorken stood up. Cliff was stretched out on the ground silent and still.

"That's enough!" I shouted.

"Shut up, Owen! This ain't none of your business! Hey, Reynolds, how about a lecture on geology? How about some history? Yeah, history! Cuz that's all you're gonna be in another minute ... history!"

He kicked Cliff hard on the side of his chest.

I knew I had to do something, but I could barely move myself.

DeWorken was laughing with delight. "How does it feel Reynolds? Huh? No comment, eh? Gee, I never thought the day would come when ya didn't have somethin' ta say. Well, I still got more ta say and I still got more ta do."

But before he could try anything else, a giant hand swooped down from out of nowhere, pulling Doug off of Cliff and suspending him in the air upside down, his leg caught between a huge thumb and two fingers. I looked up at the giant man ... a man I had never seen before.

"Oh my God!" Tinker Bell cried out. Obviously she knew who this guy was.

I felt a hand on my shoulder. It was Andy. "Are you all right, Mike? Here, let me help you up."

"Hello, Doug."

It was the giant talking ... and talking to Doug by name. The giant's voice was thunderous, kind of like Charles, only it wasn't Charles, even though I sure wished it was.

"Still talking tough?" the giant said. "Now, Doug, I thought I'd cured you of that annoying little habit. I thought that together we had learned some manners."

"Oh, my sweet Lord," Andy whispered. "We're all in trouble now."

I whispered back. "Andy, who is this guy?"

"Mr. Blake. This is Mr. Blake. He's been tracking us, and he found us."

Chapter Thirty-Two

The Day of Reckoning

I had no idea how the guy had found us. Who could be that good at tracking? It would have been quite an accomplishment even if we were still our regular size, but we were all miniatures, and he still found us! Of course, he'd been in this world before, hunting down Tinker Bell's people and capturing them for his show. I guess he knew his way around, and I guess he knew how to recognize the sound of miniatures.

"Well ... well," Blake said, sounding casual and cheerful. "Quite the reunion. New friends as well as old."

I figured he must be talking about me as the "new friend." Everyone else already knew Blake, except Caligula. Blake probably hadn't noticed the cat yet and even if he had, he wasn't likely to be expecting a cat who talks, so I was pretty sure the only "new friend" was me. It was *not* a title I wanted.

Cliff was slowly pulling himself up off the ground. His face was black and blue, courtesy of DeWorken. But DeWorken was no longer the problem. Amazing how fast a situation can change.

"Why, Cliff," Blake said in a very tongue-in-cheek manner, "you just don't look like yourself ... What's wrong? The slave market slowing down so you need to sell yourself too? That happens, son. Business takes a turn for the worst. It comes with the territory. And I imagine the terrain of your particular territory appears quite different from way down there." He laughed. Nobody else laughed with him. "Not even a chuckle, eh? Pity ... nothing a showman hates worse than making a joke in front of a silent audience with crickets chirping in the background. Hmm ... let's see ... I also recognize ... now, don't tell me ... what was the name? Andy, isn't it?"

Andy slowly nodded his head.

"This I hadn't counted on," Blake continued like a kid in a candy store. "How rewarding to embark upon a treasure hunt and actually find the treasure, a sunken treasure at that." He laughed at his own joke once again. Once again, none of us laughed with him. "But how? How did you and Cliff shrink to the same puny size as Tough Guy Doug? I must say, this mysterious world never ceases to amaze me."

"Drop dead!" Doug shouted, still in Blake's hand.

"Oh, how I've missed you, Doug. It's going to be just like old times for both of us. I'd forgotten how your courage recharges when we don't talk for a while. I do still have my cigarette lighter with me if that means anything to your thick, stubborn, skull ... But one order of business at a time."

He set Doug down and reached into his coat pocket. I expected him to pull out the lighter. Instead, he pulled out a gun. "Hopefully, I won't be needing this. When I set off on my little expedition, I packed the gun because I expected some of you to actually be the size of real, honest-to-goodness human beings. Turned out to be a much *littler* expedition than I'd anticipated." Blake stopped and glanced around the camp quickly. "But we're still missing somebody, and that's why I thought I better introduce the gun after all." He looked down at Cliff again. "Where's your friend?"

"Excuse me?" Cliff said.

"You heard my question. Where is he?"

"Where's who?"

"Don't be a fool, Cliff. You know exactly who I'm talking about. The brave one. That personal bodyguard you brought along to the carnival ... the one who knows martial arts."

"He's not here anymore," Andy said. "Ben disappeared."

Blake grinned. "Disappeared? How? Do I look like a person who believes in magic?"

"Maybe," Andy said. "Maybe it *was* magic."

"Oh, Andy. I knew you were eccentric, but this takes the cake."

"Well, how do you explain our size?" Cliff asked.

"I don't need to explain it. The lack of explanation makes for a more interesting carnival act."

"Perhaps," Cliff said. "But we still turned small somehow. How else do you explain it? In fact, how do you explain this entire world? Maybe not magic, but *something* unusual, something out of the ordinary."

"I'll give you a chance to offer a better answer. And If I were you, I'd come up with something fast."

"We don't know anything about it," Cliff insisted. "There was a weird noise out in the woods. Ben went to investigate and never came back. Maybe it wasn't magic. Maybe he was killed by an animal. We don't know."

"You don't know," Blake said, lowering his voice a little. "OK ... Well, you can at least know this. If your friend *is* around, and if he's still tall as me, and if by chance he's hiding from me and stalking me, he'd be well advised to stay hidden and out of sight. Because if I see him, I'm going to shoot him. It's just that simple." Blake raised his voice as if talking for Ben's benefit, but I was pretty sure Ben wasn't around anywhere listening. "Do you hear me, Black Belt? You show your face and I shoot your face clear off. You'll be dead!"

"He's not out there," Cliff said.

"No? Good! Well, then nobody is around to stop me. So the coast is clear to reclaim my property: Doug and Tinker Bell. In fact ..." A sneaky look formed on Blake's face. He stopped talking for a second, scratched his chin with his hand, and then continued. "In fact, why don't each and every one of you come back with me? ... Except the cat."

He'd noticed Caligula after all. This surprised me.

"A cat can't be trained," Blake said. "At least not easily, and I don't have time for the aggravation. Although, on second thought, it might be fun to see a cat the size of a grasshopper thrown into a canary cage."

A terrified-looking Caligula quickly turned the other direction and scampered up a tree. I was hoping he didn't run into a bird's nest. Blake's comment about a canary cage made me wonder about other birds, birds right here in the wild. That would be some sight, a giant bird who could turn the tables for once and eat a cat.

"Oh well ..." Blake said. "So much for that idea. It's almost as if the cat actually understood me."

"As a matter of fact," Andy started to say, but I quickly gestured him to keep quiet. If Blake knew the cat could talk, he'd find a way to get him off the tree and bring him back to the carnival for sure so that he could not only show off miniature people, but talking animals as

519

well. No sense in all of us becoming slaves.

"As a matter of fact what?" Blake said to Andy.

"Um … as a matter of fact, your first impulse was correct. Cats can't be trained."

Blake sighed. "I suppose not."

Then he pulled a thin, folded money bag out of his other coat pocket, the kind of bag where people pack hundred-dollar bills and thousand-dollar bills for bank vaults. "OK, gang. Let's all hop inside. We're going back to the carnival, where The Amazing Tinker Bell Show is going to feature a special deluxe version with an expanded cast."

Cliff suddenly got defiant. "I believe you'll find that rather difficult. There was a cave-in by the dimensional wall."

"Sure there was, junior. But guess who cleared it aside and then stepped into your little fairy tale world anyway? How do you think I got through?"

Cliff still kept going. "I understand that, Mr. Blake. Naturally you must have cleared the rocks away to get through. But what you need to understand is that these cave portals not only travel through space, they travel through time as well. You may have cleared away the rubble, but what if you return to a time before the rubble was cleared? You could materialize inside solid rock and suffocate!"

Blake's eyebrows were raised. His facial expression looked annoyed and confused. "What are you talking about? Just what kind of gibberish are you trying to pull now?"

It was strange to see Cliff being confrontational again, especially after his pitiful meltdown with DeWorken. I figured it must be desperation. Cliff liked this new world and had no intention of going back. But what could he do? What could any of us do? Our situation seemed hopeless, even more hopeless when I remembered that Charles was unavailable for any magical bailout.

The ornament was sitting next to Andy's canteen. I had taken it out of my pocket so it wouldn't break when I tried to stop DeWorken from charging into Cliff. Supposedly the ornament was unbreakable anyway, and now I wished I'd trusted Charles when he had reminded me that it was unbreakable, but I guess it's natural for people to go more by sight than promises. The ornament always looked so fragile, being made out of glass and all. So even though it couldn't be destroyed, I was still in the habit of being careful with it. If only I'd been as careful with the ornament *wishes* as the ornament itself, maybe none of us would be in this jam. Blake might have still found our camp, but three of us would be his size. Oh sure, that might not have made much difference either. Andy was no fighter. Neither was I. DeWorken had just proven that quite well. As for Cliff ... well ... I don't need to say any more about Cliff when it comes to fights ... And anyway, Blake had his gun. Still, we would have had a better chance had I not messed up my wish and turned the whole company into miniatures.

The ornament couldn't be used now anyway ... not until tomorrow, and even then we'd only get Hamartio. But thinking about the ornament did make me realize that I should at least try to keep it out of Blake's sight. So far, Blake had not noticed the ornament since it was so tiny, and right now he was distracted because DeWorken was hollering his idle threats again. I preferred to have the ornament back in my pocket since Blake was planning to scoop us all up, take us back to Earth through the cave wall, and force the whole bunch of us into his carnival act. If he did, and if somehow I could be discreet enough to pick the ornament back up and keep it hidden, we'd at least have a weapon to use, even if we had to first survive a day or two before being able to use it. But I'd already done my stupid thing for the day with that fatal wish, so if right now Blake wasn't seeing the ornament anyway, I figured it might be better to just leave well enough alone. As a giant, Blake was already in complete control. Just imagine how much worse it would be if by trying to pick up the ornament, I ended up doing nothing but bringing it to Blake's attention! Of course, there was always that risk anyway. Sooner or later he was bound to look the entire camp over, but I decided that if Blake did discover the ornament, it wasn't gonna be on my account, even though I guess it still would have been since I had been dumb enough to take it out of my pocket even when it wasn't really necessary. How frustrating ... thinking about how careful I had been this whole trip to do the right thing and how I kept striking out anyway.

And then, all of a sudden, another idea hit me. *The ornament was not our only magic device.* Neither was the stone, even though I now had a pretty good idea that the stone had turned red in the woods to warn Cliff that Mr. Blake was coming. If DeWorken hadn't drawn our focus

521

by beating up on Cliff, maybe we'd have listened to Cliff, heeded the stone's warning, and hidden ourselves in time.

But anyway, there was still another device, one that I hardly ever thought about: the key chain. Of course! The key chain! I reached into my pocket to make sure it was still there.

It wasn't. My heart sunk. This was the final nail in the coffin. Charles had trusted me to hold on to the key chain. If that key chain were still in my pocket, maybe Charles would be able to help us after all, if only indirectly. Hadn't Charles given me the key chain for protection? He said we would find ourselves in a desperate situation where only magic could help. Here we were, without Ben, facing a very menacing man who could squash our entire party with a few good stomps from his shoes. If magic didn't save us, nothing would. But how could this key chain help? I still didn't understand, and I sure as heck wasn't figuring out any riddle. A tiny sword ... That's all there was to the key chain. And it would have been even tinier had it stayed in my pocket and shrunk with me. What good would it have done? I had no idea, but that didn't give me the right to lose the thing!

How did I lose it? I never once took it out of my pocket, at least not on purpose. I remembered there *had been* times on the trip when I noticed the ring of the key chain accidentally attached to the ornament's hook during some of the times when I took the ornament out of my pocket to make a wish or to put it aside so it didn't break. The original hook which came with the ornament was well attached, that same hook Aunt Loureen used to hang it on our tree during our very first Christmas where she presented the ornament to my family as a special gift. It had stayed on the ornament over all these years. I had gotten used to it. The hook was part of the ornament.

Several times on this trip, when taking the ornament out of my pocket, the key chain would kind of come along with it. Each time, I quickly unattached the key chain and put it right back in my pocket. It had happened so often I never really thought much about it. It had become such a familiar, natural occurrence.

During one of those times, I must not have noticed. Probably the key chain came out with the ornament and fell on the ground. That had to be what happened. And that meant I would never be able to find it again. But wait! Now another idea hit me. If by chance, it fell out before I turned into a miniature, then the key chain and its

522

sword would not have shrunk with me. It would still be small, or at least small compared to Mr. Blake, but it would now be big enough from my point of view and much easier to spot. So where was it? My eyes started glancing around the camp. I didn't see anything, but there wasn't much chance for a thorough look because right now we were all standing still, waiting to see what Blake was gonna do with us when he finished squaring off with DeWorken. Walking around the camp to look for a sword key chain was not an option. Anyway, how did I know it was in camp anyway? It could be anyplace. Well, not anyplace. It would only have come out of my pocket when I took the ornament out. The last two times I had taken the ornament out of my pocket were a few minutes ago when I tried to stop DeWorken from beating up Cliff and back in the woods when I used the ornament to summon Charles. If the key chain had still been in my pocket when I returned to camp, it would have still been tiny, and if it was now on the ground, chances were I'd never find it, even if I had the time to look around. On the other hand, if it came out of my pocket when I summoned Charles, it would have turned big, or at least it would have looked to me like it turned big, and I would have noticed it right away. To me, it would have looked like a normal-size sword. I could pick it up and use it, even though it still wouldn't have done me any good because I never took a class on fencing. But wait! Since I didn't see the sword on the ground when I was with Charles and since Charles probably would have pointed the sword out to me even if I failed to notice it, then I had to rule out that place. So either I dropped the key chain here in camp, or there was another recent time when I had taken the ornament out of my pocket. As best as I could, I thought through our last moments with Charles, when he was trying to convince me that he'd still been merciful by allowing the ornament to shrink with me. Wouldn't he have said something about the key chain too? And with all that discussion about things shrinking with us if we held on to them or kept them in our pockets, I'm sure it would have been natural for me to reach into my pocket at that time. The key chain would not have been on my mind since I always kept forgetting about it, so an empty pocket would have gone unnoticed, but a key chain in the pocket would have jumped to my attention because I would have been grateful for one more magic object that I could still use. None of that happened. So it hadn't fallen out when I was with Charles. Neither was it still in my pocket when I was with Charles ... which meant it was no longer with me when I came back to camp either … which meant that I was not looking for a tiny key chain. That key chain had stayed its original size. If it was still in camp, it should be easy to spot. But we had traveled for days, and there had been previous camps. What reason was there to believe the thing was in *this* camp?

I tried to think back even more. It did not fall out the last two times I took the ornament out of my pocket, so when else had I recently taken it out? Ben! I took the ornament out of my pocket when I gave it to Ben! And that was at this same camp since we had decided not to break camp until Ben turned up!

But could I have lost it some other time, days ago, long before I gave it to Ben? Could I have lost it in one of our previous camps or along the trail? No! No, I couldn't have! The first time I summoned Charles with the ornament, that time he went over all the new rules, he also talked at length about the key chain. If during our talk I hadn't felt it in my pocket, right where it had been our entire journey, I would have noticed right away that it was missing. True, I was constantly forgetting about the key chain throughout the duration of our journey, but certainly I would have reached for the object while Charles was going on and on about its importance, all the while giving me additional clues. That would have been the natural thing to do. This had to be correct. I started concentrating as hard as I could, thinking back to that moment with Charles. Yes. Yes, I'd still had it on me. There was no longer any doubt. I remembered. I was actually able now to recall reaching for the key chain in my pocket, taking it out, and studying it while Charles talked about its riddle. Funny how the mind works, how we can fail to focus on something that goes on in the background while we have conversations but still be kind of aware of it in the back of our minds. And later, what was in the back of the mind can be brought to the front! And so, there was no more guessing. Now I knew. If the key chain fell out afterwards, it had to have been attached to the ornament when I gave it to Ben, and that was in this same camp. It would have been hooked to the ornament like other times, and then it would have dropped on the ground. I wouldn't have noticed because of the dark. And Ben *would have noticed* had it not fallen off, had it still been attached to the ornament once the ornament was transferred into his hand.

OK, so if the sword was here, why didn't I see it, especially since it would no longer look like a key chain and instead look like a real, honest-to-goodness sword? Well, one reason I might not have seen it so far was that I hadn't been looking for it. Like I said, for most of this trip, I hardly ever thought about the key chain. It was not on my mind when DeWorken and I returned to camp. I was thinking about ornaments and angels. I was thinking about other people in our party who would be mad at me for making a stupid wish. I was thinking about a lot of stuff, but not once had I thought of the sword key chain.

Still, even if I didn't think about it, the others would have. The whole reason they had immediately figured out that they had shrunk was on account of objects in camp turning bigger, or at least looking that way to their eyes. So they would have noticed it, but they noticed a lot of other stuff too, like our food being big and our canteens being big ... stuff that would have been more important to them than the sword.

When Andy met up with DeWorken and me before we returned to camp, he talked a little about the group figuring out together what had happened because of the larger-size objects. Probably Andy himself would be the one who remembered what, if anything, had been done with the sword. The others wouldn't have given it much thought. Cliff would have been too worried about DeWorken, and I doubt he would have thought much about the sword for protection since, like me, he had never taken a class on fencing and, in his hands, the sword would have been clumsy and worthless. So the sword wouldn't have mattered to Cliff, and Caligula wouldn't have cared. But Andy ... Throughout our strange adventure together, he had seemed to notice the little things.

Andy was still standing next to me. DeWorken was still threatening Mr. Blake and getting nothing but laughter in return. Since Blake wasn't looking at me, I whispered in Andy's ear. "The sword ..."

"What?" Andy whispered back as discreetly as he could.

"That key chain which was in my pocket ... Did you see it?"

"Behind the table," Andy said. "But what good can it do? It's too small to have any effect on Blake."

"I'm not sure. Just wanted to know where it was."

Andy had asked a good question. Would good *could* it do?

If things were different, if Blake had also turned miniature like the rest of us, then the sword on the key chain might have done a lot of good. Even if none of us knew how to use it, Blake might just hesitate since he wouldn't know for sure whether we were good at fencing or not. Besides, a sword could be dangerous enough, even without all the fencing skills. One quick thrust might be all it took. But anyway, all this was a moot point because, although the sword was now fully proportioned for me and for the rest of our group, it would still be a dinky little key chain to Mr. Blake.

But wouldn't Charles have known that Blake would be a giant when he found us? Maybe not. I had already found out today that Charles didn't know nearly as much as I'd thought. But the key chain was different. Charles knew all about the key chain. This had to be the moment. There was no escape from Blake without magic, and the only magic in range was the key chain. But how could I use it without figuring out the riddle? No answer to the riddle ever came to me anyway, even when all was calm. And who could think right now in the midst of terror? Then it occurred to me that I was doing quite a bit of thinking anyway, considering that all of us could die or at least get kidnapped at any time. Like I told you before, I do this a lot, think about stuff right when I'm in the middle of a strange situation. OK. So if I was thinking, why couldn't I think of an answer to the riddle?

And then, as if somebody had turned on a lightbulb in my brain, I suddenly realized the problem. *The charm was not for me.* It had been *given* to me, and I was the one who needed to solve the riddle. But all this time I had been holding on to the charm for somebody else: DeWorken. Oh sure, this conflict involved all of us, but it was mostly between Blake and DeWorken, and as soon as I remembered that, the rest of the mystery unraveled.

Once the mystery was solved, everything happened awfully fast. I think the best way to explain what happened is to first describe what I decided to do, and then after you learn about all the action, I'll go back and tell you how I knew ahead of time what role the key chain would play.

Since I was involved, since it had been my responsibility to figure it all out, it was also up to me to get this sword into DeWorken's hand. DeWorken could never figure out a riddle. His mind didn't work that way. Neither would he and I have time to talk and figure it out together. But Charles had understood that there would be no time when he had described a desperate situation. So thinking about the riddle by myself and solving the riddle was only one-half of the way this particular charm worked. The other part was a desperate situation in which we were expected to use the charm as a quick emergency device. That's what Charles had pounded into my head ... a quick emergency device ... Quick action means thoughtless action. That's where DeWorken came in. Thoughtless action was the very definition of Doug DeWorken. He handled desperation by acting on impulse. This was what I figured out, and I was sure ... or ... well ... mostly sure.

And so, in order to make the charm work, I had to get it to Doug. Doug would use the device, but I was the "custodian of the charm," as Charles had put it.

"Where are you going?" Andy whispered.

"Just keep looking straight ahead," I said, "as if nothing is going on. I'm going behind the table to get that sword."

"Don't do it, Mike."

"Ignore me. Keep looking ahead, Andy, like you're interested in those things DeWorken is saying."

"So just like I gave it ta Reynolds here," DeWorken bragged, "your day will come too, Blake. Just you wait and see! I ain't scared of ya! Even if ya try ta burn me again, I ain't scared, cuz I don't think you'll really burn me ta death."

"Oh, no?" Blake said calmly and casually, like one in complete control of a situation.

I started moving toward the table. So far so good, Blake was still focused on DeWorken.

"If ya kill me," DeWorken said, "that's the end of your act! And I know how much ya love show business!"

I reached the back of the table. There it was! The key chain! Only it no longer looked like a key chain. I was facing a real, true golden sword attached to a chain and with a big circular clasp. I picked it up quickly. It was light in my hand.

Blake continued talking. "Now, Doug. I already knew you to be one who shoots off his mouth without thinking, but I honestly wasn't prepared for just exactly how stupid you truly are. If I kill you, I lose my act? Seriously? I've had many miniatures in my act over the years. Most of them couldn't handle the situation. They didn't survive. They're dead now, but the money I made from them still sits safely in the bank."

He reached down and picked Doug up again. I didn't see it because I was still hiding behind the table, but I heard Doug shout, "Put me down! Put me down, you creep!"

"How about if I *throw* you down, Doug? Hard on the ground! Would you like that? If you die, I still have the magnificent, one and only Tinker Bell. I also have some bonus performers. I'll bet Cliff over here could master a good soft shoe. I might even be able to teach one or two tricks to my old friend Andy. Except for those annual carnival stops at Wendover, where he's already known as the town character, he'll work out just fine. Nobody from any other town will recognize him. And then there's also ..." Blake stopped short. I could tell he was looking for me, and I was scared out of my wits. "Where did the other boy go?"

"What other boy?" Andy said.

Still holding on to DeWorken with one hand, Blake moved toward Andy and sat on the ground so close to him that he could eat the poor guy. I witnessed everything again because now I was peeking out from behind the table.

"Did you actually say, 'What other boy?' Oh, Andy ... Save your cunning for idiots like Doug. Don't go insulting *my* intelligence. Now I'll ask you only one more time. And please consider the consequences before you decide to play dumb. You can answer me or you can be my first canceled booking. I'll smash you right here, Andy. You look too old to dance anyway. Catching on?"

Andy nodded.

"Good," Blake said. "Then I'll assume you are ready for what might be the very last question you're ever asked should you answer in such a way that I don't care for your answer. Andy ... Where's the other boy?"

It was time to test my theory about how the charm would work.

I felt pretty sure, but I also felt petrified. Once again, I needed to remember Aunt Loureen's words about how courage means doing the right thing regardless of how you feel. I couldn't let Andy die for me, and I needed to get this sword to DeWorken one way or the other. Maybe it was a long shot, but if I didn't try, we'd either all die anyway, or we'd all live as slaves. What did I really have to lose?

I came out from behind the table. "Here I am!"

Blake looked pleased. "Hello, Short Stack!

"The name's Owen. Mike Owen."

Blake smiled. "Your name is whatever I decide to name you. And your mouth no longer exists for any reason other than to answer my questions. So here's your question, albeit it an obvious one. What's that in your hand? Is that a weapon?"

"Not at all."

"Hold it up. Stand still ... Stay where you are and don't move a muscle except the one muscle in your hand while you hold it up."

I raised the sword high in the air. The gold chain dangled in front of my face.

Blake's smile got even more devious. "Not a weapon, eh?"

"It's a key chain," I said.

"It's a sword," Blake corrected.

"Yeah," I answered. "A sword the size of a key chain. It can't possibly hurt anybody."

"Then you won't mind handing it over, will you?"

"Of course not, Mr. Blake. Take it."

Blake squatted again and reached down in my direction.

But I kind of faked him out. It looked like I was handing the sword to him. Instead, I stuck it in DeWorken's hand, which wasn't too hard because DeWorken was in Mr. Blake's other hand. This was my moment of faith.

"DeWorken! Use it! Use the sword!"

Most people would never have tried it. After all, how could a sword the size of a key chain hurt a full-grown man? But DeWorken was different. There was nobody else like him, and that's exactly what I was counting on. Odds didn't matter as far as DeWorken was concerned. This was the guy who mouthed off to everybody no matter what their size, whether they could kill him or not. As a miniature, he had already mouthed off to Mr. Blake and a larger-than-life Cliff. He had even mouthed off to Caligula when Caligula, by comparison, was more dangerous to him than a lion or a panther. At that time, Caligula could have pounced on DeWorken with all the skilled speed of a cat, and eaten him just as quickly.

So of course DeWorken was gonna try it. His act of taking the sword was going to be as desperate as my act of handing it to him. Even without thinking of any magic charm, he would try it. At least, I was gambling that he would. Sure … of course he would. Nobody else would be that careless, but DeWorken wouldn't view it as being careless. He'd view it as being fearsome. It was part of his nature. The more I thought about it, the more I realized that DeWorken couldn't possibly do anything else. Otherwise, he wouldn't be Doug DeWorken.

His impulsive use of the charm, along with my faith in handing him the charm, would fulfill Charles' words. We would be delivered from a desperate situation where only magic could help, and it would help by acting as a quick emergency device, bringing about poetic justice.

Anyway, Doug didn't disappoint me. He grabbed the sword at once, looked up toward Blake's face from the palm of Blake's hand and shouted, "Die, you pig!"

Blake started laughing again, only this time he laughed so hard, it looked like he would never stop.

"Oh, Doug … this is too much. This is too rich. You never let up! Planning to kill me with your sword, Doug? Is that what you plan to do?"

"You ain't never gonna hurt me again!" Doug cried out.

"No? What are you gonna do, Zorro? Cut my finger with your little needle and cast a spell on me like Sleeping Beauty? Go ahead, Doug. Use it. Use your sword."

Without the slightest hesitation, without taking another moment to even think, Doug thrust the blade straight down next to his own foot, as if plunging the sword into the ground, except the only ground was the palm of Blake's hand, and the hand was now punctured.

"Was that it?" Blake said with enjoyment. "Ouch ... that really hurt, Doug. But not nearly as much as you're about to hurt. I guess it's time to terminate our association, Doug, *terminate* being the operative word. Sorry ... I hate to do this. After all, you do have hutzpah. But I'm afraid I must use you as an example to your friends. It will make my mutual relationship with them run ever so more smoothly in the long run."

But before Blake could do anything, he was surrounded with blue smoke, the same kind of blue smoke that came with Charles, only Charles never materialized. Instead, right before our eyes, Blake disappeared ... or ... actually ... he just looked like he was disappearing. When the smoke cleared, he and DeWorken were facing each other, both the same size. Blake had become a miniature like the rest of us.

Blake's mouth was wide open with astonishment. "What the ... How did you?"

"Well, whaddaya know?" DeWorken said. "Now we're the same size, Blake. Now we can have a fair fight."

"Careful," Cliff said to Doug. "He still knows karate, no matter what size he is."

"So? If he tries any karate, he'll get it with this sword."

It didn't take Blake long to compose himself.

"All right, gentlemen. I must concede that some kind of magic is indeed taking place."

I would have thought that anybody who suddenly found himself changed to a size smaller than a slide ruler would be frightened out of his socks. Like I said, Blake did look astonished at first, but in no time at all, he was talking as if his transformation was a mere hiccup to his plans, or a small bump on the road which would soon be smoothed over. He still spoke politely, still acted like he was in complete control of the situation, and still had bits of sarcasm woven in and out of his words. Maybe this came natural to him as a carnival showman. All I knew was that the others didn't seem to be fazed by these odd mannerisms, probably because they all knew Mr. Blake from the past and were used to the way he spoke. But this was my first experience with the guy. To me, he seemed as stubborn and as fearless as DeWorken, but with more composure and a better vocabulary. And like DeWorken, he also seemed oblivious to danger.

Anyway, Blake continued talking as if he had nothing to worry about, as if *we* were the ones still in trouble.

"I'm not sure how you're working these feats of magic, but I'm guessing that all powers can be reversed. So I suggest that whoever changed me change me back immediately."

"Can't be done," I said.

"Oh, no?" Blake pulled the gun out of his pocket again. The gun had been reduced right along with him, just like the ornament had shrunk with me. I wondered why Charles had allowed this since he said the reduction of the ornament had been an act of mercy. Why was he allowing mercy for Mr. Blake? Then again, I couldn't be sure this had anything to do with Charles. Sure, Charles had pointed me to the charm, but he wasn't tied to the charm like he was tied to the ornament. Maybe this was just a natural thing for the key chain's power, the way the ornament shrinking was natural for the ornament's power, even if the ornament's "naturalness" had been created by Charles.

"So ..." Blake continued. "It can't be done? I tend to disagree. Something around here reduces people. That same something is capable of an antidote. I want that antidote within literal seconds, or I start shooting every member of this little party, one at a time."

"Mr. Blake," I said, "believe me, if there was a way to turn tall again, we'd have found it ourselves by now. Do you think we enjoy being this size?"

"I won't ask you again." He pointed the gun at DeWorken. "I assume the magic lies with you, Doug, since nothing happened to me until you cut my hand with your sword. Now then, be a nice, cooperative athlete and turn me back to my normal size."

"I wouldn't help ya even if I could!"

"Sure you will, Doug. You'll help me right now. You'll help me, and then I'll be willing to forgive this entire unfortunate incident."

"I ain't takin no more orders from ya, mister. Never again! Far as

I'm concerned, ya can take your new size and go live in a turtle shell."

"Really, Doug … You must do something about your manners. Perhaps you need a different kind of incentive." He aimed the gun at Tinker Bell. "Now then, Doug, will you help me? Or do I send Tinker Bell to Never-never Land?"

That was the last straw for DeWorken. He charged over to Blake without thinking. Like I said, DeWorken did everything out of impulse, and his impulse was to save the woman he loved. A thinking man would have realized that by not being careful, he was putting Tinker Bell's life in more danger, for Blake seemed like the kind of man who could shoot her and still sleep well that night. But since I was counting on Doug's instinctive reactions and because I figured the magic sword charm was also counting on Doug's instinctive reactions, I had a feeling Doug would still succeed. My guess was only seconds in length, and I saw the conclusion immediately. Still facing Tinker Bell while pointing the gun at her, Blake was caught off guard by DeWorken, who swiftly thrust the sword into Blake's side. Blake quickly turned and fired the gun, but he was wounded and taken by surprise. The gun misfired on the ground. Tinker Bell screamed. Blake was down on his knees, but aiming the gun again, this time at Doug. He was obviously a man of quick impulses, but probably the magic charm had helped Doug by making sure that those crucial seconds of action which could have gone either way went Doug's way. Doug kicked Blake in the face. Blake fell over, still clenching the gun tightly in his hand. As his hand reached up from the ground, DeWorken stepped on his wrist and forced the sword into Blake's chest at the same time. Blake cried out again but with a weaker voice than before. In no time at all, his voice turned into wheezing and coughing until he went silent and completely limp, lying dead on the ground.

Tinker Bell rushed over to Doug. "You fool! You could have been killed!" Then she smothered him with kisses.

"Wow!" Andy said. "I've never seen anything like it."

Cliff cautiously moved toward the body and felt Blake's pulse to make sure he was really dead.

My own heart was racing a mile a minute. But it was over. I had figured it out. For once, I had used a magic charm properly. Hopefully this would make up a little bit for my blunder with the ornament, but

Doug still deserved all the credit. It was his bravery, or maybe his fierce stupidity that just happened to be convenient at this particular moment because we were using a magic device that functioned by partnering with fierce stupidity. Whatever the reason, Blake was no longer going to be a problem.

OK, before I continue and talk about what happened next, let me do as I promised and explain how I figured out the riddle.

While looking at the sword and thinking about Charles' clues, I thought even harder about Charles himself. Charles worked his wonders with tricks, by being sneaky and cunning and by imitating Hamartio. That's what he'd said and that's what he'd done. Before I even started this journey, he'd planted a weapon on me: the magic key chain. I wasn't assuming that Charles necessarily created the key chain, but I was at least sure he knew everything about its abilities before handing it to me. He gave it to me back on Earth, back in that strange souvenir shop, not long after he'd been released from the ornament as a result of Cliff's "separation" wish but before he and Hamartio had become tied to the ornament again, during those special days when he had some extra freedom to look after me. And he said that the weapon would work like a sneaky loophole. Those had been his exact words. All this time, I thought the loophole had been for me. But I was wrong. It was for DeWorken. That's what Charles meant when he used the phrase *poetic justice*. As Cliff had put it, DeWorken received poetic justice because Cliff, the guy he picked on, became bigger than him. But it worked the other way too. Mr. Blake, who had picked on DeWorken, would receive poetic justice if he became the same size as DeWorken. And if the magic charm made that happen, DeWorken would be holding a full-size weapon in his hand! That was the loophole. While still suffering the effects of Cliff's wish, some of that "fine print" in the world of magic would at least give DeWorken a consolation prize, the equivalent of a full-size sword! The rules of magic would still be honored because of Cliff's wish that DeWorken could never change back to his normal size. The loophole would be that, as far as Blake was concerned, *DeWorken didn't need to turn back to his normal size.* And the activation for the magic was me, figuring out the riddle. That's how I knew that the sword was not only going to slay Mr. Blake, it was going to first shrink Mr. Blake and prepare him for DeWorken's deadly thrust!

Tinker Bell would not stop kissing Doug, but Doug didn't look too happy with himself. Everything had happened so fast, I think it was just finally hitting him and catching up with him.

I sat down next to them. "You OK, Doug?"

"Of course he's OK," Tinker Bell said. "He's my hero! My knight in shining armor!"

It was strange to hear another familiar phrase from somebody of a different world. *Knight in shining armor* was an Earth expression, although it did seem to apply since we were probably in the Middle Ages of this new planet, or at least a time comparable to that time in Earth's history when knights in shining armor actually existed. I guess when Blake taught Tinker Bell to speak English for his act, he must have also taught her some of our common expressions.

Anyway, whatever words she used, she was absolutely right. Doug did act like a knight in shining armor, even if he only had a shiny sword without the armor. I suddenly felt jealous and also frightened, but this was a different kind of fear. We were out of the current mess, but sometime soon Marla would be entering this world, according to Cephalithos. What would happen then? Would I be able to protect my own girlfriend the way Doug had just protected Tinker Bell? I tried to feel better by telling myself that I wouldn't have been so stupid as to rush a man with a gun. But deep inside I also knew the real truth, that I simply wouldn't have been *brave enough* to rush a man with a gun. Still, I had at least shown *some* bravery. After all, I was only guessing with the key chain charm. If it hadn't worked out, Blake might have killed me. But then, he might have done that anyway, so I wasn't really sure what to label my actions. I took comfort one more time in Aunt Loureen's definition of bravery: doing the right thing, scared or not. And yet, that definition didn't seem to apply to Doug. I saw no evidence that he had been scared.

Anyway, even though I was feeling jealous of Doug, Doug himself did not seem to be enjoying the moment.

"I killed him."

Tinker Bell was staring at Doug in adoration. "Yes, my love. You killed him, and in doing so, you saved us all."

I guess I wasn't gonna get any credit for my part. Oh well.

"I killed him," Doug repeated, looking down and not even facing Tinker Bell.

"Well done, young man," Andy said. "You have our gratitude."

Suddenly Cliff reached down next to Blake and picked up his gun.

"Hey!" I shouted. "What do you think you're doing?"

"This gun might come in handy. We could use another weapon."

I knew Cliff better than that. He wanted the gun in his hand in case DeWorken decided to go after him again.

"You don't know how to use a gun," I said to Cliff. "None of us do. Maybe we should just bury that thing in the ground right next to Mr. Blake."

"Not a chance," Cliff said.

"We don't know how to use it, Cliff! Have you ever handled a gun in your life?"

"How hard can it be?"

"Put it down."

"Once again, Mike, I don't recall placing you in charge."

"We all put him in charge," Andy said. "And I agree with Mike. There's been enough bloodshed for one day. Put the gun down."

"You're both crazy!" Cliff shouted. "Why not view this as a blessing in disguise? Now we have two weapons, a gun and a sword."

But there *was* no more sword. The enlarged ring of the key chain was still lying next to DeWorken. The sword itself had vanished. We all noticed at the same time since Cliff had glanced in the direction of the sword while talking about the sword.

Cliff looked quite puzzled. "What the …?" He ran over to the key chain ring and picked it up while still gripping the gun tightly in his other hand.

"It turned blue," Tinker Bell said, "and then disappeared. Just moments ago. I saw it happening while the rest of you were arguing about the gun."

Cliff shook his head. "I don't get it."

"Well, there's a first," I said. "But I think I *do* get it. That sword was part of a magic charm, and Charles told us it could only be used once. Then it would be disposable."

"True," Cliff said. "Charles did talk about the key chain as being very temporary, to be used only one time. OK. Fine. Well … then all the more reason to hold on to an alternative weapon."

The next thing Cliff knew, he was rolling on the ground. Doug had reached up from the ground and grabbed his leg, causing him to lose leverage. In no time at all, the gun was out of Cliff's hands.

"No more weapons!" Doug shouted. He cocked the gun open, grabbed the remaining few bullets, and threw the gun back down. Then he got up and ran toward the brook.

"What are you doing?" I called out to Doug.

"Gettin' rid of these bullets!" he shouted back while throwing them into the brook.

"Are you out of your mind?" Cliff yelled.

I couldn't believe Cliff had the nerve to talk that way. Doug froze for a moment, looking at Cliff differently than I had ever seen before. Then he slowly approached.

"That gun almost killed the woman I love."

"I know," Cliff said. "But it also could have protected us in the future. I would have been careful with it."

"Careful? Like I'm gonna trust a weasel like you with a gun."

Cliff was shaking again, but he still managed to say, "It wasn't your call to make."

DeWorken clenched his fist, as if being ready for round two with Cliff, but he looked more sad than angry, and I wasn't surprised when instead of hitting Cliff he unclenched his fist and sat down on a large boulder by himself. I had not noticed that boulder before, and then I remembered that the reason I hadn't noticed it was because it wasn't really a boulder, just a rock which now looked the size of a boulder.

"Even if you guys didn't want to trust *me* with the gun," Cliff said, "*somebody* should have kept it. That gun would have come in handy."

"Not without a lot of target practice," Andy said. "Doug did the right thing. Somebody might have been killed."

"Somebody *was* killed," Doug said, and this time he was crying. "Mr. Blake was killed, and I killed him! I killed a man!"

The poor guy started weeping uncontrollably. Never in my life, would I have imagined this: the mighty Doug DeWorken, football jock and bully, crying like an infant. Only he wasn't crying for the same reasons as an infant. In those bursts of emotion, I could hear his pain and remorse. He sounded like he was literally being tortured. I guess Doug had a conscience after all.

Tinker Bell rushed to his side again.

I also walked over and put my arms around his shoulders. "There was nothing else you could do, Doug. He was threatening your girlfriend. And he would have made slaves out of the rest of us. You had no choice."

"But Owen ... I never killed a man before. Oh sure ... I've been in fights ... Lots of fights. But I never really hurt nobody. Not really!"

"You had no choice," Tinker Bell said tenderly. "And I'm proud of you."

"Proud of me? Me?" He buried his face in his hands and started sobbing again. "I'm a murderer! A murderer!"

"Young man," Andy said. "You are *not* a murderer. A murderer is somebody who kills in cold blood, who decides ahead of time to commit the crime. Murder is calculated. What you did was self-defense."

"He's right," Cliff said. "Our laws wouldn't classify your actions as murder, not technically. Instead, you merely committed homicide."

Within seconds, DeWorken stopped crying as if somebody had pulled a battery or turned off his plumbing. Leave it to Cliff! Another one of his know-it-all explanations! I hoped he would stop and not explain any further. Otherwise DeWorken was more than likely to stop feeling remorse for Blake and instead start imagining the joys of burying Cliff alongside him.

But if DeWorken felt any such temptation, it didn't last long. He looked at Cliff briefly, then started crying again.

Maybe there was something about seeing his enemy cry that gave Cliff a sense of confidence or a sense of sympathy even, but whatever the reason, he too sat down next to Doug. "It'll be all right, Doug. I agree with the others. You had no choice."

"Call it what ya want, Reynolds ... Call it homicide or self-defense. If I was back home, they'd still send me ta jail."

"There would be a trial," Cliff said. "Sure ... there would be a trial. But then the rest of us would testify on your behalf."

Tears were still running out of Doug's red-looking eyes and flushed face, but the crying stopped. "You would do that for me? You would testify?"

"Of course I would," Cliff said. "If we were back in our hometown. But we're not. We're in a new world. So it doesn't matter anyway."

"It'll matter if I ever go home," DeWorken said. "Maybe you plan ta stay in this world Cliff, but I ..." He suddenly stopped and looked over at Tinker Bell. "Well, actually I might stay here too. I might just stay here anyway. I ain't goin' no place without Tinker Bell."

"Either way," Andy said, "Mr. Blake was an iceman ... a cold-blooded customer. Nobody is going to miss this man. Let's bury him and be on our way."

***

The funeral service didn't take long. Usually at a funeral, somebody thinks of something nice to say. Nothing was coming to us. It reminded me of another funeral I once attended, a family funeral. Years ago, my Uncle Harold had passed away. He was the most ornery, bitter man one could ever know, with three ex-wives who all hated him. At his funeral, people tried to say positive things about Uncle Harold. It was really a stretch:

"Um, Harold really knew what he wanted out of life."

"Knowing Harold was ... well ... I'm not sure too many people really knew him, but those who did know him, knew him well."

"Harold's dog will miss him for sure."

I was tempted to stand up and thank Harold for his divorces and remarriages since it did give me three cool aunts — not as cool as Aunt Loureen, but they often brought presents, and that made them cool enough. Still, I couldn't think of one positive thing about Uncle Harold himself, so I stayed seated.

Anyway, nobody had anything positive to say about Blake either, except for Cliff. He said, "Good riddance!"

I would have expected that comment to come from DeWorken, but poor Doug was feeling so bad about Blake dying at his hand I guess he just didn't feel like saying anything at all.

After we buried Blake, Cliff tried to make his peace with Doug.

"I know you feel bad, Doug, but we do owe you our lives."

Silence.

Cliff tried again. "Look, I guess we're both in trouble with the law now, so we both have reasons for staying in this world. Maybe it's time we buried the hatchet."

I found myself hoping I didn't have to hear the word *buried* one more time today.

Doug didn't even look at Cliff. But he did say something which helped Cliff to feel better.

"I ain't gonna do nothin' more to ya."

"Thank you." Cliff extended his hand. Doug didn't take it.

"Only stay outta my way for the rest of this journey … Understand, Reynolds?"

"Sure, Doug. Sure. Anything you say."

"And as much as ya can, stay outta my sight. I don't wanna see ya. I don't wanna hear no lectures. Got it?"

Cliff nodded his head. I could see he was just glad to be alive.

Later, when the group had a chance to take a deep breath and review the events we'd just gone through, Andy and Cliff asked me how I had figured out the key chain charm and riddle. I enjoyed explaining it to them because, again, I was hoping this would help them overlook what became known as "the blunder of Mike's shrunken wish."

The rest of the day was spent arguing about our next course of action. The only thing everybody agreed to right away was that we could go nowhere until we figured out how to take the material from the larger objects around us and fashion smaller supplies. I already told you how we transferred water from the big canteens to our two smaller canteens and how we cut big pieces of meat into tiny pieces. That's all we'd had time for, but now we also needed cut material from our larger-than-life backpacks, blankets, and ropes. Like I said before, my own backpack had shrunk with me because I was wearing it when I made that fatal wish. But that wasn't true for everyone else. The ax was giant size now, but we helped each other move blankets and ropes over to the large blade and then rubbed the material back and forth until pieces of big blankets and pieces of big rope became smaller, usable blankets and rope. This sort of thing seemed to take forever. It was long and tedious. At first, Tinker Bell didn't want Doug to help out because he was limping after his ordeal with Mr. Blake, but Doug insisted on helping anyway. The idea was to work at this stuff long enough to eventually create the equivalent of new personal backpacks.

Later, while resting, we talked again about our next course of action. At first, I was uninterested in continuing the journey without Ben and felt we should make at least one more last-ditch effort to find him. But then Cliff reminded me that Charles was already out looking for Ben, which was a strange reminder since Cliff only knew this after I told him about my conversation with Charles. It figured, being reminded of something only about an hour after I had explained it myself.

"Since Charles is searching, we might as well keep on the move," Cliff said.

I still wasn't sure. "But what if Charles doesn't find him?"

"Look," Cliff said. "If an angel can't find him, what chance do the rest of us have?"

"He talks sense," Andy added.

"I ain't hangin around lookin for nobody," DeWorken said. "It's time to get on our way and see Tinker Bell safely home. Blake might be dead, but there are other giants in this world who treat her people as slaves."

I finally agreed. "OK. According to Charles and the prophet, this mission is important. So we'll leave in the morning after a good night's sleep."

"Maybe we should leave now," Cliff said.

I shrugged. "Why now? For the moment, we're out of danger. It's been a long day with enough excitement for one day. Let's relax and try to unwind a while."

"Out of danger?" Cliff said. "Hardly. If we're out of danger, why did the stone suddenly turn red again?"

Chapter Thirty-Three

The Horrible Trap

At first we just stared at each other in silence, even though everyone knew we needed to take action fast. I couldn't believe the crummy timing, and obviously the others felt the same way. Each one looked worried, except Caligula, who probably figured he could always climb a tree again if push came to shove. Finally, Andy managed to put in words what all of us were thinking.

"We never seem to get a break, do we?"

"What kind of danger could it be?" Tinker Bell asked. "Mr. Blake is gone and that evil angel can't hurt us unless somebody uses the ornament and summons him."

"You tell *us*," Andy said in a nice way, not an accusing way. "This is your world. Any idea what might be out there?"

"I'm afraid not, sir."

"Don't call him sir," DeWorken said. "We ain't slaves no more. You never have ta call nobody 'sir' again."

"I only meant it as a way of showing respect, Doug."

"And certainly you don't presume that I would ever want to make a slave out of her or anybody else," Andy added.

Cliff was still focused on the magic charm. "We'd best return to the matter at hand. If the stone is red, we need to break camp and get out of here fast."

"Which way?" I asked.

"Good question. Let me take a few steps. If the stone gets brighter red, we go the opposite direction."

"Any way of knowing if the danger is imminent?" Andy asked.

"Imminent?" DeWorken said, sounding confused.

"He's asking if we are in immediate danger," Cliff explained. "As opposed to a warning that something is off in the horizon, to be encountered later on."

"I wasn't talkin' ta you, Reynolds. Have ya forgotten our agreement already?"

"It gets lighter this direction," Cliff said, ignoring DeWorken. "So this is the direction we should go. As for how soon we run into the danger, there's no way of telling. But danger is danger whether it comes today or tomorrow, so the smart decision is to start moving the opposite way."

"That ain't the way ta Tinker Bell's country! I'm gonna see that she gets home, danger or no danger."

Cliff looked like he wanted to respond, but I could see he was afraid of what DeWorken might do to him.

Instead, Andy took on the challenge. "We can always find another route later. In time, we'll finish our mission and escort the young lady home. But the wise thing at the moment would be to first get out of danger."

"Hey, wait!" I shouted. "Cliff, look at the stone now. It isn't red. It's blue."

"What?" Cliff looked down at the stone again, still balanced in his hand. "No, it isn't. The rock is red ... Wait! You're right ... Wait!"

"It's flashing!" Andy said. "One second it flashes blue; the next second it flashes red!"

"Huh?" Doug said. "What kinda stupid help is that? I thought this thing was supposed ta warn us about stuff."

"Yeah," I said. "But that's only one of its functions. It warns us of danger ahead or tells us that something good is ahead."

"Well, then it should do one or the other," Andy insisted. "How can the road ahead be good and bad at the same time?"

Cliff held the blinking stone up as if he were examining a specimen in a science lab. "This is quite the paradox. Apparently the color flashes alternate deliberately. If we turn away from the danger, we also turn away from something good, perhaps something needed and necessary to our very survival."

"How can somethin' be both good and bad?" Doug asked.

Again, Cliff looked like he was about to answer. Again, he stopped himself, probably because he knew the question was for the group as a whole, not him specifically, and that if DeWorken heard one more word out of him, he would make him eat the stone.

Suddenly an idea hit me. "I keep thinking about Marla. She's supposed to come into this world at any time. What if this is her? What if this is it? This could be the actual moment. Maybe she's close by."

"So?" Cliff said, making sure to look only at me and not DeWorken. "What would Marla have to do with the magic stone?"

"It would explain the blue," I said. "That would be a good thing if she's here."

"Good for you," Cliff replied. "She's your girl. How does that help the rest of us?"

"Well, for one thing," Andy offered, "there's safety in numbers. And don't forget, Mike's girlfriend would still be her regular size."

I hadn't thought about that. This entire journey, all I dreamed of was holding Marla in my arms again. How was I gonna do that now? I hadn't counted on a giant Marla.

Cliff nodded. "I suppose if she's her regular size, she *will* be somewhat of an asset. But then, why is the stone also turning red?"

I had already figured that one out too. "Maybe she's here, which is the good thing, but she's in danger which is the bad thing. And we're being warned because we need to rescue her."

"I suppose," Andy said.

I continued. "Well, if she's in danger, we need to get to her right away. Let's get moving. The stone will be our guide, the brighter it gets, the closer we are."

"Hold on," Cliff said. "Aren't we getting ahead of ourselves? This is only a theory, Mike. You're overthinking. We don't know that it's Marla out there. It could be anybody or anything."

"Well, whatever it is," Andy said, "or *whoever* it is, the person is in danger and needs help. And this same person will be good for our group, according to the blue flash of the stone. Perhaps it's Ben. Perhaps the stone is leading us to Ben."

"I think it's Marla."

Cliff shook his head. "Why, Mike? Why does it have to be Marla?

Because that's what you want to believe?"

DeWorken decided he'd had enough. "Shut up, Reynolds! He can't help it if he misses his girl."

But Cliff didn't stop. "I must point out that Mike's girl is a giant. So even if she *is* in danger, what kind of help could he possibly offer?"

"That's my own business, Cliff. Hand me the stone, and I'll go find out."

"Young man," Andy said to me. "Surely you're not thinking of venturing out there alone."

"The rest of you can come along if you want. But we need to move fast. She could have died in the time we've been having this committee meeting."

"OK," Cliff said. "We'll continue in the direction where the stone flashes blue and red. But we all go together. We'll need our gear and supplies. Let's break camp and pack up."

"Look at him givin' orders ... like somebody just made him president."

"Doug ..." Tinker Bell grabbed his hand, probably to keep him from getting all worked up again.

"We don't have time to break camp," I said. "I'm going after Marla now."

"You don't even know it's Marla!" Cliff protested.

"Whoever it is, the stone is telling us that we need to help. Now I'm going out there."

Cliff grabbed my arm. "I urge you to reconsider, Mike. The last time somebody stormed off into the woods without thinking, it was Ben, and we never saw him again."

"Maybe we *will*," Andy said, "if you give him the stone. That could just as easily be Ben out there who needs our help."

Cliff was getting frustrated, like one who was positive he was taking the right approach and couldn't understand why his logical suggestions were being wasted on such an inferior rabble. "Nobody is saying we won't go. But first let's break camp."

"Just hand me the stone, Cliff. The rest of you can break camp if you think it's so important. I still think there's a really good chance this is Marla, and I need to move fast, without first tying a bunch of blankets and supplies on my back."

"It's a bad idea, Mike!"

"Reynolds, give it ta him, or the only danger you're gonna see from the stone is the stone smashin' your face!"

Cliff handed me the stone.

"I'll go with you," Andy said.

I appreciated the gesture. But Andy was an old man, and he moved slow like an old man.

"Thanks, Andy, but Cliff is right about one thing. We need our gear. But I also wanna move fast. So I'll head out. The rest of you pack up camp, and after I find whoever is out there, I'll come back."

"Sure of that, are you?"

"Yes, Cliff, I'm sure."

"Wait, Owen! I'll go with ya."

"You need to rest," Tinker Bell said to Doug. "You're still limping from your bout with Mr. Blake."

"It's nice of you to offer, Doug, but you *have* been limping, and I need to move fast."

Doug hesitated before answering me. Finally, he said, "OK, Owen. Go find your girl. But check in with us soon. Say … maybe ten minutes? If we don't hear from ya in ten minutes, we'll come after ya."

"Thanks, Doug."

Actually, I was limping too because of *my* bout with Doug. Doug had taken on everyone today: Blake, Cliff, and me. But the others didn't seem to notice my own limp, and I didn't really care anyway. I took the stone and headed off into the woods.

***

Something strange and good came over me the moment I found myself alone. At first I attributed it to the peace and quiet. Oh sure, maybe danger lay ahead, but a lot of noise and pointless arguing was behind me. It felt refreshing.

After a few minutes, I realized I was also enjoying my venture into the woods for another reason. Throughout this entire journey, I had constantly battled my fears. But right now, I wasn't frightened at all, even though the stone kept flashing a brighter red and a brighter blue the farther I walked. This was because of my love for Marla. The very thought of her in danger immediately trumped all personal fears. For the first time in my life, I was putting another human being before myself, and I was doing it out of desire, not because Aunt Loureen was poking my conscience and giving me lectures about the right thing to do. With Marla, there was nothing to even think about except her own safety. Mine didn't matter. My job was to protect her. Earlier, I had wondered if I would be able to rescue my own girlfriend the way DeWorken took care of Tinker Bell. I figured this was my answer, even though Cliff might be right and it might not even be Marla out there anyway. It didn't matter. Just the *idea* of her being in danger was enough to wake up my male instincts. I was becoming a man — a real man, not just some loopy kid.

And then, even more feelings rose to the surface. I realized I was feeling happy for other reasons. I was coming to grips with all this destiny talk, and I was completely at peace with my experiences in this bizarre new world. True, I was still worried about Ben, but if anybody could take care of himself, Ben could. Ben's whereabouts were the least of my questions. So many puzzles still needed to be unlocked, but I was starting to accept them too by thinking of them as interesting challenges or fun games.

Of course, I still wanted to be a winner when these games were over. Only a couple of mysteries had been solved, and every answer created about fifty new questions. I finally understood who Charles was, and I finally figured out that magic key chain. The main point of our mission had also been accomplished, at least the first, original task we set out to accomplish, so I didn't have to wonder anymore how that was going to go. DeWorken was rescued now, and the mad man after him was dead. But what about the rest of our mission? Even though I'd accepted my sense of destiny, I had no idea where it would take me. It still promised to be fun. Or … wait … not all of it would be fun. Now I was thinking about that disturbing prophecy. Which two of us were going to turn evil? And then there was the biggest question of all: What was I doing in this other world anyway? Why did it even exist in the first place, and why was it connected to my own world through that time cave? The old prophet had offered a few clues, but his explanations left me kind of hollow.

The stone was flashing brighter than I had ever seen it before, still alternating between red and blue. I sure liked the blue color better, but anyway, I put it back in my pocket. Whatever was about to happen was probably gonna happen fast now. I wanted both hands free, and I couldn't risk losing this stone the way I had lost the key chain.

I thought of calling out Marla's name, but I decided against it. What if she was in the kind of trouble where sneaking up behind her captor was the only strategy? Giving away my position by calling her name would blow the whole deal. Then I remembered again that if Marla was really around, she would be a giant. I would find her fast without calling her name because no giant could stay hidden for very long. And, like Cliff said, I really wouldn't be able to offer much help as a miniature. Oh well! Small or not, Marla would at least know I came charging to her rescue ... That is ... she would know if it was *really her* the stone was warning us about.

All at once, something very strange caught me by surprise. I stopped dead in my tracks, unable to move. A sticky substance was all over my hands and face. I looked down and looked around. It was a kind of silky string in a strange circular design. My clothes were caught on it too, but I only felt it on my face and hands. I tried to pull myself back but I was still stuck. Then I tried to lunge forward. Nothing! I was caught in some kind of ... Oh no! Please no! This wasn't possible. I hadn't stumbled into some new discovery unique to a magic world. This was something ordinary, yet horrifying. I was caught in a web! A spider's web! But how could a web be so big? Then I knew. I knew right away. The web wasn't big. *I was small.* I was still a miniature, and somewhere close by was a spider.

Great! Just great! Instead of some stupid fly getting trapped, I, Mike the idiot, was trapped. How much more could happen to me in just one day? More importantly, was this gonna be my last day?

I figured I was bound to survive on account of all that destiny stuff. But holding on to such hope was a matter of faith right now.

If only I could reach into my pocket and get to the ornament. But I couldn't. My hands were stuck to the gooey substance which made up this sinister web trap. Anyway, I'd already made my one wish today, so it didn't really matter whether I could get to the ornament or not. Yeah, I'd made my wish all right, and this was the result of the airhead wish, turning small enough to be trapped in a spider's web!

Even so, even if I survived until tomorrow, it was gonna be Hamartio's turn to grant the next wish. So, on two counts, the ornament was worthless. And what would I have wished for even if I wanted to trust Hamartio? I couldn't ask to be made big again. Wishes couldn't be reversed. So, on three counts, the ornament was worthless!

For the first time, I realized that I might just be this size the rest of my life. So many nonstop events had happened since that first moment when Charles enacted the transformation, from DeWorken charging after Cliff to the whole encounter with Mr. Blake. It was a nonstop roller-coaster ride. There had been no time to slow down and ponder my situation. The reality of my predicament hadn't caught up with me. But here, in this giant web, I had plenty of time to think. In fact, thinking was all I could do because I could barely move a muscle. From the moment I had turned miniature, I'd hated it, but now I was experiencing a nightmare that I hadn't even thought of before! My life was threatened in just about the most terrifying way a person could imagine. I'd have rather had Blake crush me with his shoe than to stand helpless while some giant-size spider spread his eight ugly legs all over me. It wasn't so much the fear of death. It was the creepiness! This sharp, sudden jolt that reminded me of my true size made me wonder what kind of destiny I might have after all. I found it strange that just moments ago I had been feeling better about myself. What self? I wasn't even a fifth of the person I had been when I woke up this morning.

So far, I didn't see any spider. Ten minutes later I still didn't see it. That was good but not real good, because one would be coming sooner or later. Hmm. Ten minutes ... that's what DeWorken had said. If they didn't hear back from me in ten minutes they would come looking. I sure hoped somebody was paying attention to the time. But how would they find me? They couldn't use the stone as a guide because the stone was with me. But I wasn't that far away, and they saw which direction I went. If they really paid attention to the ten-minute plan, they should be here soon.

Suddenly I felt a tug on the web, and there it was, looking even worse than I had imagined!

Ugly, hairy, eerie, hideous, terrifying! And I would have used those words to describe this creepy thing even if it was small enough to be crawling on my arm! I mentioned before how much I hated spiders. I never even went into our house attic out of fear that a dinky little spider might touch me. Size didn't matter! The smallest spider was enough to freak me out! But now I could multiply that freaky feeling by a thousand because this was a gargantuan monster almost as big as me! If I was my normal size, I would avoid it or step on it if it got near me. Now, instead of stepping on the spider, I was about to become its dinner.

I screamed so loud I must have sounded like a girl. But I didn't care. I didn't care how I sounded so long as someone rescued me. I was probably too far from camp for the others to hear. Maybe they'd broken camp and started on their way. That was my only hope, unless some miracle took place. I'd already witnessed a miracle or two in this world but the next one would have to happen in seconds, or I would be dead and never witness anything again.

I'd heard once or twice in school that spiders don't eat their prey immediately. They first inject them with some kind of poison that paralyzes them or puts them to sleep. Then they store the victim to eat at a later time. If I was gonna be put to sleep, I hoped I would fall asleep fast. I couldn't bear to look at this monster or feel its touch. Again, I was less afraid of dying and more afraid of the sheer creepiness.

The creature moved closer ... and closer ...

All at once there was a gust of wind as something sharp and shiny whisked by. It was a sword. Someone had thrown a sword, and most of the sword had entered the spider's body right below his head on the upper abdomen.

I was relieved but still crying out, almost out of reflex. "Oh my God! God! Dear God!"

"Hold still! I'm on my way."

The voice was from a man just a few feet from the web — a younger man, but older than me, maybe in his twenties. He had dark, curly hair and a clean-shaven face. He was also slender but muscular. At first I thought of him as some kind of medieval knight, but it wasn't a knight in shining armor like Tinker Bell had described. There was no armor at all, even though he did look like somebody from that era, maybe a knight without his armor. His shirt and trousers were very old-fashioned-looking and seemed to have some kind of rough burlap pattern. The color was a kind of brownish green.

"Easy, my friend," the stranger said with a warm, gentle voice. "It's all over! You're all right now."

He grabbed his sword by the hilt and started pulling. A kind of green pus poured out of the spider as the sword slid out. It looked putrid. I felt like I was watching a bad blend of movies, something along the order of *The Sword in the Stone* meets *Alien*.

"Augh! "I shouted out. "Gross! Gross!"

"Not sure I've ever heard the expression *gross* before, but I'm guessing it means you don't care much for spiders."

I just stared at him. Slowly a smile formed on his face. This had been his way of making a good-natured joke.

"That's one way to put it," I said.

Then we both started laughing. It felt good to laugh. I needed the release.

"I'll have you out of there in no time."

"Thanks," I said. Within moments, I thought of another lighthearted comment. I wanted to make the comment partly because I needed to keep laughing and partly because I was embarrassed that I had screamed so loudly. By making light of the situation, maybe I wouldn't come across so cowardly.

"And then, after you cut me free, maybe you can recommend a better hotel. I don't like the accommodations around here."

The stranger looked confused, probably because they didn't have hotels in this backward land and he'd never heard the word before. I started thinking. What were hotels called in the olden days, like the ancient days of the Bible or even the Middle Ages, where this guy would have blended in so well? Obviously he knew English, and the prophet had told us about years of crossover between people from Earth and people from this alien planet due to the time caves, so I figured this swordsman would know what I was talking about if I could just think of an older synonym.

"Hotel," I said again. "Like an inn."

"Oh, inn! Yes, all right. That makes sense now. Good to see you keeping a sense of humor ... Inn ... I like that one ... Yes, let's find you a better inn." He picked up the sword and started slicing the web around me, first freeing my hands, then my legs.

Strange to see a sword again so soon after that magic key chain sword had performed its one task and then vanished into oblivion. I wondered if this was some other kind of magic sword. It didn't seem to be, even though it obviously came in just as handy. But far as I could tell, there was no magic involved. The sword wasn't disappearing or changing color or going up in smoke — none of the special effects that seemed to accompany magic in this strange new world. So probably this was just a regular sword that worked well in the skilled hands of the stranger using it.

As for the stranger himself, I was pretty sure that he represented the blue color on the stone, just as the spider represented the red. I had no idea where he came from. Probably another citizen of Tinker Bell's country, inasmuch as he was also a miniature who could look me square in the eye.

Wherever he came from, the guy seemed very likable. Even apart from the stone, for some reason, I felt like I was catching a good vibe from him. Not that vibes should be trusted without thought, but there did seem to be something comfortable and safe about this fellow beyond the obvious friendliness and playful personality. At first I couldn't quite put my finger on why I felt that way. Then, after a moment or two, I realized I was comfortable because he seemed familiar. I had been in such shock the familiarity hadn't sunk in at first.

"Thank you! You saved my life."

The stranger smiled. "You might just be right about that."

He continued slicing off the web until I was completely free.

"Easy," he said. "Watch your step. Here, why don't you sit on that log for a minute? You just had quite the frightening experience. Take a moment and relax."

"Thank you ... Are you sure that creature is dead? Maybe you should slice it again with your sword just to be sure."

"Oh, it's dead. You can be quite certain of that."

"Yeah ... maybe ... But couldn't you hack it one more time just to be on the safe side?"

"Calm down, friend. You'll be all right. I promise. This lifeless spider could no more get up and move than that pile of rocks over there."

That didn't exactly make me feel better. As a matter of fact, considering the kinds of events that had been going on in my life lately, especially in this new world, moving rocks would not have surprised me at all. But I kept that thought to myself, mostly because this fellow sounded sincere. I sensed that he could be trusted. He was a brave man and quite skilled with his weapons. I had only known him a matter of minutes, and I already admired him. Why act like a wimp by worrying about the spider? If this guy said the spider was dead, it was dead.

"That's quite a trap you got yourself caught in. What brings you so far into the wilderness?"

"Um ... I got separated from my friends. Guess I'm lost."

"Lost? No! I'd say you've been found. I found you."

There was something about the way he talked and his choice of words. This too seemed familiar. It was only then that I noticed he had more than a sword on him. There was a bow and a pouch of arrows, which he had apparently put down on the ground before attacking the spider by throwing his sword. I noticed the arrows now because he fetched them.

"Normally I would have just shot one of these arrows from afar. I'm a good aim, and I would have hit the spider with precision, but I couldn't be sure the arrow would do any more than wound the wicked beast, and there was no time to waste. Even a punctured spider could have killed you. The sword is a more lethal weapon and a safer bet."

"Um ... yeah ... sure ... I can't argue with your choice. Whatever you decided to do, it worked."

"Allow me to introduce myself."

But before he made the introduction, I suddenly knew. *I had heard his words because I had written his words. I had seen this face because I had drawn this face.* I had drawn it in my comic book. I'm not saying this man who rescued me wasn't real. He was real, all right, but he looked exactly like my cartoon, or at least what that drawing would look like converted into a real photograph or fleshed-out into a real person. And this *was* a real person! A real, breathing, three-dimensional person! I stared in disbelief, but there was nothing to doubt. This is what my character would have looked like if he was real. And I couldn't even say "if." *He was real!*

And so, his introduction was unnecessary. But he introduced himself anyway.

"My name is Arch-Ranger."

For a continuation of this adventure experienced by Mike and his friends in the other world called Planet Telios, watch for Bob Siegel's novel:

Characters and Kings

Author's Appendix

The difference between a work of fiction and nonfiction should speak for itself, especially when the novel is fantasy. However, my story does include discussions about the Bible. Therefore, it is important to clearly mark the borders between authentic spirituality and matters invented for the sake of plot.

I do accept the Bible as the Word of God, and anyone interested in understanding my detailed theological beliefs can find abundant explanations in my *nonfiction* books and articles.

While the Bible does talk about God, angels, fallen angels, and demons, *Inside the Castle in the Glass* is imaging a different world where God's angels assigned to Planet Telios operate under alternate rules, sometimes channeling their power through the use of physical devices.

Of course, in reality, we only know about life on our own world and must accept what the Bible says about human interaction with our Creator. Scripture expressly forbids any harnessing of supernatural power aside from faith in God Himself and the miracles He chooses to display according to His own will.

The characters in this story interact with different kinds of supernatural charms. Such objects were included only to make the adventure more interesting and do NOT intend to suggest any new, genuine theology.

God does not use "magic charms." Although certain objects in the Bible (Aaron's staff, Urim, and Thummim) are associated with God, they are not described in relation to any magic. They were used as manifestations of faith in response to God's commands, and His abilities were never dependent upon them.

While the characters Charles and Cephalithos did express some concern about alleged "magic," their words (adequate within the parameters of my story) still fall short of the more sobering warning to avoid any venture into sorcery, witchcraft, astrology, palm reading, crystal balls, séances, Ouija boards, tarot cards, tea reading, etc.

Although many instances of fraud have often been uncovered with such practices, sometimes the power does in fact exist. It is the SOURCE of the power which should concern us. God's enemy, Satan, will offer seductive phenomena in order to counterfeit genuine miracles and deceive people into following his destructive path (2 Thessalonians 2, Deuteronomy 18, Isaiah 47).

It is human nature to be fascinated by the paranormal. The real God works His wonders in the context of our faith and obedience. Love, ministry, forgiveness, healing, and verifications of truth are the aim. Miracles are not to be sought as ends in themselves.

Bob Siegel

Made in the USA
San Bernardino, CA
18 October 2017